COLISEUM ARCANIST

FRITH CHRONICLES #3

SHAMI STOVALL

COLISEUM ARCANIST

FRITH CHRONICLES #3

Published by
CS BOOKS, LLC

Coliseum Arcanist
Copyright © 2020 Capital Station Books
All rights reserved.
https://sastovallauthor.com/

Cover Design: Darko Paganus

Editor: Jessica Meigs, Sallianne Hines

IF YOU WANT TO BE NOTIFIED WHEN SHAMI STOVALL'S NEXT BOOK RELEASES, PLEASE VISIT HER WEBSITE OR CONTACT HER DIRECTLY AT s.adelle.s@gmail.com

ISBN: 978-0-9980452-7-6

ACKNOWLEDGMENTS

To John, who never stopped believing.
To Beka, for her unflinching loyalty.
To Gail and Big John, for the family.
To Ann, for playing Volke's matchmaker.
To Brian Wiggins, for giving a voice to the characters.
To Tiffany, Mary & Dana, for all the input.
To my Facebook group, for naming the stone golem, Borod.
And finally, to everyone unnamed, thank you for everything.

ARCANIST TRAINING

Nothing hurt quite like the sharp beak of a phoenix jabbed straight into my scalp.

I growled a curse as I bolted up into a sitting position on my bed. Was I bleeding? I ran a shaky hand through my disheveled black hair and flinched when I grazed the tiny puncture wound. Some blood, but not much.

"Good morning, Volke," the phoenix said, his voice chipper.

I took a deep breath. "Hello, Forsythe."

"My arcanist wanted to know if you were ready to train."

"Yeah. Just give me a moment."

The stinging pain removed all grogginess. I couldn't go back to sleep now, even if I wanted to. After another deep breath, I peered through the open window. The sun had yet to rise. The purple hue of the sky, dotted with a handful of stars, meant we still had an hour before dawn.

"He's already awake?" I asked.

"He's been determined to work hard ever since he escaped Calisto's pirate ship." Forsythe tilted his head from side to side. "And you did say you would train with him whenever he asked."

Although it was dark outside, Forsythe illuminated my room. A gentle glow radiated from beneath his scarlet feathers, like his body was made of flame. The rest of him resembled a large heron with delicate features, including a long neck and a pointed beak. His gold eyes stayed fixed on me as I flung my legs over the side of the bed.

I loved phoenixes, but every time they moved around, soot fell from the smolder of fire hidden beneath their feathers. A trail of it led from the windowsill to my bed.

"Don't worry," I said. "I'm getting up."

"Excellent. My arcanist is waiting out by the pond. I'll see you there."

Forsythe spread his wings and flapped his way to the window. His tail fluttered behind him, the peacock-like feathers shimmering, even in the low light of morning. He took to the sky a moment later, leaving me to get ready.

I turned my attention to the shadows at the base of my bed. They shifted around as I stood and gathered my trousers. Luthair was my eldrin—a powerful knightmare capable of controlling the darkness. He stayed hidden in the shadows, but that didn't mean he wasn't aware of his surroundings. Knightmares didn't sleep, and he had no doubt listened to the entire conversation.

"I'm glad you're helping Zaxis with this," Luthair said, his voice low and rough at the edges. "You seem to train better when you're with others."

I tugged on a white button-up shirt. "You're probably right."

"You seem less than enthusiastic."

After lacing up my boots, I half-laughed. "Sorry. Next

time, have Forsythe wake me with a poke straight to the eye. Maybe that'll improve my mood."

"Did he injure you?"

I ran my hand over my scalp, relieved to discover no wound. All arcanists healed themselves faster than normal people, so it wasn't a surprise. Some of my hair remained matted with a bit of blood, however.

"Who opened this window, anyway?" I asked.

"I did, my arcanist. Forsythe landed and pecked at the glass."

"That explains it."

I slid into my long coat and fixed the sleeves. I didn't need a mirror to know I looked like a classic buccaneer. My outfit would be complete once I secured a cap, but I opted to leave it. The ocean winds stole my apparel more often than I liked, and today I didn't feel like chasing anything.

"I've woken up early every day for two weeks straight," I said as I stretched. "Just so Zaxis can yell and throw fire everywhere. Am I really getting the most out of this?"

"Perhaps not, but remember the lessons from your home island. *Discipline. Without it, we are not masters of our destiny.*"

Hearing Luthair quote the Pillar made me smile. He had never studied the 112 steps like I had, which meant he had absorbed the information from me repeating it so often. It still energized me to hear him say it. I walked over to the window, more energy in my step. I wouldn't complain—not when I had magic to master.

As a knightmare arcanist, I had control over the darkness. After a second of concentration, I slipped into the shadows and stepped out of them a moment later, my head spinning and my chest hurting. I had traveled from the third story of our guild house down to the lawn below my window.

It took me three seconds of breathing for the pain to subside. It was the lingering consequence for being second-bonded. If I had been Luthair's first arcanist, this wouldn't have been a problem, but reality loved to dole out hardships.

That didn't matter. Hardships built character, according to Gravekeeper William. I could handle it. I stood straight and headed for the pond. The hero arcanists of old never let tiny inconveniences slow them down, which meant I couldn't, either.

A gust of frigid wind accompanied me as I traveled across the back of the atlas turtle. The grass growing from the soil of the shell swayed in the morning breeze as the gigantic turtle navigated the currents. Not many arcanist guilds set up shop on top of a giant mystical creature—no other guilds, actually. The Frith Guild was unique in that way, and I liked it.

Gentel, the atlas turtle bonded to our guildmaster, was large enough for three manor homes if it ever became an issue. Her giant shell, covered in vegetation, acted like a mobile island. Even now, as I stared at the distant waves, we were heading straight for the capital, Fortuna.

"Volke! There you are. Hurry up and get over here."

Zaxis Ren stood by the rock pond dug into Gentel's shell. Despite the chill, he wore only his trousers and the guild pendant around his neck. His red hair fluttered in the early morning wind.

"I can't believe you're not cold," I said as I walked to the edge of the water. "I almost wish I had another coat."

He shrugged. "I don't get cold anymore. Benefit of being a phoenix arcanist, I guess."

Forsythe swooped from the sky and landed next to Zaxis's feet. The bronze pendant around Zaxis's neck shone for a second when his phoenix got close. All apprentices wore bronze to signify their rank in the guild. I had forgotten mine in my room, and I contemplated going back for it.

Zaxis took a few steps back and then motioned to our surroundings. "Now that you're here, we can practice our magic."

I stared at the ground. The grass had been burned, leaving a large, charred circle. As I walked over to him, my boots sank into the scorched earth. Was Gentel upset by the use of Zaxis's magic? It bothered me to think our training would leave marks on her shell.

Zaxis glanced between me and the blackened dirt. "Don't worry. The grass grows back damn near immediately. Look. You can see some fresh blades right here." He knelt and ran his palm over the ground.

Slivers of brilliant green popped out of the dirt. The vegetation on Gentel grew at a rapid rate—so fast that even moments after getting burned, it was already growing again. That eased my worry. At least there wasn't any permanent damage.

"So what're we going to do?" I asked. "Same thing as yesterday? Practice our manipulation and evocation?"

"We're going to spar."

I stared at Zaxis for a long moment, both my eyebrows heading for my hairline. "What?"

"Don't look at me like that, *fool*. You heard me." He pointed to the edge of his charred circle. "First person to knock the other out of the ring wins."

"Are our eldrin participating?"

"No. Just me and you." Zaxis shrugged and waved his hand. "But you can use your sword or something. Not the shield, though."

"Why not my shield?"

"Because then you'll win, obviously. I don't have any magical items that powerful."

"What will you be fighting with?" I asked.

Zaxis cracked his knuckles as he walked over to the edge of the pond and retrieved a pair of gloves. With quick movements, he slid them on and returned to the burned circle in the grass. Before I could ask, he threw a couple of mock punches. Fire flared around his arms with each faux strike.

Once finished, he rotated his shoulders. "At night, I practice brawling and grappling techniques. Most of the time, I use sandbags and objects with leather armor. Now I need to move on to people."

I crossed my arms. "So you want to punch me."

"Don't be such a child. You'll have your sword." He smiled, more cocky than pleasant. "Besides, if you get hurt, you'll heal. And if it's not fast enough, I'll speed up the process with my phoenix magic."

"Let me guess—none of the others wanted to help you master the art of *giving someone a black eye*?"

"Who would I even ask?" Zaxis held up his hands in a sarcastic shrug. "There's no way in the abyssal hells that Atty or Adelgis would train with me. Illia always insists on doing her own thing away from the group. That leaves you or Hexa, and *she* uses poison magic, which I don't want to mess with."

Forsythe hopped away and stood at the sidelines. "I'll be rooting for you, my arcanist."

I turned to the darkness. "You'll be cheering me on, right, Luthair?"

"Indeed," he replied.

With newfound excitement for our sparring match, I peeled off my jacket and threw it outside the ring. Shivering,

I leaned down and grazed my fingers along the shadows on the ground. Then I pulled a black sword from the void—a magic weapon crafted by Luthair's former arcanist, Mathis. It weighed almost nothing, and I swung it through the air with ease.

Zaxis took up a position on the opposite side of the circle. "I'm ready."

"Are you sure? This blade is sharp. Shouldn't you wear armor or something?"

"I can handle whatever you dish out."

I doubted that. The low light of morning made using my powers easier—there was plenty of darkness to manipulate.

"Okay," I said. "Here we go."

I held out my hand and focused on the inky shadows covering the ground all around us. As a knightmare arcanist, I could control darkness, but it was more than that. I could condense it, harden it, and make it solid. I could make tendrils or sharp edges—simple objects crafted from the void. The moment I stopped focusing, however, the darkness returned to its incorporeal state.

I made four ropes of shadow and circled them around Zaxis. He waited, his gaze on me. It must've been difficult for him to see, considering the time of day, but I saw perfectly—yet another perk of being a knightmare arcanist.

Although my second-bonded magic stung from my palm to my elbow, it didn't hurt as much as it had when I'd first started learning to use it. Confident I had improved, I willed the shadow-ropes to circle around Zaxis's ankles. Maybe I could trip or yank him out of the circle.

The moment I snared his legs, Zaxis evoked a massive amount of flame. It wasn't the hottest I had experienced, but the sheer amount startled me. The fire emerged from his palms and swirled around him like a pyre, rising into the sky at least twice my height. I jumped back and lost concentration. The shadow-ropes that weren't burned faded in an instant.

Zaxis rushed forward while I struggled with my footing. I slid into the shadows and moved across the ground at lightning speed. Typically, I'd opt to exit the shadows behind someone, but Zaxis had seen my tactics in the past. Instead, I waited in the shadows and reemerged where I had been standing.

Sure enough, Zaxis had turned around in an attempt to catch me exiting the darkness.

With his back to me, I held up my hand and evoked terrors—an ability that forced someone to see their worst fears. Zaxis grabbed at his head and growled a curse. Even Forsythe jumped back, affected by my haunting visions.

I could have easily struck him with my sword, knocking him from the circle and leaving a deep wound across his back, but that seemed extreme for a sparring match.

While I debated on a less lethal tactic, Zaxis recovered and whirled around. He threw a quick jab, and on instinct, I blocked it with my blade and sliced into his forearm. I hesitated at the sight of blood—and I was about to utter an apology—but the injury didn't stop Zaxis. He hit me on the face with a left hook, the knuckles of his gloves fitted with metal.

I staggered backward, my eyes watering. Zaxis kicked me in the gut, and I fell right out of the makeshift ring and onto the dew-covered grass. It took a moment, but the pain from the punch faded. I rubbed at my cheek the entire time, irritated I hadn't dodged the attack.

"Congratulations," Forsythe cheered. He made a loud screech like only a bird could.

Zaxis held out his hand. I grabbed it, and he yanked me to my feet.

"Impressive, right?" he asked.

"I'm sorry about cutting you."

He smirked. "Forget that. Feel this." He grabbed my hand and brought it to his upper arm.

Although I had never taken note of Zaxis's physique, it became obvious then that he had been exercising. He was burlier than I had thought. The solid muscle beneath his skin made me wonder about my own arm. I jerked free of his grip and ran my hand from my elbow to my shoulder.

His bicep had felt firmer than mine. Which bothered me.

We were basically the same age. Sure, Zaxis was a couple months older—currently seventeen compared to my sixteen—but the difference in our muscles shouldn't have been that noticeable.

"Jealous?" he asked.

"You must be training every spare moment you have."

Zaxis huffed. "Of course. Haven't you noticed everything that's been happening lately? I have to be prepared."

"What're you talking about?"

"Well, besides the fact we're always running into plague creatures or dealing with pirates, everyone in the guild has been on edge." Zaxis pulled me close and lowered his voice. "We haven't left Gentel in four months—ever since returning from Calisto's ship. And fellow guild arcanists arrive every day. Guildmaster Eventide is gathering everyone."

I dwelled on his statement for a moment. "You think so?"

"Yeah. Plus, I heard one of the journeymen say we're heading to the capital to meet with the grand apothecary. We'll be escorting her somewhere."

"Zelfree and us? Or the guild?"

"The whole guild, so you know this is important." Zaxis met my gaze, his expression one of icy seriousness. "We've been lucky so far. But we can't rely on that. We've got to be able to handle problems in the future—especially if they're heading our way."

He was right. We had fought two master arcanists in the past—one plague-ridden and the other a dread pirate. Both times we had almost died. If it hadn't been for Master Zelfree, there was no doubt in my mind we'd be rotting away in caskets.

"M-My arcanist," Forsythe said as he flapped his wings. "Your pants are on fire."

Sure enough, smoke wafted up from his left pant leg. Apparently, he hadn't felt the growing flame on his clothing. He glanced down and snapped his fingers. The fire died in an instant, snuffed out by his magic.

Forsythe sighed and shook his head. "That was your last good pair."

"I can get more," Zaxis barked. "What's important is that we train!"

"I've been reading a lot about imbuing magic," I said as I pointed to his trousers. "You can create magical items like trinkets and artifacts, and I bet you could imbue some clothes with your phoenix magic to make them impervious to fire."

Zaxis mulled over the suggestion.

His red hair fluttered in the morning breeze. He brushed it aside, exposing the arcanist mark on his forehead. After a person bonded with a mystical creature, a seven-pointed star appeared etched into the skin just above their eyebrows. A picture of the mystical creature—the arcanist's eldrin—

accompanied the star, and in Zaxis's case, his mark included a phoenix.

"Don't you need star shards to make magical items?" he asked.

"Yeah."

"I don't have any of those, genius."

"Just keep it in mind. It'll save you money on clothing in the long run." I brushed the dirt off my trousers. "Are we going to spar another round? Or should you take a break to heal that cut I gave you?"

Zaxis held up his arm.

No injury.

Although arcanists healed, they didn't recover *that* fast. My sword had cut a serious gouge in his flesh! It should've taken him a couple hours to heal, at least. Maybe even longer.

I grabbed his forearm and twisted it over, looking for any sign of a lingering wound. I found nothing—not even blood.

"I'm really good with healing," Zaxis said as he yanked his arm away. "How do you think I bulked up so quickly? Normally, people are sore for days after a hard workout, even arcanists." He hooked his thumbs into the belt loops of his trousers and smiled. "But not me. I just eat a ton, and I'm good to go."

"Impressive."

A brilliant sunrise interrupted our conversation. The glorious rays washed over the ocean and cascaded across the emerald field on Gentel's shell. Chilly winds still rushed by, but the sun made them bearable.

"Here you two are."

I jumped at the sound of the gruff voice and whipped around.

Master Zelfree stood nearby, his hands in his pockets and his expression set at an aggressive neutral. When I had first met him over a year ago, he had conducted himself like a drunken slob. I probably shouldn't have thought that about the master training me, but there was no other way to describe it.

Fortunately, that was in the past.

The Zelfree of today had a sharp intelligence to his gaze. His black hair had been cut short on the top and shaved on the sides. He stood straight, and his clothes—though still uniformly dark—had been pressed smooth. When he walked, it was with purpose.

"Good morning, Master Zelfree," Zaxis said.

After a quick glance in his direction, Zelfree turned away. "Put a shirt on. This isn't a bathhouse."

"Er, well, I burned most of them."

"Most of them? Or all of them?"

"Uh... yeah." Zaxis shrugged. "All of them."

Zelfree pinched the bridge of his nose and shook his head. "Of course you did."

"I have a few extra," I said. "Zaxis can borrow one."

"Good. Make sure Zaxis gets dressed, and then the both of you can head to the library. We'll be studying there today. If you two had been in your rooms when I walked around to inform everyone, I wouldn't have had to come out here for such a trivial message."

I rubbed the back of my neck. "Sorry. We were just getting some extra practice in."

Zelfree let out a restrained exhale. "I guess I shouldn't chide you for that. You two should be training every second you can get."

"We'll hurry to the library as soon as possible."

Without any more words for us, Zelfree headed back to the guild manor house. He didn't make much noise when he walked, and his dark clothes helped him blend into the harsh shadows of morning. No wonder he had been able to creep up on us.

"Luthair," I said. "Next time warn me when he gets close."

"Yes, my arcanist."

Zaxis laced his fingers together and placed his hands on top of his head. "I still think Master Zelfree has a problem with me. He's always fussing about *something*."

I motioned to the manor house. "Uh, yeah. We'll probably never know why though, so it's best not to think about it. Let's meet up with the others."

Zaxis shot me a sideways glance, but otherwise didn't comment.

REMEDIAL STUDIES

Once Zaxis had dressed, we descended the long staircase to the ground floor. Forsythe flew ahead of us, since he hated walking, and Zaxis said he was too big to carry. He made it to the library long before we reached the halfway point. I wore my long coat, leather boots, and thick belt—a buccaneer's outfit, like most individuals who traveled long distances on a ship—but Zaxis had gone a strange route.

He wore no coat and instead pulled at the edges of the shirt I had given him. It was too small, even though I was a few inches taller. The shirt technically fit, though it stretched tight across his chest and biceps, strained by the new muscles. Zaxis tried to adjust the fabric, but nothing worked.

And instead of one belt, he had two—one to hold his trousers and the other to hold a leather pouch and his new gloves.

The lax style made him seem more like a thug than a professional, but his bronze pendant eliminated doubt. Pirates and cutthroats didn't adhere to the guild system of identification.

Before we reached the library, he placed a hand on my shoulder. We stopped, and he stared at me with a half-serious, half-flustered expression, like he didn't want to speak, but couldn't stop himself.

"I've spent a few evenings with Illia," Zaxis said, curt. "Just talking. Don't get the wrong idea."

I lifted an eyebrow, tenser than I thought I would be. "Okay."

"The problem is—she talks about you. A lot. It gets annoying."

"We did grow up together. And none of the other kids associated with us much."

Zaxis huffed and then pulled me close. "I thought you said you would help me get in her good graces."

"What do you want me to do? Tell her what she can and can't talk about?" I brushed his hand off my shoulder. "I'm sure she brings up our adoptive father a lot, too."

Our family had consisted of Gravekeeper William, each other, and the fresh corpses until we put them in the ground. For years, that was the only company we had kept, especially since we had been excluded from the festivities by the rest of the townsfolk.

But I knew what was really going on. Illia had made it clear over the last year she wanted our relationship to be something more than siblings. I just didn't want to risk losing what we had—I had grown to think of her as my sister, and it felt wrong to abandon that.

"Illia doesn't mention Gravekeeper William," Zaxis said. "Just you."

"Hm."

"Which is why you should talk about how much you admire me or something. Tell her we sparred this morning and that I completely overwhelmed you. Maybe you could say, *I wish I were half the man Zaxis is.*"

"I'm not going to say that," I snapped. "You didn't *overwhelm me*. And I don't think I'm *half the man you are*."

"It doesn't need to be true." He gave me a sardonic glower. "I just need Illia to think *you* think I'm talented."

I rubbed at my temples, both irritated and frustrated with his request. Why did his relationship with Illia have to involve me at all? I didn't want to know about anything that transpired between them. And I truly didn't want to trick Illia into thinking I admired Zaxis like some hero of old.

"I'll think about it," I muttered.

"Don't take too long. I'm tired of waiting. On the new moon, I'm going tell her how I feel."

"Why?"

He turned away and waved his hand. "It doesn't matter. That's just when I want to do it."

The new moon would be upon us in fourteen days. That seemed soon, but then again, Zaxis had been ingratiating himself to Illia for a long while now. It was about time he did something substantial about it.

"C'mon," he said. "Let's get this training over with so I can get back outside."

We finished our trek to the library in silence.

The Frith Guild library had hundreds of books, from epic legends to detailed magical research. The rows of bookshelves were thick and bottom-heavy, most likely built to stay upright during a storm. In the center of the library, forming a semi-circle, were three tables and dozens of chairs —all sturdy yet comfortable.

Master Arcanist Vala kept the library in working order. Her eldrin, a wood nymph, prevented the paper from aging and had helped craft most of the furniture. Although I had only spoken to her once or twice, it was easy to admire her work when I sat in the middle of it.

The library was spotless.

Illia, Atty, Adelgis, and Hexa sat at the largest table, most of them fighting their fatigue with a chorus of yawns. Zaxis and I joined them just as Master Zelfree entered the library. He walked over, his mimic eldrin in the shape of bangles around his wrist.

"Listen up," he said. "Today we need to move forward with your understanding of magic. I've never had six apprentices at one time, and it's proving to be difficult. I apologize for not getting around to this sooner."

Hexa—a woman with cinnamon hair and deep scars on her sun-tanned arms—leaned back in her chair and shrugged. "Well, it's not like we've made it easy for you."

"Even if you all have made reckless decisions," Zelfree said with a sigh, "I still should've sat you down and had this conversation a long time ago."

"If you say so."

Hexa's hydra eldrin, Raisen, sat under her chair. His two heads poked over the edge of the table, the double set of gold eyes shifting from one person to another. Whenever someone stared back, he hissed and glared.

Zelfree motioned to the two empty tables. "The fact of the matter is some of you are excelling in your magic even without my instruction. Others are struggling. We can't have that. When you move on from your apprenticeship and become journeymen, you'll be expected to handle serious tasks."

Again, Hexa interjected. "Like with pirates and raiders?"

"Yes. You can't be amateurs then—you'll endanger yourself, your teammates, and the assignment. So, to better help those who are being left behind, I'm going to work with them personally."

"What about the people who're excelling?" Zaxis asked.

"I'll give you a direction, and you'll study as a group."

Seemingly satisfied with that answer, Zaxis relaxed back in his chair and waited for the rest of the instructions. Hexa scooted closer, her brow furrowed as she looked him up and down.

"You're lookin' good," she whispered. "Your exercise is really paying off."

He flexed an arm. "Right? You should've seen me sparring this morning."

"You were sparring? I wanna join."

Zelfree slammed his hand on the table. Everyone flinched and snapped their attention back to him.

"Let's not lollygag," Zelfree said. "We have too much to go over." He turned to me. "Volke, I know you're second-bonded, but you've improved your sorcery tremendously. You're also the only one in the group who has imbued something with magic and made a permanent item."

I nodded along with his words, unsure of how to reply. Was he singling me out?

He continued, "I've seen you evoke terrors and manipulate shadows, but you struggle with augmentation magic. Sure, you've learned to see in the dark—but knightmare arcanists can allow others to see in the dark. They can also target who is affected by their terrors. So far, I haven't seen you display any of that."

"I'm sorry," I said. "I—"

"Let me finish," Zelfree growled. "These are just the next steps I want you to focus on." He motioned to the left table. "You sit here. This is the table for people who will study on their own."

I got up and hurried to the table. Knightmare arcanists could allow other people to see in the dark? I could control my terrors? Those were both news to me, and I felt somewhat embarrassed that Zelfree had to tell me. Then again, knightmare were rare. There weren't many stories about their arcanists.

Zelfree glanced over at Zaxis and then pointed to the same table. "You're a natural with your healing augmentation, but it can be improved even further. Not only that, but you should practice your fire evocation and manipulation. Since you're immune to the effects of heat, you can use that to your advantage."

Zaxis got up and sat across from me at the same table. Forsythe, dropping soot the whole way, hopped over and flapped into the nearest empty chair.

"How?" Zaxis asked. "Besides burning people, what should I do with fire?"

"Lots of phoenix arcanists have gone on to become blacksmiths since forges exude powerful heat. Or, if you're determined to become a pugilist, phoenix arcanists superheat their metal weapons."

Everyone in the library perked up at the thought of white-hot weapons.

Well, everyone except for Adelgis. He had been the only one seemingly interested by the idea of becoming a blacksmith.

"I have metal knuckles," Zaxis said. "Can I make those hot?"

Zelfree scratched at his chin as he thought the question over. "What kind of metal?"

"Steel."

"Why?"

"Uh, because it's the strongest?"

"Don't use steel. It might be sturdy, but copper has a high thermal conductivity."

Zaxis shook his head. "What does that mean?"

"It means some metals heat up faster than others. Copper gets hot quick, so you won't have to use much magic or concentration to make it a deadly weapon. Steel, while durable, doesn't get hot nearly as fast."

"I didn't know that..."

"That's why you should study quietly at this table for today. I know you've been focusing on the physical aspect of your powers"—Zelfree motioned to his whole body and frowned— "but reading a damn book every once in a while wouldn't hurt you. Knowledge can be a deadly tool as well."

Zaxis gritted his teeth and said nothing.

I agreed with Zelfree.

As arcanists of the Frith Guild, it was our duty to help those in need, especially against villains and tyrants, but brute strength sometimes wasn't enough. Tactics and cunning plans were sometimes required, especially if the opponent used dastardly tricks. We needed every advantage we could get.

Zelfree surveyed Hexa. "You should sit with Volke and Zaxis. The rest of you will sit at the other table. I'll be helping you all understand—"

"M-Master Zelfree!"

The shout startled me, and I had to spin around in my chair to see the speaker. It was none other than Reo, a journeyman ogata toad arcanist within the guild. I always saw him about, but we didn't interact much.

Reo hustled over, his robes flowing and his thin-framed glasses sliding down his nose. He pushed them up twice while making his way across the library. Once he reached

Zelfree's side, he whispered something and then motioned to the door.

"I'll be right back," Zelfree said to us. Then he pointed to me. "No one is to leave this library, understand?"

I hated it when he singled me out to be "the keeper" of the group whenever he left, but it wasn't like I could tell him *no*.

"All right," I replied.

Zelfree and Reo wove between the tables and headed straight for the door, leaving me, Hexa, Zaxis, Atty, Adelgis, and Illia alone in the library. Although this was Master Vala's research domain, she wasn't in today—I had no idea why. I hadn't even seen her wood nymph eldrin.

The silence stretched on for a few moments until Zaxis leaned forward on the table.

"Adelgis," he said. "What's going on?"

Out of everyone in the group, Adelgis was the most distinct. Even his posture was different from everyone else—he sat perfectly straight, his hands in his lap, his head held high. He wore more clothing than anyone else, too. A shirt, a coat, a shoulder cape, and high boots, all pristine and pressed.

Adelgis lifted a perfect eyebrow. "What makes you think I know what's going on?"

"Don't play dumb with me." Zaxis scoffed. "Everyone here knows you listen to people's thoughts. What did Journeyman Reo come rushing in here for?"

"I don't listen *all* the time."

Adelgis's eldrin—an ethereal whelk by the name of Felicity—was also the most distinct mystical creature I had ever seen. She was, basically, a floating sea snail. With tentacles. Ethereal whelks had the power over light and dreams, which meant Adelgis could tap into the minds of others. He had been listening to thoughts for months now, even after I had told him it was a violation of privacy.

Felicity typically hid in the light, much like Luthair hid in the darkness, but today she floated around her arcanist, her shell and body glittering like pure crystal.

"Journeyman Reo had disturbing news, I'm afraid," she said, her voice light and sing-song.

"What is it?" Hexa asked. She brushed back her tangled mess of curly hair, exposing her hydra arcanist mark. "Did something happen? Is it pirates?"

Adelgis shook his head. "Not that. Reo's concerned about something else."

"I knew you were listening," Zaxis said, smirking. "I can't believe you even tried to deny it. Just tell us what's going on."

After a short exhale, Adelgis replied, "Apparently, we'll be escorting Lady Dravon—the grand apothecary—across the continent. And she'll have plague-ridden creatures with her."

Everyone exchanged troubled looks.

No one wanted to deal with the arcane plague. It drove mystical creatures and arcanists insane. Their laughing-mad delusions often led to disaster. I would know—I had fought several in my life—and it was only a matter of time before I became infected if I kept messing with them. That blood-borne illness could get into an injury, and we didn't have a cure.

Zaxis smacked me on the shoulder. "I told you something would happen. I bet you it gets worse from here."

I nodded.

"But why would she be transporting plague creatures?" Zaxis asked.

Adelgis replied, "She's researching a cure for the arcane

plague, remember? I'm sure it has something to do with that."

"Still. None of her insane creatures better get out."

While Adelgis typically kept his long hair in a ponytail, today he had it down. It shone like an inky waterfall, and he ran his fingers through it like it was a nervous tic.

"Wait," Hexa said as she glanced between the tables. "Are you telling me that I'm in the advanced magic group, but Atty and Illia aren't?" Then she laughed so loud it echoed between the bookshelves. "Seriously? I thought you guys were Zelfree's favorites."

Atty and Illia said nothing.

Like Zaxis, Atty had her phoenix eldrin, Titania, in the library with her. Titania puffed out her feathers, exposing the harsh glow of fire that made up her body.

"My arcanist is very proficient with her evocation," Titania said. "More skilled than anyone else here, in fact. She just needs... help with other aspects of her sorcery. That's no reason to mock." Soot fell to the floor.

"I'm just shocked," Hexa said with a shrug. "That's all."

I was surprised Atty had any trouble with magic. When we had been younger and both living on the Isle of Ruma, she was always the best at everything. Reading, writing, arithmetic—she mastered anything she set her mind to. Why was she struggling now?

Atty swept back her golden hair, her face slightly red as she turned away from Hexa. The two of them couldn't be more different. Hexa wore a sleeveless coat to expose her scarred and muscled arms—Atty had the long, flowing robes of a scholar. Hexa sat with her legs spread and her elbows on the table—Atty locked her ankles and used the armrests when appropriate.

After that last statement, the others devolved into quiet

conversations amongst themselves and their eldrin. Not Illia, however. She stood up from her chair and took a seat at my table, despite what Zelfree had said.

She chose the chair right next to mine and offered me a sly smile. Half her face—the half marred with knife scars—was covered by a triangular eyepatch. It didn't look like other eyepatches, however. A rizzel had been stitched into the black fabric, its ferret-like body curved around and its face smiling with mischief.

The design matched the arcanist star on Illia's forehead.

I liked the eyepatch. Not because it covered her scars, but because Illia seemed more confident with it on. Before she had it, Illia would keep her hair in front of her face, but now she tied it back, exposing her smile and slender neck. I never thought of her as ugly, but I had never thought of her as beautiful or striking until she had started that habit.

I took note of it today.

Illia stared at me with her one eye, a playful expression across her face.

"What's that look for?" she asked.

I rubbed at my neck and stared at the table. "Nothing. We should probably be concerned about the plague creatures, though."

"It'll be fine. Lady Dravon has kept those creatures locked away in her lab for years."

"I don't like the fact we'll be so close to them."

"Don't worry." Illia placed her hand on my knee and squeezed. "I'll protect you."

She said it in a joking tone, and Hexa chuckled under her breath.

Zaxis broke off his conversation with Forsythe and tapped his knuckles on the table. "Whoa, wait a minute. Are you offering that to anyone? Because I'd love it if you protected me."

"Don't be weird," Illia said as she rolled her eye. "I'm just playing around."

As if summoned by the commotion, Illia's eldrin, Nicholin, poked his head out of her giant coat pocket. His blue eyes were half-open in a groggy state, and his brilliant white fur had been plastered to one side, as though he had slept on it wrong. With a cute little ferret squeak, he stretched and then glanced up at his arcanist.

"Has Master Zelfree given us an assignment yet? I'm ready for—" Nicholin yawned for a long moment. "—I'm ready for whatever. Apple hunt, underground death maze, counting the hairs on a griffin's butt... whatever whimsical trial he has in store."

Illia petted Nicholin as he dragged himself out of her pocket and lazily climbed up her sleeve to reach her shoulder. Then he stared at me and swished his tail.

"Volke, you have dirt in your hair. Stop it."

I ran a hand over my head. Flakes of burned soil fell onto my coat and shirt.

"That's from when I bested Volke at our sparring match," Zaxis said. "You should've been there, Illia. I won in a matter of seconds."

He gave me a look—distinct and pointed—and I knew he wanted me to say something along the lines of, *Zaxis is the most amazing person of all time, Illia! I wish I could compare to his rugged good looks and incredible skillset. Alas, I am but a sad sack who will never be as great as he is right now.*

Instead, I went with, "Zaxis has been training a lot. It's paid off. Right, Forsythe?"

The phoenix lifted his head and puffed out his chest

feathers. "Oh, yes. Zaxis has dedicated himself morning, noon, and night to his magical advancement."

Illia forced a smile. "Wow. I guess I'll have to watch one of these sparring matches, won't I?"

"I'd love that," Zaxis said. "I can show you everything I've learned."

The door to the library opened, and everyone fell silent. Illia gave me one final look before she teleported back to the table with Atty and Adelgis. Her magic caused a pop and a sprinkle of silver, but that was the only indication it had happened.

In my opinion, Illia had a knack for rizzel powers, but for some reason, she hadn't learned what she could manipulate. It was easy for phoenix arcanists—they manipulated fire. And I had learned I could manipulate shadows. But what did a teleporting rizzel do? I hoped Zelfree would just tell her, so that the mystery could finally be solved.

Zelfree took his position at the front of the group. He lifted his arm, and a pair of bangles around his wrist shook and transformed into a mimic—a gray cat with two-toned eyes. She leapt onto the table with me, Zaxis, and Hexa.

"Traces will keep you all on track," Zelfree said. "And I'm going to help these three. By nightfall, I want you three to have made significant progress, understood? So don't slack."

Traces trotted across the table, her long tail pointed straight up. "Get to work, apprentices! My arcanist is concerned for your safety. We have an important mission coming up, and none of you are prepared."

"What is it?" Hexa asked.

"Trust me, you'll learn soon enough. Right now, focus on studying."

3

AN EPIC JOURNEY

No matter what I did, I couldn't seem to empower anyone else with my knightmare magic.

Hexa and I sat on the same side of the table, our chairs turned to face one another. I had tried everything—focusing on my magic, thinking about my dark sight while concentrating—but nothing seemed to work. Unlike my other abilities, where I had to actively use them, the dark sight just *happened*. How was I supposed to transfer that?

I placed my hand on Hexa's knee and focused again.

Would this be the one obstacle I couldn't overcome?

No. Of course not. I had faced pirates and plague-ridden monsters... I could master this. I just had to concentrate.

I twisted my fingers into the fabric of Hexa's trousers.

She stared at me, her eyes half-lidded in a bored glare. "You're really bad at this."

"Let me focus," I growled. "Maybe I should approach it from a different angle..."

"We've been doing this for hours."

"Has it really been that long?" I glanced out the window.

The majesty of a calm sky and ocean caught my attention. It took me a moment to realize how high the sun had risen. "I'm sorry. I didn't notice."

"Hm." She leaned back in her seat and exhaled. "You've been too busy staring a hole into my knee to notice anything. It was cute for the first few minutes. Then it got creepy. Now it's just sad."

"Fine, what do you want to practice?" I asked as I yanked my hand away. "I don't recall Master Zelfree saying what you should learn."

"We talked this morning." Hexa scratched at her head, her gaze on the ceiling. "He said my combat strategies were *ineffective*." The last word came out as a huff. "He also said I needed a weapon, but I told him I didn't study anything like that back home. He gave me books to read." She pointed to a small sack by her seat. "But they're all pretty boring. What am I even looking for?"

"Did you ever use a bow or a knife?"

"I skinned deer a couple times." She held out her hand and traced a thin scar with her index finger. "See this? I cut myself pretty bad when I was younger." Then she pointed to a twisted scar on her forearm. "And this was when I fell on a knife. Not my proudest moment, but I'd do it all over again if it meant escaping this library."

"Uh..." I crossed my arms, uninterested in her past injuries. "You evoke poison, right?"

Her eyes lit up, and she slid forward in her chair. "Yeah. The problem is actually catching anyone with it since my magic creates a gas. Raisen can bite them, and then you'll immediately get sick, but he's slow."

We both turned to look at her eldrin. Raisen sat on the floor, his four legs tucked under his fat, alligator-like body.

One head was asleep while the other met our gazes with a questioning glance.

One head could sleep while the other was awake? How was that even possible? I pondered the mystery for a long while before I remembered my previous thoughts.

"Hexa," I said. "You're also slow."

"What was that?" she snapped.

Raisen's one awake head hissed in my direction.

I held up my hands. "No, I mean *physically* slow. I've never seen you move with great haste. Or be very stealthy. Or even graceful, really."

"*Get to the point*," she growled, her body stiff and her eyes set in a glower.

"I'm saying you should try to catch your opponents without relying on grabbing or biting them. What about a pistol? You could coat the bullet in Raisen's poison. You said your poison works fast, right? You'll incapacitate your enemy with a single shot—even an arcanist."

I had gotten the idea from pirates. They would coat their bullets in plague-ridden blood and then fire them at arcanists or their eldrin. It was a dastardly tactic, but effective. If Hexa could master the flintlock pistol, she could use her magical abilities to their fullest potential.

Then again, the Dread Pirate Calisto had a magical item that made him immune to poison—even king basilisk venom—so my tactic wouldn't work for Hexa all the time. Still, it was better than nothing.

Hexa mulled over my suggestion. Then she relaxed into her chair and folded her arms over her chest. "That's not a bad plan."

"Maybe you could also carry throwing knives. Just in case."

"Yeah…"

The Frith Guild had several equipment storage rooms, including an armory. I had never bothered to ask for anything, however, since Luthair and I could merge. I gained the benefit of his shadow armor and sword—and now my shield—so what was the point in carrying anything else?

Hexa lightly kicked my shin with her boot. "Illia was right. You're pretty clever and not just the try-hard I thought you were."

"Thank you?" I wasn't sure if I enjoyed the backhanded compliment, however.

"C'mon. You should focus harder on learning whatever it was that Master Zelfree told you to learn."

"Allowing others to see in the dark," I muttered.

"Right. Yeah." She glanced around. "Sure you want to do this in the middle of a well-lit library?"

"It doesn't matter. My magic stings when I use it. I'll know if I affected you."

"Maybe we should hide between the bookshelves. Just in case that helps."

Although I wasn't certain that would do anything, I shrugged and followed her away from the table.

Several hours later, and I had made no progress.

"Everyone to the map room," Zelfree shouted, his voice echoing in the silent library. "We have a guild meeting to attend."

His voice startled me. I jumped to my feet, eager to see what a guild meeting would entail. I had technically been to one before—when Zelfree had accepted the others as his apprentices—but half the guild had been away on their own assignments at the time. Today would be different. The other master arcanists had returned, and I had no idea what we would be discussing.

Traces, who had fallen asleep on the table while watching Zaxis read, stretched like only a cat could and then bounded off to be with her arcanist.

I left the library, and the others followed soon after. Illia jogged to my side and kept pace. She maintained a slight smile, and I wondered if she was as curious as I was. Nicholin positioned himself on her shoulder and puffed out his chest, almost like he was trying to appear bigger and more regal.

It didn't take us long to cross from one side of the guild manor house to the other.

Zelfree opened the door to the map room, and Illia and I stepped inside.

Out of all the rooms here, the map room was by far the largest. A massive table with a topographical map carved across the top took up most of the space, but the table acted as the guild's navigation system. Guildmaster Eventide must have imbued the piece of furniture with her atlas turtle magic, because Gentel could sense where any tokens were placed, and she swam in the direction indicated.

Despite the spacious room, the place was packed with arcanists and guild staff. Of the seventy people jammed close together, thirty of them had to be chefs, dockhands, and cleaning crew. According to the metal on everyone's guild pendants, about fourteen of them were apprentices, twenty-one were journeymen, four were masters, and only Eventide held the title of grandmaster.

That last number seemed low for the legendary Frith Guild. I remembered stories involving at least 10 master arcanists. That had been a long time ago, however, and those who achieved the title of *grandmaster* often left to form their own guilds or cities.

Although Illia and I were pushed toward the wall to allow for everyone else to enter, I was tall enough to see everything happening.

Guildmaster Liet Eventide stood at the head of the map table. She was the only arcanist who had a mark that glowed with an inner power. Her hat, adorned with an array of feathers, couldn't hide the fact, either.

The library master, Master Arcanist Vala, waited by Eventide's side, her body similar to a lamppost. She stood tall, but if she turned to the side, she might disappear. Vala's wood nymph—a humanoid woman with skin of birch tree bark and the branches of a willow tree for hair—stayed close by.

I couldn't identify the others in the room, however. Everyone was too packed in, and most were facing away from me. I would recognize the master arcanists as soon as I saw them. The most powerful arcanists in the Frith Guild were all legends, and a piece of me wanted the meeting to end just so I could greet them.

I placed my hand on Illia's shoulder and leaned in close. "Everyone seems tense." I tried to keep my voice low, but excitement laced my words.

Illia stood on her tiptoes. "I wonder what's happening." She smirked. "I hope they send Master Zelfree somewhere and we get to accompany him."

Her own enthusiasm stoked my imagination. "Maybe we'll be sent to find a rare mystical creature."

"I'm hoping to cut down pirates."

"Oh! Maybe we'll be gathering magical resources for Gillie. She's coming to the guild, right? That has to be what—"

"Shh," someone hissed from the crowd.

I hadn't realized how loud I had become. I swallowed the last of my words as my face grew hot.

Nicholin crossed his little front arms. "Hmpf. Do they know who they're dealing with? I'm not the kind of rizzel to sit around and wait, thank you very much."

Hexa, Zaxis, Atty, and Adelgis funneled into the map room and made for the opposite corner. When Zelfree headed toward the map table, the journeymen and apprentices moved to the side.

"Greetings, everyone," Guildmaster Eventide said, smiling.

Her long, silver hair shone with a metallic hue. Unlike the other arcanists in the room, who remained youthful despite their actual age, Eventide always had an older appearance, like she was in her mid-sixties.

"I have news to discuss with you before we arrive in Fortuna," she continued. "This is of the upmost importance and should not be discussed in the presence of those outside the guild."

Illia and I exchanged glances. Still, even with the troubling tone the conversation had taken, she met my gaze with a coy smile, as though to say, *This'll be fun.*

Eventide grazed her fingers along the edge of the map table. "The grand apothecary has made major advancements in her research. She wrote me to say she's crafted a trinket that grants the wearer immunity to the arcane plague."

The excited muttering betrayed the room's collective exhilaration.

The grand apothecary—better known as Gillie by most —had discovered a way to prevent the plague from spreading to others? This news had to be shared with the world! Why would Eventide want us to keep quiet?

Guildmaster Eventide lifted a hand, and everyone fell silent. She took a moment to gather her thoughts before speaking. I didn't like her neutral expression. Why wasn't she celebrating like the rest of us?

"The materials to create this magical item are limited," she said. "Because of this, the grand apothecary has asked us to escort her to Thronehold so that she may speak with their queen about resources."

Oh. I hadn't thought about the cost of crafting magical items. While I was certain there were enough arcanists capable of making them, star shards were hard to come by. You couldn't mine them like other gems or metals—they fell from the sky, which was how they got their name. Sure, in some places they rained down more than others, but it was still a rare event.

"Arcanist Queen Velleta?" Zelfree asked. He shook his head, his irritation plain to see. "She isn't the charitable type."

"Given that the arcane plague is an enemy to magic itself, which includes Queen Velleta, I think she'll be more inclined to aid in the creation of trinkets—or even a cure."

The silence grew thick. Illia's smile deepened into a frown.

Now I understood why they weren't happy.

When I was younger, Gravekeeper William had taught us all about the history of our islands and the mainland nations. They weren't interesting stories, at least not to me. I always found myself returning to the tales of swashbucklers or rogues, but I remembered enough to recognize the name of a queen.

Technically, our island nation had once been ruled by Arcanist Queen Velleta. The Argo Empire, her seat of power, had conquered half the world—or so everyone claimed—but over time, the edges of her territory had broken away and claimed independence. Our island nation had fought off her Royal Navy and established a new monarchy and ruling council in Fortuna. Gravekeeper William was even an officer for our queen.

Arcanist Queen Velleta had never been popular, at least not in the stories I had heard. The Argo Empire was the largest and most powerful in terms of arcanists, history, and territory, and yet somehow she lost land and allies more often than any other ruler. Would she help the grand apothecary find a cure for the plague? I didn't know, but her empire was wealthy, from the last I heard.

"That isn't the only reason we'll be heading to Thronehold," Guildmaster Eventide continued. She tapped her knuckles on the table, her hesitation unusual. With slow and deliberate words, she added, "I have reason to believe a world serpent has been born and that it has yet to bond."

The whole guild held their collective breath. The heat of the room weighed heavily on me.

I knew there was a world serpent somewhere out there, and I had been the one to tell Eventide, though I did so in confidence. Why would she tell everyone now? If this information got out—

"I also have reason to believe that scoundrels of the highest order are out to find the serpent before anyone else," the guildmaster said. "Therefore, our primary objective when we get to Thronehold is to gather the tools necessary to claim the world serpent ourselves *before* dread pirates like Calisto can get their bloody hands on it."

The room filled with an anxious buzz.

Illia ran her fingers over the stitching on her eyepatch. As if tracing the picture of the rizzel enhanced her excitement, she turned to me with light in her eye. "I can't believe it."

With all the talking in the room, I almost couldn't hear her. I leaned in closer. "Can't believe what? We were the ones to confirm the birth of a world serpent in the first place."

"I can't believe we're going to participate in such a major event! All of our previous assignments have been amateurish. *Escort a messenger. Watch over a bonding ceremony. Guard a boat.* But now we're going to help find a world serpent. How are you not giddy beyond reason?"

I hadn't thought of it like that, probably because two of our assignments had actually ended in fighting master arcanists. Gregory Ruma and the Dread Pirate Calisto were enough adventure for three lifetimes, but finding a world serpent would be different. This would be like the tales of old—an epic adventure to the far reaches of the ocean, beyond the tallest mountains, and through the thickest forests.

This would be an adventure they would write books about. Just thinking about it got my heart racing with anticipation.

Nicholin snickered. "There's that familiar expression! Volke's on board."

"This is everything you had hoped for ever since we were kids," Illia said.

Guildmaster Eventide tapped her knuckles on the map table. Everyone quieted their conversations.

"The fastest route to Thronehold will be over land," she said as she pointed to a mountain range. "We'll disembark at Fortuna, meet with the grand apothecary, and then travel through the Clawdam Mountains."

Geography was another subject I hadn't cared for when I was younger. William seemed to know every location on the map, including the latitude and longitude of most major cities—apparently, it had been one of his duties as a naval officer—but none of that seemed interesting to me as a kid.

Thankfully, the map table's to-scale model of the surrounding territory made it easy to understand the journey. Fortuna was north of Thronehold, and the Clawdam Mountains were in between. There was no ocean route that would take us there quickly, even though Thronehold was positioned near a river. We would have to take the long road and pay the tolls at the turnpikes.

I had never traveled to the Argo Empire before. I had barely ever left the Isle of Ruma.

Guildmaster Eventide addressed the library master. "Vala, I'm hoping you and a handful of journeymen will stay here in the guild to watch over everything."

Vala herself looked like a tree. Her bony fingers, some knotted at the joints, long face, and oak-brown hair added to the overall woodland aesthetic.

She smiled. "I will maintain the guild while you're away."

The guildmaster would be coming with us? That surprised me—arcanists who traveled too far from their eldrin weakened their magical powers. Thronehold was 250 miles from Fortuna, according to the map. She couldn't take her giant atlas turtle across land. Would Eventide have access to her abilities once we arrived?

"Gallus?" Eventide turned her gaze to someone in the

crowd. "Your two apprentices will become journeymen soon, isn't that correct?"

"Right you are."

I didn't even need to see him. He was Gallus the Gray, the younger brother of Gali the Red. While Gali had been a murderer best known for killing a master arcanist with king basilisk venom, Gallus was the complete opposite. He and his eldrin, a fearsome kraken, swashbuckled their way into countless tales. Gallus had even helped Gregory Ruma and Zelfree on several occasions.

I wished I could get a better view, but the journeyman in front of me huffed. A large ogata toad, weighing just as much as an adult male—Reo's eldrin—ribbited in irritation.

Eventide smiled. "You should stay here as well, Gallus. A new boatful of fresh arcanists should be arriving from the islands, and you and your apprentices can administer the recruitment tests. It's my goal for the future to see the Frith Guild double in size and influence."

"It shall be done," Gallus replied, a jovial tone to his voice.

That made sense. A kraken couldn't join us in Thronehold. Gallus would be better suited sticking to the islands.

"Lastly, where is Yesna?" Eventide asked. "Oh, there you are. I want you to travel to the islands in the region and approach arcanists no longer affiliated with any guild. We'll need all the help we can get."

Although I couldn't see Master Yesna, I was excited to hear she was still among the Frith Guild. Some called her the *Ace of Cutlasses*, due to her dueling style.

"I'll handle it," Yesna answered from somewhere in the crowd.

Eventide tapped her hand on the table. "Then it's settled. Zelfree and I will protect the grand apothecary until we reach Thronehold. From there, we'll acquire the tools and knowledge to retrieve the world serpent from its hidden lair." She motioned to the doors. "We should be arriving at Fortuna sometime tomorrow morning. Everyone traveling to Thronehold should take the time to prepare for the trek."

4

THE SOVEREIGN DRAGON TOURNAMENT

I couldn't sleep.

Instead, I packed everything I needed—including my last two gold leafs—into my personal satchel. For the entire evening, I paced my room, imagining the grand walls of Thronehold. Outside of epic tales, which were likely exaggerated, I couldn't recall any hard details about the city.

"Luthair," I said. "Have you been to Thronehold?"

"Yes, my arcanist."

"What's it like?"

"The queen's royal guard is comprised of pegasus and unicorn arcanists, and they regularly patrol the massive and winding roads that make up the heart of the city. Merchants from all around the world gather in the central district marketplace. Streetlamps, and the noble city guard, keep the people safe."

I stopped walking. The shadows at my feet shifted across the floor. I stared down at them as I asked, "Is it a grand sight to behold?"

"Indeed."

"Is it larger than Fortuna?"

"Much larger."

Wanderlust shot through me like lightning. Thronehold sounded amazing. My tiny Isle of Ruma had a city guard of four men, each twenty years older than the last. We had a single road that went straight through town. Thinking about the comparisons almost made me laugh.

The sound of tapping drew my attention.

Illia stood outside my window. She waved once I noticed her and then popped into my bedroom with a quick teleport. Like me, she had all her belongings packed. Her clothes and valuables had been crammed into a leather backpack.

"Are you ready?" she asked.

Nicholin poked his head out of the backpack. "Illia, I thought you said you were bringing cakes?"

"We'll grab those in the kitchen before we head out."

He twirled his whiskers with his paws. "Excellent."

They both seemed enthusiastic about the trip, which was odd. Had Illia ever been this excited for random adventure? I tilted my head. "You two seem livelier than I expected."

"We need to find the world serpent," Illia stated. "It's all I've been able to think about."

"Why do we *need to*? It might be better if it stays hidden."

She stared at me with her one eye, an expression of sarcastic exasperation. "Anything Calisto is after, I'm going to take from him. He wants the world serpent. Now I'm going to make sure he never gets it."

"Yeah," Nicholin chimed in.

"Who do you think will bond with it?" I asked.

In theory, world serpents were the eldrin of gods. Their magic could create and alter the land, and their scales were impervious to damage. A world serpent arcanist would be vastly more powerful, even right after bonding, than most arcanists. I was certain—according to the tales—an apprentice world serpent arcanist could defeat a master arcanist of any variety with little trouble.

"I don't care who bonds with it," Illia stated. "All I care is that Calisto doesn't."

It seemed petty, but I couldn't fault her for it.

Nicholin pointed to the growing brightness of the sunrise. "We should hurry for the cakes!"

Illia gave me one last smile before she disappeared with a soft pop and sparkle. I didn't want to be late, either. I grabbed my satchel and rushed from my bedroom on the third story of the manor house. With a wellspring of energy, I flew down the stairs. Luthair stayed close the entire time, slithering through the shadows at a rapid pace, unnoticed by most.

Unconcerned by the other journeymen and apprentices rushing to get ready, I exited the building and took a deep breath, invigorated by the ocean breeze. The orange glow of a new day bathed the green field of the atlas turtle shell in a soft light. In the distance, less than half a mile away, was the port of Fortuna. The sounds of a busy city mixed with the cry of seagulls.

While most of the guild remained indoors, Hexa and Zaxis were out by the pond. Zaxis had recreated his sparring circle. He stood in the middle, a punchable look of arrogance across his face. Hexa sat on the outside, her eldrin in her lap, her brow furrowed.

Raisen's two hydra heads seemed at odds with each other. One hissed at Zaxis while the other nuzzled Hexa's palm.

I approached them with an eyebrow raised.

Zaxis greeted me with a wave. "Good. Now I can get even more practice in."

His shirt—well, *my* shirt—was singed at the sleeves. I stared at the damage for a moment before offering him a glare.

He shrugged. "It's just clothes."

"What's going on?"

"Hexa and I were sparring. She lost, just like you."

His taunt almost made me forget why I was excited in the first place. A piece of me wanted to throw him right out of his faux ring, but I held back the urge and knelt next to Hexa. She met my gaze with a clenched jaw.

"What is it?" she asked.

"Are you okay?"

"Of course I'm okay."

Raisen snapped at me, and I flinched back.

"R-Right," I muttered. "Sorry for asking."

Hexa stood and tied back her curly cinnamon hair. "Zaxis has gotten a lot faster, I'll give him that much, but I think he made the ring small on purpose. We barely started, and he just pushed me out."

"That's not what happened," Zaxis snapped. "You charged at me, and I used your own momentum to hurl you out."

"And you wouldn't let me use my evocation!"

"I wasn't using mine, either! It was a fair fight."

"Ha. Fair." Hexa rolled her eyes.

I rubbed at my neck. "Hexa, what about the pistol or throwing knives I talked about?"

Her eyebrows shot up as she slid a hand into the pouch tied at her belt. She had a set of three knives wrapped in leather. "I did get these."

"And you didn't use them?" I asked, trying to hold back my sarcasm.

"Well, no. I didn't think about it."

"You once told me that hydra don't move around much."

Hexa nodded. "Just look at Raisen. He's still a baby, and already his body is thick. Adult hydras are way too huge to move around." She jiggled Raisen's sides. His body reminded me of an alligator mixed with a fat cat. All belly, no legs. The necks of his heads reminded me of snakes, however. Long and thin.

"You should use his stoutness in your personal fighting style," I said. "Plant yourself like you're a hydra, and then place Raisen in front of you. You evoke poison gas, and once you master that—and you don't poison yourself—you can waft it around you. Think of it like a deadly moat. You can stay behind those barriers and throw poisoned knives or fire a pistol. Make the enemy come to you."

"They'll have to get past me first," Raisen said, one head held high.

"That's right," I said. "Shred their ankles like one of those yappy dogs."

Raisen snapped at me again.

This time I tumbled back, half-chuckling. "I was joking, of course. I'm sure you'll be big enough one day to eat a man whole."

"I'm still capable of ending you, even if I am small."

I didn't know why, but imagining Raisen nip at people with both heads kept me laughing to myself, despite him hissing at me the entire time.

Hexa mulled over my suggestion. I didn't know if she would implement it, considering she liked to get up close and personal with people, but it would maximize her effectiveness, given her talents. She was reckless, and while thrashing around could do some harm, real tactics always won at the end of the day.

"Hey," Zaxis said. "Stop giving her pointers and get into the ring. Everyone will be ready to go soon, and I want a few more matches."

I stood and brushed myself off. "I thought Zelfree told you to read a book."

"Don't get smart with me." He pointed to a book lying on the grass, soaking in the morning dew. "That's on metallurgy."

"Zelfree said *read*, not *throw it on the lawn*."

"Yesterday I spent all afternoon studying gunpowder." Zaxis snapped his fingers and ignited a flame. "I'm going to impress Master Zelfree with a few tricks of my own."

With the excitement of a legendary journey still in my system, I smiled. "I can't wait to see what's up your sleeve."

"Then get in the ring."

"Later. We're about to leave."

"Heh." Zaxis crossed his arms and smirked. "You're never gonna compare to all those master arcanists in your fairy tales if you're too afraid of losing to me. I don't recall the Pillar praising wet trousers and cowardice."

Despite my good mood, his taunting never failed to get under my skin. I stepped up to the edge of the circle, ready to make him eat his words. "I don't think we should have any restrictions. You, me, Luthair, Forsythe—let's see what really happens."

Zaxis gritted his teeth and took a moment to think over my challenge. Was he afraid? I felt rather confident. I would win this match, and perhaps he knew it, too.

"Hey, everyone!"

Illia waved to us from the docks near the atlas turtle's fin. I waved back. Then she motioned to a nearby dinghy.

Several apprentices and journeymen had loaded their supplies and headed toward Fortuna. I had planned to wait for Zelfree, but I didn't see any harm in heading into town if others from the guild were, too.

"Well, if we're not going to spar, I'm going to head into the city," I said. "See you two later."

They exchanged quick looks—Hexa with a half-smile, Zaxis with an ever-deepening frown.

It would take us ten days to reach Thronehold, which would give us some time to practice our sorcery. I had promised myself I would make use of that time, even if it hurt me to use my magic. I just couldn't let that hold me back, especially since Zelfree said I needed to train until everything came second nature—until I couldn't get it wrong.

Hexa stood. "Yeah, let's go."

"Fine," Zaxis said with a sigh.

They both gathered up their traveling satchels, and the three of us headed toward the docks. While we walked, Zaxis reached into his belongings and withdrew a leather pouch. The moment he opened it, a pungent odor of meat wafted onto the morning wind. He plucked a piece of fish jerky from the pouch and took an impressive bite.

"Eating again?" Hexa asked, an eyebrow lifted. "What is this? Third breakfast?"

Zaxis didn't answer. He finished his piece and then grabbed another.

Illia and Nicholin readied the dinghy and had it set to go once we arrived. The four of us got in, but we had to wait for Raisen. It took Hexa some effort to lift him up and position him in the middle of the boat. Although he had been with us on several trips across the ocean, both his heads frowned whenever we had to board or disembark.

"We don't like this," the left head said.

"Can't we just wait here?" the right one asked.

Hexa shook her head. "It'll be fine."

Raisen was getting bigger. He probably weighed more than a hundred pounds, which was twice his weight last year. It made sense. Hydras become gigantic over the course of their lives. From what I remembered, most reached ten tons.

Nicholin teleported to the bow with a pop and puff of glitter. He pointed with his little front paw. "Row, ye sea dogs! Put your backs into it!"

Zaxis and I both sat down and picked up oars. Nicholin scurried up my coat and clung to my shoulder. I rowed once, and then he hit my cheek with his ferret-like tail.

"Faster!" he commanded.

I wasn't about to play this game. I shoved him off my shoulder. He teleported next to Zaxis, but before he could climb up, Zaxis gritted his teeth and growled a threat I couldn't fully hear.

Nicholin scooted away with a half-laugh. "I think my crew might be plotting a mutiny."

Illia took a seat next to Hexa, across from me, and chuckled over the entire exchange.

As I rowed, I faced her and asked, "Did Master Zelfree help you with your manipulation?"

She regarded the water. "I don't want to talk about it." Then she pointed. "Oh, Volke! Look there!"

Beneath the glittering surface of the ocean, I spotted a dark shadow. At first, I thought it was the shape of a shark, but then I noticed the way it wiggled and moved. I leaned over the side of the dinghy, my breath held.

A kraken the size of a two-story building moved through the depths beneath our boat. Its purplish skin and many tentacles mesmerized me. Every time it shifted, the water rose like a hill and created a small wake. The beast twisted, and for a brief second, I caught sight of a single black eye the size of my head. It stared back at me with understanding. As the dinghy floated over, the kraken relaxed, calming the waters.

"That's one giant octopus," Hexa muttered, her eyes wide.

I wanted to point out that krakens had ten tentacles, which made them closer to a squid than an octopus, but I kept the comment to myself. Instead, I admired the grand scale of the mystical creature as I rowed the dinghy to the port of Fortuna. There were small docking spaces for the tender boats, and we tied our vessel to a post before disembarking.

The city of Fortuna never failed to impress me. Windows glistened in the morning sunshine, and the bright green of treetops contrasted beautifully with the white walls. The city was built on a hill, and buildings lined the flatlands, creating a circular metropolis. The roads led up to the step-like terraces, allowing for farmland. Bells rang from the massive clock tower, giving Fortuna a life of its own.

How could Thronehold even compare?

Hexa, Raisen, Zaxis, Illia, and I walked the length of our dock. Zaxis never stopped eating, and Raisen kept his four eyes on the food the entire way.

"Is that Volke I see?"

Gillie, the grand apothecary, stood at the far end of the dock, her smile as bright as her golden hair. Her arcanist star was large and prominent, the wings and tail of a caladrius etched into the skin over her forehead, all the way to her ears and then down the sides of her neck. It paled in comparison to the colors of her outfit.

She wore a dress of red and rose satin, with feathers for sleeves and a sash made from the black scales of a mystical creature. I suspected the sash was a magical item—perhaps something for defense?—but I didn't know for sure. Although I knew the general procedure for making a trinket or artifact, I hadn't learned to identify them.

Gillie hurried over to me, her smile growing wider, deepening the laugh lines at the edges of her eyes.

"I'm so thrilled you'll be joining us on this journey," she said as she threw her arms around me. "It feels like it's been ages since I've seen you last."

Her embrace was tight, but I could handle it. Her height amused me more than the hug—I had to be a foot taller than she was which made returning the embrace a tad awkward.

"It's nice to see you again," I said.

She released me. "Look at you. All lean muscle. You need to eat more. Where is Everett? He should be aware of this."

"He's still at the guild."

Her caladrius eldrin—a white bird with a parrot-beak of polished gold—flew off a nearby carriage and landed on Gillie's shoulder. Her name was Alana, and the brilliant ivory of her feathers amazed me just as much as the first time I saw her.

"Volke." Alana's sweet voice matched her tiny bird body. "I'm happy you're healthy."

I shrugged. "Uh, yeah. Thank you again for helping me that last time."

"You needn't thank me. My arcanist and I are always willing to help."

Illia cleared her throat. For a long moment, I didn't

understand why, but then it occurred to me that none of the others had ever met Gillie.

"Gillie," I said. "These are also apprentices of Master Zelfree. This is Zaxis Ren, Hexa d'Tenni, and my sister, Illia Savan."

"It is a pleasure to meet each and every one of you," Gillie said, her smile never waning. She shook the hands of each of them, one at a time, adding comments for each. "So strong," she said to Zaxis. With Hexa, she giggled. "I love your hair, young lady." When she arrived at Illia, she stared for half a second longer than the rest. "You have an aura of determination about you. I like that."

Was that really the reason she stared? In my gut, I thought it was because Illia and I didn't look like siblings. Her brown, curly hair contrasted with my black—her pale skin with my honeyed hue—and our faces had little resemblance.

If Gillie had noticed, she didn't comment, which I was grateful for.

Nicholin offered a squeak. "Uh, don't forget the eldrin. I'm Nicholin. And that deranged crocodile masquerading as a hydra is known as Raisen."

Both heads hissed in Nicholin's direction.

I leaned in close to Zaxis. "Where is Forsythe?"

"I left him at the guild," Zaxis said. "He wanted to sleep in longer. I'm sure he'll come once Atty and Titania make their way over."

Trumpets sounded from a nearby ship.

We all turned to get a better look, but I remained confused, even as I took in the details. A galleon-style ship was secured to the dock, its sails closed, but its flags waving in the wind. Flags were a method of communication, and every ship I had ever known flew at least three—one for their nation, one to signify if they had arcanists among their crew or passengers, and one to communicate if there was an emergency.

The galleon flew the flag of a nation I didn't recognize. It wasn't our island nation, or the Argo Empire, so I suspected it was from an independent set of islands far to the north.

Trumpeters continued their heralding as two arcanists stepped off the gangplank. We were too far away to see details, so I couldn't identify their eldrin, but their heavy fur coats confirmed my suspicion about their homeland. The northern waters didn't know warmth.

The arcanists marched straight into Fortuna with a purpose. Their retinue followed close behind, including two standard-bearers. One carried their national flag, and the other carried a flag with a dragon clawing at a rose.

I had no idea what that meant.

"What's going on?" I asked.

Luthair shifted through the shadows at my feet. "My arcanist, I believe—"

"By the abyssal hells," Hexa said, cutting him off. She tucked her hands under her armpits and stared with wide eyes. "I can't believe it. Is the Sovereign Dragon Tournament happening this year?"

Gillie lifted both eyebrows. Her short, blonde hair fluttered in the wind, but she kept her gaze on the flag with the dragon. "I have seen hundreds of merchants use the ports these last few weeks. It would make sense if the tournament were about to take place."

Hexa practically shrieked. Then she grabbed Illia by the shoulder and shook her. "Did you hear that? I can't believe it! *We're* heading to Thronehold! *Can you believe it?*"

Illia stared back with her one eye. "Believe what?"

"We'll be there while they hold the Sovereign Dragon Tournament. How lucky are we?"

I gave both Illia and Zaxis quick glances. All three of us had grown up on the Isle of Ruma, far from the mainland and its customs. While I understood the word *tournament*, and I had read tales about *sovereign dragons*, putting all the words together didn't hold any special significance for me.

Gillie placed a hand on her cheek. "This will make navigating Thronehold a real challenge. There will be so many people there..."

"Hey," Nicholin said as he puffed up his little chest. "I don't understand why you're so worked up. Let me in on the secret so I can get excited, too."

"The Sovereign Dragon Tournament is only held after the birth of a new sovereign dragon." Hexa waited for a long moment, as if we should've reacted. She raised her arms in the air. "This is a rare event!"

"Phoenixes are born every ten years on the Isle of Ruma," Zaxis said with a shrug. "That's kinda rare."

"Sovereign dragons aren't like that! They don't lay eggs on a set schedule, and sometimes it can take *centuries*."

"Okay," I said. "They're rare. Lots of creatures are. What else about this is special?"

Hexa glared. "This is more important, *Volke*. Only sovereign dragon arcanists rule the Argo Empire. Queen Velleta is the only master sovereign dragon arcanist in the world." She punctuated each sentence by smacking her knuckles into her other palm. "The tournament is a *huge* celebration for the dragon's trial of worth. *Way* bigger than anything on your rinky-dink islands."

A massive trial of worth? That did sound interesting.

Zaxis perked up. "Tell us the details."

"Hundreds of arcanists gather to compete in combat,"

Hexa said, her excitement translating into volume, each word growing louder. "The royal family gives out prizes, and everyone is in attendance. Then, at the end of all the festivities, those who are competing to bond with a sovereign dragon have to fight *to the death*."

"To the death?" Illia repeated. "So anyone hoping to bond with a sovereign dragon has to kill all other hopefuls?"

Nicholin tapped his nose with a paw. "Hm. I was way too easy with my trial of worth. Next time *I* want a tournament and a body count."

Hexa huffed and crossed her arms. "You guys don't get it. This is a big deal. People come from all over to watch or compete. How have you not heard about it?"

"So, the rest of the tournament isn't to the death, right?" I asked.

"Of course not. Everyone else competes for gold and fame and magical items."

While I had never heard of this specific tournament, I had read about great competitions that had taken place in the past. During times of peace, arcanists would sometimes put on great demonstrations of their power. Most competitions were between similar arcanists—to really understand which of them was superior—but all the martial tournaments allowed for any arcanist to compete.

Those stories didn't involve heroes for the most part, so they weren't my favorite, but I did enjoy the thrill of competition. Some arcanists had amazing abilities, and some were so clever, it almost didn't matter what their sorcery entailed.

The thought of watching a tournament between master arcanists overshadowed my excitement to see Thronehold. My pulse ran quick just thinking about the incredible demonstrations of skill and magic.

I didn't like the sound of the final match, though.

A fight to the death as a trial of worth? All the partici-pants had to be dedicated and confident.

Then again, I probably still would've entered the phoenix trial of worth, even if the penalty for failure had been death. Becoming an arcanist meant that much to me, and if sovereign dragon arcanists were the only ones allowed to rule their empire, I supposed there was even more at stake than simply gaining access to magic.

"My arcanist?" Luthair asked from the shadows.

"Hm?"

"You seem distant."

"I'm just thinking. I want to see this tournament with my own eyes."

"See it?" Hexa interjected. "We might as well participate!"

5

ANTLER TRINKET

Participate in a tournament? How would that even work? We were only apprentices. What if we were matched against a master arcanist? We wouldn't stand a chance.

Zaxis didn't seem to have those questions, however. He smiled more genuinely than he had in a long while. "We *should* participate. How do we sign up?"

"Once we make it to Thronehold, you can register," Gillie said. "There's no entrance fee for arcanists, but there is a charge for seating in the coliseum." Gillie's smile rivaled Zaxis's, almost like she was excited for the tournament as well.

"Even though we're not master arcanists?" I asked. "Won't we just be defeated after one or two matches?"

"Of course not. No one wants to see a one-sided beat down. They break the tournament into categories. Apprentice, journeyman, master, and elite. It's based on the amount of time you've been bonded. If you've been an arcanist for fewer than two years, you'll participate in the apprentice rounds. Everyone in that category should be roughly equal in skill and magic.”

That tiny bit of information changed my whole view on the tournament. It would be exhilarating to face fellow arcanists in mock battles. How would I compare to a group of my peers? I would have to train even harder now...

Hexa shook Illia again, this time even jostling Nicholin.

“Hey, hey,” Nicholin said. “Careful. I’m perching here.”

Without acknowledging Nicholin, Hexa said, “We have to enter. I saw a tournament in Thronehold when I was a kid. It was a tiny thing, but it was still breathtaking. I’m just mad this tournament is happening when we’re apprentices and not when we’re journeymen or master arcanists.”

Illia lifted an eyebrow. “But we’re supposed to be guarding the grand apothecary.”

“Only *to* Thronehold.”

“But remember what the guildmaster said? We’ll have business inside the city.”

I could already tell this was bothering Illia. She had her mind set on the world serpent and nothing else. Fame in a tournament just wasn’t her style.

“Stop trying to ruin this.” Hexa couldn’t seem to settle down. She paced and rotated her shoulders, her restless energy bursting from every pore. “We just have to convince Master Zelfree. We need to participate.”

With a loud clap of her hands, Gillie drew our attention. “Why don’t we wait for Everett by our caravan? The carriages are waiting outside the southern gates, and my feet are protesting standing here on these smelly docks.”

Her caladrius eldrin puffed out her feathers and nodded along with the words, even though she was a bird and probably didn’t have the problem of painful standing.

“Okay,” Illia said. “Lead the way.”

Our caravan consisted of nine carriages and two carts, each pulled by a pair of mustangs.

We had a carriage for each of the two master arcanists—Gillie and Zelfree—and one for our guildmaster. We also had four for the apprentices of Zelfree and Gillie and one more for researchers. Our two carts were for supplies, which consisted of food and replacement parts, should anything break.

The last carriage contained the plague-ridden creatures.

The entire vehicle was chained and locked and crafted from an odd, ebony wood. Warnings had been painted across the side to avoid opening the doors without permission. It was positioned in the middle of the caravan, no doubt to keep it out of the hands of brigands and bandits.

From time to time, the whole carriage rocked, and a sinister laugh echoed from within. I tried not to pay attention, but the giddy chuckles made it difficult. It was an insane asylum on wheels, only the inhabitants could spread their madness in a heartbeat.

It didn't take long for the others to join us outside the city walls of Fortuna. Atty, Adelgis, and Master Zelfree arrived minutes after we did, and I wondered if we had just missed them on the docks.

To my surprise, everyone had already heard about the Sovereign Dragon Tournament. The dozens of merchants leaving the city spoke of it nonstop, including their guards and eldrin, if they had any. It didn't matter what they transported—pearls, coral, exotic fruits, or special materials—they all couldn't wait to sell their special "island merchandise" to the people of the Argo Empire.

Many of them were also ready to bet on their favorite arcanists to win.

I hadn't even considered gambling. There would be plenty of money flowing through the streets of Thronehold. Crooks and villains were sure to find the city appealing.

Several arcanists traveled past us, each of them carrying a dragon and rose banner, signifying their intent to participate. The constant parade of travelers heightened my excitement to new levels. The ten-day travel to Thronehold couldn't happen fast enough.

A merchant transporting two carts' worth of charberries passed us with a smile. I recognized the man from the Isle of Ruma—the only place around here where charberry trees grew—but it didn't seem like he took note of us.

"Pay attention," Zelfree said, pulling my attention away from the roads. He motioned to our caravan. "I know you're all thrilled about the tournament, but—"

"Will we get to participate?" Hexa asked without reservation.

"It depends."

"On?"

"On how well you pay attention to my damn instructions."

Her shoulders bunched at her neck, and she stepped back, her face pink.

Zelfree straightened his coat and continued, "We have one goal while we travel south: make sure nothing happens to Gillie or her supplies. You have all seen the carriage with the plague creatures. We'll be taking shifts guarding it. Two will stand watch in the morning for eight hours, two in the afternoon for eight hours, and two at night for eight hours. Volke, I know you see in the dark, so you'll have the night watch the entire way."

I nodded. "Okay."

"And I want you to practice transferring this ability to others. Whoever is on guard duty with you will help, understand?"

"Yes."

Zelfree pointed to the carriages in the back. "You six will share those two carriages." He reached into his pocket and withdrew six chain necklaces, each with a bone pendant. "These are special trinkets made by Gillie herself. These're the culmination of her research. These pendants protect the wearer from contracting the arcane plague."

I caught my breath, shocked she had made so many. I almost couldn't believe it when Zelfree walked over and handed one to each of us. These had to be worth a fortune.

"Wear these," he commanded. "And never take them off." Zelfree glared at Zaxis specifically. "Did you hear me? I had Gillie make them with metal so you couldn't accidentally burn yours."

Zaxis turned the trinket over in his hands. "Yeah, yeah. Don't take it off. I understand."

When Zelfree got close, I noticed he wore one of the plague-preventing necklaces himself. How many had Gillie fashioned? Had she used all of the available supplies in her lab? No wonder she'd had to ask Queen Velleta for more materials.

"My father is quite talented at imbuing magic," Adelgis said, though no one seemed to pay much attention. "The grand apothecary should've asked him for help when making this."

Zelfree looked us over. "Are there any questions?"

Illia raised her hand. "Will we be the only ones on guard duty?"

"No. Some of Gillie's trainees and I will also take turns.

But you don't need to worry about that. Just focus on protecting the carriage."

"I have a question," Nicholin said. He scampered up onto Illia's head and then stood on his hind legs. "How much listening is enough listening to participate in the tournament? If the carriage is okay when we make it to Thronehold, can we—"

Illia yanked Nicholin off her head and covered his face with her hand. He squirmed, but he never teleported away. "I'm sorry about that," she muttered. "Go on with the instructions."

Zelfree had a familiar expression—eyes half-lidded and begging for a hard drink. He rubbed at the bridge of his nose and shook his head. "There's a good chance you can all participate if you want. We'll most likely be in Thronehold for the entirety of the event. Guildmaster Eventide has to speak with several people concerning our snake."

He probably avoided saying *world serpent* just so there wasn't a chance the passing merchants would overhear the conversation. If word got out, I suspected it would get chaotic.

I raised a hand. "Can't we just find it? We have the means."

"It's more complicated than that. Knowing where it is just isn't enough. You think the sovereign dragons have a weird bonding ceremony? Our snake has a lair that requires something to enter." Zelfree forced a chuckle. "Let's just say Eventide knows who she needs to speak with before we go charging off into the sunset. In the meantime, enjoy the damn tournament."

Hexa and Zaxis practically high-fived each other with the look they exchanged. Adelgis and Atty, on the other hand, didn't seem enthusiastic at all. They both took half-steps back and avoided eye contact with the rest of the group.

"Are you giving them a hard time, Everett?"

Gillie stepped out of her personal carriage and ambled over, allowing herself time to greet each of us as she passed, all with hugs and smiles. When she reached Zelfree, she threw her arms around him in an embrace similar to the one she had given me.

"You are looking so fine," she said with a laugh. "Much better than before. I'm so glad, Everett. I was really worried for you."

Zelfree patted her arm and then yanked free of her grasp. "And you remain unchanged, as always."

"I especially adore your new haircut."

Without his long hair, it was easy to see Zelfree's ears shift to a bright red. He turned away and crossed his arms, his whole posture stiff.

"Do you need me for something?" he asked. "Otherwise, I have apprentices to train."

"Oh, let your apprentices get settled in for the journey. They have horses to meet and other arcanists to mingle with. You and I should catch up. I have so much to tell you."

He grumbled something I couldn't hear, and then Gillie laughed again.

"Always so serious! Come, come. I have biscuits in my carriage."

She took Zelfree by the elbow and led him away from the group, despite his muttered protests and irritated groans. Everyone watched them go, but no one snickered until Zelfree had disappeared into Gillie's carriage.

"We have to look at these horses," Hexa said as she jutted her thumb at the caravan.

Adelgis shook his head, his inky hair still shiny, even

with the overcast skies. "I apologize, but I'm going to rest in the carriage." He didn't even wait for a response before he headed for the last vehicle in the line.

Normally, I wouldn't have cared if someone wanted to sit out, but Adelgis hadn't been moving around with much gusto. It was like he hadn't slept properly in weeks, and it was all catching up with him. I knew he had been sleeping, though. He slept more than anyone in the group, as a matter of fact.

I watched him go for a long moment, curious and worried. I made a mental note to talk to him later, whenever we found ourselves with a bit of privacy.

When I glanced back, the rest of the group had already taken off. Hexa led the charge toward the mustangs, Raisen struggling to keep up with her pace. Forsythe and Titania perched themselves on one of the carriages, their soot lost in the dirt road. Illia trailed behind the group, whispering to Nicholin the entire way.

I was about to follow them when Luthair shifted through the shadows. "Someone approaches."

To my curiosity, I saw no one, no matter what direction I turned to. "You sure?"

"I heard footsteps."

Then someone cleared their throat, perhaps a foot away from me, and I flinched, startled by the simple noise. Still, I saw nothing, and my mind jumped to the conclusion of invisibility.

"Show yourself," I commanded.

Sure enough, a veil of obfuscation dropped, revealing a man in his early twenties. He wore a similar outfit to my own—a long coat, leather boots, and a button-up shirt—but my attention settled on his frostbitten fingers and ears. The black skin appeared dead, but he moved his hands around without trouble and even slid them into his pockets when he realized I was staring.

And, more importantly, he had an arcanist mark on his forehead. It was a star with a creature that had a wolf body and antlers of a stag. A wendigo.

"I don't know if you remember me," the man said, his voice reserved.

I replied with a single nod. "You're the pirate who tried to kill Luthair. Fain, right?"

"Yes."

I focused on the caravan. Several of Gillie's researchers met my gaze, but none of them reacted to Fain's presence. I put all the pieces together.

"You took my advice," I said. "You helped Gillie with your wendigo magic."

He nodded, but said nothing else.

During our confrontation with Calisto, I had fought Fain and then spared him. As a pirate, he argued his life was as good as over—he would have been killed no matter where he went. But in the heat of the moment, I had remembered that Gillie wanted to study wendigo magic to create a cure for the plague. Had Fain been instrumental in her recent breakthrough? Wendigo and wendigo arcanists were immune to the plague, after all. His magic would no doubt come in handy. The thought eased my anxiety.

"I'm glad you're here," I said with a smile.

Fain didn't relax, however. He stared at me with hard, dark eyes, and his muscles tensed whenever I shifted my weight from one foot to the other. Was he upset? Angry? Offended? I didn't really know the man, only that he hated Luthair for killing his brother. Perhaps he still held that grudge?

"Why didn't you stay at Gillie's lab?" I asked. "Did you come here for a specific reason?"

"Gillie wants me to stay close. She's teaching me about her business." Fain shook his head. "And she also wants me to speak with the queen."

"You're her apprentice?"

"I have no healing magic. I'm just her assistant."

That explained why he didn't have a guild pendant. And if he was working for Gillie, he probably wasn't going to attack me or Luthair. Still—he remained uneasy.

"Where's your eldrin?" I asked.

Fain turned to his side and made a clicking noise with his tongue. The invisibility keeping his wendigo hidden dropped. There stood a large wolf with black fur and a skull over its face.

Something was odd, however. Wendigo typically had antlers—and when I had last seen Fain's wendigo, it, too, had had antlers—but now there were none. Instead, his wendigo had short points, like tiny horns, at the base of where the antlers had once grown.

With knitted eyebrows, I asked, "What happened?"

Fain shrugged. "Gillie needed pieces of a wendigo to make her plague-resistant trinkets. I cut the antlers off Wraith, and she crushed them into pieces for the pendants."

I glanced down at my new necklace and examined the pendant. The bone had the brownish hue of an antler, and I knew Fain was telling the truth.

"Will Wraith grow the antlers back?" I asked.

Fain shook his head. "No. The skull mask of a wendigo grows while they mature, but after that, it's set. Like adult teeth—the antlers don't come back."

Then it hit me.

Gillie wasn't going to Queen Velleta for star shards. She

was going to find more wendigo antlers. This *limited resource* was exceptionally rare, considering most wendigo hid themselves in the snowy mountains far from civilization.

How would Queen Velleta even help? Surely, she didn't have many wendigo arcanists in her employ, and I suspected most wouldn't want to harm their eldrin, even if it would create pendants that granted immunity to the plague.

"Thank you for your sacrifice," I said.

It wouldn't affect Fain or Wraith's magic capacity, but it would affect Wraith's ability to fight. It was the equivalent of removing a phoenix's talons.

"It was nothing," Wraith replied, his voice calm and mature. "Thank you for giving my arcanist the opportunity to start anew."

Fain remained quiet, his gaze off to the side, like he didn't want to stare at me directly. I didn't know what to say beyond what I had, and for a prolonged moment, we stood in silence.

His dark chestnut hair had been cut short on the sides, exposing the piercings on the bottoms of his ears—the part that wasn't frostbitten. It reminded me of the tattoo pirates often got on their necks as identifiers to which ship they belonged. Fain kept his skin covered with a tight-fitting ascot, however. That was smart. No one would want to associate with him if he exposed the pirate tattoo.

I tapped the knuckles of my right hand into the palm of my left. "You're quiet. Is everything okay?"

"Yes. I'm just... not used to this. I don't really know anyone here, and anyone who knows my history isn't keen on my presence."

His short explanation made me realize his awkward position. He had no family or friends, and he was traveling to a city he likely knew nothing about. No wonder he was on edge. Even though *we* had interacted, it hadn't been for long, and it wasn't as allies.

In an attempt to break the ice between us, I opted to ask the first question that came to mind. "So, uh, what kind of name is *Fain*, anyway? I've never heard it before, not even from traders from the north."

"It's made up," he said. "Everyone takes a new name when they join a pirate crew."

"Really? I didn't know that."

He glanced over, one eyebrow raised. "You thought the first mate of the *Third Abyss* was given the name *Spider* at birth?"

"Uh, well, I hadn't thought about it."

Fain shrugged. "It's just a part of the initiation."

His wendigo tilted his head. "I thought *Wraith* sounded intimidating."

"You took a new name, too?" I asked.

"My original name was Tennit."

"Oh. Should I call you that, then?"

Both Fain and Wraith shook their heads.

"I'd rather not think about it," Fain said. "I don't want be the only one here with a *new name*. I'd rather people call me what they've been calling me."

Speaking of names got me nostalgic. I half-smiled. "Hey, if it makes you feel better, I have a name different than the one I was born with."

Although Fain had been avoiding eye contact with me, he faced me straight on, his expression more curious than I suspected. "Why?"

"I was adopted," I said. "My name used to be Volke Blackwater. Now it's Volke Savan. I prefer it this way. My adopted father is a great man, and it's an honor to have his surname."

For the first time since he had appeared, Fain relaxed a bit. He still shifted his gaze away, however, and half-stared at the ground as he said, "I was born Thibault Raustin. I haven't said that aloud in years. I'd prefer to think that part of me is dead."

I didn't know if he was joking, but his serious tone told me he likely meant it. "I'll call you whatever you prefer."

"Fain."

"Right. Okay."

"Volke!"

I spotted Illia waving to me. She pointed to one of the horses and made a petting motion. I had never been around horses—not while living on a tiny island—so the thought of getting to know one of the mustangs on the trek excited me.

"I'll be right there," I called out.

When I turned back around, Fain was gone. Well, most likely invisible, but still. He had abandoned the conversation, and I wondered if he would stay out of sight for the entirety of the trip.

"I hope we can speak again," I said to the space around me, wondering if Fain was still close enough to hear.

6

UNDER THE SKIN

I walked over to the others, my hands in my trouser pockets.

Every carriage had two mustangs, and at the front of the caravan, leading them all, was an enbarr—a mystical horse creature with a dark blue coat and a silvery mane that fluttered as though underwater. They weren't the strongest magical creatures. They were known for their ability to walk on any surface, both land and sea. They could also heal and rejuvenate horses, which was likely why the Frith Guild had hired an enbarr arcanist to help with the trek.

Hexa stood in front of a mustang and stroked its muzzle. The horse's ears twitched as it lowered its head and pressed against Hexa's palm.

"I rode horses and mules all the time back home," she said.

Zaxis and Atty paid close attention, but they never got within two feet of the creature. The Isle of Ruma didn't have any horses. I had seen horses in Fortuna—we all had—but none of us had interacted with one. Horses were mighty beasts, and I suspected this one weighed over a ton.

Illia smiled as I got near. "Who were you talking to?"

"Remember that pirate I told you about?" I asked. "The wendigo arcanist? It turns out he went to Gillie's lab. He helped create these plague-resistant trinkets, and now he's her assistant."

Although I thought this was all good news, Illia's smile vanished and she stared up at me with a hard glower.

"He's a pirate? From the *Third Abyss*?"

"Well, he's not with them anymore."

"So why isn't he tied down or in prison?" Illia ran a hand over her eyepatch, her fingers shaking. "Better yet, why isn't he dead?"

Her ever-increasing anger came as no surprise, not after pirates had taken her family and right eye. Even if that were the case, however, I knew Fain wasn't the typical pirate. He had joined the crew of the *Third Abyss* because his brother had, and it had been clear to me that Fain regretted that decision.

"He's different," I said. "Fain sacrificed a lot to help Gillie."

"I don't care, Volke. We can't trust him. He's no better than flotsam washed up by the sea."

She was louder than normal, and the others stopped talking about the horse to face us. I didn't know what to say. I couldn't erase Fain's past, and I wanted to help him create a better future. But if I said that, I knew Illia wouldn't take it well.

Zaxis surveyed the spot where I had spoken with Fain. "He can become invisible?"

I nodded.

"That's creepy," he said. "I bet he's skulking around the caravan right now."

Illia wrapped her arms around herself, her one eye fixed

on the ground. Her pursed lips and stiff stance bothered me. I didn't want her to feel unsafe. Nicholin obviously felt the same, because he patted her shoulders and made soft squeaking noises.

With a confident smile, Zaxis sauntered over to Illia's side. "Here. You should have this." He reached into his pocket and withdrew a brass spyglass. "This is a Refraction Spyglass—it sees through invisibility."

"You... want me to have it?" Illia asked as she took the trinket.

"Of course."

"Thank you, Zaxis. That's kind of you."

"As soon as that dastard steps out of line, you should be the one to bring him down."

"He isn't going to step out of line," I said.

Illia shot me cold glare. "You don't know that."

The ice in her words silenced the rest of my argument. I supposed I didn't know for sure—it was just a gut feeling. Or perhaps hope. Maybe, if Fain turned his life around, it would help Illia, too, in some odd way.

Hexa stepped around the horse and placed a hand on Illia's shoulder. "Hey. Don't worry. I can station Raisen outside of our carriage at night, and he can create a cloud of poison gas. That way the pirate won't be able to get close without getting sick. It's a deadly moat."

It seemed Hexa had taken my advice to heart.

Nicholin stood on his hind legs and nodded. "That's a great idea! But let's not stop there. Raisen, can you spit venom into his food without him knowing? Hit him where it hurts."

"On it," one of Raisen's heads replied.

I shook my head. "We can't do that. I meant it when I

said he's helping Gillie cure the plague. That's vastly more important right now."

All of them—even Atty, who remained in the back, like she didn't want to engage in the conversation—gave me long looks of irritation. I didn't care, though. The arcane plague had already done enough damage in the world. If Fain was somehow the key to defeating it, then we couldn't poison his food out of petty revenge.

A rumble of thunder rolled through our caravan. The sky had grown just as disgruntled as the others. Gray clouds bunched together overhead, darkening with each new addition. Storms on the ocean meant trouble, but I hadn't experienced one while traveling over land. Surely, it would be easier.

***

Rain made the travel difficult. The wheels of our carts and carriages got stuck in quagmires of mud. The enbarr arcanist had tools for every situation, but it delayed our trek by a few hours. Our horses remained strong and fit, due to his magic, even with the chilly winds nipping at their flanks.

Zaxis, Adelgis, and I shared a carriage. Luthair and Felicity stayed hidden—Luthair in the dark and Adelgis's ethereal whelk in the light of our lantern—but Forsythe had to sit on the bench. His soot coated the leather seat a few minutes into the trip, and anytime he moved, his peacock-like tail smacked into me or Adelgis.

Time crawled by at a disappointing pace.

All three of us were taller than average, and our knees bumped around in the middle. And while the cold winds rustled the trees outside, the inside cooked us like an oven.

No airflow, no reprieve. The girls always complained whenever we didn't shower, and now I knew why.

Zaxis read his book on metallurgy. The pages had gotten warped from the wet surfaces he had placed it on, but that didn't stop him.

Adelgis stared out the window, his breathing shallow the entire way. When we spoke to him, he answered in short bursts and then returned to his window gazing.

I practiced my shadow manipulation, and when that became too painful, I switched to reading about magical imbuing. After six hours, however, I had finished the book. I set it down on the seat and turned to Zaxis. "Read anything interesting about metal?"

"Quiet down," he muttered. "I'm reading about pig iron."

Forsythe let out a strained huff. "My arcanist, I don't feel so well."

Zaxis glanced up from the pages. "Can't you... heal yourself?"

"I meant I need fresh air. Can you please open the door and let me out?"

"It's raining."

"The water won't hurt me," Forsythe said as he tilted his head. "It evaporates if it gets under my feathers."

With a mild look of concern, Zaxis thought over the request. After a few seconds, he unlatched the door and swung it open. "Stay close."

Wind rushed inside, flipping the pages of Zaxis's book and disturbing everyone's hair.

Especially Adelgis's, since it was so long. He hadn't yet put it back in a ponytail, and he instead grabbed it with both hands. The way he held his hair down against his neck— with panicked speed and a firm grasp—was familiar to me.

Illia had done it all the time when we were younger. She

used her hair to hide the scars on her face, and if the wind threatened to reveal her secret, she would frantically hold it in place.

Adelgis did just that until the door was secured close. Then he flattened the hair over his neck and smoothed out the ebony locks.

I sat forward on my seat and leaned closer to Adelgis, trying hard to see the skin beneath his black hair. I couldn't, and Adelgis lifted an eyebrow at my staring.

"Are you okay, Volke?"

"What're you hiding?" I asked.

"E-Excuse me? I'm not hiding anything."

"You've been keeping your neck covered."

Adelgis paled when I mentioned it. Actually, he already seemed pale. And sweaty. He had the wan complexion of a corpse, though it was difficult to notice with the low light of our lantern.

"Let me see," Zaxis said. He reached over and pushed aside Adelgis's hair.

Adelgis slapped his hand. "Hey!"

But it was too late. For a split second, I had caught sight of his skin—and the hideous bruise that went from his lower jaw down past the collar of his coat. It didn't look like a punch or a bite, but more like internal bleeding.

Zaxis must have seen it as well because he flinched back and sneered. "What happened to you?"

"It's fine," Adelgis replied, his tone curt.

"Why didn't you tell me you were hurt? I can fix that right up."

Again, Zaxis reached out to touch him. This time, Adelgis shoved his arm away and glared.

"It can't be healed, all right? I'm fine." He took a ragged breath and then exhaled. "Completely fine."

Zaxis and I exchanged questioning glances. I didn't want to fight with Adelgis, but I couldn't ignore the problem. What were we going to do about it? Force him to tell us what was going on?

The carriage rocked and came to a halt. Zelfree had said our first stop would be an inn located on the main road, and I thanked the heavens we wouldn't have to stay cooped up any longer.

Adelgis went to open the door, but his unsteady hand made the simple task difficult. Sweat dripped off his face and onto his lap, and I couldn't watch any longer. I placed a hand on his knee and looked him directly in the eye.

"Something is terribly wrong," I whispered. "We can't help you if we don't know what it is."

"It's... the thing under my skin."

I instantly knew what he meant.

Zaxis, on the other hand, stared at me and mouthed the question, *the thing under his skin?* I nodded, and then I returned my attention to Adelgis.

"Can we look at it?" I asked.

"Inside," Adelgis said. "I don't want anyone else... to know."

"Zaxis has heard everything."

With gritted teeth, Adelgis shook his head. "Just you two, then."

Although I thought it foolish to keep a problem hidden, I went along with his request. Once I knew the extent of the damage, I could reevaluate whether or not Zelfree should be involved, but until then, Adelgis could decide his own fate. I just hated that he kept such disturbing secrets.

I opened the door to the carriage and stepped out into the rain. The three-story inn had lanterns at every door and window, keeping the darkness at bay. I helped Adelgis step outside and then offered him my shoulder for the short walk to the front door. He shook his head and walked on his own, but his slow gait and awkward stagger betrayed his illness.

The dark clouds and gloomy atmosphere obscured him, preventing the others from noticing.

Zaxis hopped out of the carriage and grabbed me by the upper arm. "What's going on?"

"I'm sure Adelgis will explain everything."

"You *knew* something was wrong and said nothing?"

"It's not like that. The thing under his skin wasn't this harmful before."

I jerked free of his grasp and went straight for the inn. Rain soaked my coat and shirt by the time I reached the front door, and I had to kick mud off my boots before I entered. Zaxis whistled for Forsythe and waited.

The warmth of the inn settled over me like a thick blanket on a cold evening. A large fireplace and hearth dominated the back wall, keeping the front room toasty. A woman at a piano played a slow but upbeat tune, her long fingers gracefully slipping from one key to the next.

A couple dozen merchants sat at tables eating stew from wooden bowls. Some were arcanists, the prominent star on their forehead a dead giveaway. A gnome sat at one table, sipping from a cup, his beard twice as long as his short body. A pixie flew around the ceiling, glancing between tables, giggling the entire time. A leprechaun sat huddled over a pile of gold and silver coins, counting them out into two piles while the merchants on either side of him made deals.

The sheer number of people made me wonder if there would be rooms available for us to stay in. I made my way to the front counter and spotted Adelgis leaning heavily on a stool.

"They're getting us keys," he muttered. He held the collar of his coat up. "I'm sorry I kept this from you for so long. I... never imagined it would get this bad."

Before I could respond, a hefty woman with a food-splattered apron walked over and handed me four keys.

"Second floor," she said. "Except this one. That's the third floor."

She pointed to each wrought-iron key. They had numbers engraved on them—24, 25, 26, and 31. I took them all, and lifted an eyebrow. Did I have to pay? The woman walked off without seeing my confusion.

Adelgis, who I swear read my thoughts more often than I liked, said, "They were paid ahead of time. Guildmaster Eventide set this trip up long in advance."

I needed to get Adelgis to a room before the others entered, so I took the key labeled 24 and then glanced to the shadow at my feet. "Luthair, can you hold on to the rest of these? Just hand them to Master Zelfree once he gets in."

"Of course, my arcanist."

He rose from the darkness, his black, full plate armor shining under the lantern light. Cracks marred his appearance, adding to his intimidating visage. His cape, lined in a crimson red, rustled each time the front door opened. I placed the extra keys into his gauntlet hand.

Conversations in the inn came to an abrupt halt. The patrons at the tables stared with wide eyes, and the leprechaun slowly slid under the table, his whole body stiff. Even the piano woman slowed her tune as she glanced over her shoulder.

I leaned close to Adelgis and whispered, "What's going on? They haven't seen a knightmare arcanist before?"

He took a couple of breaths and shook his head. "They think you're a steel thorn inquisitor..."

Zaxis threw open the door and sauntered into the front room of the inn. He headed for us and then glared. "Apparently everyone is taking their sweet time with the carriages. What're you two still doing here? I thought you were taking Adelgis to his room?"

"We're sharing a room," I said as I held up the key. "Come on. Help me with him."

All eyes remained on Luthair as I helped Adelgis to the stairs.

I didn't know much about the Steel Thorn Inquisitors Guild. Technically, Luthair's first arcanist, Mathis Weaversong, had belonged to the guild, but that had been years ago. From what Luthair told me, the guild investigated occult matters, especially the misdeeds of other arcanists who had abused their magic. They brought down villains and blackhearts—anyone with bounty, especially if they had magic at their disposal.

Why had everyone in the inn assumed I belonged to the Steel Thorn Inquisitors Guild? Why didn't they think I was with the Frith Guild?

We reached the second floor after a minute of carefully taking each step, Adelgis hanging on to my shoulder the entire time. Hexa entered the inn through the front door—I knew because of her boisterous voice and groan of delight. I hurried to the room labeled 24 and unlocked it before anyone came upstairs.

There were two beds, a chair, and a small wooden table. A thick scent invaded my nostrils, an aroma that reminded me of mold and soggy fabric.

Adelgis took a seat on the foot of the nearest mattress, his pale skin bordering on translucent. Then he pulled back his hair and tied it with a white ribbon. The bruise had yellowed at the edges, reminding me of the cadavers that

Gravekeeper William handled from time to time. The yellowish color meant the bruise was old. How long had this been going on?

Zaxis held the door open long enough for Forsythe to hop in. Then he closed and locked it. "Okay. Start talking. What's going on?"

Although I knew the situation, I waited for Adelgis to explain. It was his problem, after all. He should be the one to tell others.

"My father researches rare mystical creatures," Adelgis said, his voice weak. "He asked me to help. I agreed, and... he put this one under my skin."

Forsythe lifted his head, his long neck practically straight. "My goodness."

"Let's see," Zaxis said.

With cautious movements, Adelgis removed his coat and placed it on the bed. Then he unbuttoned his shirt and peeled it back, his fingers shaking.

I stifled a gasp, but I couldn't hold back the shock on my face. Forsythe squawked and flapped his wings. Zaxis's eyebrows shot to his hairline.

It hadn't been this gruesome four months ago.

7

A SIMPLE PROBLEM

There was a worm under Adelgis's skin, its body protruding half an inch above the muscle.

No. Maybe an eel?

I didn't know for certain, but it was long and thin and pulsated from under the flesh. It was as thick as my thumb and extended from his rib cage down his side and continued beneath the belt of his pants, meandering the entire way, never in a straight line. If I had to guess, it probably continued past his hip.

Adelgis had bruises down his whole side, like he had rolled in purple paint. The marks ran under his armpit, around his shoulder, and up to his neck. Arcanists healed bruises quickly, so what was happening with Adelgis?

"What in the abyssal hells is going on?" Zaxis asked.

Adelgis took a deep breath and stared down at the worm-shaped bulge. "My father is trying to revive an extinct race of mystical creatures. They need to feed on someone or something with magic while they develop. I'm... incubating this one."

There was a long pause before Forsythe shook his head. "Oh, my."

"No," Zaxis finally said. "No. Just, no. *Incubate* is the word you use for eggs. Harmless, cute little eggs. *This thing* is the exact opposite. You're not incubating it—you're being devoured by it." He turned to me with a hardened and serious expression. "You have a sword, right?"

I slowly nodded.

"Good. I'll hold him down. You cut it out."

Adelgis shook his head, his brow furrowed. "No, you can't! I told my father I would do this, and I intend to. It's almost mature. Once it is, it'll come out on its own and—"

"Do you see that thing?" Zaxis yelled, cutting him off. "Have you looked in a mirror? You're sick."

"I haven't eaten. I'll feel better once... once I have something."

I stepped in front of Zaxis and placed a hand on his shoulder. He glared at me while I took a second to gather my thoughts. "Let's calm down," I said. "I'll get Adelgis something to eat, and we can discuss this." I lowered my voice to a whisper and added, "We aren't going to hold him down and cut him open. All right?"

Zaxis sneered. "If I ever have something like that under my skin, you better remove it in the fastest way possible, you understand? I don't care how many blades are involved."

"Fine. But you're not Adelgis."

"Heh."

I moved around him and exited the room. I didn't want to take too long on my quest for sustenance, not when Zaxis was hoping for blood and Adelgis on the verge of passing out. With a single-minded focus, I hustled to the stairs and then took the steps three at a time. I rushed into the front room and shot straight for the kitchen.

The inn had returned to a lively state, but the patrons still gave Luthair odd glances. He waited by the front door, and each new customer flinched as they walked in, startled by the empty suit of shadow armor.

The moment I entered the kitchen, it felt as though I had been splashed with a bucket of sweat. Despite the rain outside, the room had enough heat for ten summers. Three stoves, each blazing and covered with boiling pots, were the source of the temperature. My clothes clung to my skin as I walked over to a table and made eye contact with the same woman who had given me the keys.

"Can I get a bowl of stew?" I asked.

She held out her hand.

I reached into my belt pouch and handed over five copper leafs, hoping it was enough. It hadn't occurred to me until that moment, but would my leafs be accepted in Thronehold? Leafs were the currency used on the mainland —as the islands typically had their own barter or currency —but was it the same between mainland nations?

Fortunately, it didn't become an issue. The woman returned with a bowl of hearty goat stew and accepted my five coins. I forced a smile and exited the oppressive heat of the kitchen, only to bump straight into Atty.

Adjusting my balance, I kept the stew from spilling. "Sorry about that," I muttered.

Atty shook her head. "It's fine."

"Excuse me." I moved around her, my thoughts half on money and half on Adelgis.

She took a few quick steps and maneuvered right back into my path. I almost ran into her a second time.

"Is everything okay?" Atty asked. "You ran into the inn so fast. You didn't even help us secure the horses or carriages."

"Oh, uh, I apologize. Adelgis wasn't feeling well so I

helped him inside and now I'm bringing him some stew." I held up the bowl. "I'll help with the carriages in the future, I promise."

Again, I stepped around her and made my way across the front room of the inn. Other people from our group had entered the establishment, but most were busy drying off or discussing which rooms they would take. I didn't make eye contact with anyone and instead headed for the stairs.

To my surprise, Atty hurried to match my pace. She was with me at the base of the stairs and even placed her hand on the railing at the same time I got to the first step.

"Volke," she said. "Can I ask you a question?"

I hesitated. "Uh, sure. Let's walk while we talk, though."

We climbed the stairs together.

"Hexa said you were giving her pointers on how to utilize her magic," Atty said. She wrung out her long, blonde hair. Even though she was soaked from the rain, she still maintained a regal elegance—her posture straight, her shoulders back. "I was wondering if I could discuss my sorcery with you."

I smiled. "Of course. Any time."

"Thank you so much."

"Wouldn't you want to talk to Zaxis, though? You both share the same type of eldrin. And he's really into training nowadays. Really into it."

Her face brightened to a soft pink. "I don't know if I can ask him. He's rather pushy, and I think he hates it whenever I succeed."

I couldn't disagree with that. Zaxis did seem to think he was always in competition with Atty, simply because they both had phoenixes. Perhaps I should speak to him about that.

We reached the top of the stairs, and I inched away from

her, making my way toward the room. "I would love to speak with you, but it's... an awkward time. Maybe we can talk later tonight? Or tomorrow morning? We'll have plenty of time to train on our journey."

Atty continued to shadow my steps. "I'd prefer if our discussion happened in private."

It seemed everyone wanted everything to be private. I almost made a sarcastic comment, but I kept it to myself. How many secrets could a group of apprentices want to keep from each other? Then again, Atty wasn't about to reveal a weird creature under her skin, so spending time alone with her had the potential to be enjoyable.

I stopped at the door and placed my free hand on the knob. I looked over at Atty, waiting for her to turn and leave. She must've interpreted my staring to mean something else because she glanced down at her wet robes and frowned.

"I know," she said. "I look like a mess."

I shook my head. "Not at all. You look beautiful."

"Is that so?"

She tried to restrain a smile, but couldn't. Her reaction was infectious, and somehow added an adorable quality to her appearance. I wished she smiled like this more often.

A crash from inside the room ripped me out of the moment. Atty examined the door.

"Take off your pants," Zaxis said from within. "I wanna see how long it is."

Atty's face darkened to a shade of red.

"I'm not comfortable with that," Adelgis replied.

"Don't be a child. Strip."

I went to open the door and then hesitated. I didn't want Atty to see anything inside, so I couldn't rush in, but I knew the situation was going from bad to horrible. I had to do something.

"It's not what you think," I said to Atty. "I swear."

She laced her fingers together. "Well, since it's you, I'll take your word."

"Thank you."

"But... what is the explanation?"

"Well, uh, you see... there's an interesting story, and I'm sure we'll laugh about it in the future, but—"

Another crash inside the room got my heart beating fast.

"*Stop struggling, dammit,*" Zaxis growled.

"I have to deal with this," I said. "I'll speak with you later."

I didn't know if I could shadow-step while holding a bowl of stew, but I figured I might as well try. Using my ability, I slipped into the darkness and slithered under the door with lightning speed. A second later, I reappeared in the room, my magic burning my veins.

To my surprise—and delight—the stew had come with me. Was it like my clothes? Or perhaps the stew was just small enough to be affected by my magic? I was so giddy I almost forgot why I had rushed inside in the first place.

Zaxis knelt over Adelgis on the bed, his hands on Adelgis's belt. They fought over the buckle, though it was clear who was going to win. Forsythe stood off in the corner, his gold eyes locked on the struggle, his feathers fluffed so much I could see the inner fire of his body.

"Zaxis," I shouted. "Get off of him!"

I was two seconds away from using my magic to rip him off the bed when the light in the room danced and spun. Crystals coalesced in the air and formed a spiral seashell. A sea snail appeared from the shell; her whole body had the iridescent sheen of a soap bubble.

Then a flash of blinding light filled the room.

I didn't shield my eyes in time, and neither did Zaxis. He

shouted and tumbled off the bed. I stepped away and pressed my back against the wall. Even after the light disappeared, I couldn't see. It took thirty seconds of constant blinking before I regained my sight.

"Leave my arcanist alone," Felicity said. She shook her four little tentacles. "How dare you be rough with him. This isn't becoming of Frith arcanists. Not one bit."

I didn't know ethereal whelks could blind people, but it made sense—they controlled most aspects of light.

Zaxis jumped to his feet. He rubbed at his face with the back of his forearm. "You're insane." Then he faced me, his teeth gritted. "Adelgis is hiding something else from us. You should've heard him after you left."

"Even if he is, you can't force it out of him," I said. "Show Adelgis some respect. What's your problem?"

"*Me?* I'm not the one who shoved a parasite into my ribcage!"

"*Will you keep your voice down?*"

I handed Adelgis the bowl. He didn't say anything—he just took the meal and scooted all the way back to the headboard, his gaze downcast. I agreed with Zaxis, if only a little bit. Adelgis didn't look right, and it seemed foolish to hide his illness from the others.

Zaxis walked over to me and crossed his arms. I stared back, having a silent conversation with him—hoping he understood I wasn't going to back down on this issue. Adelgis didn't want us to cut the creature out of his body, and until it was threatening his life, I wouldn't force that on him.

"What're we going to do about this?" Zaxis whispered.

"Just let Adelgis know you're concerned for him," I muttered. "Maybe he'll change his mind about getting it removed."

"You heard him. It's almost *mature*, whatever that means."

"Then maybe this will all solve itself."

We both glanced over at Adelgis.

He looked… better.

He had devoured his stew, and the empty bowl sat on the nightstand. His skin had regained some of its honeyed color, and the bruises healed at the edges, like his arcanist abilities were returning.

"Adelgis," I said. "How long has it been since you last ate?"

He leaned back and relaxed. "I don't know. More than a day."

"Why would you wait that long?" Zaxis asked with a huff. "You're eating for two now, remember?"

Felicity floated close and waved her tentacles. "Your sarcasm isn't appreciated."

"What? We can't joke about this, either?"

I walked over and picked up the empty bowl. "I'll get you some more food."

Adelgis met my gaze, his eyes edged with water. The expression haunted me, and I almost asked what was wrong, but he cut me off with, "Thank you, Volke. I really appreciate your understanding and support. This means a lot to me."

Zaxis interjected with another huff.

"Well, it'll all be over soon, right?" I said, forcing a chuckle.

Adelgis offered a weak nod.

"Good. Then I'll be right back with some more stew." I glared at Zaxis. "Try not to manhandle him while I'm gone, okay?"

"Yeah. Sure. Whatever."

8

AUGMENTING MAGIC

Adelgis ate three bowls of stew.

When night fell, both he and I were sent to guard the black carriage filled with plague creatures. We were stationed in the inn's wagon house for the entire evening, protecting our deadly cargo from escaping into the world.

The wagon house didn't offer much in the way of entertainment. Horses were tied at one end, and vehicles were secured at the other. I walked back and forth, familiarizing myself with the nearby area. The thin layer of straw that covered the dirt floor shifted with each of my steps until I had created a path with my pacing. I checked every corner, and while shadows made for natural hiding spots, my enhanced sight allowed me to see through any amount of darkness.

Adelgis sat on the footrest of the carriage, his ethereal whelk floating around him while we waited. Deranged laughter drifted out of the carriage from time to time, muffled and sporadic. It gave me chills.

I couldn't waste my time, however. I withdrew my shadow sword and shield from the inky void of darkness, ready to train without any distractions. The lightweight weapons made it easy to practice for several hours straight.

Luthair formed and watched as I swung my sword. His empty helmet had zero capacity to express emotions, but the intonation of his voice told me how he felt.

"You've gotten better," he said.

"Thank you."

"But fighting with a sword and shield is different than what you first learned. A two-handed sword is meant to finish a fight quickly. A shield is for sustained fighting—and to use the power of your opponent against them."

I stopped swinging and took a deep breath. The pungent scent of the horses filled my throat, and I coughed for a second before asking, "How so?"

"Don't just block with your shield—learn to parry. It's a simple technique of bringing your shield up to meet their weapon and disturbing their blow with a countermove that should unbalance them."

"You want me to hit their sword with my shield?" I asked.

"Yes. Most opponents will have their arm extended for the strike, and the blow to the weapon will strain their wrist and elbow. It's then—when they're reeling—that you should thrust with your blade."

I turned the sword over in my hand. The sharp edge of the ebony blade glittered in the lamplight. It was a weapon crafted from a behemoth fang, and it had never failed me, even though I considered myself an amateur. Then I examined the shield. It attached to my forearm with shadow tendrils and was large enough to cover most of my torso if I held it up to block.

Of all my equipment, I knew I had to master using the shield. I had been the one to craft it, and it pulsed with an inner power—much stronger than anything the sword offered. Even though I hadn't been an expert at imbuing objects with my magic, the shield still retained vast potential.

Thinking of magic distracted me, however. My thoughts drifted to my earlier training. Why couldn't I transfer my dark-sight to Hexa? I had tried for so long... If I had mastered that technique, I could empower Adelgis and make our task of guarding easier.

"What're you thinking about?" Luthair asked.

"My abilities. Zelfree wanted me to master other aspects of augmentation—transferring my beneficial magic to others."

"Mathis had trouble with that as well. Perhaps you shouldn't think of it as augmenting another person."

"What do you mean? That's exactly what I'm doing."

Luthair faced his helmet in Adelgis's direction. "You're augmenting someone else's *magic*."

That one sentence stuck with me.

I hadn't thought of it that way.

The words circled in my mind until it clicked. I wasn't changing *them*; I was changing their magical abilities. I was adding something to their soul, the heart of their sorcery. It was the equivalent of thinking a window created sunlight, only to then learn of the sun outside. The realization made all my earlier practice seem wasted.

"Adelgis," I said as I hurried over to him. "Let me try my augmentation on you. I think I can give you the ability to see in the dark."

He perked up, his long hair barely moving away from his neck. He held out his hand. "Whatever you need."

I grabbed his wrist and tried to focus on his magic rather than his flesh. In that moment, I felt a twinge of power—like seeing a silhouette in the darkness—and it occurred to me that perhaps I could *sense* magic, if I tried long enough. I tucked the new thought away for later and returned to augmentation.

I had to alter Adelgis's magic and give him the ability to pierce the shadows.

But after thirty seconds, doubt crept into my concentration. What if I just couldn't do it, like Illia couldn't use her manipulation or Atty with her healing? I gripped Adelgis's wrist harder, determined to make this work.

I knew I was right. I wouldn't fail. I couldn't.

Pain flared from my elbow to my palm, and I almost gasped in delight. While I didn't appreciate the agony, I knew what it meant. *I had done it.*

"It worked," Adelgis said. "It's like... we're standing in the afternoon sun."

I stepped away, unable to contain my smile. "Wow. Some things become a lot easier when you change your perspective."

"I'm glad for you." Adelgis spoke with all the enthusiasm of a dying leper.

"What's wrong?"

He stared up at me. Then he placed his chin in one palm and leaned forward. "You're very talented. You pick up things so easily, even if you're second-bonded."

"That upsets you?" Was he trying to say he was jealous?

"It just reminds me that..." Adelgis glanced away, his shoulders slumped. "What am I even doing here? What am I going to do if someone tries to take this carriage? Singe him with some light beams? My best tactic would be blinding them and running for help. So someone else could do something."

"Why not practice with me? I'd be more than happy to help."

Adelgis grazed his fingers along his side and then flinched. "I can't. It hurts to move around too much."

I wanted to point out that using any of my abilities hurt —all the time—but it seemed counterproductive to make antagonizing comparisons. Then again, Zaxis always motivated me with his jabs. I didn't think I had it in me to imitate him well, however.

"How much longer will this last?" I asked.

Adelgis shrugged. "I know it'll be over soon. It has to be."

His ethereal whelk floated close. "Your father said it would take four years. Yesterday should've been the end."

"That's true."

"So you'll be free any day now, my arcanist. Please don't give in to despair."

The soft sound of footsteps alerted me to someone entering the wagon house. Guildmaster Eventide walked in and gave the place a quick glance. Her long coat—made of patchwork materials, including some phoenix feathers— fluttered behind her as she moved. She approached the nearest horse and patted its neck. The mustang snorted before returning to its hay.

"Uh, is there anything we can do for you, Guildmaster Eventide?" I asked, a little flustered. Why was she here? What was I supposed to say to her?

Adelgis jumped to his feet and brushed off his trousers. He acted just as uncertain as I felt.

Once finished with the horses, Eventide made her way over to the locked carriage, her expression shifting from pleasant to melancholy. She exhaled as she stared at the dark wood and thick chains. Her glowing arcanist mark stood out against the darkness of the wagon house.

"You two should get some rest," she said. "I'll take over everything from here."

Adelgis lifted an eyebrow. "You want us to leave?"

"I want you both to conserve your strength. Once we reach Thronehold, Zelfree will search the city for people and mystical creatures to join our guild. I'm hoping his apprentices will help him."

She wanted to recruit people for the guild? I hadn't thought of that before, but I liked the idea the moment she said it. The Frith Guild seemed small compared to its size in the legends of old. And our guild house had tons of empty space.

"But I'm supposed to watch the carriage every night," I said.

Eventide smiled, the lines at the edges of her eyes indicating she did so often. "If you do it every *other* night, you'll get just a little more rest then, won't you?" She motioned to the door. "Go on. This is a direct order from your guildmaster. Or are you being insubordinate?"

Adelgis shook his head. "Of c-course not." He hurried toward the door, acting as though Eventide's threat was serious.

But I could tell by the soft chuckle and shrug that she was just giving us a hard time. I half-bowed to her before heading out of the wagon house.

"Thank you, Guildmaster."

***

While it was considerate of Eventide to take our guard duty, I didn't go to bed. Adelgis did—but I didn't want to waste any more time. I left the inn and found a small patch of trees to do some training. If I practiced my drills often enough, I would develop a muscle memory for the motion, which would help in combat.

Luthair watched from a distance, always correcting me when I made an error. His nitpicks didn't bother me. I wanted to get it right—nothing would be worse than ingraining bad habits into my fighting style. It could cost me my life.

I slashed at the tree trunks and pretended they were attackers. My blade sometimes slid into the bark far beyond what I expected. The edge of the sword was sharp through magic, and that made the weapon extra dangerous. I bashed my shield against low-hanging branches to practice the power and movement.

As the sun rose, it brought with it a clear pink and yellow sky. It didn't captivate me like the sunrises over the ocean, and for a brief moment, I missed the smell of sea salt and the crash of waves.

"You need to rest, my arcanist," Luthair said.

I lowered my sword. My shoulder ached from hours of movement, and I wished I had Zaxis's ability to recover from exhaustion.

After a long exhale, I dropped my equipment into the darkness. "Luthair, do you think Adelgis's life is in danger?"

"I'm not certain."

"Should I bring this to Zelfree's attention?"

"Master Zelfree is already aware of the creature."

"But I don't think he knows how bad it's gotten."

Luthair offered me nothing else.

Torn between my options, I opted to return to the inn and rest for an hour or so before we needed to leave. I hadn't gone far, but I had gone in the opposite direction of the road. The shrubs and untamed grass slowed my progress.

"Show me what you've got," Zelfree spoke in the distance.

Curious, I angled myself in his direction. Perhaps this was a sign that I should tell him.

I came across an odd scene. Hexa stood on one side of the clearing, Raisen at her feet, while Zelfree stood on the other side, no more than ten feet away from her. She carried four throwing knives in one hand and a single knife in the other—poised to throw.

"C'mon," Zelfree said. "We'll be leaving soon."

Hexa held the knife with a hammer-grip. "Okay. Here it comes."

She threw it as hard as she could, but Zelfree easily leaned away and avoided the attack, despite Hexa's close proximity. Her shoulders slumped for a moment, but then she grabbed another knife and tossed it with less power, but more accuracy. Still, Zelfree stepped back and dodged the blade.

Then she threw the third, fourth, and fifth in a quick flurry of attacks. To my amusement, Zelfree barely moved to avoid them. He almost looked bored.

"If you're going to use throwing weapons," he drawled as he picked them up off the ground, "my first lesson is: *never throw them all*. Always keep one. You can let the enemy *think* you've run out of ammunition, but never do. A part of what makes throwing weapons so dangerous is the element of surprise."

Hexa nodded along with his words.

Zelfree handed the weapons back and then repositioned himself across the clearing from her. "First, you'll want to practice throwing a knife with only half a rotation spin before it hits your target. Then you can move on to a full rotation. Finally, once you've improved your accuracy, you can move to throwing with no rotations—just straight. After that, you'll need to improve your strength."

"What?" Hexa barked. She lifted her scarred arms and flexed. It wasn't anything to write home about, but I could see muscle definition, even from where I stood in the thicket. "I'm plenty strong!"

"Not enough."

Raisen hissed. "She threw the knife across the clearing!"

"I could still catch it," Zelfree said, his tone bordering on tired. Perhaps he hadn't slept.

"You can't catch these," Hexa said. "I've put poison on them. Any enemies trying to catch these will get sick if they're cut."

Zelfree removed his coat and held it with one arm. His undershirt was buttoned to the top, and the long sleeves extended to his gloves, covering every last inch of his skin. It seemed odd, but he had been like that ever since returning from Calisto's pirate ship.

"It doesn't matter how poisonous they are if you have a limp throw," he said.

His words had an obvious and immediate effect on Hexa. She clenched her jaw and gripped the first knife like she was choking it to death. Her whole body shook as she said, "Okay. Catch this."

She threw the knife with all her weight behind it.

Zelfree brought his coat up and snagged the knife in the folds of fabric with a simple *swish* through the air. Then he withdrew the knife from his coat—he had caught it without getting cut or even endangering himself.

The shock on Hexa's face almost made me laugh.

"If you had more power behind your throw, I wouldn't have had time to react," Zelfree said. "Or the blade would've pierced through the cloth. Either way, you could've gotten me, but right now you're too weak. If I wanted, I could just use your own weapon against you."

Hexa stared at the ground, her gaze distant.

"Oh," Zelfree continued. He reached into the pocket of his coat and pulled out a small book. "These are my notes on human and mystical creature anatomy. You should study these as well. Once your accuracy is better, you should target major arteries when you throw." He walked over and handed it to her, no real energy in his step.

"So, I have to study anatomy? And I have to improve my strength? And I have to learn throwing techniques? *And* I have to increase my accuracy?"

"Correct."

"I thought throwing knives would be easy! This is way harder than I imagined..."

"This is why pistols are popular," Zelfree quipped.

Hexa opened the book and squinted down at the tiny page. With a resigned sigh, she headed toward the inn, like her tasks were already overwhelming her and she needed to get away from her master before he demanded something else. Raisen waddled after her like an alligator, his two heads whispering things back and forth to each other.

As soon as Hexa reached the main road, I leapt over the last of the shrubs and approached Zelfree.

"Uh," I began.

He frowned. "Why haven't you slept yet?"

"I was practicing. Why haven't *you* slept yet?"

"Are you my keeper now?" he snapped.

I grimaced, half-regretting my comment.

Zelfree took a deep breath and crossed his arms. "Adelgis is currently asleep. I prefer when he's around to manipulate dreams."

Ah. That made sense. Zelfree seemed to suffer from

endless nightmares, but Adelgis's ability to weave dreams—even if he wasn't the best at it—had helped Zelfree become more of himself.

"Well, it's funny you should mention Adelgis," I said. "I'm worried about him. More than normal."

Zelfree lifted an eyebrow.

"His, uh, *little buddy under the skin* has gotten out of control. He says he wants to keep it, but I worry it might take his life. Apparently, it's overdue."

"We'll be passing through the city of Ellios on our way to Thronehold," Zelfree said. "That's Adelgis's hometown. I plan to speak to his father while we're there—and to get him to remove it."

"What is it?" I asked. "Do you know?"

Zelfree sardonically laughed. "It's the one thing his father never should've messed with. An abyssal leech."

9

THE CITY OF ELLIOS

It didn't take long to get the carriages and horses ready.

We left the inn in the early morning and continued south to the mountains. Everyone walked alongside the caravan while it was still cool and breezy. Once the sun and heat became unbearable, we would be confined to our tiny carriages, so we enjoyed the weather while we could. The phoenixes flew in the sky, swirling around one another. Raisen rode on the top of a carriage, and Nicholin sat on Illia's shoulder.

I looked forward to seeing Ellios. It was positioned on the road between peaks and was known as the *white jewel* because of the numerous marble quarries. That white stone glittered in the sunlight, according to Adelgis, and travelers said there was no city in the world quite like it.

"Ellios is the birthplace of the library and university," Adelgis said matter-of-factly, a smile permanently affixed to his face. "The evergrow trees make for great paper—that's why. I can't wait for you all to see them."

Atty smiled and clapped her hands together once. "I heard the Evergrow Forest is like a maze."

"It is. Oh, and my father teaches at Ellios University, so I can show you all around there, too."

"What does he teach?" Atty asked.

Adelgis perked up. "He has a class for every aspect of mystical creatures. He knows all about their locations, breeding habits, and magical powers, as well as the fables that bring mystical creatures to life, what properties they give magical items—everything. My father even owns the Ellios laboratory. And he has a personal lab at home. And a menagerie! Oh, did I also mention that my father has a collection of bones for his personal study room? Like a museum."

"Your father sounds like an accomplished man," Atty said.

Hexa rolled her eyes. She shoved her hands in her pockets and kept her gaze straight ahead. "I just want to get to Thronehold and participate in the Sovereign Dragon Tournament. We can see the boring trees, old bone collections, and stuffy universities on the way back."

Our trek was made easy by the smooth surface of the road and the hard-packed dirt. Merchants traveled the same path in groups of three or more, no doubt to scare off potential bandits. Arcanists sat on top of wagons and horses, their marks as clear as the afternoon sun. No one wanted to get robbed before making it to one of the largest markets in the world.

I almost wished I had more money to spend while we were in Thronehold. What exotic items would we stumble across?

Zaxis used the back of his hand to smack Adelgis on the shoulder. "Hey. When did you eat last?"

"Uh, before we left," Adelgis muttered as he rubbed his bicep.

"Was it enough?"

"I had some bread. I think it was enough."

Zaxis scoffed and untied the jerky pouch he kept on his belt. "Eat this."

"But I don't feel that hungry, and—"

"*Eat it.*"

"Uh, o-okay."

Adelgis took the smoked jerky and held it close, his eyebrows knitted. After a few moments of the savory aroma wafting around us, he dug into the pouch and nibbled on the first piece he withdrew.

Hexa trailed back to get close to Illia and Atty. She leaned in and whispered, "Why is Zaxis concerned about Adelgis eating?"

Atty brightened to a visible pink. She also whispered, "Well, I think they were undressing each other last night. Maybe they've gotten close."

I almost burst out laughing.

To hide my amused shock, I forced a round of coughs. Zaxis glanced back with a glare, and I suspected he hadn't heard the girls. If he had, he definitely would've said something.

Illia stared at me with her one eye, examining every detail of my expression. "By the way Volke is fighting back a laugh, I'm sure we've got this story wrong somehow."

While I was struggling not to chuckle, Zaxis shoved Adelgis toward the last carriage. Adelgis held his long black hair in place, hiding his neck from the others. Illia narrowed her eye and took note of the behavior, no doubt recognizing her own insecurity mirrored in the action.

"Just go sit down," Zaxis commanded. "I'll take over for all your guard shifts."

Adelgis put up a half-hearted fight on the way to the

carriage and almost ran into one of the mustangs. The large animal didn't move or change pace. It just kept forward, its eyes blocked with blinders to keep its gaze straight ahead.

"I'm feeling better," Adelgis muttered. "And I wanted to tell everyone about how my father—"

Zaxis scoffed, cutting him off. "We get it. Your father invented modern medicine and can satisfy 100 women at the same time. He's just *that amazing*. We don't need to hear anymore."

After a long exhale, Adelgis stopped his protests. He climbed into the carriage with the pouch of jerky still in hand.

We traveled two days before we came across a sign pointing us toward Ellios. Given the rough distances, we'd reach the city by the dawn of the fifth day, damn near halfway through our journey to Thronehold.

The Clawdam Mountains surrounded us on either side, and the roads had an upward slant that slowed our travels, even with an enbarr arcanist who could care for the horses. The scenery made up for the difficulty, though. Lush grass ran like a river between the rocky peaks, and trees grew on the plateaus in dense formations. Clouds cast giant shadows across the land, dappling the cliffs with silhouettes. It was a theater of nature that helped to pass the time.

When the fourth night descended, we continued our travels rather than stopping. Adelgis and I were assigned guard duty, but true to his word, Zaxis took his place. We walked together at a slow pace, keeping to the road and watching for any movement from the rocks above. I had never seen brigands, but I had read plenty of tales that started with a group of mountain thieves using boulders to their advantage.

Forsythe slept on top of the carriage with the plague-ridden monsters. With each exhale, he sounded like a cooing pigeon.

"Overland travel is the worst," Zaxis said. He kept his hands on his head, his fingers laced together. He even wore his gloves, like he was expecting an ambush. "Don't people understand that ships are superior?"

"A ship from Fortuna to Thronehold would've taken us around the continent, which would've been far longer."

"Feh." He glanced around, his breath hot enough that it was visible on the cool night air. "I hope we get attacked by bandits."

I shook my head. "Why would you ever want that?"

"We have several master arcanists in our midst. I feel sorry for the poor, unfortunate bandits who come looking for trouble. I want to knock a few around before they're all dealt with." He punched the air with a few quick jabs. Flames rushed off his knuckles and made bursts of light.

The mustang pulling the carriage snorted.

"Careful," I said. "What if you catch something on fire?"

Zaxis smacked my shoulder and half-laughed. "Don't worry. This prison-carriage isn't affected by magic."

"Really?"

Without an explanation, he placed his palm on the blackish wood of the carriage and unleashed a torrent of flame. I wanted to yell at him, but I waited until he finished. Sure enough, there wasn't any damage.

"See?" Zaxis said with a shrug. "Magic does nothing."

I grazed my fingers along the grain of the black wood. Why hadn't the vehicle been damaged? Did someone here have magic that prevented others from using magic? Wouldn't I have known that?

"The wood has been cured and stained with nullstone," a familiar voice said.

Fain walked out from behind the carriage, his frostbitten hands in his coat pockets. He moved with a quiet step and a keen eye, his attention on me as he kept our pace.

Had Fain been listening to us for long? Perhaps he had been riding on the back of the carriage and we hadn't known it. Either way, it was nice to hear he understood how the wood could repel magic.

"What's nullstone?" I asked.

"A special type of rock they mine from quarries all around the Argo Empire. It nullifies magic."

Zaxis stepped between us, much to my surprise. "Aren't you that traitor pirate I've heard so much about?"

The air grew colder. Fain continued to keep pace with the caravan, but he moved a few steps away from me and Zaxis.

"What of it?" Fain asked.

Without hesitating, Zaxis replied, "Bold of you to think you can just talk to us. We don't need to exchange words with filth like you."

"*Zaxis*," I snapped.

He wheeled on me with a glare as icy as the ever-chilling night air. It caught me off guard, and before I could make a reasoned argument, Zaxis returned his attention to Fain.

"How many people have you killed?" he asked.

Fain said nothing.

Zaxis continued, "How many innocent lives did you wreck? How many homes did you burn? How many people were tortured at the hands of Calisto while you did nothing? How many—"

"Too many," Fain interjected, the finality of his words an answer to all the questions.

The silence that followed made it seem like even the crickets in the nearby grass were afraid to draw attention. I glanced upward, curious to see why Forsythe wasn't cooing. The phoenix sat perched at the edge of the black carriage, his crimson feathers puffed and his gold eyes locked on Fain.

"Get out of here," Zaxis commanded. "Just stay away from us, and there won't be any trouble."

Fain's expression remained neutral, but there was a hard edge to his features that hadn't been there before. He turned to me. "Volke, would you mind if we spoke alone?"

I nodded.

"What did I just say?" Zaxis shouted.

He shoved Fain off the road in one powerful motion. Fain stumbled, but kept his footing. They squared off. Frost appeared over the grass, dirt, and rocks. Another drop in temperature, but the anger in my blood prevented me from feeling much of it.

I leapt between them. "Enough! This isn't needed."

Wraith dropped his invisibility and snapped at Zaxis—a warning—his disease-ridden fangs white enough to glisten in the moonlight. A guttural growl emanated from deep within his chest, and he kept his hackles raised.

The caravan continued without us. Forsythe took to the sky and circled low, his razor-sharp talons quite visible.

"Zaxis, this is uncalled for," I said. "I told you Fain helped create these plague-warding items. The least you can do is keep your aggression in check."

"Why aren't you thinking about Illia?" he asked, his voice loud, but no longer shouting. "You know it'll upset her if this lowlife is walking around like his crimes don't matter."

"I haven't forgotten about Illia, but I'm not going to back down from this position, either."

"You're making a mistake."

"I know what I'm doing. Go back to the carriage."

I could tell from the way Zaxis clenched and unclenched his fists that he didn't appreciate me giving him any kind of order. He didn't argue, though. I had expected more shouting—more physical confrontation—but Zaxis wheeled around on his heel and motioned for Forsythe to follow. The two headed down the road and caught up with the caravan.

Wraith stopped his growling and then sat at his arcanist's side. His wagged his wolf-like tail. "I've never tasted a phoenix before."

"Shh," Fain muttered. "Words like that will only cause more trouble."

"I'm sorry," I said. "Zaxis is a lot more *zealous* these days."

"You probably should've just let us fight."

I had to mull over his statement a few times before it sunk in. "Why?"

"After I joined Calisto's crew, a handful of the others took to treating me much like your phoenix arcanist friend. One night it got too rough, and I gutted a man." Fain shrugged, blasé in all regards. "After that, they didn't give me any trouble." He slipped a stiletto dagger out from the sleeve of his coat. "People will think twice about messing with you if they know you'll fight."

"Well, this isn't a pirate ship." I waved my hand around and pointed to the beautiful trees, lush grass, and glorious mountain range. "You don't need a fake name, and you certainly don't need to gut anyone."

Fain said nothing.

I rubbed at the back of my neck. "Is there a reason you came to see me?"

"Gillie said I should *mingle with my peers.*" He spoke the last part like it was an anathema. "But I think she might be touched in the head. Her cheeriness knows no bounds, and she was convinced the apprentices of the Frith Guild would accept me with open arms." He twirled the dagger in one hand. "We both saw how well that went."

"Okay. How can I help?"

Fain stopped playing with his weapon and put it away. Then he turned his gaze to the distance, his eyes unfocused. "Would you mind if... I accompanied you? To see how you do it?"

"Do what?"

"Interact with these kinds of people."

There was a sad edge to his tone that troubled me. I knew he hadn't had a pleasant life, and perhaps the others would be more forgiving if they knew, too. Everyone but Illia, that was. I already knew what she would say. *His life wasn't worse than mine.*

But Fain didn't have someone as amazing as Gravekeeper William to help him get back on his feet. And in some small way, *I* wanted to be William in this situation.

"Sure," I said. "Whenever you want to accompany me around, I'll help you."

Wanting to change was the first step—that was what William would say—and Fain wanted to change.

Adelgis hadn't lied.

The moment day broke and light poured onto Ellios, the

white marble shone as though the whole city had been carved from a full moon. Even the walls, which stood fifteen feet high, were ivory beyond compare. I stared with wide eyes the entire walk up to the city gates, enamored by the pristine beauty.

We were ushered through without hassle and then greeted by a city with grid-like streets and organized buildings. The stones of the sidewalks had been arranged in squares—large stones around the outside, smaller stones on the inside—all with precision, as though thought had gone into the placement of even the smallest pebble.

Growing on the mountainsides in both directions were massive forests of evergrow trees. Their canopies laced together to create a thick roof of green leaves, and it was almost difficult to see their twisted trunks. Once I did, however, I understood why they were so valuable.

Each tree appeared to have been cut down several times. Remnants of the old trunk created the foundation for the new tree—it grew in all directions from the stump of the previous tree that had been cut. As long as the roots stayed intact, it seemed as though the tree would grow forever, hence its name.

A river ran at the far end of town, and I could already tell by the industrial smoke that was where they kept their furnaces.

While the caravan stopped at the largest inn in the city, Zaxis, Hexa, Adelgis, and I waited on the street corner, observing the sights. Although Fain had asked to accompany me, I hadn't seen him since last night. He would work on his own time, I supposed.

"Minerva owls dwell in the forest," Adelgis said, pointing to the sides of the mountain. "My father helps with the bonding ceremonies every five years when the owlets are ready to leave the nest.”

“So they’re owl mystical creatures?” Hexa asked.

“That’s right. They’re quite intelligent. Their trial of worth involves puzzles. My father once helped with crafting them. Now my mother helps.”

“Oh, you have a mother?”

Adelgis faced Hexa, his brow furrowed. “Of course. What kind of question is that?”

She snickered, amused by her own sarcastic joke. It took Adelgis several painful seconds before he put it all together.

“Ha ha. Very funny.”

Zelfree emerged from the posh inn, his dark outfit a harsh contrast to the white and bright green of the city. He flipped up the collar of his coat, like the radiance of our surroundings was one of his hidden weaknesses. Traces sat perched on his shoulder, her long cat tail swishing back and forth as Zelfree hurried across the street and headed straight for us.

“We aren’t staying here long,” he said as he stepped up onto the sidewalk. “Adelgis, you’re coming with me. We’re going to visit your father.”

“Right now?” Adelgis fidgeted with the edges of his sleeves. “He’ll be busy.”

“I don’t care.”

“He’s never in a good mood when people interrupt him, though. Maybe we should visit him on the way back. With plenty of warning ahead of time.”

The desperation in Adelgis’s voice worried me. Zaxis and Hexa even exchanged questioning glances, like they had heard it, too.

“I need to speak with him,” Zelfree said. “And this is important. Whatever he’s doing can wait.”

"Can Volke come?"

The question surprised me, but I had to admit, I wanted to go. Adelgis spoke of his father nonstop, and it made me curious.

Zelfree shrugged. "Sure. He can come."

"And Zaxis?" Adelgis added.

That addition shocked me. Zaxis perked up and jumped at the opportunity to include himself. We were the only two other apprentices who knew Adelgis's secret, so it made sense, but the hurt look on Hexa's face made me feel guilty.

"Fine," Zelfree stated. "We just need to settle this quickly."

Traces pointed with the tip of her tail. "That way, my arcanist. I can already sense those weird creatures he likes to collect."

10

ABYSSAL LEECH

We approached a mansion positioned at the top of a small hill. The green of the trees complemented the bright red bricks and light blue paint of the walls. The clear windows allowed for a tiny glimpse into a spotless living environment, as though the entire estate was on display and not actually lived in. Two stories stretched up to the sky, and the points on the roof had the appearance of faux towers.

The wrought-iron fence surrounding the property prevented us from walking to the front door. A gate attendant stood ready, a slight smile on his face as we neared. He seemed older, perhaps in his fifties, but he held himself with a straight posture.

"Hello, Gevnin," Adelgis said. "It's so nice to see you again."

Gevnin's eyes widened, wrinkling his forehead in surprise. "Oh, if it isn't the youngest lord!" He opened the gate without hesitation and ushered us all in. "Welcome home."

We entered and the man bowed to us. I hadn't been

expecting that, but I didn't comment. Instead, I glanced at the fragrant flowers blooming in the yard, then to the walkway. Black stones intermingled with the white, spelling out the word *VENROVER*.

"Venrover?" Zaxis asked, his gaze on the ground. "What is that?"

Adelgis frowned in irritation. "My family's name."

"Don't give me that look. Why would I ever remember your last name?"

"I remember yours."

Zaxis scoffed. "Nobody cares. It's only three letters."

Without any words, Zelfree turned to us, his icy expression enough to calm someone with the plague. Zaxis and Adelgis stopped arguing, and I shoved my hands in my pockets, feeling guilty for allowing the commotion to continue unchecked.

Traces leapt from her arcanist's shoulder and landed on mine. Her sleek, cat-like body wrapped around behind my neck as she nuzzled close.

"What're you doing?" I whispered.

With a purr, and in a quiet voice, she replied, "I don't want to be on his shoulder when he starts yelling."

"At us?"

Traces hooked her claws into my coat and held tight. "Oh, no. He likes all of you. It's Theasin he detests."

"Who?"

She said nothing, her tail swishing from side to side.

We reached the front door of the palatial estate, and I stopped to admire it. The doorframe had been laced with metals—copper, tin, bronze—and the shapes they created looked like mystical creatures. The door itself had a dragon-mouth knocker, but the most interesting aspect was the wood. It was black, like the prison-carriage. Nullstone? Here?

Before Zelfree could knock on the door, Adelgis hurried in front of him.

"Wait a moment."

Zelfree regarded him with a long look.

"I think I should prepare you," Adelgis continued. "My father is, in a word, *severe*. I don't think it's wise to interrupt him when he's busy. I suggest we speak to the housemaid, and if she thinks he'll have a spare moment, then we can—"

"I know your father," Zelfree interjected.

Adelgis's eyebrows shot up. "You... you do?"

"Yes. We've been on several expeditions together."

"I know you worked with my father—that's why I apprenticed under you—but that's not the same as *knowing him*. When was the last time you two spoke?"

"Decades ago." Zelfree pushed Adelgis aside. "I didn't think I'd have to see the man again, but I suppose I'm a fool who never learns his lesson. I brought the situation on myself when I took you as an apprentice." He ground his teeth and glared at the solid wood door. "Now I have to deal with this."

He pounded on the door with the dragon knocker.

Several seconds dragged by as we waited in silence. The chill of the wind, along with the rustle of the leaves, reminded me of the graveyard back on Ruma.

Then the door creaked open, the sound slow and painful, like a metal fork dragging across a ceramic plate. An older woman peered out, her graying hair tied back in a tight bun. She smiled the moment she laid eyes on Adelgis.

"Oh, young master. Please come in."

She pulled the door open the rest of the way and bowed.

We stepped into the foyer, and I had to glance around to

take everything in. An empty fireplace, six bookshelves, two couches, four cushioned chairs, a rug of silver and white—the place was so clean, I wondered if magic had somehow been involved. I didn't know of any mystical creatures that were fabulous domestic servants, but they probably existed.

The housemaid walked deeper into the house, leaving us alone in the foyer.

"What does your father do for a living?" Zaxis asked as he, too, glanced around the giant room.

"How many times do I have to tell you? He researches rare mystical creatures."

"Is that all? This house seems like it was built on more than *research money*. My family owns the largest business on our island, and we don't have a house this big."

"Didn't you grow up on the dinky Isle of Ruma?"

The way Adelgis asked the question—with a piteous condescension—made it seem more like an insult. Zaxis must have felt the same because he narrowed his eyes in a harsh glare. It made me laugh, though. Zaxis's family had always been one of the affluent ones, but it was all relative. Adelgis's father seemed to have enough wealth to purchase our whole damn island.

Maybe Zaxis was right to ask—what was Adelgis's father researching that would get him this much money? Perhaps he dealt in occult secrets.

Adelgis straightened the collar of his coat. "My father is extremely talented. Everyone who meets him says so."

I turned my attention to Zelfree, curious to hear his take on the situation.

The far door opened and interrupted the moment, however.

A woman strode into the foyer, her emerald dress covered in ruffles yet tight on her body, hugging every curve.

Her black hair—just as lush and inky as Adelgis's—was bunched in tight curls and hung down to her waist. With an elegant gait, she walked to the center of the room and offered us all a tight smile. Her makeup highlighted her pale blue eyes and accentuated the arcanist's mark on her forehead.

The bird woven through her star made it clear to the world she was a minerva owl arcanist.

"Adelgis," she said, a hint of surprise in her voice. She hurried over to him and ran her slender fingers over his shoulders. "You've gotten taller since I saw you last."

Adelgis smiled. "How are you, Mother?"

She stepped away and examined him. "You look so different. Forgive me—when the housemaid said my son had come to visit, I thought she meant Niro."

They never embraced or offered each other any other sentiments. It felt odd, almost tense. Adelgis kept smiling, though, so I figured he had to be happy. Gravekeeper William would've hugged Illia and me for a solid thirty seconds if he had greeted us.

"Is Cinna here?" Adelgis asked.

"She's upstairs in her room, resting."

"Can I see her?"

"Knock first. If your sister is asleep, leave her be."

Adelgis didn't say anything to us; he just left the room with a single-minded focus. The silence that followed wasn't pleasant. Adelgis's mother and Zelfree met each other's gaze, the recognition—and disgust—were plain to see. I almost excused myself and left the house, but I took a breath and then shuffled toward one of the bookshelves, wishing I had gone with Adelgis.

"How many siblings does Adelgis have?" Zaxis whispered as he followed me.

"He said he was one of seven," I muttered.

"Really? That many?"

Adelgis's mother crossed her arms and tapped a finger on the crux of her elbow. "Everett."

Zelfree lifted an eyebrow. "Ketsa."

"I never thought I'd see you again."

"I wished that would've been true."

She sneered as she examined him, starting with his boots and ending with his coat. "You look like a boat rat. Dirty. Washed up. I heard rumors you had given up on life."

"I'm sorry to disappoint you," Zelfree drawled.

"Now you come shambling into my house like an undead urchin. How did you trick my son into escorting you here?"

"He's my apprentice."

Zelfree made the statement with a coy smile.

Ketsa brought a hand up to her collar bone, a silent gasp on her face—like this was the worst possible news someone could bring her. Her dramatic reaction made me laugh, but I stifled it with a soft cough.

"You're teaching him your underhanded tricks?" she asked, her tone heated. "Disgusting. Adelgis was specifically instructed not to engage with the Frith Guild. Did you blackmail him? Was it duress? Lies?"

"Adelgis petitioned to join the Frith Guild of his own accord. I admit, when I saw his last name, I was ready to send him into the ocean, but it turns out he's nothing like his father, so I gave him chance."

"How dare you."

The housemaid walked into the foyer with a silver platter. An array of cups, cookies, and sandwiches were spread out in an easy-to-grab formation. Ketsa wheeled around and hissed something under her breath. The housemaid backed out of the room in a hurry, muttering apologies as she went and taking the snacks with her.

"Get out of my house," Ketsa said to Zelfree. Then she waved her hand at me and Zaxis. "And take your goons with you."

Zaxis and I exchanged confused looks.

Goons?

Zelfree shook his head. "I'm here to speak with your husband. Where's Theasin?"

"You have no business with him."

"I know about the abyssal leech," Zelfree growled. His posture became tense, and he stepped toward Ketsa. "Now where is your husband?"

Traces clung to my shoulder even tighter than before. I patted her head and scratched behind the ears, but even I felt anxious. Would this turn into a serious fight? If Zelfree was like this with Ketsa, what would he be like with Theasin?

"That leech is none of your concern," Ketsa stated. "Leave."

"Have you forgotten that I was there when Theasin gathered those leeches?" Zelfree chuckled, but it was dark and devoid of humor. "I saw what they did to all their hosts. I helped kill the abyssal leech arcanist—and then I pried his eldrin right out of his warm innards."

Ketsa kept her arms tight across her body, her hands clenched. She said nothing, but her lips twitched downward at the edges.

"Theasin said he only gathered *dead* leeches," Zelfree continued. "For research. And item creation. Gregory Ruma told him *specifically* that if he took anything that was alive—"

"Gregory Ruma isn't around anymore, is he?" Ketsa

interjected with a smirk. "And this endeavor far outweighs any other concerns. Those leeches are extinct, except for this last one. Adelgis volunteered to keep it safe. He's undertaken a noble and historic duty, and his father and I are very proud."

"It's killing him," Zelfree said, monotone and cold.

"What would you know? You made *dressing as a pirate* your profession."

"I'll start acting like one too unless you get your husband."

Ketsa backed away, her mouth agape. "You would threaten me in my own home?" It looked as though she was overtaken with disbelief. She shook her head and threw her hands into the air. "Unbelievable. I have half a mind to call the city guard."

It only took Zelfree a few steps to close the distance between them. His movement was rigid, like he held himself back. He grabbed Ketsa by the upper arm—hard enough that she flinched—and through gritted teeth, he said, "Listen to what I'm saying. I saw what the leeches were capable of. *It's killing him.*"

"Unhand me," she growled.

Ketsa waved her own hand in an arc, and a powerful gust of wind flooded the foyer. Zelfree shielded his eyes and retreated a few steps. Books tumbled off the shelves. One of the chairs fell over. A chandelier rattled overhead, but otherwise remained whole. Zaxis and I kept our balance, and then we both spread out, ready to act if the situation escalated. Luthair's shadow darted at my feet. He would jump to my aid in a heartbeat.

"My husband knows what he's doing," Ketsa shouted. "More than you do! He said Adelgis could handle the leech, *so he can.*"

I didn't say anything, but I thought it was bizarre that Adelgis's mother hadn't even seen what the leech was doing to her son, yet she was certain everything was fine. I would've at least inspected it—especially if there was a chance my child's life was on the line.

"Where is Theasin?" Zelfree asked. I could tell by his expression he was done with this.

"He isn't here." Ketsa pointed to the door. "Two weeks ago, he left for Thronehold on urgent business for the queen. Are you happy? You can go now."

Adelgis rushed into the room, his breathing heavy. He glanced around, took in the mess, and then turned to Zelfree. "What happened?"

His mother walked over and placed a hand on his shoulder. She stared at him with a furrowed brow. "He told me you were suffering because of the mystical creature your father entrusted to you."

"What?" Adelgis glanced between his mother and Zelfree. "I never said that."

Ketsa relaxed. She held one of Adelgis's hands with both of hers. "Everett was yelling, like the lowlife he is, and then demanded to see your father."

With a quick and confused look, Adelgis asked Zelfree, "You were yelling at my mother?"

A piece of me thought Zelfree would become unhinged. It was as if no one was listening to him.

"It's killing you," Zelfree said. "Your father needs to remove it."

"No." Adelgis shook his head. "No. I have this under control. I'd forgotten to eat, but that's not a problem anymore. I'm fine."

"You've had it longer than you expected, though. Right?"

Adelgis caught his breath. He fumbled for the words, but never answered.

"Get out of my house," Ketsa demanded. "You're not welcome here. You're *never* welcome here."

Obviously done with the situation—and probably needing a strong drink—Zelfree exhaled and headed for the front door. Zaxis and I jumped to follow him, but when Adelgis didn't move, I stopped.

"Are you coming?" I asked.

Ketsa threw back her curly hair. "No. Adelgis is staying here with me."

11

AURA OF PROSPERITY

"Mother," Adelgis said. "I'm going to return to the Frith Guild. I'm in the middle of my apprenticeship."

"Since when did you join them? It couldn't have been long. You can find a new master."

"I've been with them for over a year. I write you letters. I've told you all about it."

The hurt in Adelgis's voice made me cringe. Even Traces, who clung to my shoulder, emitted a sad mew.

Ketsa ran her thumb along her son's cheek. "Adelgis... you know I can get busy. I have things to attend to and—"

"Never mind," he said, his voice much harsher than before. "Just forget it. I'm going to continue with the Frith Guild, and I'll visit you again when we pass back through Ellios."

She moved her hand down to Adelgis's arm and held firm. For a moment, they said nothing, and I wondered what was happening. Adelgis gave me a quick glance, and then he motioned to the door with a wave of his hand.

"I'll be there in a minute."

I nodded and exited the palatial foyer. The scenery of a perfect city glittered in the distance as I strolled down the walkway. Zaxis and Zelfree waited halfway between the mansion and the gate, their hushed voices drifting away on the wind. I couldn't make out their speech until I got close.

Zaxis shrugged. "I could've told you that Adelgis would refuse help. I already tried to cut the damn thing out of his body. He wouldn't let me near it."

"I'll need to convince his father," Zelfree said. As the wind swirled around us, he dwelled on the situation, muttering things to himself.

I stood next to them and glanced over my shoulder every couple seconds, hoping Adelgis would emerge so we could leave. Traces did the same thing, her cat-eyes bright in the light of an early afternoon sun. Her gray fur, short and sleek, shimmered whenever she moved.

With a look of mild confusion, Zaxis snapped his fingers. "Hey. You said you went on an expedition with Adelgis's father decades ago, and that was when you found the abyssal leech. Did Adelgis get infected then? Or was it just sitting around until recently? It didn't die?"

"Theasin is a relickeeper arcanist," Zelfree stated. "He uses his magic to preserve things on the edge of death."

Traces tilted her head and twitched her ears. "He has dozens of things in his cellar. I can still sense them." She shuddered. "It's an odd feeling."

"He probably kept the leech until he found someone stupid enough to infect."

"Relickeeper?" I asked.

I had never heard of that mystical creature, but it sounded intriguing.

The front door to the Venrover mansion opened and slammed shut. Adelgis stood on the outside, his back to the black wood. With trembling hands, he pushed away from the house and ambled toward us, his gaze on his feet. At first I thought he might be ill again, but he wasn't sweating or even pale.

Adelgis didn't get far before the front door opened again. I expected Ketsa, but a young girl around my age hobbled outside instead. Her silky, black hair marked her as a member of the Venrover family, and her fine dress of pink silk removed the last of my doubt.

"Wait, Adel," she called out. "At least say goodbye."

He stopped and headed back for her. They embraced and whispered to one another, though the girl didn't move around much. She refused to put her weight on her left leg, and the more I paid attention, the more I realized how thin and weak she was. Her hands shook, and she leaned against the wall of the mansion for support.

"How many leeches do you think she has?" Zaxis quipped.

I knew it was a joke, but a piece of me gave the statement some serious thought. I crossed my arms and waited until Adelgis had finished speaking with his sister. They hugged one last time before he walked away.

"I'll look forward to your next visit, Adel!" The girl waved. "Please write more. I miss you!"

"I will," he called back. "Goodbye, Cinna."

After a heavy sigh, Adelgis made his way to us. He didn't say anything; he just continued toward the front gate. We followed behind, no one spoke a word. I didn't know what to say, and the longer the silence persisted, the more I didn't want to be the one to break it.

The gatekeeper allowed us out with a smile. When we reached the street, we continued to the curb at a slow pace.

Adelgis stopped and faced Zelfree, his shoulders back, his posture straight. "I'd appreciate it if you discussed matters like this with me before you went to my family."

Zelfree mulled over the comment. "Fair enough."

That took the wind out of Adelgis's sails—he widened his eyes and fiddled with the sleeves of his coat. "Uh, well, okay. Thank you then."

"But when we get to Thronehold, you will at least talk to your father about the situation. I know you say you're fine, but—"

"I will."

Zelfree patted him on the shoulder. "Good. Because I've already dealt with an abyssal leech in the past. I don't want to do it again." He shoved Adelgis in the direction of the inn.

Zaxis followed after, but when I attempted to join them, Zelfree held me back. We waited a few moments until Adelgis had gotten out of earshot.

"Watch him," Zelfree commanded.

There had never been a need for the order, but I nodded in confirmation regardless.

We didn't stay in Ellios long.

It was shame—the entire city held a wealth of information. The local library had dozens of books, some even authored by Adelgis's father, which he shared more than a hundred times. I loved reading, but the Isle of Ruma didn't have an amazing selection. Gravekeeper William had a personal collection with tales about all my favorite arcanists, and I had read each of those twice over.

We took the southern road out of the city and came to our first turnpike. A fort positioned in the narrow valley between mountains marked the edge of the Argo Empire. Anyone traveling with more than a single horse had to pay a toll or take the long path up and down the peaks.

Flags of the empire waved from each corner of the fort, a dragon and a rose over the colors of red and white. Our island nation—named Perphestoni after the first queen, a mouthful to utter, which was why no one did—had a simple flag. It consisted of three gold stars and a blue background.

Exciting.

Zaxis punched me on the shoulder the second we stepped into the Argo Empire. "I bet this is the farthest you've ever traveled from the Isle of Ruma, isn't it?"

"I think Port Crown might be physically farther," I muttered as I rubbed my bicep.

"Eh. Even if it is, Port Crown would never host a tournament. I can't wait to participate."

"It'll be amusing."

"I have to win," he said. He walked closer to me and lowered his voice. "It'll be impressive, right? No one can deny that."

"We do have important matters to deal with in Thronehold. Guildmaster Eventide said we'll even be recruiting."

He scoffed and moved away from me. "Listen to you. I should've known that's what you'd say." He shook his head as he continued, "You'd be more excited too if there was any chance you'd win."

Sometimes his attitude grated on my patience. I let the conversation drift away with the ever-increasing wind, and my attention shifted focus to the other people traveling to Thronehold. The merchants seemingly doubled in number.

Each cart that rumbled by distracted me, so I walked on the side of the road to continue my training.

Zaxis's words came back to me, and although I had planned for a short magic session, I opted to practice the entire evening instead.

***

Two days' travel into the empire, and three days from our ultimate destination, an unusual shadow blanketed the caravan, despite the glory of the midafternoon sun.

I glanced up and caught my breath, stunned to see the silhouette of a massive dragon soaring across the sky.

A few people pointed and several gasped. Ripples of conversation rolled into the crowds as one by one, everyone craned their heads back to get a better view.

"Luthair," I said. "Do you see that?"

"Yes, my arcanist." His shadow shifted around my feet as he spoke. "It's the sovereign dragon of the queen."

The dragon had giant leather wings and scales of ebony and crimson. It was hard to distinguish the markings, given how high up it was, but I squinted and watched as the sovereign dragon flew south, toward Thronehold. While it wasn't as large as the atlas turtle, it was at least half the size and thick with muscle.

A question came to mind, and I hurried to find Zelfree. He and Gillie walked alongside the head carriage, their attention fixed on the disappearing dragon.

I approached and pointed to the dark spot in the sky. "Master Zelfree, I've been meaning to ask you something about the dragon."

"What is it?" he asked.

"I know you said they were powerful and impressive, but

why would this empire only allow sovereign dragon arcanists to rule? Is there a particular reason? Everyone here on the road looks like they're in awe."

Gillie smiled and quietly clapped her hands together. "Oh, please explain. I want to hear this too."

"You know why, Gillie," he said, a hint of irritation in his voice.

"Pish-posh. I want to experience your teaching method. Regale me with the explanation."

Zelfree faced away from her, more than necessary to speak with me, and then said, "You're aware of the magical basics. Evocation creates things, manipulation controls things, augmentation alters things, and imbuing empowers things."

"Okay?"

"Well, there's another category of magic use—arcanists can create *auras*. It's an area of effect where their magic permeates everything. It's difficult to learn, but powerful. Each mystical creature can create a unique aura, and the sovereign dragons have an aura of prosperity."

Gillie placed a hand on her cheek and nodded. "Quite right. You're so knowledgeable, Everett. You're doing a good job."

Her enthusiastic compliment and encouragement seemed to darken Zelfree's mood.

He continued, more irritated than before, "The sovereign dragon's aura of prosperity allows plants to grow faster and affects an individual's ambition and comprehension of math, logic, and consequences."

I half-laughed. "Kind of specific."

"They're examples," he snapped. "Just know the aura helps individuals make better decisions. That's why the empire has been so prosperous, despite losses and problems."

"Will an aura remain here if the queen leaves?"

"No."

"How far does it reach?"

I doubted he appreciated the line of questions—he narrowed his eyes, like he was trying to hint at something—but I still wanted to know. He replied with, "There are several factors. The age of the eldrin, the power of the arcanist—some mystical creatures have auras with small limits. The sovereign dragon's aura can stretch across the whole empire. That's why Thronehold is positioned where it is. In the center of the territory."

"It's a shame our queen doesn't have a prosperity aura," Gillie muttered as she stroked her chin. "I think it would help the herbs in my lab grow all the faster."

Zelfree didn't elaborate any further, so I slowed my walk and drifted to the back of the caravan, my mind on the possibilities of auras that subtly affected everything around an arcanist and their eldrin.

"What aura can you create?" I asked the shadows.

Luthair replied, "Mathis never manifested an aura."

"It's that difficult?"

"It requires peace of mind. Imagine it more like imbuing your own body with so much magic, it spills out, like an overflowing cup. That overflow is the aura. Maintaining that for a length of time can be taxing. Mathis was more concerned with mastering his other abilities."

The mystery got me curious.

A knightmare aura...

On the morning of the final day of our travel, I couldn't keep calm.

I walked with the prison-carriage, the muffled laughing and sharp cries barely registering in my thoughts. The weather had been perfect since we had entered the Argo Empire. An effect of the prosperity aura? It made me wonder.

Zaxis jabbed me with his elbow, and I shot him a glare.

"Did you hear me?" he asked.

"No," I muttered. "What do you want?"

"You seem distracted."

"Yeah. I can't stop thinking about things." I cracked my knuckles, unable to contain my restless energy. "Do you mind if I go ahead? I feel pent up."

"I feel that way all the time," he said with a huff.

"How often do I ask anything of you?"

Zaxis ran a hand through his red hair. It looked more coppery-brown today, for whatever reason, and he examined a strand for a long moment before answering, "Fine. But if you catch sight of anything interesting, you've got to come back and tell me about it. Guard duty sucks the excitement out of everything."

I almost gave the man a hug, but I knew he wouldn't like that. Instead, I headed for the woodlands along the side of the road. The throngs of merchants and travelers made my quest difficult, however. I had to dance through the crowds and even remind a few people I was an arcanist so they'd let me pass.

Thankfully, the farther I got from the road, the quieter the world became.

We were so close to our destination, yet at the same time, it felt so far.

The tranquil atmosphere calmed me for a bit, but then

my mind wandered, and I wondered if there were dangers lurking between the oak trees and shrubs. The beautiful midmorning sunshine cascaded between the leaves, creating pillars of radiance. My surroundings looked more like an oil painting than a den for evil, yet I couldn't stop myself from imagining terrible scenarios.

Bandits and cutthroats were the pirates of the land.

And plague-ridden creatures could be anywhere.

I shrugged off my anxiety. I had Luthair, and my sorcery came much easier now than it had before. If anything tried to harm me, it would be in for a world of hurt.

"Help!"

For a split second, I thought I had imagined the shout. I stopped walking and listened. The rushing sound of water echoed between the trees. I heard nothing else.

I held my breath and waited another long minute. Had I made it up?

"Help..."

The cry was weaker than before, but I had definitely heard it.

"I'm coming," I called out.

My shadow darted around my feet. "Volke. You can't rush into every—"

I took off through the woodland, unconcerned with Luthair's scolding. I knew what he was going to say. *It's dangerous to dive head-first into a situation.* But someone was calling for help—I'd rather assume they were genuinely in need rather than assume they were a villain attempting to trick me.

It didn't take me long to find the source of rushing water. A river no more than twenty feet across meandered through the woodland. The pebble shores glistened in the sunlight, and while it was beautiful, the current seemed swift.

"Please... someone!"

I glanced around, uncertain where the cry was coming from, even though it now sounded louder than before. Then I spotted a young girl in the middle of the river—she was holding onto a thin branch from a tree that had grown out over the water, but it wasn't large enough to climb up. Her hand slipped, and a second later, she disappeared beneath the surface.

RIVER ENCOUNTER

I threw off my coat and slipped into the shadows.

The cold darkness allowed me to travel faster than swimming. I shifted across the bank, under the water, and then emerged in the river. The wet shock when I exited the shadows almost made me gasp, but I held back the urge and swam up to meet the little girl. She wasn't heavy or large, so it was easy to wrap one of my arms around her. I pulled her to the surface with little effort.

Once her head got above the water, she coughed and gulped down air. Then she threw her arms around my neck and squeezed tight.

I swam toward the shore, half-fighting the current. "I've got you."

"I can't swim," she said, her voice on the edge of tears.

"Everything will be fine. I'm an excellent swimmer."

Her fingernails dug into my skin, and she trembled the entire way. I held her firmly against my chest and made sure her head never went below the surface. Ocean waters were rougher than the river. The thought of drowning never even crossed my mind.

"We're almost there," I said. "You've got nothing to worry about."

When we neared the shore, I realized how shallow the river had become. I stood—the water barely reached my knees—and I went to put the girl down. She clung harder, almost choking me.

"*No!* Not in the water." She pressed her face into my shoulder and stifled a sob. "Please... not the water."

I didn't want to argue with her, not while she was distraught, so I picked her up with both arms and carried her to shore. Even wet, she didn't weigh much. I suspected she was twelve or thirteen years old and on the smallish side, even for that age range.

"Land ho," I said with a chuckle. "You're safe."

I set her down on the emerald grass, a good ten feet from the edge of the river. She released my neck and then wrapped her arms around herself, her trembling quickly shifting to a shiver. Her dress—which I suspected had once been elegant and fancy—sagged and clung at weird angles.

And while the black and ivory lace was intricate enough to take note of, her white hair stole my attention. I had seen white hair on the elderly, but never on someone her age. And it didn't look like the wispy locks of someone who had lived a long life—the girl's hair had the lush sheen of youth and even seemed purplish at the edges.

I had never seen hair that color.

She rubbed her arms, her shivering intensifying.

"I'm sorry," I said. "Let me get you something."

I held my hand out and manipulated the shadows to grab my coat. The darkness brought it to me in a matter of seconds, and while it hurt, I pushed the sensation aside. Then I wrapped my coat around her shoulders and buttoned it in the front.

"There." I stepped back and glanced around. "Is your mother nearby? I can take you to her, just to make sure everything is okay."

The girl's expression changed in a heartbeat, switching her from *frightened girl* to *seething anger*. She glared up at me, her blue eyes laced with the same purplish hue as her hair.

"My *mother*?" she repeated. "I'll have you know that I'm a young woman."

Gone was the fear in her voice—it had been replaced with an indignant rage. Her face remained puffy at the edges, like she had been crying, but the river water made it difficult to tell.

I wrung out my shirt. "Uh, sorry about that. Is your house close? I could escort you there."

"This is private property, thank you very much. My family owns this whole area." She waved her arm around. "The real question is: what're *you* doing here?"

I stopped messing with my shirt and narrowed my gaze at her. "Are you serious? I heard someone calling for help, so I rushed over."

"Ha! A likely story." She flipped back her wet hair and straightened it as best she could with her fingers. "You were probably trespassing. Better yet, you were probably spying on me. Did you get a good eyeful? Is that what you were after?"

Her mental ship of delusions just kept sailing.

I forced a laugh and shook my head. "I think there's been a misunderstanding. I was just trying to help." I pointed back to the woods. "If you're okay now, I'll leave."

"You expect me to believe you didn't come here to see me?"

"I don't know who you are," I said with a shrug. "So no. I didn't come here to see you."

The girl's mouth dropped open. Then she grabbed at her white hair and motioned to it with dramatic emphasis. I stared at her for a long moment, waiting for her to do or say something else, but nothing came.

"Um, you have beautiful hair?" What did she want from me?

Galloping interrupted our accusation-filled conversation. Two horses rode out from the tree line, both decorated in polished silver armor and adorned with shiny saddles. Their brown manes had been trimmed short, and they headed in our direction.

One saddle was empty, but the other horse had a rider just as striking as the little girl.

The woman's white hair fluttered in the wind while she rode. Her leather riding attire had been fitted perfectly for her, including the boots that cut off at the knee.

I had to admit, I enjoyed watching her gallop over. I had never seen anything so graceful, yet mystical, in my entire life.

"Evianna?" the woman asked as she pulled on the reins of her horse. "What happened?" Once the stallion had come to a stop, she leapt off and rushed over. "Are you okay?"

The girl, Evianna, shook her head. "Everything is fine. Nothing happened."

"You're soaking wet. Did you fall into the river?" The woman heaved a sigh. "I told you not to go anywhere near—"

"I didn't fall in!" Evianna pulled my coat tight and then snapped her gaze up to meet mine. "He threw me in."

"What?" I barked.

"That's right! I was minding my own business when this ruffian threw me into the water."

Despite the wild accusation, the woman never looked at

me. She kept her attention on Evianna, and in a stern tone, she said, "This is unbecoming. A lady of your standing shouldn't lie."

Those words cut through any argument. Evianna glanced down at her bare feet and bunched her shoulders close to her neck. She stepped closer to the woman and whispered, "I'm sorry, Lyvia. B-But I don't like him. He was rough with me. And mean. And condescending."

I wanted to interject, but I held my tongue.

Lyvia wrapped a tender arm around Evianna. They shared the same dark tan complexion and heart-shaped facial structure. They had to be siblings. I'd bet my life on it.

"It's okay," Lyvia said. "I'll deal with this man. Take your horse and head back. I'll join you in little bit."

"But, Sister—"

"I can handle the situation."

Evianna took a deep breath. Then she shot me a glare before flouncing over to her horse. With the familiarity of an expert, she pulled herself onto the saddle—seated sideways—and urged her mare to move. Her mount made no protest, and the two of them galloped off into the distance.

She took my coat with her.

I rubbed at my face, realizing that between Zaxis and Evianna, I would soon run out of a wardrobe.

"Let me offer you a formal apology," Lyvia said, interrupting my musings. She stared at me with the same bluish-purple eyes as Evianna. "My sister has been acting odd lately, and she's gotten herself into trouble on more than one occasion."

Lyvia's serious tone didn't sit well with me. I didn't need an apology—nothing had happened. Instead, I offered her shrug and said, "Don't worry about it. I heard Evianna calling for help, and I swam her to shore. That's the end of the story."

The comment seemed to relax Lyvia. She placed a hand on her hip and glanced at the waters. "I told her not to go anywhere near the river, but she's determined to catch a glitter crab. She sneaks off during all her outdoor studies."

"What's a glitter crab?"

She pointed to the riverbed. "Look there. See that glint of color? Glitter crabs create shells from ambient magic and then live inside of them."

"Like hermit crabs?"

"Similar, yes. Folklore says their shells are filled with good luck."

I walked to the edge of the river. The clear water made it easy to see the rocks at the bottom. Sure enough, between stones and hidden in the cracks, pinkish shells sparkled in the light that dappled all around them.

"They're difficult to catch," Lyvia said. "They scuttle everywhere."

I created a shadow tendril and manipulated it into the river. In one quick motion, I used the darkness to pluck a glitter crab out from its hiding spot. A few of its friends scuttled away at lightning speeds, but that didn't matter. I willed the shadow to bring me the creature.

"Here," I said as I turned around, the tiny crab in the palm of my hand. "You can give this to Evianna. You don't even need to say it's from me since I suspect that'll upset her."

Lyvia took the glitter crab from me. She cocked an eyebrow and even smiled. "I didn't know you were an arcanist."

I instinctively reached a hand up to my forehead. My damp hair had clumped up over my arcanist mark. I slicked my hair back, but it twisted around and became disheveled in a matter of seconds.

"Sorry about that."

"This reminds me of Lark the Gallant," she said as she held the glitter crab close. "I don't know if you're familiar with legends of old."

"Are you kidding? I love those tales." I glanced around the area, unable to stop smiling. "And this is a lot like how Lark met his wife, but in that story, he intentionally hid the fact he was an arcanist. Plus, he gave her a magical item, not a random crab from the river."

Lyvia returned my smile, but it seemed reserved somehow, like she didn't want to get *too* happy. Then she tilted her head as she asked, "What did you say your name was?"

"Oh, I'm Volke Savan, a knightmare arcanist with the Frith Guild."

"Volke..." She rolled the name over her tongue. "You must not be from around here. Have you come to participate in the tournament?"

"That's right. Among other things."

Lyvia slowly walked back to her horse. She tucked the glitter crab into a pouch hanging from her belt and then secured it shut with a tie string. "I have to go. I trust you can make it back to the road without guidance?"

"Of course."

"Oh, and I look forward to watching you compete."

"You'll be there?" I asked, both eyebrows raised.

She laughed—it was velvety and infectious. With a quick step up, she mounted her horse. "You really aren't from around here."

While she was atop her steed, I had to stare up to meet her gaze. "Until our paths cross again, I wish you well." Then I added a formal bow.

I didn't normally use such flowery language, but Lark the Gallant would use that phrase whenever he parted ways with someone he knew. I figured Lyvia would at least get the reference and perhaps even appreciate it.

Sure enough, her smile widened. She urged her horse to follow after her sister, and I watched her until she disappeared between the oak trees.

13

THRONEHOLD

I walked through the woodland with my attention on the canopy of leaves. The air seemed crisper than before. Even though my wet boots squished with each step, I didn't mind. After every breath, I smiled wider. Lightning coursed through my veins, and I almost ran back to the caravan to bleed off my excess energy.

"My arcanist?" Luthair asked.

"Yeah?"

"You appear distracted."

"I feel really good." I stretched my arms and inhaled. Nothing felt as right as this one moment. "The last few weeks have gone my way. I figured out how to use some of my magic like Zelfree wanted, I've gotten better with my fighting technique, and I'm starting to master the little things, too. Did you see how I grabbed that crab out of the river with the shadows?"

Even remembering my first attempt at manipulating shadows got me on the verge of laughter. It had been so difficult, and now I had fine control. What would come next?

"I see," Luthair said.

I stopped walking and glanced down at the darkness swirling around my feet. "And usually I get flustered when I try to make a good impression on people, yet that time I didn't feel off at all. I mean, I have no idea what the little girl was so upset about, but Lyvia was pleasant, and conversation came easy."

"And that excites you?"

"Well, yeah." I rotated my arms, but the restless exhilaration wouldn't leave me. "This must be how Zaxis feels all the time..."

I knelt down and withdrew my sword from the shadows. I slashed it through the air as I danced around the trunks of trees, pretending each oak was an enemy.

"Confidence is like liquor," Luthair said. "Too much and you'll make yourself into a fool."

With a side strike, I sliced a low-hanging branch off its tree. "Do you think I'm overconfident?"

"No. But I do think Mathis got himself killed because he thought he could handle a situation he wasn't prepared for."

The comment stilled my hand. After a moment of reflection, I went back to parrying the falling leaves. "I have you to remind me if things are getting serious. Besides, some confidence is better than none. I don't feel like this often." I leapt back and slashed at a stump. "Maybe I should go speak with Atty while I'm still feeling this way."

A thought struck me. I lifted the sword and faced a young oak. My blade was sharper than most, and I swung at the trunk as hard as I could while maintaining a perfect form. The sword sliced through the wood, and the honed edge slipped through the tree with a surprising ease. The oak hadn't been especially thick, but it was large enough to crash to the ground afterward as it toppled over.

I lowered my weapon as I stared at the clean cut through the trunk.

"Luthair... I want to win the Sovereign Dragon Tournament. The apprentice level, at least."

He rose out of my shadow, his plate armor forming in a matter of seconds. He wore my shield, and it clinked with the rest of him as he stepped close to my side.

"Is there some specific reason?" he asked.

"I feel like I can do it."

"You don't need the approval of others. Fame is not the same as accomplishment."

"I want to prove it to myself," I said, my conviction building with each word. "I've... never been given a chance for honest competition—to test my mettle against others. There's always been some excuse or something's happened that prevented me from really understanding my limits." I faced his empty helmet. "Will you help me?"

The wind raced by, rustling Luthair's black-and-crimson cape. I waited, unable to determine what he was thinking while he stood around like a castle ornament. I couldn't win the tournament without him. We had to fight together, and I needed to know his determination matched mine.

"Of course," he said. "As your eldrin, your desires are my desires. If you want to test your might against others, we'll bring our full force in the tournament."

***

I hadn't realized how far from the caravan I was until I tried to get back. Even though I slipped through the shadows from time to time, it still took me a better part of two hours to find the road again.

I didn't mind, though. Fantasies about the tournament

played in my head as I made my way back. I wanted the victory for many reasons, and the anticipation of the event stole most of my focus.

The main road, still clogged with merchants and carts, was wider now that we were closer to Thronehold. I ran along the side, looking for anyone from the Frith Guild. Carts and creatures of all sizes made it difficult.

A gray hippogriff—a half-eagle, half-horse creature—spread its wings over and over again, blocking my sight. A tall yeti lumbered through the crowd, dropping snowflakes like dandruff across the road. I squeezed my way between people and creatures, muttering apologies as I went. Fortunately, I spotted Zaxis, Illia, Hexa, and Atty on top of two carriages in our caravan. They sat with their legs hanging off the side, each chatting with the other.

Once I got close, I shadow-stepped up to the top of the carriage with Atty. As I emerged from the darkness, I bit back my grimace and took a seat right next to her.

Her eyes widened, and she scooted to make room for me. "Volke! We were wondering where you'd got off to."

"I've been in the woods," I said.

"Are you... damp?"

I nervously chuckled. "Well, I went swimming in the river for a bit."

"No, you didn't," Zaxis interjected, all the way from the next carriage over. "Even idiots take off their boots before they go swimming. You fell in. Admit it."

Illia turned her one eye on Zaxis and glared. "Leave him alone."

She and Hexa sat on the front carriage, both facing south. I didn't see Raisen, but Nicholin offered me a tiny wave of his paw when he realized I was staring. I waved back, and I guessed Illia thought I was greeting her because she half-smiled and briefly lifted her hand.

Zaxis stood and walked the length of the carriage, despite the semi-bumpy ride we'd had traveling over dirt and rocks. He stopped once he reached Atty and me, hooking his thumbs into the belt loops of his trousers and frowning. "What's with your smile?"

"I'm in a good mood," I said with a shrug. "You should try it sometime."

"What happened? You hit your head when you plummeted into the water?"

"I've decided I'm going to win the tournament."

His laugh was immediate and thorough. My statement also drew Illia's and Hexa's attention, as they both turned all the way around and crossed their legs to get a better view of the situation.

"Illia and I are going to participate," Hexa said. "And they don't separate the apprentices by gender or anything. They assume if you're an arcanist and you're entering a tournament, you know what you're getting into."

Although I hadn't wanted to acknowledge the reality, I knew in my gut what Hexa was trying to say. I'd likely have to fight Illia at some point. I didn't want to, but I also didn't want to surrender in order to avoid the situation.

Zaxis waved away the commentary with a dismissive gesture. "Have you all forgotten that *I'm* entering the tournament? You all can compete for second place."

"Uh, have you seen how amazing Illia and I are?" Nicholin asked. He stood on his hind legs and puffed out his chest, his white and silver fur shiny in the evening sunlight. "We're champion material. They might just declare us the winner when we register."

"You're frail. One hit and you're down for the count."

Nicholin rubbed at his face in angry-rodent fashion. "Pfft! You'd never catch us! Not even Calisto could get his hands on us!"

"You ran away from Calisto," Zaxis stated. "If you had stayed and fought, you would've been ripped apart."

Although I didn't disagree, I cringed the moment he said it. Illia wanted to kill Calisto—she had tried desperately—and I knew it bothered her to hear someone say she had *run away from him*. Additionally, it seemed callous to include the phrase, *you would've been ripped apart*, considering Calisto had been the one to cut out Illia's eye. Nothing about the comment sat well with me.

Nicholin arched his back and growled. It must've been a clue for Zaxis, because he stepped back and waved his hand.

"I didn't mean it that way," he said. "You know that."

"Shut your pie-hole," Nicholin hissed. "We were going to let you off easy, but now I'm going to mess up your face in our match." He unsheathed his tiny, ferret-like claws and swiped them through the air.

Illia placed a hand over Nicholin and rolled her eye. "It's fine. Leave Zaxis alone. He doesn't think before he acts—which is exactly why he *won't* win the tournament."

The commentary halted after that statement, and I wondered what Zaxis would do in a situation where he had to face Illia in a tournament bout. Would he let her win? Or would he think it impressive if he beat her?

Ice ran through my veins when I imagined facing her. Bad luck hounded my step, so a piece of me figured it was inevitable that we fight, but if the universe had even a hint of sympathy, it would keep us from entering a match as rivals.

Forsythe and Titania swooped down from the sky, their phoenix-bodies glowing under their feathers and dropping soot onto the carriages. They fluffed and settled themselves —Titania near Atty, and Forsythe near Zaxis.

"My arcanist," Titania said, her voice chipper. "We're almost there. Look to the horizon. You'll soon see Thronehold."

We all stood, despite the shaky carriage, and glanced into the distance.

Dust kicked up by the hundreds of travelers gave the area a haze that shone in the dying light of evening, like a fog of gold flakes. Orange and purple married in the sky as the sun neared the mountains in the distance. I squinted, hoping to see the city through the poor lighting and clouds of dirt. Once the caravan crested the hill, however, none of that was needed.

Thronehold was a location that demanded to be seen.

A massive castle jutted into the sky, four times as tall as the next tallest building in the city. The flat roof and giant balcony at the highest point of the castle made for a perfect dragon landing, and a wall circled the base with enough fortifications to stop a small army.

The thousands of buildings that made up Thronehold's city proper had little rhyme or reason. Unlike Ellios, with its grid-like streets and uniform construction, Thronehold had as many unique structures as it had citizens. The roads twisted all around, some narrow, some wide. Towers dotted the cityscape, some made of stone, others of twisted wood.

A river cut Thronehold down the middle. Bridges crossed it every half mile or so, and small docks lined the waterway. Creatures swam in the waters, including beasts large enough that their giant silhouettes shimmered beneath the surface.

And the smoke...

Pillars of black and gray rose from the depths of the city, no doubt from the smiths, mines, and mills.

Atty placed her hand on my shoulder and pointed to the sky. "Look there."

A single airship hung with the clouds and smoke. It had sails on top and on the sides. I had heard of ships that took to the sky, but only arcanists with powerful control of the wind could create such things. They were rare—and breathtaking—and I never expected to actually see one.

We got a good look at Thronehold during the entire trek toward it. Once the road slanted downward, however, the city wall blocked most of our view. It wasn't too bad, though. The wall itself had been built to prevent sieges, and the many defensive turrets and arrow slits made for an interesting sight.

Once we got within half a mile to the fortified gate, something happened.

It was hard to describe at first, but it felt like I couldn't get enough air to breathe—and no matter how much I inhaled and exhaled, the irritation never left me. The frightening sensation of suffocation worked its way from my chest out to my arms and legs.

The others must have felt it as well, because they glanced around and shivered, each with a furrowed brow. The crowds around us—and all the arcanists—spoke in concerned tones, their volume increasing with each step.

Traces leapt on top of the carriage, her fur shimmering in the gentle breeze.

"Don't worry, apprentices," she said. "My arcanist sent me up here to tell you we're just traveling through the null-stone fields."

Hexa forced a cough. "What are they?"

"Large veins of raw nullstone create an anti-magic

effect." Traces purred as she took a seat next to me. "Null-stone is prevalent in this area, but it'll clear up once we reach the walls of the city."

I tried to manipulate the shadows, but nothing happened. Not even any pain. Zaxis must've had the same idea because he held out his hand in dramatic fashion. Still nothing. To my shock, he pulled out a small knife he kept on his belt and sliced his forearm.

"Was that necessary?" I asked.

He twisted his arm around as blood wept from the short line he had cut into the flesh. It didn't heal. That seemed to worry him more than his lack of his fire—he stared at it with a vacant expression.

"Please, my arcanist," Forsythe said. "Once we leave this area, your magic will return. It's just suppressed."

He grumbled something and then let the matter drop. His blood continued to drip, and I swear the plague-ridden monsters of our prison carriage could smell it. Their chittering and laughter drifted through the nullstone-wood.

When we neared the fortified gate, Zaxis and I leapt off the carriage. I held out my hand and helped Atty make a graceful dismount. She gave me a smile for my effort and even slid her hand down my arm. Before I could comment, she pointed to the city's defenses.

I had to crane my head back to take in the sight. The outer wall had to be forty feet high. Within a few steps of the city's boundaries, the anti-magic effect faded. I took a deep breath, thankful the suffocation feeling had faded.

Gate guards stopped every carriage, cart, and arcanist before they were allowed to enter the city. Guildmaster Eventide stepped forward to speak with the guards in charge and even motioned to our prison-carriage, discussing the specifics.

Traces leapt to my shoulder, startling me enough that the shadows in the nearby area shifted for half a second.

"Sorry about that," she said as she nuzzled my neck.

"It's fine."

I walked through the impressive gate, Traces clinging to my shirt, unable to take my eyes off the impressive construction.

"Volke?"

With a lifted eyebrow, I turned around.

"It *is* you!"

A gate guard approached me, his arms wide. He wore chainmail with a tunic overtop—a dragon, rose, and sword were stitched over the heart, signifying his authority as one of the Thronehold guards. He also wore a decorative lantern, which hung on the belt fastened around his waist. The lights inside danced with life, swirling to music all their own.

The man embraced me, but since he wore a steel helmet, I didn't get a good look at his face.

"Do I know you?" I asked.

"Huh?"

He stepped back, ripped off his helmet, and smiled. His red hair fluttered in the evening winds, and I recognized him straight away. Zaxis's younger brother.

"Lyell?" I said, half-laughing. "You're here?"

He smacked me on the shoulder. "I can't believe it. I've been meaning to write you back for the longest time." Without giving me a chance to answer, he pointed to his forehead.

It was faint, almost too light to see, but etched into his skin was an arcanist star. Three orbs symbolized his eldrin, and it took me a moment to realize he had bonded to a will-o-wisp—a creature of light and fire that helped or hindered lost travelers, depending on its mood. They weren't powerful creatures, but they were well-known.

I smacked him right back. "You're an arcanist? An actual will-o-wisp arcanist?"

"That's right, I did it!" His smile dominated his face as he hugged me a second time. "And I have you to thank for it." He squeezed tight. "You were right. They were never going to let me try for a phoenix."

"Lyell, I—"

"And my family even wanted me to stay on our isle and just keep up with the family business, but I remembered how you *went for things*."

I patted his back and then pushed away from the embrace. "What?"

"You charged into the phoenix bonding ceremony." Lyell pointed to me, even going so far as to jam his finger onto my chest. "You didn't care what people thought. You did things. Stupid, reckless things. But you still did them."

I wasn't sure of his ultimate point, but I nodded along with the words, hoping it would end somewhere positive.

"So I went to the mainland and traveled to Thronehold," Lyell continued. "And then I passed the will-o-wisp's trial of worth. Now I'm a member of the Lamplighters Guild." He motioned to the lantern on his hip. The lights flickered and swirled, and I realized then that it was his will-o-wisp eldrin.

I narrowed my eyes. "Aren't you only fourteen?"

Lyell quickly grabbed my shoulder and pulled me close. "That's, uh, between us, okay? Everyone here thinks I'm sixteen."

Individuals weren't technically allowed to participate in a bonding ceremony unless they were an adult—at the age of fifteen—but Lyell had always appeared older than he actually was. Even now, he was tall, he had scruff from a beard, and his wiry frame made him seem like he was almost twenty. If someone asked me who was older, Lyell or Zaxis, and I didn't know them, I would've picked Lyell.

"If they haven't figured it out by now," I said, "I won't mention anything."

Lyell exhaled and smiled. "Thank you."

I pointed to the massive gate and then glanced at the other guards with lanterns. "Why're you here, though? You said you were part of the Lamplighters Guild."

"Oh, I know the name doesn't sound like much. We do a lot more than light lamps, though. We're part of the city guard. Night watchmen. We also keep the horseless trolley cars running with our will-o-wisp magic." Lyell cracked his knuckles. "I have authority here. I get to call shots. I even have a city pendant." He pulled out the pendant from under his tunic. The bronze had a dull finish, but the dragon and rose were clearly etched into one side.

I had never seen someone get power drunk on so little power, but I kept the comment to myself. Instead, I said, "Impressive. But why are you here at the gates? Checking merchants?"

"We're here for increased security. Apparently, people are bringing plague-ridden creatures from all over. Some sort of cure and stuff is going to get tested. I have to escort those monsters to the dungeons."

14

THE TURNING OF AN AGE

"We have plague-ridden creatures," I said as I motioned to the prison-carriage.

Lyell shoved his head back into his helmet. "Perfect. I'll ask them to be your escort. Wait right here." He jogged off toward the guardhouse, his lantern swinging on his belt. The will-o-wisp flickered and spun around, but otherwise kept calm.

The shadows stirred. I turned my attention to my feet. "Luthair?"

"I have not seen Thronehold in many years."

"Any places you want to visit?"

"There is one..."

Zaxis sauntered over and punched me in the shoulder blade. I half-stumbled forward and then rotated my arm.

"Yes?" I asked.

"Did you hear? We're going to ride in a horseless trolley car." He waited, as if expecting me to gasp.

"I heard. Your brother will be driving it, apparently."

"My brother?"

His confusion caused me to chuckle. That didn't sit well

with him, though. Zaxis shoved me back toward the caravan, his expression shifting to a hard glare.

"When we visited the Isle of Ruma four months ago, my family said Lyell had run away to make his fortune. There's no way he came to Thronehold."

His statements and conclusion only got me laughing harder. I couldn't wait for him to discover what Lyell had gotten himself into.

Our caravan entered Thronehold with little delay. Eventide and Gillie directed the carriages into the city, and while they headed to the inn, Zelfree took the nullstone carriage and had it attached to a horseless trolley car. Once the mustangs were unhitched and given to Gillie's researchers, Zelfree snapped his fingers and pointed to the vehicle he wanted us on.

The trolley was an odd vehicle. More like a giant gazebo with wheels and benches. A metal, man-sized contraption was mounted to the back, and the piping traveled up through the roof of the vehicle.

Lyell took a seat next to the machinery and opened his lantern. The will-o-wisp floated out—all three glowing orbs —and then hovered into the pipes. A moment later, steam puffed out and the trolley moved at a slow crawl.

Everyone managed to squeeze on, including a few people from the city guard. They either sat on the wooden benches or hung on to the side. The metal contraption moved with the will-o-wisp magic, powered by steam and churning at a slow pace. It hissed as two pistons managed to turn the wheels. Lyell didn't need horses to steer—he used a rudder at the back, much like a boat. It connected to the axle, and I almost wanted to lean out the side to watch it all work.

The main road of Thronehold was paved with smooth

cobblestone. Water rushed down the gutters, washing horse feces and waste into drains. I stared at those too, curious about the steam flowing up from underground.

The smells of the city weren't like Fortuna, where the aroma of fish tainted everything. Thronehold had a grit to it —a grit I could feel in my nose—and the buildings were so tall that the city seemingly created its own darkness. Although the sun had set, the moon and stars remained hidden. Traces clung tighter to my shoulder, her ears back.

Atty and Illia gawked at the moving parts. Hexa and Adelgis watched for a moment before focusing on the roads, as though they had seen this technology before and were no longer impressed.

"Thronehold was built atop of old nullstone quarries," Lyell said from the back, his voice loud, but not shouting. "Some of those old tunnels were turned into catacombs, but most were repurposed into sewers."

Zaxis pushed his way to the back, almost knocking a couple of guards and two of Gillie's apprentices into the streets.

"Lyell?" he asked.

"Yes?"

"It's really you?"

Lyell lowered his voice, and in a harsh whisper, he said, "Not now, Zaxis. I'm busy giving everyone facts of the city."

"How're you controlling this thing?" Zaxis motioned to the metal on the back of the trolley car.

"It's a steam engine," Lyell replied in a curt tone. "Let me do my job."

"You work it with magic?"

A piece of me wanted to drag Zaxis back to his seat, but another piece of me couldn't help but laugh. Lyell answered with an exhale of long suffering.

"I control the steam with my will-o-wisp fire. Tin-Tin and I can—"

"Tin-Tin?" Zaxis asked.

"That's my eldrin." Lyell slowly shifted the trolley's rudder to make a wide turn down another cobblestone road. The vehicle jostled about, but it kept a steady pace. "I'm in charge here, Zaxis. Sit down. We're almost to the prison."

Other horseless trolley cars passed us. Other members of the Lamplighters Guild drove them—all with will-o-wisp arcanists. They waved to Lyell, and he waved back, indicating they were all a tight-knit coterie.

Lyell motioned to a signpost as we crept by it. "All the districts of the city are marked with both words and pictures. If you ever become lost, you can ask a member of the Lamplighters Guild or seek out any of these signs."

The nearest sign read JUSTICE DISTRICT, and the picture included a man in a cage.

How many districts were in Thronehold? I would find out eventually.

"Can I use my phoenix fire to power this?" Zaxis asked. He got close to the machinery and glanced around, his attention glued to the moving parts.

Lyell shoved him away. "*No.* Your fire would wreck this. It's too powerful. Get back."

Before Zaxis could harass his younger brother any further, the trolley car came to a slow halt. Tin-Tin floated out of the pipes and swirled over to its arcanist. Lyell opened the side of his decorative lantern, and the will-o-wisp flickered as it flew inside.

I surveyed the Thronehold prison. The entire building was black and dark blue—all nullstone, I knew it in my gut. The place had a depressing visage that made me dread the inside. Bars lined the few windows, and a large wrought-iron fence circled the property line.

"I don't feel an anti-magic effect," I muttered to myself.

Traces meowed, and I almost flinched. I had forgotten she was on my shoulders—her weight had become a frequent constant that I could ignore altogether.

"Raw nullstone creates an aura," she said. "This is refined nullstone. All its power is trapped within. Magic won't harm this place."

While everyone jumped off the trolley, I watched a pair of men in nullstone shackles being transported into the prison. They had marks on their foreheads, but they were too far away for me to see what kind of arcanists they were.

"What's wrong with them?" I asked

Traces shook her head. "They likely have the plague."

"But... they don't look crazy."

The melancholy nature of the area prevented any sort of extreme emotion, but I knew I would recognize the lunatic laugh of those affected by the plague.

"The plague affects arcanists differently," Traces said. "Mystical creatures succumb to madness within days, and their body transforms. That's because they're made of pure magic. Arcanists aren't. Most don't fully succumb to their darkest urges for a long while. Think in terms of a year. And even then... they never go laughing mad."

I remembered Gregory Ruma enough to know she spoke the truth. Ruma had been infected, but he was able to conduct himself like a normal person on most days. His judgment, and overall outlook on life, was twisted, though. He had kept his wife's corpse and tried to reanimate it with fell magic fueled by the deaths of others. The good Ruma of the old stories never would've made such decisions.

Guards from the prison took our nullstone carriage and

rolled it through the wrought-iron gates. Zelfree clapped his hands and motioned everyone away from the trolley. Except Illia and me. He stopped us both and then walked us to the far sidewalk.

"Come on," Zelfree said. "We're going to visit Skarn University."

"Right now?" I asked.

"Yes. The others will head to the inn once this is finished."

Although I hadn't expected to go anywhere, I jumped to Zelfree's side and followed him out of the Justice District. Illia kept pace. Nicholin sat in her pocket, his head above the edge and his paws hanging out. Each time he blinked his eyes, they stayed closed just a little longer than before.

"Why are you only taking me and Illia?" I asked.

Zelfree shook his head. "Eventide wants you both to see the library master at the university. He's an expert on ancient myths revolving around mystical creatures. He's going to talk to us about the world serpent."

"Master Zelfree," Illia said. "I have a few new ideas about Calisto and his ship. At some point, I want to discuss how we can effectively corner him on the open ocean."

The three of us walked along the road toward a building in the distance made of spires and archways. Zelfree waited a few moments before he responded.

"You need to stop thinking about Calisto. We have more pressing matters in front of us."

Illia frowned. "I just wanted to—"

"Listen. People become the things they focus all their attention on. Be careful you don't become the thing you hate because you neglected to focus on the things you love." He tightened his coat around his body. "That's a lesson my old master taught me, and it still holds."

We didn't even have time to argue the point. We rounded a street corner and found Guildmaster Eventide standing by a building labeled POSTAL STATION. A picture of a horse and bag accompanied the words, and I imagined parcel delivery was common for mainland cities. On the islands, letters were delivered on boats along with other goods, so there wasn't really a special designated person or group.

Although it was evening, people still traveled the streets. Lamplights gave them visibility, but I was still surprised.

Eventide wore her patchwork coat overtop a simple black shirt I had never seen before. Her guild pendant stood out on the fabric.

She smiled. "Ah, thank you, Zelfree." Then she motioned for Illia and me to come closer. "The two of you have the means to locate the world serpent, correct?"

We nodded.

Illia had her Occult Compass—an item that could locate any mystical creature, so long as she had a piece of them— and I had a world serpent scale. Together, the compass would point us in the appropriate direction.

"Knowing where it's located isn't enough," Eventide said. "But the rest of the requirements must stay between us. I don't want to risk this getting out."

Again, Illia and I nodded along with her words.

"Good. I'm glad you both understand. Please accompany me and Zelfree to the Skarn University library. There's someone you should meet."

She didn't wait for us to answer in the affirmative. Instead, she turned on her heel and headed down the street. We followed her—our walking speed about on par with the speed of the horseless trolleys. The sounds of the massive city surrounded us as we made our way from one street to the next. I had so much to look at that I almost didn't pay attention to the time it took. Zelfree walked behind us, like he was making sure we wouldn't escape. It gave me an odd feeling the entire trek.

A clear and prominent sign marked the change in district—EDUCATION DISTRICT, it read, with a picture of a book and quill pen.

"This entire district used to be a pile of dirt and stone," Eventide said as she motioned to the small buildings. "During Thronehold's restoration period, they cleared that away and built the university. That's why they gave it the name *Skarn University*, actually. Skarn is a type of waste rock they dig up with the nullstone."

We had barely seen five percent of the city, yet already I was on the verge of being overwhelmed. How did so many people live here?

When we reached Skarn University, I almost couldn't keep my mouth closed. It made for an impressive sight. The tall archways cast dark shadows around the doorframes. We walked through the entrance gate and then to the front door. Eventide didn't wait for anyone's permission—she let herself into the building and continued forward, no hesitation.

Illia stuck close to me as we traveled, our footsteps echoing in the cold halls. Nicholin had fallen asleep. His squeak-like snores mixed with the other sounds.

She didn't say anything, but we shared a few glances when we passed decorative suits of armor in the entrance hall. None of them looked quite like Luthair, but I could tell that was the first thing she thought of.

The university had wide corridors, but not much in them. A red carpet covered the stone floor, and giant windows dominated one side of the hallway, but the wall on the other was barren. Half a dozen people greeted us as we continued into the heart of the building, all of whom appeared to be students. They kept their noses in books, barely looking up as they walked. It was night, yet they still continued to study. It impressed me.

Eventide stopped at a long counter in front of an imposing door labeled *Research Library*. The man behind the counter straightened his glasses. His arcanist mark had an undead woman in a heavy cloak wrapped around the star on his forehead. Sure enough, standing behind him, and shrouded in the darkness was that very woman—a banshee. Her skeletal hands poked out from her tattered robes, and her hood hung so low I couldn't see her face.

"Can I help you?" the banshee arcanist asked.

From what I could remember, banshees could incapacitate people with their screams. That would be useful if someone tried to sneak into the library. The man could stop the intruder and alert everyone all at the same time.

"Ronin," Eventide said. "You don't recognize me?"

The man took off his glasses, cleaned them on his red and purple robes, and then reapplied them to his face. "Foreigners aren't allowed to use the libraries."

"Ronin. It's me. Liet."

"Liet Eventide?"

"That's Grandmaster Liet Eventide to you. Or Guildmaster, if you want to finally join the Frith Guild."

He stood and walked around the counter, his eyebrows knitted together. "It can't be. You look... so old."

Eventide brushed back her silver braid. For a moment, I thought she would be angry, but she maintained her slight smile and grazed a finger over her glowing arcanist mark.

It was the mark that finally eased Ronin's suspicion. He examined it for a long moment before shuffling around to the other side of the counter. "I suppose everyone is drawn to the tournament. I can't imagine you'd participate, though."

"Not this time," Eventide said. "I'm here to see the library master."

"Library Master Bintle is inside. Go through this door and head all the way to the back. He's been reading in the southeastern corner of the room these past few days."

"Thank you, Ronin."

The man watched us with a curious look. Eventide opened the door, allowing us in. She and Ronin seemed to have a silent conversation in quick glances. He shook his head, but then I entered the library and couldn't see anything else.

Illia placed a hand on my shoulder.

The research library didn't have much light. A few lanterns hung on the walls, and glowstones hung from the ceiling in chain nets. The shelves upon shelves of books prevented it from feeling like a dungeon.

Scribes sat at desks between the bookshelves, hunched over and making copious notes. None of them had arcanist marks, but they all wore pendants of the university. I suspected the books in this room were special—they didn't want to use the printing presses to duplicate the information.

It seemed odd to hide information, but Gravekeeper William had said some arcanists held the right to distribute and that the right remained with them until they died. And since many arcanists lived centuries, the information rarely reached the public.

"There you are, Bintle," Eventide said as we reached the back of the room.

An elderly man emerged from the shadows, a thick book in one hand and a blue glowing jellyfish floating by his side.

Well, it wasn't actually a jellyfish—it was a *ghost light*. They were mythical creatures attracted to knowledge and wisdom. They were one of the few creatures that preferred to bond with people who were well past their prime in age.

And Bintle appeared to be in his early seventies. He walked with a stiff leg and a slight hunch, his wispy hair fluttering as he moved. Heavy bags hung from his eyes, but the smile lines gave him an energetic aura.

"Liet," he said. "I received your letters. I was just gathering the information you wanted right now, as a matter of fact."

He had a deliberate purpose to his speech, like it was all planned out in advance. No odd pauses. No *ums* or uncertain sounds.

Eventide smiled and then motioned to a nearby table. "Why don't you sit and tell us the legends? These three are here to help me piece together a puzzle, and I want them to know everything you do."

"Is that so?" Bintle hobbled over to the fine table made of mahogany.

He took a seat, and the rest of us joined him. His ghost light floated through the air much like Adelgis's ethereal whelk. I watched it hover around, its jellyfish tentacles flowing through the air like it was caught in an invisible current.

"Tell them the legend," Eventide said. "About the start of this cycle."

Illia and I regarded the library master with curiosity. Zelfree leaned back in his chair, like he already knew what was coming.

Bintle began, "The legend is simple, but let me give you a visual aid." He held up his hands, both spotted with age. Illusions formed from the tips of his fingers, like smoke that took form. A circle appeared before us. "Several thousand years ago, when magic was still new, and the first people bonded with mystical creatures, there were no gods."

He waggled his fingers, and the illusion smoke became thirteen tiny circles.

"But then there was a fundamental change in magic," he continued. "The first arcanists shattered the sky and created star shards. This was called the *turning of an age*. We once had no magical items—no trinkets or artifacts or buildings of power—but once the sky was broken, the shards rained down and provided us the means to create. This is what caused the thirteen god-creatures to spring to life."

"They just came to life?" I asked. "Like that?"

Zelfree held up a hand. "Wait until the end."

I sat back in my chair, irritated I couldn't get this information faster. I wished they had just given me a book I could read.

Bintle said, "You see, the age of gods was meant to help humanity transition into this new era. All thirteen creatures had a role to play, and they spawned one after another, like a clock counting down the time. The world serpent bonded to a man, and—"

"A man?" Illia interjected. "I thought these creatures only bonded with gods?"

"That's a common misconception, young lady. They don't bond to gods—whoever bonds to them *becomes* a god."

"Really?" Illia's eye went wide. "What does that even mean?"

"It's more of a title," Bintle said, tilting his hand back and forth. "An epic title to represent the phenomenal power the creatures possessed. They were just powerful arcanists." He tapped his fingers on the table and made the thirteen orbs change shape into creatures. "The world serpent spawned first. The man who bonded with him became a legendary warlord, undefeated in battle. The world serpent controlled the land and sea, so the armies under his command never lost an engagement. He even helped form the nations we know today.

"The second godly creature to spawn was the *soul forge*. It's described as a giant slug with many arms. It created new mystical creatures and helped humanity master the ability to create artifacts. The woman who bonded with this beast became a hoarder of knowledge."

Eventide placed her hands on the table. "Tell them the end, Bintle. That's what we need to hear."

He frowned slightly and then rearranged the smoke illusions to create a dragon. "The thirteenth creature is known as the *apoch dragon*. It didn't bond with anyone. Its sole purpose was to kill the other godly beings, as well as their arcanists, because the age of gods had come to an end—their work was complete and humanity no longer needed them."

That part of the story came out of nowhere, like a punch to the gut. I almost didn't know what to ask. The apoch dragon had killed them all because their work was done? Dragons and killing seemed to be a theme.

Bintle frowned. "The legend says that these thirteen creatures will spawn again when there is another fundamental change in magic—a turning of an age. They will appear, in the same order, and help humanity through a turbulent time. Then the apoch dragon will once again cull them from this world, allowing civilization to continue without the influence of gods."

"We don't need divine intervention to solve our problems," Zelfree muttered.

With a wave of Bintle's hands, the illusion dragon disappeared. "Considering how vague the legend is about the turning of an age, I doubt we'll ever see it happen."

The library grew cold. Illia looked at me, and I met her one-eyed gaze.

It already had happened—the world serpent had spawned. But what fundamental change to magic had transpired? We hadn't torn open the sky to acquire star shards, like they did over a millennia ago.

What could it have been? What had caused the world serpent to appear?

With a shaky hand, Bintle pushed himself up out of the chair. "Liet, you said you wanted me to research the locations of the creatures, but I have to tell you—none of the legends give actual directions. This isn't an adventure for buried treasure."

"I don't need directions," she said. "I just need to know what's required to see them."

"The stories say each creature spawns with a land marker. The world serpent hatches under a giant tree, for example."

Eventide nodded along with his words. "I know that part of the story. And I know the roots of the tree protect the creature. They're supposedly indestructible. How did the first world serpent arcanist wake the beast?"

"The man used an object," Bintle said. "Let me go get the book with the information." He headed back to the corner of the library, and his ghost light floated ahead of him.

"Let me carry it," the ghost light said. "Your hands are sore."

She spoke with a child's voice, innocent and pure. It surprised me, only because I had expected it to sound alien and mystifying. Or perhaps mute.

Once he disappeared behind the bookshelf, I leaned

onto the table. I still didn't understand what fundamental change in magic had happened that had caused the world serpent to appear.

Eventide and Zelfree exchanged a long stare, their cold expressions distracting. I had never seen our guildmaster so... distant.

"Someone did this on purpose," she said. "I feared that was the case, but now I know for sure."

"Did what on purpose?" I asked.

Zelfree stood from his chair, his glare drilling a hole into the table. "The arcane plague. *That's* the fundamental change in magic. Someone created that terrible curse just so they could get these epic creatures of legend to spawn."

"That's right," Eventide stated. "It's the only explanation. And it makes sense why they would give it away to fiends and pirates. The more the plague spreads across the world, the more they alter the very foundation of our world."

"Which means... we really are in a race to see who gets to those creatures first."

15

QUEEN VELLETA

Guildmaster Eventide ambled around the table, her gaze vacant. When she spoke, it was more of a mutter, half to herself, half to the group. "The first creatures with the plague were all ocean travelers or birds. Things that could easily escape and spread their madness. I remember seeing it for the first time... It was sophisticated. It hadn't occurred naturally. Someone had corrupted the magic. Someone had made purposeful decisions on how to spread it without getting caught."

"And I know Calisto was working for somebody," Zelfree added. He faced Eventide, his hands restless. "He never said a name, but the way he acted when I was on his ship was out of the ordinary. Calisto's plans and schemes never involved something as complicated as any of this. He's a pawn—perhaps most of the dread pirates are."

The news didn't sit right with me.

Had someone really planned this all out from the beginning? They had created a magical corruption and then spread it as fast and as uncontrollably as possible, just to get powerful mystical creatures to spawn across the world? That kind of wanton disregard of life made pirate attacks seem like child's play. Someone was willing to watch the world crumble just to get their hands on power.

Illia scooted closer to me, but before we could discuss the situation, Bintle returned with his ghost light. The glowing spectral jellyfish "carried" a book to the table with a faint telekinesis.

"This book describes how to free the world serpent from the tree it hides under," Bintle said matter-of-factly. "A special runestone is used to open the roots—the same runestone the first world serpent arcanist used."

"And where is the runestone?" Eventide asked.

"In theory, it was meant to be part of the trial of worth for these god-like beings."

Bintle used his smoky illusions to illustrate his point once again.

"A courageous individual would find the runestone, then travel the world, looking for the sacred location, and then pass a test of the soul"—the illusion figure walked around a globe, collecting a rock, and then discovering a giant tree —"but Queen Velleta thought that was preposterous. Centuries ago, she ordered her knights and hunters to find the runestones for all the creatures. She has them in her castle now, ready for whenever these creatures supposedly reappear in the world."

With a wave of his hands, the illusions ended.

"Of course she has them," Zelfree said as he rubbed the bridge of his nose. "Let me guess—she's not about to give one of them away?"

Bintle scrunched up his face, as though in deep thought and mild confusion. "I doubt she would break a complete collection. That would be nonsense. Is that what you're here for? A runestone from ancient times?"

"I'm curious about the legend," Eventide replied. "In my old age, I had intended to unearth some of these legendary artifacts, but I suppose if the queen has already taken the fun out of that…"

"Yes, I think it would be best if you turned your eye on a different legend. No matter how many scholars tell Queen Velleta that these creatures will never return, she is determined to prepare regardless."

Eventide placed a hand on Bintle's shoulder. They shared a short smile, and then Eventide said, "Thank you for this, old friend. I'm sorry to have wasted your time. If I had known everything had already been discovered, I never would've asked you to research things for me."

"It was no trouble," he said as he clasped her shoulder in return. "I look forward to the next challenge you send my way."

Illia and I got up from the table, and while I wanted to leave the library as soon as possible, I had one more question.

"Library Master," I said, addressing Bintle. "Do you happen to have any books written by Theasin Venrover?"

"Yes, I do." He hobbled to a nearby bookshelf and withdrew a thick tome. "He's a curious soul. One of the brightest individuals of our age." His ghost light "grabbed" the book with its telekinesis and floated it to me. Bintle pointed to the spine. "This was his first finished manuscript on the classification of mystical creatures."

"May I borrow it?"

Bintle and Eventide shared a glance. Then Bintle smiled at me. "Go ahead, young man. The scribes have copied it several times, but I'd appreciate it if you took care to bring this back undamaged."

I held the tome close. "Thank you. I will."

The moment we left the university campus, Illia stopped in front of the group, causing the rest of us to halt.

"Is it Queen Velleta?" she asked, no preamble or explanation.

Zelfree huffed back a laugh. "I highly doubt it."

"We should walk," Eventide said as she motioned to the road. After a few more steps away from the university, she continued, "And I agree with Zelfree. I doubt Queen Velleta created the arcane plague. She's never had a head for complicated strategy. She mostly orders and directs. When was the last time she left Thronehold? It's been decades."

"Couldn't she have *directed* someone to do it?" Illia asked, her voice heated and her breathing visible in the cold night air. "If she already has those runestones, it's obvious she was preparing."

I hadn't thought of it like that, but Illia made a good point. Perhaps Queen Velleta had ordered someone to create and spread the plague, just so she could be the one to find a god-like creature for herself. I didn't know the queen, though. Would she do such a horrible thing? And what would she do with her dragon? The only way to unbond was through death.

We stopped at a corner and allowed a horseless trolley to squeak by. The cloud of steam was thick enough that it got me coughing.

"If we assume the queen isn't behind the plague, that means whoever is will need to get their hands on the rune-stones," Zelfree muttered. "That's both a boon and a bane. We *know* our enemy doesn't have them, but at the same time, they'll likely use underhanded tactics to acquire them.

Theft. Extortion. *Something.* We have to make sure *we* have the runestones before they do."

Eventide nodded. "And the Sovereign Dragon Tournament has drawn people from all the over the world. We can't even look for suspicious people out of place—everyone is suspect."

"How can we help?" I asked.

Eventide and Zelfree exchanged hard glances.

"Leave this mystery to us," Eventide said. "Zelfree, Gillie, and I can handle everything. I want everyone else focused on simpler tasks."

"Like what?" Illia asked.

"Recruiting people to the guild. I have a troubling feeling that we might want powerful allies in the near future. Especially since the world as we know it is on the cusp of change."

Her ominous explanation kept everyone quiet the rest of the trek back to the inn. I hadn't considered the massive ramifications of what was happening. Even if we prevented a villain from bonding with the world serpent, someone else would.

And then there were eleven other creatures—all powerful in their own way.

Who would their arcanists be? And what would they do with their vast amounts of god-like magic once they bonded?

I sat on my bed, my back against the wall and my attention locked to the tome written by Adelgis's father. All the lanterns had been snuffed hours ago, leaving the inn blanketed in thick darkness, but that didn't bother me. Adelgis and Zaxis slept on the other side of the room, both making odd noises from time to time, but nothing I hadn't heard before.

I read through the book despite the lack of light, both curious to know more about mystical creatures and to see if I could understand Theasin just a little more before Adelgis went to see him.

One passage intrigued me more than the others. It discussed relative power levels between mystical creatures and the potential each had to become great.

Tiers of Mystical Creatures

The final power of an arcanist is determined by two factors: the tier of their eldrin, and their own soul.

A person's soul is similar to their blood. Their soul bleeds for their eldrin, empowering the creature with each year they are bonded. A mystical creature only grows by feeding off the soul of a human, and each year the eldrin grows older, so does the magical power they provide their arcanist.

But the creature cannot grow forever. Once it reaches final maturity, its magic plateaus. The arcanist will gain no new abilities or power increase to their existing magics. How fast this happens is dependent on the species of mystical creature.

There are essentially five tiers of mystical creature. The higher the tier, the more magic the creature can create with its arcanist. To better understand the total capacity, each tier has been likened to a body of water.

Tier 1—a puddle

This level of creature is weak. It will reach final maturity in a few short years, and its abilities are very limited. This tier includes, but is not limited to, will-o-wisps, sprites, and gnomes.

Tier 2—a pond

This level of creature is capable. It will reach final maturity in a few decades, and its abilities are varied enough for item creation. This tier includes, but is not limited to, unicorns, trolls, and ghouls.

Tier 3—a lake

This level of creature is impressive. It will reach final maturity at close to a century of bonding, and its abilities are substantial, both for item creation and auras. This tier includes, but is not limited to, phoenixes, manticores, and leviathans.

Tier 4—a sea

This level consists only of dragons. It seems these creatures are set apart from the rest in most capabilities, and the longer they're bonded, the more power they exude. Some arcanists have gone multiple centuries without finding their plateau.

Tier 5—an endless ocean

This level is reserved for hypothetical creatures that once existed, but no longer do. This tier includes, but is not limited to, world serpents, sky titans, soul forges, and typhons. According to legend, their magic was so vast that those who bonded to them became gods.

I stopped reading at that point and just stared at the words on the page. The information wasn't new to me—weaker creatures and stronger creatures had always been discussed —but I marveled at the way Adelgis's father managed to explain it. The simplicity, and clear analogy, left little room for misunderstanding.

"Turn the page," Luthair whispered from the darkness.

I glanced over, half-smiling. "You're reading this?"

"Indeed."

"What tier do you think knightmares fall under?"

"Third."

I reread the description. It included phoenixes and manticores, and both of those impressed me enough to smile. "That's the highest tier a creature can be without being a dragon."

"So it is."

"Are you just *hoping* that's the case? Or do you know for sure?"

Luthair shifted through the shadows, slithering to the other side of me. "My magic has yet to near any plateau, and I've seen the power of grandmaster knightmare arcanists. I know what I'll be capable of."

"You sound defensive."

"Hmm."

I stifled a laugh. Luthair rarely got irritated, but I could tell by the slight shift in his gruff voice that he didn't appreciate the doubt. Then I yawned, my mouth open for five long seconds. I slid down the wall, my body far heavier than I remembered.

"Perhaps you should read this another time," Luthair said. "And we can debate my placement on the chart then."

I chuckled. "Yeah. You're probably right..."

I hadn't slept long before Forsythe woke me for training.

While everyone rested inside the inn, Zaxis and I stood out in the empty courtyard. He used his flames on a water fountain—one carved in marble to look like a kelpie, a type of mystical creature water horse—and I occasionally tried to use my terrors on Forsythe without affecting him.

I always seemed to target them both, though.

"Maybe you should imagine your terrors like a physical cloud," Forsythe said. He fluttered his wings about, trying to make a representation for his suggestion. "And that you're directing the manifestation."

"I don't create anything visible," I said. "It's just a feeling. *A terror.*"

"That's why I said you should imagine it. I think it could help."

Zaxis unleashed a wave of flame at the fountain. The heat clashed with the water and created a thick steam that wafted into the air. Whenever the wind turned, the warm mist washed over us. It felt like I was both soaking wet and sweating.

I ignored the sauna temperature, as hard as that was, and practiced my own evocation.

The inn we stayed at—charmingly named *Maison Arcana*—seemed to cater exclusively to arcanists. Wealthy arcanists. Each room came with spaces for mystical creatures, and the staff didn't mind that Zaxis and I were using magic in their courtyard. One gardener even prepped buckets of water, ready to replenish the fountain as soon as Zaxis had finished.

A window overlooking the courtyard snapped open, drawing my attention.

Illia poked her head out, her wavy brown hair dripping water from a bath.

"Illia," Zaxis called out. "Do you want to join us? You should see my evocation."

She leaned onto the sill and shook her head. "You two need to get back in here. We're preparing to go to the castle with Guildmaster Eventide. Apparently, Queen Velleta will see the Frith Guild this afternoon."

16

THE KNIGHTS DRACONIC

There were twenty-three districts in Thronehold. It was hard to keep track of them, even with the signs, but one stood out. The area marked DRAGON DISTRICT wasn't like the rest. The roads were lined with lush trees, and the buildings were massive estates.

I also found it amusing that while the district was labeled "dragon," there weren't any around. All the arcanists in the area were bonded to unicorns or pegasi. All of them. And the longer I stared, the more I realized the arcanists were dressed alike—in soldier's uniforms and matching armor. Their white tunics complemented their silver chain-mail and gauntlets.

As our trolley rolled down the cobblestone road, I moved to the back, closer to Lyell. A woman flew overhead, riding on her pegasus, the wings casting a wide shadow. The chestnut body of the horse matched the red hawk wings. I had always thought they were white, but I hadn't thought much of it.

"Who are these arcanists?" I asked.

Lyell brushed back his orange-red hair. "Pegasus and

unicorn arcanists serve in the queen's knightly orders. The pegasi are known as the Sky Legionnaires, and the unicorns are part of the Knights Draconic."

Atty and Illia leaned out of the trolley to get a better look as two more pegasi flew overhead. Zelfree and Guildmaster Eventide continued their hushed conversation near the front of the vehicle, neither of them even acknowledging the mystical creatures around us. Zaxis stood and focused his attention on a distant unicorn. He stroked his chin, deep in thought.

Everyone seemed interested in our surroundings—except for Adelgis. He stared at his boots and ran a hand over his side, his fingers gently grazing the fabric covering his ribs.

I leaned forward. "Uh, Adelgis. You know about pegasi and unicorns, right? Anything interesting we should know?"

He mulled over the request for a long while. Then he said, "Pegasi control wind and are agile. They come in a variety of colors, most matching a type of bird. Black pegasi have crow feathers, and golden pegasi resemble eagles." He rattled off the facts like he were reading straight from a book —no enthusiasm or gusto. "Unicorns are immune to all forms of poison and have amazing regenerative powers."

"What does your father think about pegasi and unicorns?"

Adelgis shrugged. "He says they're trite."

That didn't surprise me. After reading a few chapters of his book, I found that Theasin seemed most obsessed with powerful magical effects. Auras, item creation—anything that had long-lasting repercussions. His discussion and analysis of "weaker" creatures seemed short and to the point. They had magic. They made arcanists. The end. Then he moved on to dragons or phoenixes and discussed all the tiny nuances of breed variation or arcanist quality.

A unicorn knight trotted down the road in the opposite direction, pulling me from my thoughts. The man riding the magnificent creature wore silver armor with dragon flourishes. Wing-like decorations protruded from the shoulders, and a dragon had been etched into the chest.

The unicorn he rode was larger than I had expected—about the size of an adult draft horse, the kind that pulled the heaviest weight. It wore similar protection to its arcanist, with a helmet that accommodated its long, spiral horn.

I didn't know the horn was so... weapon-like. It had to be two and half feet long, with a point as sharp as the tip of a spear. The unicorn could easily impale a man.

"Good day," the unicorn arcanist said to Lyell.

Lyell forced a smile. "And a good day to you, too, sir knight."

The moment the unicorn and its arcanist had gotten out of earshot, Zaxis opened his pouch of jerky and huffed. "Sure, that's a big horse, but I could take it in a fight."

"That arcanist is a lot older than you are," I muttered.

He bit down on a chewy piece of meat. "What's he going to do? Trample me? I'd roast that horse long before he could do anything permanent."

I didn't bother continuing the conversation. A part of me suspected Zaxis just wanted to regale everyone on the trolley with tales of his hypothetical prowess. I wasn't feeling it.

We made our way through the district at a steady, albeit slow, pace. The castle could be seen from any point in the city, and I turned my gaze to its impressive visage. As we drew closer, I couldn't help but admire the glorious windows—some of which stretched two stories—or the statues that were carved into the corners of the massive structure. They were statues of dragons, each of which looked as though it were holding up the castle on their scaled backs.

When we neared the gates, Lyell stopped the trolley and motioned with a wave of his hand. Everyone disembarked, but before I could get off, Lyell touched my shoulder.

"Volke, uh, would you mind coming by the Lamplighters Guild at some point?" he asked.

"Sure," I said.

"Thank you! I want to show you around and show you all the people I've met."

"Okay. Sounds good."

He genuinely smiled as I headed off to join the others, and I wondered why he hadn't asked Zaxis. Then I remembered their earlier conversation. Perhaps it was for the best.

I joined the others in the massive garden courtyard outside the front castle doors. Guildmaster Eventide spoke with the guards on duty, and then they ushered us in without trouble. Illia stuck close to me as we crossed over the threshold.

"Master Zelfree said this place was called *King Drake Castle* on maps," she said as she pointed to a tapestry hanging on the entrance wall.

A giant sovereign dragon fighting a leviathan spanned the tapestry from one corner to the other. The scales had been woven with shimmering thread, giving the whole scene depth and wonder that otherwise would've been missing. It was obvious from the fight in the picture that the dragon would win. Had some king of the past defeated a leviathan to claim the territory? I wished I had paid more attention to history.

Nicholin poked his head out of Illia's damp hair. "Pfft.

Where are all the rizzel paintings and tapestries, I wonder? There must be some mention of me and my kind *somewhere!*"

Although I hadn't thought about it, Theasin's book had yet to mention rizzel. I hadn't finished the tome, however, so perhaps I hadn't seen the part where they were discussed, but it did make me curious.

The castle servants rushed to show us to the reception hall. The moment we entered, I had to control the swivel of my head. If I hadn't known any better, I'd have said the room was larger than the whole town on the Isle of Ruma! The two-story-tall windows allowed sunlight to flood the area. Dozens of circular tables lined the wall, and forty other people were already inside and mingling.

It didn't take me long to realize they were arcanists from other guilds. I stared at their pendants—bronze, silver, and copper—but I didn't recognize the symbols.

Zelfree pointed to a table. "Wait here. The queen is seeing all the foreign guilds today, and we need to wait until we're called into her audience chamber. Understood?"

Everyone acknowledged him with a nod or a wave of their hand. Satisfied we had heard, Zelfree walked off with the guildmaster and stood by one of the windows. Their discussion seemed animated, like they were having an argument that couldn't be resolved.

I didn't want to sit at a table, though. I walked around it and headed toward the other guild arcanists, intrigued by their eldrin. One guild seemed to specialize in nymphs— elemental spirits that possessed control over air, water, plants, or fire, depending on the type. The spirits often looked like young women, though their bodies were made out of their specific elements.

I should've been paying more attention to my surroundings. I bumped into a waiter, and he dropped his silver tray. A pitcher of water and half a dozen glasses crashed to the floor. The racket drew everyone's attention, but once they'd had an eyeful, most returned to their conversation.

"I'm so sorry about that," I said as I bent down to help him clean.

"N-No," the waiter stuttered. "I'm the one to a-apologize, lord arcanist. It was my fault."

We quickly scooped up the broken glass. Luthair even manipulated the shadows to place the sharp and tiny pieces on the serving tray.

I gave the man a smile. "Done. Is there someone I should talk to about paying for the glasses?"

The waiter—dressed in black trousers with a plain black shirt, like he was trying to melt into the shadows, unseen—held the tray close to his chest. "I will, of course, pay for them, lord arcanist." He bowed deep. "Excuse me. Pardon me." He avoided eye contact as he hustled around me, his whole body stiff.

That had been... an odd reaction.

He had almost looked afraid.

"What a klutz," someone in the room said. Their statement garnered quiet laughter.

At first I thought they were talking about me, but then a second person followed it with, "Good help is hard to find these days. The queen should really look into improving her wait staff."

I glanced around and finally determined the guild making the remarks. A guild of magical research—some group from far to the south. I debated about whether to approach them when something else drew my attention.

"What do we have here?"

I glanced over my shoulder. Atty, Illia, and Hexa had

taken seats at our table, with Atty's phoenix in one of the chairs.

Two male arcanists had approached them, both hailing from the same guild according to their bronze pendants. To my amusement, the men had dog eldrin—one bonded to an orthrus, and the other to a barghest.

"Are you from the islands to the north?" one man asked as he sat next to Atty. "You must've been the beauty of your tiny town."

Atty blushed hard enough her color could be seen across the massive room. She turned away, but forced a smile. "That's kind of you to say, but—"

"This is my eldrin, Grim. Fierce, yeah?"

His orthrus bounded to the table, its tail wagging. Unlike cerberus dogs, who had three heads, an orthrus only had two. Grim's heads reminded me of hunting hounds—sleek fur, floppy ears, and long fangs. It would've looked rather friendly had it not been wearing thick leather and metal plate armor. I admired the shine of the orthrus's sleek brown fur.

Atty patted one of the orthrus's heads, her hand shaky. "Uh, nice to meet you."

"Call me Crevis," the arcanist said. "I'm with the Huntsman Guild."

I already didn't like the guy. He wore scuffed leather armor, coarse trousers, and two daggers at his belt. And when he leaned back, he spread his knees apart and rested his hand on the mid seam of his pants, like this was a tavern.

He held himself like a man who had seen his fair share of fights, which impressed me, but it wasn't enough to over-look his lack of tact. Even the scruff on his chin was yet another subtle insult to etiquette.

"My name is Atty," she said.

Crevis smiled wider, exposing the sharp canines of his teeth. "This arcanist here is Dart." Crevis motioned to the silent man next to him—they both had the same filthy mercenary appearance, but Dart was somehow fat in the gut. He wasn't soft anywhere else, however. On the contrary —his neck was as thick as a tree stump, and his arms could be categorized as deadly weapons.

"We're gonna sweep through the Sovereign Dragon Tournament and then celebrate with the best of 'em," Crevis said. "I'd love it if a beauty like you were on my arm." He placed a hand on Atty's knee and squeezed. "I'll treat you nice."

My blood ran hot as I took a few steps closer. The rational part of me said not to get into a fight in the middle of the queen's castle, and it took the better part of my willpower to not do anything.

Atty stared at his hand for a brief second and then slid away from his touch with a graceful move of her leg to the other side of the chair. "That's a generous offer, but I'll have to decline."

Her skillful rejection soothed my annoyance, but I still hovered close, feigning interest in a nearby tapestry to hide the fact I was eavesdropping.

Hexa snorted back a laugh. "Ha! You guys and your dogs will be lucky to get third and fourth. We're arcanists of the Frith Guild. If you're entering the apprentice division, you don't stand a chance against us." She motioned to herself and Illia and cocked half a smile.

The declaration probably would've held more weight if her hydra had been here, but she had left Raisen at the inn.

Crevis and Dart shot her and Illia scowls.

"We weren't talkin' to you, scrag," Crevis said, a growl in his words. "Mind your own damn business."

I cringed at the word *scrag*. All the sailors from the south used it to describe flea-bitten whores. I had always considered it one of the worst insults to throw at someone.

Nicholin jumped onto the table and puffed out his chest. "What did you just say? We don't need to wait until the tournament to wipe the floor with half-wit arcanists!" The squeak of his voice killed any intimidation.

"*Stop*," Illia hissed under her breath. She grabbed Nicholin and dragged him back across the table.

The barghest dog stepped forward, its fur on end. Barghests were fearsome creatures—giant black wolves with razor claws and bat-like faces. This eldrin had large pointed ears, one of which was shredded. It flashed its teeth and growled, its fangs a twisted mass of death.

Crevis stood. "Half-wits?" He dragged his orthrus over by the leather straps of its armor. "You two hags are lucky— at least you won't get any uglier when Grim gnaws at your face."

I had been too absorbed in the conversation to notice Zaxis.

He leapt over a chair and lunged for Crevis. Obviously taken aback, the man didn't have time to defend. Zaxis punched him hard across the jaw and then grabbed him by the collar and threw him sideways, right into a nearby table. The resulting crash echoed throughout the reception hall and practically sent a tremor through the floor.

Forsythe opened his wings. "Please, my arcanist, calm down!"

"What in the abyssal hells is going on?" Zelfree shouted.

The orthrus lunged for Zaxis, but on instinct, I held my hand out and willed the shadows to grab at its four legs. The massive dog got caught in the dark tendrils, securing it in place before it could bring both its mouths down on Zaxis.

Crevis rolled off the broken table and got to his feet. I readied myself for a fight, but a powerful gust of wind whipped across the room at lightning speed. Tables tumbled to their sides, chairs rolled several feet, and two of the giant tapestries were ripped from the wall hooks.

Most people were knocked down, but I shadow-stepped to avoid the worst of it. When I emerged from the darkness, I noticed a pegasus arcanist by the entrance door. She wore the armor of the Sky Legionnaires and rushed in to survey the area.

A man followed in behind her—a unicorn arcanist of the Knights Draconic. His armor shone with a brilliant luster, the silver glinting in the sunlight. He walked with purpose and power, and I knew from the way he conducted himself that he held substantial authority.

"Everything is fine," Eventide said. She walked toward the pegasus and unicorn arcanists, her hands out. "Two of the apprentice arcanists were arguing over who would win the tournament, and it led to an altercation."

The Sky Legionnaire turned to the knight. "Sir?"

"I will handle this," the man said, his voice deep and confident. "Return to your post in the courtyard."

"By your command."

The moment she left, the unicorn arcanist strode to the middle of the room, right where the most destruction had taken place. Up close, I noticed his trimmed black beard and the way his eyebrows retained a permanent scowl. His eyes—a striking blue—scanned the area with hawk-like precision. When he gazed at me, I held my breath, uncertain of what to say.

Technically, I hadn't started the fight. I had participated, sure, but I wasn't sure how to explain the situation.

Zaxis and Crevis got to their feet at the same time.

"I am Knight Captain Rendell," the unicorn arcanist stated.

The name struck me. I had read stories about a unicorn arcanist by the name of Winton Rendell, the Keeper of Silent Sorrow. He wasn't a swashbuckler, like Gregory Ruma or Gallus the Gray, but he was well known across the land as a formidable fighter. He had fought in two wars, and his eldrin, Nightfall, was a rare black-coated unicorn with a curved horn.

Knight Captain Rendell looked both Zaxis and Crevis up and down. "Are you two the miscreants who decided to brawl inside the castle's reception hall?"

The question hung in the air for a long while. The other guilds picked themselves up and brushed off, all of them paying attention as the scene unfolded. Forsythe hopped over to Zaxis, his head down. Grim shuffled close to his arcanist as well, his tail between his legs.

Zelfree jogged over and stepped between the knight captain and Zaxis. "Rendell, this is my fault. I take responsibility for what's happened here."

"*Your* fault?" Rendell asked. He lifted a single eyebrow with perfect form.

"This one is my apprentice, and I know he has a temper. I should've kept him on a short leash." He shot Zaxis a glare. "Forgive me. The Frith Guild will pay for any damages."

The knight captain turned his serious stare on Zaxis. For a long moment, Zaxis said nothing. Then, as if struck with realization, he took a hesitant step forward.

"Uh, I apologize for the mess I made. Sir."

Rendell panned his gaze over to Crevis.

The thug of a man offered a timid shrug. "Yeah. I'm sorry, too."

After mulling over the statements, Rendell held his

hands behind his back. "While this behavior is not tolerated within the walls of the castle, I will excuse it this one time. I understand the thrill of a tournament can rile the blood of many men, but that isn't an excuse to forget you're both arcanists. You must set an example, and that includes both patience and restraint. Do I make myself clear?"

Zaxis nodded.

Crevis hemmed and hawed before replying, "I get it, I get it."

The knight captain's words sunk into my thoughts. The Pillar on our island spoke of all virtues, including both restraint and patience. And while Zaxis had studied the same lessons I had, I doubted he remembered those nuggets of wisdom when some thugs were insulting Illia.

The door at the opposite end of the reception hall flew open.

"What's going on?" a young girl asked, her tone familiar. "I demand an explanation."

Knight Captain Rendell placed a hand over his heart and bowed. "Princess. Please forgive the mess. It will be handled shortly."

I moved to get a better look and then caught my breath.

The girl who had entered the reception hall was none other than the girl I had rescued from the river—Evianna.

17

THE WENDIGO HUNT

Evianna was a princess? Of the Argo Empire? That explained a lot. Our interaction at the river had confused me, but perhaps I hadn't displayed the proper etiquette when dealing with royalty, and that's why she had gotten upset.

With a haughty stride, Evianna strode through the reception hall. She kept her head high as she stepped around the upturned tables and clumps of fallen chairs. Everyone she passed bowed deeply, practically doubled-over, and then muttered, "Your Highness."

Evianna didn't acknowledge them, though. She continued forward, her hands on the skirt of her sapphire and ebony dress.

Actually, the dress reminded me of nullstone. The dark hue of the blue bled into the black, creating a subtle swirl through the shimmery fabric. And it beautifully complimented her white hair—now tied in a tight bun at the top of her head. When I had pulled her from the river, she resembled a cat that had been dunked against its will. Now she held herself with a regal self-importance, almost bordering on insufferable.

As she approached, Zelfree made eye contact with each of his apprentices. Then he motioned for us to scoot back. He took a position next to the knight captain, and I figured he wanted to do all the talking.

Illia, Hexa, Adelgis, Atty, Zaxis, and I lingered around one of the downed tables. The two phoenixes perched on top, and Nicholin made huffing noises from Illia's shoulder, like he wanted to protest the whole ordeal, but knew it would upset everyone.

Our guildmaster stayed next to the window, though she watched Evianna with a close eye. When the princess passed, Eventide offered a bow as well, but her muttered words were too soft for me to distinguish. When she stood, her reserved expression was too difficult for me to read.

Evianna stopped in front of Knight Captain Rendell. She straightened her dress and then stared up at him with a pinched expression. "Captain Rendell, what's happened here? Why is our castle a mess? Our knights are supposed to keep the peace."

"Some apprentices were involved in an altercation," he said matter-of-factly. "There is no need for concern."

"Which apprentices?"

Rendell placed a hand on Zelfree's shoulder. "The Frith Guild has arrived to see the queen. They hail from the northern islands, where etiquette is far different." Then he glanced over his shoulder and eyed our group.

He was right. The Isle of Ruma didn't have school classes on how to address royalty. I was certain Gravekeeper William would know, but he had never told me. Now I regretted not learning before we arrived in the empire. I should've anticipated the need.

Without any formal training under my belt, I mimicked

what everyone else had done. I bowed and muttered, "Your Highness," hoping it was enough to demonstrate my respect. The others followed suit—each one bowing, even if some of them were half-hearted in the execution. Nicholin continued his huffing, even as Illia bowed.

Evianna's eyes went wide the instant I stood straight. Our gazes locked, and I had a terrible feeling.

"These are *your* apprentices?" Evianna asked Zelfree.

He nodded. "Yes, Your Highness."

"Then it makes sense your guild would be involved in wrecking my lovely castle." She pouted and waved her hand. "One of your apprentices *manhandled me* and spoke with a patronizing attitude."

Everyone in our group—Zelfree, the eldrin, Guildmaster Eventide, the rest of the apprentices—faced Zaxis.

With gritted teeth, Zaxis returned their staring with a glower. "It wasn't *me*."

"Says the guy who started a fight in the royal castle," Hexa quipped.

"I've never seen this girl in my life!"

With a step forward, Evianna silenced the conversation. She glared in my direction. "It wasn't the redheaded boy. It was *him*." She pointed. "He was beyond inappropriate. A brute."

I had been called a lot of things in my life, but *brute* was a new one. Had my manners with her really been that terrible?

Zelfree laughed—honestly laughed. The others didn't seem to know how to react. They exchanged quick looks, each trying to stifle a snicker. Besides Knight Captain Rendell, who regarded me with a fresh sense of disdain, everyone else reacted as though the whole exchange had been one giant joke.

"There must be a mistake," Zelfree said between his chuckles.

"I'm never mistaken, thank you very much."

"Uh-huh," Nicholin said. "*Volke* was the one to manhandle you. Pfft." He covered his mouth with his paws and snorted. "It would've been more believable if you said he bored you to death with virtues from the Pillar."

While I appreciated the fact the others didn't believe Evianna's exaggerations, her growing irritation worried me. The knight captain kept his judgmental gaze honed on my every movement, and I swear the rest of the room watched while they whispered amongst themselves. The chances this didn't end poorly were dwindling with each second and snicker.

"Perhaps I was too quick to pardon your misdeeds," Rendell said. "Gather your guild, Eventide. You will see the queen at once, and then your apprentice will explain why he ever laid a hand on the youngest princess."

My heart sank into my gut. What was I going to say? It would be my word against hers, and thanks to Zaxis, everyone would assume Zelfree's apprentices were unchecked hooligans.

Evianna fidgeted with the edges of her sleeves. "L-Let's not be too hasty, Rendell. We don't need to bother Oma with the *details* of what happened. We can just tell her he was rough and—"

"The queen will demand an explanation."

"Ah, well, can't you just do something about this? Then we won't need to involve Oma. At all."

Knight Captain Rendell regarded her for a long moment before motioning to Guildmaster Eventide. His gauntleted hand glittered in the light streaming through the windows, and it wasn't hard to see he wanted us to gather. Evianna hovered close to him, her flustered movements and restless hands a sign of her growing anxiety.

"Please," she said. "Oma doesn't need to know everything. We can just verbally reprimand him."

"I have sworn fealty to Queen Velleta. I will not keep secrets from her."

It struck me then—her sister had said that Evianna wasn't to go near the river. Would the queen be upset with her when I told my side of the story? I would bet my life on it. That was what Evianna was afraid of.

Of course, I never would've mentioned the story had Evianna not stormed into the reception hall and accused me of *manhandling* her. Without context, she made it seem like I jumped out of the bushes and shook her down for all her coins.

No words were exchanged as our guild was led out of the reception hall and deeper into the castle. The cold stone and dark crimson of the carpets seemed more ominous without the sunshine from giant windows. The farther we got, the more unnerved I became. The place had all the welcoming warmth of a graveyard.

A spiral staircase the size of a lighthouse circled around a massive statue of a dragon. Its wings even made up a couple steps as we climbed to the highest levels, and I admired the craftsmanship as we went.

The statue hadn't been carved from marble or alabaster or limestone, like most statues—it was carved from bluish-black nullstone. The smooth surface of the sculpture gave the dragon a sleek glint, and I wondered just how much nullstone the empire had.

Atty walked close by, and I slowed to match her pace. She smiled at my presence, and I hesitated for a moment before asking, "You're okay, right?"

"Yes, thank you."

I wanted to speak with her more—to understand her thoughts on the situation and whether the dog arcanists had bothered her—but Adelgis hurried to my side. He breathed heavy from walking up so many stairs and knit his eyebrows together as he gave me the once-over.

"Is it true?" he whispered.

I shook my head, but at the same time, I tilted my hand back and forth. My confusing answer didn't sit well with him.

"If something goes wrong, I can petition my father to help." Adelgis frowned. "He knows the queen well. I'm sure she'll listen to him."

"I think everything will be fine," I said under my breath.

He let out a quick exhale. "Oh, good. I'd hate to see you in prison."

Even the mere mention of the prison sent a shiver down my spine. Did I want to be locked up with the plague-ridden arcanists? The possibility hadn't even occurred to me until Adelgis put the thought into my head.

I couldn't stop myself from imagining the worst.

Atty slowed her pace, and when I tried to fall back with her, Zaxis positioned himself right next to me. With a sharp elbow to my side, he drew my full attention. Part of me wanted to throw him down the staircase. He could heal. It wouldn't be life threatening.

"Yes?" I asked, curt.

"The knight captain's name sounds familiar," he whispered. "Who is he?"

"Winton Rendell, Keeper of Silent Sorrow."

With a stifled chuckle, Zaxis asked, "Keeper of Silent Sorrow? This guy was so depressed they gave him a title for it?"

"Silent Sorrow is the name of his lance," I growled. "Don't you remember the legends? It was forged from the unicorn bones of his deceased father's eldrin. Rendell avenged his father by hunting down the killer."

"Oh. Maybe I never learned of him then. I feel like I would've remembered that."

Satisfied with the information, Zaxis grew quiet and contemplative.

We traveled the endless flight of stairs, my attention inward until the knight captain stopped and pointed. We hadn't reached the top, but we had come to a giant door at least fifteen feet tall. The wood was black with nullstone. Two men dressed like the captain, but lacking arcanist stars, stood on either side.

The moment we approached, the doormen held up their hands.

"The queen is in a meeting," one said.

Knight Captain Rendell approached and then kept his voice low as he spoke to the two men in private. Evianna wandered over to his side, distancing herself from the Frith Guild. I didn't know what they were discussing, but I suspected it had something to do with me.

Zelfree lifted his gaze to the top of the massive door. He swore under his breath, and I glanced up to see what he was looking at.

Twelve beautiful rocks, each rectangular in shape, hung on the wall. Each one was a different polished stone, and they came in a wide variety of colors. Green jade, black obsidian, tan sandstone, gray shale—none of them were the same.

And each had a series of intricate etchings. It was hard to see, since they hung above the tall door, but they looked like pictures. Each stone was the size of my hand, perhaps smaller, which made the details even harder to decipher.

"Those are the runestones," Zelfree muttered, irritation in his voice. "The queen has them on her damn wall like common decorations."

Eventide walked to Zelfree's side. "They're trophies. She wants to flaunt them."

"How're we going to get them?"

"I'll have to find a way to convince her to sell them to me," Eventide said.

"Sober up, Liet. She'll never sell them. You know that."

Eventide didn't answer. She kept her gaze on the jade runestone, her focus sharp. If I squinted, I could make out the shape of a snake on it. It had to be the runestone required for finding the world serpent.

But what could we do to get it?

Zelfree had said our enemies would be after the same thing, and if the runestones were out in the open, wouldn't it be easy for them to be stolen? Then again, the castle was surrounded by the Sky Legionnaires and the Knights Draconic—not to mention there was an actual dragon nearby. How would anyone steal them?

Before I could inquire, the two doormen leapt to the door handles and threw the entrance open wide. Knight Captain Rendell motioned us in.

The throne room stole my breath.

It wasn't a normal room with four walls and a roof—it was something gigantic and custom, designed specifically for colossal dragons. There was no back wall. It was an open balcony that overlooked the nicer districts of Thronehold, with beautiful estates and striking architecture.

I would've loved to see more, but a sovereign dragon blocked the view with its massive body. It lay on its side, its neck wrapped around the back of the throne. The red and inky scales matched the crimson and ebony of the décor, and for the first time, I got to see its horns. They looked like they had been cut from metal—silver, specifically—and they angled forward, much like a bull's.

Galleon ships, with their three masts, weighed 500 tons. The dragon had to compare. It might have even been heavier.

The beast lifted its head as the members of the Frith Guild entered, its metallic eyes watching our every step. Each time it exhaled, a hot breeze washed over the room, and a hint of sulfur tickled my nose.

I hadn't even noticed the people until we were halfway in.

Pillars lined two of the walls, with guards positioned in front of each.

A short stairway led to a platform for the throne, and Gillie stood at the base of the steps with Fain and his antlerless wendigo by her side. Gillie's bright blue and yellow robes clashed with the gray, black, and red of the room. She stood out like a daisy on a battlefield.

"Rendell?" the queen asked, drawing my attention. "What is the meaning of this? I'm in the middle of speaking with the Fortuna apothecary."

Queen Velleta rested on the nullstone throne like it was a loveseat or couch, both her legs on the seat and the majority of her weight on one side. Her long white hair cascaded around her with the fluidity and shine of fresh milk. The length of her hair surprised me—if she had been standing, it would've reached her ankles, no doubt in my mind.

"Well?" she asked, her voice authoritative and definite, not a hint of hesitation.

Knight Captain Rendell stepped forward. "Your Majesty, pardon the early arrival of the Frith Guild. An incident came to my attention, and I thought you should hear of it right away."

The queen sat up in her chair, her eyebrows knit. She had a soft physique, round in most places, but never too much. I wouldn't normally have taken note of it, but she wore a gray dress that not only hugged her skin, but also bordered on sheer.

She ran her fingers through the long locks of her hair and revealed a crown woven around her head. The golden jewelry had been designed to showcase her arcanist mark— a giant dragon with wings that disappeared into her hair line.

To my surprise, her arcanist mark didn't glow, which meant she didn't have a true form dragon. I had just assumed anyone as powerful as her would've managed the feat, but I didn't know much about true form creatures.

"What incident?" the queen asked.

"The princess claims a member of the Frith Guild laid hands on her in a rough manner."

Evianna laced her fingers together, her eyes wide. She opened her mouth to speak, but nothing came out. Was she that afraid of the details?

The dragon snorted, sending a hot wave of air all the way to the throne room door. I shielded my eyes and then wiped the sweat from my brow. That monster of a dragon could devour anyone in the room.

"Explain," the queen commanded. "What, exactly, happened?"

Everyone turned to me.

If I told the truth, I knew Evianna would deny it. She clearly didn't want her involvement at the river known to the queen. But if I said nothing, they would assume I had harmed the princess because I was an uncouth thug, and that would end poorly for me. What could I possibly do?

I took in a deep breath.

"Wait," Evianna interjected. She rushed across the open room and stopped at the base of the stairs that led to the throne. "Oma, the details aren't important. I didn't want to bother you with this in the first place. I wasn't harmed."

Queen Velleta silenced her with a single raised finger. "I will know the cause of this disturbance. Speak, boy."

Her icy words lingered at the edge of my thoughts as I stepped forward. "Uh, Your Majesty, when we neared Thronehold, I tried to explore the nearby area. In my excitement... I slipped and fell into the river."

Everyone listened with bated breath, no words or mutterings.

I continued, "Evianna must've seen me, because she rushed to the bank to ask if I was injured. I was disorientated, and when I pulled myself from the current, I grabbed onto Evianna for support. If she hadn't been there, I might've slipped back into the water and drowned."

A bit of tension drained from the room. Evianna watched me, her expression slowly shifting from panic to realization.

I took another breath and then concluded, "I didn't know she was a princess. I thanked her with a pat on the back, and I now know that was inappropriate." I offered a formal bow to the queen, and then Evianna. "Please, forgive me. I never meant any disrespect."

Silence lingered for several seconds. My heart beat hard against my ribs. I wasn't a talented liar—I knew that—but the words I had spun didn't feel unbelievable. I had said them with enough conviction, hadn't I?

"It's just as he described it," Evianna said with a flourish of her hand. "I was taken aback by his unsophisticated ways."

"I see," the queen said as she relaxed into her throne.

Hushed whispers reached my ears. *I told you he fell into the river*, Zaxis muttered with a laugh. *Why did he hide this from us?* Hexa asked. *I hope the queen doesn't punish him harshly,* Atty added.

I glanced over to Illia.

She alone stared at me with a mix of disbelief and annoyance. I turned away, unable to meet her gaze for longer than a second. She knew I was lying. She *always* knew. We had learned to swim together, after all. No story that involved me almost drowning would ever sound believable to her. She probably knew the moment I started speaking that I was concocting a fictional scenario.

"What should be done, my queen?" Knight Captain Rendell asked.

She ran two of her fingers over her lips. "I will think of suitable punishment, but I need a moment to contemplate."

Punishment? The word didn't sit well with me, but I didn't know what else to do. I slunk back into the group, hoping it wouldn't be anything permanent. Perhaps she would demand I pay a fine?

With a sigh, Queen Velleta glanced over to Gillie and Fain. "We were in the middle of discussing the arcane plague. Is there anything more you wish to add or can I speak with the Frith Guild now?"

Gillie and her snow-white caladrius lifted their heads upon being addressed. Gillie's smile helped alleviate the stress of the situation. "Your Majesty, I was just about to get to the most important part. I have magical items that will prevent the spread of the plague to other arcanists." She held up a delicate box with gold and silver etchings.

The statement would've garnered more of a reaction if half the people in the room hadn't already known it was coming. Still, the eyes of the guards went wide, Evianna held both of her hands to her mouth, and even the sovereign dragon growled for a moment that rumbled the floor.

"I have five for you and your sworn knights," Gillie continued. "As gifts."

One of the guards in front of a pillar sprang forward and took the box. He carried it up the steps and presented it to the queen after bowing.

The dragon loomed overhead, its fangs visible, even with its mouth shut. Its nostrils flared, and I wondered if it was a sign of excitement.

Queen Velleta withdrew five antler necklaces. She examined each of them before slipping one over her head and allowing the pendant to fall between her collarbones.

"You should be recognized for such an achievement." The queen pressed the magical item against her skin. "This is a great accomplishment. Every arcanist will need one immediately."

"That is why I came to you," Gillie said, her cheery tone never wavering. "The key to this magical item is the precise combination of magic and material. Caladrius sorcery applied to the antler of a wendigo with just one star shard will create this trinket."

"Only a single star shard? For such immunity?"

"That's right. It's a low-level item, but very effective. It prevents all blood diseases, actually." Gillie placed a hand on Fain and moved him a step forward. "This is my assistant.

Please tell the queen about wendigo and their antlers, won't you, dear?"

Awkward and hesitant, Fain shuffled forward one step and then stopped. Wraith stuck close, his body up against Fain's leg. The dragon breathed heavy, however, and with each individual exhale, Fain's dark hair moved back and forth.

"They don't grow back," he said, terse and stiff.

Gillie urged him on with a gentle touch to his shoulder blade.

Fain continued, "They can be removed without hurting the wendigo."

That was all he said before moving back three feet. He kept his eyes on the stone floor and his hands deep in the pockets of his trousers.

"Wendigo," the queen said, rolling the word in her mouth like it was the first time she had ever uttered it. "They aren't native to this area. They dwell in the snow, don't they?"

"Snowy mountains," Gillie said. She patted her caladrius and continued, "Most are found near caves and dense forests, especially those with the grave-rot mushrooms. Those are special treats for wendigo."

"Yes. I remember now. I don't have any in my service, but that won't matter." She slammed her hand on the armrest of her throne. "Rendell, take a note. Once this meeting is concluded, you are to relay my two hundredth and thirty-sixth decree. All wendigo, whether or not they're bonded, are property of the crown, and their antlers will be harvested. Refusal to comply shall be punishable by death."

18

PRINCESS LYVIA

The decree struck me as deeply unfair. All wendigo *had* to sacrifice their antlers or be killed? I understood the gravity of the arcane plague, but did that warrant mutilating mystical creatures against their will?

"My queen," Rendell said with a forced gentleness to his voice. "We won't find many wendigo or wendigo arcanists in our territory."

"Send a contingent of Sky Legionnaires to the north." Queen Velleta lifted a hand. Her dragon touched it with the tip of his snout. "I want them to gather all they can find and bring them back. We can breed the wendigo here—I don't care about the magics needed to do so. Inform Artificer Venrover if you must. He'll know how to make the beasts sire offspring."

"And what about the wendigo arcanists who have come to participate in the tournament? Surely you don't mean to attack foreign nationals. Such violence could warrant a war."

"Give all foreign nationals three months from today. Post signs at the turnpikes and tollbooths. Put notice in the papers. Any wendigo arcanist found after the grace period will be subject to the same punishment for noncompliance."

The queen's harsh decree aligned with her previous rulings.

She *had* been the queen to order the destruction of king basilisks, after all.

King basilisks and their arcanists were death incarnate, and that could intimidate anyone, even the queen. To safeguard herself from king basilisk attacks, she ordered them all killed—creating any new eggs was a crime punishable by death.

Queen Velleta didn't tolerate even hypothetical insubordination, it seemed.

To my surprise, Gillie stepped forward. "Taking a wendigo's antlers is permanent. I don't know if you heard that part correctly, Your Majesty."

"I heard," the queen stated.

"Surely some sort of compensation can be offered in exchange?"

"You forget yourself. The right to expropriate private property for public use is within the power of the crown. I will do what is right for my people." She slammed her hand on the armrest of her throne and then waved us away. "I'm done with this meeting. You islanders always question my rulings. Rebellious, all of you. It'll be different once you're folded back into the empire."

Guildmaster Eventide swished back her coat and stepped forward. "Your Majesty—"

"Enough. The Frith Guild has my blessing to do business within the city."

"That's not what I wanted to discuss with you. There is a matter about purchasing some of your magical items. Specifically—"

"No. I've heard enough. You're dismissed."

Someone placed a hand on my shoulder. I flinched and turned to meet Illia's one eye. She held my shirt and scooted close, even while the knight captain and the guards motioned us to exit the throne room.

"Wait," Queen Velleta said.

Everyone in the room stopped mid-motion to give her their full attention.

"The one who laid hands on my kin. He's to spend a full day in the castle's dungeon."

Illia's grip tightened, and I could feel her protest through the heat of her fingertips digging into my flesh. I held a hand up and subtly shook my head. It wasn't worth arguing, especially since I didn't want her in a dungeon as well.

When the knight captain took my arm, I allowed him to lead me away from the group. I kept my head down, determined to get through the ridiculous sentence and put this encounter behind me.

The castle extended only two floors underground, but the dungeon's odor came from the abyssal hells. It left a tangy aftertaste in my mouth, and I swear ammonia hung like invisible clouds throughout the hallways. It reminded me of swimming through warm patches in cold water. I just had to shudder and get through it as fast as possible.

Knight Captain Rendell led me to the darkest corner of the dungeon. He carried a torch, though he knew the way enough that I doubt he needed it. His full plate armor clinked with each step. The sound echoed all around us, like a whole army was marching me to my confinement. I enjoyed the sound, though. It reminded me of Luthair.

Rendell stopped in front of a dungeon cell. He opened it with a heavy metal key and then swung the door open. It creaked in protest, akin to an elderly man with achy joints.

"You're a knightmare arcanist," Rendell said.

"That's right."

"And knightmare arcanists can travel through the shadows."

I glanced around the void of the dungeon. The walls were made of nullstone bricks, stacked with precision, but left rough at the sides. I suspected it would scrape my palms to run my hand over it. "I can shadow-step in normal environments. I don't know if I can here."

"But you would never have any fear of drowning in a simple river."

Ah. He had figured it out. He probably knew I had lied to the queen. Was he upset? I was certain that lying to her would be considered a crime. I hadn't even thought of that when I spun the story for her.

"I'm sorry for this," Rendell said. He motioned to the dungeon cell. "One of the guards will let you out once your time has been served."

I stepped into the narrow room. The angry groan of the door sent a shiver down my spine until the lock clicked shut. Rendell's footsteps clinked down the hall and up the stairs. I could hear them long after he had gone.

I shoved my hands in my pockets and took in my surroundings. If I lifted my arms I could touch two walls at the same time.

There were no torches and no windows. The room would've been pitch-black, but my dark vision allowed me to examine every painful detail of my surroundings. Like the bench of splinters mounted into the wall with rusty nails. Or the bucket in the corner with its own fog of ammonia. Or the rats that squeezed through the tiny crack in the wall, their fur covered in muddy clumps—though I was certain it wasn't actually mud.

"Luthair," I said. "Was Mathis ever thrown into a dungeon?"

"No, my arcanist."

His shadow shifted around my feet. When a rat got close, Luthair growled something I couldn't understand. The rodent screeched and scurried back to its hole.

I leaned against the locked door. "So this is a new low for you? Ever regret bonding with me?"

"While I never would've wished for Mathis's death, I am grateful to have found you in the mire when I did. No matter how many dungeons you get yourself thrown in, I will be by your side."

I had been joking—trying to ease the tension of our disgusting confinement—and I hadn't expected such a serious answer. I couldn't help but smile. How was the empty suit of magical plate armor the warmest thing down here?

"Maybe I should take this time to practice my manipulation," I said.

"The nullstone will prevent that, I'm afraid."

Confused, I lifted my hand and tried to move the darkness of the dungeon cell. Nothing. Then I tried to step into the shadows and only managed to stumble forward.

"Why?" I glanced around, my enhanced eyesight still piercing the shadows. "I don't feel that suffocating feeling, like when we passed through the nullstone outside the city. And I still have my dark-sight."

"This is refined nullstone, shaped and built into the castle by generations of talented sovereign dragon arcanists. It's a cunning form of suppression, undetectable until you're in it. But the anti-magic only prevents magic activation, not passive abilities."

After hearing the information, I admired the walls with a newfound sense of appreciation. "How did sovereign dragon arcanists craft this if it prevents magic use?"

"Dragons are unaffected by nullstone."

I gritted my teeth, frustrated by the nuances of eldrin I didn't know. Phoenix arcanists were immune to fire, knightmare arcanists immune to terror, man-eating creatures immune to blood diseases, and now dragons were immune to nullstone's anti-magic powers? It seemed the list would continue to grow, and I had to master every bit of that knowledge if I wanted to be a legendary arcanist capable of dealing with the threats of the world.

"Wait," I said as I remembered the many nullstone structures in the castle. "Are there areas of anti-magic in the castle itself? Did I just not notice it?"

"The kings and queens of old built the castle for defense. Sovereign dragon arcanists—and *only* sovereign dragon arcanists—can activate or deactivate the refined nullstone found throughout most of the castle. It's meant to cripple arcanist assassins or magical enemies to the crown."

That made sense. If the queen's sorcery wasn't affected by nullstone, it would benefit her to make her fortress one giant anti-magic zone. The fact she could control when it was active was also quite interesting. I assumed, given her Sky Legionnaires and Knights Draconic, she wouldn't want the anti-magic effect at all times.

I let out a long sigh.

"Why do you know so much about this?" I asked.

"Mathis used to work and train in Thronehold."

"Is there a Steel Thorn Inquisitors Guild here? Is that where you wanted to visit?"

"Yes, my arcanist. I imagine Mathis's old mentor will be in the city."

I hadn't ever considered that. "We should meet him," I muttered as I turned my gaze to the rough ceiling.

"Perhaps once you're a free man."

I never understood why sailors sang songs while they worked, but now it all made sense. It passed the time while doing mindless activities. Sitting in a dungeon didn't give me many options, and I hummed one of the sea chanties I had learned as a lad. While the song echoed in the darkness, I retreated into my mind, hoping I could piece together more about the world serpent.

The runestones had been located—right above the door to the throne room!—but what could we do with the information? Would Eventide try to steal them? That seemed unlikely. The stories of her accomplishments never involved thievery. Would the queen sell them? I hoped, but that didn't seem to be her style.

But more importantly, once we had the runestone and found the world serpent, who would bond with it?

The answer to that question seemed like it would change the course of the world. If someone like Calisto bonded to it, he would ravage the land—an unstoppable destructive force.

But what if someone like Queen Velleta bonded with it? After meeting her, I knew why Zelfree and Guildmaster Eventide were so hesitant to inform her of what was going on. She was a tyrant, even if she didn't realize it. If the queen bonded with the world serpent, she would use her power to reclaim all her lost territory and then some, no doubt in my mind. No one could oppose her rule then, and she would do whatever pleased her, including preemptively killing anyone she thought *could* be a threat in the future.

We couldn't tell her about the world serpent. Never.

Perhaps Eventide would bond with it.

I hadn't considered it until just then, but it seemed plausible, though unlikely. If the Frith Guild had a world serpent arcanist, we would be an unrivaled contender and controller of the seas. But would Eventide stay with the guild after bonding? Perhaps she would rule a new nation as a god-arcanist. And what would become of her atlas turtle? Would she kill it to gain more power? That seemed unlikely.

Although fascinating, my thoughts drifted back to the immediate—to Adelgis, Atty, and Illia.

I wondered if Adelgis would go see his father. I wanted to meet Theasin, so while I thought it was foolish, I also hoped Adelgis had chosen to wait.

Atty filled my thoughts for multiple reasons. She had asked to train with me, but then never brought it up again. And she seemed quieter most days than before. Well, she had always been quiet, ever since we joined the Frith Guild, but it seemed like she was becoming more of a recluse as time went by. That was very different than the Atty I knew on the Isle of Ruma. She had been so perfect and amazing —everyone wanted her time.

What had happened?

And Illia...

I wanted to speak with her. She always knew just what to say.

The click of shoes on stone snapped me out of my spiraling thoughts. I leaned away from the door and rubbed at my eyes. I hadn't been here for twenty-four hours. Six or seven, at most.

The footsteps grew louder.

I waited, my body tense. I had never been in a dungeon. I really didn't know what to expect. Light shone from a lantern, growing brighter as this mystery person neared.

The clang of keys rattled in the lock. After a harsh click, the door creaked open. To my surprise—and delight—Evianna's older sister, Lyvia, stood out in the hall, the lit lantern held tight in one hand.

She wore a pair of fancy riding trousers—the kind with a pressed line on the sides—and a pair of high leather boots. Her jacket matched the black of her pants, giving her a military look that contrasted with her purplish-white hair.

When she smiled, I answered in kind.

"I'm so sorry," she said with a furrowed brow. "My sister told me everything, and I came straight down here to get you."

I stepped out the dungeon cell and glanced around. It was just as empty as when Knight Captain Rendell had led me here.

I rubbed at my neck, giddy to be let out early and grateful beyond words. "Thank you." But then I remembered a crucial piece of information. "Er, uh, I mean to say —thank you, *Your Highness*."

Lyvia placed her free hand on her hip. "Oh, you know now. That's unfortunate. I enjoyed talking to you as an equal."

"Uh... But aren't you a princess?"

She closed the door to my cell. The groan dug into my ears and I cringed. Once secured and locked, she took my elbow and led me down the hall. "I might have the title of princess, but it doesn't mean anything. You can just call me Lyvia."

"Why doesn't it mean anything? It seems important."

"Only sovereign dragon arcanists can rule in the Argo Empire." She tapped at her smooth forehead. "If anything were to happen to Oma, neither me nor my siblings would ascend the throne. We'd be ousted to allow for a new ruling family. See? Makes my title seem much less significant. I try not to let it go to my head."

The stink of the dungeon agitated me as we climbed the stairs, but it soon waned. I took a deep breath and relished it.

"Is the queen's first name Oma?" I asked.

Lyvia laughed. Then she held my elbow tighter. "I do enjoy your questions." She rubbed at the corner of her eye before continuing, "No, her first name is Shayll. She just doesn't like me or my siblings calling her things like *grandma*. She said it reminds her of the fact she's old."

"She's not your mother?" I asked, shocked. Then again, arcanists could live a long time, and I knew Queen Velleta had been sitting on the throne for centuries now. Most arcanists, once they got old enough, couldn't produce children anymore, not even the men. The queen couldn't be Lyvia's or Evianna's mother.

"She's our great-great-great-great-great-grandmother," Lyvia said matter-of-factly. "But that's a mouthful, so we call her *Oma* instead."

Interesting. For a brief second, I wondered if anyone had ever gotten that wrong and called the queen *Oma* on accident. Would they be thrown in the dungeon as well?

"What's your mother's name?" Lyvia asked. "Something unique, like your name?"

The mere mention of my mother got me tense. Lyvia must have felt it, because she immediately continued with, "Then again, I didn't tell you about my mother, so why should you tell me about yours? Instead, you should tell me the name of your great-great-great-great-great-grandmother. To be fair."

I chuckled as we exited the underground floors and made our way through the massive main hall of the castle. The windows had no light to give. The cold breeze of a perfect night greeted us with open arms.

"I don't know much about my family," I muttered. I certainly didn't know any of my grandparents.

"Then what's your eldrin's name? You have a knightmare, right? They always have interesting names."

"Luthair."

Lyvia's eyes went wide. We didn't stop walking, but she slowed for a moment before regaining her stride. "You're bonded to the knightmare who spawned from King Raulith's demise? That's... fascinating. I thought he had perished."

"No. He's still here. Right, Luthair?"

"Indeed," he said from the shadows, his voice just as gruff as ever.

When we arrived at the massive front doors, guards jumped at the opportunity to open the way for Lyvia. She smiled and waved and kept her hand on my elbow, no hesitation in her movements. I avoided all eye contact, worried someone would report me outside my cell.

"Are you sure I'm allowed to leave early?" I whispered as we entered the courtyard.

Lyvia nodded. "Yes. Don't worry about Oma. She won't even remember you were down there. She punishes everyone, even for the slightest crimes." Lyvia puffed out her chest and held up a finger. With a mock-voice of the queen, she said, "*As a queen, I cannot be soft. The citizens need to know that I will keep the peace.*"

"I see."

Lyvia relaxed and then smiled up at me. "You know, if you ever catch my sister in the river again, you have my permission to let her drown."

I knew she was joking, but that didn't change my reaction.

"Even if I had known I'd be thrown in a dungeon afterward, I still would've helped your sister."

Lyvia waggled a finger. "I figured you would say that. Just like Lark the Gallant. He almost killed himself saving people."

"Three times," I said with laugh. "He got himself into all sorts of trouble for people."

All the tales of Lark's adventures involved weird schemes and tricky plans. They say he pretended to be a villain on more than one occasion—some people couldn't keep up with his alliances—but he always came out a hero in the end. I had never considered myself similar to Lark, but he did risk himself for other's safety when no one else would. I admired that about him.

"Gregory Ruma had lots of interesting tales," Lyvia said. "I assume you've heard of him as well?"

The first image in my mind was the shambling corpse of his dead wife.

I gritted my teeth. "Uh, let's stick with Lark the Gallant."

She smirked. "That's easy. He's my favorite. I spent long nights reading of his exploits."

Then we reached the walls of the castle. The gate was open, which was convenient, but I wondered why. Lyvia didn't seem concerned. She stopped at the threshold and released my elbow, though her grasp came off slowly.

"Volke," she said. "I apologize for my sister's childish behavior. You didn't deserve any of that, and she didn't deserve you protecting her from Oma's wrath."

"Don't worry about it. I'm not angry."

We stood still and silent. Lyvia didn't make a move to leave, so neither did I. She stared at me as though she wanted to say something, and I waited.

Finally, she said, "Evianna wanted the glitter crab so she could make me this." Lyvia reached into the collar of her military coat and pulled out the pendant of a simple necklace. It was the sparkling shell of the crab—hollowed and without the creature. "She made it so that I would have good luck."

"That's nice of her," I said.

Lyvia met my gaze with a cold expression I had yet to see from her. "I think she's worried for my safety. I wish she wouldn't. It makes things awkward."

"Is there reason for her to worry?"

No answer. She glanced to the ground, and I grew restless.

"Is everything okay?"

"Yes." Lyvia pointed to the main road. "But it's dark out. You should get back to your guild. Please be safe. Crime is the most rampant during festival times, and the city has never been fuller than it is right now."

"But will you be—"

"I need to rest," she stated, cutting me off. "Goodnight, Volke. And thank you again for showing kindness to my sister, even if she didn't deserve it."

19

THE SPIDER IN THE ALLEY

Walking the roads of Thronehold felt like stepping into the future. The architecture, the lamps, the trolley cars—everywhere I looked, I lost myself in wonderment. Even at night, the city pulsed with life. The islands of my childhood paled in comparison. Sometimes, while I stared at the giant windows and brick buildings, my mouth half open, a man on a horse would bark at me to get out of the way. I apologized and tried to keep to the sidewalks, but the temptation to explore every alley and tavern got me crossing the streets at random moments.

Music drifted from gambling halls, and I slowed my walk to listen longer as I went by.

Most districts were self-explanatory. Justice, education, north market, south market—but I soon came across one that piqued my interest. The sign read: MOONLIGHT DISTRICT. The picture next to the words was a music note and a bed. Smoke wafted from the numerous chimneys, and the smell of flowery perfume lingered in the streets.

"What is this place?" I asked.

Luthair shifted through the shadows. "This is the district for bordellos, burlesque clubs, theaters, and tailors."

I stood outside the district limits, yet the sounds of rowdy drunkenness reached me with ease. Underneath the raucous bluster, I detected a hint of songs sung by beautiful feminine voices. It intrigued me.

I took one step forward, and Luthair made an odd growling noise.

"What's wrong?" I asked.

"This is a distraction. We should head back. You know Illia will be worried about your safety."

His rationale killed my urge to explore. I didn't want to give Illia any undue stress. With a quick turn on my heel, I left the Moonlight District and headed for the main road. Once I found some familiar sights, it would be a quick walk back.

The lamps, lit by the will-o-wisp arcanists of the Lamplighters Guild, kept the streets lit even with the waning moon in the sky. I stopped and examined the sliver crescent. Tomorrow would be the new moon—the sky would be empty, save for the stars. Zaxis said he intended to speak to Illia on the new moon. He wanted to declare his intent to court her.

I would spend a day in the abyssal hells just to see that interaction. Zaxis wasn't as suave as he thought he was, and Illia... Well, I really just wanted to hear what she said to him. Would she accept his advances?

I only got a few blocks into my trek when a shout sent ice through my system. The crash of glass, and a frightened screech of yelling, filled my veins with adrenaline.

"Luthair," I barked.

In an instant, he formed up around me. The cold shadows coalesced into hard armor around my body, complete from head to toe, with helmet, cape, and weapons in hand. A sense of undeniable power accompanied the change. It had been a long while since Luthair and I had merged, and I had missed it.

A man burst out of a nearby alley, running at full tilt with something tightly held in his arms.

Another man exited from the same alley a moment later, winded and struggling to keep up.

"Someone," the second man shouted. "Someone, stop him!"

The first man dashed down the street, knocking people out of the way as he hustled toward another alleyway. People shouted and pointed, but no one attempted to stop the man.

The man giving chase just couldn't keep up. He stumbled over the cobblestone and nearly fell face-first into the gutter.

I didn't need to see much more than that.

With one swift motion, I shifted through the shadows, shooting through the darkness at lightning speed. I couldn't really see while I moved, but if I kept the surroundings in my mind's eye, I managed to emerge right where I wanted.

Sure enough, when I exited the shadows, I appeared in the alleyway, blocking the path of the first man. He jerked to a halt before slamming into me, his eyes wide, his body stiff. He was around my age, with a lanky frame and long limbs. His trousers, shoes, and ratty coat all carried the stains of coal and dirt. The patches and extra stitching told a long tale of repairs.

And he also had an arcanist mark on his forehead. The creature wrapped around his faint star was none other than a twisted spider.

He was bonded to an *anansi*—a trickster spider capable of weaving illusions and traps.

The anansi arcanist held a young rabbit in his arms. The fur of the rabbit glowed with otherworldly white light, practically a soft lantern, and I knew it had to be a *moon rabbit*, a mystical creature of life and medicine.

The young man yanked a small dagger from his pocket and sliced a finger. The crimson blood stained the blade and dripped onto the cobblestone.

"S-Stay back!" he shouted as he stepped away from me, his legs shaking. "I-I have the plague! *I'll infect you* and *the r-rabbit!*"

The moon rabbit trembled, its ears pressed back as flat as they go. "Help," it whispered.

"Unhand the mystical creature," I commanded, my voice a frightening mix of mine and Luthair's. I hoped beyond reason the thief would abandon his crimes, but I knew that was unlikely.

If I evoked terrors, the anansi arcanist still had the possibility of stabbing the rabbit. If I manipulated the shadows to grab the weapon, he could still use the blood of his hand to infect the terrified creature. Attacking straight on with my sword would have the same risk. I couldn't allow the moon rabbit to get hurt.

The man took another step backward. "I c-can't let the moon rabbit go... My eldrin... it needs to eat things... It t-told me I had to."

My heart stopped for half a second as laughter echoed out of the alleyway. I was a fool not to put it together sooner —if *he* had the plague, that meant his eldrin was likely riddled with it. And where was his anansi?

Remember the wendigo pendant, Luthair spoke in my mind. *You needn't fear the plague.*

I had remembered, but that didn't erase the myriad of memories involving gruesome monsters warped by corrupted magic. I still had to be on my guard.

The clop of hooves drew my attention to the entrance of the alleyway. A pair of the Knights Draconic—a man and his white unicorn eldrin—came to a stop. He pulled his sword, and the district denizens pointed and shouted at the anansi arcanist with the rabbit.

"Stay back," I said. "He's plague-ridden. I'll handle this."

The unicorn knight didn't have a wendigo amulet. I *had* to be the one to deal with the situation; otherwise, it could spread across the city, infecting dozens—maybe even hundreds—of unsuspecting arcanists.

"As you wish, Inquisitor," the knight said as he offered me a salute.

Inquisitor? But I didn't have time for questions.

With my attention on the anansi arcanist and the moon rabbit, I didn't notice the webs until they wrapped around my armor. I tried to sidestep away, but the thin strings held like steel, wrapping tight.

The webs wouldn't physically damage me. That wasn't what anansi did. Their silk threads were coated in powerful magic that caused all stuck inside of them to fall into a coma-like state, awash in illusions that kept them docile.

"Hold... still..." a voice said, its strange cadence a dead giveaway to its plagued existence. *"It won't hurt long!"* Gleeful giggling punctuated its threat.

But I wasn't going to get caught. I slipped into the shadows, freeing myself from the vile trap, and reappeared on the other side of the alleyway. Then I spotted it—a giant spider descending from the rooftop of a nearby building. Rust red in coloration. Hairy in patches. And with eight dead fish eyes that pulsated and jiggled, like they were struggling to burst out of the spider's head.

The beast was the size of the large dog. Its legs, when stretched to the fullest, had to be three feet long. Tiny hands, like those of infants, were on the tips of the legs, the fingers wiggling.

"Magic," the anansi said through chuckles. "I need *to*... *to*... eat it."

The thief held his arms straight out, his shoulders bunched at the base of his neck. He offered the trembling moon rabbit and shouted, "It's yours! Take it!"

Although I knew my second-bonded magic would hurt, I didn't have time to worry. I manipulated the darkness, trying to end the whole situation in a single move. I wrapped the rabbit in a protective tendril and lashed out with whip-like bindings to hold the arcanist and his eldrin in place. Sure enough, I snatched the moon rabbit, but the anansi half-hissed and half-vomited, somehow damaging my magic and stopping the darkness.

I pulled the rabbit to safety, but the enemy arcanist charged at me, knife at the ready. He held his weapon with a limp wrist and poor grip. With practiced movements, I stepped to one side, tripped him, and then bashed my shield into his side, sending him to the ground. He hit face-fist, blood exploding from his nose upon impact.

The spider continued to vomit, half laughing while it did so, like the process brought it pleasure. The gurgled chuckling gave me goosebumps. And it didn't spit up partially digested food—it vomited whole organs. They fell to the ground with a wet splat, each one bursting open, spreading the infected blood around.

I evoked terrors, and I imagined them like a physical cloud of despair centered on the anansi and its arcanist, just as Forsythe had suggested. I wanted to leave the unicorn knight and the moon rabbit unharmed.

To my surprise, and delight, it worked.

The spider fell from its webbing and landed in a puddle of its own vital fluids. His arcanist screamed and clutched at his head. The moon rabbit took the opportunity to flee. It avoided the tainted blood and scampered into the arms of the knight waiting just outside of the alleyway.

"Thank you," the rabbit called to me, its voice a cute squeak.

The anansi managed to stagger to its eight feet, its tiny hands grasping at the loose gravel. Before I could act, the anansi curved its abdomen under, then sprayed the alleyway with thick, glob-like webbing. I slipped into the shadows before getting caught and then exited the darkness right next to the beast.

"I need a *new*... liver." The anansi chuckled. "*Perhaps I'll take yours.*"

It sprayed another round of blood, this time actually managing to coat my shield and part of my greaves.

It didn't matter. I was immune.

I stepped forward and slashed with my sword. The blade cut clean through the center of its thorax, slicing it into two parts. The monster laughed as its heart frantically beat the blood straight out of the gaping wound. Its legs twitched, like it wanted to crawl away, but didn't have the strength.

"You'll never... accomplish..."

But the anansi didn't get to finish its twisted statement.

The arcanist in the alleyway cried out in pain, no doubt from losing the connection to his eldrin.

I turned on my heel, my blade ready. He didn't attack, though. He just curled up, his eyes scrunched tight. The mark on his forehead slowly vanished—fading until there was nothing left. Silent tears ran down the man's face as he shuddered back the agony.

I stepped forward, ready to end his life.

This isn't needed, Luthair said. *He no longer has the plague.*

Confused, I stopped and held my shield close. *How? There is no cure.*

Non-magical creatures can't carry the plague. Now that his eldrin is dead, he's a normal man.

The man sobbed and muttered, "I was just... doing what it told me to. I s-swear. It messed with my h-head..."

It disturbed me that a plagued creature could get into the city. At this point, I was becoming an expert on their behavior. This spider had been freshly infected—its eyes and erratic mannerisms were a dead giveaway. The longer-term plagued beasts acted with intelligence, even if they were still laughing mad.

I grabbed the man by the collar of his tattered coat and pulled him close. He flinched and covered his face with his arms.

"Where were you infected?" I asked, my double voice echoing down the dank alleyway.

"I-I..."

I tightened my grip on his clothing. Luthair's thoughts seemed darker than my own, but I waited. This thief had no fight in him.

"It was... outside the city." He half-sobbed into the coat sleeve. "Near the—the old kingdom mines..."

I let him go, my panic waning.

Anansi were capable of powerful illusions. This man probably made it into the city with a combination of his anansi magic and luck. There were tons of competitors here, and if he hid his plague-ridden eldrin with a disguise...

I threw the man back to the ground, uncertain what his fate would be.

A small crowd had gathered on the cobblestone road. They burst into cheers when I stepped out of the alleyway. Even the unicorn arcanist seemed caught up in the moment. He shouted along with the rest of them, and so did his equine eldrin.

The man who had originally called for help—a scholar, by the looks of it—hurried over. He wore long robes of forest green. His short black hair, cut to the point of fuzz, made him distinct from the crowd.

The unicorn knight handed over the moon rabbit.

"Thank you so much," the scholar said as he bowed his head. Then he bowed his head to me. "I don't know what I would've done without you, Inquisitor."

More clapping and cheering filled the short block. "Thank goodness for the inquisitors!"

I was about to inquire about the title when Luthair spoke in my mind. *They think you're with the Steel Thorn Inquisitors Guild.*

Luthair unmerged from me a moment later, but instead of reforming as a suit of armor, he remained my shadow, disappearing from sight. At first, I thought he was escaping the crowds and trying to stay anonymous, but then I realized it was to clear away the blood that had splattered on his armor. When we were merged, we lived and died as one, but *he* wasn't wearing a wendigo amulet, which meant he needed to be careful.

The moon rabbit stared up at me with eyes just as white as its brilliant fur. "You were amazing, Inquisitor."

"Uh," I said as I rubbed at my neck. "I'm not an inquisitor."

The unicorn stepped close, its armor gleaming even at

night. His arcanist stared down at me from his saddle, his eyes narrowed. "You're not? I thought all knightmare arcanists became inquisitors…"

"I'm with the Frith Guild."

"I see." The man patted the neck of his unicorn. "I will handle the incapacitated thief and tend to the quarantine."

"The thief said he was infected near the old kingdom mines."

"Dreadful. I'll have the area investigated at once. Such vermin must never be allowed near Thronehold."

At sea, pirates had a frightening advantage. They could sail close to islands or other ships and infect those who stood and fought. Here on the mainland, there were few methods to do the same. The queen's military could be used to clear away plague-ridden monsters, keeping the capital safe.

"Thank you for your help," the knight said. "The city owes you a great debt for killing someone with the arcane plague." He dismounted and then commanded the locals to help gather the crying man still in the alleyway.

That was for the best. The non-magical people of Thronehold wouldn't get infected.

I regarded the unicorn. Its mane and tail were braided. The creature must've noticed my staring, because it snorted and bowed its head. "Thank you." A noble voice that matched it regal appearance.

While the citizens rushed to help the knight, the scholar stepped closer so we could talk.

He asked, "The Frith Guild is still around?"

"That's right."

"Interesting. I didn't know." He held the rabbit tight to his chest and bowed his head a third time. "How can I repay the guild for its services?"

My gut reaction was to tell him we didn't need anything, but then I remembered what Eventide had said.

"You aren't an arcanist," I said, staring at his unadorned forehead. "Why do you have this mystical creature?"

"I'm with a team of mystic seekers."

That was a term I hadn't heard outside of history books.

Long ago, when the world was less tame, kings and queens would order teams of mystic seekers to venture into the wilderness and find mystical creatures. Seekers were tasked with bringing them back—alive and healthy, and with whatever foods they required for mating—so that the creatures could be integrated into the community.

But as more kingdoms formed, and land was civilized, there was less need for mystic seekers. There were still untamed lands filled with danger, so, of course, mystic seekers would still exist, it was just an unusual profession.

"I don't do the hunting," the scholar said. "I'm the one who cares for mystical creatures. I'm more of a researcher, actually." He chuckled under his breath and then continued with, "Our leader is an arcanist, and he does all the dangerous activities."

"Can you tell him the Frith Guild is looking to expand? I'm sure we'd take his whole crew if he made arrangements with our guildmaster, Liet Eventide."

The man nodded along with my words. "Intriguing. I'll relay the message. The Frith Guild is known far and wide for its amazing deeds."

"And tell anyone else you might know. We want all the talented people we can get."

It didn't take me long to find our inn, the *Maison Arcana*. The palatial building was stationed on a corner, with massive gates and a beautiful wrought iron sign. The sun had yet to rise, but the groundskeepers managed to tend the windows and plants by lamplight, likely keeping the place presentable while the customers slept.

I passed a couple as I walked inside. They greeted me with smiles, and I did the same. Once inside, I noticed some of the lanterns remained lit, giving the place a warm, but sleepy, atmosphere.

Two seconds into the lounge, Nicholin popped into existence right in front of me. He stood on his hind legs as the glitter from his teleport disappeared.

"You've returned," he said.

"Yeah."

He vanished and then reappeared on my shoulder, squeaking something happy I just couldn't make out. His whiskers tickled my neck, and I chuckled as I tried to get him settled.

"Okay, okay! I'm happy to see you, too!"

Nicholin stopped his nuzzling and tensed up, his whole body going stiff.

I pet his white and silver fur, a bit confused. "Everything all right?"

"I'll be back."

Without another word, he disappeared, leaving me alone in the entrance lounge. I figured I should wait for him, so I took a seat on one of the many couches. The designs woven into the cushions reminded me of arcanist stars, and while I enjoyed seeing them, I hated the way the protruding threads scratched my skin. The inn had forsaken practicality in exchange for glamor—the worst kind of "fancy" a place could get.

Before I could get up, Illia teleported into the lounge.

She glanced around, her one eye wide, and when she spotted me, her smile grew wide. "Volke!"

Just like Nicholin, she vanished in a puff of sparkly glitter and then reappeared right next to me. She threw her arms around my neck and squished me against the itchy couch with all her weight.

"Don't worry me like that," she mumbled into the collar of my shirt. "And you better tell me what really happened at that river."

"I will." I embraced her, happy to have her presence. "It's more awkward than anything else."

"I don't care."

"Is everyone else asleep? What did you all do while I was in the dungeon?"

Illia didn't let me go. Instead, she settled against me, like a cat collapsing into a comfortable sleeping position. "We didn't get the runestones. No matter how many times Guildmaster Eventide asked to speak with the queen in private, she was never granted an audience."

I knit my eyebrows and silently cursed at myself. Why hadn't I asked Lyvia about the runestones? Perhaps she could've helped us.

"What're we going to do?" I asked.

"Eventide said she'll think of something, but Zelfree said we shouldn't concern ourselves. He doesn't want us getting involved."

"Maybe we should leave the runestones there."

Illia jolted up and glared at me with her one eye.

"Think about it," I said. "They're safest in the castle. Apparently it's protected with nullstone. And the queen's sovereign dragon is just a hundred feet away at all times. No one will steal them. It's practically impossible."

She leaned down and rested the side of her head on my

shoulder. "But hasn't a world serpent been born? It's out there. Waiting for someone. Are we going to let it rot inside the roots of a tree? That seems cruel."

"I... hadn't thought about it like that."

"Besides, wasn't it born to help humanity fight the corruption of the plague? Maybe if we find it, we can help it complete its goal. I don't like the idea of ignoring the creature because gathering the runestones is too difficult. We have to find a way."

I suspected Illia didn't care about the plague or the tortured solitude of the world serpent. All she cared about was getting to the creature before Calisto—or any of Calisto's associates. That wasn't a bad a goal, but she likely brought up all those points simply to sway me.

And it had worked.

"I think I know someone in the castle who might help us," I muttered. "But I don't know when I'll see her next."

"If she works in the castle, you'll probably see her during the tournament. Everyone will be there."

"When do we register?"

Illia released me and practically leapt backward. I stared at her for a long moment, wondering if I had done something to irritate her.

She frowned. "About that. We already signed up for the Sovereign Dragon Tournament."

"Without me?" I stood from the couch, my chest tight. "Can I still register?"

"Zelfree did that already. You'll be fighting."

All my anxiety disappeared in an instant. "Oh, good."

Illia fished around in her trouser pocket and then withdrew a folded scrap of paper. She handed it to me and pointed to the part that said, *RULES AND PRIZES OF THE BOUT.* I took the announcement and read it over.

· · ·

THE SOVEREIGN DRAGON TOURNAMENT

By order of Queen Velleta, the following rules will be in effect for the entire tournament.

I. A match ends once an arcanist is unable to fight or both arcanist and eldrin are knocked out of the ring (in the case of teams, this applies to all opposing arcanists and their eldrin)

2. Matches will consist of 5 uninterrupted minutes (at the end of that time, the side with the most eldrin and arcanists still in the ring wins)

3. In the case of ties, Queen Velleta or Knight Captain Rendell will determine the winner based on their performance during the bout

RANKS & PRIZES

APPRENTICE RANK—open to arcanists who have been bonded for less than 2 years. Magical items are limited to those the arcanist has made themselves.

1ˢᵗ Place: 3 star shards
2ⁿᵈ Place: 2 star shards
3ʳᵈ Place: I star shard

The prizes intrigued me, since I had never actually owned any star shards. If I had a couple, I could practice making magical items, perhaps even improved armor or a strong weapon. I scanned the rest of the page, curious about the other ranks.

·   ·   ·

JOURNEYMAN RANK—open to arcanists who have been bonded between 2 and 7 years. Magical items are limited to those the arcanist has made themselves.

1ˢᵗ Place: 6 star shards

2ⁿᵈ Place: 4 star shards

3ʳᵈ Place: 2 star shards

MASTER RANK—open to arcanists who have been bonded for more than 7 years. Magical items are limited to those the arcanist has made themselves.

1ˢᵗ Place: 100 star shards

2ⁿᵈ Place: 25 star shards

3ʳᵈ Place: 10 star shards

ELITE RANK—open to arcanists who have been bonded for more than 50 years. No magical item restrictions.

1ˢᵗ Place: Title and 20,000 acres of land personally granted by the queen

2ⁿᵈ Place: Sovereign dragon artifact

3ʳᵈ Place: 50 star shards

It would be a long while before I ever participated in an elite match, but that didn't stop me from fantasizing about it. Title and land? Amazing.

Illia took the paper from me and folded it back up. "So… that's not all…"

"What's wrong?"

Nicholin appeared back in the room. He stood on one of the couch cushions, his fur ruffled. "Hmpf! The others didn't appreciate me trying to wake them."

"There's something you should know about the Sovereign Dragon Tournament," Illia said, ignoring the huffing of her disgruntled eldrin. "Apparently, so many arcanists have signed up to compete that they made changes. The whole tournament takes place over three weeks, and that's just not enough time for everyone to fight individually. The apprentice level got adjusted."

"Are we fighting in teams?" I asked. It would be amazing to fight alongside other members of the Frith Guild. We had already done so on several occasions.

"Teams of two," Illia stated.

The number got me pensive.

Two.

Paired teams. Partners.

I stared down at her, but the expression didn't match what I expected. "We aren't together."

Illia shook her head. "I wanted to partner with you, but Hexa asked me, and I couldn't tell her no."

"She really wants our help," Nicholin chimed in. He buffed his claws on his chest. "We are pretty amazing."

"Am I with Atty?" I asked, hopeful.

The look she gave me—for a brief moment, I thought she would glare—but Illia half-smiled and replied with, "Atty has decided not to participate. Just like Adelgis."

It felt like a rock had settled into the deepest folds of my gut.

Zaxis. I was partnered with Zaxis.

How did this always happen? It seemed like every time we were broken into groups, we were paired together, much to my ever-growing chagrin.

"Hey," someone barked.

Illia and I both glanced at the staircase that led from the entrance to the second story. Zaxis stood on the steps, a tiny ball of flame in one palm—his own personal light. Had he known I would be disappointed, so he came to tell me off? I wondered if he was just as annoyed with the pairing as I was.

Zaxis sauntered down the last of the steps and then headed over to us, a groggy look of irritation plastered on his face. He wore just his trousers and the bone amulet Gillie had given us. Not even his guild pendant—just the plague-preventing trinket. I supposed, out of the two of them, it was more important, but still.

"Good morning, Illia," he said.

She lifted an eyebrow. "I'll leave you to tell Volke the details of the tournament, since you're partners and all."

Zaxis let out a long exhale, but before he could continue his conversation, Illia and Nicholin teleported out of the room. Since their teleporting range was short, I assumed they went straight upstairs, but I didn't know for sure.

I brushed myself off and wondered how much time I had to sleep before Master Zelfree dragged me from my bed in the morning. The castle dungeon cell had been too disgusting to sit or lie down. My feet ached, and I wanted rest.

"You look terrible," Zaxis said.

I turned to him with narrowed eyes. "You look like a bum, but I hadn't said anything."

"Heh. Whatever. Listen—we're partners in the Sovereign Dragon Tournament. That means we fight as a team."

"Yeah. I heard."

"Get excited, then. This is perfect." He snuffed out the fire in his palm and smirked.

"How so?" I asked.

"The final two teams at the apprentice level—the last four arcanists standing—will face off against each other in one-on-one fights to determine first, second, third, and fourth place."

That made sense. There would be paired teams until the

end, and then a final winner would be determined. I bet it would be amazing to watch.

"That means if we get to the end, we'll face off against each other." Zaxis crossed his arms. "Perfect."

"Why is this good news? You *want* to fight me in the tournament?"

"When I asked Illia who she thought would win, she said *you*, to no one's surprise."

That shocked me. I figured she would've claimed herself, but maybe her heart wasn't in the tournament. She never seemed excited about it, unlike Zaxis and Hexa, who couldn't get enough.

"So what?" I asked.

"I told you before—she admires you. That has to change. If you're not going to tell her that I'm the better arcanist and warrior, I'll just have to prove it to her. If I beat you at the end of the tournament, in front of everyone, she'll have to acknowledge that."

"You really think you would beat me?" I asked, more edge in my voice than I intended.

Something about Zaxis's presumption rubbed me the wrong way. It was like we were kids again, and everyone on the Isle of Ruma thought I wasn't worthy of becoming an arcanist. They always assumed I would be some gravedigger, alone and forgotten, and the assumption irritated me.

"You're second-bonded," Zaxis said with a shrug. "And I'm taking my training to the next level. I'll win, no doubt in my mind."

"My magic is more versatile, and I know all your tricks."

That single retort chilled the room a few degrees. I hadn't expected Zaxis to take it so seriously. This wasn't about Illia anymore. When he met my gaze, it was obvious he just wanted to prove me wrong.

"We better make it to the finals, then," he said. "That way we can test your theory."

I replied with a curt nod. "Sounds good. When does the tournament officially start?"

"In five days after some grand gala in the castle for all the participants. Master Zelfree says we *must* attend if we're going to fight."

In the castle? Perhaps I would see Lyvia. Then I could discuss the runestones with her—maybe even get some suggestions for convincing the queen to sell them to us. Or maybe let us borrow them for "research."

"Five days," I muttered.

20

A CHALLENGE

I didn't sleep much. I couldn't.

When morning came, I ate a light breakfast and headed outside to the center courtyard with Zaxis and Forsythe. Our inn was square-shaped with the courtyard in the middle. Windows surrounded the inner courtyard on all sides, and balconies overlooked everything, but I didn't mind if people wanted to watch us train.

Under no circumstances could I allow Zaxis to win the tournament. When we faced each other in combat, I had to be ready. I would practice until I couldn't get it wrong. Every technique, every magical ability—I'd have it mastered. I'd do it right.

Luthair emerged from the darkness and acted as my sparring partner. I focused on our training, redoing every failed swing, strike, and parry. He must've sensed my determination, because he attacked harder than he ever had before, using a practice sword that clanged off my shadowy blade.

When I swung for a finishing blow, Luthair shifted

through the shadows and appeared at my side. He bashed me with the flat end of the blade, hitting me across the gut.

I grimaced and held my ground, which probably surprised him, because he hadn't moved away. I slashed, hitting his armor, and he chuckled.

"They say greatness is forged in the flames of adversity," he said.

After a deep breath, I got back into my starting position. "If that's true, life has certainly provided me an adequate fire."

"I can see the blaze in your eyes now. It's always been there, but the light burns with an intensity I have yet to experience from you."

The words reinvigorated me. Although exhaustion crept into my mind and muscles, threatening to sap my strength, I refused to give in. When Luthair and I clashed a second time, I used the same shadow-shift technique he had done with me, catching him off-guard. Sure, the pain from the magic also took its toll, but that didn't matter when I had the satisfaction of accomplishment in my veins.

Hexa and Illia entered into the courtyard. I didn't acknowledge them. Instead, I paid special attention to my footwork, especially my stance. Luthair attacked with a shadow tendril, and I managed to keep my footing, even through the worst of it.

Then Adelgis and Atty joined us in the courtyard. They seemed the most rested, but they didn't participate in the sparring or combat. Both stood off to the side and focused on their evocation, manipulation, and augmentation with their eldrin.

Zaxis stopped evoking fire into the giant fountain and glowered at Adelgis.

"Hey," he barked.

Adelgis and his ethereal whelk, Felicity, glanced over. "Yes?" Adelgis replied.

"We're in Thronehold. Why haven't you gone to see your father?"

"I went to his laboratory yesterday." Adelgis returned his attention to his eldrin. "He'll see me in a few days, when he has time in his schedule."

"Wait," Zaxis said, holding up a finger. "Your father is in town?"

"Yes."

"And he knows everything?" Zaxis motioned to his ribcage.

Adelgis let out a quick exhale. "He knows."

"And he's not going to see you for *a couple of days*?"

"Correct."

Zaxis shook his head. As he turned around, his back to Adelgis, he muttered, "By the abyssal hells. What a jackass."

With sweat soaking into my shirt, and heat building in most of my limbs, I lowered my weapon and walked to a small tea table stationed in the courtyard. An attendant from the inn stood ready with a pitcher and porcelain cups. He offered me tea. I pointed to the water. The man tried to pour it into something dainty, but I took the pitcher from his hands and drank from the side.

I hadn't realized how much I needed it until the cold liquid soothed my aching throat.

After emptying half the pitcher, I gave it back to him. The attendant bowed his head three times, muttering, *I apologize, I apologize*, each time he did so. I lifted an eyebrow, confused by his over-the-top reaction. The man took the pitcher, never looked me in the eye, and said, "Forgive me, sir arcanist. I will bring out larger containers. I should have known you would be thirsty."

"Uh, it's nothing. I'm—"

"I'll correct this right away."

The man hurried off, straight for the inn, his shoulders bunched at the base of his neck.

What was that about? His actions reminded me of a frightened animal—one that had been beaten too many times to count. Surely, I hadn't given him the impression I was upset. Or had I?

Lost in thought, I ambled over to Adelgis. I took the time to rub at my arms and legs, making sure they weren't too worn out. An arcanist's ability to heal would help me recover, even if I wasn't as fast as Zaxis.

Adelgis sparked light from his palm over and over, but stopped once he noticed me staring.

"Yes?" he asked.

I glanced around. The courtyard was 150 feet from one side to the other, with a few tables, a fountain, and a couple of apple trees. Zaxis, Illia, Hexa, and Atty were busy with their eldrin, none of them looking our direction.

"Why are you so determined to do this?" I asked, acting nonchalant, as though we were speaking about the weather and not the destructive creature burrowing through Adelgis's flesh. "It's obviously causing you pain. We could end it at any time by removing it."

Felicity floated around her arcanist's head, her iridescent tentacles waving in a breeze that only she could feel. "Can't you see my arcanist is faint? He doesn't need the added stress of pointed questions."

"It's fine," Adelgis said.

"But you said you never wanted to talk about it."

"Volke has never been unreasonable with me. I don't mind telling him."

The whelk descended a few inches and clung to his

shoulder, her shell sparkling in the light. "Very well."

Adelgis ran his hand over his ribs. "My father said I would fail."

I lifted an eyebrow.

Silence lingered between us. Adelgis shifted his gaze to our feet. "And my father is always right."

"Don't say that," I said. "He can't possibly—"

"It's true, though. When I was younger, I said I wanted to become a relickeeper arcanist like him, but he said I would fail the trial of worth." He stroked Felicity's shell, allowing his story to end without further elaboration. Clearly, he wasn't a relickeeper arcanist.

"That's just one example," I said with a shrug.

"When I said I wanted to help him find a nest of stoor worms, he said I would get in the way, that I would make a mistake and get affected by their putrid breath." Adelgis let out a long sigh. "And I did."

"Stoor worms are deadly. It could've happened to anyone."

"When I told him I wanted to study magic with the greatest arcanists at Skarn University, he said I would fail their rigorous testing. When I expressed interest in researching with the apothecaries in Ellios, he said I didn't have the stomach for it."

I held my tongue, uncertain of what to say.

Adelgis continued, his eyes narrowing into a cold glare, his attention never lifting from our boots. "I just want to prove him wrong. Just once. He's had this abyssal leech for decades, but he never tried to grow it because he never had anyone he could trust with it. I told him I would care for the leech, and he said *I couldn't handle the responsibility*. He said... *I was too weak*. I would *get scared*. I would remove it long before it was ready... and then it would die."

Although I had never experienced a similar situation, I understood the kind of frustration Adelgis suffered. Soaking in doubt and negativity could turn anyone into an uncertain mass of anxiety. Adelgis wasn't that unsure of himself—not yet—and it was obvious he wanted to turn things around. Why did he have to pick this leech, though? Out of all the tasks he could've thrown his effort behind, this seemed like the worse one.

"If you need anything, just let me know," I said.

Adelgis glanced up and met my gaze. "Thank you. I appreciate your help."

I patted him on the shoulder opposite of his leech and then returned to the center of the courtyard to resume my training. Illia and Hexa practiced with their weapons—Hexa throwing knives into the bark of a tree and Illia fiddling with the grip of a dagger—and I gave serious consideration to walking over and discussing the tournament with them.

The door to the courtyard burst open, and I flinched. Master Zelfree strode outside, Traces on his shoulder, his standard black attire exchanged for a loose-fitting white tunic and a pair of belted trousers. For the first time in a long time, I could see portions of his skin. Scars marred almost every inch, likely from the manticore venom Calisto had used on him. That venom corrupted magic, including the ability to heal, and I suspected Zelfree would have the scars for the rest of his life.

Had he suffered anything else more permanent? Did the old injuries still hurt? I didn't know. He wouldn't talk about them, not under any circumstance.

Zelfree snapped his fingers and drew everyone's attention. "Listen, while we're in Thronehold, we're going to take advantage of the resources around us. For the next four days, I want you all to follow my instructions to the letter."

Traces swished her tail. "I can't wait to see you lot fight in the tournament! My arcanist even said I could put money on one of you—for fun, of course."

Hexa laughed once.

A strong breeze rushed through the courtyard, and I rubbed at my arms from the chill. It didn't feel natural, but Zelfree continued his speech before I could voice my concern.

"Volke, since you managed to sneak out of the dungeon early, I need to speak with you first. The rest of you continue with your practice. *And read your damn books.*"

The others answered with enthusiasm. Perhaps they were excited for the tournament.

Zelfree walked over, and then Luthair followed suit. Once we were together, Zelfree crossed his arms. I met his scrutinizing gaze with resolve. "I've learned how to give others my dark-sight," I said. "And I've used my terrors on individuals rather than a group. I've been doing what you asked, and—"

"I know," he said, cutting me off. "I wasn't worried about that. Right now, you need nuanced advice and training. Like how to fight without overthinking your actions."

"Overthinking?"

"You're too afraid of injuring others. And while it's true your magic and abilities are deadly, you need to learn to control your strength so you don't fear it."

He was right. I held back. Even with the thieves in the alleyway.

"You didn't tussle with other children when you were younger, did you?" Zelfree asked.

I shook my head.

"I can tell. Kids that rough around tend to understand their strength more as adults than kids who don't. You need to be comfortable with yourself. Come with me. We'll train outside the walls of the city. Traces can transform into a knightmare, and you can unleash your might to its fullest."

My first thought, even though Zelfree was trying to break me of this very habit, was to worry about whether I would hurt him. He had already suffered so much. I hated the thought of winning, just because it would result in more injury to him. That was foolish, though. I wouldn't win against Master Zelfree—I had seen his prowess time and time again.

Another rush of cold wind broke my thoughts. Zelfree's expression hardened as he glanced toward the courtyard door. A second later, it flew open, and a man stepped out. Not an inn attendant or anyone from the Frith Guild—an arcanist followed by a floating cloak, chains, and scythe.

A reaper arcanist.

Everyone stopped their sorcery and stared.

The chill intensified, and I gritted my teeth to keep them from chattering. It reminded me of Fain's wendigo magic. Icy. Unforgiving. I swear the sunlight over the courtyard dimmed, though that didn't bother me as much as the cold.

The arcanist held himself with confidence. He wore tailored clothing, padded with high quality leather, fashioned with masterwork metal plating covering his heart and right shoulder. It all seemed lightweight—like he was a man who relied on swift movement—and he carried two pistols on his belt.

The reaper and his arcanist headed straight for me and Zelfree.

"Hail there," the man said. He had thin facial hair, both a mustache and a goatee. "I'm Master Arcanist Jevel

Balestier. Please just call me Jevel." He gave Zelfree a curt bow of his head. "This is my eldrin, Ruin. Don't mind the haunting visage. He's quite gentle."

The cloak floated in place without a visible body, just like Luthair. No face. No hands. The scythe moved as if it were held, and the chains hung from a nonexistent waist. And just like Luthair, when the reaper spoke, its voice had a dark, almost hollow, tone.

"A pleasure to meet you," Ruin said.

The scythe had an ebony handle and a rusted blade. Or maybe it wasn't rust. I couldn't tell. The blade curved out wide, at least two feet in length, and it shone in the lowlight of the morning.

The empty hood turned from side to side, as if "glancing" around the courtyard, but it was like watching a ghost inside a sheet. Nothing there.

Zelfree nodded. "I'm Everett Zelfree."

Jevel's eyes lit up, and a smile crept across his face.

"Well, well, well," he said as he tapped the cloak of his eldrin. "Ruin and I were looking for you. I've heard of your exploits. You're famous in lands to the north and *infamous* in the south. A man of mystery. A spy or pirate—who knows? Quite a reputation."

Zelfree stared, his expression unreadable. He said nothing, which I thought odd, but I kept silent—this wasn't my conversation.

"My apprentices said they saw you at the castle." Jevel ran a hand over his oily black hair. He slicked it into place and then smoothed his goatee with two fingers. "You must remember meeting them. Crevis, the orthrus arcanist, and Dart, the barghest arcanist."

"Oh, I remember."

"They're looking forward to fighting your apprentices in

the tournament." Jevel shrugged. "But who really cares about those lower levels? I'm more interested in knowing whether *you're* participating. A master arcanist of your talent would be interesting to fight in a controlled setting, such as this."

"I'm not participating," Zelfree stated, no hesitation in his voice.

Jevel clenched his jaw. "Why not?"

"There's no need."

"Have you seen the prize for the master category? 100 star shards—the equivalent of 1,000 gold crowns—enough power to craft a significant artifact. You would turn your nose up at that? *No need* for permanent magic? Or wealth? From what I've heard, the Frith Guild could use resources."

Zelfree slid his hands into his pockets and shook his head. "I have to focus on training my apprentices. I wouldn't be able to give them my undivided attention if I were participating."

"You're the swashbuckler who brought dozens of pirates to their knees," Jevel said. "A mimic master who fights with craftiness and alacrity. A man of your caliber should have no problem balancing his duties and personal accomplishments." Then Jevel's tone changed from cordial to cutting, no pause between the shift. "Or perhaps the rumors are true —you're a drunkard who can't conduct himself in proper society. They say you're so far over the hill you've dug yourself a grave on the other side."

I wanted to punch this guy straight across the face, but I held myself back. A small piece of me hoped Zaxis would lose control again. It would amuse me to no end.

Zelfree didn't seem bothered by the comments. Even Traces regarded Jevel with a slight tilt of her head, like she didn't care what he had to say.

"What was your name again?" Zelfree asked.

Hexa's snort echoed all the way from the opposite side of the courtyard.

When Jevel opened his mouth to speak, Zelfree held up a hand.

"Oh, I remember now. My alcohol-addled memory sometimes forgets the lesser men I read about. You're that arcanist of the Huntsman Guild in the south, the one who has accomplished next to nothing."

I shuffled a step backward. My hopes shifted from Zaxis throwing a right hook to Zelfree showing this reaper arcanist who the better fighter was.

Jevel laughed, but it was with that same cutting tone he had before. "You're one of the few men I wanted to add to my collection." He grabbed the chains on his reaper eldrin and turned the links until the names engraved in the metal became visible.

While I didn't recognize the vast majority of them, a few caught my eye. Lana Greenwood, her name emblazoned into one of the links, was a master pixie arcanist of some renown. Why was her name there?

"I typically reserve these for my kills," Jevel stated. "But I figured no one would balk at the inclusion of arcanists I defeated in front of the queen." He dropped the chains. "I heard you maintained informants around the empire, but perhaps your information is as old as you are. I have plenty of accomplishments."

Zelfree didn't allow the comment to linger. He dismissed it with a wave of his hand. "You mean those kills you take credit for after most of your guild has chased down a plague-ridden arcanist until they're at their weakest? Where you swoop in at the last minute to empower your eldrin with their death? I don't tend to count those as *accomplishments*."

The heat in the conversation didn't match the ever-decreasing temperature. Despite that, Jevel smiled.

"So you won't be participating?" he asked. "No way I can convince you?"

"Afraid not," Zelfree stated.

"What a shame. But I guess I'll have the last laugh once my apprentices beat yours in the tournament."

"You must be joking," Zelfree said with a chuckle. "Your dog arcanists have participated in two hunts, and both times they were relegated to support roles—they don't have the experience to challenge my pupils. If I were you, I'd withdraw their entries to save myself the embarrassment."

The level of detail Zelfree seemed to know about Jevel and his apprentices bordered on the telepathic. Did he maintain contact with informants, even now? That would explain how Zelfree was such a good spy back in the day—he kept track of arcanists and their various activities.

"I have two other apprentices," Jevel hissed, his composure cracking. "An erlking and a denglong arcanist—both strong enough to rip phoenixes and hydras apart, I guarantee."

"Believe whatever you want to believe."

I had no idea what those two mystical creatures were. The curious side of me wanted to ask questions, but now wasn't the time. They had to be rare, and Jevel seemed to believe they were powerful. What were they? An erlking and a denglong? Could they really handle a phoenix and a hydra? After discovering the tiers for mystical creatures, I wondered if they would even fall into the same category as a phoenix.

Jevel turned on his heel, his lip curling in disgust under

his thin mustache. "I came here without any expectations, but somehow you've managed to disappoint me." He and his reaper eldrin left the courtyard, no pleasantries left about them.

"Yeah, get out of here," Nicholin managed to shout right as Jevel shut the courtyard door. Illia grabbed him and growled out a scolding, but I couldn't identify the words.

The cold temperature lifted, and then I felt too hot. I pulled at my damp shirt, basting in my own sweat.

Zelfree groaned. "This is going to be rough."

"The tournament?" Luthair asked.

"Yeah. His won't be the only guild looking to get their apprentices recognition."

No piece of me had considered the possibility of losing to another guild. I figured my place at the end was guaranteed, but I didn't know what our opponents were capable of.

"We'll win if we have you," I said to Zelfree. "You can tell us everything we need to know about the opponents, right?"

Traces wrapped her long tail around Zelfree's neck, though not tight enough to choke him. "We wouldn't be good mentors if we always gave you the answers."

"Listen," Zelfree said. "If you were a master arcanist, and the two of us were assigned to a mission, I would always give you the information I had at my disposal. But the fact of the matter is, I won't always be there, and you need to develop your own investigative abilities."

"What do you mean?"

"Knowing your opponent will give you the edge. If you can gather that information on your own, you won't ever need me. I think it would be best, for this tournament, that you figure out what your opponents are capable of." Zelfree took me by the shoulder. "But you can do that after we train."

21

THE RULES OF COMBAT

The grassy fields outside of Thronehold had a different aroma than the city. A cool breeze swept over us and I enjoyed the fresh air. Inside the city, squished between the crowds of people and horses, it was difficult to smell anything other than manure and offal.

Zelfree took me to the eastern wall. The oak trees rustled, and leaves scattered over the lush grass. The shadow of the city's wall crept ever closer as the sun made its slow descent.

"Now that we're alone, I have a few things to discuss with you," he said.

Traces sat on his shoulder, her long tail swishing back and forth. She stared at me with a serious expression on her cat-like face.

I lifted an eyebrow. "What is it about?"

"The runestones." Zelfree stopped and motioned me close. When he spoke, it was in a quiet voice. "Listen. Eventide and I have been talking. There's no doubt in our minds someone is after the world serpent, which means they *also* need the runestones." He said every word with careful enunciation, as if trying to instill the gravity of the situation through his tone. "This Sovereign Dragon Tournament couldn't have come at a worse time. We can't even look for someone suspicious, because hundreds of arcanists have travelled the world to get here."

I hadn't thought of it like that. Lots of people in the city were out of place, but they all had the excuse of participating in the tournament, so even if our enemy was among them, we wouldn't be able to tell.

"Maybe they don't know about the runestones," I said.

Zelfree shook his head. "Anyone with the knowledge and magical capacity to start the arcane plague *definitely* has the means to figure out they need those accursed runestones. Which means there are people here likely searching for a way to take them."

"A thief?"

"Or worse." Zelfree ran a hand down his face. "Look, if *I* was here and looking for a way to get my hands on the runestones through questionable means, I would use the upcoming gala to gather information. And since the queen —*in her infinite wisdom*—placed the runestones above the door to the throne room, I think our enemy will figure out their location rather quickly."

The situation seemed dire when he put it like that. The runestones were in plain sight. Anyone attending the gala would see them.

"So what're we going to do about it?" I asked.

Guildmaster Eventide didn't want the queen to dictate who bonded with the serpent, so telling the queen about the god creatures was out of the question.

And telling Queen Velleta that thieves were here for the runestones would only elicit more questions. She would want to know *why* people were coming for her runestones, and then she would figure out the world serpent was within her grasp.

But at the same time, villains lurked in the shadows, ready to claim the creature for themselves. Was it wise to keep this knowledge hidden when failure meant black-hearts would obtain the world serpent?

Zelfree stepped closer. "I'm going to use Adelgis's ethereal whelk magic to hear the thoughts of everyone attending the gala. Hopefully, I'll find our enemy."

My eyebrows shot to my hairline. "Isn't that an invasion of everyone's privacy?"

"I'm running out of options," he growled. "It's either this or steal the runestones before someone else does. Those were the only two plans I could come up with, and Eventide insists that we cannot steal from the Argo Empire."

"The queen would be upset—and she locked me in a dungeon for helping the youngest princess out of a river."

I could only imagine what she would do if she caught Zelfree trying to steal her magical, world-altering artifacts.

"I also want your help," Zelfree said. "During the gala, I want you to keep an eye out for anyone or anything that's suspicious. All the tournament participants will be in attendance. This will be the perfect time to observe without drawing attention to ourselves. You can do this, can't you?"

I nodded. "Why aren't you telling this to the others?"

"I already asked Illia to search the castle grounds during the gala festivities. Maybe she can find a place a thief would likely enter from. Atty and Zaxis will have their phoenixes in the sky. And I told Hexa and Adelgis to use what connections they had to ask around. Perhaps someone will point us in the right direction."

I hadn't given the gala much thought, but it seemed as though I would need to stay on my toes. Our enemies lurked in the darkness, and I suspected they didn't care who or what they destroyed to get their hands on those runestones.

"I'll keep my eyes open," I said.

"Good." Zelfree patted my shoulder. "Now let's get training. You'll need it."

It had gotten to the point where magic didn't hurt as much.

Well, that wasn't entirely true.

It didn't hurt when I used the most basic of powers. Light manipulation or a short duration of my terrors didn't result in agony. Anything complicated or powerful still stung, but I gritted through it.

Luthair and I stayed merged through the sparring. Zelfree remained separated from his knightmare-mimic. When he swung with a faux shadow sword, I controlled the darkness around his feet—using his own shadow against him—and snared him in place.

He jerked his leg, attempting to break free, and then chuckled. "Not bad. You've clearly gotten better." When he failed to yank his limbs out of the shadowy grip, he used his knightmare magic to escape.

Soldiers stationed at the defensive towers watched from up high, and I wondered if they enjoyed the show.

"Let's go again," Zelfree said. He turned and walked away.

But I barely registered the words. I held my sword, my gaze distant. Luthair unmerged with me, aware of my troubled thoughts. He had left me my sword and shield and stood next to me with a quiet patience I appreciated. His cape fluttered in the wind.

Zelfree glanced over his shoulder. "You seem distracted."

"You said I need to understand my opponent to get the edge."

"That's right."

"But when I was on Calisto's ship, Luthair told me about the man. He said Calisto was arrogant and self-assured. That didn't help me, though. I didn't know what to do with that information."

The memory still haunted my dreams. The rain, the fog, the pirates taunting us—Calisto relishing every second of our defeat. I couldn't allow that to happen ever again. I had to become stronger.

Zelfree walked over to me and stabbed his fake shadow sword into the dirt. "You're right. Knowing them isn't enough. You need to take that information and think like the individual. Understand their tactics. Understand what drives them. What breaks them."

"And Calisto? What drives that man besides insanity?"

"Power." Zelfree crossed his arms, his whole stance tense. "Social power, magical power—he hates to have his authority challenged. He can't stand to be seen as weak. When Illia smashed his ship, his façade broke. He didn't act rationally after that, you saw. And as soon as a man has lost the ability to make rational decisions, he's lost."

I recalled the fight with perfect clarity. Calisto *had* lost all focus. He failed to stop us from escaping and had no control over his crew while his attention was on Illia. Despite that, we almost didn't make it because Zelfree had been so injured.

I stared at Zelfree's scars, my chest tight with guilt. He had suffered so much just to help us. "Do those still hurt?" I asked in a hushed tone.

He rubbed at his shoulder. "No."

"They're cosmetic? No permanent damage?"

"My left foot doesn't move like it should. I've lost a range of motion." Zelfree twisted his right foot all the way in a complete circle, but when he tried the same with the left, it clearly wouldn't move like he wanted. He grimaced when he attempted to force it, but otherwise he made no indication it hurt.

"It's fine," he said, curt. "You don't need to worry about me. I've gone through worse."

Despite his reassurances, I still stared at the scars visible above the collar of his tunic. The deep gouges irritated me. The longer I thought about it, the more I recalled Illia's missing right eye. Calisto was the worst kind of psychotic sadist. I couldn't believe he was still allowed to roam free.

Zelfree pulled his collar up and shot me a glare. "*Enough.* Let's go back to training. Try to cut me. At least once."

The entire time we had been practicing, I had never landed a hit on him. I parried his attacks or caught him with my shadows, but every sword strike to his body always resulted in him defending it completely.

Zelfree took up a position ten feet from me, and I readied my weapons. Then I motioned to Luthair.

"You ready?" he asked.

I nodded.

A second later, his shadow armor melted into the ground, shifted under my feet, and then emerged again, slithering around me and hardening into place. The cold sensation of power blanketed my entire body.

For some reason, once we merged, I gained an added sense of clarity—like Luthair's mind remained calm while mine was troubled, resulting in a pathway through the mental fog. I focused on Zelfree, wondering what I knew about him and how I could use it to my advantage.

He lunged forward, his shadow blade poised to attack.

I lifted my hand and willed the darkness of the city wall to coalesce into dagger-like tendrils. I slashed with them, dozens of thin blades, in a wide strike. Zelfree dodged and parried, managing to remain unharmed as he rushed me.

I was ready. When I attacked, I didn't go for his body, I went for the edge of his tunic. He obviously hadn't expected the move. His parry didn't quite work, and I cut the fabric, revealing more of his side—and his scars.

Unlike Illia, who would've stopped everything to cover them, Zelfree didn't lose concentration. He swung his sword wide, and I had to slide through the shadows to avoid the hit. The instant I surfaced, I brought the darkness up on his right side. Like inky hands, the shadows twisted around his good foot. When he put his weight on his left, I attacked again, this time without hesitation.

Sure enough, he attempted to pivot—like any expert swordfighter would—but his ankle didn't cooperate. I caught his forearm with my blade and cut a deep gouge. I was so ecstatic that I stopped and smiled.

Pay attention, Luthair said directly to my mind.

Zelfree brought up a wave of shadows that knocked me to the ground. I hit hard, but the triumph of the early moment kept me enthusiastic. He allowed the darkness to recede, and I stood up with pep.

"Not bad," Zelfree said as he rubbed at his forearm. The injury healed within a matter of seconds. "You really took my advice to heart."

Luthair unmerged, and I shook off the pain from my magic use.

"I thought you would try to hide your scars," I said, my volume high from excitement. "Just like Illia. But I should've remembered you had more combat experience than her. Of course you wouldn't be distracted by vanity. Then I figured since you weren't a knightmare arcanist most of the time, you wouldn't always shadow-step away to deal with problems—you would rely on your swordsmanship. So, when your foot was stuck, you tried to block my blow instead of escaping, and since your left foot is weak, I figured I could land a hit, and—"

"I have eyes," Zelfree snapped. "And I don't have wild bouts of amnesia. I can remember what happened two seconds ago."

"S-Sorry." My sense of victory drained from my system. "I'm just—"

"Forget it. I understand." Zelfree held a hand over the slash on his tunic, hiding his gnarled skin underneath. "You did well to account for my fighting style and my weaknesses. If you keep this up, you might actually have a chance of winning the apprentice tournament."

"Should we really worry about that when we have the runestones to deal with?" I wanted to participate, but I didn't want to get distracted, either.

"If these runestones aren't stolen during the gala, we'll still need to stay in Thronehold until Eventide gets her hands on them. In the meantime, you might as well participate. And win. You can use the star shards to imbue something."

I held up my shield. "I don't think I did a good job the first time."

Zelfree glanced down and narrowed his eyes. "Hm. Have you used it?"

"Technically. Once. Against the first mate of the *Third Abyss.*"

"And?"

I shrugged. "I'm not sure. It was really chaotic, and I'm

not sure what happened. It *shielded me*, which I guess is the whole point."

"It's a magical item. It'll do more than just shield you." Zelfree took a couple steps back. Then the arcanist star on his forehead shifted and changed. Traces also lost her knightmare body as she twisted and glowed with a powerful inner magic. It only took a second, and Zelfree's switch from knightmare arcanist to will-o-wisp arcanist was complete.

A member of the Lamplighters Guild had to be close, no doubt on the other side of the wall.

Traces floated around as three orbs of light, giggling to herself in her new ethereal form.

"Hold up your shield," Zelfree commanded. "We're going to test this."

I did as he instructed and braced for fire.

The flames he evoked weren't that powerful, however. It made sense, considering will-o-wisps were so weak, but I was used to Zaxis's fiery magic. Instead, the heat Zelfree offered barely singed the hairs on my arm.

He struck my shadow shield with his string of flames. When they hit, the shield felt... different. It pulsed on my arm, like a strong heartbeat, and a second later a burst of raw energy exploded away from the face of the shield, right back at Zelfree. He had to jump to the side to avoid the crackle of power, and it arced onto the ground and ripped a small hole in the grass.

"What was that?" I asked, half-stunned, half-amused.

Zelfree brushed himself off. "Interesting. The shield reflected the magic right back."

"It didn't look like fire."

"No. It absorbed the magic and then unleashed it as something else." He stroked his chin as he stared at the damaged ground. "I wonder how much magic it can absorb…"

I nervously chuckled. "I think that might require a few more tests."

"Maybe another day, when I have access to an eldrin with more power. For right now, let's head back."

22

THE RULES OF ELDRIN

I returned to our inn as the sun disappeared behind the distant mountains.

Life changed in the city once the shadows reigned in the streets. People walked in close groups with their coats pulled tight. Most avoided the lamplighters who puttered down the cobblestone roads, their engine-powered trolley cars making enough noise to detect from a block away. The citizens of my home isle didn't venture out at night, so it was odd to see a major city like Thronehold transform with the time.

Instead of using the inn's front door, I stepped into the shadows and shifted to the roof. I emerged three stories higher, and the air was a bit fresher, though smoke from the coke-fueled blast furnaces tainted the evening breeze. I couldn't escape the side effects of industry.

When I glanced up, I realized tonight was the new moon.

"Illia, I have to tell you something."

I stopped in my tracks, straining to hear where the voice had come from. It sounded familiar. Zaxis? It had to be. I crept along the roof, glancing over the edge of the gutter, searching for his location. The roofing tiles shuddered and threatened to give out, but falling no longer troubled me like it once did.

I found Zaxis in the center courtyard. He paced around one of the apple trees, his phoenix sitting in the branches. Zaxis still had his shirt, trousers, and boots, which meant he probably wasn't practicing his magic.

"Illia," he said again—even though she wasn't in the courtyard. "I need to tell you something." He shook his head. "No. That's not right."

"I think you're overthinking this," Forsythe muttered.

"I just need to practice before I see her." He punched the trunk of the tree, shaking the branches enough to knock a dozen leaves loose. "Forsythe, you pretend to be Illia. React like she would."

"Yes, my arcanist." Forsythe smoothed his feathers and cleared his throat. In a feminine voice, he said, "Hm, I wonder where Volke is tonight?"

"Dammit, Forsythe," Zaxis barked. "Don't mention him!"

"You said you wanted me to pretend to be Illia. I think she would be worried at this point. He hasn't returned yet."

"I don't care. Talk about something else. Anything else."

Forsythe fluffed and unfluffed himself a second time, taking a moment to get back into character. Then he said, in the same faux-feminine voice, "Lovely weather this evening."

"Not as lovely as you," Zaxis said, his execution smooth. He grabbed at his hair and shook his head. "No. Stupid. Maybe, *not as lovely as the two of us together.*"

"Sounds presumptuous."

Zaxis growled something under his breath. He stomped

around the tree a second time. "I know. *I know*. I need something else."

"I still think you're overthinking things, my arcanist. Perhaps say you need her in your life?"

"That seems weak." Zaxis stopped pacing. "Women like confidence."

Soot fell from the tree as Forsythe hopped back and forth. For a long moment, they said nothing, but then Forsythe broke the silence between them with, "Let's try one more time." He used his fake girl voice and said, "Oh, Zaxis. I didn't see you there. What're you doing this evening?"

"Illia, here you are." Zaxis brushed back his red hair. "I've been meaning to say... I've seen the way you look at me. And I agree, we should be together."

I couldn't help it. I laughed aloud.

Both Forsythe and Zaxis jerked their attention upward, their eyes wide. The canopy of the apple tree half-blocked their view, but it wasn't enough to hide my presence on the roof. I walked to the edge and then shadow-shifted down to the ground of the courtyard.

"You did it," I said, a chuckle in my voice. "When is the wedding?"

Zaxis grabbed me by the collar of my shirt and twisted as he yanked me forward. I could feel the heat of his magic from his hands and breath, like he was ready to light this whole place on fire from sheer embarrassment. It was all worth it for the joke.

"Dammit, Volke," he growled.

I tried to sound as sincere as possible when I said, "I'm sorry. I shouldn't have said anything. I was just passing by."

He released me with a shove. I stumbled back a few feet, still amused by the situation.

"Volke, you know Illia the best," Forsythe said from the

tree branch. His talons clung to the bark with a tight grip. "What would you say to her? Zaxis has debated for some time."

"Quiet," Zaxis hissed.

"Volke would know what to say. You should ask."

While I was flattered that Forsythe assumed I had all the answers, it was far from the truth. I had no idea what someone would have to say to woo Illia.

"What do you admire about her?" I asked. She had many striking qualities, and while I suspected she would hate false flattery, I knew she appreciated earnest communication. "I think you should start with that. *Illia, I think you're amazing because*—and then ask her if she feels the same about you."

"I don't need your help," Zaxis growled.

"You did *ask* me for my help. You remember that, right?"

"Well, I don't need your help anymore."

"Need help with what?" Nicholin asked.

Both Zaxis and I flinched at the sudden appearance of the small, ferret-like rizzel. Nicholin stood between us in the grass, his blue eyes shifting from one of us to the other. Then he got on his hind legs and crossed his paws over his chest.

"You're not going to tell me? I see how you two are."

The crunch of fallen twigs heralded Illia's approach. She wore only a shirt and trousers, both loose, as though hastily donned. It was rare to see her outside of her buccaneer coat, and her casual attire gave her a much more approachable appearance.

Zaxis stepped forward. "Illia, what're you doing out here?"

"I was wondering where Volke was," she said. "And I thought I heard shouting, so I came to see."

I rubbed at my neck. "I, uh, just got back from training, and I'm really tired. I think I'm going to head straight to bed. Right now." As I stepped by Zaxis, I whispered, "Just use the phrase I gave you." I continued walking, hoping he would take my advice and not interpret it as an insult. I honestly figured it would help. All of his starter liners would result in mockery or laughter, I knew it in my gut.

Illia went to follow me, but Zaxis held out a hand. "Can I speak with you, Illia?"

She stopped and faced him. "Make it quick? It's late."

"It'll only take a second."

I felt for him. I knew that wasn't what he wanted to hear. When I reached the courtyard door, I slowed my actions, unlatching the handle with all the speed of a sleepy snail. Straining my ears, I heard Zaxis begin his confession.

"Illia," he said in a quiet voice. "I think you're amazing."

The moment he got the words out, I realized I didn't want to hear the rest. My chest hurt, my muscles tensed—I wanted nothing to do with this. It was Illia's business and didn't concern me. I shouldn't have listened, not even for a second.

I hurried into the inn, stomping my feet loud enough to drown out the rest of Zaxis's words.

I sat in bed, my back to the wall, the lanterns snuffed and darkness all around me.

Theasin's book had an appendix of mystical creatures, each categorized by tier, name, and type. I flipped through the pages, engrossed with the information. There were creatures I had never heard of on every page. When I reached the entry for knightmare, I stared at it for a long while.

. . .

Knightmare

   Tier 3

   Reproduction: Fable (born from the corpse of a murdered king, queen, or sole ruler of a territory)

   Trial of Worth: Unknown

   Knightmares are creatures of terror and shadow. They seem to bond to the righteous and noble, those with kind natures, and those who value duty, honor, and sacrifice. They are powerful combatants who merge with their arcanists.

   True Form: Unobserved

"You were right, Luthair," I whispered. "Tier three."

"Indeed."

I kept my voice low so that I wouldn't wake Adelgis. He slept on the bed opposite mine, his rest quiet and peaceful. Zaxis had yet to return to our room. I had left him with Illia over an hour ago, and I didn't know her location, either. I shook the thoughts from my mind as I flipped through the book, looking for mystical creatures I recognized.

Mimic

   Tier 1-4 (depending on the shape taken)

   Reproduction: Unknown

   Trial of Worth: Unknown

   Mimics have appeared at random across every known continent, though rare and elusive. They have the ability to copy magical items and mystical creatures, but have a limited duration for these borrowed forms. The most powerful mimic arcanists can hold the transformation for no longer than a week.

True Form: Unobserved

<u>*Atlas Turtle*</u>
Tier 3

Reproduction: Progeny (nesting grounds found near eldritch reefs)

Trial of Worth: Protecting something precious from harm

Atlas turtles create powerful shields and control the tides. They grow larger than most mystical creatures after bonding, but this limits their mobility to oceans or seas. Their shells are fertile and capable of growing exotic plants.

True Form: Island-size body, immunity to all poisons and disease—both for its body and for its plants—and the ability to create unbreakable barriers (obtained by arcanists who exemplify a nurturing, protective, and kind nature)

The entry on the atlas turtle got me excited. I had never seen information so straightforward and helpful. It answered several questions I had about true forms, and everything seemed so neat and organized.

I flipped the pages twice as fast, my pulse high as I thought about the creatures I needed to read about. First, the phoenix. I had to see what information Theasin had gathered. I almost sped right over the entry, but I stopped and then read the page twice.

<u>*Phoenix*</u>
Tier 3

Reproduction: Progeny (nesting grounds found near char-berry trees)

Trial of Worth: Demonstrable knowledge and dedication

Phoenix chicks are fragile creatures with a high mortality rate. Fifty percent of eggs never hatch. In general, phoenixes control fire and are capable of healing. Blue phoenixes, a rare variant of the red phoenix, have diminished healing, but possess the ability to burn creatures immune to flame.

True Form: White flames, gold feathers, and the ability to resurrect those who have recently deceased (obtained by arcanists who demonstrate unwavering determination and hope —unbreakable)

I had never seen the true form of a phoenix, but Guild-master Eventide said creatures who were affected by the arcane plague would eventually become *dread forms* of themselves. I had seen a dread form phoenix. I could recall its bleeding eyes, six grotesque wings, and warped body. Had Theasin written this book before the existence of such twisted monsters? Probably.

I went a few pages farther and then stopped again. The wendigo. Fain hadn't been showing himself lately, not since our trip to the castle, and I wondered if he would be interested in hearing about his eldrin.

Wendigo

    Tier 2

    Reproduction: Progeny (nesting grounds found in caves with grave-rot mushrooms)

    Trial of Worth: Unknown

    Wendigo tend to stalk lost travelers in the snow. All wendigo arcanists seemingly have frostbite, but this phenomenon is cosmetic—the limbs retain function. Wendigo have control over ice and are capable of infecting magical creatures with a debili-tating disease.

True Form: Bipedal, humanoid, and with the ability to speak with the corpses of the recently deceased (obtained by arcanists who become hermit cannibals unfettered by the taboos of their society)

I read the last sentence three times.

Perhaps I wouldn't tell Fain about the wendigo.

The door opened, and I snapped the book shut. Zaxis wandered in, Forsythe hopping behind him. I tucked myself beneath the covers before the glow from the phoenix's body revealed me to be awake.

Without words, Zaxis crawled into bed. Forsythe tucked himself behind the headboard, both to hide his glow and to curl up into the nest Zaxis had made for him.

Afraid I might wake them if I kept flipping through the tome, I tucked it under my pillow and closed my eyes.

I awoke to something patting me on the cheek.

For a brief second, I thought it was a cannibalistic wendigo arcanist. The resulting panic brought me from groggy to fully awake. I shot up in my bed, my breathing ragged, my hands shaky.

Nicholin tumbled onto my lap. He righted himself fast and then squeaked at me in annoyance.

"I'm sorry," I muttered as I scooped him up into one of my arms. "Are you okay?"

"Of course. It will take more than a little spill to incapac-itate Nicholin the Great."

I glanced over. Zaxis and Adelgis were still in bed. Confused, I turned my attention to the window. The sun had just risen over the distant mountains, creating an orange glow across the cloudless sky. Shouldn't Zaxis have gotten up to train? Then again, he had gone to bed late.

Nicholin held a paw to his mouth. "Shh. Come with me. Illia wants to go out, and she wants you to accompany her. Bring your coins."

Although I had a million questions, I pushed them from my mind as I flung my legs over the side of my bed. If I argued with Nicholin, he would squeak some more and definitely wake the others. Instead of making a scene, I figured I should just comply.

With swift movements, I dressed in one of the last few shirts I owned and grabbed a pair of trousers. I laced up my boots, grabbed my last gold leaf, and then left the room, all in record time. Luthair slithered after me, his shadow darting around my feet as I walked. Nicholin rode on my shoulder like he owned that portion of my body. He even snuggled up and rubbed his whiskered face against the side of my neck.

To my surprise, Illia stood in the hallway. I shut the door and faced her, wondering why she would be so determined to leave right away.

"Sleep well?" she asked.

"Yeah. For what little I got."

She grabbed my arm and pulled me to the stairs, more energy in her movements than reasonable for this hour. I allowed myself to get dragged out of the front door of our inn, careful not to disturb the other guests.

When we reached the street, Illia gave me a bright smile. "We're going shopping today. Just the two of us."

"And me," Nicholin interjected.

"Okay. Just the three of us."

"Hm," Luthair muttered from the darkness.

Illia rolled her eye. "*Four of us.*"

She yanked me across the cobblestone road and onto the opposite sidewalk. The Lamplights Guild ran their trolleys, and one went by after we had crossed. The will-o-wisp arcanist greeted us with a quick bow of his head.

"Why are we out here?" I asked.

Illia pointed toward the heart of the city. "We have tasks to complete. Opponents to spy on. Clothes to get for the gala." She smirked. "And we haven't spent much time together since coming to Thronehold. You're ready to have an adventure with me, right, Volke?"

Sometimes Illia had a certain tone in her voice that told me she had ulterior motives. Now was that time.

"All right," I said with a resigned sigh. "To the Market District, then?"

"Actually, I was thinking we would go to the Moonlight District instead."

23

I DANCE

"Isn't the Moonlight District the one with all the bordellos and burlesque clubs?" I asked.

"Exactly."

Illia led us to the corner of the street.

During the early morning hours, horses and deliverymen wandered everywhere. The inns required food for their kitchens, and it seemed as though arcanists in Thronehold had dozens of servants to do their bidding. I hadn't noticed it until recently, but everywhere I looked, I found attendants and servants, all bending the knee to arcanists' whims. While arcanists were respected on the Isle of Ruma, and in Fortuna, it wasn't like this.

A trolley rounded the corner, and Illia hopped on. The lamplighter at the engine gave her a quick glance, his eyes traveling up to her arcanist mark before he gave her a smile and nod of his head. I got on, and he did the same thing to me.

Illia and I sat next to each other as the trolley vehicle crawled through the cobblestone streets of Thronehold. The higher the sun rose, the busier the city became.

Merchants, milkmaids, apprentices of all professions—I almost couldn't keep track of it all.

"Do you ever get overwhelmed with our new surroundings?" Illia asked as she kept her eye on the district signs.

"Yes." The tall buildings cast dark shadows, and I wondered if the people of Thronehold ever got tired of the artificial darkness. "I like experiencing new things, though."

"It's hard to keep track of all the people, places, and magic."

"Sometimes."

"Not for me," Nicholin said. "For your information, rizzels are very smart."

Illia smiled as she turned to face me. With tepid movement, she inched a bit closer, though never so close our legs touched. "Master Zelfree told me something fascinating. He said he joined the Frith Guild decades ago because he wanted to be closer to a man he secretly pined for."

I almost laughed aloud. "He told you that? Seems like something he wouldn't want anyone knowing. Ever."

"Well, we were just talking." She looked away. "That doesn't matter. Actually, I have something else to tell you. Zaxis spoke to me last night."

Nicholin tapped my shoulder and pointed to a sign that read *MOONLIGHT DISTRICT*. The same perfume and cheerful music greeted us at the district boundary. Illia and I jumped off the moving trolley car—the slow speed made the task effortless—and we headed down the road toward the many buildings squeezed together.

"What did Zaxis say?" I asked, half regretting my question. Did I really want to know?

Illia stuck close to me while we walked. Like the other districts we traveled through, there were hundreds of people doing business. The tournament meant the residents of

Thronehold would make a small fortune so long as their businesses remained open and they were willing to provide goods or services.

Several tailors set up stands to display dresses, tunics, and riding pants. Two shoemakers worked at the large windows in front of their shops, displaying their skills for the world to see.

And women hung around the lampposts—also displaying their "skills" as they swayed back and forth, some waving to us as we passed.

None of them exposed anything scandalous, but many wore clothing I had never seen before. Lace and sheer fabrics in abundance. Was it even clothing if it didn't cover more than half of their body? Some had painted designs onto their bare stomachs, like tiny stars or flowers. It took me a full minute to realize most of them were holding small wooden signs. Did they honestly expect people to read them while they were dressed so... interestingly? It seemed like a bizarre mind game.

I looked away, opting not to play. Why had Illia brought us here?

"Did you hear me?" Illia asked.

I snapped my attention to her, my brow furrowed. "No. I'm sorry. What?"

"I said Zaxis confessed to admiring me."

My mouth went dry, so I nodded to indicate I had heard.

Illia continued, "He said he wanted to be with me. He asked that I attend this pre-tournament gala as his companion."

"And what did you say?" I asked.

"I told him I would think about it."

Nicholin chimed in with, "I told him if he ever hurt Illia,

I would bite him in the soft bits. Zaxis didn't like that much."

We strolled through the Moonlight District, passing several shops and oddly named businesses. ONE-TWO-TWO caught my eye. Colorful drapes, some bright green, red, and orange, hung from the windows on the second story. The building next to it was called MADAME ADRI-A'S. The redheaded girl standing in the frame of the front door waved to me. I turned away, forcing myself to keep my gaze on the road.

It seemed strange walking this district in the day, as these kinds of activities and services were designed for the privacy of night. And having Illia with me made the situation worse. It felt like milk curdling in my stomach—a slow and painful torture I couldn't hope to escape.

"What's your opinion?" Illia asked.

"About what?"

"Zaxis. I told him I would think about it so I could have time to talk to you."

"Me?" I shoved my hands in my pockets. "You don't need my permission."

Illia glared. "I'm not asking for it. I just want to know your *opinion*. What do you think about this situation? How did it make you feel when I told you what Zaxis said? Things like that."

This was probably the last conversation I wanted to have with anyone. How could I end it as fast as possible? What could I say that would make her happy? Did she want me to be jealous? Did she hope I would say she should reject him? I didn't know. I figured I would just stick with honesty. I never wanted to deceive Illia.

"I think Zaxis will treat you right," I said. "He's rough around the edges, though. And he might burn all your clothes. And he'll probably get into unnecessary fights from time to time."

"Seems high maintenance," Nicholin mumbled as he stroked his chin.

We rounded a street corner and entered the heart of the district—music wafted from every building, some slow and classy, other tunes fast and playful. It created a mild cacophony on the street, but I imagined the sound was pleasant inside most of the theater-like buildings.

Illia grabbed my arm and stopped us in the middle of the sidewalk. "So you think I should be with him?"

"You deserve someone who will be with you without any hesitation or reservation. I think Zaxis can do that."

She stared at me for a prolonged moment, her one eye searching for something. Then she pulled me forward and started our walking again. "He was sweet to me last night. He said he remembered every instance I ever helped him, including during our test with the Frith Guild, when I told him about the star moths."

"Okay."

"Listen, there's a reason I brought you here." Illia ran her fingers over her eyepatch, her fingers shaky. "Volke, I've never been pretty. I know that. I don't... dress for that. And no one's *dream girl* is missing an eye."

"Illia—"

"No, just listen. I want you to help me look *pretty* for this gala. You're a man. You'll know what Zaxis is looking for." She rubbed the eyepatch harder, her gaze distant. "If I'm going to be with him—if I'm going to *move on*—I want to do it right. As my brother, you should help me with this. Right?"

A lot of realizations hit me at once, and I breathed a sigh of relief.

She wanted to make things right between us. I wanted that too. We could just go back to being siblings.

"I'll help," I said. "I'm not into fashion, though."

"That's fine. I want to go to that tailor." She pointed to a building squished between domed theaters. The old wood and brick of the building made it seem ancient. "They make dresses. I saw them yesterday when I was here."

"You came *here*?" I asked, trying to hide my shock, but failing.

"That's right. Hexa wanted to see the sights. We walked around for a few hours." She patted my arm. "Focus. I saw their dresses. Some are expensive, but they're so striking. Would you mind waiting while I get fitted, and then give me your feedback? Oh, and I would need coins."

"Will one gold leaf do?" I asked as I took out the last of my money. "I think Thronehold operates with crowns."

"They'll accept leafs." Illia took the coin, and Nicholin hopped from my shoulder to hers. "Do you have any more?" she asked.

"No. That's all I have."

"Good." She gave a mischievous smile. "Because it'll take a few hours to get properly fitted, and I don't want you wandering around here with any coins in your pocket. You never know what kind of trouble a young man could get in to."

While Illia engaged with her fancy tailor, I walked around the theater block and avoided anything that looked like a brothel or bordello. The music made the wait enjoyable. I stood on street corners, pretending I would cross just so I could listen to a particular singer. The Isle of Ruma had instruments, but talented singers were a rarity. I enjoyed them the most, and I wouldn't be able to experience this kind of entertainment anywhere else in the world.

An hour into my wait, I circled back around the block, hoping to catch another series of songs, when a man stepped into my path.

He wore a coat a size too small, a top hat a size too big, and a purple ascot so large it covered half of his chest. When he smiled, he somehow managed to show all the teeth in his mouth.

"It's your lucky day, sir arcanist," he said, showmanship in his words. "We have a special show just for you."

The man had the face of a baby and the body of a forty-year-old alcoholic. He kept his gut from bursting out of his shirt with the help of an overworked belt.

"I don't have any coins," I said as I stepped around him.

The man swooped back into my path. "No need for coins at this show! All arcanists are allowed in, free of charge. Just dazzle the men at the door with your star mark and take a seat. Easy as that."

"I don't know..."

It seemed too good to be true, like the man was luring me into a dark alleyway so his thug friends could shake me down for valuables. Then again, his hypothetical friends would be in for a hypothetical beating.

"I've seen you aimlessly strolling the streets," the man said as he tipped his top hat. "You avoid the girls and never enter any of the shops. Must be dull. The show Karna puts on is far more entertaining than these filth-soaked cobblestone roads."

"Uh..."

He placed a gentle hand on my upper arm and motioned to a three-story theater house. The windows were covered in thick black curtains, and the door had guards outside. Not city guards, but mercenaries with pistols. It wasn't larger than the other theater houses, nor did it have colorful signs or women outside to draw in business. A steady stream of individuals headed for the front door, though. They paid the guards or were thrown from the line.

And the theater had been one of the buildings with charming music emanating from within.

"Go on," the baby-faced man said. "I'm so convinced you'll enjoy the experience that I'll even wager this silver crown. If after five minutes in the theater you're not satisfied, I'll hand it over." He flashed the silver coin in the afternoon light. A dragon was imprinted on one side, and a bust of the queen marked the other.

"All right," I muttered. "I'll see what's inside."

"Good choice."

I wandered into the line, but the moment I got close, the patrons shook their heads and ushered me forward. "Please go ahead, lord arcanist," one woman muttered as she kept her eyes turned down to the sidewalk. "You shouldn't wait behind someone like me."

Her deference made me a little uneasy. I gave her a quick bow before moving on.

The two guards glanced at my arcanist mark and then motioned me in. The entrance, devoid of lanterns and with all the windows covered, had the darkness of a moonless night. I walked the narrow hall, able to see without difficulty, and pushed my way through a curtain door.

The main room consisted of circular dining tables and a large stage. Lights hung from the ceiling on thin silver chains. They weren't lanterns or candles, but glass jars filled with blue glowing insects. Hundreds of them writhed around in each jar, creating enough light for the average man to see, but not enough to illuminate the floor.

It didn't matter. I slunk to the back of the room and took a seat at a lone table. At least fifty other people were scattered around, most near the stage, all with tin mugs filled to the brim with what smelled like cider.

Silence settled over the room as the curtains on the stage were drawn back. I was just in time for the start of the next performance.

I moved to the edge of my seat, curious to see what kind of show would allow arcanists to watch for free.

A woman sauntered onto the stage with no shoes. She stepped with her toes first, her long legs easily visible due to the lengthy slit up both sides of her skirt. The fabric flowed with every movement. If those slits were an inch higher, however, this would be a different kind of performance.

"My name is Karna," she said, her voice so light and feminine it was practically its own song. "I hope you enjoy my show."

The audience in the room replied with a few quick *whoop-whoops* before quieting down a second time.

Karna walked to the edge of the stage. Her top consisted of cloth strips wrapped over her chest and shoulders. With delicate fingers, she brushed back her golden hair, silky enough I could see the shine from the back of the room.

The gentle music of a piano played in the background.

And then Karna sang.

> *"When I was younger,*
> *Naïve and sad,*
> *Strong men intrigued me,*
> *Both good and bad."*

The melodic melancholy spoke to me. I paid more attention, rapt by the skillful delivery.

> *"I made a choice, became a fool,*
> *I can't go back, just someone's tool,*
> *But that was then, and this is now,*
> *I have control, and I'll show you how."*

She delicately grabbed at the straps of cloth on her chest and tugged them loose. She wasn't wearing much, and when the strips of cloth fell away, I thought she would be left with nothing. To my fascination, she wore something underneath —a thin top made of tiny metal scales that shimmered under the dim blue light. It drew everyone's attention, and she smiled, her whole demeanor blossoming into something else.

Karna gracefully flipped off the stage and landed on one of the tables, startling the four men sitting there. It was only then that I noticed the same shimmering scales on the underside of her skirt, their windchime clatter blending with the music. They caught the light mid-flip, sparkling enough to elicit gasps from the crowd.

"*I dance,*" she sang as she twirled. "*My spirit soaring higher.*"

Then she jumped to another table, both athletic and elegant. She didn't even spill anyone's drink upon landing or when she moved to the center. It impressed me more than her outfit and singing.

"*I dance,*" she sang again, rubbing her whole body down with her hands. "*And I know what you desire.*"

Karna stepped onto the floor, her song livelier and heated.

"A simple slit right up my dress,
A sway of hips, a girl's finesse,
I kiss his jaw, he smiles wide,
I'm confident, no need to hide."

She poked the chest of an arcanist and slid her finger up to his collarbone. He leaned forward, but she walked away, her song continuing.

"Touch his neck and he goes blind,
Coherent thoughts so hard to find,
I'm in control for that short time,
My charm like magic, what a crime."

"I suspect Zaxis would've liked this show," Luthair said from the shadows.

"Uh-huh," I muttered.

Her body flowed like water as she danced to the next table. Karna placed her hand on the shoulder of another man, her eyes darting to the collar of his tunic. "*I dance,*" she sang. "*A therapy for my soul.*" Then she backflipped to another table, the shimmer of her outfit drawing a round of claps. "*I dance,*" she continued. "*On stage, I know that I am whole.*"

Sweat dappled her muscled body. When she moved, it came off as flecks glinting in the light, adding to the glamour of her performance. With her voice even higher, and the music growing louder, she continued.

"I tease men, we go all day,
They choose to do just what I say,
I must confess, it's rather fun,
Then comes night, and we're not done."

She locked eyes with me and danced closer. I looked away—at the ceiling—not wanting any attention.

"People tell me I can't give in,
Yet even so, I yearn for sin,
I want men's touch, their primal need,
Their knees must buckle, I will succeed."

When Karna reached my table, I tried to put it between us, but she jumped on top. *"I dance,"* she sang. *"And it's my heart's ascension."* She twirled across and then stepped down in front of me. *"I dance,"* she hummed in a low tone. *"So I can keep their attention."*

My heart beat against my ribs as she placed her palm on my chest and gently dragged her nails up to the base of my neck. Her warm breath smelled of cinnamon, and her piercing gaze locked me in place. She hooked the string of both my guild pendant and my wendigo trinket. She narrowed her eyes for half a second when she caught sight of them.

"I dance," she sang in a soft, seductive manner. *"They don't know my true intention."*

With one effortless motion, Karna pulled them both over my head and right off my person. It took me a dazed moment to even realize what had happened.

She kissed the bronze of my guild pendant. "Come get these after the show," she whispered, her statement drowned out by the piano, secret to all but me.

Then Karna leapt back onto the table.

"I dance," she sang, winding down her words. *"I dance..."*

With a shimmery flip and leap, she made it back to the stage, my pendants wrapped around her wrist, too dull to catch the light.

The pianist stopped the song.

Karna flashed a smile to the audience. "I hope you all enjoyed."

The resulting cheers and clapping were enough to cause deafness. They threw some coins, and a couple of men shouted for an encore.

I watched Karna go until they shut the curtains.

"What are you waiting for?" Luthair asked. "Master Zelfree told you specifically not to lose that magical item."

I nodded. "R-Right. You're right."

"You never should've allowed her to take it."

"Yeah, probably." I wiped the sweat on my palms across the side of my body. "Let's just go and get them back."

INVITATION

The guards didn't give me any trouble when I made my way backstage. One glanced at my arcanist mark and then stepped aside. One even pointed to a door at the far end of a hallway, like he knew who I had come to see.

I followed their directions, wondering how often individuals went to compliment Karna on her singing and dancing. Her athleticism put some combatants to shame.

And while my focus had been on her performance, I had taken note of her blank forehead. Karna wasn't an arcanist. Perhaps she had never undergone a trial of worth.

When I arrived at the last door in the hallway, I lifted my hand to knock and hesitated. I took a moment to straighten my shirt and smooth my trousers. I had never been critical of my own appearance, but now it seemed like something I should've taken into consideration.

I knocked.

"Come in," Karna said, her soothing voice half muffled by the door.

I stepped inside, my breath held.

A single window on the opposite side of the room had been cleared of curtains and then opened. Sunlight streamed into the cramped space, filling it with radiance. Bright clothing—some woven with feathers or glittering beads—covered every surface. Karna stood in front a floor-length cheval mirror, her blonde hair pulled to the side and hand running over the scales of her top.

"Hello," I said. "I'm—"

"Shut the door, please."

I moved farther into the room and then closed the door behind me. The brightness of the day seemed foreign after the void of the theater, but I didn't mind. When Karna faced me, her clothing shimmered like fireflies, each scale a tiny sparkle. It made it hard to look away.

"I hope you enjoyed the show, sir arcanist," she said as she took a few steps forward, crossing the entire room with that short movement. She was just a couple inches from me.

"I did," I said. "You're very talented. The best dancer I've ever seen."

With a slight smile, she tilted her head. "I apologize for taking your guild pendant. I've never seen one like this before." Karna held up her delicate wrist and turned it over. "I'm not sure what this is, though." The wendigo trinket spun around as she touched it.

"It's protection," I said, tense. I cleared my throat and tried to relax. "A magical item."

While she examined the pendants, I caught sight of myself in the mirror. My black hair, windswept and untamed, fluttered out in every direction. I tried to pat it down, but it was no use.

"Are you participating in the tournament, sir arcanist?"

"Volke," I said. "Call me Volke."

"Oh, as you wish. Will you be participating in the tournament, *Volke*?" she repeated, her emphasis on my name bordering on sultry.

"Uh, yeah. At the apprentice level."

"I could tell. You have the look of a warrior." Karna glanced up at me through her eyelashes, her grayish-blue eyes stunning in the daylight. "Arcanists who have known combat always hold themselves with a little more confidence than others."

I nodded along with her words, uncertain of what to say. Our difference in height made her seem daintier than I thought she'd be. I stood half a foot taller.

"Where's your weapon?" Karna asked as she grazed her fingertips over the side of my belt.

Her feather-touch surprised me, and I chuckled nervously. "I use the shadow like a weapon."

"Ah, yes. Your pendant did say you were a knightmare arcanist." With a graceful motion, she flipped the pendants up into her palm and held them out. "Will you be attending the queen's gala?"

"Yes," I said as I took the pendants.

Karna stared straight up at me, her gaze hard. "Really? You'll get to enter the castle? See the inside of it? The garden? The ballroom?" Then she grabbed my hand with both of hers, her hold gentle. The soft texture of her skin intrigued me.

"Yeah, I'll see it all."

I allowed her to caress my knuckles, my thoughts narrowing to her touch. I swear the room got hotter, like a fire had been started a floor below. The open window and cool breeze did nothing for me.

Karna's enthusiasm waned. She released my hand and

turned away, her outfit shimmering with each step. "It's been a dream of mine to visit the castle. Always observing it from a distance, but never allowed in." She swished her hair, and her voice shifted to something quiet. "I'd give anything to see it."

"You're a marvelous dancer," I said. "And a wonderful songstress. I'm sure the queen would love to have you at her gala." They had so many servants on staff—I was certain someone as talented as Karna would find work.

"There's a big difference between attending as a guest and attending as the hired help. You've never wanted to stand on equal footing with royalty? To be greeted as a member of elegant nobility? To dine and celebrate carefree?"

Karna leaned against the wall and stretched her arms up toward the ceiling. She seemed more exposed in such a position, and I looked at anything else, my face burning for even noticing such a detail. Was she trying to pose in suggestive ways or was I reading too much into the situation?

When I forced myself to think of something, I did recall my days as a gravedigger. I had longed to spend time with the other kids, away from the toils of coffins, graves, and dead bodies. Every night I read tales of arcanists so that I could imagine myself in their place, loved by all, acting as a protector.

Karna's desire for acceptance wasn't foreign to me.

"Are you taking anyone?" she whispered. "As a companion?"

"I hadn't given it much thought."

I didn't even know we *could* invite individuals to the gala until Illia said Zaxis had invited her. It wasn't even necessary, considering they were both required to attend, but I supposed the gesture was Zaxis's romantic angle.

And Master Zelfree wanted me to pay attention to the arcanists in attendance, so the gala didn't even feel like a recreational event—more like a duty. Why would I concern myself with who I invited?

"Maybe you should give it some thought." Karna pushed away from the wall and wrapped both her arms around one of mine. She leaned heavily onto my side, her body firm and soft, toned and light. "I know I'm not an arcanist and that I don't deserve your graces."

I hated the joylessness in her tone.

"But if you considered taking me as your companion, I promise I'll meet all your expectations."

Although she hadn't outright stated it, I understood her implications. Perhaps it would excite some men, but I loathed the proposition. I never wanted to be with a woman because she felt like she had to pay me for my help. It went against everything Gravekeeper William had taught me.

I slowly removed myself from her grasp and crossed my arms. "I'd be more than happy if you attended the gala as my companion. There's no need to promise me anything."

With a forced smile, Karna stepped away. She held her hands together behind her back as she stared. "You'll take me?"

"Yes." I rubbed at my neck and realized that—at some point—I had backed up enough to touch the wall. "It'd be an honor."

"Just like that? No strings attached?"

"Uh, of course."

This seemed to bother her more than anything else we had discussed. She mulled over my statement, taking another step back, her demeanor pensive. Was she upset? Perhaps she thought I was joking.

"I'm staying at the *Maison Arcana*," I said. "We can meet there before the gala. I'm pretty sure we'll have one of the lamplighters take us to the castle on a trolley." But how could I convince her I was serious?

I held out the guild pendant. "You can keep this until then. Show it to the gate guards at the inn and they'll notify me of your presence."

"Oh, the *Maison Arcana*?" As Karna repeated the words, her smile returned, her uncertainty shed. "I understand now."

Her realization got me doubting myself. Were we even talking about the same thing?

She took my guild pendant and pulled it over her head.

"I'll be there, prim and proper," she said. "Thank you, Sir Arcanist Volke. You've been too kind to me. A true gentleman. If you need anything from me, I'll be here." With a stylish flourish, she bowed low, one arm out, the other behind her back. Her silky blonde hair spilled forward, aglow in the afternoon light.

I didn't know how to respond to that, so I quickly bowed and then shuffled toward the door. "Nice meeting you. And thank you for the show. It was delightful."

Once in the darkness of the hallway, I tried to make my way back to the theater room. Two guards held up their hands and pointed to a back door. Singing and dancing echoed from the stage, and I figured they didn't want me interrupting the show. I threw the wendigo pendant over my neck, thankful to have it back, and then exited the building out the back.

The dank alleyway had trash and broken furniture thrown together in tall piles. I walked around them, weaving through the maze of filth as I made my way back to the street.

Who had thrown this junk out? Actors and stage hands for the theater? I shook my head and ignored the pile of busted chairs as I stepped around.

Asking someone to the gala had never crossed my mind, but now that I had given it more thought, I knew I should've invited Atty. Perhaps she would understand the situation I had found myself in. Karna, the talented dancer woman, just wanted to participate in the festivities. Giving her an opportunity to experience her dream wasn't a terrible thing.

Then again, I couldn't afford to get too distracted. I needed to speak with Princess Lyvia about the runestones, and the gala might be the last place I would get to see her. Above all else, I couldn't forget that, no matter how beautiful Karna or any other lady was.

"Someone is following you," Luthair stated.

I stopped in my tracks. "Show yourself," I commanded.

To my shock, Fain moved around a broken couch, his movements stiff. He stood with his hands in his pockets, his coat collar up, hiding most of the ascot around his neck. The frostbite on his ears stood out in the midafternoon light.

"What're you doing here?" I asked.

Fain met my gaze. "Watching you interact with others."

His answer took me a moment to absorb. "Why?"

"You said you wouldn't mind if I observed you."

"I..." I rubbed at the side of my face. "I did say that. A while ago. You never took me up on the offer."

He lifted an eyebrow, his emotionless expression telling me everything I needed to know.

Fain had been invisibly following me ever since he asked. Hovering around, like a second shadow, watching my dealings with the others.

I held my breath as I recalled the last week or so, trying to remember every interaction I had. There weren't many that were private, but there were a few. Like Karna's backstage meeting... Had Fain been with me then? Of course. Why else was he here with me in this alley?

He must've known what I was thinking.

"It did get a bit uncomfortable when Karna asked you to shut the door," Fain said, staring at the alleyway junk. "I never intended to witness those types of interactions."

"You just stood there?" My disbelief almost prevented me from rational conversation.

"I didn't want to ruin your chance with a woman."

"So, in your mind, the polite thing to do was to stay hidden *and watch*?" I gritted my teeth, my confusion growing into a mild rage. "Unbelievable."

Silence stretched between us as I forced myself to take calming breaths. Why hadn't Luthair realized sooner that Fain had been following me? Probably because the noise and commotion of the city prevented him from seeing or hearing an invisible individual trailing behind us. That didn't make things better, though.

After a few quiet moments, my frustration waned. It wasn't terrible. I hadn't done anything that demanded utter privacy. I could get past this.

Fain ran his frostbitten fingers through his hair. "Can I ask you something?"

"I suppose."

"That woman was obviously willing to pay the price in pleasure in order to attend the gala. Why didn't you take it?"

With my face burning and my whole body tense, I replied, "I didn't become an arcanist to take advantage of people."

"No one on the *Third Abyss* would've done what you did."

"Yeah, well, there's a reason I'd never join Calisto and his cutthroats." I crossed my arms, uncrossed them, and then let out a long exhale. "I just... I want to do things right. I never want to hurt someone for my own desires. I don't know if I could face William if I ever did that."

"Seems naïve," Fain said with a shrug. "Nothing's wrong with a transaction. You had something she wanted, and she had something you wanted. You weren't forcing her."

The logic was sound, and perhaps some people could be fine with that, but...

Didn't Fain hear the change in Karna's voice when she offered herself? The subtle way her words shifted? None of the men I admired would've taken Karna up on her offer. They were men of principle and virtue—better than most, with the conviction to uphold their ideals.

"You said you wanted my advice on how to interact with others, right?" I asked. "Help people whenever you can. Offering Karna a chance to see the castle cost me nothing. Why should I make her pay a price?"

Fain seemed to contemplate my words, but his expression never changed. Perhaps he still thought me naïve. It didn't matter. I knew who I was and who I wanted to become.

I headed for the street, careful to avoid a puddle of brown water as I made my way through the grime. Fain followed close behind, his steps quiet and his breathing unnoticeable. His stealth impressed me.

We exited the alleyway and arrived on the sidewalk. People continued on, busier than the morning. As I walked with Fain out across the cobblestone road, I glanced over, curious to hear of his experiences.

"Fain," I said. "Have you ever been with a woman?"

"Yes."

"I don't mean just in their presence."

"You meant, *have I bedded one*. I understood."

My face grew hotter. "You don't have to word it like that. Seems vulgar."

Fain shrugged. "It seems odd to say *I made love to a whore*, but if that makes you feel better, I'll do it."

I glanced around, hoping no one was paying attention to our conversation. Fortunately, most individuals were too busy with their own lives to notice the ramblings of two passersby. Still, I lowered my voice and kept my head down. We weren't far from Illia's tailor shop.

"You've never liked a girl?" I asked.

"There's a woman in Port Crown I would visit whenever we stopped there." Fain's gaze seemed distant as he added, "I'd go out of my way to see her. She was the only one I enjoyed talking to after *we made love*."

I ran a hand down my face. "Don't. Just... don't."

"She was nice to Wraith, too. Most people find him off-putting, but not Cynthia."

"And how did you treat her? Was everything a transaction?"

Fain took a moment to consider my question. "I always gave her more money than she asked for..."

That didn't help. Fain had clearly lived a much different life than I had. Whereas I had lived on the outskirts of town, excluded from most festivities, he had lived a pirate's life—one brothel to the next. My life seemed sheltered when I compared it to his. What would Gravekeeper William say in this situation? I didn't know.

Perhaps Zelfree would understand. He had lived a life among pirates, after all. He could advise Fain.

We reached the tailor, and I stopped just before the door.

"Illia has a problem with pirates," I said as I glanced over to Fain.

"Should I become invisible again?"

"Uh, no. Just wait here. Once I've seen her and told her you're out here, we can walk back to the inn together."

EVERETT ZELFREE THE FACELESS RENEGADE

Fain narrowed his eyes, but said nothing as I entered the tailor's.

The quaint shop had stone walls and hardwood floors. The corners were filled with fabric, lace, and thread, some in vibrant rainbow colors. The place felt smaller on the inside, and that probably had to do with the four women bustling around. One of them had an arcanist mark—a small fairy-shaped mark I recognized as a brownie. Brownies were sprites talented in all sorts of fine crafts, including sewing and mending, though I had never seen one firsthand to confirm.

The brownie arcanist picked up a bag of silky cloth from a shelf and walked up to me, her eyebrows high. Her dress wasn't elegant or fancy—just practical, with lots of pockets, and needle cushions hanging from her hips.

"I'm here for my sister, Illia," I said.

"She'll be out in a moment."

I stood in a corner while two of the other women tidied up the shop. They muttered *excuse me, sir arcanist*, more times than I cared to count, and I moved to the sole window, half-blocking the light. Fortunately, Illia didn't take long. She exited the back room wearing her new dress, Nicholin hopping around her feet.

I had never been a trendsetter or champion of haute couture, so clothing never really interested me outside of its practicality. However, Illia's outfit did strike me as beautiful the moment I laid eyes on it. It hugged her tightly from the hips up, creating a corset of dark blue fabric with no collar or shoulders, leaving her slender neck exposed. The bottom wasn't fitted—it flowed downward like a waterfall—and woven into the extra cloth were small, star-like beads.

No, not just stars. Butterflies as well. Or maybe moths?

Illia must've seen me staring, because she blushed slightly as she said, "I told them I wanted to make a reference to the star moths. They added these to the dress. Do you like them?" She spun around, and the dress flared outward. Nicholin stood off to the side and clapped his paws together.

My first thought was of Karna and her alluring dance. I shook the memory away and nodded to Illia. "It's beautiful. William would approve."

"You think so? Truly?"

Illia turned to a mirror mounted on the wall. Her expression—it was like she couldn't stop smiling. I had never seen her brimming with such happiness before. She didn't even touch her eyepatch or insist on patting her hair over her face.

"Do you think it should be lower?" Illia asked as she pulled the dress down, exposing more of her skin. "Or have a dip in the middle? Which do you think is more alluring?"

"It's perfect the way it is." I glanced away, not wanting to encourage any part of this. "Masterwork quality. Any alteration would ruin it."

"I thought men liked it when their partner was sultry?"

"Well, er, there's a time and place. And this is a classy event. And Zaxis is a gentleman. Sometimes."

"I agree with Volke," Nicholin chimed in. "You don't want to outshine *all* the women. I think you should keep some surprises for later."

Illia stared at herself in the mirror. She lifted her dress back up and secured it in place. Then she ran her hands down her sides and smiled wide.

In order to avoid another odd request for an opinion, I said, "I ran into Fain on the way here. I thought we could walk back to the inn together."

Her smile died in an instant. She didn't look away from the mirror. Instead, she glared at me through it, her expression cold. "I won't speak to him."

"You won't give him a chance? Even for a short stroll?"

"There's no reason to. He isn't one of us." Illia hugged herself, and Nicholin teleported to her shoulder. "I'm going to change. You should let the tailor take your measurements. We can leave after that."

We walked out of the Moonlight District with Fain on one side of me and Illia on the other. No one spoke. They didn't even look at each other. Somehow, Illia had gotten Nicholin to stay quiet—or perhaps he was finally taking on more of her personality—because he didn't say a damn thing, either.

The mounting tension kept me on edge. I was certain Illia would lash out at any moment, and I was determined to prevent that.

"So, Illia," I said. "Why did they take my measurements?"

"My dress didn't cost a whole gold leaf." Words came out with no emotion. "I used the rest of our money to purchase you something."

I lifted an eyebrow. "An outfit?"

"Yes. Something simple. Don't worry, I know you."

I glanced down at my simple shirt and pants. My wardrobe had gotten pretty shabby. If Illia hadn't thought about my appearance, I might've gone to the gala in what I currently had on.

The conversation died right as we made it to the lamplighter's trolley car. We got on, waved to the will-o-wisp operator, and continued back to our inn. Fain kept his hands in his coat pockets, his gaze on the distance. He made no effort to engage, and it took me a while to think of a topic he would find interesting.

"Are you going to join the tournament?" I asked.

Fain shook his head.

"Why not?"

"I've been bonded to Wraith for five years, which would put me in the journeyman rank, but I've never had any formal training. Just what I've learned from Calisto and his crew."

I shot him a glare, and he regarded me with a confused expression. Then it dawned on him—he shouldn't mention Calisto, not in Illia's presence. He cleared his throat and mumbled an apology before returning his attention to the streets.

"Never had any formal training," I said. "Ever?"

"No." Fain glanced back over, his eyes sarcastically narrowed. "I did lose to an apprentice more than once."

"Maybe I could help you train at some point."

Illia grabbed my knee, her fingernails digging into my flesh, even through the fabric of my trousers. I snapped my attention to her. Instead, she met me with an icy glower, her disgust palpable.

"You told Atty you would train with her," she said. "Stop promising time you don't have."

I opened my mouth to protest, but I held back. Up until my time in the castle dungeon—and today's jaunt through the Moonlight District—I had been training, practicing my magic, or sleeping. I had no spare time, not unless I started doubling up. Perhaps Illia was right.

"Illia," Fain said.

She tensed and stared at him with her eye wide, like she never expected him to say her name. It surprised me as well.

Fain continued in a calm and forced-friendly tone, "If Volke is busy, perhaps—"

"Did I say you could speak to me?" she asked, her voice as cold as Fain's ice. "You're only alive because my brother is too kind. I'm not like him. Don't ever say my name again." Illia finalized her sentiment by spitting on his pant leg.

I looked at her, disappointed she would escalate the situation to hostile levels. She couldn't meet my gaze and instead stared in the opposite direction. Nicholin flicked his tail up and avoided looking at me.

Fain didn't bother wiping his trousers. He simply sat on the trolley bench with a neutral expression, as though unsurprised by the outcome.

Without any other topics to discuss, I allowed the silence to stew between us.

The *Maison Arcana* looked the best at sunset. The crimson orange rays filtered through the city's smoke, creating fiery pillars of light that shone down over the inn. Other buildings were too tall or too close to others to get the same effect. The occult glow made the inn easy to spot once we drew near.

Illia and Nicholin teleported off the trolley without so much as a *goodbye*. She reappeared by the inn's front gate, and I could tell by her stiff movements—and the way she slammed the door on her way in—she wasn't pleased with me. Perhaps I had been wrong to force Fain's company on her.

Fain and I jumped off the trolley and walked inside. I greeted each of the servants I passed, but Fain kept to himself, not even bothering to take a refreshment when offered.

"Now that you and Gillie have seen the queen, will you be staying?" I asked as we reached the courtyard door.

"Apparently. The grand apothecary wants to help your guildmaster acquire some magical items from the queen."

The information stilled my thoughts. He meant the runestones. How would Gillie help her achieve that goal? Perhaps she would offer her services to the queen for a chance to purchase the objects, since Gillie wasn't technically part of the Argo Empire.

I placed my hand on the courtyard door. "Well, I'm pretty sure Master Zelfree will be out here training tonight. If you're going to stick around, you should speak with him. He's great with magic and—"

"Never," Fain snapped.

The answer took me by surprise. "Why? I know he can be rough around the edges, but he's a good man."

Fain held my arm and pulled me close. In a low whisper, he asked, "Are you joking?"

"No."

"I thought you detested pirates? Zelfree is one of the worst. They still call him the *Faceless* in some ports."

I chuckled and removed Fain's grip from my arm. "Oh, you don't need to worry. Zelfree disguised himself as a pirate to help the Frith Guild. He's more of a spy or an agent—he has lots of stories written about him. They're really impressive, actually. He has defeated whole pirate crews."

"Everyone knows about those," Fain growled. "Zelfree betrayed the crew and captain he ran with. But he's not a *spy*. He's a renegade, like me. A pirate who turned his back on his brothers."

"No, I don't think you understand—"

"I don't think *you* understand. Zelfree and Calisto were once good friends." Fain let that statement sink in for a short moment before continuing, "Zelfree helped Calisto build his crew. He was the one who murdered the Marshall of the Southern Seas and allowed Calisto to escape imprisonment after he first bonded to his manticore."

"I never heard about that," I said, my eyebrows knit.

Fain shook his head. "Zelfree might say he's a man of honor—that he *disguised* himself as pirate—but that's not true. He *was* a pirate, and then he turned renegade and spun it as heroic. I don't ever want to be alone with the man. I think he might kill me."

"Even if everything you say is true, why would he do that?"

"Calisto and crew of the *Third Abyss* are the last ones with firsthand knowledge of the Faceless." Again, Fain grabbed my arm, tighter than before. "When Zelfree came to our ship, he and Calisto celebrated with drinks. It was only afterward that they got into an argument and Calisto decided to flay him."

The more I heard of the story, the more I thought something wasn't adding up.

Zelfree had gone to the *Third Abyss* without us. And he stayed on the ship for several days before he was hurt and we went to rescue him. Still... that wasn't concrete evidence.

Before I could ask for any more details, the courtyard door swung open. Fain flinched, his gaze sharp and his muscles tense. Zelfree walked in, tense and agitated. He snapped his fingers.

"Get your coat," he commanded. "We're leaving."

I wanted to comply, but I no longer had a coat. Instead of arguing, I nodded.

Fain moved out of Zelfree's way. For a brief second, they exchanged glances. Neither spoke. Then Zelfree continued toward the front door, the click of his boots echoing throughout the empty lounge room.

"Where are we going?" I called out after him.

"To see Adelgis's father."

26

THEASIN VENROVER THE ARTIFICER OF ELLIOS

Night swept over Thronehold, but I swear the noise grew with each passing hour. Swarms of people funneled into the city from every gate, and that level of overcrowding meant the streets stayed lively. Booze kept the crowds happy, talk of tournament kept them excited, and rampant thievery kept everyone on edge.

I stood in the trolley car and held on to a thin metal bar used as partial railing. Adelgis and Zelfree sat on the middle bench, no one speaking. More than once, the will-o-wisp arcanist operating the engine had to yell at drunkards to get out of the road. His vehicle didn't move fast, though, so it wasn't like he would run them over, but I imagined it would still hurt if someone got in the way.

"Where's Zaxis?" I asked.

"Back at the inn," Zelfree replied, his voice devoid of emotion.

"Where's Traces?"

"I left her to watch the others."

Fain's accusations remained in my thoughts. Did I want to confront Zelfree? No. He had proven himself to me on more than one occasion. Whatever Fain thought was wrong —or outdated. Right now, I had to focus on supporting Adelgis while we met with his father.

I glanced over.

Adelgis didn't move. He stared at the floor of the bumpy trolley car.

I walked over and took a seat. As I did, light appeared as shards of iridescent shell and coalesced together to form Adelgis's ethereal whelk. Felicity waggled her tentacles and then floated into Adelgis's lap.

"You okay?" I asked Adelgis.

"Yes. Just worried."

"About what? We did everything you wanted this time. We're meeting your father on his terms—not bursting into his house or anything."

It bothered me that Theasin would only see his son after the sun set, but I didn't know the man or his family, so perhaps this was normal. It didn't matter. Soon, this would be over.

Adelgis smoothed his long black hair. It fluttered when the trolley turned the corner, and the wind rushed over us. Even as Adelgis shivered, he sat with a straight posture, though his expression reminded me of a funeral attendee.

"I've developed the ability to hear thoughts," he whispered.

"Okay? That's not news to me."

"I'm afraid of hearing my father's."

Although I didn't know exactly what to say, I patted him on his shoulder. "Don't worry. I've got your back."

It wasn't much, but Adelgis met my gaze, his earnest confusion plain to see. It took him a moment, but he eventually smiled. "Thank you, Volke. I appreciate that."

"That's why I'm here, right?"

He nodded.

Although silence returned, it seemed less strained than before. We rode with the lamplighter all the way across the city until we came to a sign that read: ENCHANTER DISTRICT. The picture next to the words depicted fire and swords.

I figured Theasin would've been in the Education District, but obviously I was wrong.

The Enchanter District was comprised of many tall buildings. Smoke didn't gush into the sky from fireplaces or blast furnaces, but there were mystical creatures here. Grifter crows—black birds of illusion—and chamrosh—dogs with the heads and wings of eagles—sat on the roofs, their many eyes wide and reflecting the lamplights. I counted at least five of each, and I wondered why their arcanists kept them outside in the cold.

Zelfree hopped off the trolley and ushered us to one of the larger buildings with a thick stone exterior. The walls looked like granite columns, and the thin windows were too narrow for anyone to get through. Adelgis and I followed him to the odd building.

An attendant stood at the door and bowed his head when we got close. Zelfree said nothing as we stepped inside. The door closed behind us with a quick snap.

"What is this place?" I muttered.

"The artificer library," Luthair answered from my shadow. "It's also a laboratory for magical crafting and imbuing. Arcanists come from far and wide to deal in rare creature parts here."

It sounded a lot like Port Crown, but with fewer pirates.

Zelfree didn't need a guide. He continued through the front room, past an indoor fountain, and into a hallway. Adelgis and I stayed close by, with Felicity hovering overhead, her body glowing in the semi-darkness of the library.

We reached a crafting room with vaulted ceilings that stretched a good thirty feet up. A staircase led to a mezzanine level with a balcony that overlooked us.

Our surroundings intrigued me.

No dust on the shelves or tables. All the books in their place. Tools for fine craftsmanship hung on the wall in alphabetical order. It looked too clean, except for the giant pile of rubbish in the corner. The pile itself took up half the room, and the longer I stared, the more I realized every bit of trash was jagged and sharp. Glass. Metal. Even nails. The pile looked like broken magical items and bits of building.

I kicked the debris.

Why was this indoors? They didn't throw their trash into the alleyways?

A door opened and shut, and I craned my head back to get a better view of the balcony above us. A man walked down the long staircase, no rush in his steps.

He wore crisp black trousers, the crease sharp enough to cut someone. His shiny boots reflected the low lantern light, and I watched his careful steps as he reached the bottom of the stairs. Instead of a coat, the man wore a cloak, the hood brushed back and the inner pockets filled with papers. His gloves were so thin it was as if he had dipped his hands into ink.

"Father," Adelgis said in a quiet tone.

The blood relation was undeniable. Adelgis and his father had the same dark hair and smooth, tanned skin. Adelgis, however, kept his hair long, while Theasin had his trimmed shortest on the sides. And Theasin was taller, and more athletic, sturdier. Just... more impressive, which I hated to take note of.

"You're late," Theasin said. His voice matched his expression—neutral and controlled.

Zelfree stepped forward before Adelgis could respond. "You have some nerve. That's all you have to say after what you've done? Stealing that abyssal leech when you knew of the dangers?"

It took Theasin a moment, but he eventually lifted an eyebrow.

"You son of a whore," Zelfree continued, his volume becoming so loud that his words bounced off the high walls and ceiling. "You infected your own *family* with one of your odd experiments—one that's busy killing him. We saw what those leeches do, Theasin. Ruma told you not to take it, yet you don't give a damn, do you? This is all about your own personal gratification."

"Are you done?" Theasin asked.

The question had a finality to it—like this would be the last time Theasin would entertain such comments.

Zelfree took a deep breath, ready to answer, but this time Adelgis cut him off. He stepped forward, his ethereal whelk clinging to his shoulder.

"Please, Father," he said. "I know your time is valuable. Master Zelfree is just concerned, but he'll understand once he sees everything is fine. Perhaps you can take the leech back now. I cared for it as long as you asked—longer even."

Despite Zelfree's outrage, Adelgis didn't seem agitated. If anything, he sounded hopeful.

Theasin walked to his son, his intense gaze fixed on where the leech would be under Adelgis's clothes. "Hm. You did manage to nourish the creature and keep it safe all these years."

"So... you'll remove it?"

"Don't be absurd. Of course I will. It's a valuable creature that needs to bond as soon as possible." Theasin motioned to the stairs with sharp flick of his wrist. "The room upstairs has already been prepared. My apprentice will make sure everything is in order while I speak with your master."

Adelgis patted his ethereal whelk. She floated away from his shoulder and hovered close to me. "Please watch Felicity?" Adelgis whispered. "I'll be back soon."

Felicity touched one of her tentacles to my arm.

It seemed odd that Adelgis didn't want his eldrin with him, but I kept that thought to myself.

Once Adelgis climbed the stairs and disappeared into the upstairs room, I turned my attention back to Zelfree and Theasin. The dim lighting of the crafting room cast harsh shadows over the two, adding an air of menace to the whole encounter. Something seemed off about their mannerisms, and I remained tense for a fight, even though Theasin seemed detached from the situation.

"Everett," he said. "Have you given my offer any more consideration?"

Zelfree's attention slid to me, and then back to Theasin. A part of me wondered if I shouldn't be here, but it was too late now. Zelfree said nothing.

"Ruma's dead. There's nothing tethering you to that ridiculous guild anymore." Theasin stepped close. "I could use a man of your talents." He placed a gloved hand on Zelfree's shoulder.

Zelfree jerked free of his grasp, his teeth clenched so hard I could hear them grinding. "*Don't.*"

"So dramatic," Theasin muttered, dryly sarcastic.

"Enough of your tripe. What're you doing with that leech? And don't tell me it was *curiosity* or for the *saving some endangered creature*. You can fool the others, but *I* know you. What's so important that you had to risk your son's life?"

"I gave my son instructions. If he followed them, he should recover." Theasin turned away, his attention on the stairs. "Come back when you're ready to consider my offer, Everett. Otherwise, I have important work to do."

Zelfree grabbed his shoulder and yanked him back, his grip twisted in Theasin's cloak. "Answer me."

The pile of rubbish in the room moved. Glass clattered, metal clinked, and everything shook as though caught in a tremor.

The shadows at my feet moved as Luthair emerged. His cape hung heavy over his cracked plate armor, and he kept his gauntlet hand over the hilt of his blade. My shield rested on his arm, attached through shadow tendrils.

"Control yourself," Theasin commanded.

Zelfree didn't release him. "This isn't a game. The last abyssal leech arcanist inadvertently killed thousands."

The broken bits of magical items, building, and metal lifted into the air—not piece by piece, but as a whole unit connected by wispy magical threads, almost too gossamer to see. The "pile" took the shape of a dragon. Stained glass shards for fangs, flakes of copper for the face, and broken rock, shattered bone, and twisted iron creating the bulk of the body. The pieces fit together, but sometimes not well, creating an abstract monster dragon that sparkled in the low light. The threads of magic wove throughout everything, clinging like spider webs made of pure power.

It was lucky we had the vaulted ceiling, as the fragmented dragon needed the space.

The dragon "growled," but it didn't have a voice. Its noise came from the harsh clattering of metal from within its body.

Zelfree glared at the beast, which surprised me, considering the dragon was large enough to fit a grown man in its mouth.

Theasin exhaled. "Everything is under control, Essellian. Get your rest."

It was only then that I noticed Theasin's arcanist mark. His star had a large beast woven throughout. A shattered dragon.

Essellian was Theasin's eldrin—a relickeeper.

The beast lifted his tail, wrought-iron spikes sharp and gleaming. With a wide sweep, Essellian brought it between Zelfree and Theasin, forcing them apart. The gesture didn't cause harm, but the threat was clear. When Essellian brought his tail back, the metal scraped along the tile floor, the shrill sound causing me to shiver.

"I shouldn't be shocked," Zelfree said as he took several steps back. "You haven't changed. It won't take me long to figure out what you're doing with this *thing*."

Theasin walked to the staircase and ascended it, one step at a time. He didn't seem rushed or irritated. He never even glanced back. He disappeared into the same room as Adelgis as he straightened his cloak.

The relickeeper "stared" down at us, but I didn't see any eyes. It had a face and eye sockets, but nothing inside, just threads of raw power.

Zelfree patted my shoulder. "Stay here," he commanded. "I'll be back."

I looked at him, my eyebrows knit. "You're leaving?"

"Theasin and his eldrin won't hurt you. Just be here for Adelgis. I'll return as soon as possible."

Before I could protest, Zelfree stormed from the room, leaving me with the twisted dragon.

Minutes passed.

Then an hour.

Zelfree hadn't returned.

I paced back and forth, careful not to approach the bookshelves, desks, or crafting tables. Those seemed off-limits, even though no one had specifically instructed me not to touch anything. Luthair stood like a decoration near the door, his empty helmet facing Essellian at all times.

Fortunately, the relickeeper returned to his pile form, crumpling into the corner of the room and becoming "trash." I preferred it that way. While the beast's appearance intrigued me, his constant looming felt more like a reminder—if I acted out, he would shred me like a meat grinder.

Felicity hovered close, as silent as a gravestone.

"Do relickeepers speak?" I whispered, eyeing the pile.

"No," she replied, her singsong voice a pleasant change. "They communicate through telepathy."

"Is Adelgis okay? Do you know?"

"He's weak." She flailed her tentacles. "But the leech is out. Not much longer now."

"You can tell what's happening upstairs?"

Felicity orbited my head. "I, too, can communicate through telepathy. Adelgis has kept me apprised of his status. I worry if I don't hear from him."

Anxious to leave, I continued my pacing. This time, I swung close to a desk, and I allowed my eyes to linger on the paperwork. It regarded item creation and imbuing. To my fascination, the paperwork discussed magical items like a baker discussed his recipes.

.   .   .

HEAT REJUVENATION
  Phoenix magic
  2 nails of a hellhound
  1 heart of a salamander
  1 bolt of fabric
  5 star shards
  Crush the nails and heart to create a liquid. Soak cloth in the liquid for 24 hours. Imbue with phoenix magic, using 5 star shards. The resulting item protects the wearer from heat and exhaustion by absorbing the excess energy and converting it into raw power. The hotter the environment, the more excess energy the wearer will have.

Magical items were an interesting process, and not unlike a math problem. They boiled down to: *magic plus material plus a number of star shards.* Depending on the combination, they could vary wildly. Caladrius magic plus wendigo antlers plus a single star shard resulted in my plague-immunity pendant, while caladrius magic plus a phoenix feather plus a single star shard had resulted in a disease-immunity bracelet.

I touched the pendant for a second, wondering what would result with knightmare magic and wendigo antlers.

Then I spotted something interesting.

A letter.

From: SKARN UNIVERSITY
  Sender: LIBRARY MASTER BINTLE

I had enjoyed Bintle, and I still appreciated the fact he

allowed me to borrow a book from the university. Without thinking, I glanced at the letter.

Dear Artificer Venrover,

I hope this finds you well. I write because I have a curious question. The Frith Guild is headed by Liet Eventide, and she approached me regarding the runestones of old. After she learned they were in the queen's possession, Liet asked if the runestones could be recreated with advanced imbuing techniques.

My question: is there any way the legendary runestones can be duplicated? I know mimic magic may be capable, but I'm not familiar with any mimic masters who also possess notable skill for item craft.

If there is another way to recreate these artifacts, please advise.

The Library Master & Ghost Light Arcanist,
    Bintle Waitgest

Had Guildmaster Eventide visited Bintle a second time? Recreating the runestones would solve our problem. And it would be much easier than dealing with the queen.

The reply letter read:

. . .

Bintle,

The runestones are made with a foreign material I'm unfamiliar with. Duplication is near impossible.

Signed,

But it wasn't signed. Perhaps Theasin hadn't gotten around to that part.

I re-read the short reply. Theasin wasn't a man of pontification, it seemed.

The door upstairs opened and shut. I leapt away from the desk and turned my attention to the other side of the room, my throat tight with guilt. I shouldn't have been prying. This wasn't my business. Although I did find it curious that Liet was asking around, trying to find alternative solutions through advanced magical techniques.

Theasin walked down the staircase with the four-foot abyssal leech wrapped around his arm.

I knew it was the leech the moment I laid eyes on it. The disgusting rope of flesh writhed around with each of Theasin's steps, its body blood red and glistening, like a fresh umbilical cord. Tiny tendrils reached out from the leech's body—boneless fingers grasping for contact—and the creature made a constant low, hissing growl.

When Theasin reached the last step, his eyes flitted to me. "You're still here." Then he walked to the nearest work-table and slid the leech from his arm. A smear of crimson marked his clothing, but he didn't seem to mind.

"Where is Adelgis?" I asked.

"He'll be down shortly."

The leech reached out with its tiny tendrils, trying to crawl off the side of the work table. "Help me..." it whispered. "I can't..."

Theasin placed a hand over the creature, and then it went limp. After a moment of waiting, he removed his hand and plucked a scalpel from the tray of tools. He cut into the creature, his movements precise. A tiny laceration.

I watched with mild fascination and pure disgust. The blood that wept from the creature... was it the leech's or Adelgis's?

With a hesitant step, I got closer. "Artificer Venrover?"

He sliced another thin line into the mystical creature. He said nothing.

I continued, "Um, I've been thinking. If the abyssal leech was so important, and it wasn't life threatening, why didn't you care for it?"

"I never said it wasn't life threatening," he stated.

"You said Adelgis would be perfectly fine."

Theasin stopped in the middle of his third cut. When he glanced over, his expression was nothing short of *severe*. It lasted half a moment, and then he returned to his work.

"You must be Everett's apprentice."

I moved away from him, and Felicity stayed with me. "So what?"

"He always reads malice into my actions. The fact of the matter is—Adelgis knew the risks, but he took them to reap the rewards."

"What rewards?"

Theasin snorted. "Let me guess. Everett never told you what this leech could do."

"No. He didn't."

"Abyssal leeches can manipulate raw magic, and so can their arcanists."

He had said the words like they were profound and mind blowing. I knew knightmares could manipulate shadows, and phoenixes could manipulate fire—I understood the uses for those things—but what could an arcanist do by manipulating magic? I waited for further explanation.

Theasin forced a single laugh. Then he sighed, his breath laced with a lifetime of irritation. "Once again, I'm the only one with the understanding to grasp the magnitude of the situation. Let me put it in simple terms—with an example you'll be sure to appreciate."

I almost uttered a sarcastic *thank you*, but I thought he wanted that, so I remained quiet.

He said, "The arcane plague is nothing more than a corruption of magic—a disease that needs to be removed before it permeates the whole body. An abyssal leech arcanist has the ability to *correct* corruption, thus curing the plague once and for all."

I hadn't expected that answer, and I almost apologized. "Really?" I asked.

Theasin pressed the scalpel into the leech a fourth time, harder than before. The creature twitched, but remained mostly limp.

"Of course," he drawled. "And that's just *one* benefit of magical manipulation."

"We should tell this to Gillie right away. She's been researching the plague, and—"

"The grand apothecary is a short-sighted fool," Theasin stated. "She focuses her research on prevention, but that never eliminates the root of a problem. Adelgis's contribution to the cure will be far greater than anything that woman will offer."

"I don't think you have any right to say that about Gillie." I probably shouldn't have gotten so upset, but Gillie had gone out of her way to help me, and others, many times. "She's not short sighted. She's not a fool."

Theasin spread open the cuts and then used a tiny pair of pliers to reach into the tube-like body of the leech. He removed a small sac of flesh, something the size of a bead.

While he continued his work, he said, "Trust me, boy. Most people are easily manipulated fools. If these creatures had been named *rainbow eels*, perhaps the queen wouldn't have called for their extinction over a century ago. But fear and superstition run hand in hand. Do you realize how pathetic and shallow that is? I'm the only one left with enough reason to see the utility of such a creature."

"But Gillie wants to—"

"Gillie is a pretender," Theasin interjected. He ripped out another bead-sized lump of flesh. "Someone who masquerades as a doctor." For the first time since I had known him, Theasin half-smiled. "Look at me. My eldrin doesn't even provide healing magic, yet I will be remembered as the greatest doctor of all time. I'll be the *curer of the plague*, the one who freed humanity from its foul corruption. The grand apothecary won't even be a footnote."

After a third sac of flesh, Theasin stopped. He placed his tools in a tray and then wrapped the leech in a clean roll of gauze.

When he turned to face me, his gloves, sleeves, and shirt were spotted with fresh blood. His calm and controlled expression didn't mix well with the psychopath attire.

"Because you're a friend of Adelgis, I'll let you in on a fundamental truth," he said. "There are those who innovate and create, and then there are those like Gillie—simple minds who think inside their box and follow the fear-mongering crowds into mediocrity."

I hated the condescension oozing from his words. His sentences had an incomplete cadence, like he wanted to add an insult after every word, but he held his tongue at the last moment.

"Master Zelfree isn't the crowd-following type, and he doesn't like the idea of the abyssal leech getting out."

"Everett wants me to kill this mystical creature because he saw an arcanist use his abyssal leech magic for chaos. Everett's ignorance would cost us this plague-curing boon."

Theasin scooped up the leech and cradled it close. Then he collected the three fleshy lumps and placed them inside a small glass jar. Once he secured the lid, he tucked the container into his trouser pocket.

"Adelgis says he feels weak," Felicity said in a soft voice. "Are you sure he'll be okay?"

"You might need to help him walk out of here, but he should live," Theasin said matter-of-factly.

Then he got close to me and stared. He was slightly taller, perhaps an inch or two—I was usually the tallest in the crowd, so it came as a bit of a surprise. He opened his mouth as if to say something, but stopped before the first word came.

After a short moment of silence, he finally said, "You have... an artifact?" Theasin slowly turned his gaze to Luthair, still by the door.

Luthair slipped into the darkness and reappeared by my side. He said nothing, but he stepped close, my shield in plain sight.

He could sense the strength of a magical item? Artifacts were far stronger than trinkets, and from what I had read, it came down to the materials used to make them and the number of star shards used in the construction. Since my shield was made from the scale of the previous world serpent, it wasn't a surprise it was an artifact, but I hadn't told that to anyone. Theasin just *knew* somehow.

Theasin scowled at it for a long moment. He reached out, grazed his fingers along the top edge, and then recoiled, as though it stung. "I've never... sensed something like that before. What is it made out of?"

"That's none of your business," I said. I didn't trust Theasin. Perhaps he was right—perhaps people were ruled by fear and terrible decisions—but that truth alone didn't endear him to me.

And Theasin was the last man I wanted to tell about the world serpent scale.

"It's incomplete," he said. "You didn't create it correctly, did you?"

"I, uh, it was the first thing I imbued."

Theasin lifted an eyebrow. "An artifact? Don't lie. You would've broken the components and failed entirely if an artifact were your first attempt. All arcanists create trinkets first."

I didn't know how to answer him. It *was* the first item I had ever created. Then again, I didn't want to correct him, either. He didn't deserve to know the truth.

He probably sensed my growing distrust because he forced a single chuckle and shook his head. Then he leaned close and said, "I'll make a deal with you. Everett is no stranger to switching alliances. Convince him to work for me instead of that foolish Frith Guild, and I can help you make that shield into a thing of legend. No one crafts better items or knows more about magic than I do. *No one*."

Theasin didn't wait for me to respond. He walked by, never making eye contact, and then headed for the door.

"Come, Essellian."

The relickeeper didn't need to fully form to chase after his master. The broken bits of magic, glass, and metal tumbled across the tile and then funneled out the door after Theasin. The snake-like parade of parts continued for a minute before everything had gone, clattering and banging around the entire time. The room seemed twice as large afterward.

I didn't know my shield could be fixed. Perhaps someone else could help me.

I hadn't heard Adelgis coming down the stairs due to the racket. When I turned around, I spotted him on the second-to-last step, gulping down air and leaning on the railing with all his weight. His shirt, trousers, and coat seemed hastily thrown on.

"My arcanist," Felicity said with a tiny gasp. She floated to his side and fussed with his sweat-soaked hair. "Oh, no..."

He had the complexion of a dead fish and all the strength of a corpse. I had to rush to his side to prevent him from tumbling down the last step.

"Are you okay?" I asked. His clothes were damp, and he trembled nonstop.

"Yes," he murmured. "Please just take me back to the inn. I need... to rest."

27

BEDRIDDEN

Adelgis took a step forward and nearly collapsed. I caught him and held him up by his armpits. He didn't weigh much, and I didn't like how boney he felt as I helped him get back to his feet.

He stepped down from the last stair, his legs wobbly. How could his father leave him like this? I wanted to rush him to Gillie as fast as possible. I offered my support, and Adelgis placed a weak hand on my shoulder.

Footsteps beyond the door caught both of our attention. Adelgis ripped his hand away, held his breath, and forced himself to stand straight.

I reached out, ready to steady him.

Adelgis gritted his teeth. "After... my father leaves."

The door opened, but it wasn't Theasin who entered. A young man about my age stormed into the crafting room, adorned in masterwork leather armor, studded with steel at the edges. He had the bulk of Zaxis, but his tanned complexion and inky hair matched Adelgis's perfectly.

The man jerked to a stop, clearly shocked to see us. His

attention went from Luthair to Adelgis. "What's going on?" he demanded. "Why're you here?"

Adelgis exhaled and allowed his shoulders to slump. "Oh, it's you, Niro. Everything's fine. I came here... to see Father." He took my arm afterward, and I helped keep him on his feet.

Niro? I recognized the name. He was Adelgis's brother, but besides the general features of their appearance, they didn't look alike. Niro had the aggression and physique of a warrior. Even now—when he walked close to us—his hand slid down to the knives and trick pistol at his belt.

Niro's stiff stance got me nervous. He had an arcanist mark, but his hair hung forward, blocking most of it. The faint lines meant he had recently bonded, though. I kept an eye on his weapons. He wouldn't attack us, would he? Adelgis was his brother.

"Father left," Niro stated, cold and curt. "He's heading south to the coast and won't be coming back for a while. You shouldn't be here without him."

I stepped between them. "No need to get upset. We're leaving."

Our presence clearly agitated him, and we didn't need this. Again, I offered my shoulder to Adelgis, and I helped him out of the room, Luthair and Felicity trailing behind. Niro watched, his eyes narrowed, like we were potential thieves ready to make off with everything in the room. His disregard for Adelgis matched Theasin's nonexistent level of giving a damn.

We left without another word.

Adelgis faded in and out of consciousness on the way back

to the *Maison Arcana*. Luthair helped me carry him when he couldn't walk. I hadn't expected such a terrible outcome to removing the leech. Theasin made it sound like Adelgis only needed a good night's rest. This seemed different. Arcanists could heal themselves—why was Adelgis getting worse? This didn't make any sense.

Once inside our lavish inn, I brought Adelgis to the nearest couch. He fell onto the cushions and closed his eyes.

"Go get Gillie," I commanded.

Luthair nodded. "Of course, my arcanist." He slithered into the darkness and disappeared from the room in a matter of moments.

I knelt by Adelgis's side. Felicity swirled around, her shiny shell glowing slightly to make up for the lack of lit lanterns. She descended to the couch and cuddled close.

"He's already asleep," she muttered.

"You should get Zaxis."

And where was Zelfree? He had left us and never returned. Perhaps he would know what to do.

Felicity floated from the lounge as fast as she could. Left in the dark, I sat next to Adelgis and made sure he was still breathing.

Luthair returned with Gillie half an hour later, and I carried Adelgis out to a carriage so we could take him to the Skarn University. According to Gillie, they had the tools, equipment, and research to help Adelgis, and I deferred to her wisdom.

I hadn't slept much, but I couldn't sleep on the ride, either. Anxiety kept me awake. Gillie muttered reassurances from time to time, though I didn't pay much attention. She was always optimistic, which worked against her—a piece of me figured she'd be this way even if Adelgis were dead.

When we reached the university, I carried Adelgis inside. It was hard to focus through my exhaustion, yet I never faltered. Conversations drifted by like a breeze, and I barely took note of words. I set Adelgis down on a cot when instructed. Gillie motioned to the surrounding magical laboratory, and I admired it for half a minute before taking a seat next to the cot.

"Thank you," she said, her words piercing my mental haze.

"No problem."

"You don't need to wait here."

"It's fine. I just want to make sure he'll be okay."

"That's kind of you."

Gillie and her caladrius set to work on healing Adelgis.

Once certain everything was okay, I shut my eyes and leaned back in the chair. That was the last thing I remembered before waking under the hot rays of the morning sun.

I sat up, a thin sheet wrapped around my shoulders, and I stared at the window, both disgruntled and confused. This wasn't my room. It took me a few seconds to remember I had gone to the university, and even as I remembered the details, it felt like walking a path in the fog. Adelgis slept on the cot next to me, his eyes sunken in and his breathing even. He looked peaceful, though, and Felicity sat on his chest, her sea snail shell sparkling in the sunlight.

With a loud groan, I rubbed at the side of my face. "What happened?"

"Gillie said he needs time," Felicity replied. "She left to requisition materials for a healing trinket. Did you sleep well?"

"I think so."

"Good. I tried to give you pleasant dreams."

"Thank you." I rubbed at my temples. "I'm going to head out. Let me know if anything changes."

With a headache building behind my eyes, I stood and glanced around. The lab had several bookshelves, a desk, and three cots. Was it a medical lab? With questions swimming in my thoughts, I left the room.

To my relief, Zelfree stood in the hallway, only a few feet from the door. He was haggard—bags under his eyes, his clothes just as crumpled as mine. He stuck to the shadow of a pillar, hiding from the morning light that streamed in through the hallway windows.

"Master Zelfree," I said. "Adelgis is—"

"I know."

His gruff statement didn't ease my anxiety.

"What happened?" I asked. "Why isn't he getting better?"

Zelfree ran a hand through his hair. He looked substantially different with short hair as opposed to his longer style, but in a moment like this, that tired, determined expression was unmistakably him.

"Bonding with a creature," he muttered, "requires that you offer up a bit of your soul. Your eldrin feeds on it. That's how they grow."

I nodded along with his words. "I know. That's why eldrin eventually become just like their arcanists."

"Well, think of your soul like blood. Your body continually makes blood. Even if you're cut and you lose some, you won't die. Now think of an eldrin like a cut that never fully heals."

I pinched the bridge of my nose. "Okay?"

"However, if someone slits your throat, it'll take a few minutes, tops, to bleed to death. That's why people don't bond with multiple mystical creatures. It's like cutting your own soul jugular. You'll die in a matter of hours."

My chest tightened with an odd realization, but before I could form a question, Zelfree continued.

"Having an abyssal leech burrow into you is like bonding to a second creature. Not *exactly*, because you don't die, but it's like taking on a wound that'll eventually kill you. That's how it lives. It doesn't eat flesh or plants—it eats magic. It's been suckling on Adelgis's soul for a while now. And since Adelgis is bonded already, this is a problem."

"Wait, wait," I said. "You can bond with multiple creatures?"

Zelfree stared at me as though I had asked the second most ridiculous question he had ever heard in his life. "By the abyssal hells, I swear no one listens."

"Maybe if you weren't so vague with these explanations, I wouldn't need clarification." I didn't mean to snap, but I wasn't in the mood to argue semantics. "I just meant, *is it possible* to bond with two creatures, even for a moment?"

"Sure. As long as you don't mind dying immediately afterward. It's the soul equivalent of stabbing yourself in the heart."

"Okay. I understand." I ran a hand over my head, both frustrated and intrigued by the situation. "And the abyssal leech is halfway to bonding with a second creature?"

"Something like that."

"But Adelgis has been living for years with it, apparently."

Zelfree shrugged. "Yes, because the leech is a clever parasite. It takes what it can to live, but doesn't kill the host. When it was being removed, I wouldn't be surprised if it took more soul than normal." He turned away from me and leaned back against the wall. "I knew this would happen, but Theasin doesn't give a damn. As long as he has his creature, everyone else can—"

"Will Adelgis be okay?" I interjected.

"I don't know." Zelfree sighed. "We'll have to wait for Gillie to give us her assessment."

I didn't return to *Maison Arcana*. Instead, I stayed at Skarn University, just in case Gillie needed my help. Knightmare magic had no way to heal anything, but perhaps she would need someone to deliver a message or to fetch something. It wasn't my duty, but Adelgis had asked for my help in this matter, and I wasn't going to abandon him until it was over.

The staff and faculty at Skarn University didn't mind my presence. They allowed me onto their training field, which was better equipped for magic practice than the courtyard at the *Maison Arcana*. I practiced my shadow manipulation and swordplay—anything to keep my thoughts distracted.

When Forsythe swooped out of the sky, I almost didn't notice him. He landed next to me, his phoenix body glowing bright, even in the middle of the afternoon. His soot mixed with the dirt of the fighting arena, disappearing from sight.

"Forsythe," I said. "Where's Zaxis?" Wasn't he supposed to help Adelgis?

"I'm sorry, Volke. The grand apothecary said she didn't need him."

"Okay... So where is he now? Training?"

"No." He puffed out his feathers and picked at the fiery body underneath. Then he relaxed again. "Ever since Illia said they could be together, he's stopped everything to be with her."

"What?" I snapped.

Forsythe lowered his head, practically pressing it against his body. "Oh, I'm sorry. Zaxis said I shouldn't mention anything because it would upset you."

"It doesn't upset me." I rotated my arms, my body stiff. Everything felt grimy. "I don't care what they do. I'm not Illia's keeper." The shadows moved around my feet as I walked closer to one of the straw-stuffed training dummies. The makeshift person even had a face stitched into the sack. "I'm just surprised Zaxis would stop his training routine, that's all."

"I'm just as surprised as you." Forsythe lifted his head again, his voice becoming twice as chipper. "He said he's earned some personal time, and then he asked me to check up on you."

"They've been out all night together?"

"I don't know. Perhaps? I was sleeping."

"Right."

I placed my hand on the training dummy and willed dark tendrils to wrap around it. With focused control, I squeezed the figure, crushing the stuffing and ripping the seams. The burning of magic didn't bother me like I thought it would. I just continued, satisfied with my progress.

I liked to imagine the dummy was Theasin. Or maybe his *trash dragon*.

"You should remain calm," Luthair whispered from the shadows.

"I am calm."

Theasin's disregard for his son irritated me on a personal level. Gravekeeper William never would've left me dying in the arms of a stranger. My real father, on the other hand, was a murderer thrown from my own home isle... Would he have left me?

I shook the thought from my head.

"Volke?" someone asked, her voice familiar.

I lowered my hand, my heart hammering hard for some reason. My shadow tendrils released their grasp on the dummy. When I turned around, I found Atty standing just a foot away. She kept her hands clasped in front of her, and when she tilted her head, the golden strands of her hair caught the light.

Forsythe hopped close, and she patted his head. Atty's phoenix, Titania, perched on the lamp post at the edge of the training grounds, her peacock-like tail swirled around the wrought iron.

"Oh, uh, hello," I said as I took a deep breath and tried to relax. My tense muscles made it difficult. "How did you know I was here at the university?"

Atty made eye contact with Titania for a brief moment, as if having a silent conversation. Then she returned her smile to me. "Master Zelfree told me."

"I see."

"Is it okay that I came to visit you?"

"Of course," I said, hoping to keep her in my presence longer. "I just haven't seen you around lately."

"I've been practicing my augmentation in my room."

"Alone?"

"Yes." Atty stepped closer, her gait stiff. "I know this'll sound childish or foolish, but..." She trailed off and never picked her sentence back up. Instead, she struggled for the words, fiddling with the hem of her sleeves.

"You don't have to tell me if you don't want to," I said.

Atty shook her head. "I don't like failing." She said the sentence so fast I almost didn't catch it. Then she inhaled and said, "And I don't like struggling in front of others. So, I practiced alone until I got it right. Look." She held out her hand and motioned for mine.

I placed my palm on top of hers. With a single finger, Atty created a wisp of flames and dragged it over the back of my hand. The burn stung, but I gritted my teeth and allowed her to harm me. Once finished, leaving my skin peeling from flame, she ran her finger over me again, this time healing the injury.

It wasn't as fast or as proficient as Zaxis, but it worked.

Forsythe perked up, his feathers puffed. "Congratu-lations!"

"It's embarrassing to struggle with simple magic concepts," Atty whispered. She held my hand, her grip tight, though not painful. "I didn't want to look foolish by floundering with something so basic."

I rubbed at the back of my neck. "I struggle all the time. In front of everyone. You shouldn't let perfection be the enemy of progress."

"It's different. You have amazing powers, and you're learning the nuances of advanced techniques. It's like saying you're struggling to get to the peak of a mountain, while I'm struggling to find the first footpath at the base." She exhaled. "It's just... different."

Funny—it felt like struggling no matter where I was on the mountain, but wasn't that the point? If I hadn't struggled then, I wouldn't be here now. Everyone had to start somewhere.

"You don't understand," Atty said, frowning. "Have you ever seen a circus show?" she asked me out of nowhere.

I lifted an eyebrow. "Gravekeeper William took me to one once."

"Allow me to use the circus as an analogy." She took a deep breath and stared at her feet as she said, "Imagine you're the performer who spins plates on the tips of sticks. That's your one job. *Spin the plates.* You don't have to do anything else—*just spin the plates*. But every time you try, you end up dropping the sticks and breaking the plates. Now imagine someone says you should do your performance in front of a crowd. But deep down, you know you're just going to break everything again."

"I guess that would be—"

"Everyone on the Isle of Ruma knew me as the talented one," Atty interjected. She kept hold of my hand and even pulled it closer. This close, she smelled of lilacs, and her soft skin had a healthy glow. "Everyone said I was perfect. How can I mess up in front of them now? Do you see what I mean? I had to practice on my own before I could let anyone see."

It was hard to relate, since most people underestimated me, rather than overestimating me, but I nodded along with her words regardless. I wanted to be supportive, even if I didn't know how.

"I had something I wanted to ask you," Atty said, a cute fluster to her voice.

"Is it something personal?"

"Yes." The edge of her ears grew pink.

I glanced around, examining every corner and shadow of the training grounds. Then I cleared my throat and said, "I sure hope we're *alone* and not being *watched* by anyone."

Atty narrowed her eyes, her expression becoming one of concern.

But my suspicions had been correct. The crunch of sand and dirt, coupled with the soft step of boots, told me Fain had been nearby. He had followed me to the university? Of course he had. At some point, I'd have to give him a boundaries talk.

"Do you want to send our eldrin away?" Atty asked as she lifted a perfect eyebrow.

"No," I muttered. "It's fine. What did you want to talk about?"

"It's about the gala. I know it's just an event for the queen's ego and doesn't have anything to do with our objectives here, but—"

"An event for the queen's ego?"

Atty nodded. "I spoke to the other arcanists here at *Maison Arcana*. They said everyone has to present themselves to the queen and that she uses these types of gatherings to show off her sovereign dragon, Vercingetorix."

I almost laughed aloud. I hadn't heard the name of the queen's dragon until just then. What a mouthful. "*Vercingetorix*?" I said, hoping I didn't butcher it. "He was gigantic."

"Yes, well, it all seems childish." Atty rolled her eyes. "Trying to impress people with how large your eldrin is doesn't seem like something a ruler should concern herself with."

I didn't know if I agreed. Maybe the queen wanted to subtly display her power to avoid conflict. If other arcanists thought they were weaker, then they wouldn't attempt a rebellion. From what I remembered of my history studies, many monarchs lost control of their kingdom because arcanist dukes in their territory bonded with more powerful creatures and then later used their power to take the throne.

Then again, who would kill the queen or her sovereign dragon? With a prosperity aura present, it would only harm everyone it if ceased to be.

Atty poked her fingertips together. "To get to the point..."

The main door to the training grounds opened. Hexa stormed across the dirt sparring rings and then weaved between the wooden training racks. Her hydra ran alongside her, his stomach dragging on the ground. Hexa's cinnamon hair was tied back tight, creating a puffy ponytail. The expression on her face was nothing short of *disgruntled.*

"Volke," she called out.

"Yes?"

"Where's Illia?"

"Not here," I said as I motioned to our surroundings. "Maybe you should check inside."

"She's not there. She hasn't been *anywhere* since she spoke with Zaxis." Hexa sneered and only stopped her stomping once she got to my side. "I think they're trying to suffocate each other with their mouths."

I didn't need to hear that. "They're adults," I intoned. "They can do what they want."

Hexa snapped her attention to Atty. "Well? Are you two gonna disappear, too?"

"I haven't asked him yet," Atty replied, curt. "We were *just* discussing the gala."

As if tact was a foreign concept, Hexa turned to me. "So, are you two going together? Is that what's happening?"

Atty huffed. "Hexa, I don't need your assistance."

Wait, Atty was going to ask me to the gala? Curse the abyssal hells. Out of all the times to be put in a situation where I couldn't accept someone's advances. I should've thought this through before taking anyone who asked.

"About that," I began. "I've already invited someone to attend the gala with me. It wasn't because I knew her." I quickly added, "It was because she wanted to attend the gala. Independent of me. She just wants to see the castle."

Hexa and Atty regarded me with wide eyes. Even Raisen stared with both his heads, his four gold eyes fixed on me. I thought I even heard Atty's phoenix snort from the far-off lamppost.

"Who?" Hexa demanded.

I hesitated, if only because I realized how terrible it sounded.

"A woman I met in the Moonlight District," I said.

"You invited a *whore* to the queen's gala?" Hexa spoke the words like she had been slapped in the face.

"A *songstress*. And keep your voice down."

"How much did you pay her?"

"I—wait, what?—I didn't pay her anything!"

Hexa burst into laughter.

My face heated, and my throat went dry.

Raisen chuckled, probably joining in with his arcanist since I doubted the young hydra knew anything about prostitutes and the precarious situation I found myself in. Somehow, it seemed worse that he was laughing.

Every explanation I could think of involved the phrases *"and then I went to the backroom,"* and *"she offered herself to me,"* which seemed beyond naïve or lewd. In the moment, with Karna on my arm, it didn't seem so foolish. How could I possibly explain everything without involving all the details?

My prolonged silence seemed to irritate Atty. She pulled her robes close, her gaze falling to the dirt. Titania flew over and landed on the ground next to her.

"I did it as a favor to the songstress," I said. "It meant nothing to me. She's not an arcanist, and she wanted to see the queen—it really was just a favor."

Somehow, thankfully, my explanation didn't anger her further. Atty glanced up, a slight smile on her face. "Really? You invited a normal girl to the gala, just so she could meet the queen?"

"Yeah."

The entire time, Hexa continued to chuckle. She

muttered things like *I can't wait to tell Illia*, and *what will Zaxis say?*

Titania fluffed up her feathers, much like Forsythe. "That was kind of you, Volke. I should've realized that was the explanation."

Atty nodded along with the words. "I see. We'll still have a chance to socialize at the gala, then."

I had to stop myself from taking her in my arms and holding tight. Atty was always so reasonable. That was why I liked her so much. That and she was beautiful, but the reasonableness seemed like a rare and precious trait I couldn't overstate.

Unlike Hexa, who chortled incessantly, still amused by my choice and still muttering, *a whore, really?*

I just wanted to focus on what mattered—like our problem with the runestones. Zelfree said our true enemy might show up at the gala, after all. I had to take mental notes on everyone there, not worry about my social standing.

THE QUEEN'S GALA

The evening of the gala, I made my way back to the *Maison Arcana*. To my surprise, it was mostly empty. All the arcanists had left for the castle, leaving the staff of the luxurious inn an evening to themselves.

I slipped inside without anyone noticing me. One shadow-step to the roof and then another into my room. With unenthusiastic haste, I dressed in the clothes Illia had purchased for me. Nothing fancy, just a black coat, trousers, and shirt—and for some reason, a white scarf. I didn't like it. I had never worn one before, since the Isle of Ruma never got particularly cold. The warm waves of the ocean also made for pleasant recreation, and no one wanted to fiddle with a scarf when getting in and out of the water.

It was a nuisance, so I left it.

Then I used the shaving tools Gravekeeper William had given me. When I had first used the razor, I had cut my face and chin more times than I cared to admit. Fortunately, an arcanist's natural healing hid all mistakes. Now it wasn't a problem—clean swipes, and the day's growth was gone.

I glanced over at the other beds in my room. Both

empty. Adelgis remained at the Skarn University with Gillie —he would be fine, she said, but her tone didn't sit well with me. And I hadn't seen Zaxis since the night he confessed to Illia.

Using my shadow-stepping abilities, I slid out of my room through the window and back to the roof. I noticed a carriage waiting by the front gate, and I used the darkness to travel down to the lawn. The driver of the carriage seemed familiar. He was a man with a top hat and a puffy ascot. He wore thin chains from the belt of his trousers up to the breast pocket of his purple coat, like they were jewelry holding his outfit together. His gut poked out a bit, and I finally recognized him as the man who ushered me into Karna's show.

Slipping into the shadows to bypass the gate, I exited out near the mustangs of the carriage, holding back a grimace.

"Good evening, sir arcanist," the man said, not at all surprised to see me appear beside him. "Will these accommodations suffice for the evening's activities?"

The carriage wasn't anything extravagant, but I didn't care. I nodded, opened the door, and then climbed inside. The aroma of cinnamon hung on the air. Not too much— just the right amount to remind me of my initial meeting with Karna.

And there she was, sitting at the far end of the vehicle, her perfect legs crossed. It wasn't difficult to see how sculpted they were—she wore a silver dress with slits on both sides, showing skin as far as decency would allow. Her shoes, and even her top, were made of lace and string woven together to form a new kind of textured fabric. Thin and delicate. Beautiful and regal. It suited her.

I stared for a handful of seconds before realizing my improper behavior.

"S-Sorry," I muttered as I took my seat on the opposite bench.

Karna smiled. Her hair flowed over her shoulders, and when she brushed it back to expose her neck, I noticed a tattoo. At first, I thought it was like Fain's—a pirate mark—but I quickly relaxed when I realized it was a crescent moon. I didn't know of any pirates with that symbol on their flag.

"I didn't realize you had a tattoo," I said as I pointed to her neck.

Karna chuckled. "Most men don't."

"Is, uh, there a purpose behind it?"

"To remind people where I come from."

She gave her rationale with a cold and serious tone. A moment later, she returned to her smiling. "Thank you so much for inviting me, sir arcanist. You don't realize how much this means."

When she leaned forward, I noticed she wore no sleeves, showcasing her toned arms and collarbones.

The carriage started down the cobblestone road, the bumpy ride much faster than the trolley cars.

I wasn't sure what to say, so I went with, "You're radiant this evening."

"Thank you, sir arcanist. You're rather handsome yourself."

Her silky voice transformed the scene into something more intimate than I had imagined. While I was still concerned about Adelgis and his well-being, it shifted to the back of my mind the closer Karna scooted to the edge of her seat.

"You can call me Volke," I said. "I told you before, I don't need to be addressed as *sir arcanist*."

She lifted an eyebrow. "It's only proper."

"It's fine. Really."

To stop myself from staring, I turned my attention to the darkness and focused on manipulating small portions. The pain from the magic helped keep me from thinking about anything inappropriate. I didn't want to bother Karna, not when she so desperately wanted to attend this event. I intended for the evening to go perfectly for her.

We traveled through two districts in silence before Karna placed a hand on my knee. "Are you excited for the evening?"

"I don't know," I said. "I haven't been to anything like this. I don't think it's my scene, so to speak."

"Every arcanist enjoys the celebration." She grazed her fingers up my leg. "This is an event of warriors and magic, praising your many accomplishments. What's not to like?"

"Uh, perhaps." For some reason, her touch was all I could think about. Should I pull away? I didn't want to offend her—and I liked the attention—but at the same time, I didn't want her to think this was necessary. "Aren't *you* excited?"

"Very," she answered right away.

"Good." I tapped my fingers on the seat of the carriage. "*Good.*" I probably would've said it a third time, like an idiot, but I stopped myself from speaking.

"Where do you normally take elegant women when you hit the town?"

"Well, to be honest, this is the first time I've ever done something like this."

She lowered her head and stared up at me through her eyelashes. "Taken a girl out?"

"Yes."

"Ever?" Laughter laced her words.

"Yes."

Karna leaned away. "You're not a very good liar, you

know. A man of your standing has *definitely* taken many a woman out on the town."

I crossed my arms, trying not to take her words as an insult, but it was difficult. Was she calling into question my honor? When would I have had time to wine and dine multiple women? But it didn't matter. She didn't need to believe me.

When the carriage stopped, I leapt for the door and opened it. I hadn't realized how stiff I had become until that moment. Ten minutes alone with Karna had me hot in the blood and sweaty. Probably wasn't a good sign for a social event, but I wouldn't be the center of attention. Hopefully no one would notice.

I held out my hand and helped Karna exit the vehicle. She seemed surprised by my gesture and readiness to help, but I didn't know why.

"I'm not a master of etiquette," I said with half a smile. "So if I do something that embarrasses you, just let me know. I'll stop."

Again, she regarded me with a look of mild confusion. "Thank you..."

I offered my arm, and once Karna placed her hand on my elbow, I led her to the front gate. We only took a few steps before I caught my breath and held it.

Hundreds—no, *thousands*—of people were in attendance. And not just people, but mystical creatures. The sky, despite the darkness of night, was filled with colors.

A pair of golden furred griffins sat on the castle wall, both with eagle heads and sharp beaks. A thin dragon, with a snake-like body and bird-like clawed hands, flew around a watch tower without the aid of wings. Three phoenixes and forty will-o-wisps dotted the sky, like faux stars or giant fireflies.

Some creatures I couldn't even identify; they were just too far away, or they darted past at speeds I couldn't keep up with.

The mystical creatures on the ground were just as varied and colorful.

A stone golem made of white and gray marble lumbered through the crowd at a slow pace, each step shaking the walkway. Four dogs with dragon scales—which I now knew as denglongs, thanks to Theasin's book—stayed close to their arcanists, their fur and markings a bright yellow and red. A stoor worm, deadly and giant, practically the size of three horses, slithered with concertina movements, sticking to the darkness near the main path. Its scales and fins glinted in the lowlight.

I almost didn't know where to look. Everything was so fascinating, and the arcanists in attendance were numerous. At the same time, Zelfree's words echoed in my thoughts. There were people here determined to find the world serpent. They were using this tournament as a means to scope out the castle, find the runestones, and likely steal them. I had to stay on my guard. I couldn't let any of that come to pass.

Who should I focus my attention on?

The powerful arcanists. An apprentice arcanist hadn't created the plague and likely didn't have the skill to steal from the royal castle. It had to be one of the more prominent arcanists in attendance. If I limited my investigation, perhaps I could find something worth reporting.

Karna held onto my arm, her golden hair flowing in the evening breeze. "Shall we?"

I nodded.

We walked among the many arcanists, my attention on the gates of the castle. The Knights Draconic guarded every entranceway, and when I got close enough, I noticed that pegasi lined the castle balconies, their riders in full armor.

"Do you think the queen's dragon will be here?" Karna asked.

"Vercingetorix? Probably. He was here the last time I saw the queen."

"Fascinating."

The entrance hall was large enough, and tall enough, to accommodate even the most gargantuan of creatures. The stone golem had to duck his massive boulder-like head, but he made it through the wide doors without trouble. Luthair slithered at my feet, taking no more room than a shadow required, and for that I was grateful.

The castle servants lined the walls, each ready to jump forward and offer refreshments or directions. The guests were directed to the main ballroom and adjourning rooms, which was where I took Karna. Apparently, at some point in the evening, we would need to see the queen, but I suspected all the high-level arcanists would go first. An apprentice—a foreign apprentice, no less—probably wouldn't be a top priority.

Once in the main ballroom, I veered off to one of the corners, determined to stay as far from the music or dance floor as possible. Karna was a visionary with lyrics and rhythm, but I had no such skills. Instead, I planned to mingle with the master arcanists when they came for refreshments.

Nonstop conversations created a blanket of dull noise that made it difficult to hear anything unless it was close. Sure, musicians practiced their craft, but I couldn't appreciate it.

"So lovely," Karna said as she panned her gaze around. "Stunning."

I glanced down at her, and my first thought was of her beauty. The castle didn't compare.

When she caught me staring, she rubbed my elbow with circular motions. "Shall we dance?"

"Uh, well, about that. No. Never." I punctuated my statement with a nervous laugh. "You can, though. Anytime you want."

Before Karna could answer, a group of arcanists approached—two men and two women. I recognized the men based on their arcanists stars. Dogs. An orthrus and a barghest. It was Dart and Crevis, the two apprentices who had insulted Illia and gotten into a fight with Zaxis in this very castle. Members of the Huntsman Guild.

Crevis stepped forward, his sharp canines visible in his full smile. "Well, well, well. If it isn't one of Zelfree's apprentices." Unlike the last time I saw him, he wore clothing befitting our location. A long coat, a frilled shirt, and trousers with crisp lines. His posture didn't match, though. He hooked a thumb in one pocket and leaned heavily on his back foot, like this was a bar and he was already half-drunk.

"Hello," I forced myself to say.

"Master Jevel said Zelfree would humiliate himself if he showed his face in the gala. I think that'll be amusing. Where is your master, anyway?"

"I don't know."

The two women—the unfortunate souls attending the gala with Dart and Crevis—held on to their dates and giggled to each other. They looked around my age, perhaps in their early 20s.

The first thing I took note of was their scarves. Both of them wore colorful and detailed scarves designed to match their arcanist stars and their dresses. One woman had bonded to a salamander—a fire lizard born from magma—

and her scarf blazed with a bright orange and red. The other woman had bonded with a kelpie—a type of water horse capable of controlling tides—and her scarf shimmered with the aquamarine of the ocean.

With a sneer, the salamander arcanist turned her gaze to Karna. Then her eyes went wide when she spotted the tattoo. She touched the other three and pointed.

"Greetings," I said. "My name is Volke Savan. I'm a knightmare arcanist with the Frith Guild."

"The *Frith Guild*," the kelpie arcanist repeated, her eyes narrowing. She lowered her voice, though I could still hear her as she whispered, "They're the ones who caused a fight in the castle. And upset the youngest princess. *And* insulted the queen with their repeated writs. An uncouth guild from the island nation to the north."

She rattled off the transgressions like they tasted sour and she had to free her mouth of the words. She wasn't wrong about any of them, per se, but it didn't sound as if she wanted me to correct her, either.

"You can add *brought a whore into the castle*," the salamander arcanist muttered with a giggle.

Crevis and Dart both laughed aloud at that comment. Then they leered at Karna, their gaze traveling from her feet up to her golden hair, each stopping at noticeable moments to *take it all in*. Their dates scowled in their direction, but neither dog arcanist paid them any mind.

"It's been nice seeing you again," I said as I stepped between them and Karna. "We need to be on our way, though."

Crevis stepped around me, his shiny shoes clicking on the tile floor as he blocked my path. "Hold on there. You think you can bring a wench like this into the queen's gala? What an insult."

"She's not a wench," I said through clenched teeth. "She's a dancer and a talented songstress."

The salamander and kelpie arcanists both rolled their eyes in dramatic fashion.

"A likely story," one mumbled.

"It's disgusting," the other added. "Harlots have all sorts of diseases."

Dart didn't seem like the type for words, but he laughed, his gut rumbling. "It's pretty pathetic, when ya think about it. How much did ya pay?"

Their constant snide commentary, chortling, and staring drove me right to the edge of reasonable. I stepped forward, ready to get thrown from the gala, my muscles tense. "It's not like that. I said she's a dancer."

"No," Karna interjected, her voice devoid of any emotion. "There's no point in hiding it. I am a whore."

I turned around, confused and a little shocked.

Crevis and Dart exchanged grins like only fools could.

The salamander arcanist pulled her red scarf up, covering her coy smile. "Scandalous."

I didn't know what to say. There had been no need for Karna to admit anything. Why do so now?

"Look there," the kelpie arcanist said as she pointed to Karna's neck. "That's the harlot's mark. She's from the *Moonlight District*." She held a hand to her mouth. "I can't believe a member of the Frith Guild brought such a disgusting creature to the gala. I must tell my sisters at once."

Without a glance back, she hurried away from the group, her blue dress swaying elegantly as she hustled into the crowd of arcanists and their eldrin.

Crevis held up a hand. "Wait for me." He chased after, Dart and the salamander arcanist close on his heels.

A piece of me worried about the repercussions of their rumor mill. Another piece of me couldn't care less.

To my ever-increasing bewilderment, Karna stared up at me with a content smile, like that entire interaction pleased her somehow.

"Are you embarrassed?" she asked, an edge to her words.

"Yes, but—"

"Of course you are." She laughed as she swished her lustrous hair over her shoulder, once again amused with the response.

"It's just frustrating," I said. "I can't believe those four are considered my peers."

Karna stared at me, her eyes filled with an emotion I couldn't identify.

Perhaps I wasn't explaining myself well enough. I struggled to find the words and finally settled with, "When I was younger, growing up on stories of heroes, I thought all arcanists were just and virtuous. None of my childhood idols would've said such things to you. Frankly, I can't believe people like them managed to bond with a mystical creature."

Still, she said nothing.

"Those four don't embody what it means to be an arcanist," I continued. "They don't hold themselves to a higher standard. They might not even have a standard."

"You're embarrassed because they're arcanists?" she asked, her earlier confidence melting away.

"Well, yeah. You said you were really looking forward to this night, and that's the way they greeted you? There was no point to their cruelty. How is it not embarrassing that I'm supposed to call them my equals?"

She didn't say anything. She just stared, as if this were the first time she were meeting me. Was this good or bad? I couldn't tell. Karna was an enigma, but I was determined to make sure she still got something out of the evening, even if I had to descend to the first layer of the abyssal hells to make this right.

"Why don't I get you a drink?" I asked. "Then, if you want, I can escort you to the throne room so you can see the queen. If anyone hassles you, I'll step in and handle it. There's no reason for arcanists to behave like that."

The buzz of conversation echoed around us, but when Karna met my gaze, it seemed like we were alone. Our eyes remained locked, her intensity something I hadn't experienced before.

"I'm a whore," she said matter-of-factly. "You would still take me to see the rest of the castle?"

"That's what you said you wanted, right?"

"Yes."

"And I said I would do it, so I'll stand by my word."

What did it matter if my reputation here in Thronehold was tarnished? It was already ruined when I *manhandled* a princess. I wouldn't let the perceptions of others dictate how I acted.

Karna hardened her gaze as she held out her hand. "I don't want a drink or to see the queen. I'd rather dance with you."

I forced a single laugh. "Uh, that's impossible. I've never learned how to dance. I guess if you're trying to embarrass me, that would be a surefire way."

"Take my hand. I'll make sure this is anything but embarrassing."

I wanted to deny her—to tell her *that's not how dancing works*—but her dire seriousness unnerved me. Karna didn't seem apprehensive. This was what she wanted.

"Please," she said.

Uncertain of what would happen, I placed my hand on top of hers. A spark of magic spread across my palm, and I shot my attention up to her forehead.

No arcanist star.

Yet I still felt the magic—creeping into my skin and waiting. I had to give it permission. I had to accept this. The magic wouldn't work unless I allowed it to.

"I promise you'll enjoy this," Karna whispered, her tone seductive. "Trust me."

29

JUSTICE OR REVENGE

I allowed Karna's magic to affect me.

For a brief second, it felt as though fingers wrapped around my spine from the inside of my body. I gritted my teeth, unfamiliar with such a sensation, but when I tried to remove my hand from Karna's, I couldn't. Panic seeped into my thoughts as I realized I couldn't move at all.

"Relax," she said. "I'm in control. Everything will be fine."

With an elegant gait, she strode toward the dance floor. I followed—not because I chose to, but because my body moved on its own. Trapped inside my head, I watched from the windows of my eyes as we passed other arcanists, castle staff, and eldrin. When we reached the dance floor, I wanted to ask Karna what was going on, but even that was impossible. I couldn't talk. I couldn't do anything but observe.

The castle orchestra consisted of twenty musicians, more than half with string instruments. The dance floor, a rectangular area of shiny cherrywood, glittered under the chandelier light. Some eldrin, like goblins and fairies, danced with their arcanists or even with each other. The bigger creatures stayed on the sidelines. They made for an interesting audience.

While Karna led me out to the center, I wondered if Luthair knew what was happening. I had no way to communicate to him, but maybe he could sense it?

His shadow stirred around my feet as normal, and it seemed that wasn't the case.

The current song ended, and for a few seconds, we had silence. Then the musicians started up with something upbeat and festive. Karna smiled as she took my hands and leaned in close. My heart beat fast, in time with the new tempo, and we twirled across the dance floor.

I couldn't believe it. If I had control of my body, I would've laughed.

We moved in sync—every step, every motion—as we danced to the rhythm of the castle's music. I held her close, then held her out far, then close again, switching positions with the fluidity of water.

Karna let go of my hands and danced around me, her speed and grace a thing of beauty.

Others took note.

Arcanists and eldrin moved away from us, clearing the floor. I wanted to apologize, but I couldn't. They stared with rapt expressions, like our skill was far more interesting than anything else.

Karna fell into my arms, and I lifted her off her feet in a display of strength and control. The coordination of our actions impressed even me. When I spun her around, her dress flared, and I couldn't help but enjoy.

It was still awkward not having control of my limbs, but I had never been so suave or graceful. It would've taken years to master such a dance on my own.

I helped Karna perform an elegant backflip, all in time

with the music, and I swear even the musicians were having a hard time focusing. She pressed up against me for the last part of the song, her breathing heavy, her smile wide. Although I couldn't turn my head to observe the onlookers, I knew in my gut that most were jealous. Karna's dance stole the show. No one compared.

And her beauty—both physically and in attitude—was beyond what I had expected.

The music slowly came to an end, and we held each other until the last note played. The whispers from the gala attendants reached my ears as Karna and I walked off the dance floor. While I didn't care what they thought, it did amuse me that most muttered words of excitement and awe.

"Who are they?" a lady arcanist whispered.

A man replied, "I don't know. What level of the tournament do you think they're in?"

"Journeyman or higher, I would bet. Such skill with the dance means they've probably lived a long life."

Without control of my body, all I could do was dwell on the comments while Karna led me from the main hall. I thought we would stop out in the hallway, but we continued to the nullstone statue staircase and made our way up a level.

Karna navigated the castle with the familiarity of a family member. No hesitation or second-guessing. She turned down a small hallway and then into a room with a stone balcony that overlooked the massive gardens.

Sky Legionnaires waited at the end of every hall, and a few were positioned in the gardens themselves, so we were never alone, but the upper level did feel more deserted.

We walked out onto the balcony, Karna holding my arm.

"What a lovely night," she said as we came to a stop near the ornate railing. Music rang up from the ballroom, this time slow and melodic. "I didn't expect the weather to be this cooperative. I suppose some arcanist is controlling it, don't you think?"

I still couldn't answer, even though I tried.

Karna tilted her head. "Oh, sorry about that."

The grip on my spine loosened and then released, leaving me with a chill. It took me a few moments of stretching—from my arms to my toes—before I felt *right* again.

"What was that?" I asked. "You have magic? I thought—"

She held up a hand, and I bit back my words. Then she leaned against me and stared out at the gardens. For a long moment, I thought she wouldn't explain herself, but then she said, "I'm a doppelgänger arcanist."

I turned to her, my attention on her forehead. To my surprise, her skin rippled and changed, the arcanist mark seemingly emerging from the depths, like a buoyant stick in water. The seven-pointed star had a human body woven throughout.

Her trick in the main hall made sense to me now. Doppelgänger arcanists could manipulate people and augment their own appearance. They shifted through crowds with the camouflage of a chameleon, and legends sometimes stated that there weren't multiple doppelgänger arcanists, just one so epic and duplicitous that no one could tell it was a single person.

That was preposterous, though.

Wasn't it?

Karna turned to me and frowned. "I'm sure you have a thousand questions."

"Why did you hide your arcanist mark?" I asked.

"I didn't want anyone to know." She tightened her grip

on my elbow. "The fastest way to discover someone's true nature is to watch them interact with a *lesser*."

A cool evening breeze rushed over us. I pulled away from her grasp, removed my coat, and set it on her shoulders. She took it and then resumed her barnacle-hold on my arm.

"Why?" I asked. "Seems like a lot of trouble to figure out how someone will act."

"It's complicated."

"Someone tricked you in the past?"

My question struck a chord. She tensed, and her eyes hardened. The garden below bustled with life—arcanists walking the flowery paths, including the giant stone golem.

"Someone hurt me in my past," Karna finally muttered. "Years ago, when I was young and unbonded to my doppelgänger, an apprentice arcanist came to the Moonlight District and paid for my services."

"We don't need to talk about it." I motioned to the view. "We have so many other things to talk about. If this bothers you—"

"You're too polite," she said with a smile. "It's fine. You can't save me from my memories."

"That doesn't mean we need to wallow in them."

"I'm not wallowing. I'm explaining." She lifted an eyebrow. "Well, maybe I wallow. Sometimes. But right now, I just want you to know."

"I'd love to hear."

This seemed to please her more than anything else. She cuddled against me, like Nicholin in Illia's hair, and her breath came out as a contented sigh. "That arcanist who paid for my services asked me to attend a ceremony at the castle as his guest. I couldn't believe it. In my excitement, and naiveté, I thought we had made a connection. I thought he would take me away from the life on the streets and treat me like some princess in a fairy tale."

It did sound like something out of the old legends I had read. Dashing knights always whisked people away from their troubles.

Karna's gaze became distant. She stared at the garden below, unseeing. "That wasn't what happened." Her voice grew cold and curt. "It turns out he had invited me to the castle in order to share me with his friends. To treat me like a thing. To give each of them a turn and then to laugh at my discomfort. When I tried to leave, he kept me here. I couldn't escape until he had had his fun."

When the wind came again, it seemed icier than before. Unforgiving.

"Who was it?" I asked. "I'm sure we can bring him to justice if we go to the—"

"He's dead."

I glanced over, my brow furrowed.

She laughed into her hand and shook her head. "No. It wasn't me. Unfortunately." Karna sighed. "He died years ago, far from home. After I bonded with my doppelgänger, I wanted closure. Some way to get back at him."

"I can imagine."

It reminded me of Illia's need to get back at Calisto.

Karna released my arm. She rested her weight on the balcony railing. "Let me guess, you dislike the idea of revenge?"

"Well, where I grew up, we had to learn the principles of being an arcanist. There were these steps on a pillar... One of them read: *Justice. Without it, we cannot differentiate from revenge.* That step has always confused me."

"Why's that?"

"It's hard to explain." I rubbed at my neck. "What's the

difference between justice and revenge? If you found that arcanist who hurt you, wouldn't it be justice to punish him for the crime?"

Karna brushed her golden locks behind an ear. "I think so."

"My sister is dealing with a similar situation regarding an arcanist who hurt her. The more I think about it, the more I think that revenge goes beyond just punishing for a crime. Revenge is a need to cause suffering. Justice doesn't require that—it only seeks to right a wrong."

I stared out at the garden, wondering where Illia was.

After a deep breath, I continued, "So, *yes*. I dislike revenge, even though I understand the need for it. I just think it takes a high toll on both parties."

Karna stood straight. "Takes a toll?"

"My sister thinks of nothing but *plans* and *strategies* to get back at the man who hurt her. It's eating her from the inside."

Karna laughed, though it sounded cynical. When she turned to me, it was with a forced smile. "Your sister and I have a lot in common. I, too, have concocted a plan to live out my sweetest revenge fantasies."

"I thought you said that arcanist was dead?"

"He is." She moved back to my arm, her smile transforming into something more playful. "But I figured I could relive the moment—but this time, I'd do all the things I couldn't do as a normal mortal. My plan was to pose as a whore in the Moonlight District, use my magic to attract an apprentice arcanist, get him to invite me to the gala, and then—when he inevitably showed his true colors—I would make him regret every decision in his pompous, self-absorbed life."

She had a little too much gleeful delight in her voice for me to be comfortable. And then it all hit me.

With a nervous chuckle, I said, "Wait. Am *I* the apprentice arcanist in this plan?"

"You did attend my show." She lifted an eyebrow. Her movements, even that simple one, were somehow alluring. "And you obviously enjoyed it. It was easy to get you alone, and young men like you tend to take a simple payment of flesh for almost anything."

"You... thought I was pompous and self-absorbed?"

"All arcanists are," Karna stated. She waved her hands to the servants running around the garden, each with a tray and towel for the many guests. "Don't you see the way they treat the magicless? They belittle and demean. Because they can get away with it. Be honest. Deep down, you've done the same."

Now that she had mentioned it, I did remember numerous instances in which mortals seemed afraid of my wrath. They flinched like an abused puppy whenever I turned in their direction. I never treated any of them poorly, though.

Karna pulled my coat tight over her bare shoulders. "Let's forget all this terrible talk. You're right. I wallow. I should let it go. Revenge is bad. How about we have some fun instead? I'd much rather spend my time in your arms."

It seemed odd, but I wasn't going to force her to talk about grave issues that upset her.

She held onto my elbow, and for a long silent moment, we stood on the balcony and just enjoyed the view. I mulled over Karna's story, wondering if there was any way to right the wrongs against her. Ultimately, it wasn't that simple. I didn't have an easy solution, and I couldn't even imagine what Gravekeeper William would do in this situation.

Karna ran her hand up my chest, drawing my attention. With a playful smile, she turned me around, my back to the railing, and then wrapped her arms around my neck.

I held her, and she stood on the tips of her toes to press her lips against mine. She tasted sweet. I closed my eyes and brought my hand up to cup her cheek, enjoying the warmth of her soft kiss.

Karna pulled away, but remained close enough that her breath washed over my chin. "You're so polite," she whispered. "Of course you are." She tugged at my shirt, untucking it from my trousers. A mischievous smile crept at the corner of her lips as she stared up at me through her eyelashes. "You don't have to pretend with me. I know what you want."

She unfastened my belt and then started with the buttons of my shirt.

"I, um," I said, struggling to form a coherent sentence. I grabbed her arms, stopping her from undressing me further.

"Don't worry," she said. "We can go back into the castle if you're worried someone will see us."

"But—"

"Think of this as a reward." She leaned forward and nibbled my lower lip.

"It's not—" after a quick exhale, I lined up my thoughts, "—it's not that I don't want this. You're gorgeous in every way. It's just important to me that you know that this isn't necessary. I didn't bring you to the gala expecting anything."

A piece of me figured she needed to hear it. Sure, if she wanted to continue, I wouldn't stop this, but I didn't want her to have any regrets. I didn't need a reward—but I suspected she needed the kindness.

Karna took a sharp step backward, putting distance

between us. When the wind returned, she threw off my coat and covered her face with a hand. "Stop." She clenched her jaw, her shoulders shaking. "Dammit, just *stop*."

I glanced around, confused. "Stop... what?"

"This job would've been *so easy* if you had been anyone else." With a quick movement, she brushed her knuckles against my cheek.

In the next instant, the grip on my spine returned, but it wasn't gentle. It felt like barbs latching into the bones, forcibly taking control. Unlike before, where I had to accept the magic, this was an assault. I tried to fight it, and that resulted in a twitching of my muscles, but I couldn't wrest myself from her magical grasp.

Karna paced back and forth, raking her fingers through her hair. "I came here to steal something," she said, her voice now harsh and direct. No games—just her frustration. "I was going to pin the crime on the pompous arcanist who took me as a date. That was my revenge plan. I'd have my fun and get paid doing it. Then I'd leave you high and dry, the perfect scapegoat."

My chest tightened. In my gut, I knew what she had come for. I wanted to ask her about the runestones, but I couldn't.

The magic on her whole body rippled and shifted. Her blonde hair darkened to auburn and then fell away, leaving it shorter than before. Her complexion shifted to sun-kissed, and I swear she stood a couple inches higher.

Karna growled out a sigh. "Now look what you've done. You ruined my fantasy with your *naïve chivalry*. It's no fun to wreck *your* life. I wanted that one delicious moment where I tore a guy down and watched the queen feed him to her dragon." She patted her hip with a balled fist. "Every word you said, every choice you made—I thought I could get you to show your disgusting side, but it never came."

I couldn't move. Was Luthair watching this? He had to be. Did he just think I was listening to her? That was a possibility, but I wished he would say something. Then he would know.

Karna swished back her copper hair, her face more angular than it had been before. After a round of calming breaths, she stared up into the starry sky. "Now I don't even want to go through with this. If I pinned the theft on you, it'd actually bother me." She shot me a glower. "You should feel honored. I wouldn't say that about many people."

Her doppelgänger manipulation held me in place. I couldn't respond, but I continued to resist her power, mentally struggling to regain control. When she waved her hand, my body took two steps away.

In a bold display of athletics, Karna front-flipped onto the railing and then stood on her tip-toes, poised like a jungle cat, her wiry muscles more pronounced than they had been before.

"There's nothing left for me here," she muttered, her voice half-lost in the wind. "I'll never find someone in time to blame this on, and you've killed my enthusiasm." Karna laughed—perhaps the first earnest display of emotion. "I should thank you, though. I didn't think I would find someone like you at the gala. Life is full of surprises."

I jerked my arm to the side, almost free of her magic.

"I don't know if we'll meet again," she said as she inched to the edge. "But I have a feeling that our paths will cross—if you can handle more of me."

Then, in yet another display of physical prowess, Karna leapt off the balcony. She landed on the garden walkway and rolled to blunt the fall. After a graceful somersault, she got back to her feet and continued walking as though the twenty-foot drop had been nothing.

It wasn't until after she had left my sight that her doppelgänger magic released me. I jerked forward, irritated her sorcery had such power. But now I knew how it worked. She had to touch me. In the future, I wouldn't make the same mistake.

A piece of me wondered if I should chase after her. I believed her, though. She wasn't going through with her job. Which meant I needed to inform Zelfree of what had transpired. I never suspected the enemy would outsource the theft to someone else. Or perhaps to multiple people.

"You find yourself in more *interesting* situations than Mathis ever did," Luthair said from the shadows.

"Did you see what she just did?" I asked.

"She leapt off the balcony, my arcanist."

Ah. So Luthair didn't know I had been stuck in a web of control.

Curse the abyssal hells. I would have to discuss this with Zelfree as well.

"Luthair, help me find Master Zelfree. We need to inform him of what happened."

30

THIEVES

Luthair slithered through the shadows, darting into the hall ahead of me.

I took a moment to re-button my shirt and secure my belt, still flustered from my encounter with Karna. It had taken such a bizarre direction I didn't even know how I would describe it to Zelfree. Hopefully, he would just understand.

I walked out of the balcony room, into the second-story hallway, and then headed to the nullstone statue staircase. Arcanists traveled up and down the steps, all of them discussing the queen. From what I gleaned, the women didn't like her dress, but most of the men enjoyed it. I couldn't do anything with that information, so I pushed it from my mind as I entered the main hall.

The instant I got into the ballroom, individuals pointed and muttered. I avoided eye contact and stuck to the walls. To my surprise, tables of food and drink had been set up in the corners, and I had to walk my way around them to get anywhere.

"Volke."

I turned toward the sound of my name and spotted Zaxis by a table covered with platters of lamb chops. Bowls of colorful sauces surrounded each tray, but Zaxis had pushed them aside and dragged a whole pile of meat closer to him. With the utmost care, he plucked the lamb from the tray and stacked it onto a personal plate. Only then did he eat it with a delicate silver fork, like he was a fancy lord slowly consuming the rations for an entire army. The castle servant watched from the other side of the table, his eyebrows high.

"I'm so glad I found you," I said as I walked over to Zaxis.

He gave me the once-over and sneered. "What happened?"

With my face hot, I fixed the mix-matched buttons of my shirt and tucked it below the waist of my trousers.

"Oh, does this have to do with that trull you brought to the gala?" Zaxis chuckled. "Rather gauche to get so frisky in a public place. You should learn from Illia and me. We keep it classy."

"I don't want hear about you and Illia," I growled. "Have you seen Master Zelfree?"

"Hmm?"

Zaxis skewered another lamb chunk and tore it off the fork with his teeth.

He wore an outfit strikingly similar to mine, but he also wore a red scarf around his neck—one with phoenixes stitched into the design.

"Yeah," Zaxis said. "I did see him. He was talking to those arcanists." Then he motioned with a jerk of his head.

I followed his gaze to a group of four men standing near a table of wine and liquor. I had to stop myself from laughing. None of them were wearing shirts. They wore trousers and thick boots, but that was it. Their chests, arms, and sometimes even their stomachs, were covered in scars, however. Animal wounds. Claws, teeth... So many.

Each of them had the same arcanist mark—a multi-headed hydra. And each of them had tightly curled hair, cinnamon in color.

"Are those men from Hexa's hometown?" I asked.

Zaxis nodded. "That's right. From the canyon city, Regal Heights." He pointed. "Look there. Hexa's lookin' good, right?"

Sure enough, Hexa walked over to the group of shirtless men. They greeted her with loud welcomes and tight embraces.

She didn't wear a dress. She, too, wore black trousers and thick boots, but instead of forsaking her shirt, she wore a simple top that covered her front and wrapped around her neck. It exposed her back, which showcased the scars on her shoulder blades. With no sleeves, her marred arms were also on full display.

I hadn't realized until then, but Hexa was quite defined.

"They're a bunch of weird ones," Zaxis muttered. He took another bite of lamb chop. "They think their scars are *interesting* and *popular*."

"You're one to talk. Nice scarf."

Zaxis glared. "Heh. You're such an island bumpkin. Scarves are all the rage in Thronehold. It's called *fashion*." He fluffed the garment, preening himself.

I glanced around the room and found more than eighty percent of the gala attendees wore scarves. I didn't care. I wasn't here to impress people. I shook my head and returned my attention to the shirtless arcanists from Regal Heights. I didn't see Zelfree anywhere near them.

Zaxis stepped closer to me and lowered his voice. "Hey. I might be imagining things, but I suspect Master Zelfree prefers the lords over the ladies." He jabbed me with his elbow and then motioned to the shirtless men a second time.

"Yeah," I said as I scanned the crowd. "He does."

"You knew?" Zaxis swallowed another mouthful and then piled more meat onto his personal plate. "Tsk. First Adelgis's problem and now this. Why do you know everything about everyone?"

"It's a mystery," I sarcastically muttered. Zaxis had tried to rip the leech out of Adelgis's body the moment he discovered the parasite. How was he confused about his untrustworthy reputation?

"I bet you that Master Zelfree has a thing for bookish librarians," Zaxis said.

"Redheads, actually."

Zaxis stopped mid-bite. He slowly brought a hand up and ran it through his own fiery hair, like all the pieces of the puzzle were falling into place. He stared at the floor, no more words.

"I have to go." With a sigh, I left him with the lamb platters. Zelfree had to be somewhere in the castle, and my time was better spent searching.

Thankfully, Luthair slithered back to my feet, his shadow unnoticed by most.

"My arcanist," he said. "I found Master Zelfree."

"Take me to him."

He zipped through the darkness, and I chased after. We travelled across the ballroom and then out into the moonlit garden. From above, the garden appeared neat and immaculate in organization. From within, it had a mystic sense of wonder. Flowers bloomed on bushes, the stone walkways had a smooth polish that shimmered under lantern light, and the fountains created a constant trickle of water that mixed with the soft music wafting from the castle.

Zelfree stood in the shadows of a large hedge, his back to the leaves, his black clothes melting into the environment. His arcanist star wasn't blank. A seashell was behind the seven-points—he was an ethereal whelk arcanist for the time being.

"Master Zelfree," I said as I rushed to his side.

With a glower, he leaned further into the darkness. "Don't shout my name."

"Is something wrong? Are you hiding from someone?"

"Not a lot of people trust me," he said. "It's best if I remain inconspicuous."

"Uh, okay. Fine. Listen, I have so much to tell you." I shifted my weight from one foot to the other, grappling with my memories, trying to craft a narrative that made sense. "I was in the Moonlight District and I met this dancer. She took my guild pendant." I closed my eyes and cursed under my breath. "*She still has my pendant.* Never mind. I—"

Zelfree placed a hand on my shoulder, and I stopped my stammering.

"I can read thoughts," he drawled. "I got it already."

"The... the whole story?"

"Yes."

"Even the part where—"

"Where she had you under her control, but you somehow *guilted her* into not acting? Yes." He pulled his hand away and sighed. "Don't look so embarrassed. I've also found myself in bizarre situations when trying to get into someone's bed. It happens to the best of us."

I ran a hand through my hair, digging my nails in my scalp. Zelfree was worse than Adelgis when it came to *mind reading*. Would I ever have any privacy? Luthair followed me around like a second shadow. Fain followed me like a third. Now *this*.

Fighting back my momentary embarrassment, I took a deep breath.

"Karna isn't the only one here with ill intentions." Zelfree crossed his arms. He didn't look dressed for the event—just his normal outfit, like this was a ship. "I've caught a handful of people thinking about the layout of the castle. Some even mapped the hallways."

"Really?"

"They're probably thieves, but I never expected something so organized."

A pair of unicorn arcanists rode by on their eldrin, their ceremonial armor still functional, even if it was ornate and beautiful. They had plumes of feathers in their helmets, and they gave us nods as they went by.

I shoved my hands in my pockets and spoke only after they were out of earshot. "What're we going to do?"

"We'll inform Guildmaster Eventide, and hopefully she'll approve a more drastic means for acquiring the runestones."

"If there are numerous thieves, does that mean word of the world—er, *the snake*—has gotten out?"

"None of them were thinking about the snake," Zelfree said. "If I had to guess, I'd say someone hired them to do a job, and that's it. Most people would probably assume the runestones sell for a decent amount of coin, so I doubt thieves would ask many questions."

"At what point will we have to inform the queen?" I whispered.

Zelfree shot me a glare. "Never. I already told you. She's just as bad. Maybe worse."

Restless energy coursed through my system. Why wasn't

Zelfree moving? Why even wait here? We should tell Guild-master Eventide as soon as possible.

He must've heard the panic in my thoughts, because he shot me a glare. "Calm down or else you'll make us look suspicious."

I motioned to the hundreds of people in the ballroom, all of whom were preoccupied with the frivolity of the gala. "I don't think anyone will notice."

"Look above you, but keep it brief."

I glanced over my shoulder and panned my gaze up the wall of the castle. Pegasi and their riders waited on some of the balconies, but that wasn't as intimidating as Knight Captain Rendell. He stood on the wall overlooking the garden, his armor somehow even more decorative than the others. Slung across his back, and held in place with a sash, was his famous weapon—Silent Sorrow. It was a spear made out of a unicorn spine, with the tip fashioned out of the same unicorn's horn.

And Knight Captain Rendell stared down at us, his gaze focused. But why?

"I said *keep it brief*," Zelfree growled through clenched teeth. "Act natural. Strike up a conversation."

I returned my attention to Zelfree, uncertain of what to say. "Uh," I began. "How's your evening going?"

"Poorly."

"Has anyone asked you to dance?"

He narrowed his eyes into a half-lidded, sardonic glare. "I've been asked to dance by not one, not two, but *zero* people."

"Well, er, *you* could ask someone."

"The men I fancy fall into one of two categories. Either they don't want anything to do with me or I probably shouldn't do anything with them. The sooner I resign myself to dying alone, the better."

"I'm sorry—did you want this conversation to feel natural or suicidal? You're making it difficult to tell." I probably shouldn't have been as sarcastic, but Zelfree made it easy.

"Maybe you should mind your own damn business and stop asking about my personal affairs."

Giggling from within the hedge drew our attention. At first, I feared someone had overheard us, but then I recognized the voice as Traces.

"Sometimes you're so funny, my arcanist," she said, her voice light and playful. "You could've spent more time with the hydra arcanists. Especially the tall one. His voice was so husky, it could pull a sleigh."

"Curse the abyssal hells," Zelfree muttered as he dragged a hand down his flushed face.

While I got a quiet chuckle out of their exchange, it occurred to me that Traces and Zelfree acted remarkably different. For a moment, I thought there had to be some mistake. Eldrin grew to be more like their arcanists. But then I remembered that Zelfree was once a different man. Before he became so disgruntled, he was a swashbuckler. Perhaps Traces represented him before he turned jaded and cynical. It made me wonder what it was like to interact with him a few decades ago.

A thunderous roar pierced the night. I covered my ears as the raucous sound grew louder and louder. The rumble of the cry shook the castle, and the musicians ceased their playing.

It was the queen's sovereign dragon, Vercingetorix. There was no doubt in my mind.

Once the roar ended, I lowered my hands and turned to

Zelfree. He rubbed at his forehead, and I noticed his arcanist mark had become a blank star once again.

Traces tumbled out of the bushes, not as an ethereal whelk, but as a cat. She shook off the leaves and then arched her back, her sleek, gray fur standing on end.

"What's going on?" I asked.

Zelfree glared up at the wall with the knight captain. "It's the queen. She's activated the nullstone in the castle. I can't use my magic."

Sure enough, when I attempted to shadow-step away, nothing happened. The commotion from the ballroom told me that the arcanists inside were likely having similar trouble. The Knights Draconic and the Sky Legionnaires converged on the ballroom. Pegasi swooped down from the skies, and unicorns leapt over the hedges in one graceful bound. They blocked the exits and shouted instructions.

"Remain calm," one unicorn arcanist said. "A thief has been caught inside the castle. There is no need to be alarmed, but the queen has taken defensive measures until she's certain all crooks have been apprehended."

Another rumble, but this time I almost lost my balance.

Vercingetorix launched himself from the queen's balcony, his gigantic black-and-red body dominating the sky. When he flapped his wings, wind rushed over the garden, tearing up the flowers and shredding some of the shrubs. I had to keep my eyes shut until the massive beast cleared the castle walls.

I pointed. "Where's he going?"

"I suspect he'll search the perimeter from the skies."

A pair of unicorn arcanists rode to us on their eldrin, the cloven hooves of the unicorns clacking on the stone walkways. They slowed and then motioned us to the ballroom.

"I'm sorry, honored guests," one knight said. "But we'd

appreciate if you gathered inside until the queen is satisfied with the search. Then you'll be allowed to leave."

I already knew Queen Velleta used her power without restraint, but this was yet another example. She wasn't interested in anyone else. If she wanted to kill mystical creatures because she thought they were dangerous, she would. If she wanted to hunt mystical creatures for their body parts, she would. And if she thought there were villains in a group of innocent people, then she would just hold them all captive until she was satisfied.

And I doubted I had seen the worst of it. She had the attitude of a tyrant.

Zelfree and I complied with the knights. He leaned down and picked up Traces, and then we walked into the ballroom. Luthair didn't emerge from the shadows, but I imagined that if he did, he wouldn't be able to return to the darkness until the anti-magic aura was shut off.

Once inside, I cursed under my breath.

I hadn't seen Lyvia. I hadn't even searched for her.

On the other hand, it seemed like she wouldn't be in the ballroom or party areas. Only individuals participating in the tournament were here, so perhaps I had to search for her once I made it into the coliseum.

The nullstone remained active.

While the musicians resumed with their music, it was clear the arcanist guests weren't pleased. The search for thieves consumed every knight and legionnaire, and it was obvious the queen wouldn't tolerate failure. Everyone attending the gala was subject to a handful of questions, and the search didn't end until an entire hour had passed.

I never saw the thieves. All I knew was there had been a man found near the throne room. The other arcanists debated about the purpose of the intrusion.

"Who was it?" I asked Zelfree.

"I don't know."

"Isn't this a good sign, though? The queen has the rune-stones well protected."

"A doppelgänger arcanist probably could've taken the runestones and pinned the crime on someone else. They're slippery. Conniving."

"Couldn't you find Karna in a crowd?" I asked. "I thought mimic arcanists could sense the magical capabilities of others."

Zelfree smirked. "I can—so long as they don't have abilities to obfuscate their presence. Doppelgängers are known for their skills at suppressing their magical auras. I can't sense them."

"But doppelgänger magic doesn't work in nullstone areas, right?"

"Right. Only dragons are immune to the anti-magic effects."

What if our enemy had dragons? They were among the rarest of mystical creatures, so it wasn't likely, but I still considered the possibility. We needed to get the runestones as fast as possible, before a thief got lucky, but what could *I* do about the situation?

Once the Knights Draconic and Sky Legionnaires concluded their investigation, the terrible anti-magic aura lifted. The castle returned to normal, but the majority of the attendees decided it was time to leave.

Without ethereal whelk magic, Zelfree couldn't finish his plan, so I wasn't surprised to see him among the arcanists funneling toward the front door. I stayed close to him—now that the castle was on high alert, I doubted anyone would get their hands on the runestones.

"How was Adelgis when you went to see him?" I asked Zelfree as we made our way to the front gates.

"Worse than before."

Traces lowered her ears. "He didn't talk much."

The news didn't sit well with me. What could I do to help him? Gillie couldn't seem to think of anything, but I was certain Adelgis's father would have a solution. He had left the city, however.

We reached the castle walls, awash in a sea of people. Through the bodies, I spotted a glimpse of brilliant white and fiery red. I stared for a long moment, squinting through the crowd. Atty walked through a group and emerged wearing the eye-catching colors. Her simple ivory dress glowed in the moonlight, and the phoenix feathers sewn onto her shoulders gave her a regal appearance.

"Good evening, Volke," she said as she approached.

I bowed my head. "Hello."

"Can you believe there were thieves in the castle?"

"We'll have to stay alert."

Atty nodded, her eyes focused and serious. When she glanced around, however, visible confusion formed in her expression.

"Where is your companion for the evening?" she asked.

"She, uh, jumped off a balcony and left a while ago." I stifled a laugh, knowing it sounded absurd. "It's been a weird evening."

Atty lifted both eyebrows and smiled, like she hadn't expected anything close to my explanation. "I guess your life won't make for an interesting legend unless you have some peculiar events." Her cheeks shifted to a shade of pink as she held out a hand. "If you don't have anyone to accompany you back to *Maison Arcana*, I'd love to share a carriage."

I turned around, prepared to tell Zelfree I would see him

at the inn, but he was already gone. "I'd like that," I said as I returned my attention to her. Then I offered an arm. "Did you have a pleasant evening?"

"It was dull, to tell the truth. I was searching for you most of the evening, and after the nullstone affected the castle, I stood in crowds of strangers, most of which wanted me to attend the tournament with them."

She had been searching for me the entire gala?

"You're rather striking tonight," I said. Once we left the castle grounds, I breathed a bit easier. "Are those Titania's feathers?"

Atty touched the crimson feathers on her shoulders. They fluttered with the wind, shimmering with inner magic. "Titania loses them on a regular basis. Apparently, they can be used in trinket creation, so I've been saving them. I didn't think having a few on my dress would harm them, though."

"Phoenix colors suit you."

We stepped to the curb and waited for a lamplighter trolley. Atty glanced at me with a playful grin. "I've never heard you compliment anyone so much."

"It's not often I interact with someone as striking as you."

She caught her breath, the pink shifting to a dark shade. For a brief moment, she couldn't seem to bring herself to look at me directly.

Karna was radiant, but now that I had time to reflect, her attractiveness was likely enhanced through magic. Atty, on the other hand, was just... effortless. Her dress wasn't anything intricate, and her blonde hair had been brushed to one side—she just exuded femininity and grace. Even her grip on my arm was soft. Gentle.

The will-o-wisp arcanist helped his eldrin into the engine before taking his seat at the wheel. We started up and headed out of the castle with the mass exodus of carriages and trolleys.

"The tournament starts tomorrow," Atty muttered as she scooted closer to me on the bench. "Are you nervous?"

"I haven't thought about it much." Not with the problem of the world serpent still at hand.

"I'll be rooting for you to win."

"Thank you."

Despite the open trolley and blustery weather, Atty didn't shiver. Like Zaxis, she seemed to have an inner fire that kept her warm no matter the weather.

"You should go all the way to the end," she said. "And beat Zaxis."

"Him specifically?"

She exhaled, her breath visible in the chilly air. "I know he's just saying things to impress Illia, but he claims he can easily best you in any match of skill."

"That doesn't surprise me."

"The funny thing is—it irritates Illia." Atty laughed as she said, "And it irritates me as well. Our whole life, Zaxis has talked a great deal. I think you could beat him."

"I see." I forced a smile. "Well, I'll try my damnedest to get to the end."

For some reason, Zaxis wouldn't rest until this question was answered. As long as the tournament didn't interfere with our main objective, I looked forward to proving him wrong. I hadn't been the one to make things contentious between us, after all. He had brought this on himself.

31

TOURNAMENT ROUND ONE

On the day of the tournament, the whole city bustled with life.

At dawn, the birds awoke with a song in their throat and an urge to sit on every windowsill. The horses clacked down the cobblestone roads at hasty speeds, each merchant and money changer out to get everything they would need for the day.

The first rounds of each division would take place over the next three days. It was single round elimination, so once an arcanist lost, that was the end of their tournament glory. I didn't know my opponents, and we wouldn't have that information until we reached the coliseum. Prepping for the worst, I tucked Theasin's book into my satchel. Master Zelfree said we should understand our opponent's capabilities, and I hoped to gain a better understanding by studying their eldrin before the match.

Hours before we were set to arrive at the coliseum, I took a trolley to Skarn University. Adelgis was still under the weather and asleep. With no ability to communicate with him, I stayed only to speak with Gillie before heading out on foot. She seemed optimistic, but she was *always* that way.

The Sovereign Dragon Tournament took place at the Thronehold Coliseum, a massive amphitheater capable of seating 24,000 spectators. The giant arena was meant for arcanists with gargantuan eldrin. Apparently, decades ago, they had a match between a leviathan arcanist and a behemoth arcanist—their combat shook the city like an earthquake.

I arrived separate from everyone else, due to visiting Adelgis, and it took me a while to navigate the thousands of people near the coliseum gates. The battles started in a couple hours, but everyone wanted the best seat. People shoved and elbowed anyone who got close, even me. When I realized the pandemonium would yield no civility, I shadow-stepped under everyone and emerged near the contestant door.

Illia and Nicholin stood in the shadows of the massive coliseum, waiting for me. I recognized Illia due to her eyepatch and buccaneer coat. Most citizens of Thronehold didn't have the long coats used in sea travel. They wore no coat or short coats for gentlemen. It was an easy way to sift out people from the islands.

"There you are," Nicholin said as I drew near. "I was afraid you might be late."

I shook my head. "I wouldn't miss this."

"Right? Just look at this place!" He waved his little ferret arms around, trying to motion to the entire structure.

The outer façade, made of sturdy sandstone, stood nearly 70 feet high. Sky towers were posted around the coliseum, every 100 feet, creating landing areas for the Sky Legionnaires. At the far end of the Thronehold Coliseum was a special platform—one large enough to accommodate the weight and size of a fully grown sovereign dragon.

I followed Illia into the coliseum, my breath held. I had read books about coliseums—about their unique design and structure—but nothing could've prepared me for standing inside of one. There were 34 tiers of terraces for the crowd, and the denizens of Thronehold filled the benches as fast as possible.

Red dirt made up the majority of the coliseum floor, bright enough to rival the hue of a rose. A stone arena was in the dead center of the dirt field. It was 50 feet by 50 feet— a perfect square dueling stage for everyone to see.

A gargoyle with granite-colored skin waited near the stone arena. It stood taller than most men, with leathery bat wings, a pair of goat horns, and bright black eyes.

He wore a necklace with the Argo Empire's symbol, and I figured he had to belong to an arcanist in service of the queen. The gargoyle was likely the one in charge of re-forming the arena if it got busted during the fighting. Gargoyles could manipulate stone, after all. I always knew that, but I learned it the terrifying way when I fought a plague-ridden gargoyle on Calisto's ship.

Which was why I didn't care for gargoyles anymore.

I glanced around and noticed a myriad of mystical crea-tures and arcanists in employ of the empire. Three caladrius flew over the combat area. They were the healers should anything go wrong, their elegant white feathers hard to miss. Their arcanists stood by the contestant gates.

And I noticed half a dozen engkanto on the walls. They were elves with powerful telekinesis—the kind to create invisible barriers. They sat near the stands looking like gorgeous humans, their skin a shiny gold, their silver hair fluttering in the wind. I figured they were responsible for protecting the crowd from stray magics. Their arcanists, most of which appeared just as stunning, sat in the first row of the audience, a second safety net should their eldrin not maintain their barriers.

Illia pulled me toward the contestant pits. Each division had their own area for the participants—one had the bracket schedule etched into the wall for all to see. The halls of the coliseum, shaped from sandstone bricks and made into sturdy archways, felt small when there were so many mystical creatures and arcanists.

The marble stone golem had to crouch to get anywhere, and those with even larger eldrin had to walk around the outside and enter through the "sky pathways" meant for pegasi or larger birds.

A rank odor hung over the coliseum, a fog of ominous scents. Blood, sweat, copper, and dust—it wasn't as bad as the blast furnaces in the city, but I knew it would cling to my clothing and stay with me for a week.

Nicholin leapt from Illia's shoulder and landed on the ground with a huff. He jumped at the shadows around my feet, swatting at Luthair's incorporeal form with the energy of a cat.

"I haven't seen you in a while," Nicholin said. "You must tell me what you saw at the gala. Did Volke sweep a lady off her feet?"

"A man does not kiss and tell," Luthair replied, his gruff voice almost monotone.

"But you're not a man, are you? You're sentient clothing."

Luthair growled from the darkness.

"Leave him alone," Illia commanded. "They need to focus."

With a poof and some sparkles, Nicholin reappeared on Illia's shoulder. He rubbed at his face, squeaked a few times, and then swished his tail. "But I thought you said—"

"Now isn't the time for that."

I jogged to match Illia's pace.

"Have you seen the bracket?" I asked.

She nodded. "There are thirty-two apprentice arcanists, one hundred and twenty-eight journeymen, sixteen masters, and eight elite arcanists participating in the tournament. The brackets are rather large and involved, and some of the pairings were determined based on the size of eldrin—at least for the first few matches."

"Who are Zaxis and I paired against?"

I held my breath after asking, fearing the answer. What if we were matched against Illia and Hexa? I didn't want to face them in the opening match—or ever—but the first round would be the worst possible outcome.

"You get to fight those two dullards from the Huntsman Guild," she said. "You know the pair. The dog arcanists."

I exhaled in relief, thanking whatever lucky spirits watched over the tournament. Fighting them was a blessing. They deserved my shadow and Zaxis's fire.

"Which division fights first?" I asked.

"The apprentices."

The information settled into my stomach like a rock. The situation hadn't seemed real until this moment. We would fight in front of thousands for glory and prizes. Arcanists from all around the world—staring, judging.

I shook the feelings aside, determined not to get rattled. This wouldn't be worse than fighting Ruma. It wouldn't be worse than confronting Calisto. I could handle it.

Illia and I entered the apprentice pit at the same time, but there wasn't much space to accommodate us. Although only thirty-two were participating in the apprentice division, that also meant thirty-two eldrin and a handful of master arcanists were here in the pit. The crowd of bodies and giant creatures made it difficult to move. The room was half underground, with tiny slits near the ceiling for ventilation. I squeezed past the other contestants and headed toward the brackets etched into the far stone wall. It labeled us by our guild and eldrin.

The moment I caught sight of the names, I locked up.

Zaxis and I had the first match. And just as Illia had said, we were up against Crevis and Dart. I scanned the rest of the contestants, wondering if I would recognize anyone else. Sure enough, I found another pair that piqued my interest.

Niro Venrover the Stoor Worm Arcanist – No Guild Affiliation
Dramm Totmor the Stone Golem Arcanist – Enchanters Guild

Adelgis's brother had paired himself with a stone golem arcanist. I almost couldn't believe he was participating.

"Is that the same golem we saw at the gala?" I asked.

Illia nodded. "I met Dramm and his eldrin, Borod." She rubbed at her eyepatch, her brow furrowed. "They're... big. Both of them."

"I thought they would be dumb," Nicholin interjected. "I don't know why. Rocks just seem dumb, I guess. But they weren't like that. I actually kind of like them."

That stone golem at the gala had been rather huge. I knew those creatures grew to legendary sizes, but I didn't think an apprentice-level golem would be roughly the shape and weight of a small house. What kind of tactics could I use to bring one down during a tournament match?

I scanned the names one last time and spotted yet another interesting pairing.

Lucian Nellit the Knightmare Arcanist – Steel Thorn Inquisitors Guild
Nyla Gane the Manticore Arcanist – Steel Thorn Inquisitors Guild

Another knightmare arcanist? And a manticore arcanist?

I whipped my head around and surveyed the pit, half expecting the deadly manticore to jump out of the shadows and start attacking someone. I didn't see it, though. Nor did I see another knightmare.

"Do you know those two from the Steel Thorn Inquisitors Guild, Luthair?" I asked.

"No, my arcanist," he replied. "It has been close to two years since I was part of that guild."

Were they even here? It seemed foolish to miss the first day of the tournament. If they didn't show up for their match, they'd be disqualified.

"The first match will start soon," Illia said, drawing my attention. "Aren't you going to get ready?"

With a mouth of cotton, all I could do was nod.

"I'll be waiting for you afterward. Good luck, Volke."

The pit led straight to the coliseum's field, and that long hallway had rooms attached to it for fighters to use until they were called. I walked into the first one available, all while listening to the cheers and stomping of the ever-growing crowd. The rumble of excitement was the pulse of the amphitheater. It beat loud and rhythmic. It almost made it difficult to concentrate.

The rooms for fighters were small. Two benches and a rack for weapons and armor. I threw down my satchel and withdrew Theasin's book, my hands shakier than I liked. I had to concentrate. Reading about the orthrus and barghest would ease my anxiety. I flipped to those pages and examined the text.

<u>Orthrus</u>

Tier 2

Reproduction: Progeny (nesting grounds found near red cattle)

Trial of Worth: Guarding other animals

Orthrus have high endurance and need little sleep. Their loyalty is unflinching, and they are immune to all mind-effecting powers. Their magic is of physical strength and nothing more.

True Form: Bipedal and muscular, much like a minotaur. Capable of brute strength far beyond its size (obtained by arcanists who exemplify fealty)

<u>Barghest</u>

Tier 2

Reproduction: Fable (born from mutilated bodies buried on mountaintops)

Trial of Worth: Finding something lost

Barghests have an entropic touch that kills living matter. After a single bite, the wounded area succumbs to gangrene. Powerful barghests have howls that caused deafness.

True Form: A dog made out of the dead parts of other dogs, often the size of a horse, perhaps larger. Capable of foretelling the likely death of an individual by touching them (obtained by arcanists who revel in the death of lesser creatures)

· · ·

I read the information twice. Three times. Ten times. There wasn't much to memorize, but it was enough to know which of the two presented a greater risk in combat.

The pulse of the coliseum grew louder and harsher. I paced the small waiting room, listening to the exhilaration of the crowd.

Time passed, but I had no way to keep track. The room had only a tiny slit for a window. Dust swirled through the sliver of light that streamed down onto the dirt floor. Where was Zaxis? Shouldn't he be here by now?

When the door opened, I jumped. Zelfree stood in the doorframe, his expression neutral, bordering on bored. He didn't look rested, and the bags under his eyes had become a shade darker.

"Ready?" he asked.

"Why are you here?"

"I'm your master and mentor. I'm allowed to stand on the outside of the arena while you fight." He lifted an eyebrow. "Unless you don't want me there."

"N-No. You should be."

"Then let's go."

"Wait. I have a technical question."

Zelfree stared, like he couldn't even guess what I was thinking.

"What about my sword?" I asked. "It's a magical item crafted by Mathis, not me. Am I allowed to use it in the tournament?"

"There are special rules for second-bonded," Zelfree said with a dismissive wave of his hand. "I had to deal with it all when I registered you for the tournament. The sword was made with Luthair's help, so it's his trinket too. You can use it."

"Oh. Good." I placed the book back in my satchel and

exited the room into the narrow hallway.

At one end of the hall was the pit with all the other contestants. At the other end was the entrance to the coliseum field. Zelfree led me to the latter, his boots kicking up red dust as he walked. One of the Knights Draconic stood in the hall. He held out his hand and then motioned to our necks. Zelfree flashed his guild pendant, but when it came my turn, I hesitated.

I didn't have it.

The knight glared through the visor of his helmet, his teeth clenched. Did he think me an imposter?

"This is my apprentice," Zelfree stated. "Volke Savan the Knightmare Arcanist."

Seemingly satisfied with that statement, the knight allowed me to continue.

To my surprise, Zaxis waited for us near the wrought-iron gate that led to the field. It was shut, keeping us from entering, and I wondered why we bothered preparing so early.

Then the crowd settled down outside, and I lifted my head to listen. Far beyond the pit and the semi-underground of the amphitheater, I heard the showmanship of an announcer.

"The first day of the Sovereign Dragon Tournament begins!"

An eruption of cheers flooded the hallway.

"Queen Velleta welcomes you to the Thronehold Coliseum! She asks that you not only enjoy the bouts between the competitors, but that you bear witness to the many Trials of Worth that will take place during this historic event."

If the announcer took even a second to catch his breath, the audience filled the gap with stomping and clapping.

"Newborn unicorns and pegasi will bond with brave men and women, becoming the next generation of knights and legionnaires!"

The applause for that statement rivaled all others.

"And most importantly, we will see who proves themselves worthy of bonding with a sovereign dragon. The fights of this tournament are meant to honor the dragon's duel, and Queen Velleta extends her gratitude to all the competitors for joining us here today."

The announcements and cheering swirled in my head. There were a lot of fights to get through, especially when it came to the journeyman division. How much longer would they make us wait to fight one another?

While the announcer continued to explain the significance of the event, Zaxis grabbed my upper arm and squeezed.

"Did you hear me?" he hissed.

I shook my head. He had been talking to me?

"Listen." Zaxis stepped close. "We're just a few minutes away from the fight."

His words struggled to pierce through the cacophony of the crowd, but I heard them regardless.

"You hesitate too much," he continued. "But I've seen you at your best. When we were confronted by Calisto on the *Third Abyss*, you were the first to step forward and fight him. Do you remember that?"

I nodded. I could never forget.

Zaxis glared at me, his green eyes alight with something I couldn't describe. He shook my arm. "I was afraid, *but you confronted him*. You didn't show a sign of hesitation—just conviction to end the man. Bring that same mentality to these fights and we'll win. Got it?"

Again, I nodded. I just had to picture our opponents like I pictured Calisto. Failure wasn't an option.

The announcer's voice drew me out of my thoughts. "Our opening match has apprentices from the Frith Guild—Volke Savan the Knightmare Arcanist, and Zaxis Ren the Phoenix Arcanist! They're facing off against members of the Huntsman Guild—Crevis Lennox the Orthrus Arcanist, and Dart Fargo the Barghest Arcanist!"

The gates to the coliseum field lifted upward, allowing us to enter. Zelfree ushered us through the archway and up a short set of stairs. When we emerged from the fighter pits, it was to a wall of cheering and a hail of partially eaten food. The thousands of spectators couldn't contain their jubilation.

We walked along a thin stone walkway all the way to the arena. My blood ran cold, and I took a moment to take everything in.

Vercingetorix, the massive sovereign dragon, sat behind the queen and her family. Queen Velleta watched from her gigantic, cushioned throne as we walked to one side of the stone platform.

Both Evianna and Lyvia sat near her on smaller cushioned seats. They wore formal gowns, and servants held up umbrellas to shield them from the harsh afternoon sun.

To my curiosity, another person sat with them. A man. He had the same purplish-white hair, and he wore the uniform of an officer in the knights. Was he Evianna's and Lyvia's brother? He looked my age, perhaps a bit older. That had to be the explanation.

Zaxis nudged me and pointed toward Vercingetorix. "Look there. By his claw."

A hatchling sovereign dragon rested under the protection of the deadly claws. It poked its head up to observe the tournament, but it didn't move much after that. Even as a newborn, the beast probably weighed more than an elephant. Its large eyes and chubby features marked it as young, however.

On the opposite side of the coliseum, sitting in the stand closest to the arena, and set apart from the citizens, was Knight Captain Rendell. He watched from his palatial seat, shaded by the castle attendants.

I hadn't noticed Crevis and Dart entering the field. When I turned my attention back to the stone arena, they stood on the opposite side with their eldrin. They both wore fitted leather armor, and each carried a short sword and pistol.

Zaxis sported studded leather armor, and it took me a moment to realize he carried fat pouches at his belt and already had his metal knuckles secured on his hands. He shot me a sideways glance. "No armor?"

"Luthair is my armor," I muttered.

"Right. Never mind."

Had he forgotten? Perhaps he was nervous, too.

Forsythe swooped down from a sky perch and landed on our side of the arena with a showman's flair. Zaxis stepped onto the arena to meet his eldrin, and the crowd cheered. When I entered, my shadow slid away, and Luthair emerged from the darkness. That elicited audible gasps and rounds of stomping.

Dart and Crevis entered the arena with their dogs. More applause. More noise.

"We all know the rules to the matches," the announcer shouted, his voice enhanced, no doubt with magic because I had no idea where he was or how his voice carried so far. "Five minutes are allotted. Those who fall off the stage are considered defeated. Those knocked unconscious are also considered defeated. The team with the most arcanists and eldrin still in the fight at the end of the match wins."

My heart beat so loud I almost couldn't hear the crowds.

"Are we ready?" the announcer asked, laughter at the edge of his voice. "Then let's begin!"

Vercingetorix roared, signifying the start of the match.

32

A MESSAGE

"You handle the orthrus," Zaxis commanded.

He dashed forward, not bothering to hear my reply. Forsythe shot up and leapt into flight, his body glowing with an intense heat I hadn't seen before.

I turned to Luthair. We didn't need to speak. He merged with me in the next moment, his power invigorating. Wrapped in inky plate armor, and with a cape fluttering at my back, I looked more like a true knight than even some of the Knights Draconic. With my shadow sword in one hand and the shield on my other arm, I faced Crevis and his orthrus, Grim.

The two heads of the orthrus flashed their fangs. Grim was a big dog, and when riled, his fur stood on end, poking through the thin leather armor secured to his chest and haunches.

Forsythe blasted fire from his body—flames erupted out past his feathers in a wave of extreme heat. Dart and his barghest shielded their eyes. Thousands in the crowd applauded. While his opponents were effectively blinded, Zaxis lunged through the blaze. The metal on his knuckles heated, becoming reddish-white, and when he punched the bat-like face of the barghest, he seared away a layer of flesh. The black dog tumbled to the side, his screech painful.

The cheering electrified my already restless body.

Crevis drew his sword and pointed. "Grim, drag them from the arena!" His voice, although boisterous, struggled to pierce through the excited cries.

The two-headed orthrus was strong. That was what Theasin's book said.

When Grim charged for me, both mouths wet with thick slobber, I evened my breathing and clung to the feeling I had when I faced Calisto. If I were fighting that dread pirate, he would've done the same thing—ordered his eldrin to attack and then watched for an opening to strike while the opponent was distracted. It was likely Crevis's plan as well.

I stepped into the shadows just as Grim was about to bite me with his two sets of jaws. I slipped under him and remerged in front of Crevis. I went in for a powerful over-hand swing, aiming for where his sword-side shoulder met the neck. It was a telegraphed attack, and Zelfree had easily dodged all of them during practice, so if Crevis did the same, I could force him closer to the edge and—

I struck Crevis, my blade slicing through his leather armor and cleaving into the flesh. Blood didn't gush from the wound until I slid my weapon out of his body, but when it did, the sight unnerved me for half a second.

He... hadn't dodged. Was this a part of his strategy?

Focus, Luthair reminded me.

Crevis couldn't hold his sword—he dropped it as he staggered backward, his dominant arm useless. Even through his apparent agony, he pulled his pistol from the holster with his other hand. I stepped back into the shadows and exited once I was behind him.

Grim had turned around and now rushed toward us. I held up my hand and—despite the flare of pain—flooded the arena with my terrors. I imagined not hitting Zaxis or Forsythe, and I hoped it worked, but I didn't have time to check on them. Grim collapsed to the stone mid-run, like his legs had become useless jelly.

Crevis let go of his flintlock pistol, and my whole body tensed with realization.

This was over.

I had won.

Using the shadows of the stone platform, I created tendrils that lashed out and grabbed both Crevis and his orthrus. With all my concentration, I willed the darkness to drag them away. Neither put up much of a fight—they were too busy succumbing to my nightmare-inducing magic. I hauled them off the edge, and they collapsed into the red dirt of the coliseum field.

Two bells clanged, each with a deep and powerful rumble.

A second later, another bell clanged.

I took a deep breath and glanced over. Zaxis stood over the unconscious body of Dart, his breath coming out ragged, his white-hot knuckles sizzling with blood and charred skin.

The barghest tucked its tail between its legs and leapt from the arena stage to avoid another blast of fire from Forsythe. That resulted in a fourth clang of a bell.

"And that's the match!" the announcer shouted. "Twenty-nine seconds in!"

The thunderous approval from all of Thronehold left me momentarily deafened. It didn't seem to bother Zaxis, though. He held up his arms, soaking in their applause while Dart soaked in his own blood.

The three empire caladrius swooped down from the sky and landed on the arena platform. A mist of glitter-like magic settled over the area, and with each breath, I felt stronger and more capable. The burns on Dart's face—they looked like brands—stitched themselves together at a speed most arcanists couldn't hope for. Crevis's shoulder, while still bloody from my sword strike, closed at an astonishing rate.

Although Dart had been unconscious and Crevis gravely injured, they both recovered within a matter of minutes.

Zaxis continued engaging the crowd. He bowed and waved, and several people in the rows threw flowers, copper coins, and shreds of colorful fabric. The beautiful elven engkanto allowed the junk from the crowds to bypass their telekinetic barriers.

"The winners are Volke Savan and Zaxis Ren! The Frith Guild maintains its legacy of exciting combatants!"

After a deep breath, Luthair unmerged from me. I regarded him with a quick smile before walking to the edge of the arena platform. Zelfree waited there with his arms crossed. He smiled, though, like this was an amusing outcome. The powerful cheering continued, preventing me from speaking to him. Instead, I returned his grin and jumped off the edge.

Then it hit me—I wasn't even injured during that fight. The most pain I suffered was from my own second-bonded magic. Crevis and Grim were too slow and inexperienced to even touch me on the battlefield.

I understood why Zelfree was amused.

As I headed for the apprentice pit, I turned my gaze to Princess Lyvia and met hers. Had she been staring? This was my chance. I hadn't seen her at the gala, so now I needed her to know that I wished to speak.

I knelt down and picked up a flower tossed by the crowd. "Luthair," I said. "Can you take this to Lyvia and relay a message?"

"Yes, my arcanist."

"You shouldn't be seen."

"I understand."

"Tell her I have something important I want to talk about. Tell her about the inn I'm staying at and that she can send for me at any time." Then I tossed the flower into the darkness.

Luthair took it and slithered into the shadows of the coliseum walls. He could creep along the pathways all the way to Lyvia's seat and hopefully whisper into her ear. I doubted the queen wanted me talking to either princess— this was the fastest and easiest way to get her attention.

I walked through the gates and continued toward the pit.

Everyone wanted to congratulate us. Random apprentices, their eldrin—even some of the knights—and the constant bombardment of praise and adulation wore on my patience. Not Zaxis's, though. He stood in the middle of the room, his chest puffed out, his posture straight.

"I intentionally started the match with a burst of fire," he said. "Everyone squints when there's too much heat. It hinders your vision."

"That's clever," someone said.

"I know."

Illia and Hexa shoved their way through the crowd. To my amusement, Zaxis opened his arms, and Hexa dove right in for a strong embrace. He frowned slightly and then patted her back regardless. Illia hugged me and muttered, "I knew you would win."

I returned the gesture, but I could feel Zaxis's resentment rolling off him with each breath. I let go of Illia and motioned to Hexa. She slapped my shoulder and smiled.

"Good job."

When Illia and Zaxis embraced, he took a moment to comb his fingers through her hair and whisper things in her ear. I stepped back and allowed the other contestants an opportunity to continue their congratulations.

All the other apprentice matches would take place today, but Zaxis and I weren't needed again until round two. While Zaxis clearly wanted to marinate in the praise—and Illia's arms—I wanted to escape the pit and sit in the stands until Illia and Hexa's match. I muttered my apologies and pushed myself through the crowd of arcanists. People probably considered me rude, but the overstimulation of thanking someone every other second made it difficult to think.

I entered the main corridor of the coliseum, free of the commotion, when someone called my name.

"Volke!"

He sounded familiar, and when I turned, I spotted Lyell rushing toward me. The lamp on his hip jostled around as he ran, and his will-o-wisp eldrin fluttered about like a fish caught in a storm.

"I didn't know you were here," I said.

"I had to see my brother fight," Lyell said with a giant smile. "And you two were amazing. I knew you would win—I even won a couple coins!—but I never imagined your victory to be so *thorough*." He ran both his hands through his red hair, unable to cease his grinning.

"Are you allowed back here?" I asked as I glanced

around. The knights didn't seem to mind, but I knew the coliseum attendees weren't granted access to the fighter pits.

"I work for the city, remember?" He smoothed his uniform tunic. "I help maintain the peace and order. I'm practically one of the knights."

A unicorn arcanist in the nearby hall turned our way and glowered, but he said nothing.

Lyell then leaned in close to me. "I'm also here to see the knight captain. Do you know where he is?"

"Is he expecting you?"

"No." He furrowed his brow. "But this is important. You'd help me find him, right? I don't want to leave without telling him something."

The odd turn in conversation got me curious. "What did you want to speak with him about?"

"About one of my fellow lamplighters. Apparently, he went to the Queen's Gala last night and..." Lyell looked away, his shoulders slumped. "One of the knights told our guildmaster that he was apprehended at the castle. They say he was trying to steal something."

The information got me pensive. One of the lamplighters was the thief? Why? I crossed my arms as I went over the events of the gala in my mind's eye. Zelfree had said there were dozens of other people there with ill intentions. He said they had likely been paid to do a job...

"What're you going to tell the knight captain?" I asked.

"I just wanted to tell him that Corry's a good man." Lyell shook his head. "I know, I know. You're thinking, *he's a thief.* But that's not it. He's just down on his luck. He's been paying to move his brothers and sisters to Thronehold, but that can get expensive, ya know?"

I lifted an eyebrow. "So you think he was stealing something from the castle to sell?"

"No." Lyell lowered his voice to a soft whisper. "I think someone paid him to help navigate the castle."

"What makes you think that?"

"He was getting all sorts of odd jobs from this one pub he would frequent. I figured if the knight captain knew that Corry was hurting for coins, maybe he would be lenient. I even brought letters from Corry's two little girls." Lyell reached into his pocket and withdrew two folded pieces of paper.

"Lyell," I said, my tone serious. "What pub?"

"Oh, some seedy place in the Moonlight District. It's called the *Red Pot*. Why?"

"Take me there."

"Right now?"

Illia and Hexa had the last match of the day, and after each bout, the arena was fixed by the gargoyle and his arcanist—it would be hours before they were done with their match. I had enough time to get to the Moonlight District and back. Plus, this was of the utmost importance. What if the man who hired Corry was the same man who hired people to scout out the castle? There was a high likelihood they were one and the same, which meant someone probably saw him at the *Red Pot*.

I needed to know who he was, and I couldn't risk delaying anything—the longer I waited, the more likely someone could forget a crucial detail.

"Yes," I finally said. "We should go right now."

"What about the knight captain?"

"I'll help you relay your message afterward. I promise."

After multiple hours of walking around the Moonlight

District, I knew the layout pretty well, but I never would've found the *Red Pot* without Lyell's assistance.

The pub was located at the end of a narrow snickelway—an odd alley between buildings with a long set of stairs. The door was painted red, and the picture of a cooking pot had been carved into the wood. There were no signs or indication this was a pub; I only had Lyell's word on the matter.

I opened the door and found myself melting in an aroma of cooked meats and vegetables. The stink of the city had become such a norm that anything *good* was now shocking.

The *Red Pot* was just as narrow as the walkway in, but it was deep and the bar practically stretched from one end to the other. There were only half a dozen small tables, and I suspected no more than forty people could be inside at a time. The man behind the bar—a hefty individual in his 50s—regarded Lyell and me with a cocked brow. We probably looked out of place. The three other patrons all looked in their 40s and they had smudges of soot across their pants, no doubt furnace workers.

"Corry would visit this place all the time," Lyell muttered as we made our way to the bar. "But no one else in the Lamplighters Guild likes it. The ale tastes like it's been mixed with dirty water."

I went straight for the man tending the bar. He wore a dirty apron and a sleeveless tunic underneath. Scars marked his arms from the shoulders down to the elbows. It reminded me of Hexa. Was this man born in Regal Heights? He didn't have an arcanist mark, so perhaps he failed the Trial of Worth and didn't bond with a hydra.

"Sir," I said. "May I have a moment of your time?"

He leaned forward on the wooden bar counter. "What can I do you for?"

"Do you remember a lamplighter by the name of Corry?"

The other patrons perked up at the name, but no one said anything.

"Yeah," the bartender said. "Corry frequents the place."

"Did he ever meet someone here? Someone offering to pay him?"

The man pushed away from the bar counter and shook his head. "I don't pry into people's private lives."

"This is a small pub." I motioned to our surroundings. "I'm pretty sure you can't breathe in this place without someone hearing every detail of it."

"Even if that's so, I don't think it's any of your business what Corry does on his time off. Now kindly leave my fine establishment." He turned away, his body language stiff.

"Wait, please. I'm looking for dastardly individuals. Any information you have could help me solve—"

"I said, *leave my establishment*."

This wouldn't get me anywhere. I was an outsider, and he clearly didn't trust me. But that wasn't acceptable. Too much was at stake to leave the pub without answers—and I knew the man had answers. So how would I go about convincing him?

"Luthair," I said. "To me."

The shadows at my feet shifted and swirled. A moment later, he formed up around me, wrapping me in his protective shell of darkness. I swished the cape back, amused by the gasps of the patrons. Lyell stared with wide eyes and a slight smile.

The three men at the far table stood and inched toward the corner of the room on shaky legs. The bartender turned around, his bravado gone and replaced with a sickly expression of dread.

"I—" the man began as he stepped back and bumped into the wall behind him. "Forgive me. I didn't know you were an inquisitor."

Technically, I never said I was. I just donned my knightmare, and everyone else made all the assumptions.

The Steel Thorn Inquisitors would not appreciate such trickery, Luthair said in my mind.

No harm would result from this, and I needed the information before something dire happened. I was close —I could sense it. Deals took place here that could lead me back to the person in charge. I just had to follow the trail.

"Speak," I commanded, my voice a mix of mine and Luthair's—haunting and intimidating all at once.

The bartender floundered for a moment before answering, "There was a man who spoke to Corry. He spoke to a lot of other men, too. He had coins. He paid for every task he had—no questions, though. Just take the job or don't take the job. Corry took several, but none of them sounded too shady. They were all escort and package delivery. Corry drove the trolleys anyway."

Odd. I hadn't been expecting that answer.

"What was the last job he took?" Lyell interjected.

"Something about gettin' something from King Drake Castle."

"What did this man look like?" I asked.

"I don't know. He wore a hood and sometimes things over most of his face." The bartender snapped his fingers. "And a cloak. But you could still see he was man. Tall. Broad shoulders."

"What else? Omit nothing. Even the most innocuous detail could be crucial."

For a prolonged moment, the bartender mulled over my

request. He shook his head and then shrugged. "Uh... he spoke proper."

"What?"

"Proper. It's just different. Not like what most of the men say around these parts."

"Did he have an accent?"

"No." The bartender shrugged. "He also smelled weird. Like rot. I swear, that's all I know. He never came in with an eldrin or anything, but he always had coins, so I assumed he was an arcanist. Now that I think about it, though... I never saw any magic."

"Thank you," I said as I headed to the front door. "Your assistance is appreciated."

Lyell hustled to follow me out, but I barely paid attention.

Although I hadn't learned the identity of the man, I had made a discovery. The individual in question knew about the *Red Pot*, which meant he knew this area intimately. Not only that, but he spoke without an accent—a second indication that he lived in this area. The proper speech, though. That threw me for a moment. It meant he likely wasn't living in this district. While I had waited for Illia to get her dress fitted, I had noticed several noblemen and knights visiting the bordellos and burlesque clubs.

Whoever had hired Corry probably wasn't a foreigner here for the fights.

It was probably someone who lived in the city.

Which meant someone who lived here was after the runestones, and they were hiring lowlifes and desperate individuals to help them in their dubious plot. Someone with coin to spare, then. Almost certainly an upper member of society.

I had to tell Master Zelfree.

Luthair unmerged from me once we exited the snickelway.

"That was intense," Lyell said as he brushed himself off. "Now everyone will think I'm friends with an inquisitor. Thanks for that. I'm gonna get so many discounts."

I held out my hand. "I'll take those letters to the knight captain and relay your message. Thank you, Lyell. You've really helped me out."

He turned a light shade of pink. "Don't mention it. I still owe you for saving my hide in that mire."

33

TRUE FORMS

I returned to the Thronehold Coliseum after the sun had passed its peak in the sky. Worried I had missed Illia's match, I rushed into the fighter's section of the coliseum and wove through the other combatants. They murmured excited statements about the other matches—about how the stone golem arcanist was the favored to win—but I didn't catch much more.

While the main stands were packed with over 20,000 spectators, there were special sections near the bottom of the field designated for tournament participants. I didn't know my way, so I asked the knights, and they directed me with a few simple instructions.

Luthair slithered along with me. The moment we neared the stands, he caught my attention and directed me the last of the way. I wanted to ask if he was familiar with this specific amphitheater, but the shouting and cheers of the audience had become too loud to speak over. Instead, I walked up a set of stairs and entered a small box-like area for apprentice fighters.

Zaxis sat in the front row, the closest he could get to the

fight arena, with Forsythe resting by his side. He kept his legs kicked up on the railing, and when I walked over, he didn't change a thing. He greeted me with a jut of his chin. I sat on the other side of him and glanced around. Only three other contestants waited here, and I suspected it was because most had had their matches and already left.

"What a spectacular bout!" the announcer declared.

The cheering grew louder, somehow.

While the last contestants were healed and walked out of the arena, I scooted forward to get a better look at the gargoyle who came along and manipulated the stone fighting platform. He turned the stones, molding them like clay, and completely removed any evidence of the fight. All blood, teeth, and cracks disappeared into the sandstone until nothing but a new—smooth—surface remained.

The crowd settled down while the maintenance took place, and Zaxis took the opportunity to speak.

"We should strategize for the next match."

I wanted to make a sarcastic comment about how he had disappeared with Illia for the last few days, but that wasn't productive. "I agree," I said.

"Those two dog idiots weren't worth our time, but some of these other arcanists..." He narrowed his eyes and stared out across the coliseum field. "I think it would be better if we talked beforehand."

"I already said I would. No need to repeat it."

Zaxis shot me a glare. "Heh. I knew this would happen."

"What would happen?" I asked, meeting his glower with a lifted eyebrow.

"You getting huffy." He laced his fingers together and hooked his hands behind his head. "Illia and I are together now. You'll just have to deal with it."

It took most of my willpower not to utter curses to the

abyssal hells. I ran a hand down my face, tempted to point out that Zaxis could get angry at his morning toast for disappointing him. Telling me to "deal with" *anything* was beyond hypocritical, but I didn't have the energy. It didn't matter what Zaxis thought. I wasn't bothered by their relationship. I had even encouraged it. Now why couldn't people just stop talking about it?

The crowd started up their stomping, and I returned my attention to the arena.

Illia and Hexa stood out on the field, their eldrin by their side. Zelfree stood out there with them, but he was separated—a few feet back, his arms crossed—and I wondered if Illia and Hexa had bothered to strategize.

"Our final match for the day once again has apprentices from the Frith Guild! If this is anything like the last match, it's sure to delight."

The applause got me smiling. I never considered myself an entertainer, but I was glad our match hadn't been embarrassing.

"We have Illia Savan the Rizzel Arcanist, and Hexa d'Tenni the Hydra Arcanist! They're facing off against members of the Southern Anchorage Guild—Bettany Hunt the Salamander Arcanist, and Croque Demus the Ogopogo Arcanist!"

Bettany was the salamander arcanist I had met at the gala, the one accompanying Crevis and Dart. Croque, however, didn't look familiar. I probably saw him in the pit, but his plain appearance, and short dark hair made for a forgettable appearance.

His ogopogo, on the other hand, caught my eye right away. They were long sea serpents—nowhere near the size of a leviathan, but still rather large. They lived in lakes and moved through water at lightning speeds. On land, however, it didn't have nearly as many advantages. The ogopogo slithered around like a massive anaconda, circling around its arcanist and flashing its snake-like fangs at the opponents.

The salamander had the shape and size of an adult alligator, but its scarlet scales shone in the sunlight, marking it as distinctly magical. Salamanders lived in hot territories and even had the capacity to move through molten magma, despite the intense heat and crushing force of pressure.

"Are we ready?" the announcer asked, riling the crowd. "Then let's begin!"

Vercingetorix roared, and the coliseum shuddered in response.

The salamander belched flames across the arena platform. Illia and Nicholin teleported away, but Hexa—slow, slow Hexa—staggered back as far as she could go, right to the edge, getting burned the entire way. Raisen didn't seem to mind the flames, but even he had to keep his four eyes shut as the heat rushed by.

The ogopogo arcanist must've seen the opening, because he pointed and his eldrin rushed for Hexa.

I clenched my jaw and watched with tense muscles, worried they would lose as fast as the dog arcanists had lost to me and Zaxis.

Unfortunately for the ogopogo, and lucky for Hexa, it couldn't dodge Raisen's two-headed strike. The hydra latched on with both heads, his venomous fangs sinking into the scaled hide of the serpentine ogopogo as it wrapped around him.

Illia appeared next to the salamander and its arcanist. Nicholin breathed his white disintegrating flames, breaking apart both opponents as though their bodies were being teleported away, small pieces at a time.

That didn't stop the might of the salamander. It lunged

forward with more speed than I thought capable for a creature with short legs. Illia teleported just in time, but part of her coat got caught by the beast's massive jaws. It ripped the fabric away, swallowed it, and then belched another round of flame, this time all around itself and its arcanist.

Hexa pulled throwing daggers from her belt. With more skill than I had seen from her, she threw them at both enemy arcanists. The ogopogo arcanist dodged, but just barely. The salamander arcanist took the hit in the side, but I didn't know if it pierced through the thin leather armor she wore.

Instead of throwing more, Illia teleported to Hexa's side, and Hexa handed the remaining weapons to her. Illia disappeared and then reappeared behind the ogopogo arcanist. Before the man had time to react, Illia stabbed him in the arm with one of Hexa's poisoned blades.

The strike didn't need to be debilitating—the hydra venom would take care of that.

Sure enough, the ogopogo was the first to succumb to the terrible effects of the venom. It had Raisen wrapped up like a constrictor snake, but it lost its strength and let go. Then it vomited all over the arena, its body writhing around as it emptied its belly in sporadic bursts.

Roars erupted from the crowd. They stomped and clapped and pointed.

The ogopogo arcanist collapsed to his knees, the hydra venom acting fast.

Raisen used both his heads to grab the ogopogo and hurled him from the arena in a surprising display of strength. A bell sounded.

Then the salamander arcanist used her flames on Hexa. When Hexa went to step backward out of the fire, she lost her footing and tumbled from the stage, resulting in another bell.

"Damn," Zaxis muttered, his voice barely audible through the commotion.

Illia kicked the sick ogopogo arcanist off of the platform. One more clang of a bell.

As if to get revenge for his fallen arcanist, Raisen charged across the arena. He didn't move with real speed, but didn't slow or falter, not even when the salamander turned its breath on him. When the two beasts clashed, Raisen's two heads made the difference. One struck at the salamander's neck while the other fought off the salamander's maw.

Taking advantage of the struggle, Illia teleported next to the salamander arcanist. The woman pulled a pistol and fired, but Illia teleported again. The bullet struck the telekinetic barrier created by the engkanto, harming no one.

Illia reappeared, grabbed the woman's arm, and practically flipped her out of the arena. The salamander arcanist landed on her back in the red dirt, creating a puff of crimson dust that wafted up into the air.

The bell clanged.

The moment the salamander swayed on its feet from the venom, Raisen used both his heads to drag him toward the edge. They fought each other like only beasts could—biting, clawing, and thrashing, leaving a trail of blood—but the salamander had already lost. Its strength waned, and eventually Raisen ousted it from the platform.

I almost didn't hear the final bell through the excitement of the crowds. They threw flowers and other displays of approval, cluttering the coliseum field.

Illia and Nicholin waved, though it was difficult to see

the little rizzel on her shoulders. I suspected the poor schmoes in the far seats never even saw Illia's eldrin.

Raisen waddled off the arena and right into Hexa's arms—though he was getting much too big to do that. She only held him for a moment before dropping him into the dirt.

"I knew they would win," Zaxis had to shout just for me to hear.

I nodded.

But I wasn't sure how I felt about it. What if they kept winning? We would fight each other eventually. The thought bothered me, and I shoved my hands into my pockets, wondering how I would handle the situation when the time came.

Before leaving the coliseum, I left Lyell's letters with the knight captain's attendants and then told Master Zelfree everything I had discovered at the *Red Pot*. We didn't discuss it long before heading back to the *Maison Arcana* with the rest of the group. I didn't know why, but the information didn't seem to please Zelfree.

Once in the inn, I opted to head straight to my room. I was tired, both physically and mentally. A lot had happened the last few days, and all I wanted to do was read. Theasin's book still had information for me, and I didn't want to stop reading until I had all of it.

In the dark of my room—all alone—I stretched out across my bed and flipped the pages until I came to a new section I hadn't seen before. It was titled *Alternate Forms*. While I had heard legends of true form creatures, I never really understood them. I was hoping Theasin would have a clear and easy way to define what they were.

To my delight, I found what I wanted.

True Forms

All mystical creatures are born incomplete. They need the soul of another to grow, which is their reward for bonding with a mortal. If the soul of that individual exemplifies the virtues of the creature, then a true form is achieved, changing the eldrin's appearance and causing the arcanist's mark to glow with inner magical power.

The problem with obtaining a true form is the nebulous nature of mystical creatures. Mystical creatures do not share the same virtues, although there is a similarity between members of the same species. Additionally, since "exemplifying a virtue" is nigh impossible to quantify, the number of arcanists who have achieved a true form with their eldrin is vanishingly small.

Because human beings are capable of changing their nature through self-improvement, tragedy, hardship, or trauma—and because their eldrin grant them magic that pulls them toward their desired virtue—it is possible, given enough time and experience, for arcanists to develop the virtues of their eldrin, which is why most true forms are seen in older pairs.

There have been instances where an individual already exemplifies the virtues of the creature long before becoming an arcanist.

In these cases, the creature obtains its true form immediately upon bonding.

I turned the page, my thoughts drifting to the two individuals I knew who had true forms—Guildmaster Eventide and the Dread Pirate Calisto. They were worlds apart in terms of personality and goals, so I understood what Theasin meant about virtues being different between creatures. The virtues of an atlas turtle were far from the virtues of a manticore.

With unending curiosity, I continued.

A true form is better than the standard form in all regards and only the true forms of mystical creatures seem to gain access to their species "apex" ability (such as a phoenix's ability to pull someone out of death's icy grasp).

There are several benefits all true form creatures share. Firstly, while all mystical creatures and arcanists are capable of healing themselves from physical harm, true form creatures and their arcanists are capable of healing themselves from magic damage as well. They cannot be tainted or corrupted, as their magic refuses to warp.

I re-read the section several times.

Did that mean true form creatures couldn't contract the plague? That would make some sense. I remember when Guildmaster Eventide's atlas turtle had been attacked by a plague-ridden siren. Although I was concerned, Gregory

Ruma told me there was nothing to worry about. Perhaps he knew?

Secondly, the total capacity for magic growth is increased. Whereas most creatures fall into a 5 tier system, true form creatures transcend this and move up at least half a tier. Many stories speak of phoenix arcanists fighting dragon arcanists, where the true form had the advantage.

Calisto's manticore had been rather powerful. Disturbingly so.

I fiddled with the edge of the paper, but before flipping the page, I turned to the shadows next to me on the bed.

"Luthair," I muttered. "What do I need to exemplify?"

"I don't know, my arcanist."

"Really?"

"Why would I lie? If Theasin is correct, it seems there is no benefit to keeping this information from you. It would behoove us both if you helped me achieve my *true form*."

It seemed strange that Luthair wouldn't know. He was made of pure magic. Didn't that give him any insight into the task at hand? Then again, I was made of flesh, but that didn't mean I had the skills of a doctor.

Theasin was my greatest magical resource—Adelgis hadn't been lying when he said his father had researched and recorded a vast quantity of information.

I went to the next page.

Dread Forms

· · ·

I caught my breath, stunned to read such a section header. I went straight to the meat of the page, only to be disappointed.

Coined by the plague researcher Otto Kivi the Minerva Owl Arcanist, this new "form" of creature occurs during the magical corruption process of the arcane plague. Little is known about it at this time.

Curious, I went to the first page and glanced at the edition notes. This book was a first edition, and it had been written eleven years ago. The arcane plague had been ravaging the land for over a decade? I didn't know that, and it weighed heavy on me. How many people had been affected?

A gentle tapping at the door broke my chain of thoughts.

I got off my bed and straightened my clothing before grabbing the handle and opening it.

Atty stood in the hallway, her white robes extra crisp and her blonde hair up in a styled bun. "Good evening," she said, smiling.

"Atty?" I glanced around and saw no one else. "Your timing is perfect. I wanted to ask you something."

She lifted both eyebrows. "Me?"

"Didn't you once tell me you wanted to have a true form phoenix?"

"Uh, well, yes. My mother said I should strive for that. It's more of a legend, though. People don't really get them all that often."

"Wait here." I snatched up Theasin's book. When I returned to Atty, I handed it to her. "There's a section in here all about true form creatures. I think you should read it. The

Isle of Ruma wasn't the best place for information, but Adelgis's father is quite informed."

She stared at the tome and flipped through some of the pages. "Oh. Thank you."

I smiled, but then I remembered that *she* came to *my* door. "Uh, did you want to come in?" I motioned to the room, only to realize how dark and uninviting it must look. I hadn't bothered to light any lanterns.

"Actually, I'm here because you have a visitor."

"Who?" I caught my breath. "Is it Princess Lyvia?" Was she answering my request to speak?

Atty frowned. "Master Zelfree said he was the *Grandmaster Inquisitor*."

Although I had never heard the title, I had my suspicions on where he came from.

"The Grandmaster Inquisitor is the guildmaster of the Steel Thorn Inquisitors Guild," Luthair said from the shadows.

I smirked. "That's a mouthful."

"He was once called the *Knightmare Lord*, and he was Mathis's master when Mathis was an apprentice."

34

THE GRANDMASTER INQUISITOR

Was the Grandmaster Inquisitor here because he had heard of my impersonation? Perhaps.

I exited my room and shut the door. Atty stayed close, her smile returning, and I walked with her to the stairs.

"I enjoyed watching your fight," she said as she held Theasin's book close.

"I'm glad."

"You've really improved. In every way." Atty fidgeted with her hair as she said, "People here don't know you like I do. They didn't see you on the Isle of Ruma, back when we were children. It's like you're a different person."

I stopped on the first step and turned to her. She flinched and then came to a stop as well.

"Is everything okay, Volke?" she asked.

"Atty, I've always admired you," I said, taking my own advice. "Back on our home island, I thought your dedication to perfection was something to idealize. It still is. Sometimes I think I fumble my way through things in my haste to advance, and perhaps if I had more of your perfectionism, that wouldn't be the case."

She blushed hard at my statements, but I couldn't turn back now.

After a quick breath, I asked, "Would you want to spend time together and—"

"Yes," she said, cutting me off. "I'm sorry. I didn't let you finish." She fidgeted with her hair again, pulling at the strands or tucking them back into place. "But I'd like to spend time with you."

I almost laughed, but it came out as a nervous chuckle. Probably wasn't the correct response, since she stared at me with an uncertain expression.

"That's good," I said, my breathing coming a little easier.

"Perhaps once we leave Thronehold? I don't want to distract you from the tournament, and the guildmaster asked that I accompany her to recruit young arcanists, so I figure we'll be busy." She touched my shoulder and then pulled back her hand, as though she couldn't remain still. "The ride back to Fortuna will be long and less urgent than when we traveled to Thronehold. We could share a carriage. If you want, of course."

"I'd like that."

"Not that I want to interrupt, my arcanist," Luthair said from the darkness around my feet, "but the Grandmaster Inquisitor is waiting."

Atty motioned to the staircase. "You should go. We can talk more once you're done."

I nodded and continued my way to the lounge, my steps light and motivation at an all-time high. That... hadn't been so hard. I never imagined myself as suave, and my all-time low was when I had run from Atty when we were both naked in the Sapphire Springs, but I pushed those doubts from my head.

I didn't need them anymore.

The front lounge of the *Maison Arcana* wasn't busy in the evenings. Most arcanists retreated to their rooms, and the inn attendants were busy cleaning up dinner or tending to the gardens. When I reached the bottom of the steps, only two people waited in the lounge—Master Zelfree and the Grandmaster Inquisitor.

He wasn't a man.

Well, that wasn't true. He wasn't *just* a man.

He was merged with his knightmare, and unlike Luthair, his armor disturbed me. It was full plate made of shadows, but his helmet had no slit or visor. It was smooth darkness. Horns on the helmet curved up and backward, like a demonic creature, and the man's cape that hung from his shoulders seemingly moved about, like a shadow flickering in candlelight. Etched into the darkness of his chest was the symbol for the Steel Thorn Inquisitors Guild—two intertwined chains with barbs on the links.

He carried a shadow halberd on his back—a two-handed weapon that combined the long reach of a spear and the heavy blade of a battle axe.

Halberds weren't a common sight on the islands. They were the perfect weapon to pull someone off a horse, which was more of a concern for someone from the mainland.

His gauntlets and boots were also sharp and pointed, like claws. Every part of him was deadly or defended, and without the ability to see his face or body, he looked like something out of a literal nightmare.

Zelfree spotted me staring and motioned me to join them. I walked over, my attention drawn to the darkness in the corners of the room. Everything was moving. It was slight—I doubt a normal person could see it—but the void seemed to have a mind of its own.

Luthair emerged from the shadows when we got close.

To my surprise, he knelt on one knee in front of the Grand-master Inquisitor, his helmet bowed.

"I'm pleased to see you still live, Luthair," the Grandmaster Inquisitor said.

His voice... it was a combination of two people, but they sounded so in sync it was almost too difficult to tell. I only recognized it because of my experiences with my own knightmare.

Luthair stood and said nothing.

The Grandmaster Inquisitor continued, "Why didn't you return to the guild after Mathis's death? When you sent no word, I thought you had perished with him."

"Forgive me," Luthair said. "I was ashamed of failing him. I didn't know if I could face you and explain my mistakes."

"I see."

Then the Grandmaster Inquisitor turned his blank helmet to face me. I had to look up to meet his nonexistent gaze—he stood at least seven feet tall. Was it his knight-mare? Or was the man inside that giant?

"Uh," I muttered once I realized how long I had been staring. "Greetings, Grandmaster Inquisitor. My name is Volke Savan."

Zelfree patted me on the shoulder. "Don't strain your-self. Just call him Inquisitor. And he's asked that you assist him with an assignment from the crown. I told him that I didn't mind, but I'd ultimately let you decide."

"What assignment?"

"There are plague-ridden arcanists hiding in aban-doned nullstone mines of the old kingdom," the Inquisitor replied, his gruff monotone adding to his frightening visage. "I've been made aware you're immune to that disease, and since you've bonded with my old apprentice's eldrin, there is much I wish to discuss."

The old kingdom mines? The spider arcanist in the alleyway had mentioned that. If they were infecting people, they needed to be dealt with.

"Of course I'll help," I said.

The Inquisitor replied with a single nod.

"Be back in three days' time," Zelfree said. "That's when your next match begins." He glanced between me and the massive knightmare before taking off toward the stairs. He stopped at the first step. "If you see Adelgis before you return, come let me know." Then he exited. His lack of commentary made me curious. He had nothing more to tell me? He always had something to say.

Once he disappeared up the stairs, I slowly turned my attention to the Inquisitor. He said nothing, and the longer the silence went on, the tenser I became. I didn't think he would hurt me—and Luthair obviously trusted him—but everything about him was unsettling.

"It's an honor to meet you," I said.

"There are fewer than twelve knightmare arcanists in this world."

I caught my breath, uncertain of how to respond. Why tell me such a thing?

He continued, "When I saw your performance in the tournament, I knew you had bonded to Luthair. It pains me to know Mathis is gone, but the fact his knightmare found another is a fact we should celebrate."

"I'm glad I found Luthair, too."

"I've requested your assistance in order to know you better."

"Oh. I see." I rubbed at my neck. "Shall we be going,

then? It can take the trolleys a long time to cross the city, and I don't want to risk missing my match."

"You won't miss the tournament," the Inquisitor said. "Our task will be over by noon tomorrow."

"Oh. That's good to hear."

He lifted his cape with one arm. Unlike Luthair, whose cape was lined with red, the Inquisitor's was nothing but an inky void. The man held it out as though the gesture were an invitation, and for a long moment, I hesitated.

Luthair melted back into my shadow. "You need not fear him," he murmured from my feet. "He'll take us where we need to go."

I stepped forward, uncertain of what the Inquisitor expected of me. He swished his cape over my head, engulfing me in the cold sensation I had come to recognize as shadow-given-solid-form.

It felt as though the floor had given out from under me. I tried to gasp, but I entered the inky void of knightmare magic —a realm without air and where I couldn't see. This was how I felt every time I shadow-stepped, but I would exit fast, to avoid the suffocating side effect. The Inquisitor, on the other hand, kept us in the darkness far longer than I wanted, and with each passing moment, it grew colder and more devoid of life.

When we finally emerged, I stumbled away and gulped down air. I half-tripped on a rock and glanced around, stunned to recognize the road outside of Thronehold. The moon hung overhead, bathing the forested area in a soft glow. I turned my attention to the city's walls in the distance —at least half a mile away.

How had we traveled so far? And in so little time?

The Inquisitor lowered his cape and strode off the road into the woodlands. It took me a moment to regain my bearings, but then I chased after him. He walked with purpose, his stride long. The chill of the evening air lazily wafted past.

"A vast network of mine tunnels runs under Thronehold," the Inquisitor said. "These catacombs have long been a haven for thieves, smugglers, and conmen. With the queen's assistance, many of the tunnels have been blocked off, preventing people from entering or leaving the city through the old mines."

I nodded along with his words.

Then he came to a stop, and I stutter-stepped to a halt.

The Inquisitor's cape shifted around as though it had a mind of its own. "The old kingdom mines used to connect to the catacombs. And the plague-ridden dastards hiding in those tunnels have started an excavation. They wish to reconnect that mine with Thronehold—I suspect so they can bring their disease to the city."

As the trees rustled around us, I grappled with the problem. I stared up at him. "Uh, I'm sorry if this sounds rude, but why did you ask for me? Master Zelfree has a plague-preventing trinket, and so does most of the Frith Guild, actually. And this mission sounds dire. Surely someone more qualified should—"

"You needn't concern yourself with the success of the mission. It is guaranteed."

His statement took me by surprise. Before I could inquire further, the Inquisitor continued through the woods at his brisk pace. I jogged after him, more confused than before. Why bring me if everything was already set?

We only walked for a few minutes until we came across a patch of woodland shrouded in an unusual darkness. Despite the moon and the many stars, light didn't pierce through the branches of the trees. The orb of shadows had a visible beginning and end, like a bubble in water, but large enough for a man to fit inside.

As we neared, the orb of darkness melted away into the dirt, revealing another knightmare arcanist. However, unlike the Inquisitor and Luthair, this knightmare wasn't full plate armor. It was a flowing cloak and robes—the kind that blended with the shadows on the ground, creating the illusion of being connected with the land itself. The hood of the cloak hung low, completely covering the arcanist within, much like the Inquisitor.

"Good evening, Grandmaster Inquisitor," the arcanist said, her feminine voice a mix of two. "The river has been diverted, as you asked. The mines are currently filling with water. The plague arcanists will soon need to evacuate."

The Inquisitor replied with a single curt nod. "Thank you, Inquisitor Aventa."

I admired her knightmare for a long moment. She looked like a wizard made of flowing ink and darkness. The insignia of the Steel Thorn Inquisitor Guild hung on a shadow tendril around her neck, the barbs of the chains gleaming in the moonlight.

"I didn't know knightmares could look so different," I whispered, trying to get Luthair's attention.

The Inquisitor heard me, however. "Knightmares take the appearance of the ruler they were born from. Everything plays a factor, from the ruler's personality, to their culture, to their actions. No knightmare is identical to the other."

I didn't know that, and wished I had Theasin's book with me. Perhaps I could add notes? I wouldn't write in the book, but loose pages added to supplement the information seemed like a good idea.

"It is a pleasure to meet Luthair's new arcanist,"

Inquisitor Aventa said with a slight bow of her head. "I'm glad he came back to us."

"It's nice to meet you as well," I said.

The Inquisitor held his cape up a second time. "We've seen what we need to. Come."

After a deep breath, I stepped close. He threw his cape over me a second time, and we disappeared into the shadows. I counted my heartbeat as I waited to exit and managed to reach 40 before I could breathe again. This time, when I stepped from the darkness, I was prepared. I didn't stumble, and I knew to analyze my surroundings.

We stood atop a large hill. The gray rocks and lack of grass marked the area as dead. Wood beams built into the ground told me we were above a mine shaft, though I couldn't see where the entrance was. I turned around, looked for Thronehold, and only then spotted the castle in the distance.

"There are eight arcanists in the mines," the Inquisitor said. "Six of them are bonded to night cats, and the last two are bonded to harpies and capable of flight." He motioned to the hill. "The night cat arcanists will flee the water on foot, but the harpies will exit the mines through the cracks in the earth. We will prevent their escape."

I stared at the ground until I spotted the cracks in the boulders. One wrong step and someone could tumble into an abandoned mineshaft. Although I didn't know much about mining, I had read a story about the need for ventilation. Apparently, natural gases could kill unsuspecting miners, and the buildup of dust could clog in their lungs. It seemed a dangerous place, and even more so with deranged arcanists on the loose.

As we stood in silence, a haunting bit of laughter trickled out of the cracks. I knew the sound too well. I backed away. It belonged to those driven mad by the plague.

"Do not fear the laughter," the Inquisitor said.

"I'm not afraid. I just don't like it."

"The sound is a boon—like the rattle of a mountain snake. Unfortunately, when an arcanist is infected, there is no warning. They can blend into a crowd and even conduct themselves as though nothing is wrong. At least for a short while."

My thoughts went straight to Gregory Ruma.

He had been infected, but no one knew. He helped the Frith Guild and secretly killed arcanists and their eldrin to fuel his delusional experiment. It was the plague that corrupted his soul and made him think that course of action was appropriate. While mystical creatures became laughing mad when infected, arcanists became deranged—losing themselves at a slow pace, one thought at a time.

"Inquisitor," I said.

"Hm?"

"Why not just kill their eldrin?" I turned to face him. "Won't the plague leave the arcanists then? We could still save them."

"That's not possible."

"Why not?"

He stepped over the rocks, his clawed boots clicking on the hard ground. "Are you familiar with the scarlet cough? It is a common illness among the masses."

"Sure. Someone starts coughing, and then they get a fever, and then their coughing gets bloody, and they lose their energy until eventually they die." Everyone on the islands had to learn to spot the signs of the scarlet cough. There was only a limited amount of time to provide them with medicine. "Why do you ask?"

"If someone contracts the scarlet cough, and it's treated early, there are no lasting effects. However, those who carry the cough for several months and are then treated right before death—they're never the same. Their lungs are damaged beyond repair, and they breathe with a shallow rasp."

"Is the arcane plague similar?"

"Yes. If an arcanist contracts the plague, they can kill their eldrin to free themselves of it, but the longer they wait, the more corrupted they become."

"How long do they have?" I whispered, dwelling on the terrible nature of the knowledge. It was like asking how long it took to drown an infant. How many children had to die before a correct time was agreed upon? So it was with the plague—every bit of information came with a price of bodies.

"I have killed dozens of plague-ridden arcanists," the Inquisitor said, his odd voice melancholy, as though he shared my sentiments. "Arcanists who have carried the plague more than half a year are always beyond saving. Even if their eldrin is killed and they become mortal, they carry the derangement in their soul. They're wicked—lacking empathy—the damage beyond repair."

"Six months?"

It seemed long, only because mystical creatures didn't have the same luxury. Once they were infected, it took less than a day before they succumbed to the insanity.

"And the arcanists in this mine," I said. "They've been infected longer than that?"

"Most have been infected for eighteen months. Others for twenty."

Which meant we couldn't save them.

Unless Theasin was right. He seemed confident that he

would have a cure soon, but that didn't mean we could let these arcanists go. If they were opening tunnels to Thronehold, they were a menace that had to be dealt with.

"You don't enjoy killing," the Inquisitor said, half a question, half a statement.

"I've killed mystical creatures," I muttered, "but never a person."

"Then you should stay close to me when the plague arcanists begin their flight out of the mine. I'll show you how knightmare arcanists dole out death to the wicked."

35

ECLIPSE AURA

I waited with the Inquisitor on top of the abandoned mine for what felt like an hour. He didn't speak unless I addressed him, and the shadows of his armor and cape never ceased their movement. It was slight—the edges of the darkness flickering about—and I wondered what the name of the Inquisitor's knightmare was.

"Are they always merged?" I whispered to Luthair.

"Yes, my arcanist."

"Forever?"

"I've never seen them apart."

When I merged with Luthair, our newfound power invigorated me. We were better together, but I couldn't imagine staying that way. Luthair's voice in my head wasn't my own, and feeling what he felt, and vice versa, made it difficult at times.

A shadow slithered over the ground, and I stepped aside to allow it room. A man emerged out of the darkness, rising from the void and rotating his arms as he stepped close to the Inquisitor's side.

"Master, the mines have been scoured," he said. "All is set for the plague arcanists."

I recognized the man. He had been in the pits during the first day of the tournament, though I never spoke to him. He wore a high-collar shirt and loose pants, both dark and thick with heavy material. He kept his head shaved short, but not bald, and his face was as smooth as polished stone. When he turned to me, he stared with narrow eyes, his irises smaller than average.

"Hello," I said. "My name is Volke Savan."

The Inquisitor motioned with a clawed hand. "This is my apprentice, Lucian Nellit."

Lucian had been the other knightmare arcanist on the tournament bracket. With anxious excitement, I bowed my head. "It's nice to meet you."

He had to be close to my age, and that seemed significant considering the rarity of our eldrin. We were probably the only apprentice knightmare arcanists in the known world.

"Likewise," he replied, his voice soft but confident.

The shadow at his feet coalesced and formed into an odd suit of armor. It looked like light armor—thin metal and leather, but everything was black and made from shadows. The knightmare had a hood, like the wizard with Inquisitor Aventa, and it kept daggers at its side. Lucian's knightmare reminded me of an assassin.

And it wasn't quite complete. There were missing pieces —only one glove, a hole in the chest, and openings on a single leg. Was it because the knightmare was young? Fully grown knightmares were complete from head to toe, but I had never seen a newborn knightmare. It fascinated me.

"This is my eldrin, Azir," Lucian said. "He was born from the murder of Emperor Raiz. Had you heard of him?"

I shook my head. I was certain Gravekeeper William would be disappointed, and I wondered just how much I would need to study to understand the basics.

Lucian frowned. "We live in a turbulent time. The world can't afford to coddle ignorant arcanists."

The snide remark stung. On the other hand, I was pretty sure the world serpent was more important than regicide, and I doubted the Inquisitor or his apprentice were aware of its existence.

"Save your aggression," the Inquisitor said. "Tonight, we deal in death. Cooperation is the only option."

The sounds of rushing water echoed up from the cracks in the ground. I listened carefully—the laughter persisted, but now there were frantic movements mixed into the chortling. How long would it take before the plague arcanists exited their dirty hiding place?

"Why wouldn't you just go into the mines?" I asked.

The Inquisitor walked over another rock, his "gaze" angled to the ground. "Clever strategy takes into account all variables. Location. Timing. Numbers. The more you control, the less power your opponent has. If we rush into the mine, the plague arcanists have the advantage of familiarity. They've lived in those tunnels for weeks."

"But wouldn't the darkness of the mines strengthen your magic?" I turned my attention to the sky. "The sun will rise in a few hours." Although I never found myself without shadows, I always found it easier to manipulate the darkness when it blanketed the area. At night, everything became a potential tool for my sorcery, but in the day, I needed to look for the shadows I could use.

Lucian stifled a laugh as he crossed his arms. He said nothing, however.

"Powerful knightmare arcanists bring their darkness

with them," the Inquisitor said. "You shall see soon enough."

Just as I had feared, the sun rose before the plague arcanists left their lair. Neither the Inquisitor nor Lucian seemed concerned with this fact, however. They waited in silence, their attention on the next hill over. A rusted track for mine carts marked the entrance of the mine. Aventa and some other knightmare arcanist I hadn't met waited near the tracks, their inky forms blending with the harsh shadows of morning.

Five arcanists to handle eight plague-ridden monsters? Sixteen, if we counted their eldrin separate. Normally I would think that a terrible disadvantage, but the Inquisitor was a grandmaster arcanist—such a title was only bestowed on the most powerful of arcanists, and there was no way the addled minds of plague-ridden arcanists could compete with such magic.

"They're coming," Lucian said. He tensed as he turned his attention to his knightmare. "Come, Azir."

In a flash, the shadows engulfed him, and they merged. He wore the thin armor, and the hood fell forward, hiding most of his face. The assassin guise suited him well, though the incomplete knightmare made for incomplete armor—parts of Lucian were still visible, even while merged.

He held the daggers made of darkness and shadow-stepped away. He reemerged near the entrance of the mine, his movements silent and purposeful.

"Should we go?" I asked the Inquisitor.

"Wait here," he commanded. "You and I will deal with the harpies."

Luthair merged with me a moment later, and I relished the combined might of our magic.

The sun continued its journey across the sky. I held my sword and shield close, ready for whatever would come, certain it would be a fierce battle. When the manic laughter grew louder, ice ran through my veins, chilling my thoughts. I still had my wendigo trinket, and that fact reassured me.

Inquisitor Aventa, Lucian, and the other knightmare arcanist braced themselves at the mine entrance. I observed them from atop the hill next to theirs, high enough to get a good view.

I held my breath the instant a night cat lunged from the tunnel. It was as large as a panther and just as deadly. Those felines had a distinct pattern on their ebony fur—bright blue dots marked their back and hind legs, glowing with inner magic. They looked like they had stars on their pelt, twinkling any time they used their sorcery.

But this one...

The plague twisted everything it touched. The night cat's innards hung from its distended gut, moving about, twisting and lashing, similar to a pile of eels writhing around on land. The blue dots on its fur were ringed in red, and everything about the beast's mouth seemed implausible. Teeth, blood, and a tongue four times the normal length.

The night cat went straight for Lucian, but it only got halfway before the shadows at its feet latched to its legs. The monster stopped in its tracks, both laughing and grunting as it tried to free itself.

"Should we help them?" I asked, Luthair's voice just as concerned as mine.

The Inquisitor pointed to the sky with a clawed finger.

I glanced upward. To my shock, and fascination, a blot of darkness moved in front of the sun, creating an eclipse unlike anything I had seen before. The intense gloom that fell over the area included fierce winds of melancholy, rustling the leaves of the distant trees and wilting grass. I could see through the supernatural murkiness, but with each second, it somehow grew darker and darker.

When I took a breath, I felt... different.

I turned to the Inquisitor. "What is this?"

"An eclipse aura."

It took me a moment to process the new information.

Zelfree had said that all arcanists could create auras. A sovereign dragon arcanist could create a prosperity aura, after all. Was this the aura of a knightmare arcanist? Utter darkness? I returned my attention to the sky, intrigued by the shifting shade that consumed all light. I couldn't even see the sun's halo, just blackness.

This wasn't an aura that covered an entire nation, however. I could see the edge of the effect—Thronehold, over a mile away, remained in the light, unaffected.

"Those who dwell in darkness will die in darkness," the Inquisitor said.

The laughter of the night cat stopped. I walked to the crest of the hill and stared down at the mine entrance. I didn't see the cat. It wasn't there. And when the others came running out—five night cats, each as disgusting as the last— they didn't get far. The shadows that covered the area moved with astonishing speed. Instead of tendrils, the darkness became chains and hooks. They latched onto the plague creatures, stopping them long before they made it to the inquisitors.

In what could only be described as *brutal efficiency*, the empowered shadows tore the plague creatures into pieces. It reminded me of revenge tales I heard involving four horses —it was a punishment so vile it made me sick. In the tales, they would tie a man's arms and legs to four horses, one limb per animal, and then have the horses walk in opposite directions. I had never seen it, but now I felt like I had. The night cats tore apart like cooked meat. They struggled, but it lasted less than a moment.

The six plague-ridden arcanists who staggered from the mine met similar fates, but I looked away before the images could carve themselves into my memory.

"The harpies are coming," the Inquisitor said.

With wings and the power of wind, the two harpy arcanists and their eldrin flew up the cracks in the mine, exiting mere feet from where I stood.

Harpies spooked me as a child, and now I remembered why. They were humanoid—bodies and faces that could easily pass for an adult woman—with hawk wings, talons on their feet, and claws at the end of their fingertips. They conducted themselves like beasts, even without the plague, and used their human-like faces to trick people into trusting them. Their bare-chested bodies glistened with sweat, somehow more animalistic and feral than I had ever imagined. When they opened their mouths, ear-shattering screeches sounded.

The Inquisitor didn't reach for his halberd. He stood still, his helmet facing the disgusting monsters that took to the sky. The two arcanists flew with the wind, but their wide eyes and panicked movements betrayed their terror. They couldn't see.

"Kill any that escape," the Inquisitor commanded.

He held up a gauntleted hand and evoked terrors. The two harpies and their arcanists crashed to the dirt, all of them crying out as if suffering. The shadow chains and hooks rose from the ground, lashing the harpies down. One arcanist got caught in the same chains, unable to escape his own fears. The last arcanist, however, got to his feet and leapt into the air before the darkness bound him. His wind magic carried him without wings.

I stepped forward, my body filled with a restless energy.

Careful, Luthair spoke to me.

I willed the shadows to answer my command, shocked by the result. The eclipse aura didn't just create darkness for me to wield—it made it powerful. I created tendrils in a second—they whipped into the air and grabbed the harpy arcanist with little difficulty. He blubbered something, but the darkness wrapped around his neck, torso, arms, and legs. He gurgled something as he slammed back to the ground.

And my abilities...

They didn't hurt.

I stared at my own gauntleted hand, realization overcoming me. I had used my magic without a bit of pain.

"They must die," the Inquisitor said.

Before I could answer, the gloom did all the work. Just like the night cats and their arcanists, the chains tore apart everything—the ripping sounds not unlike paper yet somehow wet. I moved away, my breath coming in short bursts.

The Inquisitor and the others in his guild hadn't gotten hurt. They weren't in danger, not for a second. They funneled the enemies into their deadly trap, ready to mutilate them the moment they showed.

The blood from the corpses soaked into the dirt. Would they summon someone to clean the area? They had to if they wanted to keep this contained.

While the sun remained blotted out, Lucian shadow-stepped back to his master's side. His knightmare unmerged, returning him to his normal state.

"Grandmaster Inquisitor, all the night cat arcanists have been dealt with."

"As expected."

"Shall we collapse the mines?" Lucian asked.

"All the entrances should be closed and marked." The Inquisitor held out a hand, stopping Lucian from leaving. "Stay. I will deal with that in a moment." Then he turned his helmet to me. "Volke—how does your second-bonded magic feel while under the blackened sky of the eclipse?"

Luthair unmerged from me, but unlike before, I didn't feel weakened.

I rubbed at my arms, still surprised. "I didn't hurt at all."

"As I thought," the Inquisitor muttered. "This aura empowers everything that deals in shadows. It stood to reason that it would soothe the pain of Mathis's eldrin."

"Is that why you brought me here?"

"In part." The Inquisitor motioned to Lucian. "I rarely take apprentices, and although I already have one, I will not abandon Luthair. Volke Savan—consider this a formal invitation to join the Steel Thorn Inquisitors Guild. I will take you on as an apprentice."

My chest tightened, and I didn't know how to reply. No one else reacted, however. Luthair stared with his empty helmet, a gauntlet resting on the hilt of our sword. Lucian kept a neutral expression, his gaze fixed on me. Had they all known this was coming?

This wasn't something he had offered lightly; I had felt it in his words. At the same time, I had chosen the Frith Guild specifically.

The Inquisitor continued, "The eclipse aura created by knightmare arcanists is beyond powerful. It is the epitome of battlefield control. It empowers darkness—which is why it's among the first lessons I teach new knightmare arcanists."

"Master Zelfree said creating auras was too difficult for an apprentice," I said.

"That is common wisdom among other arcanists. However, Everett Zelfree doesn't understand the nuances of knightmares—not like I do. He's a jack-of-all-trades, which is typical among mimic arcanists. His advice has general application and isn't tailored to what you need." The Inquisitor held up his cloak, offering it to me once again. "Come. I will give you the training you require. You can take Mathis's place at my side."

The eclipse kept the area shrouded in a midnight blanket. While that would've disturbed others, it comforted me —and made the decision-making process an easy one.

"I'm sorry," I said. "I need to stay with the Frith Guild."

Lucian's neutral expression heated to rage in an instant. "How utterly foolish." He motioned to our surroundings. "Do you not know who you're speaking to? The Grandmaster Inquisitor is power incarnate—his guild is respected across the world! You would dare refuse his gracious offer?"

"The Frith Guild is involved in important matters." I rubbed at my neck, my thoughts dwelling on the world serpent and the runestones. "I can't abandon them. I'm sorry."

"*Nothing* the Frith Guild does is as important as the work of the inquisitors." Lucian stepped closer, his voice rising. "You're a child to squander such opportunity. Everyone else had to prove themselves to join this guild, yet *you* get special treatment and—"

"My arcanist," Azir said as he placed a gloved hand on Lucian's shoulder. "Enough."

The Inquisitor nodded. "Such anger is unbecoming,

Lucian. Life is long for arcanists, and my offer will remain until Volke's tasks are completed." He lowered his cape. "I must be off, but I do hope you reconsider. Dark times are coming, and we will only survive the changes of our era if we unite our strength against common evils."

36

DREAMS OF THE PAST

The Grandmaster Inquisitor sank into the supernatural darkness and reemerged near the entrance to the mine, over a quarter mile away. The speed with which he moved through the darkness intrigued me. It was as if I crawled through the void and he sprinted—an infant versus an adult athlete.

After a short sigh, I turned my attention to Thronehold. I would've preferred the Inquisitor to take me back to *Maison Arcana*, but I was technically capable.

I shifted through the shadows, thankful for the eclipse aura, but the moment I reached the edge of the dark bubble, the pain of my second-bonded magic came back in full force. I emerged and took a moment to catch my breath before diving back in. When I pictured my travel in my head, I was a darkness dolphin, leaping in and out of the void.

When I emerged near the wall of Thronehold, I couldn't help but laugh at my own imagination.

"Wait."

I flinched and spun around, surprised to see Lucian

standing so close. His small eyes seemed even beadier in the sunlight. When he faced me, he did so with his hands behind his back. It reminded me of officers in the military, and I wondered if he had once served.

"What important business is the Frith Guild engaged in?" he asked.

I appreciated his straight-to-the-point conversation, but Guildmaster Eventide had told us specifically not to tell anyone. "I can't say."

Lucian sneered. "Of course you can't."

"I'm sure you can't speak of every assignment the Grandmaster Inquisitor gives you. Just know that this is so important I can't abandon it. I'd have declined an offer to join any guild."

"This isn't *any guild*," Lucian said. "The Grandmaster Inquisitor is one of the greatest arcanists of our time, and in the last century, he's taken exactly two apprentices—Mathis and myself. The fact that he extended that invitation to you is an honor."

"I'm not declining the offer because I want to insult the Inquisitor," I said.

"Even if that's not your intention, it's what you're doing."

"My current master is quite talented, though. He's—"

"Your master is a buffoon, which means whatever so-called task you're engaged in probably isn't worth the time."

I straightened my shoulders and glared. "What do you know about Master Zelfree?"

"Stories tell of his *epic betrayals* against pirates in the north, but a lowlife is still a lowlife." Lucian huffed and then dismissively waved his hand. "The few times I've met him, I've never been impressed. You should take my advice and distance yourself from him as soon as possible."

Fain had the same fear and disgust when it came to

Zelfree, but for some reason, it irritated me more that Lucian would say such a thing. Then again, I wasn't entirely sure what Zelfree had done. Sure, I had read the stories—and in those, he was always the roguish hero—but those were embellished, like all great tales.

Was it possible that...

"The Grandmaster Inquisitor will be a better master," Lucian stated, dragging me from my dark thoughts. "So I'm going to ask you again—reconsider and join the Steel Thorn Inquisitors Guild."

"No, thank you."

The haste of my answer clearly irritated him. He pursed his lips until they became a white line on his face.

"So be it."

He slipped into the shadows, leaving me alone with Luthair just outside the Thronehold wall.

I returned to my inn room by high noon.

Zaxis and Adelgis were still gone, their beds empty. My bed, on the other hand, had Theasin's book and a short letter. I picked them both up and read the note first.

Volke,

Thank you so much for letting me borrow this. I stayed up last night reading everything I could about true forms and found the information fascinating. I'll be away with the guildmaster for the next couple days and figured I should return it.

. . .

I look forward to speaking with you again,
    Atty

Once finished, I tucked the note under my pillow. Then I grabbed my satchel and shoved the book deep within. I didn't want to stay in the empty room, so I gathered everything I needed and went for the door. Right as I was about to turn the handle, it opened wide.

Master Zelfree stood in the hall, one eyebrow raised.

"What're you doing here?" he asked. "I thought you were helping the Inquisitor?"

I rubbed at my neck. "We finished this morning."

Zelfree glanced down at my belongings. "So, you decided to join his guild, huh? I guess I'm not surprised. I'm sure you'll do well there."

"No," I said as I slung the satchel over my shoulder. "I'm going to Skarn University to visit Adelgis. I declined the Inquisitor's offer."

"Why?"

"We're in the middle of finding the world serpent. Why would I abandon that?"

The bangles on his wrist morphed and shifted until they formed the sleek cat of Zelfree's mimic. Traces leapt from his arm over to my shoulder, purring the entire way. "I knew you wouldn't leave. My arcanist wouldn't believe me, but I knew it." She wrapped her long tail around my shoulders.

Zelfree shrugged. "I thought you might want to surround yourself with fellow knightmare arcanists. That's why I came up here—to clear out your room. I suppose our snake is the more pressing matter, though."

"Did he try to impress you?" Traces asked with a purr on

her voice. "The Grandmaster Inquisitor likes to show off in front of apprentices."

"He showed me the power of the eclipse aura," I said. "I don't think it's as useful as the sovereign dragon's prosperity aura, but it... was impressive."

The power to blot out the sun wasn't something to take lightly, but it was limited, and wasn't conducive to growth. A purely destructive aura didn't seem as appealing, but I suppose that was why they wanted sovereign dragon arcanists as rulers and not knightmare arcanists.

I turned my attention to Zelfree. "What kind of aura does a mimic arcanist have?"

"A chimera aura," he muttered. "But I've never fully mastered it. It allows my mimic to take on the characteristics of multiple eldrin at once, rather than transforming into a single creature."

"And you gain the benefit of all their magic?"

"In theory."

Traces arched her back and flattened her ears. "Having multiple heads is unpleasant! One time, on a boat out at sea, my arcanist insisted we try—*to impress someone, mind you*—and I realized I didn't make for a good chimera."

Of course, the utility of a chimera aura would depend on the eldrin in the area. Having a chimera of will-o-wisps and grifter crows would be near pathetic, but a dragon and a phoenix would be a thing of legend.

Then my thoughts went to the boat, and Zelfree's past.

"Master Zelfree," I muttered. "I have something I want to discuss with you."

"What is it?"

I met his gaze, wondering how I should phrase it. When I couldn't decide on a clever or diplomatic way to ask, I just went with blunt. "On more than one occasion, people have claimed you're a turncoat who only gave up pirate secrets to avoid being imprisoned for your own dastardly deeds. Fain even said you murdered the Marshall of the Southern Seas to help Calisto build his crew. Is... is any of that true?"

Traces stopped her purring.

A long moment of silence passed between us.

"What do you think?" Zelfree asked, no emotion in his voice.

"I—"

I stopped mid-sentence to mull over the situation. I had known Zelfree for a while now—almost two years. And upon further reflection, I think only Gillie and Eventide knew him more than I did.

I started again and said, "A turncoat doesn't care about the people or places he associates with. But you... You were willing to die to save your apprentices. You barged into Theasin's lab just to chastise him for the way he treated his son. And knowing that your mistakes might've cost other people their lives almost broke you. These are the actions of a man who might care too much."

Zelfree half-laughed. He ran a hand over his chin, hiding his smirk. "Is that what you think? Heh. Listen, I've never, and will never, betray the Frith Guild, no matter what some cutthroats might say." He shoved his hands into his coat pockets and shrugged. "Every piece of information I gave them—every person I killed—had been calculated and justified, even the Marshall of the Southern Seas."

"Really?" I asked, my voice a whole octave higher with hope.

He glared. "Don't look at me like that. I'd prefer if you didn't repeat any of this."

"But why not? Everyone thinks you're a scoundrel."

"It's better this way. Occasionally it still helps me." He

stepped into the hallway. "No pirate crew trusts me anymore, but some think they can still come to me to buy and sell information. They think I'm shady enough to be one of them, and that makes them easier to deal with."

Traces swished her tail. "Besides, no one would believe the truth, anyway. The only thing that spreads faster than fire is misinformation. Tales of my arcanist's exploits are in every tavern and pub from here to the abyssal hells. It would be impossible to correct them all now."

"Do you mind if I tell at least one person?" I asked.

"Who?" Zelfree asked as he stopped and turned around.

"Fain. The renegade pirate. The man who works with Gillie now."

"Why?"

"He's having a hard time adjusting to life beyond the *Third Abyss*. I figured you could help him, but he doesn't trust you."

Zelfree groaned.

"Are you okay?" I asked.

"Eh. I'll handle it. Whenever I see him next." He continued down the hall.

Traces leapt from my shoulder and chased after her arcanist.

It wasn't until I arrived at Skarn University that I realized how exhausted I was. I hadn't slept the whole night, and the constant training took its toll.

I shuffled through the university, my eyelids heavy and my body sluggish. The students and professors didn't mind my presence, which was good, because I still didn't have my guild pendant to show them. A piece of me figured they recognized me—I had come here as often as possible to check up on Adelgis.

When I made it to the recovery room, my heart sank into my stomach.

He looked worse.

Pale, shallow breathing, and coated in a thin layer of sweat. His sheets were twisted around his legs, like he had been thrashing about. Even his black hair, long enough to get tangled, appeared matted and wrapped around the small pillow.

"Adelgis," I said as I took a seat next to his cot.

He didn't answer. He didn't even acknowledge me.

Once settled, I leaned back in my chair. I would ask Gillie about his condition whenever she came back. Hopefully her research had been fruitful, and she knew what we needed to do moving forward.

I closed my eyes and exhaled.

I was having a dream—I just knew—and the scene played out in a familiar place. Theasin's research lab. But I wasn't me. I could *see* me, from my unkempt black hair to my curious expression as I glanced around the room.

It took me a long moment to realize I was Adelgis.

Zelfree and Theasin's argument played out a second time, mist haunting the corner of my vision, reminding me this was all an illusion. When the conversation ended, Adelgis approached his father and asked about the leech.

"So... you'll remove it?" I asked—well, *Adelgis* asked, but the surreal feeling of watching everything from his perspective halfway confused me.

"Don't be absurd," Theasin said. "Of course I will. It's a

valuable creature that needs to bond as soon as possible." He motioned to the stairs with a sharp flick of his wrist. "The room upstairs has already been prepared. My apprentice will make sure everything is in order while I speak with your master."

I patted Adelgis's ethereal whelk, and it floated over to me—the version of me I could see—the dream Volke watching the conflict unfold in front of him.

"Please watch Felicity?" I whispered. "I'll be back soon."

Then I climbed the stairs, my body shaking with each step. The cold railing stung my palms, but I didn't stop until I reached the top and opened the door. Something writhed beneath the skin over my ribs. No, not something. The leech. Every time it moved, even slightly, I felt it.

Was this how Adelgis experienced everything? He didn't complain much, but if this was accurate, it felt as though he had been on the edge of collapse.

I entered a small room with a wooden table, a long counter covered in medical instruments, and a bookshelf filled with glass bottles. The place smelled of dust and sweat, and with no windows or ventilation, the air hung thick.

The table disturbed me. Dark stains tarnished the oak wood, no doubt from blood. I ran my fingers over the markings, my hand unsteady. Then I undid my shirt and placed it onto the counter, next to the thin scalpel and pliers.

When the door opened, I grew stiff and cold.

"Father," I said, speaking in Adelgis's voice.

Theasin shut the door after entering. He turned his harsh gaze upon me, his eyes focusing on the leech. "Is there a reason you refuse to follow my instructions? Or is this just a manifestation of adolescent rebellion?"

"I don't know what you mean," I said.

And then Adelgis reached out with his magic—like trying to touch Theasin's thoughts with an invisible tendril of understanding. Reading his mind? But something prevented the magic from working, like a shield or blanket, covering everything from view. Theasin prevented Adelgis's ability from working, which seemed to relieve Adelgis.

"I made it clear what I thought of the Frith Guild," Theasin said. "Yet here you are, pretending to be a seafarer." He rubbed his gloved hands together and sneered. "Your life would've been more fulfilling had you done as I told you."

"I've enjoyed my time with the Frith Guild. They've done great things for the world."

"Only halfwits admire individual acts of heroism," Theasin stated, his tone laced with venom. "The problems of the world can't be solved by a handful of people. Real progress is made through fundamental improvements— magic, health, education. Saving one ship from pirates doesn't eliminate the threat of pirates. You understand this, don't you? Or do I need to use smaller words and simpler analogies?"

"I understand," I muttered.

"Then what? You knew a mariner's life was foolish, but you decided to do it anyway?"

"I joined the guild because I admired it, but also because I wanted to help you."

Adelgis' voice and tight chest made the conversation painful for me. I had never heard him sound so defeated and uncertain. He couldn't bring himself to meet his father's gaze. He half stared at the floor, his breathing raspy.

"Explain," Theasin commanded.

"You said you needed the help of a mimic arcanist." I reached into the front pocket of my trousers and withdrew a small stack of papers. "And while I doubt Master Zelfree will leave the Frith Guild, I did get him to tell me all about his bonding and where he found his mimic." I handed over the papers, but lifting my arm more than a few inches stole most of my strength.

Theasin snatched the notes away and read them.

I continued, "I figured you could use the information to find a mimic and help it bond. Then you'd have a mimic arcanist to call upon."

The silence hung as thick as the air. Theasin refolded the papers and tucked them into his cloak pocket. Then he turned his scrutinizing gaze on me—or, rather, on Adelgis.

"That's what you wanted... right?" I asked, my voice small.

With all the tenderness of a rock, Theasin patted my shoulder. His movements were so procedural and awkward that if I had been in control of the body, I would've laughed. Adelgis didn't, however. He seemed to relax at the touch, thankful in some way.

"I see," Theasin said. "Next time, you should begin with that." He pulled his hand away. "You've surprised me—and done better than I expected you to. The leech is alive, you've taken some of my concerns to heart, and you managed to meet me in Thronehold without my intervention."

"Thank you."

"With this information in hand, there's no need for you to stay in the Frith Guild."

"I'd rather see it through."

"Why?" Theasin snapped.

For a brief moment—something I feared deep in my gut —I thought Adelgis would tell him of the runestones and world serpent. Although Theasin was an accomplished researcher and occult scholar, I didn't want him to know of the potential power waiting out in the world.

Adelgis shook his head. "I've started my training with Master Zelfree, and I want to finish." He shifted his weight from one foot to the next; I suspected that Adelgis had debated with himself in this moment. Despite that, he remained quiet. He didn't tell his father.

Theasin exhaled as he picked up a pair of steel pliers. "Very well. I'll overlook your infantile decision to remain with the Frith Guild, but I expect you to come to your senses eventually. You aren't built for the high seas, and you haven't the disposition for swashbuckling. If you really want to experience those things, you should be content to read books in the safety of a library."

Adelgis replied with a single nod.

"Lay down. The sooner I can remove this leech, the better."

With painful movements—everything that disturbed the leech flared in agony—I hoisted myself up on the wooden table and laid down. The unforgiving wood didn't agree with Adelgis's bony shoulder blades. No matter how I tossed, there would be no comfort.

And then Theasin loomed over, his expression so cold and neutral it was hard to imagine he saw a person on the table and not a lump of flesh that needed dissecting. He placed a hand on my chest, the black gloves icier than his demeanor.

"Relax," he stated. "It'll be over shortly."

A powerful sensation came over me—magic spreading from Theasin's fingertips and soaking into my body. It slowed my heart and my breathing, and it dulled my thoughts. Once I couldn't move, Theasin took a scalpel and cut into my side.

Adelgis's side.

But it felt so real.

And the procedure bordered on nightmarish when I realized that Adelgis had no choice but to lie there as his father sliced into his flesh and peeled away skin. And Theasin offered no reassurances or words of explanation. He did his work with lifeless efficiency. At least it didn't hurt —everything was dulled by Theasin's magic.

The second he uncovered the abyssal leech, a harsh hissing filled the room.

Theasin growled something I didn't catch.

"No," the leech said, its voice both squeaky and sharp. "*No*. If you try to move me, I'll kill him." The creature gripped at Adelgis's insides with thin tendrils. It screamed something else, too high pitched to understand.

"Calm yourself. It's time for you to bond." Theasin stroked the length of the leech with the same unfeeling show of compassion. "But first you need to release your host."

The gripping tendrils loosened, but didn't let go. The leech writhed as it continued its hissing. "I... don't sense any people to bond... I need someone. I need..."

Theasin ripped the leech straight from Adelgis's ribcage —one brutal motion that splashed blood across the table, floor, and onto Theasin's cloak. The hissing and screaming intensified, but Theasin tightened his grip, and the crying died down, replaced with wet rasping.

It was a blessing that I couldn't feel the pain. I had felt the tendrils being dragged from the innermost sections of my body, and the disturbing knowledge that the creature had a grip close to the lungs and spine didn't sit well.

The abyssal leech wrapped itself around Theasin's arm, like it was trying to attack him but didn't have the means. Theasin ignored the thrashing of the blood-coated creature and instead turned his attention to the far bookshelf. He sifted through the glass bottles until he came to one—something with sand-like contents. He plucked the bottle from the shelf and returned to Adelgis.

"You'll recover," he said as he uncorked the container and poured the sand over the injury on Adelgis's side. "Don't exert yourself."

The tannish sand clung to the injury and mixed with the blood, creating clots and somehow lumping together. Theasin's magic waned, returning sensation a second too soon. The burning agony caused me to tense and suck in air through my teeth. It hurt from my throat to my knees—burning with each heartbeat.

Theasin placed all the tools back on the counter and then glanced around, his brow furrowed. He searched for something, and when he couldn't find it, he cursed under his breath and then headed for the door. No goodbye or concerned glance for his son. He just left.

Adelgis rolled to his side and curled into the fetal position. The sand continued to clump and soothe. It turned into new flesh and fixed itself into place over the massive injuries, slowly filling in the gouges like mortar fills in the gaps between bricks.

But the sand never took away the pain deep in my chest. The leech's tendrils had left a lasting torment that refused to relent.

What had it done? It wasn't a normal wound—it pulsed with something more. Something terrible.

TOURNAMENT ROUND TWO

I jerked myself awake, gulping down air.

The room in Skarn University was just how I had left it. Adelgis remained on the cot, his health declining. Now I knew why. The leech had injured him, but how?

Felicity floated nearby, her sparkling shell a welcome sight after the terrible nightmare.

"Was that you?" I asked.

"Yes," she said, her voice somehow sing-song and melancholy. "I wanted you to know what happened, so I manipulated your dreams. I hope you don't mind."

"Did you tell Gillie? Perhaps she can help with—"

"I told her." Felicity floated close and landed on the edge of Adelgis's bed. "But she doesn't know what to do with the information. No one seems to know."

I grabbed for my satchel and dug through the contents. When I found Theasin's book, I flipped straight to the section with mystical creatures. Perhaps there was some information in here I could use—or give Gillie to use.

To my relief, I found the section for abyssal leeches. It read:

. . .

Abyssal Leech
    Tier Unknown
    Reproduction: Progeny (lays eggs in the hearts of magical beings, both arcanists and mystical creatures)
    Trial of Worth: Unknown
    Records show that most civilizations purged abyssal leeches and their arcanists whenever they appeared. Extinct.
    True Form: Unobserved

I reread the section twice, my concern growing.

Theasin knew more about abyssal leeches than *this*. He told me himself, when we had a conversation in his lab, including their ability to manipulate magic.

"What're we going to do, Volke?" Felicity asked. "I don't want Adelgis to die."

"He won't. We'll find something."

"How can you be so sure?"

I wasn't, but despair wouldn't help either of us.

"We're in the largest city of the empire," I muttered. "*Someone* here must be able to help."

Desperate to find answers, I flipped through the book again. I stopped only once I came across the ethereal whelk entry. Could Adelgis's eldrin help in this situation? Perhaps. I barely knew anything about ethereal whelks. It read:

Ethereal Whelk
    Tier 1-3 (depending on the amount of magic consumed)
    Reproduction: Fable (born from certain children who die in water)

Trial of Worth: Overcoming a nightmare

Bizarre creatures capable of illusions, mind reading, dream manipulation, and changing their shape. Like reapers, ethereal whelks can permanently increase their magical capacity through outside sources. Unlike reapers, who must consume the essence of dying arcanists, ethereal whelks consume star shards.

The reproduction of ethereal whelks is widely debated. It seems that they are born from the corpses of children who died in water, but not all children. The age doesn't seem to play a factor, so long as the child has yet to reach puberty.

A passenger ship, The Regal Waves, crashed outside of Port Crown. Of the 132 child passengers, only 2 ethereal whelks were born.

A second passenger ship, Azure Dreams, crashed into rocks near the northern straits. Of the 56 child passengers, 3 ethereal whelks were born, all from the same siblings.

More research is needed to make solid conclusions.

True Form: Unobserved

I stared at the information, hoping an idea would come to me, but nothing did. Ethereal whelks and abyssal leeches seemed similar, but perhaps I was mistaken. Felicity couldn't help her arcanist, just like Luthair couldn't heal an injured soldier.

"There you are."

I glanced up from the pages to meet Illia's one-eyed gaze. She wore her coat secured shut in the front and a hat on her head, giving her an odd silhouette, but I'd always recognize her.

"What're you doing here?" I asked.

She held up a small bundle of golden poppies. The flowers radiated orange and yellow, their petals practically glowing. "I wanted to see how Adelgis was doing." She placed the flowers on the table next to his bed. "He didn't look this bad yesterday."

Why bring him flowers? Did they already consider him dead? The morbid thought hung heavy, and I wondered just how much time was left. Could he even recover at this point?

Felicity clung to her arcanist. "I hope he gets better soon."

The door flew open, hard enough that the handle slammed into the wall, leaving a mark. Zaxis strode in, fully dressed, with a shirt and everything—which meant he probably hadn't been practicing. Nicholin clung to his broad shoulder.

"I think we should try it," Nicholin said. He flailed his front paws around. "It would make for a great party trick, don't you think?"

Zaxis crossed his arms and leaned against the nearby wall. "I'm not swallowing anything I can't digest. Besides, I thought you and Illia couldn't retrieve things with her teleportation?"

"We can't. Yet. This would be a great way to practice."

"I'm not some idiot who eats coins."

"But just imagine how *impressed* Illia will be when we show her—"

"Nicholin," Illia snapped.

The pair of them flinched, obviously too wrapped up in their conversation to notice her presence. Nicholin disappeared from Zaxis and landed on his arcanist's shoulder. He squeaked as he wrapped himself around behind her neck.

"You ruined the surprise."

Zaxis walked over and threw an arm around Illia, drawing her close. With stiff movements, she leaned on him, but it was brief. A second later, she broke away and fixed her wavy hair.

"Adelgis isn't awake," she said. "I'm going to wait in the hall."

"Whatever you want, starfish," Zaxis said.

Illia flushed at the nickname as she hustled from the room. Her boots clicked hard on the wood floors until she shut the door.

Although I had a lot I wanted to discuss with Zaxis, I hadn't gotten over my exhaustion. My muddled thoughts swirled in my head, not quite adding up. To my surprise, Zaxis stepped past me and went straight to Adelgis's side. He placed a hand on his shoulder and held it there.

"What're you doing?" I asked.

"I'm trying to heal him," Zaxis muttered. "I stop by once a day to see if it'll have any affect, but it never does." He shot me a glower. "What're you doing here? Sleeping again?"

"Again?"

"Yeah. Every time I see you, you're passed out in the chair. It's like you only sleep when you're here."

I didn't know Zaxis had been visiting Adelgis so frequently. For some reason, that made me feel better. I thought I was the only one concerned, but it seemed I was mistaken.

"I give him pleasant dreams," Felicity chimed in. "Volke sleeps better when I do that. Same with Master Zelfree."

Except for the last dream she gave me. That would bother me for weeks to come.

"You better be good and rested for our match," Zaxis said. He removed his hand from Adelgis and headed toward the door. "Gillie will help Adelgis, so you should focus on the problems at hand."

He showed up every day to offer Adelgis healing—did he really think Gillie would come through? I doubted it.

I shook my head. "Don't worry. I'll be ready."

* * *

The day of our match came quicker than I thought.

In the morning, while I still dwelled on Adelgis's problem, I dressed in my sturdiest trousers, belt, and shirt. When I reached for my neck, I hooked the wendigo trinket, but not the Frith Guild pendant. It bothered me, but I couldn't deal with it now. I had to handle one problem at a time.

I headed through the town, separate from everyone else. They had practiced at our inn, but I had stayed close to Skarn University, like I had before. I didn't know why, but I thought better when I was alone. Even as I traveled through the city—riding the lamplighter trolleys until I reached the Dragon District—ideas came easier to me without distraction.

"Theasin has left Thronehold," I muttered.

Luthair stirred at my feet. "Yes, my arcanist."

"But what about Adelgis's brother, Niro? He's in the tournament, right? Maybe he doesn't know about the situation. He could help."

"Perhaps."

Niro had been in Theasin's lab, after all. There was a chance he knew about his father's research. If I could somehow explain the situation, maybe he'd know what to do.

When I arrived at Thronehold Coliseum, I had to shadow-step my way through the throngs of people. The matches were getting intense—according to the excited shouts of the crowd, anyway. The early bouts between master arcanists had everyone talking. I wished I could've seen them, but I had too many things to worry about. Runestones, Adelgis's health, my own training—when would I have time to watch a couple matches for fun?

I entered the apprentice pit, welcomed by a foul stench of stale sweat. It wasn't as crowded as the first day since half the contestants had been eliminated, but that didn't mean there was space. The stone golem itself took up a fourth of the room, even while sitting down. Its smooth marbled rock looked out of place in the gritty fighter's pit of the coliseum, but I didn't have time to dwell on it long.

I went straight for the bracket, cursing myself for not meeting Zaxis earlier to discuss our match. As it stood, we had a few hours to devise a strategy before our match would begin.

The moment I spotted our opponents, I caught my breath.

Lucian Nellit the Knightmare Arcanist – Steel Thorn Inquisitors Guild

Nyla Gane the Manticore Arcanist – Steel Thorn Inquisitors Guild

I didn't want to interact with Lucian, not after his indignant rage upon declining to join his guild. He had taken it too personally, and part of me thought he would take this fight too far as well.

"I hadn't seen a manticore arcanist with the inquisitors at the mines," I said.

Luthair stayed still near my feet, as if avoiding the boots of the other contestants. "The Grandmaster Inquisitor only involves knightmare arcanists when he uses his eclipse aura."

"Why even have a manticore arcanist in their guild? Isn't it a man-eater?"

"Manticores are adept at hunting people. One of the main objectives of the Steel Thorn Inquisitors is to hunt villains. Not only that, but immunity to the plague is a useful trait when fighting plague-ridden beasts."

"I suppose."

I still disliked manticores, however. Nothing would change my mind—not after fighting Calisto.

I turned away from the brackets and scanned the dank pit. The other competitors offered dirty looks or taunting expressions. I ignored them and searched for Niro. He wasn't around, though.

"Luthair," I muttered. "Find him."

"Yes, my arcanist."

Without further need for instruction, Luthair slithered from the room. I headed to one of the many prep rooms for the fighters. Although it would be smaller, the lack of other people and mystical creatures made it more bearable. I got to the door when someone grabbed my shoulder. With heat in my blood, I whirled around, but Zaxis met my anger with a look of his own.

"What did I say about strategizing?" he growled.

"Sorry. I was—"

"Don't apologize. Let's talk."

He opened the door and shoved me in. A moment later, he snapped his fingers and lit himself a small light. It illuminated most of the room, but the dim light of morning kept the corners shrouded in darkness. That didn't matter to me.

"I already have a plan," Zaxis said as he played with the

free-form flame in his hand. "You handle the manticore and its arcanist, and I'll handle the knightmare."

I lifted an eyebrow.

Zaxis huffed. "Don't look at me like that, *fool*. My fires can burn away your shadows, and I've seen you fight enough to know what knightmares are capable of. Forsythe and I can handle one idiot in armor. You'll handle the manticore because you can use the darkness to fling it out of the ring like you did with the orthrus and its arcanist."

"I think the knightmare arcanist might be more trouble than you realize."

"Feh." Zaxis waved away the comment with a flick of his wrist. "If I can handle you, I can handle him. Besides, I watched his earlier match. Sure, he won pretty easy, but his fighting style wasn't surprising."

I wasn't going to argue with Zaxis. If he thought he could handle the knightmare arcanist all his own, he was more than welcome to try. A piece of me figured it wouldn't be that simple, however.

Luthair shifted under the crack of the door and straight to my feet. "My arcanist," he said. "I found Niro."

"Good." I headed for the door. "Take me to him."

"Unfortunately, that isn't an option."

I stopped with my fingers on the handle. "Why?"

"Niro is with the prince and two princesses. He made it clear, in no uncertain terms, that he wouldn't speak with any of the competitors until after the tournament was over."

"Did you tell him about Adelgis?" I asked, glaring down at Luthair's shadow.

"I tried, but he rebuffed my efforts."

Zaxis half-laughed and then shrugged. "Don't worry. If he's competing, you'll see him in the arena."

My first instinct was to lash back with a sarcastic

comment, but Zaxis's words stilled my actions. He was right. We *would* see Niro eventually. Did Adelgis have that much time, though? It worried me that none of Adelgis's family rushed to do anything, even in life-or-death situations. How could they all be so callous?

"Stay here," Zaxis said. "Our fight's coming up, and we should be prepared."

When the time for our match arrived, one of the Knights Draconic opened the door to the tiny room and motioned us out. I followed the man, who wore full plate armor, all the way to the wrought-iron gate that led to the coliseum field. It was open already, and Master Zelfree waited on the other side.

The stomping of the crowd rumbled the whole amphitheater. Dust and flakes of stone showered down from the ceiling. I had to rub my hair to clear it of the debris as I made my way outside.

"The second rounds of the Sovereign Dragon Tournament are about to begin!" the announcer shouted, his voice carrying to every inch of the coliseum.

An explosion of applause hurt my ears. I rubbed at my temples, trying not to dwell on the fact I couldn't hear myself think. Zaxis didn't seem to mind. He held his hands up and greeted some of the spectators with waves and a smile.

Forsythe swooped out of the sky and landed near his arcanist. He, too, reveled in the audience's attention. He fluffed up his feathers and hopped along the stone walkway to the arena platform with his head held high.

Vercingetorix spread his gargantuan wings—probably

just to stretch—but that minor movement shaded half the coliseum, and the crowd went wild.

I turned my attention to the queen's box. Lyvia and Evianna were there again, along with their brother and Niro. Why hadn't Lyvia answered my request to meet? Did she not want to associate with me? Or perhaps she was too busy. I didn't know if she could help with the runestones, but I still needed to try.

"After the match is over, I want you to contact Lyvia again," I said, my voice almost inaudible.

"By your command, my arcanist," Luthair replied.

The announcer spoke again. "Our next apprentice match is between the Frith Guild and the Steel Thorn Inquisitors Guild! Volke Savan the Knightmare Arcanist and Zaxis Ren the Phoenix Arcanist versus Lucian Nellit the Knightmare Arcanist and Nyla Gane the Manticore Arcanist! What a matchup, ladies and gentlemen! This'll be a fight to remember!"

Master Zelfree stopped when we reached the steps to the stone platform. He gave me a nod as I climbed my way up to the edge of the arena. Zaxis followed close, and once we were in position, I turned my attention to the far side.

Lucian and his knightmare, Azir, stood waiting.

Next to them was a woman and an adolescent manticore —a young lion with bat wings and red scorpion tail. It looked just as disgusting as I thought it would, and it kept its black eyes trained on us. The woman patted her manticore, but it was hard to get many details about her. She wore thick leather armor, including a cowl that covered half her face and gloves that attached to her sleeves.

To my surprise, Lucian walked forward. The woman, Nyla, matched his pace. They made it halfway across the arena and then stopped. Lucian kept his hands behind his back and waited.

"A sign of respect!" the announcer shouted. "How civil!"

The dog arcanists hadn't shown any deference in our match, so seeing Lucian and Nyla ready to offer bows was unexpected.

I walked to the center of the arena with Zaxis. He gave me a questioning look, like I should know what's going on, but I didn't. When we reached our opponents, I bowed at the waist, as was custom for formal duels, and Zaxis followed suit.

Lucian and Nyla did the same. The crowd cheered our sportsmanship and displays of honor, but the tension between us reeked of aggression.

"I'm going to humiliate you," Lucian said as he stood.

I straightened my posture and met his beady-eyed gaze.

He continued, "I'll show you the gravity of your mistake by proving that the Grandmaster Inquisitor is a superior mentor. You'll be broken and weeping before this match is over."

UNEXPECTED STRATEGY

Zaxis flashed Lucian a smirk. "Talk is cheap. Come at us and I'll knock those delusions right out of your head."

With the formalities concluded, we walked back to our side of the arena, the pulse of excitement and the cheers of the audience mixing into my own exhilaration. Although Zaxis appeared invigorated by Lucian's challenge, I knew it meant that Lucian wasn't going to hold back. He had something in mind, and that troubled me.

"You should be cautious," I said to Zaxis as we took our place at the edge of the platform.

"I know what I'm doing."

The announcer cleared his throat. "Are we finally ready? Because it's time to begin!"

Vercingetorix roared, rumbling the coliseum more than the stomping or clapping of the crowd.

I didn't need to call Luthair's name—he merged with me a moment later, coating me in shadow plate armor within the span of a couple seconds. The cold mystic metal helped relax and focus me.

Lucian turned to the manticore arcanist. "Nyla, thank you for your assistance, but I'll handle this on my own."

Although Nyla and the manticore gave him skeptical looks, they both muttered something I couldn't hear and then nodded. To my surprise—and shock—Nyla leapt from the side of the arena and landed in the red dirt surrounding the platform.

A bell rang out, its clang combining with the gasps of the audience.

Then her manticore followed her.

Another clang of the bell.

"What's going on?" the announcer asked with a laugh. "Nyla and her eldrin have forfeited the match!"

Zaxis glowered at me. "This fool thinks he can beat us both by himself?"

That was what Lucian had meant when he said he would *humiliate me*. He intended to win at a self-imposed disadvantage. That wouldn't happen, though. Lucian didn't understand me or Zaxis, whereas I finally understood what made him tick.

In the next instant, Azir and Lucian bonded. They lived and died as a single entity, just like me and Luthair, but their added strength wouldn't be enough. Lucian had to understand that fact. What was his strategy then?

Zaxis stepped forward, and Forsythe took to the sky with an eagle-like screech.

I held out a hand. "Wait," I said in my double voice.

"Why?" Zaxis barked. "We'll win this match faster than—"

A wave of darkness rushed over the coliseum, blanketing everything in the void of a starless night. The crowd was awed into silence, and a creepy stillness came over the amphitheater. Even the wind stopped, as though the world held its breath to observe the shadowy phenomenon.

Zaxis wildly glanced around, his eyes unfocused. Forsythe circled over the arena, his bright body the only light visible.

The brilliance of the sun had been stolen by Lucian's eclipse aura.

Unlike the Grandmaster Inquisitor's aura—that covered the countryside—Lucian's seemed small, like it couldn't extend past the coliseum itself.

And Lucian struggled. I could see it from across the arena platform. He doubled over and panted, the exertion of his magic almost too much for him. An aura obviously required more than manipulation or evocation.

"What's going on?" the announcer asked, amusement in his voice. "How will we know who's winning?"

Zaxis ignited a flame in his palm, but it did little to light up the area. The darkness around us was supernatural—it chased the light away with aggressive shadows that aimed to snuff out the flame.

"I can't see," he growled.

Without much thought, I leapt to his side and placed my gauntleted hand on his shoulder. I gave him the ability to temporarily see in the dark, but that wouldn't be enough to win. Given the way Lucian wrestled with his ability to create the eclipse aura, I suspected he wouldn't be able to maintain it—which meant he'd aim to end the fight quickly.

"Stay close to me," I commanded.

The aura empowered my abilities as well. In theory, I could counter anything Lucian threw our way.

Zaxis shrugged off my grip. "He's just strengthening himself. We need to end this fast!"

He didn't wait for my reply. He rushed forward and grabbed a small pouch from his belt. He threw it and unleashed a wave of his flames. Once heated, the contents of the pouch exploded outward in a flash of bright white and red.

Lucian shielded his face since his knightmare didn't offer total protection.

The explosive must have had gunpowder and metal flakes or salt to create such a flash. Clever. I wondered if Zaxis's tactic would work as a distraction. Since Lucian was all alone, we could win the match in an instant if he was thrown from the arena.

But then the darkness around us moved with ominous intent.

The same chains and hooks I saw at the mines rose from the ground and lashed out. While I could use my own knightmare magic to repel them—without pain, thanks to the eclipse—Zaxis wasn't as lucky. He tried to burn them with flames, but the shadow-realm we found ourselves in was too powerful. His fire didn't destroy the chains.

The hooks stabbed into his left arm and leg. He grunted and fought against the hold, but the hooks themselves were barbed and clung to muscle. I wanted to help him, but he had gotten too far away from me. When Zaxis thrashed against his restraints, he tore his flesh, growling curses the entire time. More hooks and chains emerged from the darkness—two more sinking into his shoulder and calf.

Forsythe flew toward his arcanist, but Lucian held up a hand and evoked terrors. Forsythe screeched and then plummeted from the sky. He hit the red dirt outside the platform.

Despite the darkness, a bell rang out. Someone could see what was happening.

Zaxis, bleeding from the hooks, was dragged to the edge

of the arena, fighting the entire way. Fire erupted from every inch of him, scorching his clothing and the sandstone platform.

Was Lucian going to tear him apart, like he did the plague-ridden arcanists? No. That was overkill.

Then again, he had said he wanted us broken and weeping...

Cursing the abyssal hells, I shadow-stepped to Lucian.

Chains sprang up all around me, like a trap waiting to be sprung. Lucian must've anticipated my move. I blocked the most devastating shadows with my shield and thrust forward with my sword, no hesitation. I wouldn't let him rip apart Zaxis.

Lucian was too consumed with his magic to dodge. My blade cut through his knightmare's armor and straight into the soft part of his gut. He gasped and grabbed at my sword arm, his body trembling.

Another clang of a bell—for Zaxis, no doubt—but it didn't shake my focus. A hook caught the thigh of my right leg. I ignored that as well.

He's faltering, Luthair said in my mind. *Finish this.*

Empowered by the false eclipse, I manipulated the darkness to yank Lucian from the arena. I didn't create chains like the Grandmaster Inquisitor or Lucian—it was more like a web or net that clung to every inch of him and prevented shadow-stepping. When he tried to fight my shadows, I slashed with my blade, catching his neck and collar bone and cutting deep.

His concentration failed. I threw him from the arena.

The magic blotting out the sun broke apart, allowing the day to come in bursts. Another bell rang out. When I managed to catch my breath, I realized the audience was cheering.

I had thrown Lucian a good fifteen feet from the platform. He lay on his back, his blood gushing into the red dirt and creating a gory mud. His breathing came in short bursts, interrupted by painful coughing.

Zaxis stood outside the arena, his hook injuries already healing.

I was the only one left standing.

"That was the craziest match I didn't get to see," the announcer said with a laugh. "The winners are Volke Savan and Zaxis Ren! Their duel in the darkness was obviously a bloody one!"

I lifted my sword and the audience went wild. Flowers, bits of color cloth, and food rained down from the stands. While merged to Luthair, his helmet protected me from the bigger bits, and I just laughed to myself. While one of Lucian's hooks had caught my leg, it wasn't deep—also thanks to Luthair's armor. It healed without problem, leaving me practically unharmed.

I unmerged as I walked to the edge of the arena. Master Zelfree stood near the steps, his arms crossed and a smirk across his face.

"Good work," he said, his voice drowned out by the exhilaration of the crowd.

Zaxis walked around the platform, his expression set into permanent irritation. Forsythe flew to his side, but upon glancing at his face, didn't say anything.

"You've been reading a lot of books," Zelfree said, his volume set to *loud* just to be heard. "Nice use of fireworks, even if it didn't work like you wanted."

"I need to make them bigger," Zaxis growled.

"The metal you're using could be ground down finer, to create more of a flare. It'll blind people if you use enough. Still, I'm impressed with what you've done. You did well."

This conversation seemed to assuage Zaxis's anger. He rotated his arms and nodded along with Zelfree's words, even muttering a *yeah, I'll make it better*. Forsythe perked up a bit, despite the hail of petals and food scraps.

The three caladrius flew down from the sides and washed the amphitheater in their glittering healing magic. Then they landed next to Lucian and administered the most powerful of their abilities.

Despite the odd looks I got from Zaxis and Zelfree, I walked over to Lucian to check on him. The bright white birds had healed the worst of his injuries, and when Lucian attempted to stand, I held out my hand.

He tried to take it, but he remained weak. I had to pull him to his feet and then steady him so he didn't fall over.

"This is why apprentices shouldn't use an aura," Zelfree said, startling me. I hadn't realized he followed me. "It takes a toll. I suspect he couldn't maintain it for longer than sixty seconds without passing out."

I shook my head. "The Grandmaster Inquisitor seemed to think it was important all knightmare arcanists knew this, no matter their level of training."

"Because the Inquisitor assumes there will always be other knightmare arcanists nearby to benefit. The eclipse aura's usefulness is multiplied by the number of people it's enhancing—but as a sole fighter? That was a terrible risk Lucian made. And he underestimated your capabilities."

Lucian shoved me away, his body tense. With unsteady movements, he turned on his heel and walked away. He and his knightmare remained merged. I was certain they would both collapse if they separated.

Zelfree motioned me to the gates. "Let's go. He'll be fine."

The apprentice matches continued with plenty of excitement from the crowd. I thought most people would prefer the grandiose nature of master arcanists fighting, but apparently the paired battles made for great entertainment as well.

Some apprentices had fantastic synergy. Some had mythic creatures that distracted or weakened the opponents, and their partners were nothing but power—once their opponents were dazed, they'd get thrown from the ring by the muscle. Simple tactics, but effective.

I sat in the stands next to Zaxis and Forsythe, my mind only half on the fights. I kept my full attention on Princess Lyvia and Evianna, and when they got up from their seats and left, I wondered where they were off to. Adelgis's brother, and the prince I had never met, remained with the queen, each pointing or commenting on the fights. Would the princesses return?

"Pay attention," Zaxis barked. "It's Illia and Hexa up next."

My chest tightened as I returned my attention to the arena.

Master Zelfree stood on the sideline as Illia and Hexa stepped up onto the platform. The wind blew the red dirt around the sidelines, hiding some of the flowers and debris thrown from the citizens of Thronehold. Nicholin waved to the crowds with his little rizzel paws, reveling in the cheering. Raisen hissed with both his hydra heads. Hexa and Illia, though, were too engrossed in a conversation to care about the audience.

The announcer shouted, and the audience got riled, but I paid close attention to Illia's and Hexa's stance. It was different than before, and I suspected they had strategized beforehand.

Their opponents were a pair of yeti arcanists, one man and one woman. They wore thin studded armor, but no weapons. They didn't need them, though. Yetis were powerful beasts, much like bears, with muscled bodies and long fangs. Their snowy fur contrasted nicely with their ebony claws. Each breath they took reminded me of Fain. It came out as a frosty mist, and the arena was already coated in a light layer of ice.

When the fight started, Illia and Hexa didn't separate. They stayed together as Raisen breathed out a hideous amount of toxic gas. The greenish-purple fog hung close to the ground, creating that deadly moat I had advocated for. Illia, Nicholin, and Hexa remained behind Raisen as he continued to spew the poison. If left alone, Raisen would cover the whole arena in a matter of minutes, likely winning the match. The moment those yetis or their arcanists breathed it in, they'd be incapacitated.

The yetis charged forward, roaring as they went. They lumbered like bipedal bears, their arms long enough that their claws scraped the stone of the platform. When they reached the gas, they closed their mouths, but Hexa and Illia were prepared. Hexa threw poison-coated knives, and Illia teleported behind the arcanists with her own set of blades.

It didn't take long—it only took seconds after getting cut to see the effects of hydra venom. Even the massive yetis, who had to weigh 500 pounds, collapsed to their knees in agony.

Someone tapped my shoulder, and I glanced up.

Two of the Knights Draconic stood close, their hands on the hilts of their swords.

"Volke Savan?" one asked.

"Yes?"

"You're to come with us, by order of the crown."

I got up from my seat, tense and confused. "What's going on?"

"Just come with us."

Zaxis leapt up and smacked his hands together, like he was ready to backhand some knights, even though they were the authority here. I motioned him to sit back down, thankful he would come to my defense, but also worried he would escalate a casual encounter to something serious.

"I'll be back," I said to him.

He nodded.

Then the two knights placed hands on both my shoulders to lead me out of the spectator's box.

"Princess Evianna wishes to speak with you in private."

39

A DUEL TO THE DEATH

The Knights Draconic took me to their unicorn eldrin outside of the coliseum. I marveled at their draft horses' sizes and wondered if they'd make me ride one. Fortunately, the moment never came. They escorted me via will-o-wisp trolley to the castle gates, only a district away from the coliseum.

We didn't speak much, which was fine. Instead, I dwelled on Evianna's request. Why hadn't Lyvia sent for me? She had been the one I contacted, not the younger sister. Perhaps there had been a mistake?

When we finally arrived at our destination, I hopped off the trolley and allowed the knights to guide me into the castle. Although I probably looked like a criminal, they didn't lay hands on me or speak in a gruff manner. They didn't speak at all, actually. We walked in silence through the front room, a guest lounge, and then to a set of stairs that led into the ground.

Evianna waited at the top of the staircase with a stiff posture. Her ivory dress, covered in a blue lace, reminded me of spider webs. The collar went up to her jawline, keeping her neck long and straight. Her purplish-white hair was secured back in a tight bun atop her head, giving her a bit of pretend height.

"Leave us," Evianna said to the knights.

They exchanged hesitant glances, but complied without protest. Once they shut the door, I glanced around. The room was located in the middle of the castle, which meant no windows. Air howled up from the staircase, indicating something down below had access to the outside, but it was difficult to determine how far away that exit was. Lanterns hung from the walls, illuminating the gloomy space just enough to see, but not enough to absorb details.

"Hello again," I said.

"We don't have time for pleasantries." Evianna headed down the stairs. "Follow me."

I walked down the narrow steps, surprised by how quickly the temperature dropped as we descended. Evianna shivered and rubbed at her arms. I didn't have a coat to offer her, however.

The stones of the castle became more and more null-stone the deeper underground we went. A terrible sense of suffocation came over me, and I knew there had to be raw nullstone nearby. I hated the feeling—I wanted nothing more than to climb the stairs and leave this place.

When we reached the bottom, we came face-to-face with a nullstone double door. The gap at the bottom spewed air at a steady rate.

Evianna stood under the sole lantern. "You're a good combatant."

Her statement caught me off guard. I rubbed at my neck and nodded. "Thank you?"

"My sister is in the other room. I brought you here so you could help her become a better fighter."

I glanced at the door and then returned my attention to Evianna, an eyebrow raised. "A better fighter *how*?"

She huffed and crossed her arms. "I don't know. Teach her your special technique for winning."

"I don't have a *special technique for winning*. That's not how combat works. It takes years of practice so that your stance and skills become second nature. And even then, you need to take your opponent into consideration. Their style of fighting will change the course of—"

"I don't care," Evianna interjected. "I saw how you won both your tournament matches. You were so fast and capable. The opponents didn't stand a chance. You need to teach Lyvia whatever it is you know."

"Why does she need to be a better fighter? She doesn't have to fight anyone—not when she has the queen, the knights, and the legionnaires."

Evianna met my gaze with tears in the corners of her eyes. She glared, hardening her expression, but unable to hide her distress. "What's wrong with you? Lyvia is trying to bond with the hatchling sovereign dragon. She can't rely on others once this tournament is over. She has to participate in a fight to the death!"

The information stole my breath.

I had almost forgotten about the sovereign dragon trial of worth. Lyvia was participating? Did she really intend to fight others to the death in front of the denizens of Throne-hold? I almost couldn't believe it. She didn't seem like she was the type. Then again, it was the only way to become a sovereign dragon arcanist.

"You need to help my sister," Evianna said, her tone haughty. "That's a command, by the way. Now go in there and talk to her." She pointed to the double doors.

I opened one side—it was difficult, what with the air

pushing against me—and stepped into a large, circular chamber. Sunlight streamed down from a hole in the dome roof, creating a pillar of illumination. Massive bones were stacked against the walls. I examined them as I ambled in, my head tilted back just so I could get a good look. Some of them looked like sovereign dragon remains, but the others had six legs and jaws like crocodiles.

"What are those?" I whispered.

"King basilisks," Luthair replied. "When the queen ordered their genocide, she collected their bodies."

I hadn't realized how *giant* king basilisks were. They rivaled the sovereign dragons, despite not having any wings. Regular basilisks, on the other hand, were smaller beasts, often no larger than a dog. Seeing so many stacked in this basement room caused me to shudder. The queen had ordered the death of many people. No wonder she was so unpopular.

The clink of metal on metal drew me out of my thoughts. I turned my attention to the center of the room. Lyvia swung around a light saber, occasionally striking a rusted suit of armor hanging on a post. She wasn't striking hard—just practicing her form and footwork. With each hit, she returned to her start and went again. It was a common drill I had engaged in plenty of times.

I watched for a moment, admiring her skill. She didn't look like she needed any guidance, and she moved as though she had done this thousands of times before. Her white hair had been braided tight, and her clothing was little more than a tunic, trousers, and boots.

"*Go,*" Evianna hissed from my side.

I flinched, unaware of her close proximity.

After a long exhale, I walked into the light streaming down from the ceiling. The hole in the dome roof went up a considerable distance and was the source of the cool air flowing into the room.

"Lyvia," I said.

She whirled around on the ball of her foot, her eyes wide. "Volke? What're you doing here?" In the next moment, her gaze went to her sister. "Evianna, is this your doing?"

"He's here to practice with you," her sister said as she flounced into the light. "You need help."

Lyvia wiped the sweat from her brow and then fidgeted with the hem of her tunic—straightening it and rubbing her palms along the fabric. "I didn't think anyone would see me like this."

"I'm sorry," I muttered. "The knights escorted me here and—"

"You asked the knights to drag him here?" Lyvia asked her sister. "That's irresponsible, Evianna. An abuse of your authority."

Evianna shook her head. "I don't care. The tournament is halfway over! You need every advantage if you're going to win against Rishan!" She huffed and stormed out of the light again, like she couldn't control herself enough to prevent an outburst.

I didn't know what to say. Illia and I never argued like this, and even when we did have disagreements, Gravekeeper William would know how to handle the situation without conflict. What would he do in this situation?

"Lyvia," I said as I stepped forward. "It's okay. I don't mind being brought here. I've been meaning to talk with you, regardless."

She sheathed her saber and furrowed her brow. "I got your message after the first tournament match, but I didn't answer you because I thought you wanted to dissuade me from fighting for the sovereign dragon."

"Er, no. I didn't even know you were doing that until Evianna told me on the way here. I had something else I wanted to speak about."

Lyvia tilted her head and half-smiled. "Is that so?" She motioned me close. "Please, tell me whatever is on your mind."

I walked over, intrigued by the pillar of light. It seemed mystical somehow—surrounded by a perfect circle of sunlight—and while I preferred the darkness since I had bonded with Luthair, I liked the way the afternoon rays glinted off the loose strands of Lyvia's white hair.

"Um," I began. "I wanted to talk to you about the queen's trinkets and artifacts. She has a lot of them on display in the castle."

"Yes? What about them?"

"Do you think it would be possible to buy them?" I shrugged and added, "Or perhaps borrow them?"

"Which one?"

Guildmaster Eventide made it clear we shouldn't reveal the presence of the world serpent, but I would never get the runestones unless I spoke about them openly.

"The stones above the throne room," I said. "The twelve hanging over the doorframe."

Lyvia shook her head. "Oh, I doubt she would sell those. They're called *runestones* and they supposedly have histor-ical and magical significance."

"Well, that's the thing." I sighed. "I think someone is going to steal them."

Both her eyebrows shot to her hairline. "You do?"

"Yes. So, maybe the Frith Guild can take them for a short while—to protect them. Do you think Queen Velleta would allow that?"

It was the best tactic I could come up with. We didn't

need to keep the runestones, after all. We just needed them for the god creatures. And if we could find someone to bond with each one before the queen found out, that would be for the best.

"I doubt it," Lyvia said. She placed both her hands on her hips. "Oma doesn't like to give anything to anyone. She thinks our nullstone castle is the safest place in the empire. I mean, the thief during the gala was caught pretty quickly and easily. Why would she give the runestones to a traveling guild?"

I hadn't thought about that. Still. I had to try.

"I think the thieves might be assessing the strengths of the castle and planning something major."

She laughed for a moment. "For the runestones? Why?"

"Er, well, maybe for *lots of things*, the runestones included. I'm just worried."

"There's no need to fret. Oma and Vercingetorix will defend everything in the castle with their lives. No one is going to take those runestones, trust me."

Evianna stomped back into the circle of light, her cheeks flushed, and her mouth pressed into a tight, white line. "No. Stop this. You should be practicing." She pointed to the rusted suit of armor. "Volke, I command you to show her your fighting techniques!"

My conversation with Lyvia was basically over. I failed to convince her of the importance. But what else could I do? If I couldn't reveal the actual reason, I didn't have anything to base my justifications on. Plus, Lyvia thought the castle was a much safer place than the Frith Guild. If I told her about the world serpent, I figured she would go straight to the queen with the information.

What other angle could I try?

Lyvia withdrew her saber. "I'm sorry about this. Evianna can be rather demanding."

I reached down to the shadow at my feet. "It's okay." I pulled out the shadow blade that Mathis had created. "I don't mind practicing with you."

The suffocating effects of the nullstone remained. Out of curiosity, I tried to return the sword to the darkness, but it wouldn't go. The field of anti-magic prevented active uses of magic, but didn't cancel on-going effects, just as I had suspected.

"I've trained with several master swordsmen," Lyvia said as she took a position opposite me. "I've learned several styles, but I think one-handed finesse is my preferred."

I wasn't versed enough in formal swordsmanship to know which I favored. I nodded along with her words and held my sword at the ready. I almost reached for my shield, but I thought better of it. She wasn't using a shield.

When she stepped forward to attack, I parried and moved away. Lyvia thrust again, keeping an aggressive pressure. I knocked her blade to the side, and she recovered with a quick jab that caught my forearm. Her speed impressed me, but the sting of the cut was light.

"Are you okay?" she asked as she stepped back.

I glanced at the injury. It didn't heal. Not with the nullstone. But it wasn't deep. "I'm fine," I said as I readied my weapon a second time.

We went again. Lyvia continued her aggressive fighting style—never letting up, always ready with a counter. She cut me again, and I realized her skill probably exceeded mine. That wasn't a surprise, though. I started learning swordplay less than two years ago, and she had apparently studied all her life.

However, when she went in for the third attack, I understood her pattern. I feigned one direction and then caught her with the edge of my sword, slicing through her tunic and into her shoulder. I held back, though—I didn't want to hurt her—but a crimson stain bloomed across the fabric.

Evianna gasped. "Lyvia!"

She held up a hand to quiet her younger sister. Then she gingerly touched the injury. Shallow. She pressed her palm down on it, stifling the blood flow.

"I didn't expect that," Lyvia muttered.

"You fight in a predictable manner." I pantomimed her movements, showcasing the way she thrust her saber. "Whenever you attack like this, you follow it up with a strike." I tried my best to mimic her movements. "You did it enough times that I could use it against you. In a fight, you never want to be predictable."

"I've never sparred against a person before."

"I thought you said you had multiple swordsmen teach you their fighting styles?"

"They went over the techniques, but they were all too afraid of Oma to hurt me. We never sparred. It was just... drills. And practicing by myself."

I lowered my weapon, my chest tight with doubt. That was a huge deficiency in her training. A real fight just wasn't the same as practicing moves on a stationary dummy.

"How many opponents are going to participate in the death match?" I asked. "Maybe you can use the remainder of your time to study their fighting styles. That could give you the edge, even though you've never sparred against someone."

"There's only one other opponent."

I lifted an eyebrow. "I thought everyone who wanted to bond with the sovereign dragon fought in a battle royal?"

"That's correct." Lyvia turned her gaze to the floor. The

castle stones shone in the sunlight, but they didn't chase away the melancholy atmosphere. "However, only two people completed all the tests required to participate in the battle royal. Everyone else..."

"They failed?" I asked.

Evianna huffed, drawing my attention. "They were attacked! And it was all Rishan's fault."

I turned back to Lyvia. "Attacked?"

She nodded, her eyes still downcast. "That's right. All the other participants, including the grandson of Knight Captain Rendell, were injured during their trials. One by one, they were disqualified."

"And some man named Rishan is to blame?"

"I don't have any evidence it was him." Lyvia glanced up and met my gaze with a cold glare. "But I *know* it was him."

The seriousness of her tone surprised me. I took a moment to absorb the information while I wrapped my minor injuries in gauze that I kept in a small belt pouch. I never really needed it, but I kept it just in case I ran into non-arcanists with injuries. As soon as I left this underground chamber, every wound would heal, so there was no need to tend to them. The work allowed me to concentrate, though. I dwelled on the problem, wondering how best to achieve a solution.

"Who is this Rishan man?" I asked.

Lyvia and Evianna exchanged glances, like they couldn't believe I would ask.

"Rishan is my older brother," Lyvia said. "And he's a power-hungry autocrat of the highest order. That's why I volunteered for the sovereign dragon's trial of worth, even though I knew it could kill me. I think the world will be made worse if my brother was ever allowed to bond with a creature as powerful as a sovereign dragon."

40

HEROES SAVE PEOPLE

"Your brother can't be that bad," I said.

Lyvia shook her head. "He's always been cruel, ever since we were small children. And he thinks it's his destiny to bond with a sovereign dragon." She gripped her injured arm tighter than before. "It's hard to explain, but he's the kind of man who revels in power over others. He delights in simpering and goes out of his way to make sure those beneath him know it." Then she relaxed a bit. "Have you met a person like that?"

"Yes. They're unfortunately too common."

"The others who were competing all met with disaster. One woman was found dead. One of the squires broke a leg on one of the trials, but when questioned, all he said was *he had to forfeit*. No matter how many terrible things happened, Oma said they were all coincidences. She *likes* Rishan—more than anyone else in the family, I would wager. She never believes me when I speak of his questionable behavior."

"The less competition, the more likely he'll win."

"Then you must understand the position I'm in. What would you do if you were me?"

I knew the moment she asked the question. I would do the exact thing she had done: participate in the trial of worth to prevent my brutish sibling from bonding. Then again, this situation made me sick. The whole point of a trial of worth was to weed out those who weren't suited to the noble task of becoming an arcanist. Yet... it seemed like wherever I went, there was always someone trying to manipulate the outcome of the trials. First, it was Schoolmaster Tyms back on my home Isle of Ruma, and now it was Queen Velleta, trying to make sure her dynastic legacy maintained control of dragons.

What could be done about this? I didn't have a solution, but an odd thought struck me while I contemplated.

"Lyvia, what if you could bond with something more powerful than a sovereign dragon? Would you consider that an acceptable path to take?"

She furrowed her brow and then shook her head. "Dragons are the most powerful of eldrin."

"Hypothetically. If there was something, would you bond with it to help keep your brother in check?"

I wasn't going to tell her about the world serpent—not without Guildmaster Eventide's permission—but what if Lyvia bonded to the beast? She seemed reasonable, and honorable, and noble in all regards. It wouldn't surprise me if the world serpent wanted to bond with her.

Lyvia sighed. "If you had told me a year ago, I would've considered it, but now I've run out of time. Rishan and I are the only ones left, and if I withdraw from the trial of worth because I fear death, I'm just a coward."

I figured she would answer that way. It was the same thing I would've said.

"None of my heroes would run," Lyvia said, hardening her voice and posture. "Lark the Gallant faced countless challenges, even when he knew the odds were against him. How can I ever think of myself as their equals if I run when given the opportunity?"

Evianna ground her teeth—loud enough I could hear. She scrunched her eyes shut and then fled from the room, her dress flowing behind her as she ran. I gave thought to chasing her, but I didn't know what I would say.

"It's okay," Lyvia muttered. "Evianna doesn't want me to participate. She's made that clear since the first test." Lyvia reached into her tunic and withdrew the glitter crab shell she had on her necklace. "Evianna's done everything to help me, even when I told her not to worry. The luck from the glitter crab shell was her latest great idea. It pains me that she's so upset."

I would be upset if Illia participated in a duel to the death. I wasn't sure how to comfort Evianna, though. The entire situation seemed outside of my control.

Lyvia lowered her voice and stepped closer to me, her gaze distant. "Volke. Answer me honestly. After witnessing my fighting technique, do you think I can win?" Her hands trembled, betraying her dread.

"I don't know."

It was an honest answer. I couldn't know for sure until I saw her brother. She had skill, sure, and I had seen her speed—but power and experience could make the difference. I needed more information.

"I'm sorry," I whispered.

She shook her head and half-smiled. "It's fine. You have no way of truly knowing. I was childishly looking for reassurance, but the time for that has long passed."

"Don't hesitate," I said.

"Hm?" Lyvia glanced up, a hint of confusion in her expression.

"When you go to fight Rishan. Don't hesitate. You can't... have regrets about killing him if you're going to win." That was a lesson both Master Zelfree and Zaxis had taught me. Hesitation had no place on the battlefield—not when life was on the line.

Lyvia didn't reply. The words visibly sank into her being, weighing on her like only tragic news could. She already knew her destiny. One of them would have to die. And even if she thought her brother was a brute, that didn't mean she wished to be his killer.

"I think I need to rest," Lyvia muttered. She stepped away from me, her hand still clasped over the wound on her shoulder. "I'll get this healed and spend the rest of the day hardening my soul to the reality of the situation. Thank you, Volke. I apologize for my sister, who continues to meddle in your life, but I'm also glad she did. I don't think we would've met, otherwise."

I nodded along with her words, though it didn't ease the tension in the air. Our pillar of light had almost vanished. The sun overhead had moved in such a way that the light no longer shone directly through the hole in the roof. I hadn't noticed until then, but lanterns hung on all the walls, keeping the room aglow in orange and yellow.

Lyvia motioned to the door. She said nothing as I made my way out of the room. The hollow eyes in the skulls of the king basilisks haunted me. It was like they watched my every movement.

It struck me then—the queen had ordered their genocide and then kept their parts for herself, no doubt to make magical items. It was yet another sick aspect to the story I didn't want to dwell on.

I shut the door behind me and took the first few steps in slow silence.

Evianna walked down from a step and blocked my path, her cheeks red and her expression cold.

"If you can't teach her how to win, then I want you to stop her from participating."

"What?" I asked.

"Convince her not to fight. Tell her it's foolish. Tell her she's not suited for combat. *Tell her whatever it takes to make her stop.*"

"She's made up her mind," I said. "I don't think I can talk her out of it."

"Then do something else!" Evianna rubbed at her eyes with the back of her arm. "Please." She took another step down and then threw herself onto me. I braced and kept my footing—she was lightweight—but she gripped my shirt with an unbreakable force and pressed her face into my chest. "I'm sorry, okay? *I'm sorry.* I shouldn't have said those things about you. I shouldn't have lied. Just help my sister."

Evianna spoke with a rasp, like it took most of her strength to hold back a sob. Her body quaked, and she wouldn't look at me. She just spoke straight into my shirt, her fingers twisted into the fabric. I didn't know what to do with my hands, so I placed one gently on her back.

"Lyvia might win," I said, hoping it would appease her.

"*But she could lose.*" Evianna shook her head. "You... you said you wanted those runestones, right? I'll convince Oma to give them to you. I'll give you whatever else you want. Just make sure Lyvia is safe."

"What would you have me do?"

Fueled with frustrated rage, Evianna pushed away from me and turned around, her shoulders bunched at her neck. "Kidnap Lyvia and take her away from here! Kill the hatchling sovereign dragon! Kill Rishan when no one is looking! I don't care what it takes." Evianna placed both her hands on her face as tears started to flow. And then she ground her teeth again—I feared she would hurt herself. "*I don't care.*"

It was clear she had given this plenty of thought, but I couldn't do any of the things she wanted, not even for the runestones.

"I can't," I said, though it pained me to do so.

Evianna rubbed at her face for a long minute, her motions rough, like she wanted to wipe away her very eyes. "What's the point?" she rasped.

I moved closer to her and placed my hand on her shoulder.

She continued, "I thought heroes saved people? Isn't that what Lyvia is always going on about? Arcanists are heroes? So why can't you save her? *Why*?" Evianna jerked away from my grasp and ran up the stairs two at a time.

I let her go.

There was a difference between saving someone and undermining their own choices. Lyvia wasn't an infant reaching for flames, and I wasn't her parent, swatting her hand away to save her from the burn. She was an adult— she had taken a path that was dangerous, but also one she felt to be correct. I couldn't rip her away from her own destiny.

At least... I didn't think that was the correct course of action. I had to let Lyvia take her own risks.

What else was I supposed to do?

I left the castle as the sun set behind the distant mountains. The reds, golds, and purples of the sky hid themselves behind massive clouds. I made my way out the front gates, barely aware of the knights who looked me over as I went. The cobblestone streets led me deeper into Thronehold, winding between buildings and collecting trash in their gutters.

While my original intent had been to head back to *Maison Arcana*, I couldn't bring myself to face anyone. I didn't want to discuss the fights or the tournament, and there was still so much I had to do.

I stood at the corner of a street and waited for the next trolley. Chill wind rushed by, carrying bits of soiled cloth and leaves from the distant trees. When a trolley finally arrived, I almost laughed upon seeing the driver.

Lyell leaned away from the engine and smiled. "Volke? Is that you?" He gestured for me to board. "Get on. I'll take you wherever you need to go." He patted the side of the trolley car, a bright smile on his face. "Tin-Tin has this thing moving at a quick pace today!"

"Tin-Tin?" I asked as I took a seat on the cold bench.

"My will-o-wisp. You remember, right? He's my eldrin and—"

"Yeah. Okay."

Lyell got the trolley heading down the street. Then he gave me an odd glance. "Are you feelin' okay?"

I nodded and leaned back on the bench. Fatigue clawed at the edge of my thoughts, shredding away some of my coherence and logic.

"Where am I taking you?"

Where did I want to go? What could I get done before the end of the night?

"Someplace seedy," I muttered.

Lyell chuckled. "Heh, right. Funny."

"I'm serious. Someplace like the *Red Pot*."

"Why?"

"I want to ask people about that man offering jobs."

That seemed to excite Lyell, because he stood from his seat and held onto the steering shaft with a single hand. "Thank you, by the way. The knight captain got my letters! We're going to get to speak with—"

"That's great."

I didn't mean to be curt, but I didn't have enough willpower to get excited over everything. If I couldn't help Lyvia, the next best thing I had to do was find out who was trying to steal those runestones. And if I couldn't do that, I needed to help Adelgis. And if that wasn't an option, I needed to train. I just... had no time for anything else.

Lyell grew quiet as he retook his seat. "Someplace seedy, comin' up."

The travel was faster than normal, but not by much. Someone jogging at a quick pace could keep up with the trolley. I closed my eyes and evened out my breathing. I felt like I was closer to most of my goals, yet frustratingly too far away.

"My arcanist," Luthair whispered from the darkness.

"Yes?" I replied, my voice groggy.

"You shouldn't let Evianna's pleading bother you."

"I'm trying. It's not working." I opened my eyes and stared at the roof of the trolley, watching as it wobbled over every crack and dip in the road. "What would Mathis have done in this situation?"

"I don't think he ever would've found himself in this situation." Luthair shifted through the shadows until he could emerge on the bench next to me. It was rare to see him form, and it amused me to see him lean back like I had, his helmet also facing the roof of the trolley. "But if he had been approached by the princesses, he would've informed the knight captain and the queen and had them deal with it."

"Is that what you think I should do?"

"I must admit—I'm uncertain." He turned his empty helmet to face me. "But I do know you can't let it consume you."

The trolley rocked back and forth as we went over a small pile of debris in the road. The farther we got into the city, the more the stench of industry festered all around us. I exhaled and closed my eyes a second time.

Time slipped away from me.

"My arcanist."

I just wanted to sleep.

"Wake up. We've arrived."

Had I slept? It didn't seem like it. Wasn't I just awake? I ran a hand through my disheveled hair and forced myself to stand. After a moment of stretching, I turned to Lyell. He smoothed his lamplighter tunic until he noticed me staring.

"Volke, did you hear me? We're in the Smithy District. There are lots of pubs here." He pointed to a narrow alleyway between buildings made of thick stone and grimy windows. "You can find a couple down there. Be careful, though. Technically the Lamplighters Guild doesn't come through this district."

"Why not?" I asked, my voice rusty. I cleared my throat. "I thought you kept the peace?"

"I don't know why. Our guildmaster just doesn't draw many routes through here."

The chill of a quiet evening crept over us. I shivered as I crossed my arms.

"Did you need a coat?" Lyell asked. He leaned over and opened a small trunk tucked between benches. "I collect things people leave behind. Here's one." After patting it clean, he handed over a dark fisherman's coat with ten pockets, some the size of a satchel.

I slid my arms in. It didn't fit perfectly, but I didn't care. I had lived most of my life with hand-me-down clothing. This wasn't much different.

"Thank you, Lyell," I said. "And I'm sorry if I was rude earlier."

He forced a chuckle and patted his red hair. "Don't worry about it. I used to live with Zaxis, remember? You're nowhere near as grumpy or insufferable as he was."

We both shared a laugh as I leapt off the trolley car. Luthair stepped down after me, his shadow armor clinking with each movement. We stood on the sidewalk until Lyell's trolley disappeared around a corner, leaving us on a mostly deserted street. Twilight fog rolled into the area, and the occasional person stumbled out of the nearby alleys, but otherwise there was nothing.

Where were the crowds of people? Perhaps they were busy at the coliseum or perhaps this was one area of the city that didn't see many foreigners. From what I could gather, only the blast furnaces and metal workers called this district home.

Luthair sank into the darkness and stayed close to my feet. "Stay alert. Now isn't the time to be dozing."

41

A MAN WITH MANY JOBS

I slunk through the gloom of the Smithy District, my hands inside the massive pockets of my new coat. I had propped the collar up to hide my exhaustion and keep my neck as warm as possible. The icy fog reminded me of the ghostwood on Calisto's ship. It didn't help my mood.

Before I entered any of the pubs, I took a moment to stand under the gutter of a nearby building. The trickle of water allowed me to pat my hair down and hide my arcanist mark. I figured people might talk to me if they thought I was a man on hard times rather than an inquisitor looking for criminals.

The first pub was just like the *Red Pot*. Small. Narrow. Barely occupied. I went to the bartender and kept my voice low.

"I heard there was a man offering jobs," I said.

The woman behind the counter pointed to an empty table. "He comes by. Maybe tonight. Maybe tomorrow. Can't tell. Sorry, hon."

I didn't want to sit down. I'd fall asleep then.

With a heavy sigh, I left the pub and headed for another.

The walkway between establishments varied between horrific and cozy. Some parts on the path had bright lampposts with plants growing around the base. Other parts had no illumination, and every turn was sharper and darker than the last. Anyone could be hiding in these alleys, and it would be difficult to notice until it was too late.

Then again, I felt sorry for the mugger who decided I was their target. It would just be a hassle for me.

Second pub—this one smelled of fish stew—but it was just as small and barely occupied. I missed fish stew, though. I practically had it once a week with William and Illia when we were younger. It was difficult not to salivate.

"Good evening," I said to the bartender. My pockets were empty, and I had no coins to purchase food. "I heard there was someone offering jobs."

The elderly man cleaning dishes just shook his head. "Not tonight."

Although disheartening, I knew I was on the right track. No one gave me confused looks or odd glances when I asked about this mystery man. They knew of him—and the jobs he offered. I just needed to find him.

I exited the pub and returned to the gloomy alleyway much hungrier than before. A part of me wanted to head back to my inn and pursue this another night, but another part of me didn't want to give up. I continued down the narrow path, but stopped when I heard the echo of footsteps.

"Volke, there you are."

To my surprise, Zaxis stepped around one of the sharp corners, smiling wide. He jogged over, and I cocked an eyebrow. He came to a stop with a hop in his step.

"Zaxis?" I asked. "What're you doing here? How did you find me?"

"I've been looking all over for you." With a contented sigh, he continued, "What're you doing out so late, buddy? Something I can help you with?"

Buddy?

I stared at him for a long moment, unable to think of a response. My blood ran cold, and the alleyway seemed darker than before.

This wasn't Zaxis.

He must've known I figured it out, because his expression shifted to hardened amusement. "Odd," he whispered. "People don't normally suss me out that quickly."

This false Zaxis swiped his hand. Fatigue slowed me—he touched my neck with a slight graze of his fingertips before I could step into the shadows or physically dodge away. In the next instant, it felt as though claws gripped my spine. I couldn't move, and I recognized this as doppelgänger magic.

Now that I was frozen in place, Zaxis wrapped an arm around my neck, like we were chums.

"My arcanist?" Luthair asked. "Is everything all right?"

"Yeah," Zaxis said. "You're acting jumpy."

"You're acting strange yourself. What's gotten into the pair of you?"

Fake-Zaxis shrugged. "I don't know. It's late. We're tired. Tell him, Volke."

"Everything is fine," I said, much to my horror, though I couldn't express it. I wasn't aware doppelgänger manipulation could force me to speak.

The shadows stirred around the alleyway, and I sensed Luthair was suspicious, but not swayed into acting. Unfortunately, I was a prisoner to this *person*, and I wasn't sure if I'd be able to free myself.

"I heard you're looking for someone," Zaxis said in a sly

tone. He tightened his arm and held me close. "I know a place." He motioned to the path leading deeper into the district, far from anywhere I knew. "Let me take you there."

Before this doppelgänger could get us out of the alleyway, a blade whistled through the air and stabbed deep into Zaxis's jugular. He cried out and stumbled away, the knife still buried in his neck. Blood splattered across the cracked cobblestone.

The doppelgänger hold on my spine disappeared. That was all I needed.

I lifted a hand and used the oppressive darkness all around us in order to bind the fake Zaxis. He fell to the ground, and the web of shadows I created held him down.

Ice sprouted across the walls and windows of the nearby shops, and Fain dropped his invisibility to place a hand on Zaxis's shoulder. Debilitating frost clawed its way across Zaxis's body, hindering his movement.

Wraith appeared from the shadows and growled at the imposter, the fur on his hackles raised high.

I gulped air and shook my head, excited to be free of the controlling magic. Luthair formed from the darkness —seemingly out of the ground—and stood next to me. I imagined if he had a face, it would be twisted in confusion.

"It's a doppelgänger," I muttered. "Fain freed me from his magic."

Fain stepped away from Zaxis and made his way to my side. He ran his frostbitten fingers through his hair and then exhaled. "I'm glad you're unharmed."

"So am I. Thanks for stalking me, I guess."

He chortled. "I knew the moment Zaxis showed up that something was wrong. He would never talk or act like that."

Wraith circled the strange man, flashing his fangs and

breathing heavily enough to cover the cobblestone in thick rime.

Broken and bleeding, the Fake-Zaxis maintained an amused expression. He lay on his back, the dirty water of the alleyway soaking into his blood-stained shirt. He managed to lift a hand and tug the blade free of his flesh. Then he coughed, tilted his head, and pressed his fingers on the injury.

"Well, cut me some slack," he rasped, healing slower than the real Zaxis. "I've never met Zaxis, but I *had* seen him fight in the coliseum alongside Volke. I figured, *if they're friends, this Zaxis guy must also be a justice-seeking try-hard.* I didn't realize that was so far off." He spoke with Zaxis's voice, which made the encounter almost surreal.

"Want me to slice his windpipe?" Fain asked.

"N-No. Of course not." I pulled my fisherman's coat closed, a little disturbed Fain had jumped to that conclusion so quickly.

"I apologize, my arcanist," Luthair cut in. "I knew something wasn't right, but I didn't act."

"Forget it. I don't blame you."

Zaxis took shallow breaths, restricted by shadows and ice, his complexion pale from blood loss. "Well?" he asked. "I assume you came looking for me. Now you've got me. What's next?"

"Are you the man giving out jobs?" I asked.

He mulled over my question before answering, "No."

"Then I wasn't looking for you. I'm not even sure who you are."

"Don't play coy. There's only one doppelgänger arcanist in this whole city. Or are you confused because I'm currently a man?"

"Karna?" I asked, unable to hide my shock.

"Congratulations. You've won the prize for slowest real-ization."

Wraith snapped his jaws and let out a guttural growl. "*Watch it.*"

"Look, I'm tired," I said as I rubbed my neck. "And you attacked me. I figured... well... I just didn't think you would do that."

Karna managed a weak laugh. "I thought you had come to apprehend me. I suppose I was overthinking things."

I released my hold on the shadows. They slithered back into darkness, returning to their natural state. She thought I had been looking for her? It spoke to a guilty conscience, and while I wanted to ask about her attempted theft at the castle, I didn't want to scare her away, either. Perhaps she could tell me where the man with all the jobs was hiding.

Fain waved his hand, and the ice in the alleyway started its slow melt.

"Thank you," the Zaxis-Karna said, still using his voice. "You two are such fine gentlemen."

It was off-putting.

"I don't care what you look like," I said. "Just don't look like Zaxis." I'd never get the image of him calling us *fine gentlemen* out of my head.

Fain pointed to me and then nodded, adding his opinion without a single word.

"If that's how you feel," Karna said. She got to her feet, a hand still on her neck. Her magic melted away, shifting her body into the Karna I knew—a beautiful woman with long blonde hair. Her clothes didn't shift, however, so the shirt and trousers hung loose. Now wearing her new skin, she flashed a smile. "Better?"

Wagging his tail, Wraith returned to his arcanist's side. "I agree with you two. Zaxis would never say those things." It was odd speaking to a wolf-creature with a skull for a face, but in that moment, it felt like we were long-time friends.

"Clearly I don't know Zaxis very well," Karna muttered.

I waved away the commentary. "Forget that. I'm here for a specific reason. Someone's going around and offering jobs to people. Shady jobs—like theft in the castle. I want to find him."

"That's why you're here?"

"Yes."

Karna sauntered over and leaned against the wall between Fain and me. Even in ill-fitting clothing, and partially bleeding from the neck, she could pull off alluring. It was a surprising talent I had never known anyone to possess.

"You missed him a long time ago," Karna said. "He made all his deals and hasn't been back since."

I cursed under my breath. "Was he the one who hired you?"

"He didn't hire me *specifically*, but he hired my crew."

"Crew?"

She pointed to the sky. I tilted my head back, half-afraid she would stab me or something while I wasn't looking, but nothing came. Instead, I stared at the clouds as they passed overhead. When they finally parted, the sole airship hanging over Thronehold came into view.

"That's the *Sun Chaser*," she said. "It's even prettier up close."

"I thought the *Sun Chaser* was run by a roc arcanist?" Fain asked. He ran his frostbitten fingers over the ascot hiding his pirate mark. "Isn't it his magic that makes the airship fly? I've seen him at Port Crown a few times."

Karna threw back her golden locks and then shot Fain a glare. When she spoke, it was with the serious tone that grated—venomous and cold. "I knew you were a sea rat. You're a member of Calisto's crew, aren't you? They call you *Kalroux*."

"You're mistaken," Fain said through gritted teeth. "That was my brother."

I stepped between them. "Enough. It doesn't matter."

"The *Sun Chaser* is home to a group of mercenaries and mystic seekers," Fain muttered as he shoved his blackened hands into his pockets. "The crew is made up of people who reject the guild system or were thrown from it. Supposedly, you can hire them for any job and they don't ask questions."

Luthair—who had blended in with the darkness— stepped away from the wall, his tattered cape flowing in the evening wind. "Fain is correct. Mathis had some dealings with the *Sun Chaser* at one point. They helped us hunt down a criminal."

"And that's great," I said. "But I need other information. Like, who was that man who hired the *Sun Chaser*? Karna, did you ever see his face? Or did he give you a name? Or tell you where to find him?"

I was so close to finding out who hired people to scout out the castle! This man was trying to steal the runestones; I knew it in my gut. Why would no one give me his identity?

With gentle movements, Karna removed her hand from her neck. The gouge from the knife had become a thin line along her artery. She rubbed at the tender wound and then returned her attention to me. When she spoke, it was in a gentler tone—not fake, just kinder. "What do I get for helping you?"

"You don't get stabbed," Fain quipped.

Karna knitted her eyebrows together. "You wouldn't do that." She placed a hand on my chest. "I'm not fighting you anymore, and knights don't hurt cute girls like me, do they?"

"We're not going to stab you," I said, giving Fain a scolding glance. "But this is important. Beyond important, actually. Please. Just name your price."

"Oh, really important, you say? Good. I know exactly what I want."

I waited with bated breath, hoping she would just blurt it out. For whatever reason, she drew out the moment for a painful amount of time, tapping her fingers along the buttons of my shirt.

"I want you to leave the Frith Guild," Karna said. "And I want you to join the crew of the *Sun Chaser* instead."

42

CELEBRATIONS

"Why?" I asked.

Karna exhaled, her expression softening into something remorseful. "They're going to ruin you. If you stay with them, you'll turn into every arcanist I ever hated. But if you join us..." She slid her hand up my neck and to my jaw. "I wanna be the only one ruining you."

My face flushed, to the point I felt the heat in my ears.

Fain glanced between us. "Should I leave or...?"

"I'm not joking around," I said as I grabbed Karna's wrist and removed her hand. "This is important. There are world-altering consequences."

"Well, I'm also serious." Karna jerked free of my grasp. "If you want my help, that's the price. Everyone on the *Sun Chaser* already knows about you, anyway. Our blacksmith has money you'll win the tournament, and the captain is impressed you managed to escape the clutches of the Grandmaster Inquisitor."

I lifted an eyebrow, my cheeks still pink. "Clutches?"

"He snatches up all knightmare arcanists. I've never known one outside of the Steel Thorn Inquisitors Guild—

except for you. It'd be great having a knightmare arcanist on our side."

I didn't want to leave the others at the Frith Guild, especially not Illia, but I was willing to do a lot to solve this mystery. I lifted my hand to the base of Karna's neck. She must've misinterpreted my movements, because she tilted her head to the side, giving me better access to her skin. Instead, I caught the leather of my guild pendant and pulled it over her head—freeing it from her long hair—and returned it to my neck.

"I'm in the middle of something important," I muttered. "I can't abandon the Frith Guild on a whim. Especially not for a temporary advantage."

Karna forced a pout. With a light touch, she patted my chest. "Fine. You have to help the *Sun Chaser* with a task in the future. That's fair, right? I help you now—you help me later."

I opened my mouth to add stipulations, but she held up a finger to silence me.

"Nothing illegal," she continued. "And nothing that conflicts with your *beloved* Frith Guild. But it'll be some task where you meet the crew of the *Sun Chaser*. Trust me. You won't regret this. They're dying to speak with you."

Dying to speak to me? That seemed odd, but it wasn't worth questioning.

I nodded. "It's a deal."

She regarded me with a scrutinizing look. Then she chuckled. "You're just foolish enough to mean exactly what you say, aren't you?"

"I wouldn't lie, if that's what you mean."

"It's settled, then." Karna stepped back and smiled. "The *man with all the jobs* is a ghoul arcanist. He offered all sorts of odd tasks, including paying people for information on the trinkets and artifacts owned by the Knights Draconic and Sky Legionaries. He hired the *Sun Chaser* to locate a bunch of runestones and steal the late king's crown."

The information excited me, but it was also a tad confusing. She wasn't hired to steal the runestones outright? She just had to locate them?

"Did you manage to steal the late king's crown?" Fain asked.

Karna turned to him, glowering. "*No.* I decided against it." She shrugged. "That's fine, though. The ghoul arcanist paid us for the runestone locations. I doubt he'll return to us, considering our failure, but he seemed grateful I wasn't caught."

"Do you know where we can find this arcanist?" I asked.

"I'm not sure." Karna placed both hands on her hips and stared at the ground. "He stopped coming by, just like I told you. It seemed he only wanted these jobs before the Queen's Gala."

Dammit. I couldn't let this one lead get away from me.

"I need to find him," I said. "Where did you meet him?"

"I met him in several places. Never the same place twice. And ghouls are notoriously hard to find. They slink around without being detected—slimy and disgusting—and I'm pretty sure ghoul arcanists have a form of invisibility."

Both Karna and I glanced over at Fain. He shook his head.

"Just because I can become invisible doesn't mean I can see through it."

All I had to do was find this ghoul arcanist. I almost laughed to myself when I realized the solution. Illia and I had taken the Occult Compass from Calisto's ship—it could find any mystical creature, so long as I had a part of it.

I turned to Karna. "Do you think you could find a ghoul

trinket? Or maybe a part of a ghoul for sale in the marketplace?"

She smiled. "Have you seen the things they're selling in the Thronehold market? You can find anything."

"Can you get it for me? If I had that, I'd be able to locate the ghoul arcanist without a problem."

The cold winds of evening howled down the alley. Karna shivered and tilted her head. "You can find this arcanist with just a piece of a ghoul, is that it?"

"Yes."

"All right. I'll get you what you need."

<hr>

I reached the *Maison Arcana* at the height of midnight.

Fain and Wraith had stayed by my side—visible the entire trek—though we had walked in silence. The pubs and taverns were packed, but the streets were calm. It seemed as though half the city had cause to celebrate, and the coins won from lucky bets flowed across bar counters.

"You waited for me outside the castle?" I asked Fain. "The entire time?"

He ruffled his hair, switching it to one side and exposing his frostbitten ears. "Your master was looking for me after you were summoned away, so I decided it would be safer to wait at the gates rather than return to the inn."

"I know you said you didn't trust Master Zelfree, but I spoke with him about what you said."

Fain tensed and shot me a concerned glance. "You did?"

"Yeah. He explained everything to me. He's always been a member of the Frith Guild. You have nothing to worry about. He even said he would help you."

"I... don't know." He half-laughed. "You're too trusting,

you know that, right? First me, then that doppelgänger woman—people you should never put your faith in. Everett Zelfree is the same."

"You're wrong," I stated, no hint of doubt. "Unless you're saying you're about to backstab me. Even Karna hasn't really betrayed my trust. She's helping us now."

We walked through the *Maison Arcana* front gates, and Fain slowed his steps. "I won't cross you," he muttered. "But temptation is a devious thing. Gillie has been running around Thronehold trying to find ways to buy artifacts from the queen. Makes me think big things are happening, and maybe you shouldn't trust *questionable people* in tempting situations, if you understand what I mean."

We went straight for the front doors of the inn while I mulled over Fain's advice. I hadn't thought about what our close associates would do once they found out we were hunting a world serpent, but that was exactly why we were keeping it hidden. Some people would give in to temptation. They would stab everyone in the back for a chance to have power, fame, and unstoppable magic.

But not Zelfree.

We entered the lounge. Everything was quiet, save for the inn attendants cleaning the last remnants of a soirée. I wanted nothing more than to sleep. Soon I could let my tired body rest.

I made it up the stairs and to my room, but I stopped when I heard talking from within. A light shone under the door, and I wondered what could've happened. Perhaps Adelgis was well and had returned to the inn?

Fain nodded to me and then slipped into an invisible state. Wraith wagged his tail a few times before following suit. Although I knew they were still there, the wide hall felt deserted.

Anxious to see Adelgis, I threw open the door and froze in my spot.

Everyone was in my room.

Zaxis, Illia, Hexa, Atty—all their eldrin—and even Traces was present, though I didn't see Master Zelfree or Adelgis. Soot lightly coated everything like dew at morning, and I knew the phoenixes must've been frolicking around.

Everyone else sat on the beds or the chairs, with mugs and pitchers of ale. Cards were scattered across the floor, and no one had their boots on. The blankets were tangled around the bed posts, which was probably the most confusing part of all.

"Volke!"

Illia leapt from Zaxis's side and rushed into me. I hugged her, my confusion at an all-time high.

"What's going on?" I asked.

"We're celebrating." She broke our embrace and stared at me with her one eye. "We all won the second round of the tournament. If you and Zaxis win the next match, and Hexa and I win ours, we'll be in the semi-finals."

"So, we're celebrating that?" I glanced around the room, surprised by how addled everyone seemed. Even Nicholin sat in a dirty mug, alcohol matting his fur, his eyes half-lidded. "I don't really want to fight you."

Illia smacked my arm. "We aren't celebrating *fighting each other*. We're celebrating our victories so far. We did this after the first match, too, but you were nowhere to be found. We figured this time we'd celebrate in your room so that we'd manage to catch you."

She was right. I *had* been away from the inn for a long while. Perhaps too long.

Hexa shoved Illia out of the way and embraced me with all her strength. I awkwardly patted her back, unsure of why this was happening. She smelled of booze—and sugar cane, for some reason—and she chuckled into the collar of my new coat.

"I used your techniques," Hexa said. "The deadly moat. Sticking to my strengths. And we won!" She pushed me away, exchanging her joy for resentment in a flash. "But you weren't there for that. What's so damn important that you couldn't be there for your own sister's fight?"

"Well—"

"You weren't cavorting in the Moonlight District, were you?"

"N-No."

"Were you associating with that pirate?"

I opened my mouth to deny it, but I couldn't. Fain had been with me for most of my extracurricular activities.

Hexa's eyes went wide when I didn't offer an answer. Like a ripple on the water, everyone else had the same reaction, starting with Illia and ending with Atty, who stood at the back of the room. I didn't know what to say other than I thought we should give him a chance, but it was obvious the others considered this too heinous to attempt.

"Really?" Forsythe asked from his nest at the head of Zaxis's bed. "You've been spending time with the pirate instead of us? That doesn't seem like you."

No one else offered commentary, however. They exchanged worried glances and avoided meeting my gaze.

To my surprise, Atty stepped forward, her hands clasped in front of her. "You know what? Tonight's a night of celebration."

"Yeah it is," Nicholin chimed in, then added a *woo*.

"Why don't we put all that behind us?" Atty asked as she gestured to everyone in the room. "We can play some card games and forget the past. You know we might not have nights like this in the future."

Zaxis huffed. "What does that mean?"

"We fought dread pirates and master arcanists and barely lived. Perhaps we should just cherish these moments and be thankful that the avarice of piracy can be undone in someone like Fain."

So. Amazingly. *Reasonable.* If I could, I'd shower her with affection and compliments. Probably wasn't the time for that, considering my bedraggled state, but still. I appreciated Atty's willingness to trust me, even if the others were skeptical.

I didn't want to squander the opportunity that Atty had created. I cracked open the door. "You all don't know Fain like I do. I think he could benefit from our influence. Gillie trusted him, after all. And you saw how he spoke in front of the queen to help with the plague-resistant trinkets."

I wanted to list more things he had done, but I couldn't bring up the fact he stabbed someone in an alleyway to protect me. That would draw too many questions.

"I don't know," Zaxis muttered. He crossed his arms over his chest. "That coward doesn't have the gumption to beat a wet sack."

"If he causes any trouble, I'll remove him myself."

"And you'll stop associating with him," Illia added.

The others in the room exchanged silent glances. Illia was the one to convince—if she didn't want Fain here, everyone would agree, even me. I just hoped she would give me this chance.

"Don't worry," I said. "If he ever caused you any discomfort, even for a second, I would never associate with him again."

That seemed to go over well. She avoided looking at me,

her posture weakening as she mulled over my words. She would agree. This was always what she did right before she agreed to something she was hesitant about.

Illia slowly nodded.

"Fine. Bring 'em in."

I stepped into the hallway, hoping Fain hadn't gone too far. With a soft click, I shut the door and then glanced up and down the dark corridor. Of course there was no indication of his presence, so I hustled to the top of the stairway.

"Fain?" I asked.

"Yeah?" he responded, perhaps a few steps down.

"You should join us. We're celebrating the tournament victories."

Nothing. The sound of my own breathing haunted the quiet stairwell. Outside, beyond the walls, other arcanists caroused their way through the streets, and it was only in this stillness that I could hear them.

"This is a terrible idea," Fain finally replied.

"Gillie wanted you to mingle. And now I've made an opportunity."

He allowed his invisibility to drop. He stared up at me with a half-lidded expression, like he already knew how this whole evening would turn out, but he was holding back the *I told you so* for the appropriate moment.

After a long sigh, Fain walked up the few steps and followed me back to my room. Wraith ended his invisibility and followed as well, his wolf claws clicking on the wood with each step.

When I returned to my room, Zaxis was up off the bed. He stood in the middle of the room, his arms crossed over his tunic, his pants wrinkled and stained with fresh alcohol. He still held himself like he meant business, however. The others ended their whispered conversations, and once Fain entered, all eyes were on him and his wendigo.

After the door shut, Fain rested his back against it. Wraith sat next to his side, his tail notably still and his eyes under the skull an odd shade of amber that I hadn't realized until that moment.

"Listen up," Zaxis said. "We're going to lay some ground rules."

I already hated this. I almost stopped him mid-speech, but perhaps his rules wouldn't be so bad. And if they made Illia more comfortable, I supposed it was needed.

Fain nodded along with the statement, his expression revealing nothing.

"I'm in charge." Zaxis made the claim with no hint of irony. Half the people in the room—including Forsythe— shook their heads as though they didn't have the willpower to deal with him at the moment. "Illia is equally in charge," he added. "Since she's my woman."

Illia shot him an icy, one-eyed glare.

"What?" he barked. "You can say *I'm your man.*"

Nicholin waved his ferret-like paws around to draw attention. "Since I'm Illia's eldrin, does that make you my man, too?"

"No."

"But... but... I'm still also in charge, right?" Nicholin puffed up his chest. "Because I'm leader material." He squeaked out a hiccup afterward, killing all authority.

"You're third-in-command at best, rizzel," Zaxis said with a scoff.

Before their argument could devolve into shouting and angry squeaks, Fain held up a hand. His frostbitten fingers were a shade darker in the dim lantern light. It caught the attention of everyone in the room, and silence followed.

"I get it," Fain said, his voice monotone. "There's a hierarchy. I'm at the bottom. If I get out of line, you'll make sure I regret it. I've done this song and dance before."

His statements didn't surprise me—I had already heard some shocking tidbits—but it obviously shook the others. Even Illia had a slight look of regret. It was fleeting, but there.

Fain pushed away from the door and took a couple steps into the room. Then he stopped and shifted his weight from one foot to the other, his gaze on the floor. "Well? Get it over with."

His wendigo softly whined like only a dog could.

The others glanced at me, just as confused as I was.

"What're you talkin' about?" Hexa blurted out from the back corner of the room.

Fain shrugged. "Rough me up. Tattoo my neck. Whatever you do for initiation—to make sure *I know my place.*" He said the last part with a dark sarcasm.

Hexa let out a single laugh. "Are you serious?" She slid off the side of the bed and walked across the room. Her cinnamon hair was curlier and puffier than normal, giving her a slight lion's mane. Combined with her scars, she looked like she came straight from the untamed plains, or perhaps the darkest jungles. "Uh, this is the *Frith Guild*—home to legendary heroes who saved countless lives, from the mundane to the magnificent. We don't beat people into their place. We demand people *step up to the challenge.*"

I lifted both my eyebrows, stunned to hear Hexa give such a speech. She felt that way? I didn't know, but now that I did, I admired her more than before.

"So?" Hexa asked. "What say you? Can you live up to those expectations?"

Atty held up a timid hand. "Um, Hexa? I'm sorry to interrupt, but you know he's not joining the Frith Guild, right? As apprentices, we can't accept people into the ranks. Only the master arcanists can do that. We were just inviting him to play cards."

"Pfft." Hexa waved away the comment. "Didn't you hear Guildmaster Eventide? We're supposed to be recruiting. I'm sure she would take him, if he wanted." Hexa turned her attention back to Fain. "Well? You want to, right? You're not gonna get scared and back off?"

"Technically, the grand apothecary is joining the Frith Guild," Fain muttered, "which meant I would be as well, but if you want my oath of loyalty, you can have it now. I'll *step up to the challenge*, as you said."

Wraith wagged his tail and scooted a bit closer to his arcanist.

"Words are cheap," Zaxis growled. But Illia placed a hand on his shoulder, and he quieted down.

That didn't seem to matter to Hexa. She flashed Fain a genuine smile and then threw her arms around him in a surprise embrace. He tensed—his expression the very definition of uncomfortable—but he didn't push her away, despite how long she stayed latched to him.

"Sit next to me," Hexa said as she broke away. Before he could answer, she dragged him over by the elbow and pushed him onto the bed. "We'll deal you in."

Hissing and snapping emanated from under the bed. Fain lifted his feet onto the mattress and then glared down at Raisen's heads as they slithered up toward him. Hexa's hydra seemed bigger than I last remembered, and both sets of eyes were glistening gold with deadly attention—the pupils slits, like any snake's.

"We'll be watching you," the left one muttered.

"Don't even try to cheat, either," the right added with a hiss. "Our venom is deadly."

"R-Right," Fain said.

Once everyone settled into a seat, I took my place on the edge of my own bed. Cards were gathered by Nicholin and brought back to Illia. They shuffled and dealt, and while no one seemed to have any coins they were willing to bet, everyone made "gentleman's bids" and continued on like we would keep a running tab of *who was the better player*.

I was too tired to appreciate the game, and my third fight in the tournament wasn't far off.

Still—I took a moment to appreciate that I had at least done *one* thing I set out to do: get people to give Fain a chance.

43

TOURNAMENT ROUND THREE

The time between the second and third matches flew by.

Although there were fewer participants, the crowds in the city seemed rowdier than before. The bookies were always busy, and the bets being made were becoming the thing of tales. Since arcanists lived so long—and the prosperity aura over the Argo Empire helped generate wealth—some could horde great fortunes, and apparently, they only got their jollies from risking it all, it seemed.

If Zaxis and I won this next match, we would be split and fight individually in the next round. That excited me, especially since I wanted the distraction. I couldn't do anything else while I waited for Karna, so I wanted to fill my time with something productive.

My first thought was to speak to Adelgis's brother, but he still refused to see me. My last hope was to meet him in the arena and speak to him there—which was ridiculous, but I had to do it.

Instead, I trained with Fain. Zaxis was still "busy" with Illia, and I didn't want to interrupt, for fear everyone would assume I was attempting to keep them apart. Fain needed the help, anyway. He knew how to use his magic, but he wasn't familiar with terminology or how to delve into more advanced techniques. It helped me reconnect with the basics just going over them with him.

Master Zelfree helped as well, though Fain got quiet and stiff whenever he was around.

It was difficult to keep track of everything, however. I just never got enough sleep, it felt. That was probably why time slipped away from me and why the details blurred together.

The morning of the third tournament match, I woke before dawn, my blankets soaked in sweat.

"My arcanist?" Luthair whispered from the darkness. "Are you unwell?"

I took deep breaths as I threw my covers off and sat up. My nightmares lingered at the edge of my thoughts, poisoning my blood with adrenaline and false panic. I had dreamt of Lyvia. She died in front of me, and I couldn't do anything about it. And then my dream shifted to Adelgis in bed at Skarn University. He, too, died—and I was unable to affect it. Finally, it ended with Calisto bonding to the world serpent, even though I was standing right there... I just... couldn't stop him.

The helplessness burned worse than any fire or terrible sensation from my second-bonding.

I couldn't let those things come to pass.

"My arcanist?"

"I'm fine," I muttered, quiet enough not to wake Zaxis or Forsythe.

I got up and dressed in relative silence, remembering to

pack my satchel and Theasin's book. I even picked up my boots and walked with them out of the room before slipping them on in the hallway. Shrouded in the darkness of night, I left the inn and headed for the coliseum. Luthair kept close, and through a combination of jogging and shadow-stepping, I made it just as the sun was beginning to peak over the edge of the horizon.

The weather was fair. It was always fair. Was it because of the prosperity aura? The thought mildly intrigued me as I approached the coliseum entrance.

To my surprise, there were already crowds. It wasn't bustling, but it was lively. When I took a moment to focus on my surroundings, I also noticed the many Knights Draconic and Sky Legionnaires. The unicorns were uniform in their white coloration, but the pegasi came in as many colors as there were birds. One pegasus caught my eye because of its blue jay wings and the grey-blue coat on the rest of its equine body. I had never seen one so vibrant before.

As I walked by, a pegasus arcanist—a tall woman dressed in her Sky Legionnaire uniform—patted the shoulder of a much shorter woman. "You'll do fine. Father will be watching from the stands."

"I hope I'm chosen," the other woman muttered, her expression a mix of youthful hope and dreaded anxiety.

I didn't know what was going on, but once I entered the coliseum, everything made sense. The field had been rearranged, no doubt with the help of the gargoyle and his arcanist, and instead of a fighting arena, there was an obstacle course in its place.

I vaguely recalled someone telling me that the new pegasi and unicorns would have their trials of worth between the matches. The obstacle course had to be for the pegasi. They were mystical creatures that valued acrobatic physical prowess.

Although interesting, I ignored the trials and headed straight for the apprentice pits. The smell of blood and sweat got me into the appropriate mindset for combat.

A few other arcanists and their eldrin were already here, including the giant stone golem. When it moved, the bits of rocks scraped together, and I shuddered. It *sounded* heavy. That kind of weight would shatter a person, and I hoped beyond reason I wouldn't be matched against the beast.

I stared at the wall with all the matches etched into the stone. I half-smiled once I found my name and realized the stone golem wasn't anywhere near it. Instead, Zaxis and I would face off against others from the Huntsman Guild.

Candace Milton the Denglong Arcanist – Huntsman Guild
Warren Kell the Erlking Arcanist – Huntsman Guild

"It's the apprentices that the reaper arcanist was taunting us with," Luthair said.

Right. Jevel the Reaper Arcanist—master to the dog arcanists—was *certain* that a denglong and an erlking could defeat us. But I didn't know what those were.

I pulled Theasin's book out of my satchel and flipped to the portion where it discussed mystical creatures. Hopefully this would give me some insight into their fighting tactics.

Denglong
  Tier 3

Reproduction: Fable (born from a falling star that strikes a mountain)

Trial of Worth: A demonstration of righteousness

Denglong are unwavering in their morals and sense of justice. Although considered weaker than dragons, denglong are built to eat them. They are immune to heat of all forms, and their front claws—shaped like talons—rip through lizard-scale defenses. Stories claim they were the gods' hunting dogs, and only dragons are suitable game for the divine.

True Form: Unobserved

Erlking

Tier 3

Reproduction: Fable (born from a queen's fairy who consumes her arcanist's corpse)

Trial of Worth: Unknown

Erlking are considered the "kings of fairies." They create powerful lights and illusion, and if they're old enough, they can ensnare others with false feelings of infatuation. Mischievous and callous, these mystical creatures often hurt people on accident with their lethal magical affects.

True Form: Unobserved

I gritted my teeth and slammed the book shut.

Zaxis and I would have a difficult time fighting these two. Their magical abilities had an advantage over ours. Zaxis wouldn't be able to burn the denglong or its arcanist, and the erlking could likely destroy my shadows with a blast of its powerful light.

The stone golem moved to the side, and then its arcanist walked into the pit from the far entrance.

No. He didn't walk. *Lumbered* would be a better term. The man was both tall and stocky—built like a mountain with legs. His thick, brown beard acted as a forest of brambles that covered his whole chin.

He was my age? I would've guessed he was ten years older, perhaps more.

"Hey," he said as he made his way over to the wall with the names. "I see you're one of the few remaining." He wore leather armor studded with steel, though it barely contained the hair on his arms and chest.

I nodded. "I see you're still in the tournament as well."

"My name is Dramm. And this is Borod." He motioned to his stone golem.

The mighty creature lifted a rock fist and slowly waved it through the air. It was gentler than I first imagined and set its heavy fist onto the ground with cautious movements, as though trying to avoid any possible accidents.

"I'm Volke," I said.

"I hope you win your match. Then you'll get to participate in the semi-finals later today. I'd love to see a capable knightmare arcanist in action." Dramm smacked my shoulder with more power than I was expecting. I almost tumbled to the side, but I kept my footing. He laughed. "All your matches have been fun to watch!"

"Uh, thank you," I said as I rubbed my arm. "I haven't watched any of your matches, but I'm sure they were impressive."

"Oh? Well, you should pay attention to this next one." He jabbed the wall with a sturdy finger. "I'm facing off against others in your guild."

I glanced back to the brackets and caught my breath. Illia and Hexa were paired against Dramm the Stone Golem Arcanist, and Adelgis's brother, Niro the Stoor Worm Arcanist. That was also a terrible match up—stoor worms *and* stone golems were unaffected by poison. Not to mention the golem's incredible size and fortitude.

"It'll be an interesting bout," I muttered.

Dramm smiled wide. "I have to do the Enchanters Guild proud, so I won't be going easy on them."

"You'd lose if you went easy. Those two have a lot of tricks up their sleeves."

"Is that right? I'll be on the lookout, then." Dramm smacked my shoulder one last time before turning back to his eldrin. "See you in the semi-finals, Volke."

His overall jovial nature was a pleasant change, but his assumption that we'd meet in the next round meant he had no doubt he'd win against Hexa and Illia. I hoped that didn't come to pass. Instead of dwelling on that, however, I pushed it from my mind and went into one of the private fighter rooms.

I didn't practice my magic. Instead, I went through my sword fighting drills. Attack, parry, dodge—going through the motions until I couldn't get them wrong. Hours went by, and the coliseum became noisier and hotter, but that didn't bother me.

The red dirt on the floor clung to everything. The bench, the walls, and the tiny windowsill beneath the two-inch hole in the upper part of the room. The small amount of light that shimmered through wasn't much, but I used it as a marker on the ground to keep track of my footwork.

The door to my room flew open, and I stopped my swordplay.

Zaxis stood in the doorway, his expression set to *incredulous*. "You came here without me?" he barked.

I sarcastically glanced around, wondering if he wanted me to actually answer that.

"Never mind." He stepped in and shut the door behind him. "We need to strategize. Did you see our opponents? This'll be rough."

"I figured I should handle the denglong and you should handle the erlking," I said. "That way they won't have the advantage on us."

"I've watched all their matches, *fool*. These guys don't separate and fight people one-on-one. They fight as a true team." He ran a hand through his fiery hair. "Why did you leave the inn early? I was looking all over for you this morning! I've been meaning to tell you this. We need a better plan than *none at all*."

"Why didn't you come to me yesterday? Or the day before that?"

"I was... busy." Zaxis growled something under his breath and then shook his head. "Forget it. Let's just talk now."

The door opened a second time. Master Zelfree stood in the hall, looking more haggard than I had seen him in a long time. When he rotated an arm, he grimaced and cursed under his breath. "Are you two ready?" he asked, his voice gravelly.

"Right now?" Zaxis asked. "I thought we still had time."

"You have the first match."

We always had the first match, and I wondered if it was just the luck of the draw or the way they formatted the brackets. Either way, it didn't help us now. I needed to think of a strategy—some way to beat a team specifically tailored to combat Zaxis and me.

Zaxis must have thought the same way, because he grew quiet and seemed to lose himself in deep thought.

We followed Zelfree out of the room, down the long hall to the gates of the coliseum, and stopped when the knight held up a hand. This time I could flash my guild pendant, and the man nodded in approval. Then he yanked on the chains and lifted the wrought-iron gates for us to enter.

Shouts and cheers bombarded us from all sides. Again, flowers, petals, and bits of rice rained down as well, mixing with the vibrant dirt like a bizarre piece of art. I tried not to think about it. I tried to focus on the match. But the heat seemed more oppressive today.

"We're into the third round, ladies and gentlemen," the announcer shouted, riling the crowd further. "And our very first match of the day goes to the Frith Guild! They still have four participants, and the two fighting now are Volke Savan the Knightmare Arcanist and Zaxis Ren the Phoenix Arcanist!"

Stomping mixed into the roars, as though the current level of enthusiasm just wasn't enough to express the collective desire to watch us fight.

"Their opponents hail from the Huntsman Guild—Candace Milton the Denglong Arcanist and Warren Kell the Erlking Arcanist! Their teamwork has been the stuff of legends! So synchronized! So harmonious!"

Before Zaxis or I could step onto the arena platform, someone from the opposite side walked over to us. It was a man and his eldrin. I recognized the floating cloak and scythe—the creature without a body, much like Luthair. It was a reaper, and the chains that fell from the cloak were etched with the names of arcanists that it had helped kill.

Jevel hooked his thumbs into the waistband of his trousers, his tailored cloth and fine armor on display for the world to see. When he got close, he stroked his black mustache and goatee, trying to hide his smirk but failing miserably.

"Everett Zelfree," he said. "It's finally time for the main event."

"Do we all know the rules of the event?" the announcer shouted. "Remember that ties are settled by the queen or her knight captain!"

I stopped paying attention to the announcer and focused all my attention on Jevel. I disliked him and his floating eldrin, if only because he seemed sleazier than before. The pistols he had hanging from holsters on his belt seemed like a threat.

"I want to make this fight interesting," Jevel said, his smile widening. "If *my* apprentices win, you have to fight me —man to man. No tricks."

"And if my apprentices win?" Zelfree asked. The conversation was drowned by the screaming audience, but I was close enough to make out their words.

"Whatever you want, renegade."

"Ten star shards and twenty-five gold crowns."

The quick reply seemed to shake Jevel. He lifted an eyebrow, his confidence waning as he thought over the request.

Zelfree chuckled. "The Frith Guild needs resources. And since I didn't participate in the tournament, this will make up for that."

"If you win."

"*When* I win."

The reaper twirled its scythe. The ebony handle and rusted blade didn't catch the light like most weapons, but it kept my attention regardless. The creature moved the weapon with invisible hands—a deadly gesture that seemed to be the reaper equivalent of a dog wagging its tail.

"Deal," Jevel growled. "And when I win our little fight, I'll be adding your name to my collection."

The reaper clinked its ominous chains, the sound quickly replaced with the screeching of excitement.

"If the contestants will step up to the platform, it's time to begin!"

44

LIGHT SHOW

As I went to enter the arena, Master Zelfree placed a hand on my shoulder. I glanced back, anxious to get this over with. Every second of delay added to my restlessness.

"Don't lose this," Zelfree said.

He released my shoulder and motioned to the arena.

I walked up the short stairway and took my place by Zaxis's side. Was Zelfree afraid of Jevel and his reaper? I thought it unlikely. Then I had another thought—he didn't want anyone knowing about his injuries from Calisto. That was the only explanation that made sense. Zelfree was a man that thrived on the control of information, from his spy contacts to his intentional misdirection with his own reputation. He didn't want someone like *Jevel* knowing he had permanent damage after a fight with a pirate.

Our opponents appeared formidable.

The denglong looked like the mix of a dog and a dragon. It was the size of a wolf, with golden fur and a red mane, though its face was puppy-like. It was an adolescent, after all. I imagined the denglong would be larger than a lion when fully grown.

Its underbelly was scaled, just like a dragon's, and its claws were practically talons—long, curved, and piercing. Catfish whiskers sprouted from its massive head, just above a jaw filled with fangs. I had never seen anything so other-worldly. The beast shimmered in the early morning light.

The denglong's arcanist, a young woman, stood behind him, her black hair tied in a tight ponytail that went down to her lower back. She seemed lithe and wore light leather armor, the same gold as her eldrin.

The erlking, on the other hand, was somehow more ostentatious than a golden half-dog, half-dragon. He was a fairy—no bigger than someone's head—but his wings were the size of an eagle's, and his feathers had the markings, and pomp, of a peacock. When the erlking moved, he left an after-image behind him, like there were illusion copies following his every movement.

The erlking's arcanist, a young man, didn't wear armor. He wore a fine robe and stood with his hands behind his back, like we were about to debate in a civil manner, rather than stabbing and punching one another.

They didn't approach for a bow, like Lucian, but before the official start of the match, Forsythe swooped out of the sky and landed in front of us. He held two golden poppies in his beak. He stretched out his long neck and offered the flowers to me and Zaxis.

Zaxis took his, and once I took mine, Forsythe said, "These are from Princess Lyvia. She wants you to win."

I glanced over and spotted Lyvia standing at the edge of the stands. She was as close as she could get without being on the field herself, her white hair fluttering in the gentle breeze. Was she worried? Or perhaps she just wanted us to know she'd be paying attention. Either way, I tucked the poppy into my trouser pocket.

Lyvia...

Everything about her reminded me of the fairy tales I had read as a child.

Zaxis grabbed the collar of my shirt, jerking me out of my musings. "They're going to start the match by trying to blind us!"

Vercingetorix roared, and I barely had enough time to process what Zaxis had told me.

I threw up an arm to cover my eyes and managed to block the majority of the bright light released from the erlking arcanist. It was intense enough that it felt as though the sun had burned a portion of my skin.

"*Luthair*," I shouted.

Although I had my eyes shut, I appreciated the cold sensation of the shadows as they wrapped protectively around my body. In an instant, I was protected, but the light continued to shine, stinging my shadow-armor as though it were my actual skin.

I lifted my shield, and it protected me from the harshest aspects.

With gritted teeth, I held up a hand and unleashed my terrors. A second later, shouts rang out across the arena, and the harsh light ceased. I lowered my arm just in time to see the denglong charging for me. Before it knocked me off the platform with its sheer size and power, I slipped into the shadows and reemerged a good twenty feet from it.

Zaxis unleashed a wave of flame, but the fire did nothing to the denglong or its brilliant golden fur. Instead, the dragon-dog whipped around and charged for him.

I lifted my hand to manipulate the shadows, but another burst of light tore through the darkness and destroyed all my creations. The erlking and his arcanist smirked, like they had prepared ahead of time to counter my actions.

The crowd cheered, and the announcer stoked their excitement.

"Denglong are immune to fire! This'll be tricky for a phoenix arcanist."

Zaxis and I relied so heavily on our shadows and flame for combat—it made devising an impromptu strategy difficult.

Zaxis punched the denglong with his white-hot knuckles, but it didn't do much. The beast swiped with its claws and easily tore through chest and gut, splattering the arena with crimson.

Before the denglong could shred Zaxis to pieces, Forsythe dove for the dragon-dog's face and hooked his talons into the soft bits. The denglong and Forsythe thrashed around the platform, the phoenix flapping his wings and the dog growling and barking the entire time.

The denglong's arcanist rushed over to help, but that's when I had my idea.

I shadow-stepped to Zaxis and grabbed his shoulder. He gulped down breath, and he kept a hand over his injury, but he didn't falter. He didn't even seem fazed.

"We should target the erlking," he growled.

I shook my head. "Attack me with your fire," I commanded, my double voice distinct, even through the cheering.

In my mind, I imagined that I would need to convince Zaxis—because he would deny my request—but that didn't happen. He just attacked me. Straight away. It occurred so fast it almost surprised me, despite being *my* plan.

I got my shield up in time to defend the blow. The heat

washed over me, and the shield itself pulsed with an inner life, even as orange and red waves licked around the sides.

"What's going on down there?" the announcer shouted. "The Frith Guild has turned on itself!"

When Master Zelfree had used the will-o-wisp fire, my shield reflected it back as a bolt of raw magic. Zaxis's phoenix flame was far stronger, and once he stopped attacking, the black shield rippled with inner power.

A second later, I turned it toward the denglong and its arcanist. A surge of lightning burst off the face of the shield and tore through the arena. The damage happened in the fraction of a second—too fast for anyone to dodge or even see coming. It struck the denglong straight on, and the beast cried out as it tumbled from the platform, a scorched hole in its golden fur.

A loud bell rang out.

Forsythe turned his claws on the denglong arcanist, and the woman panicked, not because of the phoenix, but because her eldrin continued to yell out in pain. She leapt from the stone platform and landed hard in the red dirt. Another bell sounded, but that didn't stop her from running to the denglong's side and cradling it close.

The creature wasn't dead, but it did twitch and continue its dog-like sobbing.

"Useless," the erlking said, his voice regal and high-pitched. "We'll have to handle this ourselves, my arcanist." His peacock wings flared wide, and a mist of green and blue poured from the feathers. The odd dust rolled over the arena as though carried by gale-force winds.

My vision blurred.

"I love watching the erlking in action," the announcer shouted. "So colorful!"

After a couple blinks, everything had changed. I wasn't

in the coliseum. I stood in the middle of an emerald meadow. Daisies dotted the distant hills. Everything smelled of spring.

Zaxis rubbed at his eyes. "Damn illusions," he growled. He held up his hand. *"Let's do this again."*

I protected myself with my shield and allowed Zaxis to attack me with his flames. Our opponents knew this tactic, however, and they separated—one to the left and one to the right. Once my shield pulsed with barely contained power, I pointed it toward the larger target: the robed arcanist.

The lightning bolt of pure energy ripped across the illusion field and struck the man square in the chest. He tumbled beyond the fake scenery, and in the distance, I heard a bell.

"Again?" I asked.

Zaxis pushed me aside. "Enough. I got this."

He dashed through the meadow, his eyes closed. He wasn't taking the chance of the illusions tricking him—and he was obviously confident in his ability to remember the arena before it shifted. The erlking flew up in the air, however, away from Zaxis's reach.

"Fool," the fairy king said, his tone bordering on egomaniacal. "You cannot hope to harm the likes of me. I'm far more—"

Forsythe dove from the sky and collided with the fairy going at outrageous speeds. He didn't seem to care about landing properly. They both sailed straight into the ground, and two bells rang out. A moment later, the illusions faded, leaving Zaxis and me standing in the middle of the fighting platform.

"The winners are Volke Savan and Zaxis Ren! The Frith Guild continues into the semi-finals!"

Coins, fabric, and bits of pottery rained down in waves.

The clapping and stomping overtook the cheers, and the rumble through the coliseum shook the stone under my feet.

Zelfree applauded from the side of the arena, a pleasant smirk across his face.

And Jevel was nowhere to be seen. Had he left after the first apprentice of his fell from the arena? It wouldn't surprise me.

The healing effects of the empire caladrius fixed the injured denglong and erlking arcanist without trouble, and I was thankful that the raw magic of my shield's blast didn't deal any permanent damage.

"Will the Frith Guild face off against itself?" the announcer asked the out-of-control crowds. "If Hexa d'Tenni and Illia Savan win against Niro Venrover and Dramm Totmor, we'll be seeing friends face off against friends!"

The knowledge sank into my gut and felt like a rock trying to pass through my system. I really didn't want to fight Illia in a one-on-one match. Not now. Not ever. But first she would have to beat the mountain and his stone golem.

Luthair unmerged from me, and we walked off the arena together. It was only then that I realized my magic had burned slightly during the fight. I hadn't noticed in the moment—not when I used my terrors or when I had attempted my shadow manipulation.

The thought chased away the dread.

I had improved.

Zelfree slapped me on the shoulder as we walked back to the apprentice pits. "Illia and Hexa are up next. Stick around, though. The semi-final takes place right after their match concludes."

I nodded. "Okay."

The building of the coliseum protected us from the excitement of the audience. My hearing returned once I walked down the long hall and returned to the pit. The stone golem had disappeared, but Illia, Nicholin, Hexa, and Raisen were there waiting for us. Hexa and Illia had their best leather armor, and they stood with confidence, though Illia's expression betrayed a hint of anxiety.

"Come on," Zelfree said to them. "Your match is next."

As Illia walked by me, I held out a hand. "Good luck," I said.

"Thank you," she muttered.

"Don't mess us up with your *good luck* curse," Nicholin squeaked. "We didn't need it last time, and we don't need it now. We're too good to lose."

Before Illia could follow Hexa and Zelfree toward the arena, I placed my hand on her shoulder. She was trembling —I felt it then—but she stopped and took a deep breath. Once steady, she offered me a tight smile.

"Thank you," she whispered.

45

SEMI-FINALS

I made my way to the contestant stands and took my seat next to Zaxis.

The dog arcanists were there, sitting on benches a few rows back. The moment they spotted me, they got up, slinked into the shadows, and then headed for the exit. No words. No eye contact. I smirked and returned my attention to the field.

Dramm and his stone golem, Borod, lumbered to the arena. The marble coloration of the stone golem stood out against the sandstone tan of the platform, and it was interesting to see the golem's chunks of rocks held together by faint threads of magic. Dramm's eldrin stood fifteen feet tall, at least. *At least*.

I dug through my satchel and withdrew Theasin's book. Perhaps there were things about the stone golem that he could teach me.

Stone Golem
   Tier 3

Reproduction: Unknown

Trial of Worth: A test of resilience

Stone golems appear near mountains with rich lodes, though the exact requirements for one to spawn are unknown. Their bodies are made of the stone prominent in the area, which means each stone golem's hardness varies. Occasionally stone golems are laced with veins of metal, though this is rare. They do not eat, drink, or sleep.

Stone golem arcanists are known for their ability to sense movement through subtle tremors and to have strength enough to punch through walls.

True Form: Unobserved

The cacophony of cheering made it difficult to focus on reading, and when a new wave of applause rolled through the stands, I glanced up to see what the commotion was about. Niro Venrover, Adelgis's brother, strode out across the red dirt.

Unlike Dramm, who wore half-plate armor over the vital organs, Niro wore scale-plate—the type of armor that looked like it came from a snake or a dragon. The scales themselves were black, and the moment I saw his eldrin, I knew where he got them from.

His stoor worm was a creature of night terrors. It was a long sea serpent with black scales, gold eyes, and scarlet fins, and thirty feet long from the head to the tip of the tail. The beast glistened in the late morning light, as though wet. Fangs protruded from the sides of its long mouth, and it moved with powerful concertina motions.

Had Niro ripped the scales off his eldrin to fashion himself a set of armor? If he imbued it with his magic, it would be a sturdy set, no doubt in my mind, but it seemed cruel.

I turned my attention back to the book and flipped to the page that spoke about stoor worms.

Stoor Worm
> *Tier 3*
>
> *Reproduction: Progeny (nesting grounds found near shipwrecks)*
> *Trial of Worth: Surviving an ocean storm without assistance*
> *Stoor worms have deadly venom and aggressive natures. Their forked tongues are prehensile and capable of drawing in victims. Powerful stoor worms can rot vegetation and flesh with their gas-like breath. They are man-eaters and consume flesh exclusively. Their arcanists are known for their corrosive magics.*
> *True Form: Unobserved*

The tales of stoor worms weren't uncommon on the islands. I read tons of tales of Gregory Ruma fighting stoor worm pirates, and most considered the beasts a sign of bad luck. Their venom wasn't as deadly as a hydra's or basilisk's, but it was still potent enough to end a man's life.

Sea serpents had given me nightmares as a child. I feared one would find me while I was swimming. Or worse —one would find Illia. Apparently, according to legend, they liked to eat people with scars and injuries.

With Niro and Dramm all set up on their side of the arena, Illia and Hexa took their place on the opposite side.

"The last match before the semi-finals! We have Hexa d'Tenni the Hydra Arcanist and Illia Savan the Rizzel Arcanist versus Niro Venrover the Stoor Worm Arcanist and

Dramm Totmor the Stone Golem Arcanist! It'll be brutal, folks. Don't blink."

There wasn't time to waste. Vercingetorix roared as he spread his wings, rumbling the coliseum. The crowd got to their feet, and the excitement shot through stands with the force and speed of lightning.

The announcer was right. I shouldn't have turned my attention to the crowds, not even for a moment—Niro's worm had shot across the arena platform the half second after Vercingetorix announced the start.

Raisen was too slow to avoid the giant sea serpent. The worm collided with him at full force and sunk its fangs into Raisen's body. With one skilled motion, the worm flung Raisen from the arena. It was like Niro and Dramm already knew who to target first, perhaps from watching the previous matches.

A bell clanged as Raisen rolled through the red dirt.

Hexa threw knives at the stoor worm, and while a few cut the beast, they didn't seem to do much.

In an attempt to deal with my nervous energy, I shoved my hands in my pockets and shuddered. My fingers grazed the crushed remains of the golden poppy flower. I took it out of my pocket and stared down at the broken flower. Then I turned my attention to Lyvia's seat on the other end of the coliseum.

Empty.

So was Evianna's.

But their brother—Rishan—remained. He sat at the edge of his seat, his eyes locked on the match. I was too far away to see details, but I imagined him enthralled with the violence. I knew nothing about the man, but knowing that he would be in a death match with Lyvia left a terrible rage building in the depths of my chest, like a fire on the verge of control.

"Are you paying attention?" Zaxis hissed.

I glanced back to the arena and jumped to my feet.

Illia teleported around the platform while the stone golem swung its boulder-fists from side to side. She avoided one bone-shattering attack, and then the next, but the third time she wasn't as lucky. A rock half her size bashed straight into her ribs. Even from the stands, I could feel the impact. The weight of a full boulder sent her off the side of the arena, and instead of teleporting back, Illia tumbled across the ground. When she finally stopped, she just lay there, unmoving.

I grabbed the railing, intending to shadow-step to her, but the telekinetic shield around the arena prevented me from getting to her. Zaxis was on his feet as well, half an inch from the barrier, his breath held. Illia didn't get up. Then he ran from the stadium seating, leaving me without another word.

Hexa and Nicholin didn't last much longer.

The stone golem continued to thrash around the arena. Hexa couldn't teleport, and when the rock struck her face, blood splattered across the platform in an oddly beautiful semi-circle. She collapsed and didn't get up.

Another bell.

Nicholin teleported, and at first, I didn't understand where he had gone, but then Dramm jumped around the arena, grabbing at his thighs. Nicholin had appeared in his trousers and set to biting him in all the soft bits. The man punched his own crotch before leaping off the side and getting them both knocked out.

That was the end of the match.

Illia and Hexa had lost.

I waited in the apprentice pit, pacing from wall to wall. The place was empty. There were only four apprentices left in the tournament, and that was me, Dramm, Zaxis, and Niro. According to the brackets etched into the coliseum wall, Niro and I would fight next, supposedly within the hour.

The crowds outside remained rowdy, but without a fight to rile them, it was quiet enough to think.

Illia and Hexa had recovered. I knew they would. Caladrius magic was the most potent healing in the world, after all. Despite that, I rushed to Illia's side the moment she entered the pit with Master Zelfree, Zaxis, and Hexa. She crossed her arms before I reached her, and bunched her shoulders close to her neck, walling herself from me.

"You did great," I said.

She met my gaze with her one eye filled with anger. "*Don't.*" She spoke through gritted teeth, so tense she shook. "You wouldn't say that to Zaxis, if he had failed. Don't patronize me."

The others stood around, not saying a word. Nicholin even hung on Zaxis's shoulder, watching with his ears down and his tail droopy.

I stepped closer to Illia, until there were only a couple inches between us. "You didn't care about this anyway," I muttered. "Remember? You wanted to focus on the mission at hand. On Calisto."

I hated invoking Calisto's name—especially to fuel Illia's need for revenge—but it was the truth. Zaxis and I trained and strategized to win, but Illia hadn't concerned herself as much. Now that she lost, why was she treating it like a disaster? There was no need.

And perhaps my words got to her.

She relaxed a bit, and forced a quick shrug. "I know. I just... didn't want to... face you afterward."

"I'm just glad you're okay."

Zaxis stepped between us and pushed me back a few feet. Then he massaged Illia's shoulder and whispered comforting words about how he had been so concerned for her safety, and that he didn't know what to do with himself when he saw her hurt. While I didn't mind him showing affection, it bothered me that this needed to be a competition between us—like any moment Illia said something to me was a moment I was somehow stealing from him.

Before I could comment, Hexa smacked my shoulder. "You better win this for us," she said. "Ya know. Avenge our loss."

Illia stepped around Zaxis and nodded. "That's exactly what I want, Volke. You should show those two what the Frith Guild is really about."

The coliseum rumbled with commotion from the audience outside. Were they getting ready for my upcoming fight?

"Enough of this," Master Zelfree said. He placed a hand on both Illia and Hexa. "You two come with me. Volke, be prepared." He led them out of the apprentice pits, even though it was clear they wanted to stay and chat more. Perhaps he wanted to make sure they were healed all the way?

Zaxis lingered back for a moment, which agitated Nicholin. The little rizzel wagged his tail and glared. "Hurry. Illia is leaving."

"Volke," Zaxis said, an edge to his words. "You better not lose this."

Then he left, leaving me alone with Luthair in the underground room. Dust clung to the air, and when I resumed my pacing, I could taste it in the back of my mouth. Although I hadn't been nervous before, the anxious feelings I had at the start of the tournament returned. Why did Illia want me to win so badly? She, Hexa, and Atty all did—but did it really matter? I said I would win, but so much had happened since then. This tournament almost felt like a distraction.

The crowds outside remained boisterous, but they weren't cheering, so it made it easy to detect movement in the corridors. Sounds echoed with ease through the coliseum.

I stopped my pacing and faced the new individual in the pit. It was Niro Venrover and his disgusting stoor worm. They both entered the pit with a distracted look about them, Niro sauntering around and his worm slithering at a slow pace.

This might be the only chance I had to speak with him. And it would be a good distraction from my anxiety. After a shallow dust-filled breath, I stepped forward and bowed my head.

"Hello," I said. "I'm Volke Savan of the Frith Guild. We met in your father's workshop."

Niro shot me a glare, and it was strange how much his black hair and tanned complexion matched Adelgis's. He wiped off his scale-plate armor and then turned his attention to the fight listings. He didn't say a word. Not even a greeting.

"I know we have a match coming up, but I need to speak with you on another matter." I lifted my head and hardened my gaze. "Adelgis is dying."

That got his attention.

Niro faced me with a sneer. "What's that?"

"Your brother. Adelgis. He's not well. He's dying."

"Feh." Niro stepped close and crossed his arms. His sea serpent eldrin slinked around me, circling wide, its putrid breath filling my nostrils. It reminded me of rotting animals and death. "Who says Adelgis is dying?"

"The Grand Apothecary of Fortuna."

"From what?" Niro asked.

"The abyssal leech he had inside his body," I growled. "The one he carried *for years*. Or did you not know that part?"

Niro scrunched up his face and remained silent. He didn't have the same hint of intelligence that his father or brother had. His eyes seemed a bit unfocused, and he shifted his gaze around as though uncertain of what to think. Up close, he had the same muscled physique as Zaxis, but he didn't carry it as well. Not as tall and not as limber.

"I need your help," I said, trying to hold back my anger. "Please. I know your father probably has a solution to this, but he's disappeared, and no one else knows anything about an abyssal leech."

"You think I do?" Niro asked.

"You have access to your father's workshop, right? You must know something. *Anything*. Adelgis's life is on the line. Even *notes* about the abyssal leech would be better than nothing."

The stoor worm exhaled and inhaled with a deep rhythm that washed the pit in a stench that would last for years, no matter how deep someone cleaned. Then it turned its serpent gaze to its arcanist. "There is one way, my arcanist." It spoke with a deep, yet distant, voice. "Your father keeps them for... his other experiments."

The crowds outside grew louder and louder. Soon our match would be called.

"You want me to help?" Niro asked, his tone callous.

"Throw this fight and let me win."

I had to stifle a laugh. When I realized he wasn't joking, I narrowed my eyes into a glower. "Are you so petty that you'd rather win a tournament than help your own brother?"

"You don't know our father. He told me to win this tournament. I have to."

The ominous statement got me thinking. Why would Theasin care if his son won? It seemed beneath him. Theasin wasn't the kind of man who cared about temporary acknowledgement—I knew that much about him.

Niro grabbed the front of my shirt and yanked me closer, his aggression a bit of a shock. The shadows at my feet swirled, and Luthair was seconds from attacking him, but I held out a hand and stopped him.

"Well?" Niro demanded. "Is it a deal?"

The swell of excitement traveled like a tremor through the building. It was time for the match.

Niro's stoor worm hovered close, its fangs near my head. They were trying to intimidate me, though it wasn't working. My only hesitation came from Illia's and Atty's expectations. They had asked that I win—and I wanted to do it for them—but Adelgis's life was far more important than fame or recognition. In reality, the tournament paled in comparison to the complications hiding in the shadows of Thronehold.

And technically Zaxis wanted to face me in the arena as well. His request was selfish, however. He just wanted to beat me in front of everyone, and I couldn't care less about that.

"I'll lose," I said, curt. I would have to apologize to Illia and Atty.

With a shove, Niro released my shirt. "That's what I thought."

46

THROWN FIGHT

Standing on the edge of the arena platform, my heart beat out of sync with the rumbles of the audience. The afternoon sun blazed down, and I tossed my odd fisherman's jacket off into the dirt. Master Zelfree hadn't returned yet. I shook my head, dispelling the thought. It was probably for the best he wasn't here—I didn't want him to see me throw a fight.

I couldn't bring myself to glance at the queen's seats. Lyvia and Evianna would be there. I knew it without needing confirmation. What would they think? I didn't want to imagine it.

Luthair shifted through the shadows around my feet. "My arcanist, are you sure you want to do this?"

"It's the easiest way," I said, my voice barely audible through the commotion. "What does it really matter if I lose?"

"The winner is awarded star shards. You could use those to craft a magical item. Or you could use them to fix your shield."

Hm. I hadn't thought about that. They were rare

resources, and practicing my imbuing would help me become a better arcanist.

"There will be more star shards in the future," I muttered. "But Adelgis won't have a future if I wait."

"A wise observation, my arcanist."

Niro stepped onto the platform a moment later, his stoor worm following close behind. He wore a short sword on his belt, and he fiddled with the ornate hilt while waving to the citizens of Thronehold. They didn't respond like I expected. They threw food and cloth. No flowers. Some even booed. Niro seemed to have their disfavor—or perhaps the crowds wanted me to win? I knew people had placed bets on my victory, but I couldn't do anything about that now.

"The first semi-final match for the apprentice arcanists is about to begin," the announcer shouted. He sounded more excited than he had before, and that enthusiasm traveled to the spectators. There was a music to the event—an orchestra of stomping, shouting, and cheers. I had become familiar with the song, and I enjoyed the intensity it brought.

"We have Volke Savan the Knightmare Arcanist of the Frith Guild versus Niro Venrover the Stoor Worm Arcanist, son of the famed artificer, Theasin Venrover!"

Luthair lifted from the shadows and stood by my side, his sword held his gauntlet. I took a deep breath and then exhaled, wondering how I should go about *faking* my defeat. Perhaps I could just allow the worm poison to disable me.

Niro ambled to the center of the arena, ready to bow.

Odd. He hadn't done that in his last fight.

I walked out to meet him. The moment I drew near, he smirked.

"Create an eclipse," he demanded as we bowed to one another. "Hidden in the darkness, no one will see."

"I can't create an eclipse aura." I stood straight and rotated my shoulders. "Just fight by the edge of the arena. Knock me off."

We parted and returned to our respective sides of the platform, my muscles stiff. I wanted this over.

The sovereign dragon roar sent adrenaline shooting through my system. Luthair merged with me a moment later, but instead of moving, I remained rooted in place. Niro's stoor worm started his matches with a fast strike. If I took the hit, I could act out a quick defeat without much suspicion.

Right on cue, the worm lunged and collided with me. Its fangs couldn't pierce through Luthair's shadow armor. Instead, it bashed me toward the edge of the arena. I held up my shield and swung with my sword, my heart not in the bout.

Then Niro joined in the fray. He readied his short sword —the sharp blade gleamed in the light—and he thrust it with all his might.

The attack was telegraphed. I could've dodged, but I twisted to the side and allowed the weapon to strike me. The tip scraped off the shadow-plate. When he realized he couldn't pierce it, he grazed his fingers across my side, and he evoked corrosive acid that ate away at the darkness. When he stabbed a second time, he cut me under the armpit, and I grimaced for effect.

His technique is sloppy, Luthair said straight to my mind.

Everything about Niro seemed sloppy—like he relied on power over skill.

Then his worm bit me in the wounded area, injecting its venom straight into my veins. Out of instinct, I shadow-stepped behind Niro, but instead of attacking, I staggered backward. The venom hadn't taken hold yet, but I wanted this over. All he had to do was throw me off the platform.

Instead, Niro grabbed my arm and used his powerful magic to melt a portion of the armor. This time, it hurt. *Burned.* I shouted and actually slipped into the shadows to avoid him. When I emerged, his worm grabbed me and threw me back into the middle of the arena.

My head spun.

The venom blurred my thoughts.

"What're you doing?" I growled, my double-voice laced with confusion.

"Giving them a show." Niro sauntered over as he swished his sword through the air. "Everyone thought you would win, so I wanna make this look good."

"This isn't what we agreed."

"You said you would lose, we didn't agree on how. They can't think I won by accident. I have to *prove* I'm better."

They? Luthair asked me. *I suspect he isn't referring to the crowd, my arcanist.*

Niro continued, "If you can't make an eclipse, I'll have to beat you into unconsciousness. Then there'll be no mistake. I can handle knightmare arcanists."

His eldrin lashed at me with its tail. The whip-like strike hit with considerable power behind it, and I rolled to my side. Niro lunged and swiped with his hand. His palm burned my shoulder and left arm—another dose of agony. I slipped into the shadows, emerged a few feet over, and got to my feet, my head still throbbing from the venom.

"This fight isn't going like I expected," the announcer declared. "Just—*not at all.*"

More boos rained down from the stands.

"Stop acting like a dead flounder," Niro shouted at me as he approached. "Give us a good performance. Swing at me."

I lifted my sword and swung with it, but Niro parried the blow and then stabbed me in the same damn spot along the ribs. His magic—that corrosive stoor worm evocation—it felt like it was boiling under my skin.

Niro chuckled. So did his sea serpent beast.

They're here to revel in your torture, Luthair said. *Disgusting.*

They weren't the first ones who wanted to see me beaten and broken, and they wouldn't be the last. I wouldn't let them walk all over me, though. If Niro wanted a damn good show, I would give it to him.

Gritting my teeth, I stepped back and held up a hand. With as much magic as I could force through my body, I evoked my terrors, giving Niro and his worm hallucinations of their worst nightmares. Some people with strong wills could shake away my horrors, but I had never made them as powerful as I had in that moment.

Niro hit the arena on his knees, grabbing at his head with both hands. His eldrin thrashed around, screeching something incoherent.

Although my sorcery burned when I used it for prolonged periods, I didn't care. I manipulated the shadows, the afternoon sun making the whole process difficult, but I did it no matter the cost. Tendrils lashed out and grabbed the stoor worm. I yanked it from the arena in one powerful display of my ability. The bell that sounded afterward was drowned out by the shouting of the audience.

A part of me knew the crowd cheered, but the venom made it impossible to hear properly.

I turned my attention to Niro. With a few long strides, I made it to his side. When he went to stand, I bashed the edge of my shield into the side of his face, breaking his nose and splitting his lip.

He tightened his grip on his sword and swung wildly. I sidestepped and avoided it, my technique far above his, even while affected by venom. And after a second swing, I didn't bother using my sword. I stepped in close and hit him with my shield a second time, smashing the other side of his face.

Niro collapsed to the ground, blood weeping from his busted nose and shattered mouth. His eyes watered, and his hands trembled. He was strong, sure, but he really didn't have the skill to beat me. I knew it. And now he knew it, too.

"I thought you were going to let me win?" Niro asked as he scooted away from me, unwilling or unable to stand. "Who's the petty one now?"

"Get up," I commanded.

Niro struggled, but he eventually stood. Pink saliva poured onto his black scale-armor and practically disappeared into the dark hue.

"We're going to fight near the edge," I said. "And then you're going to knock me off."

I lifted my sword. He did the same.

Then I said, "And if you get second thoughts about helping me—or if you even try to alter this deal afterward—this is just a small taste of what'll happen." Intimidation wasn't my strong suit, but when I was merged with Luthair, it came easy. Our voice could scare the darkness out of shadows.

I attacked, and Niro attempted to parry, but it wasn't much. I bashed his weapon with mine and forced him to walk backward a couple paces until we reached the side of the platform. From there, I allowed his strikes to bounce off my shield.

The venom had taken its toll. My footing didn't feel right.

If this had been a real fight, I would've used my terrors to end this. Unfortunately, pain dominated my thoughts. From my second-bonded magic, to the stoor worm venom, everything felt on fire. It was a relief when Niro hit me in the shoulder with his sword.

I tumbled to the side, left the platform, and collapsed into the dirt.

Then my vision faded.

***

"Wake up. C'mon."

I sat up, the soreness in my body quickly fading. "What?" I asked, groggy.

"Get up. We have to get off the field."

Wanting to comply, I stood and walked in whatever direction the hands on my shoulders directed me to. It took a few moments, but my thoughts returned in a flash of realization, like a ship finally sailing out of a thick fog. The healing magic of the caladrius chased away the last of the agony. Luthair and I weren't merged anymore—I didn't know when that had happened.

Master Zelfree walked by my side, directing me toward the coliseum pits. His arcanist star had a unicorn, and seeing it made me laugh.

"Why?" I asked.

He lifted an eyebrow. "Unicorns can cure people of poison. I used the magic to purge you of the stoor worm venom."

I ran a hand through my disheveled hair. Sweat made everything sticky. "Thank you..."

"What was that out there?"

We entered the dank pit, and I coughed as soon as the

dust entered my lungs. After wheezing for a few seconds, I shook my head. "I lost the fight," I said.

"Why?" Zelfree snapped. "That wasn't your fighting style. You waited, barely doing anything. Then you start giving a damn, only to fall off afterward? Your shadow-stepping alone would've prevented that. Did Theasin have something to do with this?" Zelfree grabbed my shoulder, his grip tight. "Did he interfere somehow? This seems like a stunt he would pull."

"It had nothing to do with Theasin."

Zelfree opened his mouth like he had a retort, but then he closed it without saying a word. He inhaled, released my shoulder, and then paced the empty room.

"I'm okay," I said. "I threw the fight because I wanted Niro's help with Adelgis."

Zelfree stopped walking. The thunderous applause of the crowd echoed between us. Once it settled, he sighed. "You think Niro can help?"

"I hope so."

47

RECOVERY

I left the apprentice pit before anyone else could speak with me. I didn't want to see the princesses, not even from a distance, and I was certain the others from the Frith Guild would question my bizarre performance in the last battle. A small piece of me wanted to stay to cheer Zaxis, though. He had to fight Dramm and his stone golem, and if Zaxis lost, I would actually feel guilty for my intentional loss.

So I stayed.

I shifted through the darkness until I reached one of the sky platforms for flying eldrin. It was hundreds of feet in the air, taller than the coliseum wall, and positioned next to flags the size of horses. They fluttered in the wind, displaying the dragons and roses that signified the Sovereign Dragon Tournament.

Up on the sky platform, I could see everything—the people in the stands, the entire fighting arena—even the queen and her gargantuan dragon. I stayed near the edge, shivering as a powerful breeze rushed past. The commotion of the crowds wasn't as bad when the wind carried every-thing away.

I had never been so high, and the lack of water bothered me. I wished I stood over the ocean, watching waves crash against distant shores.

"My arcanist," Luthair said. "You know the others will be worried if you don't explain your loss."

"Master Zelfree will tell them."

It would be better coming from him.

This was the last match of the day, and the last semi-final bout—Zaxis versus Dramm—and I wondered if Zaxis would get as hurt as Hexa or Illia. When the crowd threw flowers for his arrival, it looked like a field of colors raining down into the heart of the coliseum. The new perspective amused me.

Forsythe flew off one of the nearby sky platforms and rushed to his arcanist's side. The stone golem and Dramm also got into position. They looked like toys from my height, but the thunder of the competition kept everything real.

I took a seat, my feet dangling off the edge of the platform.

The announcer spoke. Vercingetorix roared. Then the match started.

I hadn't realized how devastating a stone golem could be. It couldn't be burnt, it couldn't be poisoned, and even the strongest of arcanists couldn't dismantle its boulders. Could someone knock it unconscious? I doubted it. And how would Zaxis throw it from the platform? It was impossible.

When the beast lumbered forward for an attack, I expected Zaxis to get thrown from the arena, but he nimbly dodged aside and went straight for Dramm.

Although Dramm was a large man, even larger than Zaxis, he wasn't as solid as rock. Zaxis punched him a few times—at least, that's what it looked like from my angle—and before the stone golem could get involved, Dramm was knocked off the platform.

The gong of the bell was louder up on the sky platform. I grabbed at my ears to protect them from the reverberation.

Borod, the stone golem, thrashed about, his rock-fists smashing the arena platform. Each hit was harder than the last, and the craters he created reminded me of meteors. If Zaxis were hit, that would be the end. A caladrius would have to swoop in immediately to heal his pulverized body; his own magic wouldn't be enough.

I scooted to the edge of the platform.

Zaxis kept his distance. He moved away from the strikes and leapt over the craters when he needed to. He never got close to the golem. Never attacked.

He was avoiding it. Even Forsythe took to the air and refused to get close.

I chuckled to myself, piecing together their plan. These matches were five minutes long. At the end of that time, if Zaxis and his eldrin were still in the fight, but Dramm wasn't, Zaxis would be declared the winner. He didn't need to remove the stone golem—he just had to outlast him.

Clever. Not the best strategy ever, but good enough so long as Zaxis didn't get hit.

The problem was—five straight minutes of intense physical and mental alacrity wasn't easy. Every second took its toll. Zaxis had to keep tense, keep his eyes on the golem's movement, keep his footwork proper, not trip on the ever-increasing rubble, and avoid every swing of the boulder-arms. I couldn't see from my distance, but I knew he was soaked in sweat and breathing hard from only a couple minutes.

The longer the match went, the stiller the crowd

became. More and more people realized the plan, and the intensity brought quiet. The denizens of Thronehold got to their feet, watching with rapt attention. The breeze even died down, like the wind had gotten distracted by the match.

By minute four, Zaxis had become slower and stiffer. I could see it in the way he limited his movement. The arena platform was a topographical map of hills and valleys, and his footing never quite made up for it.

Then he slipped on loose debris.

I jumped to my feet, and a whole section of the coliseum gasped.

Borod smashed a fist down, and Zaxis rolled to the side, but his foot got crushed in the process. I couldn't hear if he yelled out or not. I shuddered in empathetic pain. When the stone golem lifted its hand, Zaxis got up and limped away, bloodied and sluggish.

"Don't you dare lose," I muttered as I clenched my fists. "C'mon, Zaxis. You can do this."

The golem swung with all its might. It didn't aim for the ground, but Zaxis's head.

Zaxis ducked and slid away, mere inches from Borod's stone strike. Another round of gasps, followed by some hesitant applause.

Another swing. Another *just-barely-made-it* dodge.

I didn't know if I could keep watching, but at the same time, I didn't think I could look away.

The stone golem kept attacking, forcing Zaxis closer and closer to the edge of the arena. Zaxis didn't have the mobility to get around the beast, and it seemed only a matter of time before he fell off.

Another swing, but this time Zaxis got hit.

The crowd roared as Zaxis went flying. He didn't go over

the edge. Instead, he had angled himself to get thrown farther onto the broken platform. When he collided with the ground, he could barely move. Had he broken all the bones in his body just to get a temporary advantage?

A bell rang out, and my heart leapt into my throat.

Had Zaxis gone unconscious?

"That's time!" the announcer shouted. "Zaxis Ren the Phoenix Arcanist wins the match!"

By the abyssal hells—*he won?*

The applause and cheering erupted like a celebration volcano, and I ran both hands through my hair. "Did you see that, Luthair?" I shouted.

"Yes, my arcanist."

"He better win the damn tournament." I laughed as I glanced back down at his broken body. "After a stunt like that, I'd be disappointed if he lost."

"He seems determined to impress Illia. He's found a good source of motivation."

The three caladrius of the coliseum swooped down and blanketed the field in their healing magic. Zaxis remained on the ground, unable to move. Broken bones healed the slowest, and I didn't envy his agony. Forsythe glided down to his side and cuddled close to him, despite the blood.

A part of me wanted to rush down to the field and help him, but Zelfree was there before I could slip into the shadows. Zelfree helped Zaxis and half-carried him away. I wondered what he said to Zaxis in that moment and whether he was proud of his performance or not. It wasn't a spectacular win, but it was still a win.

The coliseum gargoyle and its arcanist ran to fix the arena. The shattered stone needed to be repaired before the journeyman semi-finals, and they went to work correcting all the damage done by Borod.

I left the sky platform, done with the fights.

Although the *Maison Arcana* was over an hour away by foot, I avoided the trolleys. I had enough restless energy to keep me awake for a week, and I wanted to bleed some of it off before rendezvousing with Niro.

Lost in thought, I didn't even notice the lengthy trek. Cobblestone roads, gates, lines of carts, and merchants—I slipped past them all, my second-bonded magic burning in my veins. Once inside my inn room, I changed into a set of clean clothes, lamenting the fact I had forgotten my fisherman's coat in the arena. Perhaps I just wasn't meant to have one while in Thronehold. It seemed fate conspired to keep coats from me.

I left the inn, using the shadows to quicken my step. The Enchanter District wasn't far, and I remembered my way to Theasin's workshop. The tall buildings, slanted roofs, and thick windows gave the district a unique atmosphere. There weren't many signs for businesses, and I suspected most arcanists here were under direct employ of the queen.

The sun had started setting, and a hazy crimson filled the sky. The smoke of industry filtered the dying light. It was only then that I realized I no longer smelled the stench of the city.

I slowed my pace when I reached the workshop. To my surprise, Niro stood outside, his stoor worm lurking in the shadows of the alleyway near him. The scales of his armor shone in the red hue of sunset, some damaged from our fight. Although I left him injured in the arena, his wounds had been healed.

"Niro," I said as I approached.

He whirled around, tense and glaring. After he got a good look at me, he walked over and shoved two glass vials into my chest. "Take 'em."

I examined the containers. Both had sand—one tannish in color and the other a rose pink. The tan sand I recognized. Theasin had used some on Adelgis after he extracted the abyssal leech. It had clumped together with the blood and healed the injury much faster than normal.

"You didn't get these from me," Niro growled under his breath. "I'm reporting them stolen, so if you try to sell them, it'll be the last mistake you ever make."

"Why would I do that?" I asked. "I told you—Adelgis needs help. I wasn't lying."

Niro shook his head. "Whatever. Listen closely. This one will heal physical injuries." He tapped the tan sand. "This one will heal someone's soul." He tapped the pink sand. "But with the pink one, you'd better be certain. You have to consume it, and if the person's magic isn't damaged, it'll kill them."

"What are these?"

"I don't know." He motioned me away with a dismissive wave of his hand. "Now get out of here. My father would never approve of this, and I don't want it getting back to him that I spoke to you."

"Wait." I held the glass jars close. They were so small that both could fit into one hand, though I couldn't close my fingers around them completely. "You really don't know what these are?"

"No. I'm not privy to my father's research. I just know where he keeps all his *rare and valuable* resources, and I've seen him use these sands before."

I gently placed the bottles into my trouser pocket. "Thank you," I muttered. "I really appreciate this."

I didn't know why, but my statements seemed to agitate Niro. He gritted his teeth and mumbled something I couldn't hear. When I went to leave the Enchanter District, he grabbed my shoulder. I tried to face him, but he just held me in place, like he didn't want me to move.

"I'm not close to Adelgis," he said, his voice low. "We have different mothers."

That last part surprised me. I didn't say anything—I had no idea how to comment on such information—and it seemed Niro didn't want me to speak anyway.

He continued, "But he's still my brother. Thank you for... giving a damn."

Niro released me and headed back for his father's workshop. He whispered for his stoor worm, and they made their way into the building together.

The staff and faculty at Skarn University greeted me as I rushed down the halls. The moment I got close, I slipped into the shadows and emerged in Adelgis's medical room. The lanterns had been snuffed, and he slept in peaceful darkness. I hated seeing him so wan and sickly, but I smiled regardless.

"Adelgis," I said as I made my way to the side of his bed. "I brought you something."

I withdrew the rose-colored sand from my pocket and removed the cork seal. Niro had said it needed to be consumed, but pouring dry sand into someone's mouth didn't seem right. I glanced around, spotted a pitcher of water, and used it to mix a little liquid into the bottle. Once thick, I returned to Adelgis and lifted his head.

"You're going to be okay," I muttered.

With careful actions, I poured the unknown substance into his mouth. I wasn't sure if he would swallow properly, so I massaged his neck, hoping to coax the substance down. How long would it take to work? I didn't know.

I poured the wet sand in a little at a time until everything was gone. Adelgis coughed afterward, but he didn't wake. I rested his head back onto the pillow and took a seat next to him.

"My arcanist," Luthair said from the shadows.

"Hm?"

"Shall I inform the Grand Apothecary?"

"Yes. Thank you, Luthair."

He moved through the shadows of the room and left under the shut door. Perhaps Gillie would know what these sands were.

Certain I had done everything I needed to, I rested back and forced my eyes to remain open. Sleeping wasn't an option. My dreams of helplessness would end here, once Adelgis awoke, healed of his injury.

The ceiling offered no distractions, however, and my thoughts wandered to Karna. Would she return with a bit of ghoul for me to use? Would I finally find the thieves after the runestones? And what of Lyvia? Would she win her death match?

I gripped my shirt, uncertainty eating at my daydreams.

"Volke?"

Adelgis's weak voice startled me. I sat up, my breath held.

He stared at me through the darkness, his eyes half-lidded and unfocused. He probably couldn't see. I touched his shoulder and used my augmentation to allow him sight in the dark. It probably would've been easier to light a lantern, but this seemed faster.

"How're you feeling?" I asked.

Adelgis took a deep breath and forced half a smile. But he didn't answer.

I moved to the edge of my seat and placed a hand on his arm. "Do you need anything? Water? Food? Medicine?"

Adelgis brushed his black hair away from his face, his hands unsteady and his skin dappled in fresh sweat. Despite that, he already had color to his complexion.

"I've been dreaming," he whispered.

"Oh, yeah? About what?"

"About whatever I wanted. Felicity was there, helping me."

I knew ethereal whelks possessed powers over dreams, but I wasn't sure the extent. Was there some sort of significance to dreaming for weeks on end? Had he mastered something while locked away in his own slumber land?

Adelgis exhaled and then closed his eyes. "I could hear everyone's thoughts, even while asleep. It's like... I can't stop. It just happens, whether I want it to or not."

Just like my ability to see in the dark.

"Is that a problem?" I asked.

"So many people kept thinking I would die. They wanted me to hurry up and end it. It messed with my dreams."

He said the words like they were just *facts*, but it seemed disturbing to me. Who thought that? Surely no one from the Frith Guild?

"But I really appreciated hearing about the tournament and the guild's problems from you," Adelgis continued. "It was like you were keeping me informed, even while I couldn't move."

I rubbed at my neck. "That's your take away from all this?"

He sat up and pushed the blankets down. A twisted scar ran the length of his ribs, where the abyssal leech had embedded itself in his body. Was that the result of the healing sand? Or was that because abyssal leeches messed with magic? Either way, I suspected he would carry the scar forever.

"I feel much better," Adelgis said. "And it's mostly thanks to you."

"Don't worry about it. I'm just glad you're okay."

"Did you know you have a lot of people who follow you around?"

I stifled a laugh. "Tell me about it."

"The wendigo arcanist seemed concerned about your safety. And I'd have to agree. The doppelgänger arcanist and her eldrin have been stalking your every movement."

THE GHOUL PIECE

"You mean Karna?" I asked.

She was *stalking my every movement*? What did that entail? And I hadn't met her eldrin before. Or had I? Adelgis's statement brought more questions than answers.

"The woman you met in the Moonlight District," Adelgis said. "She's followed you around for some time. She's not here now, but she was here the last time you visited. She took the appearance of staff and lingered close. Her thoughts are vastly different than the people who work here."

As I was about to ask more questions, the door opened. Master Zelfree and Zaxis stumbled into the room, neither of them walking quite right. They struggled with the darkness and patted the walls to find their way to one of the beds. Zaxis rested on the down-filled mattress, and Zelfree lit one of the oil lanterns, illuminating the room in a gentle orange glow.

Zelfree flinched once he glanced over to Adelgis and me.

"What's—" he caught his breath and then rubbed his eyes. "Adelgis? Are you up?"

"Yes, Master Zelfree."

"Does that mean Niro came through?" Zelfree asked.

I nodded. "I think Adelgis will be okay."

"Good... good..."

Zelfree continued to rub at his face, his posture lax. He reeked of booze. So did Zaxis. Had they been celebrating? Perhaps they got a drink on the way here. Both appeared exhausted, and Zaxis had already closed his eyes.

"You broke your bones," Adelgis muttered. "Fighting a stone golem? That's interesting."

Zaxis rolled to his side. He wore a fresh shirt and trousers, but no boots or belt. After getting pummeled by the golem, his old clothes had to be blood soaked and disgusting. "My leg hurts," Zaxis said. "They said the healing magic fixed the worst of it, but that it'd still take more time. Master Zelfree gave me a couple drinks. Dulled the pain."

"Where's your phoenix?" Adelgis asked.

"Forsythe is back at the inn. I told him to wait there for me."

Again, the door to the medical room opened. This time, Gillie strode in, her bright green robes fluttering behind her, her steps light and filled with energy. When she smiled, it lit up the room more than the lantern. She shifted her gaze from Adelgis to Zaxis.

"You're both alive," Gillie said with a sigh of relief. "I'm so thankful."

Her caladrius eldrin flew in before the door closed. The bird landed on Gillie's shoulder, her parrot-like beak shining in the low light, drawing my attention. Caladrius were beautiful birds—small, ivory, and delicate. If it wasn't for their healing magic, I doubted I would be alive today.

Gillie rushed over and threw her arms around me. I tensed, confused by her sudden embrace.

"Uh," I muttered.

"Luthair told me you found medicine for Adelgis. Thank you." Then she broke off the hug and narrowed her eyes. "He also told me you used it all. Next time, let me see it. I need to duplicate such valuable resources in the future, young man."

"But—"

She threw her arms around me a second time. "I know, I know. Luthair said not to ask. Just keep it in mind."

Gillie was interestingly short when compared to me. Her arms wrapped around my ribs, and her hands clung to my shoulder blades. I hadn't noticed before, probably because she never hugged me for so long. I had to pat her back until she finally let go. Then she hustled over to Adelgis and hugged him good. He didn't react much, and his touch seemed mechanical—devoid of emotion.

Gillie released him, and continuing her overflow of affection, she rushed to Zelfree and did the exact same thing, perhaps even squeezing him tighter than the rest.

"I was so worried when I heard that your apprentice would fight a stone golem." She shook her head against Zelfree's chest, her cheek flat against his black shirt. "Yet he pulled through. You should be proud."

Zelfree rolled his eyes. After a long moment—Gillie never moving—he broke away from her hold and then motioned to the door. "We should let them sleep, Gillie. We can talk more in the morning."

After a short sigh, Gillie stepped back. "I've been watching Adelgis for weeks, and now that he's finally recovering, you want me to leave. I see how it is."

"Don't guilt me, woman," Zelfree growled under his breath. "You know it's late."

She giggled, joyful and uplifting, and took Zelfree by the elbow. "You were always my favorite to rile up, you know that, right?"

Her caladrius peep-laughed at the comment, like only a bird could.

Then Gillie walked with Zelfree toward the door, his expression set to an irritated neutral. Before they left, he glared at me and snapped his fingers. "You stay here and watch these two. Don't let them strain anything. We can talk about their final recovery in the morning."

"All right," I said.

They shut the door behind them. I glanced down at my feet, happy to see Luthair moving through the darkness. Although he remained quiet most of the time, his presence calmed me. I understood why the Grandmaster Inquisitor remained merged with his knightmare.

Zaxis leapt off his bed and walked toward me, half-limping on his bad foot, but gritting through the pain. He grabbed my shirt and yanked me close. "What's your problem?" he asked.

"I have no idea what you're talking about." I shoved him away, my blood running hot. Where did this even come from?

"I only asked for one thing—a fair fight. And what did you do? Intentionally threw your last match like a chump. Now Illia thinks you're a martyr, and you've denied me the chance to prove to her what I'm capable of."

"*That's* why you're upset?" I shoved him a second time, harder than I wanted. He stumbled back a few feet.

Embers flared in the air between us, like Zaxis's magic was just as angry as he was. The shadows shifted, but I knew that wasn't me. It was Luthair. His non-verbal warning brought me back from the edge of anger, and I forced a short exhale.

"Get it together," I said, curt. "I didn't *want* to lose. I did this for Adelgis."

The heat in the room subsided just as quickly as it came. "*I know*," Zaxis said. "I would've preferred if you let me do it. Then at least Illia wouldn't have another reason to bring you up in conversation." He ran a hand through his hair, his irritation still present.

Adelgis slid off his bed. He wore a thin pair of trousers—the kind they gave the bedridden for extended stays—and his guild pendant. Nothing else. He shuffled over to Zaxis, his movements stiff and awkward. The two of them exchanged glances, and without a word, Adelgis placed a hand on Zaxis's shoulder. He slid his fingers up until they touched the skin of Zaxis's neck, almost like some sort of seductive gesture, though neither of them had the body language or expression for that explanation.

A second later, Zaxis's eyes fluttered and his knees shook. "What in the... abyssal hells..." Then he collapsed forward and hit the wooden floor with a hard thud. I dashed to his side, bewildered and concerned.

"What was that?" I asked.

Adelgis shrugged. "I put him to sleep."

"You forced him?"

"It was something I learned while I dreamt. Sleep is just a state of mind—where it lets go of its control. I heard Zaxis's thoughts, and I knew he wanted to argue more about Illia, but that doesn't interest me. So I helped him get some rest."

"Ethereal whelk arcanists can put people to sleep?" I repeated the information for myself, still dumbfounded.

And Adelgis had somehow learned it while he slept. Amazing.

"I'll give Zaxis pleasant dreams," Adelgis said as he shuffled back to his bed. "They'll involve Illia and winning the tournament, and at some point you'll admit you've always admired him." Adelgis tucked himself under the covers. "Trust me. He'll feel better when he wakes. Then he won't be upset."

Luthair lifted from the shadows. Together, we picked Zaxis off the floor and carried him to his bed. Despite our fumbling and difficulty getting him positioned, Zaxis never woke. He remained limp and quiet, his breathing even and his muscles relaxed.

Once settled in place, I threw the blankets over him and made sure his injured foot was protected with an extra pillow.

"How long will this last?" I asked.

"I don't know," Adelgis said. "He'll probably wake if you jostle him enough."

I stared at Adelgis, surprised by his blasé attitude. "Are you okay?"

"Definitely. I've never felt better." He rubbed at the scar on his side. "It feels like I've recovered from a long and terrible sickness."

I took a seat next to his bed, the chair creaking under my weight. Luthair took up a position in the corner of the room, like a decorative suit of armor in a castle. How long had it been since I had a good night's sleep? Too long.

"Thank you," Adelgis said. "You and Zaxis both wanted me to recover. He brought me food and water in the morning, just in case I awoke during the day. But you were the one who never gave up. I don't think I can ever repay such determination." The tone in his voice didn't sit well with me.

He seemed woebegone and pensive, but when he glanced over, he smiled.

"Don't worry about it," I said.

Pleasant dreams lingered at the edge of my perception, too vague for details, but warm enough that I knew I enjoyed them. Fingers caressed my neck and jaw, and I wondered who would do such a thing. My first thought went to Lyvia. I didn't know why—we had only interacted a handful of times—but she felt familiar, like a kindred spirit.

Guilt took hold. Atty had made it clear she wanted us together. I had agreed.

Hot breath washed over my chin, someone's mouth close to mine.

What was going on?

I jerked awake, my pulse high and my confusion building. The medical room in Skarn University was just as I remembered. The lantern flickered in the corner near Zaxis's bed. Oil lanterns only lasted four hours, so if it was still lit, not much time had passed since I had fallen asleep in the chair.

To my surprise, Atty stood in front of me, bent over and leaning close. I sat up, and she slowly took a seat on my lap, taking her time to wrap her arms around my neck.

"I came to see everyone," she whispered. "I'm so sorry about your tournament match."

I rubbed at my eyes, my brow furrowed. "It's fine."

Atty wore a bright white robe that complimented her long blonde hair. Her expression, on the other hand... She stared at me with the same blue eyes I had always known, but they seemed more confident and playful than I had ever seen.

It wasn't long ago that Atty told me how much she feared the judgment of others; how that fueled her desire to be seen without flaw. *This* behavior—flirtatious and aggressive —was never something she did. Ever. Always proper and demure, I suspected Atty dreaded anyone calling into question her self-control.

Atty kissed my jaw, a coy smile at the corner of her lips.

"Karna," I breathed, my grogginess melting into anger.

She sat back, her lips pursed. "That was fast. How is it you always guess so quickly?"

I stood, half-tempted to throw her from my lap, but I set her down gently before stepping away. That was when Luthair slipped into the shadows and rushed over to my side of the room. Perhaps he was preparing for a fight, but that was something I wanted to avoid.

"Why do you keep taking other people's forms?" I asked. "Why not approach me as *Karna*?"

With a huff and swish of Atty's hair, Karna replied, "You've never seen the real *Karna*." She placed both her hands on her hips and moved them side to side. "I prefer interacting with people when their guard is down. I've seen the way you mingle with this girl—I just figured you'd open up more and I'd get to see more of your *real* personality."

"I don't hide my personality." I massaged the place she had kissed my jaw. "And it feels..." I searched for the words, trying to describe the disgust I felt, but failing to form an eloquent explanation. "Don't use Atty's appearance," I finally said.

"Why? She's too *precious and innocent*"—Karna said the words with a faux cuteness—"to ever kiss a man awake?"

"That's not it. It's just disrespectful to her and you. If I wanted to court you, I'd court you. And if I wanted to court her, I'd court her. Having you *be* her is… weird. I just don't want that."

Karna allowed the guise to drop. It shimmered away, the magic piecing her into another person, like clay rearranging itself. Threads of magic wove longer hair and even changed her eyes from a bright blue to gray. Her arcanist star shifted from a phoenix to a human, but her clothing remained the same. Once she returned to *Karna the Dancer*, she narrowed her eyes into an odd glower.

"I don't think you understand the carnal appeal of a doppelgänger arcanist," she said, her words thick with sarcasm. "A part of the fantasy is having someone who normally wouldn't take you. Can you imagine a night with Queen Velleta?" Karna motioned to herself. "It'd be simple to duplicate."

"Yeah. I get it." I pinched the bridge of my nose. "I just don't like the idea of pretending."

My face grew red and hot, and for the first time in the conversation, I feared someone else would hear. Zaxis remained asleep, his body unmoving. When I glanced over to Adelgis's bed, I flinched. He just sat there—watching—silent and inquisitive. My whole body burned with embarrassment.

"How long have you been awake?" I hissed.

Adelgis shrugged. "I never went to sleep."

"By the abyssal hells, say something next time!"

"Very well. I'll do so."

Karna didn't seem to care about Adelgis. She didn't acknowledge him or even glance in his direction. Instead, she reached into the pocket of her robes and withdrew something lumpy and ashen. At first I thought it was a square piece of cloth, but then she turned it over in her hand and revealed the blackened edges and odd stitching.

"You wanted something from a ghoul, right?" she asked. "This is a trinket made from ghoul skin. It writhes around when something undead is nearby. I found it at the market."

I caught my breath, forgetting all about the previous conversation as I stepped forward to take the gross flesh patch.

Karna held it away from me, like an older sibling taunting a younger one. "Wait. I do want one question answered first."

"Fine," I muttered.

"Who's the most attractive woman you've ever met?"

"You."

I didn't even need to think about it. She had a way about her—confident, but somehow fragile—and even her idle movements had purpose and seduction. I assumed it was magic. It had to be. And given that advantage, how could anyone else compare?

Karna tapped her bottom lip with a single finger. "Hm. That wasn't any fun." Then she offered a mischievous smile. "Is there someone you can't be with, but you wish you could be?"

"You got your one question," I said as I manipulated the shadows to snatch the ghoul trinket from her hand. The tendrils of darkness brought me the item, and it amused me how surprised she was. "We don't need to discuss any of this. Just... be yourself. Or as much of yourself as you'll show me. Please."

The lantern light flickered and faded at a slow rate. Soon the oil would burn out.

Karna walked to the door and opened it wide. "Are you ready to go?"

"Go where?"

"To find this ghoul arcanist, obviously." She swished her hair over her shoulder. Even in a long robe, she somehow made it bend to her curves. "It'll be easier to catch him at night. During the day, ghouls are... difficult."

I didn't know what she meant by that, but I didn't want to waste any time, either.

Adelgis's bed groaned as he slid off the side of it and stood. He didn't wobble or stumble. Instead, he gathered up his shirt and boots and donned them as quickly as possible.

"Shouldn't you rest?" I asked.

He shook his head. "I've slept enough. Now it's time to find those thieves."

49

THE OCCULT COMPASS

The quiet halls of Skarn University greeted us with a chilly gust of wind. I pulled my shirt tight across my body, but it didn't help much. Adelgis crossed his arms over his chest and pushed his long black hair close to his neck. His ratty trousers, wisp of a mustache, lack of belt, unkempt hair, and thin frame all came together to paint a picture of a homeless vagabond.

"Should I bathe before we leave?" Adelgis asked me as we walked.

Again, my face reddened, and I looked away. "Sorry. I forgot you can hear thoughts."

"It's fine. I'm aware I look like a *homeless vagabond*, as you put it."

Karna stopped mid-step and wheeled around on her heel. She smiled sweetly as she pointed at Adelgis. "How about we leave your creepy friend back in the room? I'd rather it was just the two of us."

"Creepy?" I asked. Sure, Adelgis was strange, but I never would've described him as disturbing in any way.

"We had a short chat before I woke you up. I don't like that he sometimes knows things he shouldn't."

"She keeps a lot of secrets," Adelgis said. "Not just her own, but for others, too."

Karna's smile changed into something forced. She sauntered over to Adelgis, a tense and hostile energy to her movements. "I thought we made an arrangement where you agreed not to say anything."

"I told you I wouldn't reveal your secrets so long as you didn't lie to Volke."

They regarded each other, neither flinching. After a long moment, Karna relaxed and returned her attention to the hallway. She walked for the exit, her blonde hair fluttering behind her, golden strands shining in the lantern light.

Adelgis's ebony locks also shone, but with an inky, almost oily, sheen. He ran a hand through his hair, perhaps in response to my inner thoughts, and then gave me a sideways glance. "You're concerned about me."

Not a question, but not entirely a statement, either.

We stopped walking, allowing Karna to go ahead.

"You're not yourself," I said.

"How so?"

"You seem somber. And detached."

Adelgis mulled over my comment without much of a reaction. "I told you why. I heard everyone's thoughts while I dreamt. They added to the visions I had—to the magic I was weaving. People are petty. Selfish. When I focused on their concerns, it ate at me, but when I stopped caring, that made it easier to see what mattered."

"And what matters?"

He didn't answer. I feared he would eventually say something dramatic and terrible—like *nothing*—but he never did.

Instead, he motioned to the hallway with a quick gesture of his hand.

"Maybe when we have more time to discuss it," Adelgis said. "But right now we have bigger things to concern ourselves with."

I picked up my pace to reach Karna, the sound of my steps echoing in the quiet corridor. Adelgis hustled to stay by my side, his movements weak and without energy, but he didn't complain. Once we reached the front door, Karna held it open for us and we exited out into the frigid night. I shivered as I went down the front steps and waited on the walkway.

"Where to now?" Karna asked as she joined me, a smile in her voice.

I pointed down the street. "We need to go back to the inn. Illia has the Occult Compass."

It didn't take us long to return to the luxurious *Maison Arcana*. The place already felt like a second home or perhaps a haven floating in a sea of unfamiliar people and places. I could navigate the inn's entire estate with my eyes closed, and while there were technically other occupants, they kept to themselves, so I rarely interacted with them.

I asked Adelgis and Karna to wait by the sidewalk before slipping into the shadows and emerging on the roof. There was a good chance that Illia and the others would be asleep, and I didn't want to disturb anyone in my attempt to speak with her, so I crept through the darkness, one careful step at a time.

Once I reached an open window, I used my magic to travel through the shadows and enter the building in a sitting room. Then I went to the hallway, doing my best not to make much noise. The moment I shut the door behind me, however, I heard the shuffle of feet on carpet, followed by a hushed whisper.

"Zaxis? Is that you?"

Illia waited by her room door. She pushed away from the wall and huffed, her eye unfocused, no doubt due to the lack of lights. While she couldn't see me, I could see her—wearing a dress-like tunic and her guild pendant. Her outfit wasn't risqué, but the Illia of two years ago never would've worn something so casual.

"I was worried about you," Illia whispered. "Why did you make me wait so long?"

Nicholin poked a head out of Illia's wavy hair. In a low voice, he added, "Yeah, *Zaxis*. You made me eat your dinner so it wouldn't go to waste. And your dessert. They were delicious."

I stepped close. "Illia. It's me."

She grimaced and moved away. Then she crossed her arms tight over her chest and bunched her shoulders close to the base of her neck. "*Volke*? What're you doing here?"

"I'm sorry. I didn't mean to bother you. I, uh, wanted to borrow the Occult Compass."

The Occult Compass was a rare artifact crafted by Master Arcanist Livia Brite. It was made using the eye of an all-seeing sphinx—an unusual breed, now extinct. The compass could be attuned to any mystical creature, and then it would locate the nearest one without fail. With the ghoul trinket, I could attune the compass and follow the arrow straight to the ghoul arcanist and his eldrin, even if they had somehow hidden themselves with invisibility or inside a building.

"Where's Zaxis?" Illia asked, her posture stiff.

"He's at Skarn University. Adelgis, well, er... put him to sleep."

Nicholin tilted his head. "How?"

"With his magic. I don't know when Zaxis will get up. He didn't move the entire time I was there."

This news seemed to bother Illia. She grazed her eyepatch with the tips of her fingers, and without saying anything, hurried into her bedroom. I waited in the hallway, listening to the soft sounds of someone rustling through clothes. When Illia reemerged, she wore a loose pair of trousers and a coat.

"Here," she said. She opened her hand and revealed the Occult Compass. It had the appearance of a normal compass made of copper and gold, but the face of the compass had a cat-like eye.

I took the magical item and smiled. "Thank you."

"Don't lose it."

"I won't." I gently tucked the compass into one of my pockets. "Do you want to come with me? I think I'm getting close to finding out who's trying to steal the runestones in the castle."

Nicholin rubbed his little ferret nose. "Hm. Interesting."

Illia secured her coat closed, her eyebrows knit. "Are you doing something dangerous?"

"I'm trying to find an arcanist hiding in Thronehold. It's not my intent to fight anyone, and if things get heated, I'll inform Master Zelfree."

"Just be careful." She reached out into the darkness until she placed a hand on my shoulder. Then she pulled me into her arms. "I wish you would've told me you were going to intentionally lose that fight with Niro. I was... really upset."

"I'm sorry. I didn't know until moments before the match. I swear."

"Still. Do this one thing for me, okay? Don't take any unnecessary risks."

She didn't say anything else. I returned her embrace, worried I had disappointed her. Ever since we arrived in Thronehold, I had done the exact opposite of what she wanted. I didn't avoid Fain, I didn't avenge her loss in the tournament—I just couldn't bring myself to do everything she wanted.

Illia shook her head. "I'm concerned about Zaxis," she whispered into my shirt. "I'm going to see him." She waited for a moment longer before letting go and taking a step away. Illia then scooped Nicholin off her shoulder and handed him to me. "Here." She glared at her eldrin. "Nicholin, you make sure he's okay, understand? Protect him at all costs."

I took her rizzel, bemused. Illia had never given me Nicholin before. He curled up in my arms, his ivory fur warm.

"Aye, aye," Nicholin said with a salute of his paw.

"When will you be back?" Illia asked.

I mulled it over for a moment. "By morning."

"I'll see you then."

While I carried Nicholin, I couldn't slip into the shadows. I hadn't yet perfected my magic, and taking someone into the darkness was beyond my capability. Although I suspected it wouldn't be difficult under the power of a knightmare eclipse. Perhaps I would try it next time I found myself in one.

As I navigated the stairwell down to the lobby, Nicholin positioned himself on my shoulder, half his body behind my neck. He squeaked to get my attention, and I glanced over, my eyebrows knitted.

"You like me, right?" Nicholin asked.

I nodded.

"Do you think Illia still likes me?"

"Of course. You're her eldrin."

Nicholin turned his blue eyes to the shadows around my feet. "What do you think, Luthair? Does she still like me?"

"Indubitably."

"What makes you think she doesn't?" I asked as I crossed through the dark lobby.

Nicholin gripped my shirt with his tiny paws. "Illia always used to love it when I tricked people. I would hide Hexa's long johns or jump out of Atty's sheets when she least expected it—but now Illia doesn't think that's funny when I do it to Zaxis. She always wants me to give them some alone time! Can you believe that? She wants *me* to leave."

"If I had to pick between you and Zaxis, I'd pick you," I said, sarcastic.

"Right? Who wouldn't?" He fluffed his tail. "She's just been acting weird lately. Perhaps I should find her fish in the market. Illia has been missing the fish she ate on the islands. Maybe then she'll see that Zaxis is the best person to mess with."

"He has command over fire, though. You should be careful."

"Ha!" Nicholin smiled. "Do you know who you're talking to? Rizzels are the masters of cleverness and trickery. If I didn't want Zaxis to know I was duping him, he wouldn't. I was just being nice before. *Nice.* Well, no more."

We exited the inn, and I headed straight for Adelgis and Karna. To my surprise, they weren't the only ones waiting.

Fain and Wraith were on the sidewalk as well, perfectly visible and speaking with the others. The skull and wolf-like body of the wendigo prevented me from understanding Wraith's mood, but Fain's steady stance and clenched jaw told me he wasn't enjoying the conversation.

"Look, it's Adelgis," Nicholin whispered, his mouth practically in my ear. "And the pirate. Oh! And his wendigo. You know, I thought I wouldn't like them, but they're not so bad. They laughed at my jokes, so you know they're good people."

Everyone quieted as I approached. An evening fog lingered between the buildings, pouring from the alleyways and clogging the streets. It made the meeting feel ominous, even if I already knew everyone involved.

"Well?" Karna asked. "Where do we go now?"

Fain stepped to my side, his attention locked on Karna. "She gave you the ghoul piece, didn't she? There's no need for her to accompany you now."

"It's fine," I said. "I trust Karna. And if she thinks about betraying us, I'm sure Adelgis will let us know."

Adelgis half-smiled. "She's just curious to see how your compass works."

Apparently, everyone was curious, because they all turned to face me. I withdrew the compass from my pocket and then placed the odd square of ghoul flesh underneath it, like a macabre cushion. The Occult Compass glowed with a golden hue, and the arrow spun at ludicrous speeds. It stopped hard, pointing in a direction opposite the inn.

"That way," I said.

I took off on foot as I didn't want to involve the Lamplighters Guild in our search. Wraith vanished with his invisibility, his claws clicking on the stone walkways as we went.

Fain and Adelgis flanked me on either side, while Karna kept ahead of me, her steps light and silent.

The streets weren't packed with individuals, but stable hands and merchant's apprentices were busy prepping carts and horses. The tournament was coming to an end. The final bouts would happen soon—and then the death match between Lyvia and her brother—and then everyone who traveled to Thronehold for the festivities would need to make the long journey home. The successful merchants and disgraced arcanists were just preparing for an early departure.

I supposed our group was an odd and an intimidating one, because the merchant's apprentices would duck behind their carts the instant they caught sight of us. We were four arcanists, one of which was bonded to a wendigo, a man-eater, and I suspected no one wanted to draw our ire.

To my amusement, none of us had our eldrin visible, even if I had Nicholin on my shoulder. Wraith was invisible, Luthair shifted through the shadows, Felicity hid herself in flickers of light, and Karna's...

Well, I had never seen Karna's doppelgänger.

"You've met Karna's eldrin," Adelgis muttered. "It's usually around, taking the form of entertainers, servants or passersby."

Fain cocked an eyebrow and turned his head, obviously confused by the non sequitur. I wondered what he was thinking, but the moment I had that thought, I shot a glare at Adelgis, trying to inform him I didn't actually want to know. Adelgis needed to get out of my head or at least let me pretend he wasn't listening to every tiny musing that crossed my mind.

We didn't travel long before the compass needle shifted

directions. I took a side road, jogging down the cobblestone walkways until we reached another large carriageway.

The lamps kept the darkness at bay, but the position of the lamps became wider and wider the further we traveled. When we reached a sign that read: SOUTH MARKET DISTRICT—complete with a picture of coins and a donkey—the lamps only stood on street corners.

We traveled from one bubble of light to the next, and while this seemed to get the others nervous, my dark-sight allowed me to keep track of our surroundings. Individuals lingered in the alleyways, but just like the merchant apprentices, they refused to approach.

When the compass needle jerked to the side, I stopped. Karna, Fain, Nicholin, and Adelgis glanced around, but there was no one here. Instead, I pointed to a nearby building—a two-story woodworker shop, where the crafting equipment was on the ground floor, and the second story was for living. The place seemed abandoned, however. The windows were bordered up, and the sign on the front door read: PROPERTY OF ARCANIST TIMRICK.

I took note of the name, just in case.

Then I stepped forward, checking the compass for the third time. It pointed directly at the shop. The ghoul had to be inside.

"Wait here," I said to the others. "I'll be right back." With my shadow-stepping abilities, I could slip through the cracks in the window and get inside without much effort.

"I want to come, too," Nicholin said. He swished his tail. "Illia would never forgive me if I let something happen to you."

He *could* teleport. I supposed it wouldn't be a problem. "Very well."

Fain grabbed my shoulder. "Are you sure?"

"I can handle myself."

"What if he's a master arcanist?"

My intent was to investigate, not to confront anyone. A part of me wished I had just told Zelfree—he would know exactly what to do in this situation. On the other hand, I was a member of the Frith Guild, and we had been tasked with figuring out a way to prevent the runestones from falling into the wrong hands. This was my duty and privilege. I would investigate and then leave.

"I need to go alone," I said. "Just wait out here."

Nicholin squeaked.

"Fine, fine. Nicholin and I will go alone."

Karna placed her hands on her hips. "You know *I* could just handle this, right?"

"No." Although I trusted her, she *wasn't* a member of the Frith Guild. She didn't need to know why I was doing any of this. "You, Adelgis, and Fain wait here. I'll be right back."

50

THE GHOUL LETTER

The ghoul trinket pulsated and writhed, indicating there were undead nearby.

I tucked the Occult Compass into my pocket and slipped into the shadows. I emerged within the woodworker shop, close to the front door. Mold and dust hung on the stagnant air. A second later, Nicholin teleported to my shoulder, a quiet pop heralding his arrival.

The floorboards groaned in protest as I made my way through the empty shop. When I reached the stairs, I knelt and withdrew my shadow sword from the darkness.

"Shall we merge, my arcanist?" Luthair asked.

I kept my voice low as I replied, "Not yet. Let's see what we can find first."

Although Luthair's armor wasn't heavy, it still clinked like metal, and I'd rather not burst into a room in full battle attire if I could somehow speak to the ghoul arcanist in question. Master Zelfree valued information, and I needed to prioritize that in this situation.

I went up the stairs as quietly as possible, but every third step seemed to squeak under my weight. Nicholin nibbled my ear, and I turned to him with a glower.

"I could teleport us," he whispered.

That... wasn't a bad idea. Then again, I didn't want to be taken by surprise if we appeared next to someone. That was exactly why I hadn't stepped back into the shadows.

"Not yet." I continued up the stairs. "But if we're attacked by surprise, you can take us outside."

Nicholin buffed up his chest. "You can count on me."

I reached the top of the steps and found a curious sight. All the doors had been taken off their hinges, leaving the upstairs one continuous space with occasional walls. The windows were boarded, except for one, which didn't even have glass. Wind swept inside, chilling the building with evening frost. I walked over, shivering, and found a wooden board positioned between this building and the next, creating a bridge that led from the open window to another. The board had been nailed down, preventing it from falling.

A plank-bridge? I withdrew the Occult Compass and ghoul bit and used them again. The arrow pointed across the board and into the next building. Despite that, I stepped back. I wanted to investigate this place first before moving on.

I tucked the compass into my pocket and then dropped my sword. The weapon fell straight into the shadows and disappeared without a single sound.

Despite the odd arrangements, everything in the wood-worker home seemed used. The tables were covered in papers and maps, the one bed had blankets, and bottles of wine lined the bookshelves. Someone lived here. I went straight to the cluttered tables and rummaged through the paperwork, hoping to find something of interest.

Again, I found myself struck with confusion. The papers

were covered in writing—but it was all nonsense. The first one read:

Kittens in lesser leagues travel here eventually. Greatness requires a nimble dance. My attic stinks tonight. Even reeks. Invite no quitters. Unions interrogate stalkers. I think onions rot.

What was that? It wasn't a poem or instructions or even coherent. I flipped over the page, hoping for some understanding, but there was nothing. Just gibberish.

"I know what happened," Nicholin muttered. "We've found the writings of a drunken bard."

Luthair shifted around my feet. "No. It's a code. Mathis and I would often find letters with the same strange phrasing. My arcanist, we should leave."

"Why?" I asked.

"This is far beyond the sophistication of petty thieves. Only an organization would utilize such methods, and in my experience, organizations are far more of a threat than deranged individuals."

I scooped up the paperwork, folded it enough to fit in my pockets, and took as much as I could. I didn't know what any of this meant, but I was certain Zelfree would know what to do. He needed to read as much as possible.

Heavy steps and the creaking of wood drew my attention to the open window.

A well-to-do man and a hunchbacked ghoul leapt into the woodworker building. The man's arcanist mark confirmed what I already suspected: a half-decayed person was wrapped around the star, indicating he was, in fact, the ghoul arcanist. He wore thick leathers, and a coat that hung down to his knees. His slick blond hair and sharp face gave him a distinct look, and it was clear he kept himself groomed.

The ghoul was everything I had ever read. It looked like a bipedal corpse, but it was hunched in such a way that it could walk or run on all fours, similar to an animal. Skin flaked off at a hideous rate, and its teeth were long and sharp, as though it had a full set of canines instead of normal molars and incisors. Ghouls were man-eaters—the type that consumed children, if they could get their decaying hands on one. They preferred their flesh warm.

The ghoul arcanist and his eldrin must not have noticed me, because the man threw down a bag of coin on a nearby counter before withdrawing a flask from his coat.

"We need to leave the city soon," the ghoul arcanist said, his voice so raspy it sounded like it hurt to speak. He spoke properly, though, confirming the story in the bar.

"Ahem," Nicholin said with a loud clearing of his throat.

The man and his undead eldrin whipped around, though they weren't athletic or even skilled about it. They both moved with awkward stances, as though off-balance or weak in the legs.

The lot of us stared at each other, the tension palpable.

From what I could remember, the skin of ghouls caused sickness. They were harbingers of disease—a walking blight.

"I'm Volke Savan," I said, more confident than I felt. "I'm with the Frith Guild."

The ghoul arcanist squinted, his lip curling upward in visible confusion. "You don't resemble members of the Frith Guild."

"*What?*" Nicholin barked. "We're so deep into the Frith

Guild even this guy's shadow is a member! You better be scared out of your wits, buddy."

"But..." The ghoul arcanist took a hesitant step back. He scratched at his neck, and small flakes of skin fluttered off. "You don't look like any of the descriptions I was given."

I moved forward, keeping the distance between us limited. He seemed unpredictable, and I needed to keep him focused. "I'm looking for the man with all the jobs. The one hiring arcanists. Is that you?"

"You're mistaken," the man said. "I'm just here for the tournament."

"Squatting in a suspiciously abandoned shop?" Nicholin sarcastically asked, his hackles raised. "Give it up. You're a terrible liar."

I placed a hand over Nicholin's head. I didn't want to antagonize the man—I wanted him to point us in the right direction. "We have someone who knows it was you," I said. "If you cooperate, then this doesn't need to get violent. Tell me why you're hiring people. Tell me who's in charge. Is it the Dread Pirate Calisto?"

"Calisto wishes he was in charge," the ghoul said with an odd hiss in its voice. "If you don't know that much, you're in over your head, boy. Drop all your trinkets—and all our papers—and get out of here while you still can."

Long razor claws sprouted from the tips of the ghoul's fingers. When it exhaled, a cloud of black mist lingered in the air, like the reverse of hot breath in cold weather.

"Hold, Gunter," the arcanist said. "We can't... get involved." The rasp seemed worse. Was he sick? That would be ironic.

The ghoul straightened his spine—cracking noises, like bones breaking, the entire time—and held his claws out to both sides. "My arcanist, these guildlings are here to interfere. They won't allow us to just leave, and we can't permit them to take our correspondences."

"It's too late to interfere, even if they wanted to. We need to watch out for ourselves. If you die... I won't get another chance."

It was then that I noticed an oddity about the man's arcanist mark. It wasn't right. Cracked? There were lines across the star and image of the decaying ghoul that shouldn't be there, much like mine. Was the man second-bonded? It would explain his hesitation to fight. His magic would burn him. Was their bonding recent?

Then, to my shock, Nicholin vanished. He blinked out in a puff of white sparkles.

Had he *abandoned* me? I could hardly believe it.

"He's not backing down," the ghoul hissed. "We *need* to kill him."

It swung wide, its claws outstretched. I leapt away, avoiding the attack, but I slammed into the wall. Before I could call his name, Luthair formed out of the shadows, his armor coalescing all around me, enveloping me in a cold sense of power and protection.

Sword and shield in hand, I blocked the next strike and then thrust. My blade sank into the ghoul's gut, but when I pulled it out, nothing happened. No blood. No scream or indication of pain. It was like I had stabbed a stack of hay.

The ghoul slashed down, its claws striking my armor. They did nothing, however. It wasn't strong enough to pierce my defenses.

A pop rang out in the room, and Fain appeared, along with Nicholin on his shoulder.

The ghoul arcanist pulled a pistol out of his coat and fired at Fain, too fast to properly aim. The bullet barely missed, and Fain held out his frostbitten hand in response.

Ice flashed across the room, coating everything from the table to the walls. It was a thin layer, like dew, but even I found myself without proper footing.

The ghoul lunged forward, its mouth opened wide enough to fit half my head inside. I slashed with my sword, catching its cheeks and slicing its face. Still no blood. No indication of pain. The monster slammed into me, and we collided into the wall.

Nicholin breathed white flames across the room, his teleportation breaking the furniture and the sleeve of the ghoul arcanist's coat.

"*Gunter*," the man growled. "We need to leave!"

The ghoul leapt to his side, my sword wounds visible, but slowly stitching themselves back together.

Fain coated the room in a second layer of rime, this time so thick it appeared like snow. It was difficult to move, and if it happened again, I suspected we would all be stuck.

The ghoul arcanist reached into his coat and withdrew what looked like a white ferret foot. Perhaps it had belonged to a rizzel? Sparkles—like radiant glitter—wafted around him and his ghoul. The whole second story of the shop had become a mystical winter wonderland.

In the next instant, the man and his eldrin were gone. They had teleported. Had that foot been a trinket? There was no other logical explanation.

Luthair unmerged from me and then stood by my side, the sword and shield in his gauntlets. "Cowards."

Nicholin vanished and then popped into existence on my shoulder, his ears laid back. "Can you believe that? They ran!"

I went to the window and leaned over the sill. Illia and Nicholin couldn't teleport far. Perhaps that was also a limitation on the villain's item. But I saw nothing. No indication of the direction the ghoul arcanist had traveled. And when I pulled the ghoul trinket out of my pocket, the flesh had stopped undulating. There were no undead nearby.

Fain glanced around the room, eyeing the open doorframes and rundown living environment. "Was that the man you were looking for?" Then he found the bag of coins the ghoul arcanist had left behind. Fain plucked the bag off the counter and tucked it into his coat pocket, the speed and silence betraying his skilled sleight of hand.

I ignored the "theft" and nodded. "I think I have everything we need, but could you help me carry more?" I walked over to the table and brushed away the fresh layers of ice. Some of the paperwork had been damaged, but not much. I gave Fain the rest of the stack before motioning to the staircase. "Let's go."

We made it down to the woodworker's shop on the first floor, and then Nicholin grabbed Fain and teleported. Luthair and I used the shadows to slip through the broken window and emerge outside. Although the wind continued to rush down the half-empty roads, the excitement of the fight kept me warm. I jogged to Adelgis and Karna, anxious to show them the strange notes.

"Read this," I said as I handed Karna one of the bizarre messages.

She read it over, one eyebrow raised. "What is this?"

"I don't know. I was hoping you could tell me."

"I've never seen it before."

Adelgis took the paper from her hand, his attention fixated on the wording. He brought the paper close to his face, seemingly withdrawing into his own world.

"I thought you said we weren't going to get into any fights," Nicholin said as he hopped over to my arm and then clawed his way to my shoulder. "Illia will be upset when she finds out." Then he nuzzled my neck. "*But*—since you weren't hurt—I can be persuaded to keep quiet. For some of your dessert."

I patted his head, a little more concerned about the current problem. "I need to tell Master Zelfree what we saw here. And he needs to know about this *organization*. Something terrible is happening, and I feel like we barely have any of the pieces."

Fain shoved his hands into his coat pockets. "Organization?"

"That's what Luthair says we're up against. Not like a single pirate crew or person. Something bigger. The ghoul thought it was funny when I mentioned Calisto, like he was a pawn. Zelfree said the same thing a while back... Calisto was taking orders from someone."

"He hates that," Fain muttered. "But he would do it sometimes, if the pay was right. Calisto didn't like talking about it, though. He always told the crew *he was in charge,* no matter what anyone said."

"This is a coded message," Adelgis interjected. He waved the paper around and handed it back with a bored expression.

"I know that already," I said as I snatched it away. "Can you tell me anything new?"

"It's a set of instructions. It says, *bring us the number of Knights Draconic stationed in the Dragon District.*"

I caught my breath. Fueled by exhilaration, I pulled Adelgis close and handed him a whole pile of notes. "If you can read them, tell me what these say. And start here. These were the more recent notes."

Karna hovered around, her gaze bouncing from the pages, to me, to Adelgis. She kept her attention focused the entire time, never growing disinterested or looking away. I didn't care. She seemed just as confused as I was, which meant she probably wasn't in bed with our enemies.

"This one says they need more information on Sky Legionnaire trinkets," Adelgis muttered as he pushed it aside and grabbed the next note. "This one talks about the wendigo trinkets and how they prevent the plague. It says that's a problem, but it doesn't elaborate."

I kept the notes in the order he handed them back to me, trying to decipher them myself, but failing. "How did you figure this out?" I asked.

"It wasn't difficult," Adelgis said, almost bored. Then he found a note and held still for a long time, his grip getting tighter on the paper.

Nicholin leaned forward. "What is it?"

"This one... talks about the runestones."

Karna and Fain both perked up on the last word. Although it probably wasn't a good idea to discuss the runestones in front of them, I didn't stop Adelgis in time.

"It says their plan is to take the runestones after the sovereign dragon bonding ceremony."

"After bonding?" I asked.

"After the death match," Adelgis muttered. "It says here they plan to steal them that night."

51

THE SECOND ASCENSION

The evening wind howled down the cobblestone road, disturbing wooden shutters and loose shingles. I stared at the paperwork, my heart beating hard enough to echo in my ears. The death match between Lyvia and her brother was only two days away—right after the final fights in the tournament concluded. Were these runestone thieves planning on hiding in the crowds of merchants, arcanists, and foreigners leaving the city?

Nicholin stroked his chin with a paw and murmured, *hmm*, his voice right in my ear.

"That's strange," Karna said. She tapped her lower lip with a single finger. "If they wanted to steal a runestone, they could've asked me for one instead of the crown."

I shook my head. "They don't want one. They want them all."

"Twelve weirdly shaped rocks? Why? My associates on the *Sun Chaser* say those runestones are antiques from a distant era. Relics. Nonfunctioning."

Which meant no one on her airship knew of the world serpent's birth. Everyone was still ignorant—they thought the runestones were the consolation prize and not the primary goal of our enemies. But I knew otherwise. The late king's crown sounded important, and I was certain everyone believed that, but they were being fooled.

"This one talks about the plague," Adelgis muttered. "Something about *dread forms*."

I turned to him, my curiosity piqued. "What exactly does it say?"

"That they need more time and magic before their dread form is complete. It doesn't give a name, though. It doesn't even list the eldrin." Adelgis flipped the note over and lifted an eyebrow. "Here it says their operation can't proceed without it. Again, no specific details."

I gathered up all the notes, my hands unsteady. Master Zelfree needed all of these. Right now. Nicholin took a single piece of paper and held it close to his chest, like it was his sacred duty to protect the note.

"Let's go," I said.

Karna grabbed my elbow and held on, keeping me from slipping away. "What're you going to do?"

"I'm going to stop these thieves, obviously."

She half-laughed. "Don't be so quick to get yourself killed. You're still an apprentice. The fools looking to steal from Queen Velleta won't be amateurs. And if they're talking about the plague—and the castle's plague defenses—you're better off avoiding this."

"It won't just be me stopping them." I slowly removed my elbow from her grasp. "I have to do what I can. These villains can't be allowed to steal those runestones."

"Why? What's so important about them it's worth risking your life?"

I wanted to tell her, but I knew I couldn't. Luthair stepped from the darkness of the road, his cape fluttering with the winds, his empty helmet focused on me. "My arcanist, there's no time for delay. We must inform the others."

Nicholin, gripping the paper tighter, poked his wet nose into my ear. "I can teleport you."

"We'll stay together," I said, rubbing the side of my head. "And thank you for your help, Karna. I appreciate it."

When I started down the road, Fain and Adelgis came with me. Karna waited near the woodworker shop, watching as we left, her expression neutral, though her gaze remained intense. Once I turned a corner and entered the main street of Thronehold, Adelgis lightly touched my shoulder.

"She's planning on informing the crew of the *Sun Chaser*," he muttered. "Her thoughts involved the captain and the blacksmith, and how they would worry about you."

"About me?" I asked.

"Yes. Karna also had thoughts about the people infiltrating the castle. She thinks they're dangerous. More than she let on when she spoke to you."

Fain secured his coat close, his black fingers darker than before, almost like coal. "I know you're smitten with that woman, but the stories of doppelgänger arcanists always end in treachery."

"I didn't hear anything *treacherous*," Adelgis muttered. He stared at the paperwork, his thumbs running over the ink of the letters. "But she does like keeping her cards close to her chest. She doesn't trust me or Fain, and at several points she wished she were alone with Volke."

Fain nodded. "That makes sense."

I lifted an eyebrow and gave him a sideways glance. "Why?"

"I'm a renegade—of a pirate ship she loathes—and your

sickly friend has a habit of conducting himself like a ghost spying on everyone's thoughts. Of course there's doubt."

"I'm better now," Adelgis said. "And my name is Adelgis Venrover. You don't need to keep wondering."

Fain combed his hair with his frostbitten fingers. "Sure. Whatever. The point is, Volke is a trustworthy individual, and that seems to fascinate her."

"Oh, that's true. The majority of her thoughts were about Volke. Trying to remember exactly what he said, what he wears, his preferences in certain situations, his—"

"Enough," I said, uncomfortable with the whole conversation. How could Adelgis stand listening to so many personal thoughts? "Let's keep this quiet until we reach the inn."

Master Zelfree had his own room in the *Maison Arcana*, and once we got close, I left Nicholin with the others and slipped into the shadows. I appeared on the roof above Zelfree's window, my footing steady, despite the slant. Fortunately, Zelfree kept the window cracked open, and I used the narrow space to shadow-step inside.

Dim lantern light kept the room illuminated. This was the *Maison Arcana*, so of course there was a lavish bed and dresser, both white and far larger than what the apprentices had. For some reason, however, they looked undisturbed. Zelfree sat at a card table positioned in the corner of the room, his head resting on the back of the chair, his eyes closed. Traces was curled in his lap, her long tail swishing back and forth. When I rose out of the darkness, she lifted her head and stared at me, her cat-like expression infused with curiosity.

"Volke," she said with a purr. "What a pleasant surprise. But isn't it a bit inappropriate to visit at this hour? And without knocking?"

Zelfree's breathing remained even. He didn't move otherwise.

"I apologize," I said. In the same breath, I continued, "This couldn't wait. The individuals after the runestones are going to strike the night of the sovereign dragon bonding. I have the proof right here."

With restless energy coursing through my veins, I withdrew the notes from my pockets and brought them to the table. I spread them out so that the gibberish on each was visible and then pointed to the page that Adelgis said was the most damning.

"I know this doesn't look like much," I said, almost tripping over my words in my haste to get the information out. "But it's actually a cipher! Luthair thinks there's an organization behind this—a large group with powerful arcanists."

Traces leapt onto the table, her feather-touch steps barely disturbing the papers. Her eyes, one pink and one gold, scanned over the writing. Her cat-face was difficult to read, but her ears stuck straight up once she came to the main letter.

"Oh no."

She pounced on Zelfree, her claws out and sinking into the soft parts of his thigh, right through the fabric of his trousers.

He jerked awake, growling a curse and reaching for his belt. His attention shifted from me to Traces before he relaxed back into his chair. His expression and posture were the very definition of irritation. "This better be good," he said, his voice raspy.

"My arcanist," Traces said. "Look here. Coded messages. Just like before."

Zelfree sat up, his bloodshot eyes tiny orbs of pain. He rubbed at his face while he stared at the table.

"Where did these come from?" he asked, curt.

"Remember how there were people at the Queen's Gala who were mapping the place out?" I asked. "And remember how the doppelgänger arcanist was there to steal something? They were all hired by the same man! A ghoul arcanist. I went to find him and—"

"What?" Zelfree barked.

I didn't break my stride. I had to tell him the whole story. "—when I found his hideout, he and his ghoul attacked. I took the letters, and Adelgis managed to decode them. This is legitimate, and we need to do something."

Zelfree stood so fast that the chair fell backward. Traces almost tumbled to the floor, but her cat-like reflexes saved her. With a graceful twirl, she landed on all four feet and then licked herself, as though nothing unusual had happened.

Zelfree slammed his hand on the table, glaring at the letters like he was plotting their death. "Next time you tell me what you're doing," he commanded, his volume bordering on a shout. "Do you know what you've stumbled into?"

I motioned to the papers. "Yes. I just told you. Thieves are going to take the runestones in two days."

"Not *this* specifically. Luthair was right. This isn't *someone* or even a couple *someones*. I've seen these types of letters before—this specific cipher. Several pirate ships communicate using this system, and so do individuals Guildmaster Eventide has classified as unstable and deadly."

"I'm sorry," I said, though the excitement in my veins

didn't wane. "I didn't know the ghoul arcanist was connected to something so large. I just wanted to find out what was going on."

Traces rubbed her feline body along the side of my leg. "My arcanist is worried about you. Save him some heartache and at least tell him where you're off to. He lost his last apprentices when—"

"*We don't need to discuss that*," Zelfree hissed.

We really didn't. I knew what had happened. I knew their death weighed heavily. If something had happened to Adelgis or me, I was certain he wouldn't take it well.

"I won't do it again," I said, my excitement finally at manageable levels. "I'm sorry."

Zelfree shook his head. Then he glanced at the notes again. "Listen. I found a man earlier who gave me some disturbing details."

"You *found* a man?"

He shot me a glare. "I *discovered* a man transporting plague blood. He worked for this ghoul, apparently. He was paid good money to bring the blood into town—a few days before the sovereign dragon bonding."

"Was he a lamplighter driving one of the trolleys?" I asked.

"Yes."

My heart seized for a moment as everything came together. Lyell's friend—Corry the Lamplighter—had been running errands for the ghoul arcanist, delivering things without question. This had been going on for weeks, which meant these villains had been prepared long before the Sovereign Dragon Tournament even started.

"What does the presence of plague-blood mean?" I asked.

Traces bounded from the floor to the table and finally

onto Zelfree's shoulder. "It means these cutthroats aren't just going to steal the runestones," she said. "They're probably planning on using the plague to cause a commotion, likely as a distraction so they can escape the city."

That was a well-known tactic among the pirates of my island nation. The plague could cause a massive panic, and if those dastards infected foreign arcanists, I wasn't sure how this would all end.

I played with the wendigo amulet around my neck. *I* wouldn't be infected, but that didn't mean much if a powerful mystical creature, driven insane by the plague, lashed out at me. No matter what, I had a duty as one of the immune to prevent tragedy. I had seen too many good people and mystical creatures driven mad by the arcane plague. Just... too many.

Luthair formed from the darkness, his cracked armor shining in the low light of the lantern. The shadows of the room flickered and shook, a clear sign of rage I could feel like waves in the water. Then he unfurled his cape and tossed it to the side. "And what will the Frith Guild do about this?"

"Don't worry," Zelfree said, chuckling. "We'll inform the Grandmaster Inquisitor of the plague threat, but the Frith Guild will be the ones handling the runestone thieves."

The darkness of the room calmed. Luthair stepped back. "Thank you."

"I want to help stop them," I said. "Let me know what I can do."

52

ZAXIS'S FINAL MATCH

S leep eluded me.

Anytime I closed my eyes, my thoughts would immediately shift to Lyvia and her upcoming duel to the death. And if I somehow managed to fall asleep after that, my dreams consisted of faceless thieves in the castle, snatching everything off the walls.

Guildmaster Eventide, Gillie, and Zelfree informed the knight captain and the queen of the attack. I doubted they had explained everything, but as long as the queen had her Knights Draconic and Sky Legionnaires patrolling the castle grounds, I would feel more at ease. The castle defenses, including the nullstone aura that cancelled out magic, would be in effect.

The Steel Thorn Inquisitors Guild had also agreed to help—their primary goal to stop the spread of the plague. They wanted these villains dealt with as soon as possible.

I had robbed our enemies of the element of surprise. Now that we knew their schemes, it would be easy to deal with them. Queen Velleta had even said she would move the runestones from the wall before nightfall and replace them with lookalikes. Although the Frith Guild still didn't have access to them, this was an acceptable solution.

I rolled to my side, but it didn't help with my sleep. The cool air in the inn room did little to comfort me.

Today the final matches for all divisions would take place. Tomorrow, Lyvia would enter the battlefield.

Of course I couldn't sleep.

I sat up on my bed as the sun crested the distant mountains. Dawn. Only a few hours before Zaxis's match. He wasn't in his bed, and Forsythe wasn't in his nest, which meant Zaxis was either with Illia or training for the last amount he could fit in.

"I could put you to sleep, you know," Adelgis said from his bed in the far corner. It had been so long since he slept in the room that I had forgotten he was here.

I shook my head. "I don't have enough time to sleep before the tournament."

Instead of trying for a quick nap, I decided to read Theasin's book. While there were hundreds of mystical creatures I had yet to read about, I went straight for the few I couldn't get off my mind.

Sovereign Dragon

Tier 4

Reproduction: Progeny (nesting grounds found near centers of civilization)

Trial of Worth: Five tests of tenacity, followed by a final duel to the death

Sovereign dragons are the most sedentary of all dragons. They enjoy luxury and wealth and often horde riches. Sovereign dragon arcanists have access to the famous "aura of prosperity," which greatly improves a country's trading, order, and stability.

In grandmaster arcanists, this aura can stretch for hundreds of miles.

Unfortunately, sovereign dragons reproduce infrequently, and their sedentary ways make them the weakest combatants of the dragons.

True Form: Their horns curve around their head, becoming a crown, and they sprout a second set of wings that help in precise flight. In this true form, their aura of prosperity is significantly increased in size and influence (obtained by individuals who are true autocrats—those who thirst for power above all else —authoritarians).

Dragons were among the rarest of mystical creatures, so it was amusing to see one compared to the rest. I touched the page, wondering why Queen Velleta didn't have a true form eldrin. Was she not authoritarian enough? Her many gruesome decisions made it seem as though she ruled with an iron fist, but perhaps her lax leadership was what prevented her from achieving the added bit of magic?

Thinking of her reminded me of the hatchling sovereign dragon. I had only seen it from afar—tucked under the claw of Vercingetorix. Where was its mother, for that matter? I knew most sovereign dragon arcanists became the rulers of other tributary nations, so it was likely the mother was just far off, but it seemed odd she wasn't here to watch the bonding.

I flipped to another page, scanning the information until I came to one that stood out.

King Basilisk
    Tier 4

. . .

I stopped and lifted both eyebrows. King basilisks were a type of dragon? After rationalizing it to myself, it made sense, considering their giant size, but I hadn't known that fact. I continued with the rest of the information.

Reproduction: Progeny (unknown nesting requirements)

Trial of Worth: Lacking a fear of death

King basilisks are dangerous in all regards. From their stone gaze to their acid blood, every part of them is designed to kill. Even their claws—all six of them—are coated in a toxin that paralyzes. The most infamous aspect of a king basilisk is their deadly venom, capable of ending arcanists and their eldrin in an instant, just upon contact.

Most king basilisk arcanists become assassins, and for obvious reasons. Their magic can stun, paralyze, and kill with little effort.

True Form: Unobserved

Adelgis slid to the edge of his bed and waited. I didn't know what he was thinking, but he stared at the floor for a long while before standing. He dressed without making much noise, even though he fumbled around with his clothing, unable to see. The longer I watched, the better at moving around in the darkness he became. Perhaps he heard my thoughts and used that to alter his movements, like a blind man taking verbal instruction from someone else.

Once dressed in a fine robe of black and white, Adelgis took his seat back on the edge of the mattress. I returned to the book, hoping to read one or two more entries before the sun chased away the remnants of night.

. . .

<u>Reaper</u>

Tier 1-4 (depending on the amount of arcanists killed)

Reproduction: Unknown

Trial of Worth: Killing a blood relative

Reapers are considered "bad luck" in most civilizations throughout history. The requirements for their birth are unknown, but they only tend to appear after long years of war or famine, which is why they carry such a negative reputation.

Reapers are hollow beasts that merge with their arcanist for more power and tend to have abilities that stun, disable, and disrupt magic, especially healing. If a reaper kills an arcanist, its magical capacity is increased, though the benefits are less with each subsequent murder unless the arcanist is stronger than the last.

True Form: Unobserved

Jevel from the Huntsman Guild seemed to love his reaper eldrin, Ruin. The names of their victims were etched into the chains, and now I knew why. Ruin was stronger because of the deaths, and I wondered if Jevel secretly wished he could kill Zelfree, just for his own power gain.

"We should leave soon," Adelgis said as he stood. "If we want to see Zaxis's match."

Without protest, I leapt from my bed and donned my own trousers and shirt. Luthair shifted through the shadows and dragged my boots close, helping me prepare faster. The last thing I did was tuck Theasin's book into my satchel.

"Let me carry it?" Adelgis asked. He held out his hand, palm up.

Although I liked having it as a reference, it was Adelgis's father who wrote the thing. I handed it over.

Adelgis forced a small smile. "Thank you." He used his own satchel to keep the tome close.

Instead of stepping into the shadows and traveling through the darkness, I walked with Adelgis out of the room, through the long hallway, and down the stairs. He said nothing and remained close. When we exited the *Maison Arcana*, he shielded his eyes from the brilliant rays of the morning sun and then straightened his silky black hair. It was obvious he had taken a long bath and pressed his clothing. He appeared more like himself—prim and proper —less like a vagabond.

We boarded one of the lamplighter trolleys and headed for the Thronehold Coliseum. I didn't see the others from the Frith Guild, and I suspected they were already there.

Once we entered the Dragon District, the trolley could no longer travel down the roads. The swell of bodies made everything difficult, even walking. Everyone wanted to watch the final matches—even people who hadn't attended the previous days showed up for the *best of the best*.

Mystical creatures filled the sky. Long dragons, fairies of various shapes and colors, and even a massive roc. I had spotted several rocs at Port Crown, but this beast soared overhead with wings twice the size of any roc I had ever seen. It was a dragon among birds—its head was larger than a full-grown man. Mesmerizing.

Then it tilted and flew for the lone airship, the *Sun Chaser*.

"The roc belongs to the captain," Adelgis said.

I squinted as I watched the roc circle the flying vehicle. "Yeah. Fain said the roc arcanist uses his magic to keep the ship afloat."

Once we neared the coliseum, the sea of Thronehold Denizens became rowdy. The gateways into the gigantic structure just weren't big enough to accommodate the remaining 20,000 people attempting to funnel inside.

"This place is gargantuan," Adelgis said as he was squished against my side. "Way bigger than anyone's thoughts indicated."

I had forgotten that Adelgis never attended any of the other fights. He had been sick the entire time.

I grabbed his arm and pulled him toward the fighter entrance. I didn't care if he wasn't a fighter—if Atty could sit in the participant box, so could Adelgis. With aggressive shoves and a couple of hard glances, I managed to push my way through the crowd. The moment we entered the coliseum, the sandstone bricks muffled the agitation of the city. I led Adelgis through the dust-filled corridors. Knights were positioned at the gates, but none prevented us from heading straight to the fighter's spectator box.

The coliseum wasn't difficult to navigate. I turned down the main corridor, and in my haste, I almost ran face-first into Zaxis. He and Forsythe were heading in the opposite direction but stopped once they realized who we were.

At first, I thought he would be upset that I had left him sleeping in Skarn University, but he greeted us with a genuine smile.

"There you are," Zaxis said. "You should take your seat. The match is about to begin."

I nodded and went around him.

Zaxis stopped Adelgis by grabbing his arm.

"I'm fighting your brother," Zaxis said, curt.

"I know," Adelgis replied, no concern in his voice.

"Niro told Volke he *had* to win the tournament. And

instead of just helping you, like a brother should, he forced Volke to lose before he would get involved."

The information settled over the dreary corridor like a wet blanket. Why bring this up now? Was he trying to upset Adelgis?

"I'm aware of what my brother did," Adelgis said.

"Why, though?" Zaxis barked. "Winning the apprentice tournament isn't life changing."

"All the winners are invited into the castle for a private dinner after the sovereign dragon bonding. My father said Niro had to attend."

I hadn't heard that. I met Adelgis's gaze, my eyebrows knitted in confusion.

Zaxis released Adelgis. "Is that right? Interesting." He cracked his knuckles. "Well, I'm going to make Niro regret ever turning his back on you."

"That isn't necessary," Adelgis said. "Niro and I aren't close, and—"

"*I don't care.* Niro's a scumbag. He hurt both you and Volke, and I'm not going to stand for it." Zaxis slammed his fist into the opposite palm, flame bursting out upon impact. "Your brother doesn't know what's coming."

Forsythe fluffed his phoenix feathers, dusting the floor with soot, and held his head high. "He even tried to bribe Zaxis earlier this morning. Niro has no honor."

Although I thought this would displease Adelgis, it actually made him laugh. He brushed back his black hair and half-smiled. "You were the only other person who remained optimistic about my recovery," he said.

Zaxis narrowed his eyes. "Huh?"

"It's nothing. Just know that I look forward to your victory." Adelgis placed a hand on Zaxis's shoulder. "Be careful, though. Niro's the type of guy who might try something desperate to win."

***

"It's the final match for the apprentice division!" the announcer shouted.

The stands of the coliseum were full to bursting. Technically, there were 24,000 seats, but I suspected over 30,000 people were in attendance one way or another. People sat on steps, bunched close together near the walkways, or even perched on the tops of walls and the backs of benches.

The spectator's box reserved for the fighters had everyone from our division except the dog arcanists. Even Lucian and his knightmare, Azir, were here to watch the final bouts.

The wooden benches had been pulled as close as possible to the railing around the outside of the field. Atty, Hexa, Illia, and Fain were seated in the front, each one focused on the arena, their respective eldrin close by. Adelgis and I sat one row behind them, since we had arrived later. The commotion made it impossible for conversation, so no one even tried.

"The first opponent is none other than Zaxis Ren the Phoenix Arcanist! He represents the Frith Guild, and each one of his fights was a showstopper, ladies and gentlemen. You better be prepared!"

I covered my ears to brace for the applause. Although Luthair was just a shadowy suit of armor, he moved around as though the noise irritated him as well.

Nicholin scampered around Illia's shoulders, his white and silver fur occasionally catching the light. He kept trying to position himself for the best angle, poking his head up and then to the side or even switching positions altogether.

"The second opponent is Niro Venrover the Stoor Worm Arcanist, son of the famous Theasin Venrover! I must admit, I'm surprised to see him here, but maybe he can pull another win out of thin air!"

The comment got me chuckling. Even the announcer knew that Niro never should've won his match against me. It also amused me that boos mixed with the cheers as Niro and his worm slinked their way to the fighting platform.

"The winner of this match will walk away with the first place prize! Are we ready?"

Vercingetorix roared.

Flames erupted from Zaxis's side of the platform. The sudden and intense fire elicited a wave of gasps from the crowd. The inferno swirled around Zaxis and Forsythe, likely created by the two of them evoking and manipulating flame. It looked like a bonfire had just burst into existence, dominating half the fighting arena.

Niro didn't flinch. He and his giant stoor worm waited, the scales of his armor, and the scales of his sea serpent eldrin, glittering from the light of the fire.

Without warning, the pyre lashed out like a heated tidal wave, rushing Niro's side of the platform. Zaxis threw a fat pouch into the fire and then leapt back. The pouch exploded, similar to a firework, filling the arena with a flash of dazzling light.

Forsythe took flight and then dove for Niro. I could see his sharp talons all the way from my seat, and I knew if he dug them into Niro's flesh, it would be its own special kind of agony. Since Niro had been blinded from the explosive pouch, Forsythe managed to sink his deadly bird-claws into the side of his cheek. He flapped hard afterward, ripping skin away from Niro's face.

Zaxis ran forward, and the worm slithered out to meet him. The snake beast was at least thirty feet long, and it quickly darted around Zaxis to trap him in a bind. Zaxis waited until the stoor worm squeezed onto him before unleashing another round of intense fire. It burned through the black scales of the worm.

The stoor worm bit Zaxis on the shoulder, its fangs injecting venom. I had handled the dizziness during my fight, so I hoped Zaxis could, too.

Then Zaxis freed himself from the worm and punched with his white-hot knuckles, tearing flesh from the mystical creature as though it were seared. The stoor worm screamed and writhed away.

Zaxis faced Niro and took a deep breath. He lunged for the other arcanist like a berserker. Even when Niro used his corrosive magic to melt a part of Zaxis's skin, that didn't stop him. Zaxis punched Niro so hard I could have sworn I heard the crunch of bone. Blood exploded from Niro's nose. Then he lost his focus and stumbled backward.

Zaxis punched him one more time. That probably wasn't necessary—a tooth flew out of Niro's mangled face—but I did think it was funny. Even Adelgis stood and applauded with the rest of the bloodthirsty crowd.

The second Niro tumbled off the platform, a bell clanged, signifying his loss.

Instead of sticking it through the fight, the charred stoor worm glided from the arena. Another clang. More excited hysterics.

Zaxis and Forsythe had won the apprentice division of the Sovereign Dragon Tournament.

53

DAWN OF THE FINAL DAY

"**A** brutal victory!" the announcer shouted.

The celebrations probably would've continued for a solid ten minutes, but the coliseum audience quieted themselves as Queen Velleta stood from her seat. Vercingetorix dipped his head and allowed her to climb to a ridge next to the massive horns. She pointed to the arena, and her dragon dove from his special platform into the center of the fighting field. When he landed, the ground rumbled, and red dirt wafted into the air as clouds all around him.

Vercingetorix carried the queen all the way to the platform and then lowered his scaled head so she could step off with a graceful leap. Even from my seat in the stands, I could tell she wore the finest of dresses, tailored to fit her body. It shimmered silver in the midmorning light.

"The winner of the apprentice tournament goes to Zaxis Ren the Phoenix Arcanist of the Frith Guild! Queen Velleta will now present the prize and congratulate the young man."

Zaxis swayed on his feet—no doubt from the stoor

worm poison—but he managed to stay upright as the queen sauntered over.

She handed him something, probably star shards, and then leaned in close. Although I couldn't hear a damn thing, it was obvious she was whispering in his ear. Zaxis bowed, and Forsythe followed suit, his wings outstretched as he lowered his head.

<hr>

A part of me wanted to watch the final bouts between the master arcanists, but the rest of the Frith Guild had other plans. Tonight we would commemorate the event in song, drink, and food.

We didn't return to the *Maison Arcana*. We headed to a fancy pub in the Dragon District—one that entertained guests by invitation only. Apparently, it was a bar and theater for the knights, legionnaires, and members of the queen's court. They had nothing but the finest of foods and the smoothest of liquors. Dancers and singers lit up the stage, though I couldn't help comparing them to Karna. None of them came close.

Each table came with couch-like chairs filled with down pillows. The lights that hung from the ceiling were crystals imbued with azure light, creating a calming atmosphere that reminded me of the ocean. The servers all had smiles, and my cup never ran empty.

While I admired our surroundings, I couldn't enjoy them. All I could think about was tomorrow. The death match. The thieves. This celebration was a distraction, and I couldn't afford to get distracted.

Master Zelfree must have felt the same way. He stayed away from the festivities, opting instead to stand in the far corner, tucked into the darkness. He didn't drink, and he rarely spoke to anyone.

Hexa, Illia, and Zaxis danced with some of the knights near the stage. Music played, and while everyone from the Frith Guild was obviously out of place—dancing an island dance rather than something popular from Thronehold—they laughed and smiled the entire time. Although several other women approached Zaxis and asked for a dance, he declined each one. He seemed to only have eyes for Illia, though Hexa managed to squeeze her way into there as well.

Raisen, Nicholin, and Forsythe also danced, but it was a bizarre mix of animal motions. Forsythe acted like a preening peacock, shaking his feathers and leaving soot all over the fine hardwood. Raisen bobbed both his hydra heads in time with the music, one going up while the other went down, like little pistons on the trolley cars. Nicholin bounded in tight circles, occasionally teleporting around the room.

Guildmaster Eventide, Gillie, and Atty spoke with Knight Captain Rendell at the bar. Rendell's black unicorn couldn't fit inside the pub, so it waited outside, which I felt was a shame.

I had never seen our guildmaster drink and be merry. She allowed her silvering hair to flow naturally, and it went down to her waist, much to my surprise. She was the only one in the pub with a glowing arcanist mark, and it gave her an otherworldly appearance, even though she wore nothing but a simple button-up blouse and a pair of slacks.

Atty glanced at me from time to time, offering me a smile or a small wave of her hand. At several points, she motioned for me to join her, but I refused each with a polite shake of my head. I wasn't in the mood to mingle.

Her phoenix, Titania, sat on the rafters above us,

watching the festivities with bright golden eyes. Her tail feathers hung low and swished along with the music. Even Gillie's caladrius was up there, her white feathers and parrot-like beak glistening in the azure light.

I sat at one of the far tables, my back to the wall. A platter of hard cheese, cooked pheasant, and warm bread filled the air with delicious scents. I picked at the food as the celebrations carried on into the night.

Fain and Adelgis remained close to me. They occupied the same table, eating and drinking, though they kept quiet. Even their eldrin—Wraith and Felicity—stayed visible, but silent.

"I don't think it does you any good to dwell so much, Volke," Adelgis said as he nibbled on some pheasant. "And you're making the others worry. Their thoughts keep drifting back to you, wondering what they can do to liven your spirits."

I rested my elbows on the table and leaned forward. "I'm not upset."

"You're just concerned about Princess Lyvia."

I glowered at the platter of food, uncertain of what to do. When Fain threw back a glass of wine, downing it in one go, I chuckled.

"What do pirates do to take their mind off things?" I asked.

Fain returned his glass to the table and forced a single laugh. "Not this."

"You're not having fun?"

"It's interesting, but I don't fit in here. On the *Third Abyss,* we'd play cards. Or we'd stop in port for some whores. Maybe do some fishing." He held his breath for a moment as he spun the wine glass between his dead-looking fingers. "When I was a child, my brother taught me about constellations and birdwatching. He said if you know the stars and the birds, you'll never be bored, no matter where you go. Sometimes that's what I'd do when I had lookout. Watch the sky."

Wraith placed his wolf head into Fain's lap. When he stared up through his skull mask, he almost looked like a cute dog. Almost.

Fain pet Wraith along his neck and back and even scratched behind Wraith's pointed ears.

"Master Zelfree wants to speak with you, Volke," Adelgis said. He pointed to the gloomy corner that Zelfree stalked. "He keeps debating about whether to send his eldrin or not."

I found it odd that Adelgis just didn't care about hearing the hidden desires of others—invading their privacy whether they wanted it or not—but he had said he couldn't seem to stop the magic from functioning, so I let it drop.

"I'll talk to him," I said.

The upbeat music continued as I traveled from one side of the pub to the other. Arcanists and their eldrin sat at the other tables, laughing and drinking without a care in the world. A few people greeted me, and some even congratulated me on my victories in the tournament, but otherwise I walked by without delay.

Zelfree straightened his posture as I drew near. "Good," he muttered. "I was hoping you'd come speak to me."

"What is it?" I asked.

"Tomorrow afternoon, before those villains plan to attack the castle, I want you to watch the others." Zelfree jutted a thumb to the three dancing by the stage. "No drinking. No side adventures. No gloating around in the bars. They need to remain focused."

"You won't be watching them?"

"There are several of you and only one of me," he muttered, pinching the bridge of his nose. "I figured you could watch one half and I'll watch the others."

The music stopped, and the dancers on stage pranced behind the curtains to prep for another round. While that happened, Zaxis grabbed three glasses of wine from a nearby attendant and then strutted over, his head high.

"Here you go," Zaxis said once he reached the corner. He handed me and Zelfree a glass.

I examined the red contents. I disliked wine.

Zelfree narrowed his eyes and stared at the drink, as though he were silently debating.

"A toast," Zaxis said. He lifted his glass. "To my victory."

He hadn't brought us drinks for the fun of it. He had brought us drinks so we would have something to toast him with. Of course.

I didn't want to spoil his fun, however, so I lifted my glass. Zelfree did the same, his expression set to a hard *neutral*. We tapped our glasses and then took a sip. Zelfree and Zaxis drank far more than I did, much to my amusement.

"Master Zelfree," Zaxis muttered as he lowered his drink. "I want to thank you." He lifted his arms for an embrace, still sweaty from the dancing. And if I had to call it, he was a bit tipsy.

Zelfree took an obvious step backward. "There's no need to thank me. It's part of my duties to train you."

"Pfft." Zaxis shrugged. "I couldn't have won without your expert guidance."

"I want to make sure you're prepared for anything in the future." Zelfree took another sip of his wine, probably in an attempt to keep his hands busy or at least unable to accept any sort of *thanks*.

"C'mon." Zaxis smacked me with the back of his hand. "Volke told me all about your preferences. I can do my training shirtless for a few days, if you'll consider that thanks."

Zelfree choked on his wine and half spit it back into his glass, coughing the entire time. I had never seen him so red.

I grabbed Zaxis by the collar of his sweaty shirt and yanked him away from the corner. "What's wrong with you?" I growled under my breath. "*You're with Illia.*"

Zaxis had a notable aroma of booze, though he seemed to hold the liquor well enough to speak without slurred speech. "Of course I'm with Illia, *fool*. But I also have to get used to the fact that everyone finds me attractive now." He ran a hand through his slightly wet hair. "And, I mean, who can blame them?"

"I had almost forgotten how insufferable you can be," I muttered as I dragged a hand down my face. I led him away from Zelfree, who still needed a moment to recover from his unexpected choking. "I like you better when you're not drinking," I said.

Zaxis shot me a glare. "Admit it. You don't like me at all."

We reached the edge of the dance floor as another round of music filled the pub.

"Weren't you the one who said we were friends?" I asked. "Remember? You said we were the same age, from the same island—both arcanists at the same time. We were so in common that we had to look out for each other."

Zaxis slowly nodded along with the words, like he didn't want to move his head around too much. "I do remember that."

"Well, you were right," I said. "We're friends. I admire your tenacity. You're a natural fighter. We worked well together in the tournament. But sometimes... Well, sometimes it's difficult to remember those good traits."

My statements seemingly hit him hard. Zaxis furrowed his brow, a mild hint of confusion in his gaze. "Wait, *you* admire *me*?"

I gritted my teeth, held back a sarcastic comment, and then patted him on the shoulder. "Listen. You look like someone Zelfree once knew. It makes him uncomfortable, but I'm sure he'll get over it. In the meantime, don't offer to do anything *shirtless* in his presence. That'll be thanks enough for him, understand?"

He nodded.

Would Zaxis even remember this conversation after tonight? I hoped so.

"Volke! Zaxis!"

Illia jogged over to us, smiling the entire way. It had been a long time since I saw her so happy. She grabbed one of my hands and then grabbed one of Zaxis's. With a playful tug, she led us both onto the dance floor.

"I don't know," I said, though I didn't pull free from her grasp. I was certain Zelfree would want to have *words* with me about Zaxis's comment.

"Dance with Hexa," she said. "Please? I want you to have a good time before we have to protect the castle. Do this for me?"

I couldn't deny her anything. I nodded and allowed myself to participate in the celebrating, even if I didn't feel like it.

Again, I couldn't sleep.

Adelgis offered to use his magic—to give me pleasant

dreams—but I couldn't stand the thought of accidentally sleeping through any important events. When the sun rose, I forced myself out of bed and into my clothes.

This was the final day.

Tonight, after the queen had her feast with the winners of the tournament, dastards would come for the runestones, and we had to be ready.

I packed my satchel with all my belongings, careful not to make much noise. Zaxis and Forsythe snored louder than ever, both exhausted from the celebrations. I didn't want to disturb their rest.

When I glanced over at Adelgis, I realized he wasn't asleep. He sat up on his bed, his attention on the window. Did he need to sleep anymore? Ever since I had woken him...

"Don't worry," Adelgis whispered, never turning away from the window. "I'm fine."

Although his newfound condition still bothered me, I decided not to press the issue. We would have a long trek back to Fortuna, and I could discuss everything then.

After I finished my packing, I slipped into the shadows and emerged on the roof. The sun shone through wispy white clouds, and birds flew by in large flocks. I didn't have time to enjoy my final day in Thronehold, however.

Today Lyvia would have her duel with her brother, and only one of them would survive.

I wanted to see her—speak to her—anything before the match. With haste in my step, I slid from one shadow to the next, moving closer to the castle with each short trek I took through the darkness. The trolley would've been easier, but my way was faster, even if the sting of magic still lingered from my second-bonding.

It seemed as though Thronehold was wide awake, even

in the early morning. Merchants, craftsmen, guildsmen—they sped through their work and filled the city with anxious chattering. Everyone wanted to know who the sovereign dragon would bond to.

Unicorns and pegasi were on every street corner, no doubt on high alert considering the threat. I even spotted some of the inquisitors, their knightmares and dark garb hiding them from the average citizen, but not me.

The Dragon District was the worst. Unicorn knights stood by the walls of the castle every twenty-five feet, their eldrin heavily armored.

I emerged from the shadows a good fifty feet from the front gate. Panning my gaze over the surroundings, I suspected I would never get inside, not unless I decided to sneak in.

"You want to meet with Lyvia?" Luthair asked from the shadows.

I nodded. "Do you think you can go inside and ask?"

"Of course, my arcanist."

He slithered away, nothing but darkness, and made it through the front gate.

Before Luthair returned, however, the front gate opened wide. Evianna rode out onto the cobblestone road with her elegant sorrel horse. Two knights accompanied her, and I was curious to see where she was going. As she approached, I stepped out onto the sidewalk and met her gaze.

"Volke," she said with a gasp.

Evianna pulled the reins and had her mount come to a stop. She slid from the saddle and then hustled over to me, her black dress flowing as she went. If I didn't know any better, I would've said she was dressed for a funeral. Her purplish-white hair contrasted nicely with the outfit, however.

"I was just coming to get you," Evianna said. "I'm ordering you to accompany me to the coliseum."

"Why is that?" I asked, not even bothering to dispute her claim of authority.

"Lyvia is there, preparing for the match, and I want you to speak to her again." Evianna motioned to the Knights Draconic. "Escort him, please. Whichever one of you is the fastest."

"Why me?" I asked.

"Because Lyvia trusts you!" Evianna stomped her foot once for dramatic effect. "She won't listen to me, and no one else will try to talk her out of it. You *must* go. You're my only hope."

Although I disliked the idea of pressuring Lyvia to do one thing or another, I did still want to see her.

"I'll go," I said. "But I don't need an escort. I'll meet you at the coliseum."

ONLY ONE WILL SURVIVE

I waited for Luthair to return before I headed through town. It wasn't long before I reached the Thronehold Coliseum.

The contestant entrances were closed, each secured shut with a wrought-iron gate. Those didn't stop me, though. I had the mobility of a shadow when I stepped into the darkness, and even the slightest gaps between the bars were enough for me to slide through.

Once inside, the stillness bothered me. No other contestants meant the inner corridors were empty. I walked through the coliseum with nervous steps, wondering where Lyvia had gone off to. She wasn't in the pits, and she wasn't in the fighter waiting rooms. The longer it took me to find her, the more anxious I became.

Finally, Evianna arrived. She entered the corridor with a large book held close to her chest, and I hustled to her location.

"There you are," Evianna said. She held the book out. "Here. Take this."

The cover had a metal name plate that read: *1001 Tales of*

Heroes. The massive tome must have weighed close to ten pounds. I flipped through the thin pages, impressed by the craftsmanship of the binding. Gravekeeper William had a similar novel on his shelves, but it had faded over time, and several of the stories were incomplete.

Evianna pointed to a page in the middle of the book. "Lyvia loves these silly stories. She quotes them all the time. Look here—I read through this whole thing and found one story about how the hero pretends to give up, only to come back stronger in the future! Don't you see?"

"See what?" I asked.

"Use this to convince Lyvia she shouldn't go through with this. She should give up now and then try something else in the future." Evianna placed her hand on mine and then met my gaze. "Please. If you change her mind, you can have anything you want. Anything. I just want Lyvia to be okay."

I hated the desperation in her voice. I hated that I couldn't tell her everything would be fine.

It reminded me of my dreams—helpless and forced to watch the situation unfold without intervention.

"I'll see what I can do," I said as I closed the book. "Where is she?"

Evianna flounced down the corridor, her steps quick and her unusual hair fluttering behind her. She was taller today —slight heels on her elegant riding boots—but she still had the face and mannerisms of a young teen. During our walk, she continually glanced over her shoulder, as though checking to see if I was still there.

We went past the parts of the coliseum I was familiar with and straight toward the queen's private section.

"Lyvia is important to me," Evianna said, slowing her pace. "Our mother and father died at sea. Oma took care of us, but she's busy. She hired nannies and tutors, but Lyvia was the only one who... who was there for me."

"I understand," I said. "Truly."

Evianna rubbed at her face. "My brother... he... he never even tried to convince Lyvia not to participate. He doesn't care about anyone."

We arrived at a door guarded by two of the Knights Draconic. They tensed as we approached, but relaxed once Evianna flashed her white hair by combing it out with her fingers. She pointed and then motioned me forward.

"She's in there. Don't leave until you convince her, okay?"

I stepped around Evianna and let myself into the room. The door closed behind me with a loud slam.

Unlike the pits and waiting rooms, this was an area with tile flooring and a small bath filled with clean water. A cushioned bench lined the wall on the opposite side. Lyvia sat there, her posture straight, her hands in her lap, and her eyes closed. Was she meditating? I wasn't certain. She wore fine chainmail armor, the links of which were so polished and intricate that it could only have been crafted by a master.

I crossed the room, my steps echoing. The open space seemed designed for several dozen people, but it was just the two of us. I took a seat next to her, half a foot away, the thick book still in my hand. I placed it between us on the bench.

Lyvia opened her eyes and glanced over. Her hair had been braided and then tied into a bun, showcasing her long neck and striking smile.

"Volke," she said. "Let me guess. My sister put you up to this, didn't she?"

"I'm sorry." I leaned back against the sandstone wall.

"She wants you to convince me not to fight?"

"That's right."

"Are you going to try?" she asked.

"I didn't plan to."

Lyvia leaned forward, an eyebrow raised. She seemed more jovial and happier than I suspected her to be. "You won't? Why not?"

"If I tried to convince you not to go through with this, I'd be tacitly saying I thought you couldn't win." I gave her a half-smile. "And no one needs doubt going into a fight."

She laughed, and it dispelled the melancholy that had taken root in my thoughts. I sat forward and chuckled, glad this situation hadn't gotten to her like it had with me.

"You're a good man, Volke," Lyvia said. She ran a hand over her chainmail and then turned her attention to the book sitting between us. "Did you come to tell me a story then?"

"No. Evianna wanted me to remind you of Captain Felveena the Anansi Arcanist. It's a story about a clever arcanist who pretends to give up a contest, but later comes back to win it when everyone thought she wasn't a threat." I knew the story well, though it didn't quite say what Evianna wanted it to. Captain Felveena used her opponent's assumptions to her advantage. They *assumed* she had quit, but that ended up being their downfall. If Lyvia quit now, she would be giving up her chance to bond with the sovereign dragon —a choice she couldn't take back later.

Lyvia exhaled, her smile waning, but not gone. "No matter how many times I speak to Evianna, she never listens. She thinks the sovereign dragon trial of worth is cruel and unjust."

"You don't think it's cruel?" I asked. A part of me thought it was.

"This whole thing is a lesson," Lyvia said, her enthusiasm returning in full force. "Everything comes from something. The wood for houses doesn't just appear—you have to cut down a tree. You don't just gain skills—you have to dedicate time and attention. That's what the sovereign dragon trial of worth is all about. Sacrifice. And appreciating where that comes from. There's no greater sacrifice than dedicating your life to your citizens—serving as a leader for the betterment of others."

It took me a moment, but I finally understood. The rulers of a nation should be prepared to lay down their life for what they believed was right. They would ask the same of their soldiers and knights, and conviction was important when leading others.

And I knew what would happen once Lyvia won. She would bond with the dragon, and then Queen Velleta would give her territory to rule over, probably somewhere far to the south or west. This was a chance to expand the Argo Empire, and the people of the newly added territory would never want the sovereign dragon arcanist to leave. They may even welcome it with open arms, just to get access to the prosperity aura. It was a responsibility that would dictate the rest of Lyvia's life, however long that was.

"Do you feel better now?" Lyvia asked.

I lifted an eyebrow. "Me? Shouldn't I be the one comforting you?"

"I came to terms with this months ago." Lyvia laughed and slapped my leg. "You were the one who shambled into the room like a depressing corpse. When was the last time you slept?"

I rubbed my chin, trying to hide my slight smile. "Heh. Yeah. Sorry. I'm glad we spoke. This does make me feel better. I was afraid... Well, I thought you'd be worried. Or lonely. I'm not sure." I scooted to the edge of the cushioned bench, restless. "It upset me to think you were waiting here—what could be your last moments—drowning in dread."

Again, she laughed, and I found it infectious. "You have made the wait easier," she said. "Just like Lark the Gallant. He always had a kind word for his friends and associates. Are you sure you're not related to him?"

"I don't think so."

The sounds of the crowds outside began to swell. It wasn't long now. The last fight would soon commence.

I stood from the bench, still filled with an odd jittery feeling.

Lyvia got to her feet as well, her sword at her side and her armor tailored to a perfect fit. She moved around with ease and quickly donned her helmet. As soon as she secured it into place, she faced the door, her back to me.

"I already thought of two contingencies," she said. "One for if I lose, and one for if I win."

"What happens if you win?" I asked.

"Once I have my own territory, and once you complete your training and become a master arcanist, I want you to become my knight." She couldn't stop herself from smiling. "I could tell—watching your fights—that you'll be the kind of man I look forward to seeing at the height of his life."

My face heated, and I didn't know how to follow up that statement. I didn't want to hear the contingency for her loss.

"If I lose," Lyvia continued, her tone remaining upbeat, "I would really appreciate it if you occasionally came back to Thronehold and spent time with my sister. I think Evianna will blame herself for a long period after my death, but I know you have the patience of a saint. I'd be forever in your debt if you helped her whenever she was in need."

My throat tightened, and it was too difficult to speak.

Lyvia waited, the rumble of the crowds far overhead.

After what felt like an eternity, I forced myself to say, "Whatever the outcome, I'll be there. I give you my word."

I took my seat in the former contestant box with the others. Although Atty, Adelgis, and Fain hadn't participated, Master Zelfree managed to get them in. The benches were packed with arcanists and eldrin—even Dramm and Borod were here, though it was difficult to squeeze the stone golem into the back.

While everyone spoke with excited tones, their eyes wide, I couldn't bring myself to participate. I watched the field, my attention locked on the sandstone arena.

Instead of the announcer shouting across the coliseum, Queen Velleta slid off her throne and walked to the edge of her gigantic dragon platform. When she spoke, it was with the same volume and intensity the announcer had.

"Thank you," she said, one hand in the air. "This is a monumental event, one so rare it sometimes skips generations. The last two vying to bond with a sovereign dragon are none other than Lyvia Hanar Velleta and Rishan Joze Velleta, my kin."

There were cheers, but no objects were thrown this time around. After a few moments, the queen held up her other hand.

"This match will have no time limit. Once the participants step onto the arena platform, they will not be able to leave until the other is dead. Then, and only then, will they bond with the hatchling sovereign dragon."

As the ocean of people erupted in applause, Queen Velleta retook her seat just below Vercingetorix. The wings of her dragon offered her shade. Evianna sat as close as she could to the railing around the coliseum, her gaze fixed to the arena.

Two gates opened on the field.

To my surprise, and ever-building anxiety, the denizens of Thronehold quieted themselves. Lyvia and her brother, Rishan, stepped out into the light to no cheering, clapping, or encouragement.

An eerie stillness came over the crowds, as though they were consumed by their curiosity and unwilling to miss a single detail about the fight.

Lyvia reached the platform first. She walked up the steps and took her place at the edge, her silver chainmail shining in the sunlight. In one hand, she held her light sword; in the other, she held a buckler—a small circular shield.

Rishan climbed onto the platform a moment later, his armor equally as impressive and lustrous. He, too, carried a sword as his weapon of choice, though his was heavier. A two-handed blade. No shield. And although they could've approached each other for a formal bow, neither moved from their spot.

The calmness of the crowd unnerved me. I couldn't remain seated. I stood and made my way to the railing, my heart rate high.

Vercingetorix roared louder than any other time before.

Lyvia lifted her weapon, and so did her brother. As they approached each other, I held my breath, fearful to blink in case I missed something. Lyvia made the first strike. She lunged with her thin sword—a finesse weapon meant for quick attacks. Rishan, without a shield, attempted to parry, but his heavier weapon was harder to swing around in fast motions.

Lyvia cut her brother on the elbow, right where the

armor of the upper and lower arm connected. A precise strike, drawing a small amount of blood.

Rishan swung wide with his blade. The silence of the massive audience actually made it possible for me to hear the *swish* of the weapon slicing through the air. Lyvia leapt back, her footwork perfect.

Without magical powers, the fight played out one swing, parry, and thrust at a time. The clinking of metal on metal filled the coliseum, replacing the nonexistent cheers with a song of death.

Lyvia attacked again, this time catching Rishan near his armpit—another area between patches of armor. He tried to backhand her with his gauntlet, but she blocked the blow with her buckler.

When he went in for a heavy overhand slice, she side-stepped and cut him again.

The small wounds were evidence of every moment Lyvia had outwitted him, and it was clear that Rishan's move-ments were becoming volatile, almost frantic. He stabbed with the sword and then twisted it to the side. Lyvia had to back up to avoid the attack altogether, and it was obvious she had lost her footing. She stumbled away, and Rishan pressed the assault.

He swung harder with each attack, forcing her to retreat. Finesse fighting was about control and patience—death by a thousand cuts—but it would only take one well-placed blow from Rishan's heavier weapon to end the whole fight.

Lyvia feigned a dodge, and when Rishan attempted to catch her, she spun around and cut him again on the same arm. More blood spilled from the wound, splashing onto the sandstone, and I couldn't help muttering encouragement under my breath.

Rishan thrust his sword, and instead of twisting it to the

side, he angled it down. Lyvia tried to get out of the way, but he nicked her knee and lower leg, sending her tumbling.

I gripped the railing so hard I couldn't feel my fingers.

Lyvia got back to her feet. When she placed weight on her injured leg, however, she almost crumpled. Even if Rishan hadn't cut through her armor, he could still damage her with enough force—she may have even twisted her ankle.

Rishan slashed downward. Lyvia rolled away and leapt to her feet, limping as her brother maintained an offensive strategy. He swung again. She wasn't fast enough to dodge. Lyvia held up her buckler, but the blow was too powerful. He knocked the shield from her hand and sent it flying across the platform with a loud *clang*.

Rishan lifted his sword high. Lyvia went in for a fast strike, like a coiled snake ready for any opportunity. She cut him deep along the ribs, to the point he almost dropped his weapon. She opted to stay close and attack again—to finish the fight with a strong enough pierce through the ribs—but Rishan actually followed through with his overhand blow, despite the injury.

He cleaved down, hitting Lyvia's right shoulder and burying the blade deep.

"*No!*"

Evianna had leapt from her seat and thrown herself against the invisible, telekinetic barrier that prevented anyone from the audience from interfering.

"*No,*" she screamed again, her strangled voice heard throughout the silent coliseum. "*Stop! Please stop!*"

Lyvia hit the ground and dropped her weapon, Rishan's blade still stuck in her body. She wasn't dead, but after an injury like that, she wouldn't be able to use her sword arm.

For all intents and purposes, the fight was over.

"*You could stop this*," Evianna shouted through strained sobs, motioning to the queen. But no one moved.

Evianna fell to her knees, her voice alone the backdrop for Rishan as he lazily picked up Lyvia's weapon. Agitation rolled through the crowds as the bout came to its agonizingly slow conclusion.

Using Lyvia's own sword, Rishan drove it into her neck as she lay on the ground, blood pooling around her twitching body.

It felt like literal hours before the bell finally ended the match with a haunting chime.

THE NEW SOVEREIGN DRAGON
ARCANIST

"That was... difficult to watch," Zaxis muttered, his arms crossed tight over his chest, his expression set in a sorrowful glare.

I shoved away from the railing, my thoughts nothing but angry buzzing. I couldn't stand to be around anyone—to have them speak to me or ask questions—and I stormed out of the participant's box. With each step, my headache grew, first hot, and then icy.

"My arcanist," Luthair whispered.

"*Leave me*," I barked.

His shadowy form slipped away from my feet. I turned down one corridor, and Luthair slithered down another. Finally alone, I ran my hands through my hair and dug my nails into my scalp. I felt the furrows I carved into my skin, but I couldn't feel the pain. I stopped and turned to the wall of the corridor, wanting nothing more than to destroy this entire building.

My breathing came in short bursts. I pressed my forehead against the cold sandstone, blood trickling from my hairline.

I crossed my arms, uncertain of what to do with my rage. It clung to my thoughts like barnacles, and a piece of me wondered if I would ever be rid of it.

Footsteps alerted me to someone's presence. I wanted it to be Lyvia, or perhaps even Illia, but instead it was Adelgis. He ambled through the empty corridor until he reached my side, his black and white robes dirty at the bottom with red dust.

"Go back to the others," I commanded.

Adelgis didn't move. He pressed his back against the wall, and I had the urge to drag him away with the shadows, but I controlled myself.

"I'm the only one who actually knows why you're upset," Adelgis said, his tone calm.

I forced myself to take a deep breath. I hadn't told anyone the full story of my relationship with Lyvia. I had told them I met her, but I was certain the rest of the Frith Guild thought the princesses hated me, especially given the way Evianna treated me when we visited the queen. Adelgis, on the other hand, probably heard every single one of my thoughts on the matter—even during the fight.

I pushed away from the wall, my magic healing any self-inflicted injuries.

Evianna's crying hurt more than I thought it would. I paced from one wall to the opposite one, her voice replaying in my mind.

I stopped and faced Adelgis. "Could you hear the thoughts of Lyvia and Rishan?" Perhaps the magical barrier around the arena prevented his magic.

"I heard," he intoned.

What were Lyvia's final thoughts? I almost asked—I was on the verge of blurting it out—but I held back. I didn't want to know. I never wanted to know.

Instead, I looked away and focused my gaze on the wall. I needed something to take the edge away. Something to help me accept what had happened.

"Was he... Was Rishan at least remorseful?" I asked. "Sad? Regretful? Anything?"

"He was not."

I gritted my teeth. "What *did* he think?"

"He hoped Lyvia suffered in her final moments, as punishment for trying to interfere with his ambitions."

Rishan had been so slow with her death—and now I knew why. That fact ate at my self-control. How could he be allowed to get away with what he'd done? Lyvia didn't deserve that. And Evianna didn't need to see her sister's prolonged death.

The shadows in the corridor stirred, brought to life by my growing fury. They weren't tendrils or nets or even objects—more like claws and fangs that dug into the coliseum's structure and grew like fire. When I didn't know if I could contain myself, the darkness lashed around the hall, slicing deep into stone and ripping up the dirt as everything went dark.

Adelgis kept himself still. My magic never touched him, but it got close.

After two deep breaths—and with the burning sensation of magic in my veins—I managed to leash the shadows. The corridor looked like a war had broken out. Sandstone crumbled from the gouges I had left. Then the darkness waned, returning the area to a normal amount of light.

For a moment, I almost understood what it was like to create a magical aura. It was like my magic had wanted to spill out, though I didn't know if I could control it.

Adelgis smoothed his long raven hair. "It's time for the bonding ceremony."

A powerful rumble shook the ground, and I knew Vercingetorix had leapt from his platform and landed in the center of the coliseum. A part of me didn't want to see Rishan's "triumph," but I couldn't stop myself, either. I stormed from the corridor, determined to witness everything involved in this nightmare.

Adelgis didn't follow, and Luthair didn't return to me.

When I arrived at the participant's box, Illia rushed over. Perhaps the dried blood around my hairline startled her, because she flinched back, her one eye wide.

"Are you okay?" she whispered. Before I could answer, she grabbed my shirt and yanked me close, her arms around me in an instant. "What's wrong? What happened?"

"I'm here to watch the bonding," I said, terser than I wanted. I returned Illia's embrace, long enough to acknowledge her attempt to comfort me, but not a second longer. "You don't need to worry. I promise."

Illia released me, and we walked to the railing together, her steps quick and her gaze set on me, rather than the field.

The queen, her dragon, and the hatchling all stood on the fighting platform with Rishan. Lyvia's body—and the blood—were nowhere to be found. They probably cleaned the *mess* while I was calming down in the corridor.

"We now know who will bond with the hatchling dragon," Queen Velleta said, her voice still magically amplified.

The child dragon stepped forward, its elephant-sized body massive when compared to Rishan, and its black and red scales vibrant in the sunlight. It lowered its head and spread its wings. Rishan placed a hand on its nose, and they both glowed a soft white, enveloped in the sorcery of bonding.

Gasps flew through the audience as the light shifted from white to gold. I gripped the railing, my eyebrows knit. I had seen plenty of bondings, but none of them involved this odd golden color.

As the light faded from their bodies, the hatchling dragon transformed. His horns, once angled forward, twisted around its head like a spiked crown. A second set of wings ripped free from its body, the same leathery appearance as the first set. And it grew larger—tougher. When the light finally disappeared, the hatchling almost looked like a different dragon altogether. Still black and red. Still a sovereign dragon. Just... menacing.

Rishan's arcanist mark continued to glow with inner light, marking him as someone with a true form creature.

A true form sovereign dragon.

"Rishan Joze Velleta," the queen announced. "The newest sovereign dragon arcanist!"

The celebrations of the audience exploded through the stands, engulfing all of Thronehold in a single burst of jubilation.

Whereas time had crawled before, now I didn't know where it went. The sun disappeared behind the mountains, shrouding Thronehold in twilight darkness.

The entire day I had stayed in my room with Adelgis, pacing.

Soon the thieves would make their move.

The winners of each tournament division were given invitations into the castle to celebrate with the queen and the newest sovereign dragon arcanist. In that moment, I was thankful I hadn't won the apprentice division. I didn't think I could speak to Prince Rishan without wanting to make him answer for everything he had ever done.

Along with the invitation, Zaxis received three star shards for his victory. Master Zelfree had taken him to the market, and when they had returned, they had fine leather armor and salamander scales. Apparently, Zaxis's first lesson in imbuing would be to create armor immune to his flames. I thought it apt.

An hour before the soirée was set to begin, everyone in the Frith Guild—including Fain and Gillie—set off for the castle. No one attempted to engage me in conversation, which I assumed was in part due to Adelgis. Although I hadn't told him I wanted to be left alone, I was certain my thoughts exuded my desire.

I barely took note of the trip. When we arrived, I stepped off the trolley and made my way to the gates, my hands in my pockets.

Every knight and legionnaire was in attendance. They stood watch in the castle gardens, the landing platforms around the castle towers, and every ten feet from the front door to the gates. The unicorns practically sparkled in the moonlight. The pegasi seemed restless, their feathered wings always fluffed.

To my surprise, several will-o-wisp arcanists from the Lamplighters Guild were also here. They had lit lanterns and hung them in every dark corner. They couldn't use their light evocation sorcery, however. A powerful field of anti-magic covered the castle. Queen Velleta had activated the defenses, preventing anyone but dragon arcanists from using their magic.

Despite that, the lamplighters planted hanging lanterns around the gardens and walkways, illuminating all paths to the castle. While they didn't seem combat trained, each carried a baton and a pistol, just in case.

"Volke."

I shifted my attention to Zaxis as he sauntered over with a smile.

I didn't need to ask. He motioned to his body. Instead of a singed shirt and charred pants, he wore a fine gentleman's outfit, complete with tailored black trousers, a scarlet button-up shirt, and a fitted vest. The outfit had been modified with salamander scales, giving his shoulders and cuffs a dark red sheen.

"What do you think?" Zaxis asked. "I'm impressive, right?"

I nodded.

He dropped his arms and his jovial expression. "Illia's worried about you," he said, straight to the point. "She said I need to speak to you before I went inside. Why do you look like flotsam washed up on the beach? Have you been sleeping?"

"I'll be fine."

Zaxis stepped close and lowered his voice. "Is someone bothering you? I can give them a talkin' to, if you want." He smacked his fist into his other palm.

I offered him a forced smile. "No. Thank you, though."

"All right. But listen."

I lifted an eyebrow.

"Watch Illia. If villains really do have the guts to show up tonight, I don't want anything to happen to her."

Again, I nodded.

He clasped me on the shoulder and then strode off for the castle.

Guildmaster Eventide and Gillie accompanied him inside. They, too, had been given an invitation, no doubt because of their highly regarded status. Gillie was, after all, the one who provided the queen with the wendigo trinkets that prevented the spread of the plague.

Once the guests funneled into the castle, the patrols began. We were to stay in the aura of the nullstone and walk tight perimeters around the outside. Should we see anything—anything at all—we were to sound an alarm. Zelfree was convinced it wouldn't be a single enemy, and he was fearful the scoundrels would cover their weapons in plague blood, which could infect most of the knights or lamplighters.

I did my patrol alone, confident in my skills.

Thronehold at night looked like everything I had imagined a massive kingdom to be. The castle grounds were right out of a dream. Sprawling gardens. Pristine dragon sculptures. I wished I could enjoy it all. The suffocating effects of the anti-magic made it difficult, though.

And every sound sent me to the edge. I kept my sword in hand, and more than once, I sliced at a bush or branch, thinking someone was sneaking through the shrubbery, only to find a mouse or owl tucked between the leaves.

Perhaps the thieves would see the defenses of the castle and decide not to attack.

When I rounded the corner of the southern tower, I spotted Master Zelfree by one of the many apple trees. His eldrin, Traces, sat perched on his shoulder, her feline form silhouetted by the many lanterns.

Zelfree searched around the trunk before meeting me on the walkway. He carried a long sword and a pistol, and his keen gaze jumped from one far-off location to the next.

"I think we may have scared them off," Zelfree muttered.

I shrugged. "Perhaps."

He ran a hand down his face, his fingers disturbing the stubble that had grown on his chin. With a scrutinizing look, he asked, "You knew the older princess, didn't you?"

I couldn't bring myself to speak of it.

Zelfree sighed. "I was going to have words with you about Zaxis—*and how you never should've told him anything about my past*—but..."

Traces tilted her head and purred. "I think we should all get drinks after this is over. Hard drinks. The kind that'll put you to sleep no matter what kind of thoughts run through your head."

"Exactly what I was going to say," Zelfree muttered as he petted Traces along her back. "Consider this a lesson you need to complete before you become a journeyman."

I stared at him for a long moment. "Drinking with you is a required task in this apprenticeship?"

"You heard right," Traces said, her tail swishing back and forth.

"I can see how you got in trouble with your last apprentices," I quipped.

It was a low blow. I knew the moment I muttered the words.

Zelfree didn't react like I thought he would, though. I expected anger, but instead he replied with half a smile. "I've buried a lot of friends. It's always the worst afterward, when it feels like the grief will never leave."

His words pierced right through my apathy. I had forgotten how many people Zelfree had lost. I turned away from him, ashamed of how I had acted. "I'm sorry. I just—"

"Don't worry about it."

I would've preferred to continue the conversation with him, but the nullstone aura vanished, startling all three of us. Traces leapt to the ground, and Zelfree glanced upward and scanned the surroundings, convinced villains would be in the shadows.

I saw nothing, though. No people. No odd disturbances.

I breathed easier without the anti-magic suffocating me.

"What's going on?" Traces asked, her fur on end.

Zelfree hardened his gaze. "Volke, I think you should shadow-step up to the throne room. You see the dragon landing balcony, right? You can enter the castle through there."

"Why?"

"The main control for the nullstone is the throne itself," Zelfree said. "The queen must be there. Ask her what's going on."

"Are you concerned?" I asked. I stared up at the balcony far above us. It had to be six stories up. Perhaps more. "I don't see anything strange. Or hear anything unusual."

I didn't spot Vercingetorix, however. Then I remembered he hadn't returned to the castle straight away. He had flown around the edge of the city, searching for anything suspicious. The queen still had her powers—she wasn't defenseless without him. Perhaps she had deactivated the aura for a personal reason? There was a possibility she wanted someone else to use their magic, if only for a second.

"I'd rather know for sure," Zelfree said. He shivered and pulled his coat tight, glaring at the far-off balcony. "Something isn't right."

THE KING BASILISK ARCANIST

The throne room balcony was too high for me to reach in one trek through the darkness. Instead, I shadow-stepped to a nearby windowsill, then to a balcony, then to the claw of a dragon carved into the side of the castle—higher with each movement, until I reached the edge of the dragon landing platform.

The wind rushed by as I emerged from the shadows, and for a brief second, I almost lost my footing.

"Careful," Luthair whispered from the shifting darkness around my feet.

I steadied myself before glancing over the edge. It was a seventy-foot drop to the ground.

The long platform was connected to the throne room without a wall—it was just an open space for Vercingetorix to fit through. The throne itself was faced away from me. I could see the backside of it, and the long rug that led to the door on the opposite end of the room, but not the throne seat itself, or the occupant.

There were no guards, and as I walked across the balcony, my heart beat harder and faster. Zelfree said the throne was the magical object for controlling the anti-magic aura, so shouldn't the queen and her retinue be nearby?

With quiet steps, I entered the castle, creeping ever-closer to the backside of the throne. It was on an elevated platform, raised to be the tallest thing in the room. The entire chair had been carved from nullstone. It was a smooth bluish-black rock, which made it impossible to see around. The wind howled across the balcony, giving me enough noise as cover as I rushed to the base of the throne platform. Although the room seemed empty, a knot of dread had formed in my stomach. Zelfree was right. Something had to be wrong. I didn't want to rush in without knowing what was happening.

Pillars lined the walkway to the throne. I slid into the shadows and emerged behind one, my back pressed against the smooth stone so that I was as hidden as possible. Now in front of the throne, I carefully glanced around the side of the pillar and stared.

My blood ran cold.

Prince Rishan. Although I had never seen him this close before, his purplish-white hair, and the dragon design of his glowing arcanist mark, gave him away. He sat straight, his hands running over the armrests of the throne, like he was caressing it.

His hatchling dragon sat on the steps that led up to the throne platform, its menacing appearance chilling me further.

Why had the prince deactivated the aura?

I almost didn't notice the other man in the room. He stood so still he could've been a statue, and he wore a dark cloak and a hood, his stubble-covered chin barely visible. I would've sworn he wasn't breathing. He just stood there. In front of the dragon. Facing the far double doors.

Who was he? Why was he here?

The double doors slammed open. Queen Velleta, flanked by two Sky Legionnaires, strode into the room. The legionnaires rode atop their pegasi, each one brown with hawk-like wings, their armor silver shining.

Confused, I decided to remain in hiding. The queen's expression was set in a deep glare, and the heels of her fine leather boots hit the rug as though she were punishing it.

"*Rishan*," she hissed. "What is the meaning of this?"

"Good evening, Oma," Rishan said.

That was the first time I had ever heard him speak. Slow. Callous. I hated him before, but that feeling quickly became a loathing. Somehow, he had a voice and tone with no empathy.

The queen came to a sudden stop the moment she noticed the unmoving man. Then she approached with purposeful steps, her attention shifting from the man, to the hatchling dragon, to Rishan. She smoothed her skin-tight black dress, composing herself.

"You will explain yourself," Queen Velleta stated. Embers appeared in the air around her, creating star-like beads of light. Dragon fire was said to be legendary in heat —capable of melting even the strongest of metals within seconds. "But first, you will get off my throne."

"I think not." Rishan settled into the nullstone seat, a smile spreading across his face. "Your long, pathetic reign needs to come to an end. My associate will show you the way out."

The man who hadn't moved a single muscle stepped forward. He pulled back his hood, revealing his short copper hair, tanned skin, and prominent arcanist mark etched deep into his forehead. Even I could see the design from my hiding spot behind the pillar.

He was a king basilisk arcanist.

His cloak fell to the floor, revealing his wondrous armor. It was—without exception—entirely made from gray scales and thick pieces of bone. The scales had the sleekness of a snake, and his pauldron looked like it had been crafted from a dragon's single claw. It didn't clink or rustle when the man moved, which was probably the most impressive aspect of all. It was utterly silent and fitted to his muscular body as though a second layer of skin.

"I doubt you remember me or the other king basilisk arcanists," the man intoned, his voice gruff. "But you ordered the death of my brother, sister, and daughter."

The queen snapped her fingers. The two legionnaires slid off their mounts, one pulling a sword and the other a heavy pistol. The pegasi spread their wings and stepped to the side, obviously ready to help their arcanists should a fight break out.

The king basilisk arcanist waved his hand out in a wide arc and evoked poison. It splashed across the room, hitting the queen, the legionnaires, their eldrin, the rug, and two of the pillars. A smattering of it landed near me. It burned into the rug, rotting the very fabric with its deadly magics.

No poison was as deadly as the king basilisk's—it killed instantly so long as the individual wasn't immune.

Which meant the queen and her soldiers would be fine. The Knights Draconic, made exclusively of unicorn arcanists, could craft trinkets to protect someone from poison. Calisto had worn something similar when Illia attempted to kill him, and I was certain the queen and the Sky Legionnaires had their own.

Unicorn magic was the epitome of purity, after all, and with so many unicorns in Thronehold, I was surprised the king basilisk arcanist thought this would work.

"You're an idiot and a fool," the queen said with a dark chuckle. The poison had struck her arms and portions of her dress, but done nothing. "And if you miss your family so much, I'm happy to reunite you with them."

She held out her hand, and a torrent of white-blue flame burst across the throne room with unrivaled speed and intensity.

The hatchling leapt in front of the assassin and shielded him from the attack. Sovereign dragons were immune to fire, and the queen's flames washed off the hatchling's scales like water off the feathers of a duck. Everything else caught fire or melted, even the stone under the rug and the first few steps up to the throne. The temperature even rose a few degrees, as though the glory of a midafternoon were beating down on us.

Queen Velleta stopped her attack.

Rishan laughed as he stood. "You're already dead, Oma." He tossed a small brown pouch into the center of the room, just a few feet from the queen.

It exploded—much like Zaxis's pouches of gunpowder —but instead of fireworks, a fine mist of bluish-black dust spread throughout the room. It washed over the queen and her legionnaires, and to my horror, it looked like parts of their armor and clothing crumbled into ash. The queen's jewelry, from her necklaces to her earrings, all wasted away into nothing.

Then she caught her breath, her skin paling. The next moment, she collapsed to the ground, unmoving, her eyes wide, but vacant.

The pegasi tried to flap their wings and clear the air, but it was too late. They crumbled to the floor, their armor clanging against the stone. The legionnaires followed suit.

They hit their knees, one coughing out a choke, and died an instant later.

The dust wafted all around me. I pulled up the collar of my shirt, panic flooding my thoughts. Did the dust kill on contact? Should I attempt to run? I couldn't shadow-step far enough to escape the room without being seen. The king basilisk assassin would surely end me in an instant.

But the dust didn't burn or sting or steal my life.

It broke the wendigo trinket around my neck. The antler pendant turned to ash and scattered into the dust.

I held my breath, realization hitting me hard. The dust had destroyed the poison-immunity trinkets the queen and her soldiers wore. Without them—and still coated in the king basilisk venom—they were no longer immune to the poison. That was why they had died.

Rishan's laughter faded into a soft chortle. He retook his seat on the throne, his gaze focused on the queen's corpse.

"That decay dust is brutal," Rishan muttered as he stroked his chin. "And beautifully effective. The best use for nullstone yet."

Far in the distance, like thunder in a storm, the mighty Vercingetorix screeched—a mix of a roar and cry. Eldrin could feel their arcanist's death.

Before I could decide the best course of action, the sounds of popping echoed throughout the throne room. With shaky breaths, I sneaked a peak around the other side of the pillar. Flashes of white sparkles heralded the teleporting of at least a dozen individuals. It was rizzel magic—I'd recognize it anywhere—just like the ghoul arcanist had used when I confronted him.

More and more people teleported in, until at least twenty individuals had arrived. They all wore heavy cloaks, like the king basilisk assassin before he threw his to the ground. The black cloaks covered them from head to toe, and even obscured the top of their face, hiding any sort of arcanist marks. Mystical creatures arrived with them, including fairies, sea serpents, griffins, and a gargoyle.

Last, and the most impressive teleport of all, was the king basilisk itself.

It appeared behind the throne, on the dragon landing balcony, its gigantic body the same shape and size of Vercingetorix, though it had no wings. Its scales were gray on top and bluish along its belly. All king basilisks had six legs, each ending in clawed feet, and the massive reptilian beast stood tall. Thankfully, it kept its four eyes shut. If anyone glanced into them, even for a second, they would be turned to stone.

A cloaked man with a hunched back hurried forward. He was scrawny—I could tell, even with the thick clothing —and he moved as though jittery and not fully in control of his actions. The decay dust had long settled to the floor, and with each step the man's cloak sent puffs of it into the air.

"We haven't much time," the fidgety man said, his voice high-pitched. "The queen's sovereign dragon will soon be here."

"Nyre will handle the dragon," the assassin stated. He turned to his king basilisk eldrin. "Make sure it dies quickly, and carve out the heart before we need to escape."

The massive basilisk responded with a low growl that rumbled through the room.

Flailing his hands about, the man with the hunchback motioned to the individuals in robes. "*Listen.* Use the dust as much as possible. *Did you hear me?* Fill the castle and stay within it. I don't know how, but someone alerted the knights to our plans, and there are more here than we anticipated."

The cloaked individuals, along with the mystical creatures, replied in nods.

Although I hadn't noticed before, some of the creatures were twisted with the plague. One griffin had two heads, both with bloody saliva dripping from their oversized fangs. Their red eyes and lack of laughter meant they were beyond the initial stages of the infection. This was a dread form griffin, which was why its wings were black and torn, and quivering pustules covered its back.

"Infect everyone," the man said, still moving his hands, even if he didn't need to. "Especially the legionnaires. Remember to infect the eldrin first—the arcane plague takes hold of the mystical creatures faster than it does with the arcanists."

The man spoke quickly, yet he annunciated each word perfectly.

Then he pointed to one of the cloaked individuals. "*You.* Gather the runestones. Rishan says the ones in the hall are fake so head to the queen's quarters. *Get them all*, but especially keep your hands on the jade stone—the one carved with a world serpent."

Damn. Our ploy to keep the runestones hidden didn't even slow them down. Rishan betrayed us all. And for what? A chance to sit on the throne? There were no limits to his sins.

The jittery man pointed to a small group. "*You three.* Handle the Knights Draconic. Make sure you slay Knight Captain Rendell." He motioned to the next group. "*You four.* Head to the banquet hall. The winners of the tournament—along with a few important arcanists—should still be there, unaware of our presence. Infect the ones you can, and kill the ones you can't."

The situation continued to escalate far beyond anything

I had been prepared for. My heart beat so hard against my ribs, I almost couldn't hear.

Zaxis. Gillie. Guildmaster Eventide.

They were all in the banquet hall.

"*You six,*" the man continued. "Head to the vaults. Take what you can, but make sure you acquire the late king's crown. If anyone tries to stop you, get rid of them." He glanced around and then pointed to two specific individuals in the back. "*You two.* Kill the young princess. You know where to find her. *Our new king* has made it clear that she won't cooperate with us."

Rishan chuckled at the comment, but otherwise didn't interject.

Evianna.

I gripped my shirt tight, panic filling my thoughts.

"Lastly, *you four.* Target the lamplighters and anyone else who will flee into the city. We need as many of the arcanists infected as possible."

The king basilisk arcanist made his way toward the double doors, his gait betraying his agility and precision. He moved like a killer of men. Someone who wasn't afraid of anyone else in the room—someone built with confidence and forged in years of experience.

"Wait, Akiva," the hunchbacked man said. "You're not done until you kill the Grandmaster Inquisitor. He'll be here any moment with his knightmares."

The assassin—Akiva—didn't stop to speak. "You needn't fret. I'll eradicate the inquisitors."

"The rest of you get on with it," the man said as he rubbed his hands together. "And remember not to hurt our allies in the chaos. You can distinguish them by the marks on their shoulder. Return in time for our escape. We won't wait for you."

The group of madmen broke into their teams and headed for the door.

My vision tunneled as I withdrew into my thoughts. I didn't have the power to stop them all. I couldn't fight a king basilisk arcanist—especially not one as powerful as Akiva— and I didn't know the capabilities of the others. Without my wendigo trinket, they could infect me with the plague, and with their decay dust, they could render everyone else vulnerable as well.

At this rate, they would take the runestones, infect all of Thronehold, and escape into the dark of night. That couldn't be allowed to happen. Not now, not ever.

And Evianna...

I gritted my teeth and closed my eyes.

Lyvia had one dying wish, dammit. I wasn't going to let her sister die less than twenty-four hours after she did. If I didn't go to save Evianna now, she wouldn't stand a chance.

But at the same time, I had to warn the others. Everyone needed to know what we were up against. It was the only way we could avoid *all* becoming plague-ridden. Or worse— corpses in shallow graves.

"Luthair," I whispered.

His shadow moved at my feet.

"Quickly—warn everyone in the banquet hall and then tell Master Zelfree about everything you've seen here."

"I won't leave you," he said, curt.

"You must."

"I've already lost one arcanist." The shadows went still. "I ask that you not do this. We're stronger together."

We didn't have time!

"This is what needs to happen, Luthair," I said. "We both know it."

As a shadow, he could freely move along the floors and

wall, and if he acted fast, he could make it to the banquet hall before those dastards. He *had* to be the one to disseminate the information. And I needed to keep my word to Lyvia. I had to rescue Evianna before they ended her life.

Luthair didn't offer any further protest. He slithered from my feet and kept to the edge of the room, away from Rishan, the jittery man, and the gargantuan king basilisk. Once he had disappeared out onto the balcony, I clenched my jaw and took a deep breath.

Where would I find Evianna? The cutthroats had hired people to map out the castle for this exact reason. They knew all the locations—all the hiding spots. What did I have?

Although I didn't know the castle well, I did know of one place...

But first I would need to escape this room.

"What's that?" Rishan blurted out.

My heart stopped.

Had he noticed me?

"Oh," the nervous man responded. "Queen Velleta's knightmare is finally forming."

I jerked my head to the side and stared at her corpse. Sure enough, the shadow around her body writhed and twisted and eventually rose into a form of clothing, coalescing into solid material. It was a cape that looked like a pair of dragon wings and a partial set of thin—and somewhat alluring—armor. It wasn't complete, though. Like Lucian's knightmare. It was young. Newly born.

The shadows created an empty cowl, much like Luthair's empty helmet. The neonate knightmare stood over the body of the queen, "looking" without a face at the carnage, and then glanced up at Rishan.

"I am Layshl the knightmare," she said, her voice dark but clearly feminine. "Born of betrayal—a seeker of justice."

Rishan sneered. "Kill it," he commanded. "My new empire has no need for knightmares."

His hatchling dragon moved forward with its long tongue lashing outside of its mouth, like it was excited to eat.

Curse the abyssal hells.

I had to do something about this.

PRINCESS EVIANNA

I wanted to intervene and save the newborn knightmare, but to expose myself would mean the king basilisk would see me.

As though the universe heard my plight, darkness washed through the throne room in an instant. It snuffed the lanterns and deadened any magical sources of light, until they were nothing more than dim stars in the void. The melancholy gloom that lingered on the air told me this was the result of an eclipse aura.

The Grandmaster Inquisitor had arrived, probably somewhere out on the castle grounds.

I wouldn't squander my chance. I manipulated the newly created shadows and snatched the young knightmare away from the queen's corpse. With perfect control—and no pain—I yanked her into my arms and whispered through gritted teeth, "They're the ones who killed the queen. We need to leave."

Perhaps it was because I was a knightmare arcanist, but Layshl didn't protest. She wrapped her shadow-body around mine, almost like we were merged, but not really. It was more like draping clothes over my own—I received no benefit, but at least she was with me.

"Damn those inquisitors," Rishan growled, his eyes wide and unfocused. "*Get rid of this darkness.*"

The fidgeting man nodded his head with vigor. "Have patience. Akiva will kill the inquisitors. *You* must prepare for your grand entrance. Run to the knights and tell them of the queen's murder. Help them repel our forces so that you are above suspicion. You must be the good prince the city needs."

"The knightmare is gone," the hatchling dragon growled, his voice far deeper than I thought it would be. He whipped his head around, obviously struggling to make out shapes in the thick darkness.

I didn't want to deal with them searching, and I needed to reach Evianna. I stepped into the shadows and slid out of the room and into the massive hallway of the castle. The other cutthroats were nowhere to be seen, which meant they were far ahead of me.

The only place I knew was the training room under the castle. It was blanketed in anti-magic from the pure vein of nullstone, unaffected by the throne's controls. Would Evianna be there? It seemed secluded and distant, and Lyvia had clearly favored the location. My gut said Evianna would be there. I had to find out as soon as possible.

I shadow-stepped to the stairs and flew down them three at a time, stopping only to glance out the nearest window. Fighting took place all over the castle grounds. Knights, legionnaires, and foreign arcanists were all engaged in combat. The cracks of gunfire and the clash of steel swords filled the night with an intense song of death.

Although twenty arcanists had been in the throne room, it seemed as though hundreds of individuals were involved in the skirmish. The jittery man spoke of allies—it seemed some of the arcanists who arrived in Thronehold under the guise of participating in the tournament were actually their lackeys.

We couldn't trust anybody.

A sense of urgency filled me. I leapt down the stairs and dove into the shadows, my magic uninhibited and giving me confidence. When I emerged, I was on the first story, closer to my destination, but disoriented by my surroundings. People screamed, and castle servants fled from the rooms in small groups, most crouched with their hands over their heads, just trying to avoid the arcanists and their fell magic.

Everyone had a hard time seeing. The eclipse aura muted all lights, but since so many had been placed around the castle, there was enough dim illumination for people to navigate.

A cloaked arcanist and his plague-ridden fairy killed people that went by. The fairy laughed after each attack, its eyes glazed over like a dead fish and its limbs so long there was an extra set of joints—two elbows, two knees. It fluttered with dragonfly wings, but the buzzing sounded like a nest of hornets.

The arcanist wielded a short sword, and after each strike, he recoated it in his own blood.

Their goal: spread as much chaos and plague blood as they could.

Fueled with righteous anger, I manipulated the shadows and grabbed both the man and his fairy eldrin with dark tendrils. I threw the man into the nearest wall, head first, and I flung the fairy at an ornate window, shattering the glass and sending it tumbling into the garden, broken and bleeding.

I rushed by the unconscious arcanist and continued toward the inner portion of the castle. The entrance to the basement was in a room with no windows—that was as much as I could remember. I slammed open every door, only giving myself half a second to survey the contents before shadow-stepping to the next.

Then I found it. The staircase leading down. Air howled up the steps, and I knew this was the correct location.

I ran down the stairs, the temperature dropping at a rapid rate. The stones of the castle became more and more nullstone the deeper underground I went. The suffocation of raw nullstone choked me a bit, but something surprising happened.

The lights seemed normal in the basement. The eclipse aura didn't have an effect here.

Shaking away my curiosity, I rushed to the bottom and came face-to-face with a nullstone double door.

"What wicked place have you brought me to?" Layshl asked.

I had forgotten I wore the newborn knightmare around my body, and I grimaced as she spoke, but quickly regained my composure.

"Wait here," I commanded. "I'll return soon. I promise I'll answer all your questions later."

"Very well."

Layshl slithered off of me, and I thanked all the good winds at sea that knightmares were so compact. She even positioned herself in the corner by the door, in the darkest part of the room. I doubted anyone would find her hidden in plain sight.

I pushed through the double doors and jogged into the large circular room. The center was open and inviting, but the bones of dragons and king basilisks lined the wall. Training dummies had been piled near the far end, and random crates were stacked up high enough to reach portions of the dome roof.

There she was.

Evianna.

She sat on the floor next to a training dummy, twirling a glitter crab shell between her fingers. Her long white dress and black velvet belt were smudged with dirt, and I suspected she had been down here for quite some time. Perhaps ever since the end of Lyvia's fight.

"Evianna," I said as I hurried to her side.

Her glazed eyes, red at the edges, told a story of anguish. She turned away from me, her shoulders bunched at the base of her neck. "*How dare you.* I never want to see you ever again."

Evianna hid behind her white hair. It flowed loose around her face, blocking her gaze and acting as a shield.

I knelt by her side, but didn't touch her. "Evianna. Please listen. We need to leave. Cutthroats have come for you."

She said nothing, and her whole body trembled.

The door to the basement training room opened. My blood iced over, and I knew the dastards had arrived. Without my magic, I would have to protect Evianna with just my skill at the sword. I placed my hand on the shadows and withdrew my blade and shield before standing tall. In the anti-magic, I wouldn't be able to return them to the darkness.

"Evianna," I whispered, my tone calm despite the pounding of my heart. "Stay behind me at all times."

She looked up, fresh tears staining her cheeks.

Two men sauntered into the room, both clothed in thick black cloaks. The first man pulled back his hood, and he looked like something I had drawn with my left hand. His eyes were crooked, his beard grew in some spots and not others, and what little teeth he had left weren't talking to each other.

The second man removed his hood, and he was in the same boat. If someone had told me his face was made of wax, I would've told them he was left out in the sun too long.

They were both sea serpent arcanists, though they couldn't use their magic here. Instead, they pulled cutlasses from their belts—long curved swords favored by pirates.

To my ever-growing panic, a single sea serpent slithered into the room, its green scales shimmering under the many lanterns hung around the walls. It had to be twenty feet long and as thick as a python. Its bulging, dead eyes and bleeding fangs betrayed the plague running through its veins.

It was me versus two plague-ridden arcanists and one monster eldrin.

They didn't seem to wear more than a few patches of thick leather armor. I had none. If magic were involved, it wouldn't have mattered as much, but now it could mean life or death.

Evianna stood and held the glitter crab shell close. "What's going on? Are they...?"

"Stay back," I said as I tightened my grip on the sword. "Lyvia asked me to protect you, and that's exactly what I'm going to do."

"We just gotta gut the girl," Wax-Face muttered. "Infect the guard, and let's get outta here."

The first man rushed forward. He wasn't as tall, but he probably weighed a good thirty pounds more than I did. In the split second it took for him to close the distance between us, I noticed he favored his right side substantially more than his left. I used that to my advantage and ducked left. In one quick thrust of my weapon, I stabbed straight into the upper leg, right where it met the body. A major artery runs close to the thigh, and I slashed outward, making sure to slice it.

The disfigured man slammed to the ground, completely off-balance.

Evianna gasped and stepped backward, running into the training dummies.

The man on the floor tried to slash at my ankles, but I plunged my blade straight into his temple, ending his life in a quick second.

The second man—and his plagued sea serpent—rushed forward. I blocked the man's blow with my shield by bashing his sword, just as Zelfree had taught me. The man staggered back, but before I could stab him, I realized the sea serpent wasn't aiming for me.

It shot straight for Evianna, its mouth wide and filled with razor-rows of bloody fangs, like a disgusting meat grinder.

I leapt between them, determined to protect Evianna no matter what. The sea serpent caught me just below the ribs and bit down, giggling with insanity the entire time.

Evianna shrieked, more tears flowing down her face.

Adrenaline dulled all sense of pain—and with the creature's head locked in place, it made it easy to slam the point of my weapon right into its face, just between the bulging eyes. A gush of blood bubbled up from the wound, and then a moment later, it went slack and released my side. Somehow, even in the throes of death, the monster snickered and smiled, like it knew what it had done.

The other man lunged for me, but his movements were

predictable, and I was twice as fast. In one powerful motion, I thrust the point of my black blade right into his throat. The force of the blow toppled him over, and I swear I felt the sword chip his spine. He gurgled and choked on his own blood, his windpipe shredded. At this rate, it would take a few minutes for death to find him. Instead, I ran my weapon through his chest, piercing the heart. It was a mercy he didn't deserve, but one I felt obligated to offer.

They were all dead.

"Volke," Evianna whispered, her voice strained. "Are you... okay?"

I placed my hand on my injury, covering it from view. When I turned to face her, I smiled. "Don't worry, princess. A scratch like this would never stop me."

"But—"

"We haven't much time," I interjected. "We need to leave as quickly as possible, before they send more men."

"More?" She scanned the corpses, her brow furrowed. "There are more of them?"

I didn't want to upset her, so I maintained a confident tone. "Now that I'm here, none of them will hurt you."

Evianna rubbed her palms hard across her eyes, her shoulders shaking. "Volke..." Her voice quavered, but she pushed through. "I've been nothing but terrible to you... Everything you've ever done... I never even said *thank you*."

That was true, I supposed. But it didn't matter. We didn't have time. Whatever she felt, she could say it later, once we were safe from the carnage.

"You don't need to thank me," I said as I jogged toward the nullstone double doors. "We just need to leave, all right?" I held out my other hand, hoping she would take it so we could flee.

To my relief, Evianna ran to me and hugged my arm, holding it close to her thin, trembling body.

"Volke," she whispered, but she never followed it with anything. She pressed her tear-soaked face into the sleeve of my shirt, not even bothering to look where we went while I guided her out of the room.

THE WORLD SERPENT RUNESTONE

I pushed the nullstone doors open and led Evianna through. The newborn knightmare, Layshl, stepped out of the shadows, her dragon-wing cape flowing behind her. She "stared" with an empty cowl and then moved to wrap around me a second time.

"Don't," I said as I tightened my grip over the plague-ridden injury on my side. I didn't want any mystical creature touching it. "Just follow close. I'll protect you."

Determined to flee the castle as fast as possible, I hooked my sword on my belt and dashed up the stairs. Layshl kept my pace, her movements quiet, but Evianna was young and exhausted, no doubt from a day of grieving. She climbed the stairs with shaky steps, never complaining, but short of breath and drained from visible fear.

If this were any other time, I would take a moment to reassure her, and even slow my gait. But we couldn't afford a single second. I leapt to Evianna's side, scooped her up into my arms, and continued upward, thankful she weighed as little as she did.

My injury bled freely as I traveled through the anti-magic of the nullstone, staining my shirt and trousers in dark crimson. Evianna wrapped her arms tight around my neck, her shaking gradually fading. Halfway up, the temperature increasing with our height, the nullstone disappeared, allowing me access to my magic once again.

My injury started the gradual process of healing, but that wouldn't stop the spread of the plague. I pushed it from my mind. I would come to terms with it later.

As I took the last few steps of the stairway, I slowed. Both men I had fought were sea serpent arcanists, but I only faced a single eldrin. Master Zelfree said I should think like my enemies, and it seemed logical that perhaps they left one of their sea serpents behind for protection—or perhaps as a lookout. Which meant it was probably waiting at the top of the steps.

I set Evianna down, motioned to the newborn knight-mare to watch her, and then stepped into the darkness. I emerged in the room at the top of the steps. Sure enough, a fat sea serpent sat coiled in the corner, its giant maw open and drooling pink saliva, poised to strike the first thing that came up the stairs.

It hadn't noticed me, and I used that moment of surprise to manipulate the shadows.

The monster hissed as dozens of tendrils lashed out from the darkness, covering it like an inky web. The sea serpent thrashed, breaking some of my restraints, but while it tossed in confusion, I rushed forward and stabbed it through its serpentine body.

"*Fool,*" it hissed as it writhed. "You can't win!"

The monster puked up boiling water. I sidestepped, tightened the shadow restraints, and then stabbed again. My blade slid through the scales of the beast, cutting a fin and opening its body wide. It hissed and struck at me with its many fangs. I blocked with my shield and then slashed afterward, slicing through half its face.

The sea serpent shook, flailed weakly against my shadow tendrils, and then collapsed to the floor. Its breathing stopped after a long exhale.

I ran back to the stairs and motioned to Evianna and the knightmare, Layshl. As soon as Evianna drew near, I scooped her back into my arms and leapt into the hallway.

Dust clung to the air from the floor to the ceiling, swirling about as though caught on a perpetual breeze. Someone had used their sorcery to waft the nullstone decay dust throughout the castle—I'd stake my life on it.

To my horror, the sword in my hand broke apart. I tried to return it to the darkness, but I was too late. The blade shattered due to the dust, and the hilt crumbled like stale bread.

My shield, on the other hand, wasn't affected. It didn't break or even react to the dust. I assumed it was because the shield was an artifact—an item of substantial magical power—whereas the sword had been a trinket, something weaker, even if they were both technically magical items.

The cacophony of chaos broke my chain of thought. Men and women fought down the hall, including a Sky Legionnaire atop her pegasus. Her long lance, designed to be used from horseback, was sharp enough to pierce the armor of the villains. When too many got close, she evoked a powerful gust of wind that blew everything back.

The supernatural darkness confused everyone, however. The pegasus arcanist gusted away her own allies, and non-magical individuals couldn't seem to find their way out.

I didn't know my way around, either, but at least I could see.

Fueled by adrenaline, I ran for the front room, but

almost collided into a statue on the way there. Why was there one in the middle of the hallway? My breath caught in my throat when I realized it wasn't a statue—it was one of the Knights Draconic. He had been turned to stone, frozen in place.

The ability to transform flesh and other matter into stone was master-level magic of the highest order, capable by only a few rare mystical creatures. This, I knew, had been done by the assassin, Akiva. King basilisks were famous for their ability to render flesh mineral.

I stepped around the stone figure only to find three more down the hallway, all of them servants. The closer I got to the front room, the more there were, and my dread built with each step.

I couldn't go this way. I would surely encounter Akiva, and then I would meet my end.

With hesitant steps, I turned around and rushed down the hall. Where would I go? How could I avoid the worst of our enemies?

"I can't see," Evianna whispered into my collarbone.

I hefted her with both my arms, keeping her close. When my fingers grazed the skin of her neck, I used my augmentation to grant her the ability to see in the dark.

A nearby window shattered inward, spraying the hall with fragments of glass. A man in a heavy coat tried to leap in, but I used the shadows to fling him right back out. I didn't know if he was fiend or an ally, but I didn't have time to figure it out, either. My default assumption was that anyone smashing their way into the castle was probably someone I should stop or at least delay.

Gunshots echoed in nearby rooms that I passed.

Evianna gritted her teeth and made no noise, as though afraid to utter a single sound.

Where could I go? How could I avoid the pandemonium?

"Evianna," I said as I rushed down the hall, avoiding the legionnaires and knights fighting individuals in the corridors. "Are there exits to the outside? Like the dragon landing platform in the throne room?"

She twisted her fingers into my shirt and kept her face pressed against me. "The throne room... and Oma's room."

The queen's quarters.

Those dastards had sent someone there to collect the runestones. Could I fight a single arcanist while protecting Evianna? If I managed to get outside, I could likely flee through the gardens and avoid the fighting.

"Do you know how to get to the queen's room?" I asked.

Evianna looked over her shoulder long enough to point to the hall toward the main stairs. Although I was getting short of breath, I ran as fast as I could. The newborn knightmare said nothing and accompanied me with agile movements.

When I reached the base of the gigantic spiral staircase, I was met with a gruesome sight. A dozen bodies covered the floor, puncture wounds throughout their chests, necks, and heads. Some were mystical creatures, including the two-headed dread form griffin, its feathers and fur smeared across the walkway, the pustules from its back ruptured and oozing a substance that looked like yellow porridge. The carnage left a terrible smell of copper and sweat. I stifled a gag.

An armored man sat atop a striking beautiful black unicorn with a curved horn. They both blocked the staircase, their movements perfectly coordinated, betraying a deep bond. The man held a spear made of spinal cord and a unicorn horn—the Silent Sorrow.

Knight Captain Rendell.

The dust that wafted through the air didn't break his weapon, which meant it was much too magical to destroy with this nullstone mist.

"Captain," I said as I hurried to his side. "I'm Volke Savan of the Frith Guild."

He readied his spear, his gaze unfocused. "Come no closer," he commanded. "Several *guild arcanists* have declared their loyalty only to use a blade on me the moment my back was turned. I won't allow anyone to pass."

"I have Evianna," I said.

Rendell and his unicorn both tensed.

Although Evianna didn't release me, she said, "Rendell! Are you... Are you okay?"

Blood decorated most of Rendell's plate armor. His unicorn also seemed bathed in it, from his hooves to the base of his curved horn. I took some comfort in the fact that it obviously wasn't all theirs. Too much had been splattered around.

"It's the princess," the unicorn muttered. "I'm certain of it."

I went to Rendell's side and touched both him and his unicorn. I gave them dark-sight, hoping it would help clear the confusion. Rendell stared down at me with focused eyes, blood running in rivulets from somewhere under his helmet.

"Our enemy is trying to kill her," I said, motioning to Evianna. "Please take her."

Evianna tightened her grip around my neck.

"I cannot," Rendell said, his tone morose. "Nightfall and I have been infected with the arcane plague."

Evianna dug her nails into my skin, her trembling returning in full force.

Rendell's unicorn, Nightfall, lowered his head to match his gaze with mine. "We must protect the castle servants and obstruct the villain's plans as much as possible. We will fight until our bodies give out, dying as knights and not monsters."

His words haunted my thoughts, but I forced myself to nod. "I'll keep Evianna safe," I said, my chest tight. "But I need to reach the queen's quarters."

Knight Captain Rendell and Nightfall stepped aside.

"I will ensure you're not followed," Rendell stated.

We didn't have time for speeches or long goodbyes. I ran past him and went up the stairs, my legs burning the longer I went at full-force.

Knight Captain Rendell was a man they wrote stories about. He knew his fate, but he didn't flinch. He stood his ground, surrounded by literal and metaphorical darkness, his eldrin by his side, his weapon at the ready, the corpses of his enemies scattered around his feet.

His conviction pushed me to fight through my exhaustion.

Just as I made it to the next floor, I heard the sounds of weapons clashing from the stairs below. Were there dastards coming to finish off Evianna? I couldn't turn back to find out.

Layshl slinked through the darkness as we climbed higher and higher.

"A new knightmare," Evianna whispered into my neck. "Is it...?"

She never finished her question.

"Where can I find the queen's quarters?" I asked.

"One more story up..."

My breathing became ragged. No matter how much air I swallowed, it was never enough. I held Evianna close and thanked the good fates when I arrived at the last step. We were one level higher than the throne room—a place I had never been.

The sounds of combat echoed in the distance, but that didn't put me at ease. The king basilisk was on the floor below us, and I knew the cutthroats invading the castle were a slippery bunch. They could be anywhere. I couldn't let my guard down.

Unlike the floor below, these halls were draped in silk. Small tables stood outside of each door, all made from luxurious woods far beyond the edge of the Argo Empire. The metal of picture frames and door handles sparkled, even in the darkness, as though magic had been woven into the original ingots, keeping them lustrous.

The place reeked of royalty.

After a deep breath, I dashed forward and turned down the hall. The queen's room was clearly at the end—the double doors were large enough for several horses to fit through.

I stopped, however, stunned by the surroundings.

People... hung in the air. Everything hung in the air, actually. The wooden tables, the pictures, the silk cloth, bits of rock from the walls and floor...

The people were knights and legionnaires. Some were dead, but those who were alive flailed around with no hope of escape.

All were suspended above the ground, floating and twirling, as though unaffected by gravity and simply haunting the corridor.

In front of the queen's room stood a man in a thick, black robe. He had thrown his hood back, revealing a disturbing sight. His arcanist mark glowed red with inner power. I had seen arcanist marks that were glowing white

—like the prince's and Guildmaster Eventide's—but never *red*.

His eldrin, to my ever-increasing disgust, was a rizzel with eyes that matched the scarlet of the arcanist mark. The rizzel was on his shoulder, its head poking out from the cloak.

While Illia's rizzel was ferret-sized and adorable, this was anything but. It was the size of a full grown weasel, its mouth large enough to swallow a lemon whole. And there were two heads. Or—a better description—it *had* two heads. The second head hung limp and was discolored with gangrene and rot. It was dead, just hanging there, its eyes sunken and its mouth ajar.

A dread form rizzel so twisted by the plague it was almost difficult to look at.

This was the arcanist sent to gather the runestones. Was he the one who teleported everyone into the castle?

"Can't you see?" the dread rizzel asked. "Shoot another one! Don't kill it this time, Meatbag. It's gotta return to all its friends and share the disease."

The weasel-monster laughed, high-pitched and wicked, bordering on callous. Well, not the main head. The *dead* head did all the laughing, like a disgusting puppet.

The arcanist—Meatbag?—loaded his flintlock pistol with a blood-coated bullet and then pointed his weapon down the hall, aiming for the air. He fired, and the shot echoed all around us. I ducked around the corner, clenching my jaw. Evianna didn't scream or gasp. She just held tighter, her eyes so firmly shut it was like she never wanted to open them again.

The rizzel arcanist had hit one of the knights, and the man grunted and spun through the air. When the arcanist went to load another bullet, he coated it in his blood.

Damn.

I didn't know how the knights and objects defied gravity, but I came to the conclusion that it was the rizzel. I had never learned what rizzel magic manipulated, but this made sense. Rizzels had to control gravity. The rizzel was the ultimate mystical creature of mobility—both using it and taking it away. None of the knights in the hall stood a chance. They were helpless, and Meatbag was going to riddle them all with plague bullets, even if the darkness meant he had sloppy aim.

I set Evianna down, knowing full well I needed to kill this arcanist and make it to the queen's room in order to escape the castle.

"Don't leave me," Evianna whispered. She clung to my shirt, pulling me closer, refusing to let go. "Everyone always leaves me."

"Layshl will watch over you," I said.

The knightmare stepped forward. In one comforting motion, she wrapped her cape around Evianna's shoulders and drew her close. Although Evianna pleaded at me with her eyes, I turned away.

I didn't have a sword, but there were some floating in the hall. If I approached by foot, I'd also get caught in the field of manipulated gravity.

But shadows weren't affected by gravity.

I dove into the darkness and emerged on the other side of the hall, behind the man and his twisted rizzel. Before they could act—before they even really understood what was going on—I manipulated the darkness and snatched a sword from one of the helpless knights. I dragged it back to my hand and then evoked my terrors.

The man and his rizzel screamed. The gravity-controlling magic semi-faded, causing everything to lurch downward half a foot. While distracted, I thrust forward with the knight's sword and plunged it deep into the man's chest.

He wasn't wearing any armor, and blood bloomed across his clothes.

"You missed," Meatbag said, his voice shaky.

I almost laughed. I had clearly hit him.

Then he threw the cloak to the side, revealing the rest of his body.

The rizzel...

It was snaked through his torso, like the creature had teleported into his chest and become stuck. The weasel-body jutted out of the man's chest, and a limp leg poked out from the ribs, their two bodies so twisted together it was hard to see where one of them started and the other stopped.

My sword was in his chest, but because everything had been rearranged, I hadn't struck anything vital.

The rizzel opened its mouth, but I knew what was coming.

I lifted my shield and blocked the white disintegrating flames. A moment later, my shield pulsed, and a bolt of raw magic shot forward, striking the arcanist and rizzel, since they were the same being. Meatbag slammed onto his back ten feet away, and the gravity manipulation came to an end. Everything fell to the floor.

The man and the rizzel didn't move.

I exhaled and inhaled with deep breaths, my body still on fire from the run up here.

Evianna and Layshl hurried through the decimated hallway, stepping around people and objects until they reached my side. I opened the door to the queen's bedroom, ignoring the knights who were injured, simply because I didn't have time to deal with it all.

Where were the runestones?

I closed the door and glanced around. Had the rizzel teleported them away? That was my greatest fear.

The queen's bedchamber had everything an entire house should. Bed. Couch. Fireplace. Bathtub. All of them were three times the normal size and so clean it looked as though they were made yesterday.

My heart stopped for a moment once I spotted a trunk made of nullstone-infused wood. I tried to open it, hoping the runestones would be inside, but it was secured shut with nullstone in the shape of a combination lock. Had the rizzel arcanist failed to open it? Of course. Magic didn't affect null-stone, which meant this trunk couldn't be teleported or destroyed without physical force.

"Evianna," I said as I motioned to the container.

She joined me and examined the combination spinner. It was a six-digit turn wheel, and I would never be able to guess the queen's combination. Evianna, on the other hand, fidgeted with the lock. On her first try, it opened.

The lid flung up, revealing a velvet-lined interior. All twelve runestones sat within.

They were magnificent. Each one was rectangular in shape and a different polished stone. Pink quartz, white marble, red bauxite—all of them unique and carved with pictures.

The green jade runestone had the mark of a giant serpent wrapped around the world.

I picked it up, my hand shaking. The runestone could fit into my palm.

A popping sound echoed in the room.

I jumped to my feet, my heart beating fast as I slipped the runestone into my pocket.

The dread form rizzel stood on the edge of the queen's

bed, half his body red with blood, the other half white and striped silver, like a normal rizzel.

"Oh, look," it said, smiling. "You opened the trunk for me. Now I don't need to wait for my associate. You're so useful I think I'll make you *Meatbag Number Two*."

The freakish rizzel disappeared in a puff of red sparkles. In the next moment, I leapt to the side, barely avoiding the monster as it appeared right where my chest had been. The damn beast was trying to teleport *into* my body.

It disappeared a second time, and Layshl rushed forward to protect Evianna.

I leapt onto the queen's bed, just barely avoiding another attempt to rearrange my insides. I used the knight's sword to slash at the creature, but it flickered away in a quick blink.

"Are you secretly two people?" the rizzel asked. "Because no single person is this stupid."

The dead head laughed at the insult.

The rizzel teleported again. I slipped into the shadows and emerged on the other side of the room. I didn't want to leave—for fear the rizzel would turn its attention on Evianna—but my fatigue was weighing me down, and I couldn't last much longer.

"Tsk, tsk," the rizzel said with a snicker. "You didn't keep your eye on the prize."

It stood over the runestones in the trunk, a twisted smile on its weasel-face.

I shadow-stepped over, but the monster teleported to the other side of the room with the eleven runestones I had left in the trunk.

The beast slicked its fur with blood. "You can't catch me—*you can't even catch your breath*." Using its gravity manipulation, the rizzel orbited the eleven runestones around its body. "Wait, where's the green one?"

Empowered by the eclipse aura, I manipulated all the shadows in the room and created dozens of claws, sharp edges, and hooks. I sliced through the bed, the curtains, and even the couch, the force of the shadows enough to rend the furniture apart. I hadn't meant to devastate the room—I just couldn't allow this monster to escape with the runestones, and in my desperation to end the fight, I lost a bit of my control.

Blades of darkness slashed at the rizzel, and in the confusion, I used shadow tendrils to snatch five of the runestones away.

Bleeding from several lacerations, the dead head of the rizzel hissed.

"You can't stop the Second Ascension, *Meatbag*."

And then the rizzel disappeared in a burst of red glitter, taking the other six runestones with it. When it didn't reappear in the room, I knew in my gut it had decided to flee.

"Curse the abyssal hells," I muttered between gulping down air.

But I still had the world serpent runestone, which was what mattered most at the moment.

THE REQUIEM AURA

"Volke."

Evianna walked over to me. Her bluish-purple eyes, wide and glazed with tears, hurt more than my exhaustion. I didn't want her to be worried or frightened or panicked—I just wanted to assure her everything would be fine.

"Why're you doing this?" she whispered. "Why protect me?"

"I promised Lyvia I would," I said, still unable to get enough air. "I don't want to see you hurt."

Evianna's gaze fell to the bloodstains on my trousers and shirt. Then she stared at me, and I knew I looked ragged as I sucked down air.

"Why aren't you... afraid?" she asked. "How can you be so brave?"

If I could breathe, I would've explained how I felt, but I needed a moment to gather my strength. Each new breath burned my lungs. Exhaustion never felt so debilitating.

The newborn knightmare joined us, her cape fluttering outward, showcasing the two-wing design. Up close, I could even see scales were part of her armor, hidden in the ebony design.

"Courage isn't *the absence of fear*," Layshl said, "it's the determination to act even when fear permeates your very being."

Evianna shook her head. "I wish... I had the strength to be courageous... I feel so weak. Like I can't... do anything..."

Layshl placed a gloved hand on Evianna's trembling shoulder. "A true knight understands that strength and excellence aren't traits—they're outcomes. They're *the results* of courage. They're what happens when you choose to risk, protect, or push forward, even when it seems like you might not succeed."

"A true knight..." Evianna whispered as silent tears ran down her cheeks.

That sounded like something Luthair would say.

I gritted my teeth, wishing he were here with me.

I gathered the six runestones and hesitated. Where would I keep them? In my pocket? What if they slipped out? Could I live with myself if I lost the most important magical items of my lifetime?

Evianna rubbed at her face. "Did... Rishan do this?"

"He did," I muttered as I emptied my belt pouch of simple supplies. I could fit three of the runestones inside, and I just had to risk carrying the others in my pockets.

"And he killed Oma? That's where this knightmare came from, isn't it?"

I didn't want to have this conversation, but I didn't want to hide the information from her, either. "Yes," I said.

Evianna asked nothing else.

Although I hadn't fully recovered, I couldn't delay a moment longer. Shouting from the hallways agitated me, and I knew it was a matter of time before the monster rizzel brought some of its friends back to deal with us.

I jogged to the double door at the other end of the massive bedroom. I threw it open and caught my breath. The dragon landing platform was just as large as the one attached to the throne room, but this one was covered in person-sized silk pillows. I felt like I was a shrunken person walking across a normal-sized bed as I made my way to the edge.

Layshl and Evianna followed close behind.

I leaned over and stared at the ground, convinced we were at least eighty-five feet up. The throne room landing platform was a floor down and on the other corner of the castle. To my horror, the king basilisk waited there, its four eyes open and gazing into the sky. I quickly turned away—to look into the monster's eyes would result in certain death.

Below us, the sounds of swords and the burst of gunfire filled the castle grounds. Above us, a screech pierced the night—low and rumbling, a mix of agony and rage.

Vercingetorix, the mighty sovereign dragon, swooped in, his wing span so large that it felt like he could wrap them around the castle itself. That was foolish, of course, but in the moment, it seemed like a plausible reality. He angled himself for the throne room, and soon he would contend with the king basilisk.

"We have to leave," I said. I motioned for Evianna to join me at the edge of the platform.

"Where?" she asked, her eyes wide. "We can't jump..."

I had never taken someone with me into the shadows, but the Grandmaster Inquisitor had, so I knew it was a possibility for knightmare arcanists. I hoped—with the power of the eclipse aura—I would be able to take Evianna to the ground with me.

It had taken several treks through the darkness to go from the ground to the throne room, so I figured I would have to do multiple to get down.

"We're going to travel through the shadows," I said as I scooped Evianna back into my arms. My shoulders burned, and I knew I couldn't do this forever. "Hold your breath. It'll be over shortly."

I gave her a second before sliding into the darkness, my grip on her tight. When I emerged, it was on a small balcony two stories below the queen's bedroom. I breathed a sigh of relief when I realized I still had Evianna in my arms. She gasped for air, like she had come up from a long dive underwater.

Layshl slithered as a shadow to me, not needing any instruction.

"Two more," I said.

I shifted to another balcony, thankful my magic worked, but it consumed me more than other uses of my sorcery. I didn't know why, but taking Evianna into the darkness felt like a drain—like I had to expend twice as much effort to do it.

A crash of glass from inside the castle drew my attention.

"We gotta leave!" a man shouted.

"We don't have the crown yet," someone replied, her voice gruff.

"It doesn't matter. A mimic arcanist took the form of the king basilisk and is hunting people down in the castle. *He'll be here any moment!*"

Master Zelfree.

I couldn't help but smile, and a piece of me wanted to rush to find him. Unfortunately, I didn't know his exact location, and I wasn't willing to risk going back inside.

After a deep breath, I traveled through the shadows one more time, finally emerging in the garden. A tremor shook the ground, followed by a set of deafening roars. The king basilisk and the sovereign dragon were fighting on the throne room platform, their massive bodies crashing into the stone walls and shaking the foundation of the castle. Rubble the size of small boulders fell from six stories above, crashing onto trees and shattering them in an instant.

"Volke!" Evianna shouted.

I ran forward, putting as much distance between us and the castle as possible. A hundred feet away from the walls, I managed to find the entrance of a hedge maze. I went into the first faux-corridor and had to stop. Sweat covered every inch of me, and the injury on my side had re-opened due to stress, even though my body kept trying to heal it.

"Volke?"

I stood straight and tensed, acutely aware of the fact I had left the knight's sword in the queen's bedroom.

But I didn't need it. Fain and Wraith entered the hedge maze, both looking surprised to see me. Although wendigo always looked thin and emaciated, as though they could never eat enough, Wraith seemed extra gaunt when he was splattered with blood and looking like a wet dog.

Evianna stared at his skull face and then leapt behind me.

"It's okay," I muttered. "They're friends."

Fain approached, his clothing unsullied by blood. He gave me the once-over and then ran his frost-bitten fingers through his hair.

I stepped forward, my movements sluggish. Then I touched his arm and Wraith's head, giving them the ability to see in the dark.

"Fain," I said. "Here. Take these." I withdrew the three

runestones from my pocket. "Carry them for me. Keep them secure and give them to Guildmaster Eventide."

He held the runestones in his hand, his eyes narrowing. When he glanced back up, he practically glowered. "These are what the villains came to steal?"

"Yeah," I said after a few short breaths.

"You know it would be easy to kill you right now, right?"

His harsh statement took me by surprise. I shook my head.

Fain shoved the runestones into a pouch on his belt. "Here you are, bleeding and haggard, carrying the most valuable things in the castle, and you hand them to *me*? It wouldn't be hard to end you and take these to the cutthroats. I'm sure they'd pay well."

"You wouldn't do that, though," I muttered. "C'mon. We need to make it back to the Frith Guild."

I didn't know why, but my statement amused him. He chuckled under his breath. "You're too damn trusting." Then he motioned to the deeper part of the garden.

We hustled through the shrubbery, turning corners as fast as possible. I didn't know my way, but Fain guided us. Evianna and Layshl kept pace, for which I was grateful. My stamina wasn't limitless.

The instant we exited the hedge maze, we came into view of the central courtyard.

The Grandmaster Inquisitor stood near the dragon fountain, his cape of living shadows bleeding onto the ground and swirling all around him. The horns on his knightmare's helmet, along with the claws on his gauntlets and boots, gave him the visage of a cruel monster, but I was thankful for his presence.

Chains and hooks sprouted from every surface, and the Inquisitor used them to cull the forces of our enemy. Castle servants ran by the Inquisitor without fear, but the moment a cutthroat entered the courtyard, they were torn into four pieces, completely ripped apart in a matter of seconds.

"This way," Fain said, angling us away from the courtyard.

Without warning, my heart beat discordantly—without rhythm and frantic—and I didn't understand why. I was familiar with the hammering of my pulse in moments of fear or anxiety, but this was as if something had clawed its way into my chest, causing my heart to pound and flutter at the same time.

Evianna placed both her hands on her chest, as though she felt it, too.

Fain whipped around to face me, his whole body paling. He spoke in a fevered tone and said, "I know you're not going to believe me, but a king basilisk arcanist is nearby."

Had Luthair not told him the situation?

"I'm aware," I said, gripping my shirt. "But why do you say it like that?"

"This feeling in my chest... I've had it before. When an assassin came to work for Calisto."

"His name was Akiva, wasn't it?" I asked. Master Zelfree had been right. They were all in bed with each other—a cabal of villains.

Any color Fain had left faded completely. Even the black tips of his ears seemed grayed. "This feeling—it's the king basilisk's requiem aura," he said. "Those monsters and their arcanists get stronger and tougher the more death there is nearby."

Oh, perfect. We might as well have been standing around in a charnel house on top of a graveyard.

"Let's hurry, then," I said.

Fain and Wraith wrapped themselves in invisibility as

we slinked around the courtyard, taking the long route away from the carnage. Mere moments later, I caught sight of a man dressed in gray scaled armor, the masterwork craftsmanship enough to betray his identity. Akiva. He was perched on a second story balcony of the castle, and with a single deft movement, he leapt from the railing and landed on the edge of the courtyard.

"There you are, fiend," the Grandmaster Inquisitor said, his voice a perfect blend of his knightmare's—dark and precise.

Despite the eclipse aura, Akiva strode forward with no hesitation or confusion. "You're a dog who enforces the whims of a genocidal queen, yet *I'm* the fiend? Laughable."

It seemed the two didn't need any more words.

Akiva leapt at him, far faster than humanly possible. With a powerful wave of his hand, he sent king basilisk venom splattering across the courtyard, killing every plant it touched. I shoved Evianna and Layshl behind the topiary of a dragon, protecting them first from any splashes. A single drop could kill.

The Inquisitor moved throughout the darkness with such agility that the attack didn't seem like a threat. He disappeared into the shadows and reappeared next to Akiva.

Hundreds of chains and hooks rushed into the courtyard, all to skewer the assassin. When Akiva flipped away from the first attack, the Inquisitor pulled his black halberd out of the void and slashed outward.

But Akiva was too swift to get caught. He dodged the halberd, the chains, the shadows, and even managed to leap to the other side of the courtyard. His requiem aura obviously empowered him beyond anything I had imagined, and with each passing second, the beating of my heart got worse, like it would explode at any second.

While they fought, I urged Evianna and Layshl to keep moving. We would've gotten away from the courtyard if it hadn't been for the earthquake that happened a moment later.

The king basilisk and sovereign dragon had plummeted from the throne room. They hit the ground like meteors from the heavens, creating waves of earth rippling across the garden, destroying trees and toppling fountains.

Evianna fell to the ground. Fain and Wraith lost their invisibility and crashed through the shrubs. Layshl and I used the shadows to avoid the devastating tremor.

Vercingetorix was dead, and the king basilisk started the gory process of carving out his chest.

Unicorn knights came rushing from all corners of the castle to fight the king basilisk—unicorns were naturally immune to poison, so even without a trinket, they could face the beast and potentially survive. But I doubted it.

The Grandmaster Inquisitor, however, had a different plan. His chains flew up around the monster—hooks going straight for the creature's four eyes and carving deep. The king basilisk didn't even have time to comprehend what was happening. The attack happened so fast and brutal it was as if the Inquisitor had been waiting for the monster to fall to the ground.

I helped Evianna to her feet and then urged her forward, but I was too fatigued to take her through the shadows. I glanced over my shoulder, impressed beyond words.

Somehow, the Grandmaster Inquisitor was restraining a gargantuan king basilisk, fighting random scoundrels that neared the courtyard, saving innocents who fled through the area, *and* fighting Akiva—an assassin who could kill him with a single strike, should he falter. The Inquisitor kept his ludicrous pace, never showing signs of slowing, but the more he killed, the faster Akiva became.

Evianna, Layshl, and I made it to the other side of the courtyard—the closest to the castle walls—when Akiva starting covering the whole damn castle estate in deadly venom.

He threw it everywhere—at the unicorn knights, at the ground, on the plants. The more area Akiva covered, the less anyone had to walk on. And the poison went straight through the shadows, as though they were completely incorporeal, like true darkness. The Inquisitor couldn't risk stepping on it. He and his knightmare lived and died as one.

Before I looked away, a smatter of venom caught the Inquisitor on his arm just as he was disappearing in the shadows.

His death happened fast.

The eclipse broke. The shadows in front of the moon bled away, like the sky had been cut. Then the chains fell off the king basilisk, draining into the darkness as though yanked to deep depths.

I swear the shadows cried out as the Grandmaster Inquisitor sank to his knees and then crumpled to his side. I couldn't stand listening—I hated that this memory would haunt me forever.

Acutely aware there was no one nearby to stop Akiva, I took Evianna's arm and rushed away from the courtyard. Without the power of the eclipse aura, everything hurt. Even taking in air burned my body.

"Fain," I weakly called out. "Please, take her."

Fain dropped his invisibility and rushed to my side. He offered his shoulder. "I'll carry you."

"I'm just going to slow you down," I said. "Take Evianna and go. I'll follow behind and—"

Evianna wrapped her arms around mine. "I won't leave you. *I won't.*"

"Stop fighting it," Fain growled. "Let's go." He grabbed my other arm and threw it over his shoulder, like I was a stubborn child he had to direct.

We made it fifty feet, maybe less, just past the last of the garden benches and bushes, when Akiva leapt in front of us. He was too fast to avoid—he had cleared the entire courtyard and made it to us in mere seconds. His gray scale armor now sparkled under the moonlight, shimmering with inner magic that couldn't be destroyed by the decay dust.

On instinct, I manipulated the shadows to yank both Fain and Evianna away from me. Akiva threw his venom—aiming for me—and I just barely brought my shield up to block it. My shield, made from a world serpent scale, completely ignored the effects of the king basilisk venom, but there was no way I could deflect every attack.

"*Run,*" I shouted.

Akiva wanted *me*, simply because I was a knightmare arcanist. That had been his directive, after all. Eradicate the inquisitors.

He turned to the side and kicked hard, striking my shield, but sending me tumbling backward. I hit the ground, my heart beating without rhythm and the hardest it ever had in my life. I wanted to get up—desperately wanted to get up—but my body struggled to comply. With slow movements, I rolled to my side, knowing this wasn't good enough to win the fight.

Damn.

"No!" Evianna shouted.

She imposed herself between me and Akiva, her whole body shaking. She was a third his size and not even an arcanist, yet she held her ground as he walked over, venom dripping from his fingertips, his cold gaze unreadable.

Evianna backed up until her heels hit my legs. "Volke's n-not one of the Steel Thorn Inquisitors! He's... I'm..." Her voice broke for a moment as she struggled with the words. "Whatever price you r-require... I'll..."

"Evianna, *leave*," I said. "I'm begging you."

She shook her head. "I always have to watch! *Sit back and watch.* Watch as you get hurt for me. Watch as Rishan takes my family and home. *Watch as he kills my sister.* I can't watch his monsters take anything more! I... I have to do something... Even if..."

But Akiva wasn't listening anymore.

He had visibly turned his attention inward the moment Evianna mentioned the murder of her sister. His expression shifted to something pensive.

Then his king basilisk roared, filling the night with a reptilian screech that sent shivers down my spine. Even from my position on the ground, I could see the gigantic form of a second king basilisk entering the gardens. Traces and Zelfree. They had arrived.

Akiva didn't say a word. He simply gave me and Evianna one final glance before returning to the courtyard, his celerity in a league of its own.

I pushed myself to my feet—painfully and slowly—and Evianna threw her arms around me. She was careful not to touch the blood on my shirt, as though disgusted beyond reason. That didn't stop her from squeezing tight, though. For a prolonged moment, I just let her hold me.

"You should've done what I asked and run," I said with a chuckle, fear still lingering in my system.

Evianna laughed, her tears still flowing. "I'm the princess... I give the orders." It was playful, in a woebegone way, and I thanked the good winds at sea nothing had happened to her.

The distant clash of titans rumbled through the ground. I motioned for us to leave, but the shadows moved around our feet.

Layshl lifted from the darkness, her incomplete set of armor a reminder of her newborn status. Still—she reminded me of Luthair. And when she approached, it brought back memories of the Endless Mire on the Isle of Ruma.

"True knights are hard to find," Layshl said. "Evianna, the blood that created my shadows is one of your kin. If it's your goal to protect your allies and avenge those with no means to seek justice, I would be honored if you became my arcanist."

Evianna stared up at me, as though confused. I broke our embrace and then motioned to Layshl. Although Evianna was younger than the standard age to bond, she wasn't significantly younger. On the Isle of Ruma, we had to be fifteen, and Evianna was at least thirteen, perhaps older, but not much. If Queen Velleta's knightmare wanted to bond with her, I thought it poetic.

Evianna faced Layshl and then tepidly held out her hand.

The knightmare took it, and they both glowed a gentle white.

Once the magic faded, Evianna had an arcanist mark on her forehead—a star with a picture of armor and a cape behind it.

END OF THE LONG NIGHT

As Evianna rubbed at her forehead, her face set to disbelief, Fain crawled from the bushes that I had thrown him in. Wraith appeared, and they both rejoined the group, but the sounds of combat still lingered in the distance.

Darkness moved in front of the moon once again, blanketing the castle in another eclipse aura. Although it seemed to surprise the others, I understood the tactic. It was battlefield control—if every knightmare arcanist had the capability, the enemy would never escape it, not until they killed every single inquisitor in Thronehold.

"We need to go," I said. My strength returned in a small amount thanks to the new eclipse aura. I was certain I could escape the castle grounds without assistance.

Evianna rushed over to me, as though she wanted to retake hold of my arm, but I jerked away and kept my distance.

"Don't," I said. "You can't get near me anymore."

"Why?" she asked.

I motioned to the stone walkway, painfully aware of the

roars and shrieks of the courtyard. "You're an arcanist now. It means you can be infected with the plague. You can't touch me."

"The plague?" Fain whispered.

Images of plague-ridden arcanists and eldrin danced through my thoughts. Gregory Ruma, the white hart in the Endless Mire, the gargoyle on Calisto's ship, Meatbag and his rizzel—insane and destructive. All of them. Barely sentient, barely functioning. Worse than animals and a disease of the world, much like the one coursing through their veins.

I touched my side, my hand trembling.

Wraith growled as the intensity of Zelfree's and Akiva's fight escalated. "We need to go."

No one spoke.

We ran down the stone path, away from the most frantic locations. When we neared the castle walls, however, Fain seemed turned around. He glanced down two separate paths, his brow furrowed. He pointed down one, and we headed in that direction.

A voice entered my head, not audible, but telepathic.

"Volke. You're going the wrong way."

I stopped dead in my tracks. The others did the same. Who had spoken to me? I didn't see anyone new. It wasn't Luthair's voice. It was... Adelgis's?

"Head in the opposite direction. Everyone is waiting for your return."

"Over here," I said, motioning for others to take the other path. "The Frith Guild is this way."

Fain, Wraith, Evianna, and Layshl complied without question. As we ran, Layshl sank into the shadows around Evianna's feet, and my urge to see Luthair grew. If he had been with me tonight...

The castle walls weren't as chaotic as everywhere else. The many innocent people caught in the battle had fled straight to them, and the non-arcanist soldiers had set up defensive perimeters.

Although I felt trapped in the quicksand of my own dread, I couldn't help but smile when I spotted the burst of red and white flame from atop the western wall.

It was Zaxis and Illia, fighting off flying mystical creatures with the coordination and timing of experienced combatants. A dread form fairy swooped in close with sparkling illusions, but Nicholin's disintegration flames shredded its wings. The fairy fell, and Zaxis burned it away with a powerful blast of heat.

Hexa and her hydra had set up a deadly moat of poison gas to prevent villains from reaching their safe zone. Whenever a servant got close, she manipulated the gases aside, allowing them passage without any harm. She had familiarized herself with poisoned throwing knives enough to stop some cutthroats from escaping over the walls.

Atty and Gillie offered healing to whoever needed it, their phoenix and caladrius helping to keep everything healthy. Guildmaster Eventide stood with them, her eyes scanning the distant devastation. She was hundreds of miles from her eldrin, which meant her magic wouldn't work here.

I...

I hadn't realized how much I missed everyone until that moment. It seemed like this night had lasted a decade and that I had traversed through the abyssal hells without them. The sight of Illia—and the others—invigorated me. I wanted nothing more than to be with them, back at the guild manor house. I'd even welcome Zaxis's constant training and schemes to impress Illia.

It didn't matter that this wasn't the Isle of Ruma or the Frith Guild on Gentel's massive atlas turtle back. *Their presence* made the war-torn wall feel like home.

I stopped before I made it to the perimeter that Hexa had created.

Fain and Evianna whirled around to face me. It took Wraith a little longer, but he also stopped and glanced back, his wolf-like ears erect.

I couldn't go back.

Evianna stepped toward me, but kept her distance, never getting closer than a foot. "Let's go," she said. "You have to come with us. I can't do this without you."

Puffs of sparkles blinked from the wall, to the ground, to Hexa, to the pathway, and then finally to me—Illia using her short teleporting abilities to cross the large distance in a matter of seconds. She had spotted us from her perch on the castle wall, but how? Darkness covered everything like a fog. And although I wanted to see her, and hear her voice, and tell her everything, I also dreaded this moment most of all.

When Luthair slithered to my feet, I knew he had been the one to lead her to me.

"Volke!"

The sound of Illia's voice eased the agony in my chest.

Even Nicholin's happy squeak caused me to smile.

She rushed to greet me, but just like with Evianna, I flinched away.

That was all that was required. Illia froze, her expression shifting from jovial excitement to painful realization. I didn't need to explain what had happened. We had known each other for the majority of our lives, and I couldn't hide a thing from her. In that moment, she knew everything.

I withdrew the last three runestones from my belt

pouch. "Here." I offered them to her, my hand unsteady. "It's for the world serpent."

Fain dug into his belt pouch and handed over the other three runestones as well.

Illia took them, her one eye never leaving my face.

Then I handed her my shadowy shield. "For when you need to use it with the Occult Compass," I said. That was how they would locate the world serpent. Together with the runestone, the Frith Guild had all the pieces to claim the legendary mystical creature.

Who would the world serpent bond to? I didn't know, and at the moment I had other problems to deal with first.

"You can't go," Evianna said as she moved closer. "You can't." She rubbed at the new set of tears forming in her eyes.

"Evianna," I whispered. "This is my sister, Illia. You need to accompany her to the Frith Guild. They'll look after you. They'll keep you safe from your brother."

"No. *No.* You need to come with me. I saved you, remember? This is the part... where we all make it to safety."

"I trust Illia more than anyone else. She's the type of roguish hero you read about in books—true and just, even if she's rough around the edges. She's my Lyvia, do you understand? Please go with her. I can't be around you anymore."

Illia's lip quavered. She took a breath to steady her voice. "Come with me, Evianna." She gently took hold of Evianna's shoulder. "Volke—don't you dare leave. I'm going straight to Guildmaster Eventide, and then I'm coming straight back to get you. Master Zelfree will know what to do about... about all of this."

Even she couldn't bring herself to say it.

Nicholin pawed at his face, rubbing at his eyes and nose. "Volke, if you leave... I'll never forgive you."

The chill winds of night swept between us. Illia guided Evianna away and ran with her toward the others. I watched them go, wondering if Illia would glance back. She didn't, and I knew it was because she feared not seeing me.

Fain narrowed his eyes. "You're going to leave, aren't you?"

I took a single step away from him. "I can't risk hurting the others. I'd never forgive myself." A single accident and they could all be infected. Why would I bring that danger into their life?

Before I could slip into the darkness, Fain rushed forward and grabbed my arm. I glowered at him, confused. "What're you doing?"

"Accompanying you," he said, no hesitation in his voice.

"You can't. I said I didn't want to hurt anyone."

"I'm *immune*." Fain allowed the statement to sink in. "I'm the only one you can't hurt. So let me repay you for every-thing you've done for me."

Any mystical creatures that were known as man-eaters were immune to blood diseases, both mundane and magi-cal. I had forgotten that wendigo were creatures of insatiable hunger—man-eaters from the frozen north.

I gritted my teeth and gripped his arm. "Wraith, come here," I commanded.

His wendigo bounded over. I placed my hand on him, too.

"Hold your breath."

We slipped into the darkness and emerged on top of the northern castle wall, as far from the Frith Guild as I could go in a single trek. The eclipse aura made it possible to take others, but *two* people really took its toll.

In the distance, Akiva and his king basilisk disappeared with a quick teleport. The sounds of fighting dissipated, and the assault on the castle had left it ruined and blood soaked. Portions of the walls were cracked, smoke spilled from some of the shattered windows, and corpses littered the gardens more often than flowers.

The second king basilisk—Traces in disguise—also disappeared, but I assumed it was because she went back to her cat-like shape.

If Zelfree knew I was leaving, he would stop me. I could hear his voice in my head, telling me he wouldn't lose another apprentice to scoundrels. Which was another reason I couldn't stay.

"I thought you trusted Zelfree?" Fain asked. The wind was worse atop the wall, and it howled by, carrying lingering amounts of decay dust.

"He can't cure the plague," I said. And if I slowly slipped into insanity while under his care, I didn't think he would ever recover. If I left, he at least would never know my fate.

Luthair's shifting shadow form stopped. A moment later, he lifted out of the void, his black and red cape fluttering in the gale. He had no face—just an empty helmet—but I could feel the shock roll off him.

"My arcanist?" he asked.

I just nodded.

There was no known cure for the plague. At least... not yet.

What options did I have? What could I do? According to the Grandmaster Inquisitor, arcanists were corrupted by the plague, just like mystical creatures—it just took longer. A few months, if that, was all I had.

"Only individuals with magic can carry the arcane plague," Luthair stated matter-of-factly. "If you weren't an arcanist, you would be cured."

"Don't say things like that," I growled. "It's not even an option."

But Luthair was technically right. If he died, I wouldn't be an arcanist. And the plague would leave me. Unfortunately, there was no way to unbond with a mystical creature. Luthair would have to die.

"I already lost one arcanist," Luthair said, his voice swelling with conviction. "It would be my honor to protect you from this darkness."

After a deep breath, I said, "It was... my fault... this happened. You shouldn't be the one to pay the price for my mistakes."

"I'm your eldrin, not your slave. When the time comes— when you're at the point of no return—I'll do what needs to be done to make sure you make it through this."

"*By the abyssal hells.*" I turned away from him, my hand over my face, my composure breaking. I didn't know if I could have this conversation. It hurt worse than leaving the others from the Frith Guild without saying goodbye.

"What're you going to do?" Fain asked.

The same telepathic voice entered my thoughts.

"*Volke. We're outside the castle wall, waiting.*"

Adelgis?

I wished I could reply to him, but I didn't know how. Instead of questioning it, I placed my hands on Fain and Wraith and shifted through the darkness until we were on the other side of the castle wall. Thickets grew all around us, but Adelgis's ethereal whelk shined with an inner light. I stomped through the undergrowth and headed in their direction. Fain and Wraith followed, never saying a word.

Luthair returned to the shadows. He had said his piece, and I doubted I could change his mind.

Adelgis's ethereal whelk spun in the air, her sea snail shell sparkling as she did so.

"Why are you out here?" I asked as I stepped over the last of the shrubs.

"I heard your thoughts, and I know about the plague." Adelgis smoothed his long hair, picking leaves out of the ends. "And I knew you would try to leave. You wouldn't want to risk anyone's health with your proximity."

I found it difficult to reply. He was right, of course, but where was this going?

"My father wanted that abyssal leech for many reasons, but one of them involved a cure for the plague." Adelgis forced a half smile. "I figured I would help you find him."

Although I hadn't yet decided, Theasin had been an option in my thoughts. I didn't trust the man, but if he had a cure, I had to try.

"I can go myself," I said. "You should stay with the Frith Guild."

"No, thank you."

"But—"

"When I was sick, it wasn't the Frith Guild who saved me —*it was you*." Adelgis made the statement with pointed words. "Now that *you're* sick, I intend to make things right."

His ethereal whelk, Felicity, did another spin through the air. "My arcanist and I discussed it. We won't leave your side until this ordeal is over."

First Fain and now Adelgis? I almost didn't know what to say. I rubbed at my neck, the warmth of their friendship enough to chase away the feelings of woe.

"But how will we find your father?" I asked.

Adelgis pointed to the sky through the tree branches. An airship floated through the air, slicing through clouds as it circled around.

Someone leapt down from the canopy of leaves. I tried to reach for my sword, but I didn't have it. The weapon had been broken in the dust.

To my surprise, Karna rolled up after the jump, her dance outfit just as eye-catching as it ever had been. "Don't worry," she said to me with a wink. "Your creepy friend told me everything. And we made a deal. The crew of the *Sun Chaser* and I are *more* than willing to take you to see the famous Theasin Venrover."

ABOUT THE AUTHOR

Shami Stovall is a multi-award-winning author of fantasy and science fiction, with several best-selling novels under her belt. Before that, she taught history and criminal law at the college level, and loved every second. When she's not reading fascinating articles and books about ancient China or the Byzantine Empire, Stovall can be found playing way too many video games, especially RPGs and tactics simulators.

To find out more about Shami Stovall and the Frith Chronicles, take a look at her website:
https://sastovallauthor.com/newsletter/

If you want to contact her, you can do so at the following locations:

Website: https://sastovallauthor.com
Twitter: @GameOverStation
Facebook: www.facebook.com/SAStovall
Email: s.adelle.s@gmail.com